THE MYSTERIES OF NEW ORLEANS

The Longfellow Series
of American Languages
and Literatures

Marc Shell and Werner Sollors,
Series Editors

Baron Ludwig von Reizenstein, his wife and daughter, in New Orleans. Date uncertain (circa late 1870s). From Schloss Reitzenstein, Bavaria, reproduced by gracious courtesy of Baron Konrad von Reitzenstein.

By Baron Ludwig von Reizenstein

TRANSLATED AND EDITED BY

STEVEN ROWAN

The Johns Hopkins University Press

Baltimore & London

Printed in the United States of America
on acid-free paper

2 4 6 8 9 7 5 3 1

The Johns Hopkins University Press
2715 North Charles Street
Baltimore, Maryland 21218-4363
www.press.jhu.edu

Library of Congress Cataloging-in-Publication Data
Von Reizenstein, Ludwig, 1826–1885
[Geheimnisse von New Orleans. English]
The mysteries of New Orleans / by Baron Ludwig von Reizenstein ; translated and edited by Steven Rowan.
p. cm. — (The Longfellow series of American languages and literatures)
Includes bibliographical references.
ISBN 0-8018-6882-3 (pbk : alk. paper)
I. Rowan, Steven W. II. Title. III. Series.
PT2547.V92 G4413 2002
833'.7—dc21

2001003733

A catalog record for this book is available
from the British Library.

Contents

Book · III

Book · IV

Book · V

Preface and Acknowledgments

This edition began as a whim and ended as an obsession. The memory of Reizenstein and his notorious book was preserved primarily by J. Hanno Deiler.[1] It has long been known that Ludwig von Reizenstein wrote a book about New Orleans which offended the taste of its time and was quickly withdrawn from circulation; more could not be said. It is safe to assume that the book, *Die Geheimnisse von New Orleans,* remained unread for more than a century until 1990, when I managed to reconstruct almost all of it from the microform files of the *Louisiana Staats-Zeitung.* It was not until a trip to New Orleans in 1990 that I was able to confirm the existence of two copies of the publication, one version including almost all of the first four books (in the Louisiana Collection of the Tulane University Library) and one complete version (at the Historic New Orleans Collection). These were surprising discoveries, as there is no mention of Reizenstein's book in the standard reference work on New Orleans publications. [2]

The edition that follows is based on the book as serially published in the *Louisiana Staats-Zeitung* as well as the sometimes slightly different fascicles of the book publication in 1854 and 1855. The translation is a modern English rendering of nineteenth-century German prose, although obvious linguistic anachronisms have been avoided. Terms of ethnic abuse are rendered in a historically accurate manner, as is sexist and otherwise colorful language. Reizenstein's notes, usually making an arch point, appear as footnotes, while all of my annotations can be found in the Notes at the end of the book. Words or passages given in spread type (*Sperrdruck*) in the original are usually rendered here in *italics.* In my annotations, I have tried to explain references that the author probably expected his readers to know or enhance the reader's comprehension of the text. Many names, however, were simply included as part of the atmospherics of a dense narrative style, so I have not tried to resolve everything. It is clear that Baron Ludwig intended that some of the obscurities of his *Mysteries* should never be clarified. That is part of why one can glean new information with every reading.

...

A project that connects such fascinating towns as Munich and New Orleans has to incur interesting debts and obligations. Don Heinrich Tolzmann, director of the German-Americana Collection of the University of

Cincinnati has continued to be helpful even after the completion of our joint effort on an Emil Klauprecht novel. In New Orleans, the Historic New Orleans Collection has always been obliging, particularly the former director, Dr. Jon Kukla, and the former reference librarian Jessica Travis. The current reference librarian, Mrs. Pamela D. Arcéneaux, has been invariably quick and helpful. Joan Caldwell of the Louisiana Collection of Tulane University Library also read the translation at an early point and shared helpful notes on New Orleans localities. Ellen C. Merrill provided more than will be obvious in the notes, since I eventually passed over her translations to the original sources. During the final period of my research, it was my good fortune to come into contact with Professors Werner Sollors and Marc Shell, and I was introduced to the program of the Longfellow Institute during an idyllic return to Harvard University in the spring of 1996 and autumn of 1998. They have provided a perfect setting for the revival of Ludwig von Reizenstein. Caryn Cossé Bell of University of Massachusetts–Lowell has helped to remind me of the often bizarre Creole dimension behind these writings. The Mercantile Library, now at my own institution, the University of Missouri–St. Louis, has helped me reenter the America of the mid-nineteenth century. Its director, John Hoover, has been ceaselessly generous and helpful. In early 2000, when I was in New Orleans as a guest of the Jean Lafitte National Historic Site, I was able to make the acquaintance of Sevilla Finley of the German-American Cultural Center, who showed me the community of Gretna, which Reizenstein surveyed when it was called Mechanicsburg.

In Germany, I was able to do research at the Stadtarchiv München, the Hauptstaatsarchiv München, the Staatsarchiv für Oberbayern, the Universitätsarchiv, the Universitätsbibliothek, and the Bayerische Staatsbibliothek. Professor Dr. Berndt Ostendorf of the Seminar für Amerikastudien of the Ludwigs-Maximilans-Universität was supportive, as was his former colleague Professor Dr. Hartmut Keil, now of Leipzig University. Dr. Hans-Joachim Hecker of the Stadtarchiv brought me into contact with current members of the baronial house of Reitzenstein, particularly Dr. Helene Freifrau von Reitzenstein. It was my pleasure and privilege to visit Konrad Freiherr von Reitzenstein at Schloss Reitzenstein in the Franconian Forest in late October 1992 to enjoy his hospitality and advice. My resurrection of Baron Ludwig appears to have the blessings of a noble house.

Financial support for early phases of this project was provided by the College of Arts and Sciences of the University of Missouri–St. Louis, as well as by the Chancellor's Fund for Innovation in the Humanities.

The first publication of Book II, Chapter 7, "Lesbian Love," was in the *Antioch Review* 53, no. 3 (summer 1995): 284–96, for which I must thank Robert Fogarty, its editor and a true friend. It has since been republished with the German text in Marc Shell and Werner Sollors, eds., *The Multilingual Anthology of American Literature: A Reader of Original Texts with English Translations* (New York: New York University Press, 2000), 185–209. Small excerpts dealing with St. Louis were also published in "'Smoking Myriads of Houses': German-American Novelists View 1850s St. Louis," *Gateway Heritage* 20, no. 4 (spring 2000): 30–41.

My wife, Marilyn, has been most patient while I pursued this project, which often threatened never to be realized.

Introduction

Searching for a Key to *The Mysteries*

Who Was Baron Ludwig von Reizenstein?

The only available sketch of the life of Ludwig von Reizenstein consists of tantalizing fragments and suggestive scraps, some of which resonate with his surviving work. J. Hanno Deiler provides a rough outline that has to be corrected in many of its details.[1] Ludwig von Reizenstein was born in Marktsteft am Main on 14 July 1826, the eldest son of Baron Alexander von Reitzenstein-Hartungs (1797–1890) and his first wife, Baroness Philippine von Branca (1800–1864).[2] The Barons von Reitzenstein were Franconian Imperial nobility of ancient lineage, counting high ministers (most notably Sigmund Freiherr von Reitzenstein, chief minister of the Grand Duchy of Baden in the Napoleonic era) and twenty-four generals in their number.[3] At least three members of the house served during the American Revolution as officers of German auxiliaries in British service.[4] As Baron Alexander explained in his memoirs, which have recently been published, Ludwig's birth excited hopes destined for disappointment:

> Another delivery by my wife that took place on 14 July 1826 increased my household by a son, who received from his godfather at his baptism the name of "Ludwig," after the reigning king. The intention of the namer in bestowing this on his grandson was to place before him an example of a continuously striving spirit. Indeed I attached the most splendid hopes for the future of my house to this event . . . In my mind I conceived of my firstborn son as the refounder of the dignity and splendor of my house, risen to high honors and married to a wealthy heiress, recovering one of our ancestral estates.[5]

Baron Alexander's line had lost all its estates by the end of the eighteenth century, and the Baron had to rely on his income as a bureaucrat.[6] Baron Alexander had worked his way through the ranks of the Bavarian army in the last phases of the Napoleonic wars, losing an eye in a training accident and being awarded a Prussian decoration for bravery in battle at Bar-le-Duc.[7] Although a Protestant, he married the Catholic Baroness Philippine von Branca in a love-match in Straubing in 1821 (confirmed legally only in 1823), and he entered the Bavarian customs service in Franconia. He served in various towns along the northern and eastern frontier of Bavaria until

1837, when he was called to Munich. He received a patent as a royal chamberlain as early as 1824, but this was a ceremonial court rank shared with hundreds of others—the printed roster of chamberlains for 1846 runs to eighteen closely set pages.[8] Baron Alexander's chief claim to fame was his energetic work in organizing the border patrol (*Grenz-Wache*), which won him a position on the supreme council for customs (*Ober-Zoll-Rath*) in the Finance Ministry. Decorated with the Order of the White Falcon by the (Protestant) Grand Duchy of Saxony-Weimar for his negotiations over the Zollverein, Baron Alexander did not receive any significant decoration from the Bavarian state until 1852.[9] He retired for health reasons in 1863. In all, Baron Alexander had a successful but hardly brilliant administrative career for someone who was a Protestant noble in Bavarian service.[10]

Baron Alexander's brood of children—all baptized Catholic—amounted to two sons and at least ten daughters born between 1822 and 1840. The long inspection trips demanded by his position began taking a toll on his wife after 1841, when she started to show signs of depression and alienation. She also fell under the influence of the wife of a "Colonel von J." in Munich: "a lady who obviously did not have a spotless past. This woman exercised the worst influence on my wife, who possessed an imagination easily excited, as well as hot blood. Soon I was aware of a surprising change in her entire nature, since she always acted as she felt and was incapable of dissimulation, due to her lack of self-control."[11]

This sudden change of attitude led to a confrontation and a confession by Baroness Philippine of her "guilt," the exact nature of which is never made clear in the memoirs. She might have been accused of lesbianism. A petition to the king written by the chief customs administrator on Baron Alexander's behalf provides more detail: Baron Alexander returned from one of his border tours to find "his wife sunk in the deepest immorality, his eleven children delivered over to seduction by their own mother, and his house robbed of almost all its valuable objects by the same hand." Baron Alexander himself described his wife's "intense and sensitive temperament" as leading her to "steps which . . . not only suspended the marital fidelity she had preserved through nineteen years, but also injured my honor."[12]

With royal aid, Baron Alexander managed to repair his finances, and in response to pressure from his wife's relatives and others he reunited with his wife. Yet two years after the original crisis, in 1843, he returned home from another tour to find his wife once more "fallen into bad company and gradually drawn down into the most extreme moral decadence. After she had squandered all objects of any value, not excepting even the best, she ran away, leaving eight children in the house, plundered and helpless."

Baron Alexander estimated the cost of restoring basic household furniture and such supplies as linen at no less than 1800 guilders. A divorce was soon obtained, and the woman's father shared with Baron Alexander the expense of supporting Baroness Philippine, who quickly deteriorated from mere irresponsibility to true insanity.[13] She was placed in a convent, but after the nuns refused to take further responsibility, she was put under the personal supervision of an elderly priest. She died in these circumstances in Untergriesbach on 6 February 1864.[14]

In the autobiographical sketch at the beginning of Book III of *The Mysteries,* Ludwig von Reizenstein makes much of his putative Italian heritage, claiming to have spent much of his childhood in Italy. His father's memoirs show that the Italian idyll is a fabrication, but a fabrication with significance. The claim of Italian birth and culture not only brought Ludwig von Reizenstein into line with the Italianate style of the Bavaria of Ludwig I, but it also constituted a silent vote for the ancestry of his mother over that of his father. The Barons von Branca were an old noble house originating at Cannobio, near Milan, and had been granted a patent as German nobility in 1775 for services to the elector of Bavaria. Hence, although the von Branca house originated in Italy, it had been thoroughly Germanized by the nineteenth century, and had Protestant as well as Catholic branches. Baroness Philippine herself had been born in Wetzlar, Prussia, and she had met Baron Alexander in Straubing, where her father was a government official.[15] There is no evidence that she ever saw Italy, let alone brought her son there.

After the trauma of divorce and the institutionalization of their mother, the older children were placed under personal pedagogues (*Hofmeister*). Ludwig, as the eldest son, was assigned to a theologian; his sole brother Ernst (born in 1827) was already in military school. Two daughters took their turns as stipendiaries of the prestigious St. Anna Foundation in the Munich *Altstadt,* thanks to grants by King Ludwig I, which provided a much-needed boost to strained family finances. As early as 1843, Ludwig began giving signs of being a problematic child: the year 1843 was a period of care and distress, Baron Alexander wrote, "because my son Ludwig had been expelled from the Holland Institute, and I was only able to get him into the Educational Institute at Neuburg on the Danube with much effort and the most pressing intervention of Abel, the [Prime] Minister."[16]

In 1845, family responsibilities compelled Baron Alexander to remarry, and he took a Protestant spinster as a wife. This marriage would remain childless. Due to the poor air in the city, the baron's new wife soon withdrew from Munich, settling with the younger children in a newly purchased property in Streitberg.[17] This left Baron Alexander alone in the capital, where he was in the habit of changing apartments more than once every year.[18]

> In the meantime my son Ludwig had completed the *Gymnasium* at Neuburg on the Danube, but owing to his inclinations and my own frequent absences from Munich, it was not held to be prudent to have him enter the University there right away. Instead he obtained a place at the *Lyceum* at Freising, where I placed him under the control of Freudensprung, the able rector of this institution. He remained there for a year, and only then did he transfer to Munich for specialized study. Since he was unsteady and variable in his character, he could never come to a decision as to what career he would chose. First he wanted to be a jurist, then a physician, then he simply wanted to train as a writer. In this manner a year passed, during which he attended the courses of the University in philosophy when I was in Munich, skipping classes when I was out of town. This was my son, who otherwise had so many abilities, who learned and grasped everything so quickly, and it caused me so much concern that I looked to the future with nothing but anxiety.[19]

Baron Alexander consulted various authorities to see what to do with this wayward, unsteady young man, and they recommended placing him under stricter ecclesiastical discipline. Ludwig rejected this suggestion, since it ran against his nature.

By the start of 1848, Baron Alexander had already decided Ludwig had to leave. He petitioned the king to permit Ludwig to enter the military service of the British East India Company, arguing that Ludwig was "talented but frivolous to the highest degree" and that he was in no position to control his son's conduct; during his last absence of three months, the young Ludwig had managed to run up seven hundred guilders in debts. Since Baron Alexander could not afford to place his son under continual surveillance, his solution was that "he must go at once to a distant quarter of the world." The strict discipline of such a post, far from any chance of family aid, would perhaps help bring him around. The king was asked to release Ludwig from his obligation of Bavarian military service and allow him to apply his student stipend to travel costs so he could go abroad.[20] Just under the surface of this petition is the father's obvious fear that his son might be retracing the downward path into insanity already taken by his institutionalized mother.

During the outbreak of revolutionary tumult that swept Germany in March 1848, which before the end of the month would precipitate the abdication of King Ludwig I, Baron Alexander was sent to the Rhenish

Palatinate to report on the state of popular opinion. He soon had another unpleasant surprise: "On returning to Munich from my mission, I found my son Ludwig absent, and it was only after several days of searching in town that he was at last discovered in Brunthal, a resort for residents of Munich, where he had quartered himself together with a friend of his persuasion, a young Count Voltolini, and both of them had been living it up for weeks at my expense."[21] This passage is the only one hinting that Ludwig might have been homosexual, since the phrase *seiner Überzeugung*, here translated as "of his persuasion," could be interpreted that way. The delicacy with which Baron Alexander danced around the subject was precisely the same way he had handled questions of his wife's sexuality five years before.

What is missing from this confession of family sorrows is any indication that Ludwig von Reizenstein was involved in the political troubles in Munich of 1847–48 surrounding Lola Montez, the "favorite" of King Ludwig I.[22] In later years, Ludwig von Reizenstein would claim to have been a member of the Alemannia Corps, a student fraternity that served as Lola's personal bodyguard at the end of 1847 and in the early weeks of 1848. Led by Fritz Peissner, the corps had promoted the establishment of a secular state that would reduce the role of political Catholicism in Bavaria; several members of the corps joined Lola on the first stages of her exile from Munich. The records of the Bavarian government, however, including those dealing directly with the Alemannia Corps, never mention Ludwig von Reizenstein, nor do police records cite him as one of those expelled from the university once the fraternity had been banned.[23]

Whether or not Ludwig von Reizenstein had been involved in the "Lola Affair," his father remained convinced Ludwig had no future in Bavaria. When a Herr Steinberger from Bayreuth recruited Ludwig to run his farm in America, Baron Alexander agreed to ship Ludwig there: "[Ludwig] eagerly agreed to this, since he always loved change in his life, worshiped the ideal of the free spirit, and expected to make mountains of money in the New World." Steinberger, however, died of cholera on the passage to America. Soon Ludwig ran out of cash and had to go to work.

> At the outset he split oysters on the shore, watched cows for a farmer, then he also edited a newspaper for a time, an undertaking which he soon gave up, since he lacked capital . . . then he traveled through most of the American states selling birdcages, coming finally to St. Louis, Missouri, where he met a relative, a Baron Eglofstein, who ran a surveying office. He finally felt more suited to this occupation than to any of the others he had yet tried, and he soon learned it and established himself in New Orleans as a civil en-

gineer and architect, a business that brought him sufficient income to raise him to the level where he could obtain a house and garden in his last place of residence.

If I had not left him on his own, had I supported him occasionally as he desired, he would never have achieved autonomy or grasped the necessity for a man to lift himself by his own efforts. He also found a wife to support him on the course he had chosen, a women he said was the daughter of a Colonel Schröder, who appears to have brought with her a considerable dowry of understanding and strength of character. These were qualities that gave needed support and persistence to our ever-trembling reed. In the first years he gave me considerable news of his efforts, but later he no longer concerned himself with his relatives living in another part of the world. He did not care whether his father, mother or siblings still lived, and he only gave any sign of life when I demanded a statement on a matter of business.[24]

Although the father seems to display a grudging pride at his son's eventual self-mastery, Ludwig's obvious disinterest in the fate of his relatives in Germany provoked Baron Alexander's scorn. It was the second son, Ernst, who carried on the traditions of the Reitzenstein-Hartungs line, even though Ernst's military career had been blighted by dubious loyalties in the revolutionary year of 1848.[25] Ernst went on to marry a factory owner's daughter and fulfill, on a modest scale, the expectations his father had harbored for his older brother. In his will, published after his death in 1890, Alexander von Reitzenstein felt bound to grant only a minimal portion of the estate to the family of his eldest son, since Ludwig had pursued democratic political imperatives, even marrying in America without his father's permission.[26]

Ludwig von Reizenstein's ambivalence about his family and social rank is indicated by the evolution of his own name in the course of his life in New Orleans. In the 1850s, soon after the heyday of the democratic forty-eighter immigration, he was simply Ludwig Reizenstein, then by the late 1860s he had become Ludwig von Reizenstein, and by the end of his life he was known as "Baron von Reizenstein."[27]

On 12 May 1851 Ludwig von Reizenstein entered the public record in America by launching a weekly German newspaper, *Alligator,* published by a group of reptilian "saurians" in New Orleans and its suburb of Lafayette. By the next year he was living in Pekin, Illinois, near Peoria, and on 23 March 1852 he circulated the prospectus for a paper called *Der Pekin Demokrat,* in which he promised he would soon publish a novel entitled *Die Geheimnisse von New Orleans.*[28] He is mentioned serving as secretary for an assembly hastily called in Pekin in late April 1852 to hear an address by the German revolutionaries Amand Goegg and Ernst Violand.[29] He must have left Pekin within months, since he first appeared in a New Orleans city directory for 1853, published in late 1852, and would continue to be listed as a New Orleans resident until his death.[30] Following his failed efforts to launch his own journal, Ludwig von Reizenstein wrote first for the *Louisiana Staats-Zeitung* (1850–66), the more radical of the two major German dailies. Its rival, the *Deutsche Zeitung* (1848–1915), was also anticlerical and Unionist but tended to defend the status quo (specifically the institution of slavery) in New Orleans and Louisiana.[31]

Despite his episodic involvement with journalism, Reizenstein usually stated his profession as draftsman, architect, engineer, surveyor, or civil engineer,[32] although much of his income appears to have come from surveying or preparing illustrations of property posted at auctions (an occupation for marginal artists, which he describes in detail in Book II of *The Mysteries*). The Notarial Archive of Orleans Parish preserves a large number of Reizenstein paintings, most of which display only perfunctory skill. He changed residences with a nervous frequency exceeded only by his father in Munich, moving from the uptown area to the French Quarter and back, sometimes relocating only a few doors away from one year to the next.[33]

Reizenstein's obsession with the insects and plants of Louisiana was already blooming in the pages of *The Mysteries* and would bring him a quiet sort of local scientific renown, but old associates also recalled with dismay his vain efforts to find a mathematical formula for winning the lotteries in Havana and Louisiana.[34] As will be seen, his quick, broad intelligence never allowed him any rest.

Publishing *The Mysteries of New Orleans*

The novel that Reizenstein completed in December 1853, *Die Geheimnisse von New Orleans,* had clearly been on his mind since early 1852, when he announced it in his prospectus for *Der Pekin Demokrat,* but later commentators argued that he had been moved to publish it by the horrors of the yellow fever epidemic during the summer of 1853 or by his disgust at the reception that the social world of New Orleans accorded Duke Paul of Württemberg in the autumn of that year.[35]

In 1852 a French-language novel entitled *Les mystères de la Nouvelle-Orléans* began publication in *La Semaine littéraire,* an occasional supplement to *La Semaine.* The author of this novel-in-progress was the French-born radical Charles Testut (ca. 1819–92). There is no obvious link between that novel and Reizenstein's effort, other than title, location, and a similar fascination with occultism and decadence. After the publication of the first two "volumes" (actually fascicles of about a hundred pages each), the French novel misplaced its narrative threads so that volumes 3 and 4 became exclusively concerned with Testut's current hobbyhorses of spiritualism and religious sectarianism, especially Mormonism.[36]

Publication of *The Mysteries of New Orleans* began on 1 January 1854, headed by a "Note to the Reader" dated December 1853. It began running in tandem with a novel by Alexandre Dumas. In a note dated 12 January 1854, the editors announced that Ludwig Reizenstein had taken over editorship of the literary section of the paper due to the great response the newspaper had received from the new novel. They promised not only that the novel would be continued, since interest was likely to rise as the novel unfolded, but also that "additional sketches with a political, religious and artistic content" would be added.[37] After this point, Dumas was relegated to the back pages and *The Mysteries* occupied the right two columns of the first page, sometimes with a few verses to fill out the space. At the end of the first month of publication, Reizenstein published a mocking "Monthly Report of the Literary Editor," thanking his women readers for their support and taking account of criticisms of the novel voiced by writers of the competing *Deutsche Zeitung:*

> For several weeks the seven-star-constellation of the *Deutsche Zeitung* has swung through all the bars and coffeehouses of New Orleans, spreading stardust and accusing the *Louisiana Staats-Zeitung* of being a "courtesans' paper." If these gentlemen possessed any intellectual or literary education they would see that this comment is more a compliment than an insult to the companions they so hate. Lais, Aspasia, and Nanon de l'Enclos [*sic*] were all courtesans, and they were the very focus of the artistic and intellectual efforts of their day. Since the existence of a "courtesan's paper" assumes a readership of courtesans, we can indeed be very proud of our paper. If the *Deutsche Zeitung* really insists so much about "decency," "good morals," and its "moral, country-oriented" nature, then it will only be read by shy, superannuated virgins unwilling to look any man in the eye. In that case, we leave our colleagues to take over the eunuch's office for these odalisques, and we shall not enter any chamber where someone else's slippers are already on the threshold.[38]

The *Deutsche Zeitung,* meanwhile, reprinted this "monthly report" together with the protest of a contributor against the corruption of young women by such publications. Even if such a literature might have a right to exist, the contributor argued, it still was highly improper to market it in a newspaper that entered private homes at the cost of pennies:

Ne Omnibus Omnia [Not All Things to Everyone]

Mr. Reizenstein will not hold us to be a Jesuit on account of this motto, but he will have to admit this principle on esthetic grounds. His response to supposed attacks by another newspaper on his serial has flowed from such an unesthetic pen that we must recall Mr. Reizenstein's conscience earnestly once more with this phrase. Alongside his lack of esthetic feeling, Mr. Reizenstein violates a veritable host of journalistic duties with his serial.

It must ever be the mission of anyone involved in entertainment journalism not to be used as a cover for immoral reading . . . We would recall Mr. Reizenstein that there are other aspects to life than the wanton wiles of a lusty Negro courtesan, and whoever announces how a man quivers in response to such charms is betraying a lack of propriety that borders on moral decadence. We are not miserable rigorists, for we do recognize that once in a while in some bar a coarse comment can and may be made, but whoever makes wit of such things before unprepared ears and allows his muse to bathe in the vicious waters of *Venus vulgivaga* is immoral. Perhaps all things are pure to the pure, Mr. Reizenstein, and we would not wish to suspect his morals on account of his immoral pen, but we only remark that even the purest gets dirty in mud.

It is a sad sign of the times that a trained pen exercises itself in portrayals that have their charm only in sensation, using locales only to excuse their esthetic worthlessness. There can be no distinction in being the writer of things that young girls devour all too gladly with glowing cheeks, burning with the desire to discover what is kept quiet, which their innocent souls did not yet know. There can be no distinction in creating a bordello literature with such books, introducing lustful premature development to female youth, which besides poisoning the soul will lead them never to find satisfaction in married life with one man (Mr. Reizenstein should know this himself). If such a literature must exist, then let it be sold in the form of books, since a writer does have to live, but it should not be brought into the family for a few cents, entering a reading world that hitherto had kept far from such things. Most of all, the editors are to be chided for promoting such things simply because they hope they will "draw." In sending Mr. Reizenstein these words, we assure him that there are hundreds of Germans in New Orleans who look upon his entire serial with disgust and reject it. *Sapienti sat* [Enough to the wise].

S. H. Lützen[39]

Reizenstein responded that the opposition was not so upset by the text as it was by the intent of the stories, which was to assault hypocrisy. In a world where dreams of cotton, molasses, and codfish filled the souls of youth, sensuality and spirit were needed correctives. Soon a stage version of *The Mysteries of New Orleans* was announced at the American Theater, starring noted local thespian Don Arias. By the middle of February, Reizenstein was fielding guesses from correspondents about the true identity of some of his characters. Was Count Emil the young Count Seckendorf, then working as a plantation overseer in Texas? Was Orleana actually a daughter of Madame Pontalba? He teased his readers by telling his correspondent, "We could not find a place for your other comments about *The Mysteries of New Orleans* because they penetrate too deeply into the affairs of well-known families, and we do not feel entitled to violate our discretion in this direction."[40]

As a sop to those who felt that the novel was too steamy for family circles, Reizenstein began publishing an alternative offering alongside it, so those offended by *The Mysteries* still had some poetry to read. Repeatedly throughout the publication of the novel, Reizenstein described his readership as being almost exclusively female, leading him in one of his "Monthly Reports" to celebrate the creation of a true "gynaeceum" of energetic, spirited women, reaching in spirit from the courtesan Aspasia to far Lesbos.[41]

The first three books of *The Mysteries* were completed in continuous daily installments, but at the end of Book III, Reizenstein announced that there would be a delay of a week, for reasons he claimed were already known to German readers, particularly the ladies. He promised that Books IV and V would confound those who saw the novel as nothing more than a theater of libidinous extremes and warned that the devotees of morality would lose their sleeping caps and be put to flight. In the meantime, the space previously occupied by *The Mysteries* was taken by a new tale by Alexandre Dumas and an exposé of Russian foreign policy in the Crimean War. The following week did not see a return of the serial, however; instead, a new serial novel replaced the Dumas story, which had run its course. It was not until 20 July 1854, after an interval of almost three months, that Book IV began. Even then, the excerpts were shorter than before, and the book was not completed until the end of September. After another interval of more than two months, a notice appeared in mid-December, in time for readers to renew their subscriptions, declaring that the fifth book of *The Mysteries of New Orleans* would begin the next day and appear serially without a break until finished. The preface to Book V, which speaks of the Kansas-Nebraska Bill of 1854, was clearly added to the text after the novel's putative date of completion in December 1853, so at least some changes were made to the text after publication commenced. The book finally concluded on 4 March 1855.[42]

According to J. Hanno Deiler, the author soon withdrew the book from circulation and had the copies destroyed. It is certain that the newspaper columns, divided into book pages, were reissued as volumes of the novel as soon as serialization of each book had been completed. According to Deiler, the author repented of what he saw as a "sin of youth" and made his amends by suppressing the book.[43] The book's apparent offense was its portrayal of openly named or thinly disguised residents of New Orleans, together with the scandalous nature of the goings-on. None of the sources mentions radical politics or the problack theme of the book as a reason for its withdrawal.

After *The Mysteries*

At the very height of the secession crisis in spring 1861, Reizenstein appears to have accepted the collapse of the United States as inevitable, and on 20 March 1861 he wrote to the *Deutsche Zeitung* to urge Germans to make the best deal they could in a secessionist Louisiana by organizing their own militia units under German commanders.[44] Reizenstein eventually did join up, becoming a member of a Louisiana militia unit. There are no details on his service other than the fact that he was transferred from the line to the medical service, and his earlier sympathies suggest he would have been a reluctant Confederate.[45] When federal forces occupied New Orleans, he remained in the city and made his peace with the new dispensation.

The suppression of *The Mysteries* did not put an end to Reizenstein's work as a novelist. On 29 September 1861, in Confederate New Orleans, he began publication of a series of columns in the *Deutsche Zeitung* entitled *Wie der Teufel in New Orleans ist und die Dächer von Häusern abdeckt* (The devil in New Orleans, and how he lifts the roofs of houses), a theme touched on in *The Mysteries,* inspired by Le Sage's *Le diable boîteaux.*[46] His movement to the rival *Deutsche Zeitung* from the *Louisiana Staats-Zeitung* might indicate his adoption of a more "southern" stance.

In contrast to the *Mysteries,* Reizenstein managed to finish his only other major literary undertaking in no fewer than eighty-five chapters, published on Sundays in the *Deutsche Zeitung* from April to December, 1865. Entitled *Bonseigneur in New Orleans, Or a Thousand and One Scarlet Threads,* it dealt with the impact of the Civil War on a mythical Creole family, but Reizenstein placed the stress on the collective guilt borne by this class for having introduced slavery to both the Caribbean and the American South. It gives the impression of having been left unfinished, breaking off in the middle of a promising narrative.[47]

Even before publication of his last New Orleans fiction, however, Reizenstein's enthusiasms appear to have shifted definitively to the natural world. His collection of rare insects became the most extensive in the state, although he sold it through a lottery in 1862 following a series of public lectures.[48] In 1863 he published a ten-page pamphlet entitled *Catalogue of the Lepidoptera of New Orleans and its Vicinity.*[49] It is a simple list of species of butterflies and their feeding places in the New Orleans region. Further works on the flora and fauna of Louisiana published in the *Deutsche Zeitung,* which had become the sole German daily in New Orleans, fitfully kept Reizenstein's name before the German-speaking public over the following decades.[50]

It was as an entomologist that Ludwig von Reizenstein came to the attention of the novelist George Washington Cable in the early 1880s, just as Cable was launching his literary career while working at the New Orleans Cotton Exchange.[51] Reizenstein presented Cable with a case of fine insects, and, when he discovered a larva at Spanish Fort on Lake Pontchartrain that developed into a new species of moth, Reizenstein generously named it *Smerinthus cablei* after his friend. Cable then intervened with his own editors so that Reizenstein was able to publish a brief illustrated essay on the discovery of the moth in *Scribner's Monthly.*[52] Reizenstein followed this with a series of English-language essays on the flora and fauna of Louisiana in the New Orleans *Times-Democrat.* Ironically, Cable never mentioned that the unworldly, obsessive amateur entomologist he knew in the 1880s had once done some writing of his own, and in Cable's own specialty of local-color fiction.

Cable did recall Reizenstein as a colorful New Orleans character, and he would incorporate elements of Reizenstein's speech and persona in German figures in his stories. The Reisens in *Dr. Sevier,* a novel set in New Orleans during the period before and during the Civil War, are thought to have been patterned after the Reizensteins.[53] *Dr. Sevier,* like *The Mysteries,* contained gruesome accounts of the treatment of the sick poor at the Charité in the 1850s, although Cable excised the most disturbing portions before publication on the advice of editors.

A character inspired by Baron von Reizenstein was the primary focus of *The Entomologist,* a novella Cable published in 1899.[54] This title character was unflatteringly portrayed as a dried-up, obsessive pursuer of bugs and butterflies:

> He was bent and spectacled, of course; *l'entomologie oblige;* but oh, besides! . . .
>
> It would have been laughable flattery to have guessed his age to be forty-five. Yet that was really the fact. Many a man looks younger at sixty—oh, at sixty-five! He was dark, bloodless, bowed, thin, weatherbeaten, ill-clad, a

picture of decent, incurable penury. The best thing about [him] was his head. It was not imposing at all, but it was interesting, albeit very meagrely graced with fine brown hair, dry and neglected. I read him through without an effort before we had been ten minutes together; a leaf still hanging to humanity's tree, but faded and shrivelled around some small worm that was feeding on its juices.

And there was no mistaking that worm; it was the avarice of knowledge. He had lost life by making knowledge its ultimate end, and was still delving on, with never a laugh and never a cheer, feeding his emaciated heart on the locusts and wild honey of entomology and botany, satisfied with them for their own sake, without reference to God or man; an infant in emotions, who time and again would no doubt have starved outright but for his wife, whom there and then I resolved we should know also. (99–101)

Always adept at dialect, Cable reveled in rendering the entomologist's guttural speech: "'Vhat?' said the entomologist. 'Go avay? Mien Gott! No, I vill not ko avay. Mien gloryform! Gif me mine gloryform! Dot Psyche hess come out fon ter grysalis! She hass drawn me dat room full mit oder Psyches, undt you haf mine pottle of gloryform in your pocket yet! Yes, ko kit ut; I vait; ach!'" (128–29). In the end, however, Cable's entomologist does not cut a very proud figure: he becomes involved with the sexually aggressive wife of a neighbor, and he dies of yellow fever, a fate hinting at something like divine retribution.

Ludwig von Reizenstein, by now once more styled "Baron," died on 19 August 1885, barely fifty-nine years of age, and his widow, Augusta von Reizenstein, followed him in death on 2 September 1886, at the age of sixty-two.[55] Ludwig von Reizenstein was buried in Cypress Grove Cemetery II, a burial place for indigents which has since been obliterated by the extension of Canal Street.[56] In 1890, after the death of his father, Alexander von Reitzenstein, retired Major Ernst von Reitzenstein wrote to Ludwig von Reizenstein's surviving daughter, Mrs. Berthelson, to express the affections the German family continued to feel for its relatives in distant New Orleans.[57]

The Mysteries of New Orleans and the German-American Urban Mysteries

One of the most obvious gaps in American English-language fictional writing in the period before the Civil War is the almost complete lack of an urban novel genre. One result of this is that our vision of American culture in that period is dominated by descriptions of rural and frontier regions. Other than the work of George Lippard or Ned Buntline, little fiction deals directly with the booming cities of the Eastern Seaboard, not to mention the nascent cities of the South and Midwest.

It might come as something of a surprise to many that there was indeed a vigorous genre of American urban novels in that period, written in German according to a French model. The so-called urban mysteries derived their form from the serial novels of Eugène Sue (1804–1857), first his *Mysteries of Paris* but also *The Wandering Jew.* These novels were published serially in the lower, or "street-level" (*rez-de-chaussée*), columns of newspapers over long periods, boosting circulation by encouraging people to subscribe. Only later would these works be reprinted as multivolume novels, finding their way into subscription libraries as well as bookstores.[58]

The basic genre of the "urban mystery" dealt with an existing city, well known to its readership but portrayed as a sinister place where events are steered by forces beyond the control of ordinary mortals. Individuals are tools in the hands of conspiratorial entities, whether for good or ill, struggling for generation after generation in unresolved conflict. The interaction of all levels of society, from moneyed aristocrats to the most desperate poor, is steered by persons and institutions invisible to the casual observer. Above all, professional criminals and princes are shown to have more in common than they would let on. Verisimilitude is provided by using real persons to interact with the fictional characters, against the backdrop of genuine buildings and neighborhoods and in the context of concrete political history.

Sue's novels were immediately seized by the European Left as demonstrations of the misery of the poor and the unworthiness of the aristocracy and bourgeoisie. Marx and Engels denounced Sue's need to uncover a secret conspiracy when real economic exploitation was easy to see.[59] Others on the Left hailed Sue as an ally, a man "made a socialist by his own book," seizing his genre as a means of opening European society up to criticism. It was, above all else, a suitable instrument for portraying the essential criminality of existing power structures.

The Sue vogue was particularly strong in Germany, and it was rapidly transferred to the German emigration after the failure of the Revolutions of 1848–49. In 1844, Heinrich Börnstein, editor of the Paris *Vorwärts!,* gleefully noted that mysteries were in the process of being written for every little town in the country, to the distress of the authorities, who feared exposure.[60] Not only were several translations of the original *Mystères de Paris* circulating in Germany by the mid-1840s, but virtually every community soon seemed to boast a *Geheimnisse* novel of its own, written by someone with at least a specious interest in social progress.

Sue's *Mystères* appeared in ten German translations by the end of 1844, including two in the United States. Don Heinrich Tolzmann observes that Sue's image of the city as a "swarming mass of signals" that was "dense, obscure, undecipherable" appealed particularly to German-American readers. Werner Sollors feels the books functioned "as a tour guide to slummers who were ready for the descent, for initiation into the underworld, in the age of nascent tourism."[61]

Sue argued his fiction was an urban sequel to James Fenimore Cooper's *Leatherstocking* novels, but instead he presented "other barbarians different from the savage tribes depicted so well by Cooper." Inhabitants of the underworld had "customs of their own—a mysterious language, full of dark images of bloody and disgusting metaphors."[62] Sue addressed social issues, combining the reader's need for romance and adventure with a sort of reformist realism.[63] The social message, which sought to decipher the obscure motivations of otherwise inexplicable events, provided a vehicle for communicating sensational and scandalous material to a bourgeois audience, particularly a female bourgeois audience.[64]

In 1850 an anonymous author in Philadelphia published *Die Geheimnisse von Philadelphia* (The mysteries of Philadelphia), the first original German-American urban mystery novel.[65] The surviving first section describes the black quarter of Philadelphia in telling detail, concentrating on the life of a free black seamstress, Miranda. The salient features of this novel include elements of local description found in later German-American urban mystery novels. Although some critics have stressed the role of the genre in dramatizing the immigrant experience and its dislocations,[66] in fact these novels deal with much broader subject matter, making them part of a specifically American genre.

The German-American urban mystery novel is an interesting witness even beyond its obvious function of describing the immigrant experience in the pre–Civil War era. The German writers showed much more sensitivity than their English-speaking contemporaries to the ethnic diversity of the United States. The novels teem with Creoles and foreigners, and the black population of America, both free and slave, is described with a detail and a lack of false sentimentality that is unique for the time. For instance, a novel's detailed description of a free black hotel in downtown Cincinnati led to the discovery by scholars of that very hotel in the surviving property register of Cincinnati.[67] The automatic sympathy the authors had for the Native American population, continuing a German tradition already established by Charles Sealsfield, is a harbinger of the "Old Shatterhand" tradition of Karl May's popular adventure stories.

In 1851 Heinrich Börnstein, now resident in St. Louis,[68] published his famous *Geheimnisse von St. Louis* (*The Mysteries of St. Louis*), which tells the story of the involvement of the immigrant Boettcher family in a net of underworld intrigue entwined in the history of St. Louis.[69] It was translated quickly into English, French, and Czech for St. Louis newspapers, and it would be reprinted in Germany into the era of the *Kulturkampf,* when Bismark attacked the authority of the Catholic Church in a united Germany in the 1870s.

In 1853, Peter H. Myers published a novel in New York entitled *Mysteries of San Francisco,* followed in 1854 by Rudolf Lexow's *Amerikanische Criminal-Mysteries, oder das Leben der Verbrecher in New-York* [American criminal mysteries, or the life of criminals in New York]. The fascination of German-American writers with urban mysteries novels would continue into the later nineteenth century.[70]

The most successful representative of the classic urban mystery genre in German America is probably *Cincinnati, oder Geheimnisse des Westens,* by Cincinnati artist and journalist Emil Klauprecht.[71] This vast novel recapitulates the history of the Ohio Valley over a period of seventy years, epitomized in the person of a young man who is heir to the title of the land on which the city of Cincinnati was later built. As in other urban mysteries, the young hero, Washington Filson, is a pawn in a struggle between two conspiracies, an evil conspiracy led by the Jesuits, and a benign, patriotic one led by former Missouri Senator Thomas Hart Benton. In the conclusion, Filson refuses the offers of both factions and decamps with his German sweetheart for Davenport, Iowa, to live as a farmer among the Schleswig-Holsteiner immigrants there.[72]

The Mysteries of New Orleans can be epitomized as an extension of the *Mysteries* genre into territory that had hitherto been left utterly unexplored. Although the usual translation of *Geheimnisse* is "mysteries," in deference to the familiar *Mystères* of Sue, a better translation would be "secrets." The book details the secrets of a community, of an entire social order. Its reputation was as a sexually indiscrete book, but its root sin was vastly more serious: it staged a frontal attack on the ethos of the entire American South. Unlike the rather wan philanthropy of Sue, Börnstein, or Klauprecht, Reizenstein's tale foretells the descent of a bloody retributive justice upon the American South. Slavery is a massive sin that would soon be made right by a bloodbath, heralded by the birth of a black messiah, a deliverer of his people. This messiah would be born of a black prostitute and fathered by an epicene German aristocrat. Without false sentimentality or hopeful liberalism, Reizenstein portrayed the coming revolution in frankly apocalyptic terms, as a stroke of fate which transcended the morality of ordinary men and women. Instead of melodrama, Reizenstein provided horror on the scale of E. T. A. Hoffmann, both retail and wholesale. In the coming storm, the virtuous will not only go without reward, they shall suffer obliteration along with the reprobate. The executioner of this malign fate, the cadaverous Hiram the Freemason, a man over two centuries old, is a nightmarish superman before Nietzsche's time, beyond good and evil.

Unlike most writers of mysteries, Reizenstein was concerned with writing a serious book rather than a potboiler, and the work demonstrates both care and skill in building a coherent image of horror laced with absurdity and comedy. His style is carefully calculated to promote an atmosphere of mystery and ambiguity, telling parts of the story out of order and keeping the identity of some persons obscure until the moment is right. Like Dickens or any other good storyteller of the time, he exploits stock characters and episodes, but he does so with an a complexity that always surprises.

The language is often poetic and evocative, with purple passages and portrayals of place as if time were suspended. The oddest feature of Reizenstein's style is his use of strange, unexplained phrases repeated almost as an incantation: Jenny and Frida live in *das wunderliebe Häuschen* (translated here as "a lovable cottage"), a small earthly paradise obliterated at the end of the story with casual cruelty. The leading comic character, Caspar Hahn, is *der Büchsenspanner* (literally "shotgun-cocker," here translated as "Cocker"). These *Leitmotive* are never explained, they are simply repeated without variation wherever they are needed, like a Homeric tag. As his sources, behind the stock authors of the German Biedermeier, or the racier novels of Goethe, stand not only popular French authors such as Sue but also the Marquis de Sade and others of a more dangerous shade. The great German writer of horror and humor in weird combination, E. T. A. Hoffmann, is the most obvious model for Reizenstein's work, although Reizenstein's consistent social realism sets him apart from his Prussian archetype.

Above all else, the book is saturated with the presence of the city of New Orleans, whose history and organization Reizenstein knew intimately. In the novel, New Orleans is the "palmetto boudoir" of Louisiana, a sinkhole of every delicious vice humans are heir to. Reizenstein himself celebrated the "daughters of Sodom" who populated its streets, mostly mixed-race girls in their early teens. The sweaty brothels and dance halls of the Crescent City are his favorite venue. Looming over the city is the continual threat of visitations of yellow fever, attributed by Reizenstein to the poison of a strange plant, *Mantis religiosa,* said to bloom at the mysterious source of the Red River in distant Texas, where Hiram, the nemesis of the South, dwells.

The South is not the only target of Reizenstein's fury. At the start of the final book, Hiram presides at an allegorical trial of three villainous beasts, a bald eagle (representing American racism and rapacity), a Nebraska owl (the Kansas-Nebraska Act) and a pelican (the mournful bird of Louisiana). He foretells a dreadful fate for all of them, since they have managed to combine inhuman cruelty with cowardice. Reizenstein's approach is metapolitical rather than political: his condemnation of American life is so total that he prescribes no practical solution, no sop of socialism for the poor. He even eschews the usual facile anti-Jesuit polemics: he loathes individual priests for their hypocrisy, but he sees no point in denouncing whole orders when there is bigger game to hunt.

The mover of the story, Hiram, remains a puzzle throughout, since his goals are expressed in nearly incoherent ravings. Hiram is clearly the master of the situation, the puppet master over all the figures in the drama, but his purpose, his mission of bringing to birth the "black messiah," is that of a midwife of fate. Although Hiram obscurely celebrates the glory of "*Nigritia,*" his main purpose is to punish whites for their historic crimes against African-Americans.

The story is moved along by agents other than Hiram, though they are less aware of their motivation and goals. The diabolical Hungarian Lajos, a gentleman criminal in league with the sadistic old Catholic preacher Dubreuil, commits most of the more heinous acts in the book. Neither Lajos nor Dubreuil appears capable of profiting from their many crimes: time and again, the profits of their escapades flow away, leaving them empty. Lajos represents an evil so radical that only a bolt sent down from heaven can eradicate him. The story also displays a dark fringe of episodes suggesting that all the protagonists have Doppelgängers pursuing alternative lines of story development, reflecting the tentative nature of visible reality, even if it simply may be a sign of the author's shaky grasp of reality.

Lastly, Reizenstein challenges the platitudinous moralism of his freethinker colleagues by gratuitously stressing the peculiar sexuality of most of his characters. It is easy to say that the only sympathetic lovers—really the only "straight" people—in his entire story are the tender lesbians, Claudine and Orleana. They represent an alternative lesbian society flourishing in New Orleans as nowhere else in America. This particular vision of lesbian communal utopias derives from a masculine pornographic-voyeuristic tradition that ritualizes the sexuality of "others" in society, whether they are repressed monks or women ensconced in harems. When projected specifically on women, such ideal communes recur throughout the history of American popular culture, from fictionalized seraglios to the Amazon community that was home to Wonder Woman. Despite its dubious parentage

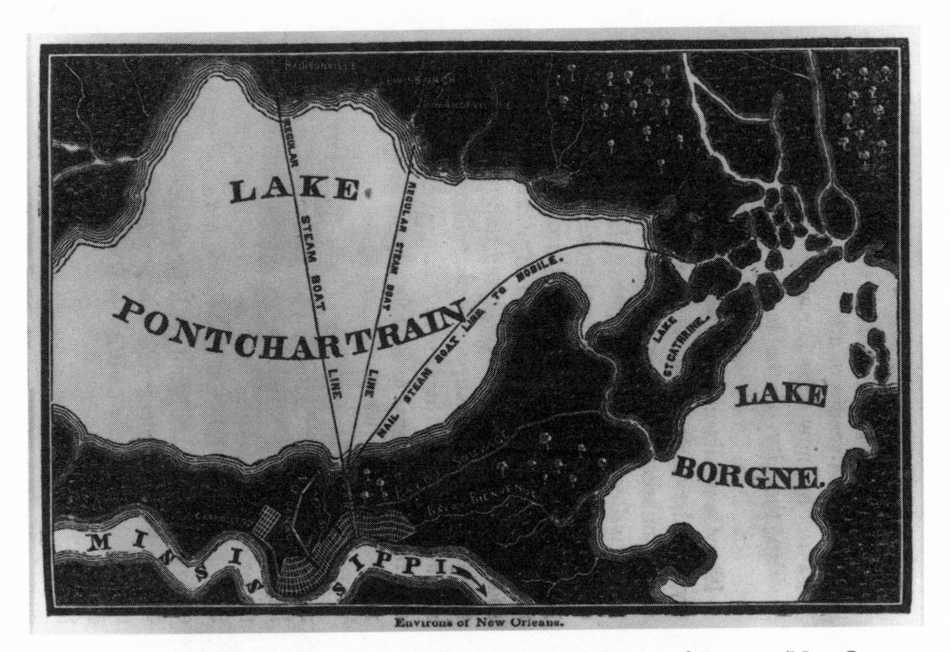

"New Orleans and Environs," from *Norman's New Orleans and Environs* (New Orleans: B. M. Norman, 1845), 190. From the Collections of the St. Louis Mercantile Library at the University of Missouri–St. Louis.

and progeny, Reizenstein's celebration of same-sex love remains a landmark in the portrayal of homosexuality in American fiction.[73] Reizenstein does not hesitate to see the love of Orleana and Claudine as a revolutionary act, a gentle revolt against the domination of males over females, against the domination of property over want, against the domination of oligarchy over virtue, and even against the domination of humans over other animal species. The lesbian episode appears to have had some deep personal importance to Reizenstein, since it serves no purpose in moving the plot forward. Needless to say, Reizenstein would have had to wait a long time to find the audience for such a message.

Virtually everyone else in his book displays perverted sexuality: the effeminate cross-dressing dandy Emil, the equally effeminate architect Albert, Emil's amoral hooker-lover Lucy, the drunken sexist "Cocker" Hahn, the murderous, sadistic priest Dubreuil, the necrophiliac rapist Lajos, the timorously incestuous repressed lesbians Frida and Jenny, and even the naive North German cook Urschl (who becomes in all likelihood the only white female in nineteenth-century American fiction to have her sexual encounter with a black male portrayed as a comic episode).

"View near the Head of the Ke-Che-Ah-Que-Ho-No," now known as Palo Duro Canyon. This and other illustrations in a report by Randolph B. Marcy adumbrated Reizenstein's description of the mythical Mesa in Books IV and V. From Randolph B. Marcy, with George B. McClellan, *Exploration of the Red River of Louisiana in the Year 1852, with Reports on the Natural History of the Country, and Numerous Illustrations,* House of Representatives, 33rd Congress, 1st session (Washington, D.C.: A. O. P. Nicholson, Public Printer, 1854), lithographic plate no. 8, by H. Lawrence of New York, from the Thomas Jefferson Library of the University of Missouri–St. Louis.

Reizenstein certainly had major flaws as a writer. His book, like most subscription publications, is too long, although it is strikingly short on the irrelevant storytelling found in abundance in such other writers as Emil Klauprecht. Just as critics of a few years ago would have been shocked at Reizenstein's sensuality, decadence, and openness to alternative sexuality, readers today will be bothered by a whiff of anti-Semitism in his portrayal of Gabor. The same present-day readers will tend to overlook the quite pornographic anticlericalism; this is a sign of our own hypocrisy, not his. Still, bigotry of all varieties issues from the mouths of his villains and fools, which are many. In this he was recording the world around him to condemn it, certainly not to endorse it. He also has a superfluity of characters, some created only in order to be snuffed out in particularly colorful and ghastly ways. Even when boiled down to the minimum needed to carry the story, there are still too many characters to keep straight or to effectively move the story forward.

After all of this, Reizenstein's peculiar vision of New Orleans is worth resurrecting precisely because it crossed the boundaries of acceptable taste in nineteenth-century German America and squatted firmly on the other side. By writing a dark comedy about the dreadful fate of America, he cut through confused sentimentality to reveal the roots of a clear and present danger. By challenging the platitudes under which freethinkers sought to give lip-service to Christian values while challenging clerical authority, Reizenstein reveals the hypocrisy of a lukewarm semihumanism. By neglecting to reward the virtue of individuals in order to lambaste the criminality of an entire social order, Reizenstein highlights the shallow compromises made in the other exemplars of the urban mysteries genre. By articulating his dreadful fantasy of a coming cataclysm, Reizenstein documents beyond a shadow of a doubt the historical existence of a very real southern nightmare. Above all else, this work makes us realize how limited our notions were of what could be conceived by a fertile American imagination in the middle of the nineteenth century.

Perhaps the best thing to come from this resurrection of *The Mysteries of New Orleans* is Baron Ludwig himself, a wanderer between the worlds with more than a superficial resemblance to his fellow European-American lepidopterist Vladimir Nabokov. He could also be seen as a bizarre Teutonic avatar of Tennessee Williams. Like his heroine Orleana, the baron in the end had become the arch-representative of a whole new ethnic category, the German Creole. It is high time he came home to us and told his tale. This time, we just might listen.

The Mysteries of New Orleans

A Novel by

Baron Ludwig von Reizenstein

Impavidum ferient ruinæ

(ruin awaits him who does not take heed)

Memoranda

for the SYMPATHETIC READER

Ever since Eugène Sue's delicate Fleur-de-Marie resisted the enticement of the "wedding night" with a prince, preferring to end her young life in a cloister, Fleurs-de-Marie have lost their charm, and since they are what blooms in the garden of mysteries, mysteries have ceased to be fashionable.[1] It is a decade too late to sow Fleurs-de-Marie, all the more so because, as every lover of flowers knows, they can only produce seeds for two years.

All of the subsequent mysteries were thus more or less like one of the Gerolsteins,[2] even if the former lacked princes, Viscounts Remy, or Marquises D'Harville.

The disreputable novelist Ned Buntline launched the literature of mysteries on American soil and thereby utterly killed all their enchantment as well as any interest in them.[3]

The "Mysteries of St. Louis" flowed from a German-American pen and is of importance only insofar as its appearance coincided with the struggle of Germans at that time against the attacks of Jesuitism.[4] H. Hassaureck's "Mysteries of Cincinnati"[5] are a pale reflection of the *Mysteries of Berlin* or *New York,* and they unfortunately contain too much that is familiar for a well-read man.

Despite all this, the author has given his work the title of *Mysteries* because it is based on a true event that would be hard for anyone in this generation of our city to be aware of unless he happened by accident to obtain a transcription of Lakanal's "Narrative of an Ursuline Novice in New Orleans."[6] In the days when Baron de Carondelet was still governor of the province and the areas around Canal and Esplanade Streets consisted of plantations,[7] an ominous person lived on the plantation where Talbot's slave depot is now located. This person was summoned before the Inquisition of Louisiana, and then suddenly vanished before the eyes of everyone, leaving dreadful traces behind in the city.

Although common sense rebels against all that is fabulous and mysterious, extraordinary events often give us the key to the unbelievable, and what is most improbable becomes true.

Thus in the following work.

New Orleans, 25 December 1853
THE AUTHOR

Prologue

NO CITY of the old or new continents, save perhaps for San Francisco and Calcutta, displays a greater panorama of peoples than New Orleans, the Queen of the South, ruler of the majestic Gulf of Mexico. Louisiana's most radiant city already had a stable, highly defined character when still under Spanish jurisdiction, and it retained that character under French rule beneath the scepter of Napoleon Bonaparte. The Castilian idiom, with its deep earnestness and quiet craving for pleasure, was never really more than a monochrome painting in contrast to the noisy disorder and flippant nonchalance of the French. Only after the Americans had solidly set foot here, after 1804, followed by more energetic trade and manufacture, did the character of our city melt into a desolate chaos of morals, languages, and customs. It became a true world city, taking on a thoroughly cosmopolitan appearance.

New Orleans is the spring from which so many thousands have drawn their wealth, but it is also a bitter cup of suffering, misery, and despair. New Orleans is now the prima donna of the South, the whore insatiable in her embraces, letting go of her victims only after the last drop of blood has been drained and their innermost marrow of life sucked dry. New Orleans is the great gambling den at whose roulette and faro wheels excited players consort day and night with the goddess of luck, from whom they receive in the end only a stab in the back. It is a vast grave for poor immigrants and the homeless, who can never extract themselves in time from the arms of this prostitute. Here the chains of a maligned race rattle day and night with no advocate for their human rights; they can expect such only from the North. Only rarely is there heard in this southern clime a weak echo of the shouts of revenge in the grove of Abington. No angels have yet appeared to our *Negritians* to announce the birth of a Toussaint L'Ouverture!

Poisonous mists arise from the palmetto swamps, and from the mighty live oaks ominous "Spanish moss" hangs like the hair of an old man, blowing in the wind. Up to Natchez and as far west as the source of the Red River, this marks the region of *yellow fever.*

How many hearts have beat their last here? How many tears have been poured out here? How many have looked about hopeless and despairing, feeling themselves alone and abandoned amid the chaotic hustle and bustle? New Orleans is the tree with the forbidden fruit; here the old snake extends its three-forked tongue as far as the Gulf shore and licks its frothy waves. Here life and death dance continuously with each another, each sinking into the other's arms. Whoever has not yet seen sin, come hither!

...

Horrid foolishness! I dreamed
I was Messiah,
And that I bore the great cross
With patience and fidelity.

Impoverished beauty is sore pressed,
But I shall make her free
From blame and sin, from torment and
want,
From the filthiness of the world.
[Romanzero]

New Orleans had not seen so magnificent a night in ages. The sickle of the waning moon seemed to float blissfully in the midst of the immeasurable sea of stars, and it held the entire city as if embraced in a golden frame. Happy was he who could lean over the veranda of his house on this enchanting night and look down on his garden to breathe in the scents of magnolia blossoms, kissed by the moon, or who could stand at the stern of his boat, spying through a sextant the light of his life in the midst of the forest of masts—they are to be envied tonight; they are the fortunate ones who are privileged to carry the starry train of the Queen of the South and view her face in its full glory. He is a nasty usurer with his feelings indeed who demands more of his life than to be truly happy for one night. For the one will be carried to the grave before his magnolias wither; and the other will soon float in rings around his wayward boat, a ghost, and he will be the herald of his own death on seeing his own flag flying at half-staff. What does it matter? They *were* happy once.

This evening is the first gift of a miserly divinity in several months; stars are being embroidered on a dark blue baldachin to shine on graves and paint the emptied streets with pale figures.

It was the 27th of April, 18—.

A tired pony trotted down Magazine Street bearing a figure on a loose saddle whose long legs almost scraped the ground, in complete contrast with its short upper body.

Despite the southern climate, the figure wore the head covering of a farmer from northern Missouri, a stiffened fur cap with hanging earflaps, a buffalo-hide vest covered by a wool blanket, high sportsmen's boots reaching to his thighs, and a red wool shirt whose open collar was marked at the corners with the crude insignia of a sailor's jacket.

He negligently let the reins lie loose on the neck and shaggy mane of the horse, which seemed to know the way precisely.

At this moment he turned at the next row of houses, suddenly revealing his face, illuminated by the moonlight. Just as suddenly, he shrouded his face in the darkness of the blanket, as if he feared to show himself, and he drew his fur cap down over his eyebrows. Then he lowered his head, pressing a kiss on two rosy lips and murmuring: "Diana Robert will already be in bed—we are there, my child—I cannot see any lights at the windows, we should go back and pass the night in the open."

"Oh, let's ride through the passageway and knock on the window, Hiram," a sweet voice responded. "I haven't slept for three nights—and I am deathly tired," it added with a sigh.

"Be still, my child," the cadaverous figure responded, "don't be upset with my excessive caution—consider that I am all too well known in this city—six years ago we only escaped from our enemies with great difficulty.

"Now, to be sure, it seems we have been forgotten, for once again, sin has spread its luxuriant tent, and many a beautiful young life will be sacrificed on the scaffold of its passions.

"Have patience, my child, you will be given back to the world, and—"

A soft arm wrapped around his neck suppressed his words. The rider now came to a complete stop.

He found himself before an old building with cracked columns and capitals eaten away by storm and weather. The windows were broken and weathered, and the interior rooms, where gold had once been counted, weighed, and discounted, were abandoned and desolate.

It was the Atchafalaya Bank,[1] two doors down from the Canal Bank,[2] but at the time these lines were written it was already gone. Two stately four-story brick buildings have replaced it, and in their interior the goods of the wealthy Mr. James are stored. Nemesis itself ruled over New Orleans only a few months ago, where merchandise now is being stored and bartered. Why was the building of the Atchafalaya Bank torn down? Was it speculation or—a whim? Neither of the two.

The building had to vanish, along with the lodgers who had lived in its rear room. On tearing it down, a worker discovered under the rubble a three-foot-high cross of iron, engraved with the insignia and symbols of the

Freemasons. This cross now decorates the grave of a great tolerator, a noble philanthropist much mourned by his brothers in the Order, who has only lain in consecrated soil for a few months.

His face is turned to the sun.

On finding himself in the courtyard, the rider dismounted and, his burden on his arm, carefully approached one of the small doors that led through a side passage into the main building.

The moon had now sunk below the horizon, and deep darkness enshrouded him.

"I have to turn them out of bed," he murmured to himself as he tapped his ring seven times on the windowpanes, forming a cross. Then he listened carefully, leaning his left ear against the crack in the window.

"God preserve us all!" he heard a choked voice. "That is *Hiram and his child*!"

"Keep quiet—we're not letting him in!" whispered a second voice.

"No! I'll open the door to him, otherwise he will take his revenge on us!"

In a few seconds the door groaned and the blanket-wrapped figure entered, still holding his burden on his arm.

"God preserve us all! Look at you, Hiram! You have a yellow mask over your face.

"Hiram, Hiram, you are up to no good. You are once more bringing great misery on our city! . . ."

Instead of answering, the gigantic, emaciated figure lifted the blanket from his child, and the black inhabitants of the room fled like shadows of the night before the splendor of this gleaming sun.

Outside the night had vanished; but as the sun-god rode his steed out of the bottoms of the Mississippi, his golden face was bedecked with a black veil.

Wringing her hands, a pale woman streaked through the streets of New Orleans, prophesying disaster.

The Queen of the South shuddered herself awake.

Book
I

Lucy Wilson

It is well known to most people who have lived for a long time in New Orleans that, with the arrival of darkness, no one is permitted to carry a bag or even a small packet on the streets, and only the most impressive credentials will spare one from the hands of the police and a night in the calaboose. It is a wise measure, since no city in the Union provides thieves more opportunities to rob and plunder than does this one.

Despite this, such illegal activities occur all too often, particularly in the western portions of the Second and Third Districts, since the strictest oversight is often not exercised here and the watch in this region is often in cahoots with the loafers and rowdies; still, this ban does restrain burglary and theft to some extent.

Just as is the case with all branches of legislation, where people endeavor with energy and slyness to subvert laws in a *legal* way, this is all the more so with the rules for conduct at night, and there are people in certain classes of society in New Orleans who consider it a great accomplishment to deceive the watch with the greatest possible impertinence or to defy them with limitless boldness.

One of these practiced violators of the law was a slender, tall young man with a trunk over his shoulder, who had rushed up Royal Street and run right into the arms of a watchman just as he was about to turn onto Orleans Street.

"How's it going, Jim?" the young man called out, not allowing himself to give the slightest sign of confusion at this unwelcome encounter. "'Tis almost two years since I saw you last, I'm back from California—don't want to leave my things on board overnight—here you can't trust anybody—'tis a damned den, that New Orleans! This loafer-trash would be in the position to take my hard-earned dollars right from under my head—I'd rather take it to my brother-in-law! Well, tomorrow you will be able to visit me first thing—no time now to wait here—you know my apartment, next to Colonel Macpherson!"

These words, spoken with cleverness, did not fail to have their effect. The watchman actually believed he had encountered an old friend, returned from California, though he could not recall his identity at the moment. The confident, friendly address, the "you can find me next to Colonel Macpherson," eliminated every possible doubt, so that the idea did not even occur to him that he was being deceived.

But after this supposed friend from California had called out another loud "Goodbye Jim!" he shot up Orleans Street like a fox being chased by hounds, despite his heavy load, disappearing into a run-down house that looked more like a den for bears or wolves than a dwelling for human beings.

This house, generally falling apart, had a large gabled roof dating back from the time when the first French had settled, and it was the anchor of a chain of houses or tenements in the French colonial style, which followed one another the length of the street.

Every stranger developed an odd feeling as he approached these dwellings, looking at their weathered house fronts with their flaking green paint and thinking of their time of origin.

A white face is seen only here and there in this area, for blackness alone sets the tone here. Whole houses can be rented here for a song, and no one should take too literally the half-torn notes, *"chambre garnie"* (furnished room), hung over the entrances, since the total furnishing usually consists of a humpback bed with a mosquito net of blue or sulphur yellow. Washing utensils have to be obtained every morning from the landlady—the managers are invariably women, usually widows.

The renters have to be single men, since these widows will not rent their rooms to a married person or even to a family.

Many a man who has come into this quarter with his better half to seek a cheaper place of rest has had to depart without success, upset after doors were slammed in his nose and he was heaped with curses. *"Seulement pour un garçon!"* is the motto here.

But it is now time for us to return to the house into which we saw our nightbird slip with his luggage.

This house, which directly fronts Orleans Street, is bordered on two sides by a fence consisting of coarse pickets, but it is overgrown with evergreen climbing vines, which permit no view into the inner space. The moon, which had hitherto been hidden, had just emerged from a black cloud in all its marvelous clarity, radiating a stage of strange coloration and complection.

In the courtyard is an image of the greatest disorder and neglect: a mess of washbasins, washboards, brooms, coffeepots, broken chairs and tables, a child's overturned cradle, etc.—all of it in colorful confusion, scattered across the entire courtyard.

On the gallery, which spread to a tasteless width at the rear of the house, two figures can be discerned: one of them that of the young man we saw enter, the other that of a woman between fifteen and nineteen years of age. She is of striking beauty and surprising height, and she is just now tying a long green scarf, which she has thrown over her head to protect herself from the rising wind. A long white blouse of *mousselin de laines,* much loved by the fair sex in New Orleans, is almost entirely covered by a ruby red silk shawl whose fringes touch the ground. Her raven black hair covers her shoulders with luxuriant fullness and slides down to her full breasts, only lightly covered, which continually move up and down in response to the slightest movement.

The dazzling whiteness of her face would lead a superficial observer to conclude that she was of white ancestry, a fact that a finer connoisseur would doubt on seeing the dark cloudiness of her fingernails and the mother-of-pearl coloration at the corners of her eyes.

And in fact *Lucy Wilson*—for that was the name of this beautiful woman—is the daughter of a planter on the Grand Bayou Caillon, a few miles from Lake Quitman, who had sired her with his favorite slave and freed her shortly before his own death, in keeping with a provision of his testament.

Lucy had been ten years old then.

She then went to Houma, a little town on the Bayou Petit Caillon, where she soon married a free mulatto by the name of Jean Aimé.

Both of them decided to go to New Orleans together to start a small business. But before she arrived in New Orleans, the inconstant Lucy fell in love with a Frenchman, and on her arrival in the great seaport she ditched poor Jean and vanished with the Frenchman.

In 1844 we find her living as Madame Wilson in Esplanade Street, owner of an important house that the Americans call the "Mulattoes' Settlement" on account of the yellow faces of the girls continually glimpsed through the windows. The upper floor, decorated by an iron verandah, shines with the most brilliant lights on winter nights, and from the street people can see the shadows of dancers sweeping against the red damask curtains. Madame Wilson gave the most magnificent balls, and she always had the best musicians.

Not everyone was allowed to set foot in the ballroom, and even the privileged were carefully searched to check for a hidden Bowie knife or revolver or any other dangerous weapon. Any that were found had to be handed over to the lady of the house.

When the Mulattoes' Settlement, then the most sought-after venue for gallant adventurers in New Orleans and the gathering place of the wildest Don Juans, burned down in 1846, Madame Wilson took the run-down house on Orleans Street, a dramatic contrast to the splendid Mulattoes' Settlement.

Even neighbors were unable to say what her source of income might be. Some believed that she held deposits for old, crippled slaves who were useless to their masters and were thus given to persons who would agree to care for them for sums as low as a hundred dollars. Others believed that she made her living stealing small Negro children, whom she was very good at winning over. Most people spoke of her as living by selling her charms, since she was occasionally able to exploit the wealth of a lovesick fool.

Now we find her together on the gallery of her house with the young man.

"Emil," Lucy began, turning to him, "you promised to be here before eight—what kept you so long? Did you perhaps have to make another important visit to Algiers?"

These words were spoken in a strong voice as she aimed her flashing eyes at his face, turning the corners of her mouth down in a mocking frown.

Visible embarrassment was printed on the facial expression of the young man. He seemed to consider something for a moment, for he passed his hand across his forehead, stamping a foot on the floor.

"That is your German character, Emil," Lucy continued, "since I do not have the best of reputations, people have pangs of conscience over me. Pangs of conscience, Emil! What connection does that have with your life otherwise?—That's how all you Germans are! On the one hand, you commit error after error, and on the other hand you fall into endless depression without being able to decide to do better. It is as if you commit sins entirely in order to have new material for worry and self-torment. Your brother was like that, even before he had the great misfortune that led to his death. He would be as easy-going as a Gascon market woman, and then—suddenly—at a wonderful party at our settlement, where everyone was dedicated to providing happy and joyous faces, he would hang his head and pursue his unhappy reveries—if you want to improve yourself, good! Go ahead, give up your unclean source of income and work along with the niggers on the plantations of proud, nasty Creoles. There you'll have a golden life—an unending source of enjoyment of all kinds! Then every evening you'll have the fine consolation of having earned your bread the whole day by the sweat of your brow, in keeping with the prescriptions of the Bible—oh, how blessed!"

"You speak as sanctimoniously as a Father of the Church," Emil responded without much thought.

"Still, Emil," Lucy continued, "whatever you want, want it *whole;* halfways have always disgusted me, whether in virtue or in vice. If I were a judge, I would only punish moderation—consistent, systematic scoundrels would have nothing to fear from me! Moderation is the greatest crime, and it should be punished the most severely.

"I would like to get to know your parents; you said they were coming across the ocean."

"Leave my parents alone!" Emil responded darkly.

He leaned against a post of the gallery, now seeming to inspect Lucy's beautiful breasts, then seeming to drift off into another world of his own thoughts.

It surprised Lucy that Emil, who in the past had always fallen into a rage when he was the object of such preaching and irony, now kept his peace and let all the references directed at him pass by. She was also surprised that he did not precipitate another one of those scenes in which they grew upset with each another only in order to enjoy the excitement of reconciliation. And what exactly was it that she was trying to accomplish with her harsh words? She loved the ecstasy. The rancor soon dissolved into oaths and kisses. To her, ordinary wooing and fondling were repellent; she scorned the individually launched rockets of a languorous encounter—with her powerful sensuality, she could only find satisfaction in a full barrage.

She was about to give her mute friend a new provocation to break his peace, but he abandoned his previous position with the words "Tonight I still have a duty to perform!" and ran off in haste.

"Fool!" Lucy thought to herself as she watched him go down the stairs as swift as an arrow. "He still has a duty to perform!—For whom? For his sentimental wife, or the pale shadow of his mistress?—Fool, robbing himself of such a beautiful night and preferring to go lie in official arms!—Pah, I concern myself too much for these German vagabonds—he is not worth the love of a real woman!"

She stood moaning for a few moments, closing her marvelous eyes as she tended to do in the divine play of an assignation, then opening them wide to spew lightning, bold as an infuriated maenad.

Was she tormented by injured pride or jealousy? Was it the hellish suffering of a supernatural sexual intoxication that raged in her? What could be the source of the flames that shot lightning from her eyes?

Lucy was as cold, sly, calculating, and sleek as a snake; she loved gold, she loved intrigue—but often she was stormy and unrestrained, particularly when she was prepared to enjoy an act of love.

So she had prepared for her friend's arrival today; for certain reasons she had even had him haul his necessities to her house under cover of darkness. She had so prepared herself all the day for the joys of this night that she now found it unbearable to have to renounce them due to her friend's stupid turn of mood or moral scruple. She had to divert herself. To the theater—St. Charles? Variétés? The French Opera? To the ball at the Hamburg Mill? Louisiana Ball? Fandango in Frenchmen Street?

Every imaginable enjoyment passed before her fantasy—but she could decide on nothing.

If she was to enjoy herself tonight, then it was necessary that Emil be her *cavaliere servente.* McDonogh himself would not have been able to gain entry to her tonight,[1] even if he were to weigh out his words in gold. All at once a baroque thought crossed her mind. She stepped back from the gallery into the room where Emil's trunk stood, and she tried to open it.

She was unable to do so. Recklessly giving in to her mood, she took a hatchet and split the lid in two.

Pieces of clothing, underwear, haberdashery, lacquered shoes—everything was torn from the trunk in haste, spread over the carpet, inspected and inspected again.

"So! That would be the proper wardrobe for me!" she cried as if mad, once she had set aside a complete man's outfit. "Everyone in the city recognizes him in these clothes; his wife recognizes him in this suit, and so does his pale shadow!—Wait, Emil, Lucy will have her revenge on you yet today!—Your sense of duty will cost you plenty!"

She stripped quickly, and in a few moments a second Emil stood in front of the mirror. She lacked only the blond hair and the comfortless German eyes.

"I shall meet you yet, somewhere or other," she said to herself, as she left the house and passed down Orleans Street, a polished dandy.

Chapter 2

The Masquerade

Lucy had no idea that, at the very moment she closed the courtyard door and left her house, she had been spotted and recognized by the very person for whom she was staging this carnival game.

Enthralled by the sweet obsession to play a truly great trick, she went her way.

Emil had in fact gone nearly halfway to his intended destination after leaving Lucy so precipitously, but then he had turned around and rushed back up Orleans Street.

He was one of those men who makes a decision quickly but is as likely to throw it aside just as quickly. Despite the fact that he had been glowing a few moments before to conscientiously fulfill some sort of obligation, he had now cooled off, and his thoughts drew him back to Lucy.

He inhaled deeply. Then he proceeded with slow steps, retracing the path he had taken in such a rush.

"She will laugh me to scorn," he said half to himself, "that she has always managed to triumph over my heart in all the accidents of life!

"What will my poor wife say when I keep my promises so poorly? Still—that could just as well take place some other time—she was able to live without seeing me for half a year, so her heart won't break this time. The prince of W[2] will be able to console her."

He sought to excuse himself in this and similar ways, in order to give free rein to his feelings for Lucy Wilson.

"How's it going, old boy?" a powerful voice greeted him in the midst of his revery. It came from a jovial young man who was shaking his hand in a rather abrupt manner. "Why does one see you so seldom these days?" he continued, "Where are you hiding yourself? What drives you about all the long night?—Only yesterday people were asking about you at Cassidy's[3]—I can assure you this, that Cassidy still has the best oysters in New Orleans—come along—first I have to pick up a nice pretty child—come on, come on, accompany me to her—We'll take her along to the Ladies' Salon and have a big meal of oysters and London porter—take one of these cigars—by jingo, Laborde and Caballero do have the best cigars in New Orleans—a damned fine leaf, that—huh?"[4]

Emil took the cigar, lit it on that of his talkative friend, but put the lit end in his mouth.

He corrected his error quickly, without his comrade noticing, with as much finesse as if he had not burned his lip.

"Yes, and just imagine, Eliza ran off last week with three hundred dollars. A pretty little sum, that—what? But I did not grow any gray hairs over that, I earn as much in two times twenty-four hours—one of us is not so green as to torment himself for weeks over a pittance of fifty dollars—Isn't that a pittance for a whole week of work?—what?—Yes, and just think, old buddy, we just gypped a couple perfect greenhorns, one of them had only been in America, that is, New Orleans, for two weeks (for one of us New Orleans *is* America)—and one of the greenhorns is a splendid young man—has all his pockets filled with gold! He cannot live without me now—he is of the opinion that he is fortunate to have found such a good friend immediately on his arrival in America—tell me, old friend, isn't that extraordinarily lovable and childish—no, there is nothing nicer than Germania's sons—you can always find heart and poetry with them."

"The greenhorn is dumb enough!" Emil declared phlegmatically.

"But damn it!" the other went on, "I thought you were asleep."

"I haven't been feeling well for several days," Emil said.

"An aorta surely burst in your heart, old Don Juan!"

"It is remarkable what you . . . look, look," he interrupted himself suddenly, rushing right across the street, "our Cocker!"

As the two of them made their way to safety on the other side of the street with as much dignity as possible, Emil quickly used the opportunity to relieve himself of his comrade, who was inconvenient at the moment.

He swiftly turned the corner and blended in with the crew of a fire engine, which had just rattled down the street. When he saw a second and third engine follow, blocking his way, he swung himself over one of them, perhaps to demonstrate he had once been a member of one of the crews.

Since he had made his acquaintance with Lucy Wilson, he had cast aside his red jacket and black belt, for the fire signal awoke him from his wonderful reveries too frequently. He preferred to play Adonis, and also he had enough to do controlling the raging elements within himself. He was much missed by his company, for he was one of the boldest and most daring fellows, and he never failed to elicit general amazement when he balanced on the narrowest gables, at a dizzying height, nimble as a cat, hose in hand, directing water on the most threatening point.

Emil went straightaway to the house, or rather to Lucy's old tenement. He was hardly three steps away when he saw a figure slip out of the courtyard door.

The blood that shot to his head when he saw her soon returned when he made a quick turn to the center of the street and recognized Lucy in his own clothing.

He first thought to follow her, but then he had a better idea.

After a bit of consideration, he had no doubt that she was seeking him in this costume in order to embarrass him or to play some trick on him. If that was the case, then she would visit the Hamburg Mill, where he regularly went at ten o'clock when he did not pass the evenings staying with her until one or two in the morning.

It was not long before he made a similar decision. He wanted to make the same gallant metamorphosis in order to await her at the same Mill, where he would probably meet her soon.

Her clothes fit him—he knew that; after quick musing, he measured his own waist with his hands, then checked himself from head to feet. His not overly wide but arched breast was also contemplated.

Anyone who saw him in such a pose, with such gesticulations, would have taken him for a young actor who was preparing himself for his first starring role and had gotten drunk the night before the performance. But, as it happened, no one noticed, with the exception of a few rats that ran across his lacquered shoes.

The whole undertaking would be easy to carry out after this inspection. There was only *one* problem in the way, which was how he was to get over the fencing of vines and thorny roses in women's clothing, for Lucy had taken the key.

It would be easy to climb in, he could see that. But after he had changed, it presented significant difficulties for him to get out without tearing to shreds the dress, petticoat, and other appurtenances of the fair sex.

He could not get into the rooms on the lower floor to climb from there through the windows, since these were barred and he had no idea where the key was kept. It seemed dangerous to him to let himself down from the upper story, on account of the night watch.

What was he to do?

After long musing, he finally decided, for want of an alternative, to lower himself from the upper story and risk being caught by the night watch.

As he was crossing the fence, he lost his hat, which remained hanging on a branch reaching over the street.

He seemed not to notice this in his zeal.

In order not to cause undue alarm for Lucy's gray-headed Negroes, who lived in a shanty pitched in the courtyard, he informed them of his plan.

The old niggers were entirely amused by their young master's notion, particularly since he pressed a Spanish dollar into each one's hands.

When Emil found his trunk so pitilessly split and its contents scattered all over the floor, he froze for a moment, stunned. He was as surprised as he had been when he had first glimpsed Lucy costumed, since he had not considered how she had come into possession of his clothing. He was offended at her high-handed manner with his property, which he had placed under her protection. But this upset only lasted a little while, and then he continued carrying out his plan with the same liveliness with which he had first made his original decision.

Emil was pretty. Perhaps too pretty for a man. Even Apollo's clear, pure face would have turned yellow with envy at the sight of this ideal body with its elastic shape and roundness of limbs. Phidias would have thrown away his mallet in shame, and the Venus de Medici would not have hidden her charms with her hands, or rather she would have fallen about Emil's neck at first glimpse.

If Lucy had seen him now, standing half-naked in front of the full-length mirror, moving his upper body back and forth on his elastic, full haunches as he sought to press his arm through a sleeve that was a bit too narrow for a man's arm—she would have gone half mad. And Emil? Emil had not lowered his thyrsus-staff, and if Leda's swan had been female this time, Juno rather than Zeus would have abandoned Olympus and descended to earth.

True beauty always deserves our wonder, whether it gleams from a woman or a man. It's all the same! Whether it is a whim or a perversity of Mother Nature, she bestows her full gifts only on those who are regarded in social life as decadents and ne'er-do-wells, who waste their lives wandering from one day to the next in careless indifference. Who has ever seen a beautiful banker, a beautiful grocer, a beautiful established citizen, a beautiful newspaper editor, and so on? Certainly no one.

Vice has to have a beautiful exterior on this earth in order to put virtue to shame. So heaven has glittering stars, sun, moon, and comets as its court, in order to hide the empty spaces of its interior . . .

Emil had completed his ensemble.

A straw-colored dress of satin with an extended, segmented bodice set with black lace and beads was most becoming on him. His blond hair had been parted in the middle, combed on both sides so as to cling to his forehead, and from there descended to his ears. He almost had a problem with Lucy's shoes because they were—too large for him. Lucy had small feet, but Emil's were even smaller.

The head covering he chose was entirely in keeping with the rest of the ensemble in its elegance. He looked like a young lady of the court, pretty as a picture, suitable to be led on the arm of a dutiful chamberlain into the chamber of her mistress.[5]

Everywhere prose—which is epidemic in America—has invaded the halls of poetry. It was unfortunately the case here as well.

Downstairs, a savior of his country, which the Germans so charmingly call the *Nachtwatsch,* was already awaiting our friend with impatience.

He had seen him pass over the fence, and he had already seized his hat, which had been left on the outward branches. Since he was sure that something evil was afoot—for, incidentally, the watch was obsessed with keeping an eye on Lucy Wilson's house—he waited patiently for a little while for some fruit for this leaping. Finally he grew impatient and was about to knock on the courtyard door when he saw one of the windows to the street open and a feminine figure appear and start to let herself down on a rope. Even before Emil touched the ground with his feet, he felt a muscular arm around his bodice, which, incidentally, was not making his tender acquaintance for the first time.

Chapter 3

Two Sisters

Several weeks have passed. January 8th,[6] the most celebrated day in New Orleans after the Fourth of July, could not be observed this year with the proper pomp, since a steady rain had continued for a month and undermined all preparations for it. The fireworks that had been planned to close the joy and celebrations of the day, under the direction of Professor Müller, had to be omitted, and due to rain and wind it was cannons alone that proclaimed the undying glory of our beloved general. All the houses in Jacksonburgh were illuminated, and the rich planters whose holdings lay between Bayou Bienvenue and the left bank of the Mississippi left their proud cottages and villas and came to Versailles, where they celebrated with their equals a day immortal in the annals of the South. In New Orleans itself, people could make out little of the celebration other than the sounding of cannons and the frequent display of the Star-Spangled Banner. Only the youngsters fired off thousands of firecrackers and blasted away with their guns and pistols on the open streets until early morning, doing what they pleased the whole night through.

Today, however, would have been perfect for a festival, for New Orleans had not seen such a beautiful, clear sky for many weeks. Merry busyness and pushing predominated once more in the French Market. Here the nations buzzed together like an anthill. Black, yellow, white, brown, and red families—all colors mingled together like a colorful mosaic And it was still early in the day; the sun had just risen from the hollows, breaking through the mists in its peculiar violet glory. A fresh morning breeze stirred, and soon the sun rose with all its royal splendor, spreading its purple mantle and dropping it in the yellow flood of the old stream. The air vibrated with joy. People quickly forgot the many dark, rainy days—nothing but happy and cheerful faces as far as the eye could see! The first ray of the sun conjured up life in an instant from all directions. Now we want to concentrate on *one* image, since it is impossible to traverse the entire city at this early morning hour. We mean the *French Market.*

Despite the winter month, Pomona had generously emptied out her cornucopia. From the tiny hickory nut to the hairy fruit of the coconut palm, from the fine apples to the splendid golden orange, from the short babas to the bunches of pisang figs or bananas, shaped like grape-clusters; apples, pineapples, lemons, oranges—all presented in great pyramids, with bobbing diadems and garlands of large Levantine figs in between. Costly flowers flourished among aromatic vegetables of all sorts, seducing many a buyer through their beauty to linger here a bit longer, causing their gaze to move from the flowers to the vegetables, for the floral decorations had been placed with that in mind. Several rows of cactus stood like stern guardians around the smaller flowerpots; a gigantic *Cereus grandiflorus* stood sad and closed among her sisters. Perhaps she dreamed of her coming splendor as the enchanting queen of the night!

Everywhere women were selling, but rather few men were present. Broad-shouldered Negro women with their orange-colored, bright red, or green-striped headcloths; Mulatto and Negro girls with their swiveling gait and precocious gaze; grotesquely made-up French women who violated the usual quiet, cursing one another or throwing pieces of fruit; Indians offering healing herbs, their women hiding much in baskets on their backs, holding a suckling baby as they crouched on the stone floor of the market hall, only half-covering their nakedness, allowing the curious to gape and inspect their bodies. There were German girls, working their way shyly through the colorful press with their little market baskets, soon departing the market hall in disappointment because they could not find the ingredients for German cuisine. There were Irish women with copper-colored noses and swollen mouths, who cursed and shouted in competition with fat, thick-necked Negresses. There were drinkers of coffee, tea, and chocolate, contemplating themselves reflected twenty-fold in the mirrors opposite them during breakfast before bustling away, leaving their chairs for others, and so on. All of this rotated about the head of the onlooker like a wild carousel.

Among those lucky enough to have completed their purchases and be on their way home were two elegantly clothed ladies, followed at a respectful distance by a Negro youth with a basket on his arm and a net in one hand. Besides various baked goods, some oranges and bananas were in the basket, probably destined for dessert. In the net were a few bunches of red radishes, which looked cheerful and inviting in the midst of green, fresh lettuce. The youth followed, singing and whistling to the young ladies, who were proceeding along the levee to await the return of the ferry that would take them to Algiers.[7]

As the boat paused on the opposite shore, the little Negro was subjected to a brief examination from one of the ladies.

"Tiberius," began the younger one, who had beautiful black hair and dreamy eyes of deep blue, "put down the basket and the net on these cotton bales and come closer." The Negro did it at once what he was bidden. He approached the two ladies with his cap in his hand.

"Tell me, Tiberius, whether you met Mr. R* at his home when you delivered the note?"

"Yes, Madame!"

"Can you recall what this gentleman was doing, and whether he was dressed to go out?"

"I know nothing except that he was stretched out on the sofa in shirt-sleeves, leafing through a little book—while a tall lady sat at the window weeping, for her eyes were quite red, and she turned her head away as I entered."

The two ladies looked at each other in shock. Then the same one spoke again: "Did the gentleman say anything further to you when you left?"

The short fellow was silent a moment, then he finally stuttered: "Massa said to me as I went out to say nothing about the lady I saw with him. I had to promise him that I would say nothing."

"So you broke your word, you little scoundrel!" she threatened him mockingly with her finger.

"Then you shouldn't have asked me, Madame," Tiberius responded naively.

"Well, if you go back there, and he asks you whether you revealed anything, what will you say?"

"Then . . . I'll say . . . that I said nothing about the lady."

"That is improper, Tiberius, you must always speak the truth!"

"So I am allowed to say that to Massa?"

The lady was distressed by this question, and in order to put an end to the discussion she ordered the little fellow back to his place. Then she turned to the other, sighing and speaking with a strained, sad voice, "So she is with him again—and he had promised you so solemnly not to see her again! Oh how unhappy I am!"

"Console yourself, dear sister," the other began, "what I always predicted has come to pass. Never believe he will give up that disreputable woman so long as she is in the vicinity. I know him all too well. He could promise it to you a thousand times over, reinforced by the holiest oaths—once he turns his back to you, he will forget everything. Look—my precious Jenny, follow my well-intentioned advice at last and let's go back to our country. Your sick heart can only recover health on native soil, and there you will be safe from shame and misery. Dear, good Jenny, we are both companions in sorrow! I with my husband, who has abandoned me so callously and has not sent me a word in two years—without any concern for whether I am well or whether I am ruined, and you with your own husband, who continually proclaims his love to you through his hot tears and promises to do better, and then—oh—we are both unhappy creatures!"

"Oh, don't talk about leaving, dear sister! How could I bring myself to leave my husband? No matter how bad he is, he remains my husband—perhaps he loves me yet—only his frivolity makes him so often untrue. Oh, he will yet come to himself and become a faithful, loving husband! There are so many examples of such men. Do you know the story of Count A*—it was exactly that way with *him,* in the first years of his marriage he was wild, clumsy, committed indiscretion on indiscretion . . . they began speaking of divorce, and now neither can live without the other. You read it to me yourself in the letters from Germany . . . What, isn't that so?"

During the conversation, the steamboat had returned to the near shore, and the two sisters boarded along with little Tiberius, and in a few minutes they were in Algiers, where they had chosen to reside only a short time before. We will escort them home.

Barely a hundred feet to the left of the landing, not far from the bank of the Mississippi, a lovable cottage stands separated from the other buildings. It is located in the midst of a large garden, decorated by a significant number of orange trees, all their branches groaning under the burden of their golden fruit, together with *arbor vitae* trees, shaped like pyramids, and slender oleanders. The orange trees formed a shadowed pathway to the front door, separating there to the right and left before rejoining at the back of the house. Between the orange trees stood luxurious rosebushes with the lushest green color and the fullest of blossoms. The splendid landscape offered a most surprising sight to passers-by. If a stranger came here from the eastern or northwestern states, where everything was frozen with cold and buried in heavy snow at this time of year, he would think himself touched by a magic wand and imagine that a generous fairy had taken residence here. With joy he would breathe in the vanilla aroma of the tea-rose, displaying its most wonderful blossom. He would look in longing on the bright red, violet, or white balsamins, so sensually called "lady slippers" in

English. He would also not overlook the dark red lychnids, the significant "bachelor buttons," which is the American woman's favorite flower. Wherever lady slippers and bachelor buttons are to be found together, rest is assured! The greatest order and neatness reigns in such a garden. There is no grass or weed, hardly even a stray leaf to be seen on the clean, hard-rolled garden paths. Following both good taste and poetry, the paths are not set with bricks, such as one finds in all American gardens, which always gives even the most beautiful layouts a hint of stiffness and lifelessness. On the north, next to the cottage, whose exterior is painted a silver-gray and supplied with bright green shutters, stands a water tank of dark green, bound with heavy iron bands, into which a gutter of the same color, running around the entire house, delivers rainwater, which can then be tapped by a cock on the bottom of the tank. Other than the Mississippi, rainwater is the only drinkable water in New Orleans and its environs. We are taking the greatest care to mention every detail concerning this place, since it will be the theater for so many events in our *Mysteries.*

The two sisters, *Jenny* and *Frida,* had just entered the open garden gate and, after giving Tiberius some duties and orders for the house and kitchen, they passed to the upper story via a narrow but quite elegant stairway whose steps were covered with carpet worked in green and red—the standard decoration for steps of fashionable homes. The side walls and the stairwell were covered with pale green tapestry. On arriving above, the sisters were greeted by their emerald green parrot, who hopped from ring to ring in his massive, palatial cage, energetic and happy. "*Estrella mia—guerida mia,* ho, ho, ho—*Señor Caballero,* ho, ho, ho!—ho, ho, no understand!" Then he squawked and twisted his tongue, as if wanting to laugh.

"Just you wait, *Papchen*!" the sisters cried out, as they stepped up to the bird's cage almost at the same instant, threatening him with their fingers. The loudmouth must have understood, fearing a severe lesson, since he rubbed his head on the bars, bowed his body, and shrieked, "Good morning, lovely ladies! How are Jenny and Frida today?"

"That's right, *Papchen,*" both of them chattered away with the bird, "You shouldn't speak Spanish anymore!" As they said this, each stuck a little finger through the brass bars and let him chew at them, which was no small repayment to the parrot and must have been stimulating to the ladies as well.

"But the sun is shining in *Papchen*'s face," Frida, the blonde, began, "I'll put the shawl around his cage—there, there—that's right—now you can sleep a bit, little parrot."

"Sleep—good night!" the little parrot squawked. "Ho, ho, ho—*Señor*

Caballero, ho, ho, ho!" he screamed once more after the sisters, though they had already reached the drawing room.

"Was Emil here?" Jenny began with bated breath, looking at her sister, "*Papchen* chatters too much today about a *señor.*"

"How could you even think that?" Frida responded with an emphatic tone she did not believe herself, "What would he be doing here? And—besides, he would not dare come here, since he knows I'm here, and he would be afraid of my reproaches. If only that bird could quit saying *Señor!* It continually reminds me of the silly obsession your husband had about playing the Spaniard, yet—let's not talk about that—what, Jenny? You're weeping again? Jenny, come and kiss me, but don't cry!"

With tears of concern in her eyes, Frida approached her sister, who had sunk down into a rocking chair. She stroked Jenny's somewhat loosened hair back from her pure forehead and planted a kiss there. "You are too concerned about it, dear sister," she continued. "Come and sit down at the piano and sing me the pretty little song you learned from little Elise. I like it all too much, although I usually cannot stand to listen to English. This fits our current mood so well—and you sing it so beautifully!" she added as a compliment. "Good sister, do it to please me, please?"

"Out of love for you I shall sing it, although I would rather weep," Jenny declared, raising herself with charming effort and stepping to the open piano. Frida sat with her sister, rolling over a small chair.

The sister now sang with profound feeling, with the enchanting purity of a developed voice:

> Bring back the days, the sunny hours,
> Of girlhood's thoughtless glee;
> The placid stream, the opening flowers—
> Oh! bring them back to me,
> The noontide walks, the hallowed eve,
> The loved, the lost—That brow
> On which love sat like sunset's leave . . .
> Oh! bring them to me now.
> Where is my home . . . my girlhood's home
> Of sweetness? Has it fled!
> Alas! 'tis gone! The . . .

Here the unhappy singer broke into tears and fell on Frida's neck. After she had calmed herself somewhat, her sister asked her to finish the song. After some resistance, she resumed the interrupted verse, repeating the last lines with determined voice:

Alas! 'tis gone! The joyous tone
Of its lost cadence dead.
Bring me the happy scenes, which there
Passed like a summer's dream . . .
The soft'ning tints of memory,
Ere sorrowing o'er me came.
O, let me dream I see it still,
With bird and sun and flower;
'T will serve to soothe a treasured will
In this and trying hour.
Home of my youth . . . farewell . . . farewell!
Once did I hail your glee;
Painful as in the bosom's swell . . .
Oh! bring it still to me!

When she had completed these verses, the two sisters sank into each other's arms, kissing with stormy enthusiasm. They loved each other so much, and when one did something pleasing, the other sister always had a garland for the other's brow. Each doted on the other's beauty: while Frida admired her sister's dark eyes, Jenny forgot her unhappy fate and her trying plaints over a faithless husband with a glance at Frida's bright eyes, from which shone a whole heaven of blessedness. In short—the two were totally crazy about each other, as people were accustomed to saying.

Seeing them at this instant, bathed in the green shimmer of light created by the blinds, on whose linen surface was painted a dark, primeval forest with a Turkish city in the foreground, from which numberless minarets of mosques peeked, one would be forced to think of the charming sisters Scheherazade once described in the sultan's bed in *A Thousand and One Nights.*

On a round table that stood in the middle of the room lay an album with a chrysalis-green binding of Moroccan leather, open to reveal a watercolor landscape of southern Germany, a castle built in Renaissance style on a high cliff, about whose base sprang a dark evergreen forest through which ran a small river, threading through a lovely valley of lush meadows and ripe grain. To one side of a small bridge could be seen a weathered stone cross on which hung a wreath of colorful wildflowers. The entire landscape was permeated with a gentle rose-colored mist, which could hold a connoisseur's gaze for hours. At the bottom on the right, in the dark shadow of a copse of trees, the name Frida with the year 1845 could be read.

Next to this album, several butterflies were pinned to a red satin pillow with great care, including two "argonauts," splendidly gleaming in the deepest lapis lazuli blue. Next to these was a jar with bugs who had found their death in the alcohol it contained. On the stopper of the jar was pinned a mass of small *neuroptera* and many-colored flies. The sight of these creatures would be enough to convince anyone that the lovely inhabitants of this house were entomologists. This was not true. These insects had been gathered for Prince Paul of Württemberg, who was wont to visit Algiers from New Orleans to receive them from the charming hands of these collectors when he returned from his hunts for flora and fauna. Since Citizen Paul had not visited for some time, the collection had grown significantly.

The sun rose ever higher and higher in the eastern heaven, and now it bore down on the cottage with its full force. Outside in the garden, hundreds of grasshoppers and cicadas chirped and shrieked. When this was added to the monotonous droning of flies at the window who had lost themselves in the curtains and could not find their way out, it lulled the two sisters to sleep. They had made the long trip to the French Market and back, and they had not been able to recover adequately at the piano. Frida with her head pressed into her sister's lap, Jenny with her lips on Frida's full neck—thus they had fallen asleep. Repeated knocking on the door soon awoke them from their slumber.

They shrank back in shock.

Chapter 4

A Night after the Honeymoon

Before we allow the person who knocked on the drawing room door and disturbed the two sisters' sweet slumber to enter, we must present to the reader's intellectual eye a domestic scene that took place on one of the most distant streets the night before, across the river from Algiers in New Orleans. We bring the reader to that part of the town which happens to be the place of residence and nursery for thousands of goats, who wander about undisturbed, taking their sparse meals on the edge of streets and in the scattered green squares. This quarter, which seems dedicated to Esmeralda, supplies the entire city with the milk of these particular beasts. Led by a lady or a small girl, they are brought to the doorsteps of their customers so that everyone receives his specific ration milked directly into a vessel made for that purpose. This way, the customers receive their milk pure and unadulterated, and none need fear that they have been cheated. This goat district lies in the First Municipality, and it reaches from Claiborne Street west to the furthest two streets parallel to it, limited by Bienville and Conti Streets.

It was one of those magnificent nights normally found only in the tropics, when the moon shines in full, majestic clarity in the sky, so that the night is made almost into day, and the stars, the moon's silent companions, enchant the heart with unending longing through their planetary glow. A warm zephyr blowing from the Gulf, causing one to forget what time of year it was, played in the rows of trees that pass down Claiborne Street, slipping over the wall of the nearby churchyards and kissing the tops of the lilacs and cypresses there. It was one of those nights when the loving heart feels so happy that it flees its restrictive home and flies out into the great pure arch of the heavens in order to struggle against its own inclinations, far from vanity and distraction, to reveal its secret desires to a nature undefiled. Along the wall of one of the churchyards there slowly walked a slim female figure of medium height who presented an enchanting sight in the full glow of the moon. Under her snow white bonnet, whose two ties swayed back and forth in the gentle breeze, one could see a finely carved face of the most beautiful proportions, whose pure paleness reminded one of an ancient cameo. Her dark blonde hair, braided à la Fleur-de-Marie,[8] compensated somewhat for the moderate thinness of her face, insofar as it provided a frame a good two inches wide, making her face appear fuller than it in fact was. In one hand she held a simple palmetto fan, covering her face with it from time to time to hide from passers-by the tears streaming from her large, bright blue eyes. About her shoulders was draped a gray silk mantilla, which she mechanically held in place with her left hand.

A man was walking several paces ahead of her, now and then murmuring a word and blowing out long plumes of blue smoke from his Havana into the warm night. A small Panama hat with a black silk band sat far back on his neck, showing his high forehead, over which he frequently passed a hand, witnessing to his considerable vanity. His total ensemble consisted of a cravat loosely thrown about his collar, a light brown coat, and broad trousers of the same material. A full, tanned face with short black waxed mustache, an open shirt that revealed almost half his naked chest, and long hair in a disorder that seemed intentional all gave him a free and unbounded appearance. Every time he removed his cigar from his mouth, replaced it, or flicked off ash with his index finger, he gazed at his own fingers with obvious self-satisfaction.

The two had probably been walking this far apart for a good quarter hour without exchanging a word between them. It was obvious that they knew each other and must not be mutually indifferent. They were a pair of lovers who were upset with each other, for whatever reason. The tears in the woman's eyes allowed the conclusion that there had been a quarrel, which the young man's affected behavior only confirmed all the more. Any doubt that they belonged together disappeared at once when the young man suddenly stopped and allowed the woman to catch up with him.

"But Claudine," he began in an irritated tone, "you are going so slowly that we will need another hour to get home. I should long since have been at my work, since it is supposed to be completed tomorrow at noon, and besides that I made the most precise promise to the two ladies in Algiers—I see already that I must once more give you my arm, otherwise we will never get underway." At these words, he drew out his watch, looked at it, and impatiently put it away.

The young lady silently hung on the arm of her companion, who rushed forward without paying attention to her own smaller steps.

So they went for several hundred more steps, until they reached the block where their home was located. The house, which also contained another family, of Irish origin, lay all the way at the back of a courtyard whose entrance was blocked by a large gate made of pickets. On the inner side of the gate was a bar as thick as an arm, which was usually placed there at eleven to block the entrance. People must not have noticed the couple was gone and thought they were sleeping, as they found the door blocked. After the young man kicked the gate several times with his foot and rattled it with his hands, several dogs began barking and ran to the gate. Their alarm was stilled the instant they recognized the new arrivals. A light could be seen in the room of the landlord, a bachelor who lived in the building, and soon they were able to enter and cross the courtyard into their own home. On the stairway they met a little girl who had fallen asleep in their absence, and she apologized for not having lit any lamps, since she had misplaced the matches. Soon they were able to find what was necessary, and the young *married couple* sat at a table that had been set for them three hours before, on which was placed a tea maker that soon brought its water to a boil with a spirit lamp. In a silver basket there were some cut pieces of a cake the wife had baked herself yesterday—and on top of it was the young woman's embroidery.

"Claudine, take that embroidery out of the basket; it doesn't belong there. I've often told you I cannot stand this sort of disorder," the young man said, interrupting the silence.

"Albert," the young woman responded, "don't be so irritable, and don't get upset over such unimportant matters. You only started to be quite unpleasant to me again today, while we were on our walk; if that's how you are going to act, then I'll never go out with you again—be sure of it!" As she spoke, she took on a threatening manner, a pose that happened to be her very favorite.

"You are talking," Albert responded, forcing a smile, "as if I had to convince you to go out. Wasn't the truth that you would not leave me in peace until I put all my work aside in order to comply with your pressing wishes? Look how clever you are! Now you want to turn the matter into its opposite."

The young woman, who could be described as genuinely beautiful—for no one had a more lovely or charming mouth, no one had smaller or more gleaming teeth, no one a whiter or more truly aristocratic hand—fell silent for a moment, then responded in a depressed tone, looking her husband directly in the face:

"For several days now, I no longer understand you, my dear Albert; so cold, so rejecting, always an ironic smile on your lips, no more hearty acceptance, not the slightest sign of the attentions with which you showered me before—everything has vanished! May God grant that it is only a transitory mood, since otherwise I am in despair! If I seek even a small kindness, you are both irritated and hostile. Once, when you were on your way out, you first gave me a kiss; when you returned home, you overwhelmed me with tenderness and could not kiss me often enough. And now—now you barely tell me goodbye and often stay out late into the night and are irritated when you still find me out of bed."

"You know, of course," her spouse remarked lightly as he stood and selected a cigar from the mantel, "marriage is the grave of love. I will bring you my favorites, Saphir and Oettinger, from Schwarz's lending-library tomorrow and read you a chapter on this subject.[9] Are you satisfied, little Claudia?"

That was simply more than this good-natured woman, who had been utterly committed to her husband up to that time, could bear.

Such phrases as these could easily be used in the course of a delicately managed conversation in a completely harmonious mood, but when they are suddenly blurted out without any preparation, and at a moment when it had still been possible to turn the mutual disharmony of their feelings into something tender, they will injure a sensitive soul. In fact, the memory of something like this can linger for a lifetime. In any case, it was not meant all that seriously, but it still demonstrated a great deal of indifference and coarseness on her spouse's part. In fact, if we assume it was not on purpose, it showed a complete ignorance of the female heart.

We will later see what momentous results this blurted-out "truth" would have on the domestic life of this married couple. In critical moments, nothing injures so much as the truth, for it hurts more severely than a lie. One can easily imagine this woman's position, who, out of her concern for her husband's indifference, consoles herself with the hope that his attitude is only a passing phase, and that his earlier affection and intimacy would return. Now she sees cold words resolving the riddle of marriage and love. She would not have been more fatally wounded by an Indian's poisoned arrow.

Albert was, on the whole, an ambitious and hard-working man who took care of a husband's financial obligations faithfully, and he sat night after night at his architectural plans and other sketches. But that was all. He had been spoiled in early youth and was a roué in the extreme, so as soon as the magic of the honeymoon had dissipated, he returned to his old phlegmatic state, from which only a fresh beauty could rouse him. Perhaps he already bore another's image in his heart, and so he played the tormenting and exhausting role of an adulterer of the spirit. Although honorable of character, strong, and experienced in carrying out his plans, in erotic matters he was one of those protean types of which there are thousands in the effeminate classes of Europe's aristocracy. His energy and iron persistence in matters of business had thus far saved him from the moral abyss into which unemployed roués unfailingly fall. His restless activity, supported by his robust health, protected him from shortage of money, so that he had never had occasion to enter into a dishonorable business arrangement. But we will soon see him in a situation profoundly different from his present one, and he will be almost beyond recognition.

Something else must still be mentioned here, something that would eventually have dealt a deathblow to the love of this man, who often made overly great pretenses concerning the fair sex, even if he still loved his wife with the same intensity and dedication as before. Albert was of German origin, and Claudine was French. With a husband such as Albert, only spirited engagement could have prevented the utter cooling of their love, and he could not manage this with Claudine. Although he spoke excellent French, he usually failed to strike on the most spirited phrases. Once the first rush of sensuality is past and love cannot speak in its native language, there is a natural inclination to lower the temperature. One speaks in vain of the beloved's worth, since an alien language cannot completely make it known, and distrust or indifference eats ever deeper into the heart. One learns little or nothing of the positive qualities of the other, and in short husband and wife remain foreigners to each other even in marriage.

It is extraordinarily rare for spouses to be happy when they do not speak the same language. They normally function as little more than automata on public display, bound together by an arbitrary contract, and the children of such parents are always odd, at best traitors to their national self-awareness.

But enough of philosophy; we would rather take up the romantic threads once more.

Pale as a marble statue, Claudine rose from her chair and sat down on a love seat in the corner. She was deeply offended. Total contempt had taken the place of her pain, and her features expressed this attitude all too clearly. In the spirit she searched her past and came to understand that this man had never really loved her, that his wooing of her had simply been a matter of plucking a fragrant flower just so that it would wither without his attention. She was now assured of the truth to the words he had just spoken, and in the place of her contempt there grew a sense of injured pride she had never known before, for she had taken to her breast a man she thought had loved her.

Albert, who had just risen from his chair to return to his usual work, noted with astonishment the proud glare and cold contempt that expressed itself in her pose when he happened to catch his wife's eye. He, the smooth, slick lover, who normally had a thousand tricks up his sleeve to soothe an irritated woman and bring her back into his arms, now did not dare speak even one word to her. He went into the neighboring room, where he told the maid to prepare the large crystal lamp and to make ready another small fireplace, since he had been suddenly chilled as the north wind replaced warm Gulf breezes. Then he ordered the girl to prepare a couple of glasses of grog and bring them to his room. He assumed this drink would reverse his cross mood, putting him into a positive frame of mind for his drawing. He was totally wrong about this. The liquor guided his imagination in precisely the direction he wished to avoid, and in lurid colors it painted the horrors his reckless behavior might bring. Then he felt painful stimulation in his limbs, and desire rose up in revenge with all its enchantment and magic. As if he were bathed in welling mists of incense, sensuality now clouded his eyes. He let fall the pencil he had taken up several times to finish his drawing, and now he brooded, head sunk on his chest, over—*the beauty of his wife.*

She had never seemed more beautiful to him—even on their wedding night, her virginal charms had not injected greater excitement into his veins than did *his wife* at this moment. He loved variety in his physical enjoyments. Until now he had held a love-intoxicated Venus in his arms, but now he even wanted to embrace once more the cold marble she had become. His wife now seemed more beautiful than ever, with her proud stare and cold contempt, than she had with enticing eyes and burning lips. His eyes flickered, and his head seemed ready to burst at the thought of a liaison. He pressed his head with all his might against the sharp corner of a table, as if he were trying to squeeze the blood out of it; he let his lips hang open, and he wallowed in a decadent chaos of images of every sort. He felt that he could no longer endure this condition. He had to make a rash decision. In his mind he was already throwing himself at the feet of his disdainful Claudine and beseeching her to forgive him and grant him her love once more.

Then he suddenly stood erect and pounded his forehead with his clenched fist, breaking into a Satanic laugh: "Greenhorn that I am," he started to converse with himself, "that I still am, I cast up the most wonderful, overheated images, torment myself with the most fantastic images of what divine enjoyment I would have if I could still take her in my arms this evening, and I don't even consider that to win this boon she would first have to forgive me, in which case I would have the same old friendly eyes and normally colored cheeks before me. Nature is indeed cursed with eternal contradictions and deceptions! First nature shows me a goddess chiseled out of alabaster with a strict, cold stare and proud countenance, shows me an earnest Minerva who turns back into a waiflike Venus in my arms. If only one could enjoy that creature we know as woman in all her phases! This cheat nature, who grants us her most beautiful gifts only in our imagination and never in naked actuality! Yes, we are only born with our powerful sensuality in order to rave unceasingly about love—otherwise it is nothing! Love does not grant us an ordinary pleasure for once, such as we might have at any well-set table. It is enough to drive one mad!"

In this manner he disputed with himself for a while longer before turning to his work, seemingly satisfied. But he didn't manage to get anything done. He reached for the compass instead of a T-square, and instead of an ordinate he drew a circle. Indeed, in his preoccupied state he took up an old casting plan long since set aside, and he set about calculating the gears of a machine that had been figured months ago, whose models were already at the foundry. He threw it all aside in disgust, sank down in his chair, and thoughtlessly stared at the half-closed door that separated him from his wife's bedroom.

He sat musing for a while, then he thought he could hear the closing of the other door of the bedroom, which led to a hallway. He listened carefully. The light in the bedroom was gone. At the same moment he heard the door of the outer room open and quietly close. He picked up the tall crystal lamp and opened the door. Everything was gone. Neither the maid nor his wife were there. As he looked around he saw that one pillow was gone too. The down comforter his wife normally covered herself with was also not to be seen. She must be making her bed in the outer room this evening. He set the lamp on the table and went to the window, which he opened, allowing the fresh air to cool the burning fever of his brow. He was still undecided about whether to speak with his wife this evening. After long consideration, he decided not.

Before he went to sleep—midnight was long past—he reached into his bookcase and fetched Lord Byron, his faithful but perilous companion since his wedding. He opened to his favorite canto in *Don Juan,* feeding heart and soul with the bright, shining mirage of this poet:

> How can a wife still satisfy lust,
> Since sin cannot be found in a wife's kiss?
> Could Petrarch love his Laura as wife—
> He never would have written a sonnet in his life!

When we look in on Claudine, we find her sealing a letter, which the maid is to take with her in the morning on her way to the market. From the following laconic lines, the reader can see the decision she has made and learn much of both spouses' futures:

Madame
la baronne Alma de St. Marie Église
New Orleans, Rue de Bourbon no. 135.

Dear aunt!

I want to speak with you as soon as possible concerning an important matter. If you would be so good as to have an hour to spare in which I might visit you? Prepare to learn something extraordinary, and stiffen your courage until the moment of our meeting. There are situations in life for which one can never be adequately prepared. In any case I believe that you will once more be a rescuing guardian angel with your usual openheartedness and goodness. With deepest respect I kiss your hand, your

Claudine R——n
née de Lesuire

The person to whom these lines were directed is an old, respectable lady who, besides a few of the minor failings of her sex, has the great weakness of being somewhat obsessed over her aristocratic origins. Whoever violated her aristocratic pretensions even in the slightest immediately lost her favor. Although she could not really be called rich, she owned three houses in Bourbon Street and a *volante* with two horses. A mulatto she just obtained through an inheritance completes her half-dozen slaves. She belonged to that French clique in New Orleans that could still boast of the hereditary titles they brought with them in the period of the emigration. This considerable clique of French aristocrats, which excludes even the richer Americans from its circle, since they are regarded as not of equal birth, plays the same role in the small circle of New Orleans that the grandees of South Carolina play in the whole United States. Many of them rush to Paris in the summer—at least this was the case until 1848[10]—to enjoy full recognition of their old splendor. They then return to New Orleans at the end of autumn, with their experiences in the great capital providing material enough for the soirées and tea dances of the winter season. A truly aristocratic enjoyment, this life of wandering between the salons of two different hemispheres!

When the sun rose from the dark shadows of the hollows in the morning, Claudine rose from her bed enriched by experience but poorer than ever in love, desires, and hopes.

Chapter 5

A Welcome Guest

Jenny and Frida had barely been able to put their hair back in order in front of the mirror, and they were standing with burning red cheeks as the man repeatedly, energetically pounded on the door.

"Tell me, sister," Jenny turned to Frida and said, "where could Tiberius be hiding that people may enter so freely without being announced in advance? We might have been most embarrassed to be found sleeping in broad daylight. We would be considered to be good for nothing. But listen! I think the person has gone back down the stairs, so that we can see who it is in the shadowed walk."

They both went to the window and lifted the shades wide enough for them to lean out. On the stairs could be heard a man's footfall, cushioned by the carpet, and soon a man emerged from the front door of the cottage and stood on the stone steps, frequently looking back at the entryway, often making a step forward as if listening to hear if anything stirred in the house.

"Who could that be?" the sisters asked one another as they searched the face of the man standing below.

"It isn't Albert, the young architect?" Frida continued.

"What could you be thinking about? Look now, as he turns about—he has a full, red beard, so one can hardly see his face, and that's supposed to be Albert? You must be quite mistaken, little sister."

"The red beard wasn't visible before, and you really must admit that he looked exactly like the young architect from the back; he had the same free and unrestricted movement, the same size, see—even the same coat . . ."

"Indeed, and the same red hair," Jenny remarked ironically, "look how it rolls out from under his gray hat. That's a coarse fellow! How happy I am that we slept through his coming—who knows what troubles this person would have caused us."

"Ever since young Hagen repaid our hospitality so poorly last year, I no longer have the same trust in people of that sort, who announce themselves and make themselves into guests in an instant. Things here are different from Germany."

"But we're talking like children, dear little sister. Is it established that this man wants to become a guest? Perhaps he is here for an utterly trivial matter. Look, he's still standing down there—look, look, now he's finally moving—for God's sake, sister, now he's seen us!"

The two sisters shrank back from the window, holding each other's hands and standing in the middle of the room on their tiptoes as they listened at the door to hear the sound of footsteps on the stairs. Their anticipation was all too justified. The man came up the stairway even more rapidly than he had gone down, and in a few moments he was at the door of the drawing room. He had seen and *recognized* them, blonde Frida thought; she was convinced that he must be an acquaintance of some sort, since a stranger would have perceived the awkwardness of his visit and left. Only a close relative or an acquaintance would have allowed himself to rush right up the stairs on seeing them. That would be inexcusable for anyone else.

The stranger had not yet reached the top step when the parrot, who had been napping in solidarity with the sisters, began to squawk with all his might, letting loose with a long tirade of all the words and phrases he had learned, including his notorious "*Señor*" and the names of his mistresses.

"So, I really am in the right place!" the stranger said to himself, after he had heard the names Frida and Jenny more than twenty times. "My dear cousins really do live here—they won't recognize me all at once. The long voyage, the large beard, the tanned face—all of this makes me unknowable." He stepped up to the bird's cage and began to chat with it and to pet it. He didn't do that for the bird's sake, or to have a little enjoyment with it, but only to give himself time to consider how he was to approach his cousins and whether or not he should identify himself at once. Then he saw that the shawl hanging beside the birdcage was the same one he had bought for Frida the previous year. Now all doubt had vanished. The cousins must be in the next room, where he had glimpsed them from the street. Besides, the bird continued tirelessly to shriek out the names Frida and Jenny—there could no longer be any doubt.

In the meantime, the two sisters conferred on how they were to greet the man still a stranger to them, since he had to be received in the drawing room rather than in the parlor on the lower floor, owing to little Tiberius's negligence.

Under the prevailing circumstances, it would be difficult to observe the proper decorum there, since various feminine articles that should have been cleared away lay scattered about, and the stranger was likely to enter at any instant . . .

After a few moments had passed, however, the sisters were hanging on the neck of their *cousin* and kissing him, storming him with questions, and he was replying to their charming attentions in kind, kissing them back heartily and twice over.

Once the stormy first moments of the reception had passed, the sisters began speaking about their domestic situation, which they related gently and hesitantly to their astounded cousin. He was quickly initiated into the two young women's difficult position, and they agreed that he should stay in their home during his sojourn in New Orleans, sharing good times and bad.

"Now I'm on my way to the kitchen to teach our negligent Tiberius a little lesson," the businesslike Frida declared, after she had recovered from the excitement of her cousin's arrival and the revelations he had made—which must be kept from the reader for a while—were past, making way for quiet reflection. "Besides, it's almost noon and our cousin must be hungry."

"Dear cousin, how can you believe that I should think of food in the presence of such lovable ladies; that would be quite an improper thought," their gallant cousin Karl remarked, holding Frida's hands in his so as to prevent her from going. "Besides, now is no time for me to be concerned with eating."

"Everything at its proper time, dear cousin, but I would like to see how you would fare if we let you starve for several days. You would certainly tire of our presence in the end—but you certainly don't mean that. You men always want to think us women to be ethereal beings who can live off a pretty face and poetry, and you cannot imagine our feelings might be injured by that." After saying this, she slipped out of her cousin's hands and sprang rather than walked down the stairs, finding the kitchen in perfect order but without Tiberius. The black cook must not have been long gone, however, since the recently beheaded hen on the floor still gave evidence of life, forlornly flapping its wings against the planks.

The young residents of the cottage had no domestics left save young Tiberius, still in his teens. Everything went through their own hands, separately or together by turns. Jenny, the younger of the two, had not yet passed her eighteenth year, one year less than Frida, and she was all the more unprepared for taking care of and doing for herself because her husband had provided her with two mulatto servants, besides Tiberius, who was his own. Since her unhappy separation from him, she had shared with her sister all those small cares and concerns, which even the smallest household supplies, with an empathetic spirit. They were reasonable enough to see the need for sisterly cooperation, all the more so due to their disgust with men, of whom one had utterly vanished and the other had been amusing himself with whores and courtesans.

Since the new arrival will often concern us in the course of this novel, it would be proper to sketch him with a few strokes right at the outset, paying some attention as well to his physical appearance. Accustomed from his earliest years to the inequities of material life, and growing to manhood struggling for a free existence, he had learned to bear the changing fortunes of life and had adopted the stoic good humor one finds with men whose powerful, lively constitution views misfortune not as a burden but as a source of future activities and enterprise. Let us add that he completely lacked that gift of reflection which torments and obsesses a person when contemplating his own fortunes and problems, so that we could describe him as a happy man, even if the experiences he would relate might appear dark. He was seized by an unlimited lust for travel, seemingly born to wander forever. He was a natural adventurer, which is to say that he was an adventurer by necessity and instinct, not driven to it by an artificially adopted philosophy of life.

He was like a passenger pigeon[11] or the mysterious flamingo, whose freedom to wander has become a necessity, a law, but who must suffer much at the hands of greedy hunters. The rage to travel that possesses money-grubbing Americans, meanwhile, is all too similar to that of the buzzards on the Mississippi and the Ohio, who set themselves down on any carcass thrown up by the waves and, once their hunger has been stilled, return with fattened belly to their nests to rest a while and sleep with open eyes, lest any booty escape them during their slumber. The proper comparison between full-blooded Americans and our German guest is that of a buzzard to a passenger pigeon, between naked reality and poetry. It should be said in praise of the American, however, that they are birds of prey with gourmet tastes, and they do not settle upon just any carcass, but only on fresh, fat meat. The reasons we describe them as buzzards is best left to the reflection of the sympathetic reader, whose patience we do not wish to try any further with images of these birds.

Our guest would already have been placed in a dubious light, so far as his German countrymen are concerned, by his service as chief agent of an important southern slave market. Yet, considering that he took this position at a time when he was in great financial need, it should not cast any shadow on his character. After the material discomfort had been somewhat relieved, one would hardly expect him to leave the agency right away and place himself in distress once more just to yield to childish scruples. In fact, he was often rather pleased with himself over what he himself described as a wildly romantic career. He was often nagged by his cousins over it, and there were all sorts of philanthropic skirmishes and duels, which Karl always won in the end. So the following brief conversation developed between him and Jenny while Frida was busy in the kitchen. It would soon be interrupted by a man known to us from the previous chapter.

"Dear cousin, how nice it would be," said Jenny, sitting at her embroidery, working on the design of an antique vase showing Agave in her glory,[12] "if you found a permanent position in New Orleans, like our young architect from Saxony. Then you could visit us several times a day, brightening us through your happy temperament and sweetening many a bitter hour. How much finer an existence it would be for all of us if you could stay with us for a while. Your life is continually exposed to accidents on steamboats, and we are always worried that we shall lose you forever. Besides, dear cousin, yours is such an ugly business! Traveling salesman in woolly-heads! Just think, this does not match at all your character and sensitive heart. If I didn't know you better, I would have despaired for you."

"You are a little egoist, cousin," Karl responded, "I am supposed to give up a prosperous business and renounce travel, even endanger my health—since travel is second nature to me—all in order to remain close to you? I would never be able to settle down the way you want. But let us assume I would, what would I do? Tell me—perhaps I should roll cigars like my friend Schlicht in Valparaiso, or even become a barkeeper?" he added laughing. "No, I would be destroyed in no time at all by such boring occupations. So far as my present occupation goes, everything but the travel repels me, and I would exchange it for another in a minute if I could get the same money. We are, after all, in America, my dear, and money is not at all unimportant. Besides, you know that I do not love money for its own sake, but only in order to guarantee me a free existence in the future."

"More than a Jesuit," Jenny called out in jest, "for you the ends justify the means. If only Frida had heard that! She would hate you forever!"

Instead of denying this, Karl confidently looked at her with his large blue eyes and pressed her hand meaningfully. The lively cousin responded to his pressure by whispering, "What I read in your eyes makes me surrender to the sweet hope that you have come to New Orleans to stay with us forever."

"You are a clairvoyant, Jenny; your prophecy is correct and true."

"Now look at the bad man who talks that way!" the charming young woman said with a light blush. "One would think that he was sacrificing the favor of his women-friends to a whim."

Karl and Jenny loved each other like siblings. The guileless eyes that attached themselves on her cousin had darkened when he spoke of leaving. Karl was anything but handsome, indeed he was rather to be called ugly. A disproportionate stump of a nose and a mouth no smaller deformed his strong and vigorous face, shadowed by a strong red beard. But whoever looked into his eyes had to love him, and after spending time with him one completely forgot his ugliness. Besides, he possessed a supple and mobile body, which will always win more victories with women than the most handsome, regular face.

Karl had long been composing plans for the future in secret. He of course did not want to give up his position as agent, but he did want to cease traveling for a while and take the subordinate position of second agent in New Orleans, which was always open to him. He would make less money, but there was the positive prospect of being able to recover from his repellent business in the company of beloved and loving persons.

The arrival of the architect, who had just entered with Frida, disrupted any further intimate conversation. One could describe Karl's greeting as quite friendly, even loving, but Albert greeted his friend in a cold manner. The architect apologized to the ladies that he had been unable to complete the drawing by the agreed time, saying he had been indisposed. He continued the conversation without warmth, speaking monosyllabically, and Albert soon excused himself despite pressure from both the sisters and Karl to spend the afternoon with them. His tanned face looked pale and distorted today, and a careful observer would have been able to read more from it than mere indisposition.

Following the catastrophe already noted, Albert had gone to bed in the morning hours and awaited the break of day with impatience. Claudine did not appear at the usual hour, and he had breakfast alone. When he asked why she did not appear, the maid informed him that her mistress was unwell and would be spending the entire day in bed. At first Albert was determined to go to his wife, but he changed his mind after some consideration. A perverse pride prevented him from making the first move to a reconciliation. He remained in his room and occupied himself with trivial things. Although he had already conceded that he could not keep his promise to the ladies in Algiers, since the plan still lay complete, he did not want to miss visiting them; he in fact decided to spend the whole day with them in order to have some petty revenge against Claudine for not appearing at breakfast. The unexpected appearance of Karl had upset his plans. The vain man could not stand having to share the sisters' attention with him. In addition to that, Albert knew of Jenny's attraction to her cousin; when he encountered Frida emerging from the kitchen and learned from her that her cousin had arrived and was with Jenny upstairs, jealousy seized him in no small way.

Unbeknownst to Jenny, the architect had conceived a feeling for her—she who had been condemned to widowhood even while her husband was alive—a feeling so tender that it disturbed their calm. The young, beautiful widow was infinitely attractive to him, and he had already been conceiving a more intimate relationship for some weeks. But now his clumsy imagination immediately painted everything black, and he saw in the cousin a dangerous competitor. So we can see him leaving the sisters' house after the usual formalities of courtesy and wandering the streets of New Orleans. Fortunately for him, his rapid departure raised no remark, since his own comments about indisposition provided an explanation. Even Jenny could see no more than that in his frosty conduct.

The rest of the day passed like a beautiful dream. With music and song, with joking, kissing, and hugging, the evening loomed without anyone noticing it, and it seemed that they had not passed such untroubled hours in such beautiful and pure harmony in a long time. Through a westward window one could see the sun already halfway beneath the horizon, bathing with its rosy light the furry sheep that were accompanying it to sleep. The warm evening breezes nuzzled with the dark leaves of orange and magnolia, rustling the drapes at the open windows. The parrot stilled its cries, and in the place of songbirds the nocturnal butterflies pierced the warm air, striking the walls of the cottage and zigzagging back and forth through the tops of the *arbor vitae* trees and the lilacs. In the east, the moon rose, hanging like a cheerful fireball above the highest mast of a majestic merchantman. Hundreds of little barges and sailboats plowed the Mississippi, rejoicing in the beautiful evening. But within the cottage, the occupants huddled closer together, bidding one another farewell with handshakes and kisses.

Chapter 6

Don Juan in Hell

By the Cid! One must see her in her
  white
Nightgown, that splendid figure!
You must see it, this beating, biting,
When once she raves and bites at a
  kiss,
Raving strange words!
. . . .
Up, Page, follow my footsteps!
Forward to the sound of tambourine!
This evening I will serenade
So that the Alcaldes shall curse me
All the way to the Guadalquivir!
  [Alfred de Musset[13]]

Everyone agrees that there is only one New Orleans in the world. London is too smoky, New York too Yankee-Doodleish, Boston and Philadelphia too calculating, and Cincinnati, the Queen of the West, eats too much pork.

"New Orleans is paved with Negro skulls," says one American author. He would have done better to say that New Orleans is paved with beautiful women, although this would not disqualify the first observation.

In the garland of women woven about the brow of the Sovereign of the Gulf are to be found all possible blossoms; alongside the flaming tuberose and crown imperial gleams the seductive camellia, who bids us stand before her door on a winter's night without pity; the soft, white magnolia, who allows us no more than to lay a lovesick head in her lap; the bachelor button, so perilous to married men; and the evergreen Adelaide d'Orléans, whose glimpse can cause even a wholesale grocer to burn with love.

Only two flowers are lacking in this colorful flora. They are rarely to be found here. Those who seek them should fly to the banks of the vineyard-crowned Ohio. They are called Measured Love and Male Fidelity.[14]

Where are there more troubadours and paladins than in New Orleans? Only Madrid, Seville, and Barcelona have any right to compete as rivals.

Among the knights of love ever ready to break a lance for the lady of their hearts, there are many Germans. It is only too bad that German clumsiness and ungainly prudishness often rip up the tender threads spun by the notes of a mandolin.

Our *Cocker,* whose superficial acquaintance has already been made by our lovely lady readers, was precisely this sort of bad-luck bird.[15]

Since Eliza had fled his friend with three hundred dollars, and Shellroad Mary had gulped down four dozen oysters and five bottles of London porter at Cassidy's on his account,[16] bankrupting him, he has taken it seriously and decided not to blow money on tambourine girls and dancers; he did not understand how useful it can be to run through his money that way.

From then on, he drank his cocktails alone, unless a friend was paying for it.

Since he still felt an irresistible urge to show his adulation for the fair sex, and since he often observed *caballeros* and *messieurs* of New Orleans under the windows of their beloved armed with guitar or mandolin, serenading, he wanted to try his luck this way, too. He saw at once that this could be useful, and it would also save him money.

He had a guitar, and he was also a poet, and he had attended lectures on esthetics at Tübingen—he had only learned cocking shotguns since coming to America. He was a born fool, a student unfit for state service.

He was about thirty-two years old, and although he insisted that he had been quite slender in Germany, he is not to be trusted on this. He could not have grown fat in New Orleans, which he had not left since his arrival in the New World. He had often used this assertion to exploit the gullibility of women when they remarked on the extent of his girth.

The Cocker's most attractive feature was his teeth, and in fact he thought himself quite handsome when he stood in front of the mirror and formed his coral lips into a sweet, pining smile.

Often he was still somewhat concerned about his obesity, and on such occasions he would console himself by mumbling: "Well, even if I am not handsome, I am at least interesting, and how many times does one find that the most beautiful, celebrated women prefer ugly, interesting men to those who are handsome and uninteresting." The fact that beauty makes one interesting, and that handsome, interesting men do exist, appears not to have occurred to him in his reflections.

His gray eyes were not as small as they might seem at first glance. They were pressed together by the overhang of fat pressing down on his lids. Flat and sparkless when he was calm, his eyes glittered after he had taken on several brandy cocktails. At such a moment, he was capable of anything—that is, capable of whatever a good-natured man such as the Cocker would be able to do.

He could make a scene, was easily irritated, boasted, and would go directly at the throat of anyone who injured him, naturally without doing his enemy any real harm. He made do with threats and noise, and his sword always remained in its sheath.

One would have done him an injustice assuming that his corpulence came from too much eating. Actually, he ate very little, as is the case with anyone whose second nature is perpetually to drink too much.

He would fall head over heels in love at the sight of a skirt, and a calf, even when wrapped in a stocking, could push him over the edge. For that reason he would hang halfway out of the window when it rained and the dirty streets forced the gentle sex to raise their skirts. There he would smirk with happiness and wish the sun would stay away.

Although he thought himself a man of the world *comme il faut,* and he often compelled his friends to listen to his opinions on theater and music, often in the most pressing manner, still he had only been to the theater once in his seven years in New Orleans. On that occasion he did not even wait for the curtain to rise before lounging about in the barroom buffet, spending so much time there that his friends had to send the old chum home in a cab.

The next day he could not censure the play severely enough, and he bestowed the most dramatic phrases on the despicable efforts of French actors.

For several months *Orleana,* the most beautiful German Creole maid* who had ever seen the light of day in Louisiana, had been living in Toulouse Street.

*It is a great error, committed even by Washington Irving, to use the term *Creole* exclusively for those of French blood. If one considers the original meaning of this word, which indicates someone "raised over here," then it is no contradiction to speak of Spanish, Ger-

Her parents, both born in New Orleans, had been taken away by yellow fever in a day, and besides a prospering business, which Orleana gave over to other hands, they left her several valuable properties located in the busiest parts of town.

A mere two months after her parents' death, Orleana turned all the properties into cash at a considerable profit, bought a house after her own taste in Toulouse Street, and lived off the substantial interest of the remaining capital.

If it is true that our reading betrays our level of education, then Orleana must have had a good education indeed, for her mantel boasted the poetry of Mrs. Hemans and the St. Helena memoirs of Las Casas, while she had Goethe's *Propyläen* on her lap.[17] A splendid Viennese horn, with a guitar hanging over it, attested to her musical sense.

Orleana lived a quiet, chaste life, caring for her little household with the aid of an elderly female slave she had inherited from her parents. Her heart was still free, and no man could boast of having received the slightest preference or favor from her.

She had several wealthy relatives in the city, whose company was always a burden because their only purpose was to convince her to accept an advantageous marriage. The sons of two respected merchants felt themselves particularly entitled to make claims on her hand. Yet she always managed to keep these pressing suitors at a suitable distance.

Orleana was rich, young, and beautiful, qualities people were well able to hold in esteem.

Even the Cocker had heard of Orleana, and since she was, as he would say, a compatriot, he believed he had all the more right to rave for her and compete for her love.

"For," he declared to himself, "though it is conceded that I am not handsome, I am at least interesting, and on top of that a compatriot—what more does one need to win her heart?"

Today he was determined to serenade his beautiful, wealthy compatriot. But first he must place himself in an elevated mood, for a song sung from a dry throat would not reach the heart, so far as he believed.

But with what song should he surprise his compatriot? What would make the greatest impression on her?

---

man, and Indian Creoles. Applying the term *Creole* only to the descendants of the French colonists, as usually happens, reflects poor knowledge of our relationship of races. A child *born in Louisiana* of German parents is a Creole. So is a child born of the mixture of a white man and an Indian woman—but not the reverse, for *only the white color of the father* makes a child a Creole.

He was not short of songs, printed or written, for he had a veritable mountain of fraternity songs, including several fiery commercial ballads. He pored over his entire treasure, choosing now this, then that, for the serenade, and then rejected them all, until he thought he had found the right one after an hour of consideration and sweating. "Es zogen zwei Burschen wohl über den Rhein!"[18] must exercise a magic without equal on her innocent heart, and he hummed and whistled the melody to himself several times. "'Es zogen zwei Burschen wohl über den Rhein': how full of feeling, how sensitive!—properly presented, to the accompaniment of a guitar, it has to make an indelible impression on every spirit not yet defiled . . ."

Thus he philosophized for a long time, taking a hearty swig from his demijohn from time to time.

When he tried to tune his guitar, he discovered to his distress that two strings had broken, and—horror of horrors—the sounding board had a long crack.

This crack had appeared last night, when he returned home in a rather spirited state and used his guitar to kill a rat.

If the Cocker had not looked so often at his demijohn, he would have come to the conclusion that the serenade for Orleana was out for this evening.

We have already remarked that the Cocker was also a poet; but he often committed the unforgivable impropriety of bestowing no garlands on his hippogryph.

So he commenced reasoning in the following manner:

"Since it is of no small poetic worth in praising my darling that my heart is broken rather than happy, or to have a split in my heart, which is the same, and since singers and paladins describe their 'broken heartstrings' in hundreds and hundreds of songs, it would only be a perfect symbol of my love for me to serenade my compatriot with a broken guitar."

Now there was another quaff from the demijohn.

If up to now he had been a poetic pedant, now he became a frivolous Abbé Chaulieu.

What an effect the consumption of liquor can have! It makes the dumbest of us witty, the most phlegmatic genial.

The Cocker was ready to go, his guitar under his arm, a Hecker hat cocked fantastically on his left ear.[19]

"Es zogen zwei Burschen wohl über den Rhein!" he whistled away as he stepped out the door into the street.

The streets were already still.

The fresh night air had such an enlivening effect on him that it was as if he had wings on his feet; in truth, it seemed as if the gaslights, the houses—everything—rushed with him toward Toulouse Street.

He passed from whistling to declamation, and one must really confess that here he outdid himself.

"Beautiful women of New Orleans!" he let his imagination rip, "I love you because of the knavish glances with which you so often tempt me—I—I love you because of your naive sins—I love your children, the representatives of selfless love and sensuality—I love you for the prickly heat on your silken shoulders, when gleaming *helios* has wounded you with his kiss—I love you for the white powder I get on my shirt-front—I love you for the eau de Cologne on your blouses and stockings—most lovely—most lovely blossoms in the palmetto boudoir of Louisiana, I love you with all the passion of a botanist; for the wilted stems and petals in my herbarium are the gospel of my trans-Atlantic love . . .

"Toulouse Street? Hm, hm—that must be Toulouse Street!" He tottered about looking for someone he could ask.

"Damn'd! I'm already too far—yet—stop! Here—here is the Rheinpfalz, here is the Stadt Mannheim, and here is Victor's Restaurant—now it's sure that I've come too far—and where does my compatriot live?—so, so, there's still a light at Victor's—I must have a quick one along my way."

The Cocker pounded two, three, four times on the restaurant door, but in vain. No one would open.

"I will bankrupt the lout—just you wait, you scoundrel—I'll be damned if I have supper with you ever again," he threatened the closed door with his fist.

The Cocker now entered the phase in which a drunk begins to become brutal.

His self-deception grew extreme.

He no longer spoke of the deification of beautiful women, but rather he swore like a guttersnipe.

When he reached the office of the German Society,[20] he pounded his guitar on the door and roared:

"Well, if you know anything, you in there—you German Society—where is my beautiful compatriot?—You, you are my people—you, you? You'll take a couple dollars in advance, and then you'd still not lead me to her. Don't look at the nest! It is so filthy, so infamous and greasy, that a decent person is ashamed just going past it—hah, hah, German Society—get out—where does my compatriot live? '—Oh, she is never at home—adieu . . .'"

Sometimes stumbling, sometimes leaping high when he encountered something, waving his guitar in the air, he went several squares further.

If the sound of a piano had not reached his ears now, he would have gone right past Orleana's house a second time.

"Halt, halt—here—how beautifully my compatriot can play," he declaimed, not quietly, once he had had a sufficient look at the house—doors, balcony, and all.

Then he called out the name of his compatriot with the greatest pathos several times, at last so loudly and piercingly that it was no wonder that Orleana ceased playing and woke her slave woman.

He was about to begin his "Es zogen zwei Burschen . . ." when he was hit by powerful blows, and he would have fallen if a nearby wall, which his head struck, had not held him erect.

"I'll beat you to death, you lout, if you don't leave this place immediately and never return!" thundered a voice in French.

Although the Cocker had never learned a word of French in seven years in New Orleans, he could suspect why he was treated thus, and he hauled himself away as best he could, not going home at all but spending the night in the calaboose.

The next morning, after he had paid his last cent in a fine to the recorder, he wandered home in a dreadful mood, swearing to revenge the injustice done him and to discourage his competitor from forbidding his serenade.

Despite this hindrance, his desire for Orleana had grown even more intense.

Chapter 7

Parasina Brulard-Hotchkiss

Now we lead the reader into the Third Municipality, where he will see crimes committed that, although they are rather common in and around New Orleans, are still horrifying and debasing. Robber's Roost and similar hiding places and dens of vice in St. Louis are temples of the fairies compared with the home of the infamous *Negresse* Parasina Abigail Brulard, or Hotchkiss—as the Americans call her—in the eastern portion of the Third Municipality.

Anyone to whom the shameful, immoral activities of the colored people in New Orleans is no longer a secret will not shudder too much when I lead him to a place where the most unnatural sins are practiced as everyday activities and where vice emerges in all its glory and splendor. It is no wonder one sees the untrammeled frivolity of African beauties, who boldly leap over the boundaries of decency set by civilization and innocent nature, drowning in the white-hot stream of a throbbing volcano of sensuality. But for those who have encountered nothing in the South but the golden fruit of the orange tree and the bright blossoms of the chaste magnolia, and who know no greater horror than the growl of an alligator or the poisonous bite of the congo snake—those people might find the colors of my painting a bit garish. They will surely doubt the truth of what is portrayed and accuse us of violating the sovereignty of the human spirit or of having trod its dignity in the dirt.

We will ask these innocent children of paradise to pass over this chapter and the eighth, and to bide their time until the ninth comes.

We have long considered whether it is not too daring to permit this chapter in our novel, since many still worship a veiled portrait without having the courage to lift the veil. Those of our times have long since arrived at the philosophy that there is no further profit to be gained from veiling things and that knowledge is by no means as dangerous as the lies of a negative religion would have it. Even if we find human beings to be degenerate beasts under this veil, it is still better that we see them in their full ugliness than hear their howling and gibbering and fearfully hide ourselves behind our nursemaid's skirts. Vice, when painted in its nakedness, leads to a knowledge of human beings; mere allusion and gentle veiling leads to confusion.

In the eastern portion of the Third Municipality stands a large building built of brick in the form of a long parallelogram. The many large doors on the front of the house, which faces south, are always barred, and malice has dirtied them and covered them with so many caricatures and slogans that the original green paint can only be discerned in a few places. This building, with no windows on the ground floor, was once a tobacco warehouse, and in 1847 an auction brought it to its present owner, the free *Negresse Parasina Brulard.* It was had at that time for the enormous price of fifteen thousand dollars. Considering that the entire first floor consisted only of a single room in which there were only naked piers, devoid of decoration, and considering as well that there were a great number of small rooms on the second floor made of planks of the most indifferent construction, without any hominess or comfort, no one expected a buyer to use this building for any other purpose than as a warehouse. At first it was thought that Madame Brulard would rent out the lower floor or exploit it in some other speculative manner. But a whole year had passed, and the building still stood empty and quiet. There was none of the previous business, no drays, no clerks, no agents—nothing of the sort of thing which had once been common in and around the building. People could think what they wished, and the black woman had the right to do with her property what she wanted. A rather roomy courtyard on the back of the building was enclosed by a wall thirteen feet high, penetrated by a small door that was reached by a step three feet high. That was the sole visible entry, since the doors on the front were never opened, as mentioned. We do not wish to linger on the external description of this place longer but to turn our gaze into the interior.

The great hall on the ground floor, which occupied the entire width and breadth of the building, and whose view was not disturbed by any partitions or divisions, had been transformed by Madame Brulard into a sleeping hall, with hundreds of straw mattresses covering the floorboards. In surprising contrast to the more than cynic simplicity of this mammoth dormitory, whose bare walls were not even painted and whose ceiling revealed raw beams and planks, there were several clothing mirrors a good six feet high, which were always placed two by two, so that a woman dressing could see herself from both the front and the back. Each of these mirrors hung between two commode tables, in whose recesses were located the materials for lighting the dormitory. Light was absolutely necessary; the place was otherwise so dark that one could barely see the outline of a body. These commodes took the place of the columns usually used for such mirrors, and they had the extra advantage that the light did not create disturbing reflections for the person making themselves up.

It was Sunday morning. Utter, uncanny silence ruled in the dormitory, only broken here and there by the quiet murmurs of a few girls, barely roused from sleep, as they softly exchanged words with one another. Most were still sunk in slumber or groggily tossed on their colorfully quilted blankets.

Two of them must have just entered, since their complete clothing and disgruntled faces indicated that they had spent the night elsewhere. More and more were being driven out of bed by impatience, and they stood in their most low-cut negligées in front of the mirrors, trying to put their hair in order. They were all young girls of eleven to fourteen years of age: Negresses, mulattos, mestizas, quadroons—in short, all the shadings of colored blood. Whoever might appear at this hour without knowing the reason for these girls' gathering would have doubted his own sanity, believing instead that his senses had been clouded by some sort of trickery from the wand of an evil magician. If he then listened in on the soft conversations of the awakened girls, he would have realized, to his horror, that no magic or fantasy was afoot but rather that all of this was true and genuine. He would have come to the dreadful realization that he had entered a shameful den of vice, and that the bodies of these pretty maids were being sold and rented. He might have throttled *the woman who owned* these girls in his rage, little suspecting that he would never leave this pit alive.

The two who had just arrived sat down on one of the empty beds after having taken off their clothes and put on long shifts. They were registered in their mistress's name list as *Pharis* and *Elma.* They were of middle height, and their pitch black hair wound about their full brown shoulders. Their deep black eyes, their dark red lips, their glittering white teeth—which made every word they spoke to each other visible—the round, swelling contours of their body, all welled up with the warmth of life, which had not yet been stilted by the poisonous pall of habitual prostitution: these were all positive qualities that Parasina Brulard understood how to exploit. When she was in a good mood, she called these two her dear "gold chickens," a term of endearment not worthy of them. They were highly regarded by the other girls, and anyone who disturbed Pharis and Elma had reason to fear mistreatment at the others' hands.

"Pharis," Elma said, so quietly that the others could not hear, "do you really believe we can trust the young gentleman?"

"What could he intend with us, Elma?" Pharis replied in a concerned tone. "If he doesn't keep his promises to us, we could hardly end up in a situation worse than we are in now. I will follow his proposition, come what may."

"But just consider what torments we will endure if we are brought back! Madame will not rest until she has us in her clutches, and her connections with rich gentlemen will make it easy for her. I do not know the laws, but Celia, who came to us from a plantation a few weeks ago, tells me that her brother fled to Boston due to his massa's brutality, and that he was brought back and had to endure the most dreadful tortures. I haven't forgotten that!"

Pharis seemed to think for a moment, then she responded in a relaxed voice: "They can force us back into slavery, Elma, but they cannot force us to lead such a shameful life. We will make a complaint against Madame and get justice!"

"Make a complaint?—Get justice? Don't you know," Elma continued, "that we have no rights and cannot lodge a complaint?"

"Why not? What are the courts for, the lawyers and all those white gentlemen? If I have suffered an injustice, why can I not make a complaint? Does color make a difference there, *too?*"

A loud knocking, which seemed to come from the upper story, interrupted the conversation, and all eighty girls leaped up from their mattresses as if at a single command, dressed themselves in their long white shifts, and slipped on their shoes. Then they washed and did their hair in front of the mirrors, and in an instant they stood ready, lined up in two ranks along the whole length of the dormitory.

This maneuver had a particular purpose, as we shall soon discover.

Pharis and Elma had placed themselves in the first row.

"Madame," the first whispered, "will get no sin-money from me today; the young gentleman promised to pay me next Saturday. I hope that Madame will not be upset as a result."

"I have no idea," Elma remarked in a somewhat louder voice, "what Madame's attitude is right now. Ask *Hyderilla,* who will tell you what was done to her in a similar situation."

"What are you saying about me?" a girl of about eight called out with a bright child's voice.

"Elma thinks that you were severely punished by Madame when you extended credit to a rich planter's son for a whole night."

"Yes I was," declared the mestiza, barely out of children's shoes. "Now I have them all pay in advance. I could not bear this punishment a second time. Oh, how it burned and stung!—And I could not cry out, since they had bandaged my mouth. But you all know how badly I was hurt then."

"Poor Hyderilla!" another remarked sympathetically. "She could have died of it."

Madame Brulard entered with a purse in her left hand and a pocketbook under her right arm. At her side was a slim little man.

Anyone who encounters the personality of this woman for the first time has to be amazed. It would be pointless, a mere Tantaluslike hunt for proper words, to portray the full power that Parasina exercised on her poor victims simply by appearing. A glimpse of a holy shrine, *prostituted* by a priest to a faithful crowd, could not have summoned up such devoted silence. One could distinctly hear the breathing of the black and brown hosts. Their eyes flitted anxiously back and forth, barely daring to rest upon their mistress. Whoever has an imagination that can fly high enough to conjure up the Whore of Babylon and fix it in memory would have found Parasina her double.

Madame Brulard was a powerful figure, a full six feet in height, whose large and mobile breasts emerged from a negligently closed dress. Her skin color, the blackness and crispness of which competed with satin and ebony, could easily be compared with dark pitch gilded by the shining rays of a tropic sun. Her large, black eyes, like the second hand on the white disk of a clock, left the slow minutes behind, continually twitching forward, shadowed by a crown of long lashes in which the bold son of Cythere had taken his residence. From her half-open mouth of bright red glittered the enamel of her faultless teeth. Her breasts heaved and rolled like the ocean in a hot night's tempest. About her head was a sort of turban of carmoisin-red silk with fine black stripes. Her ears bore golden rings, which hung to her half-naked shoulders. The long shift, already so often mentioned, of the purity of new-fallen snow, was bound under her bodice with a rope of green silk, set with gold thread, whose tassel hung below her knee. Her feet were covered with moccasins decorated with bright blue bows and beads. On her little finger sparkled a diamond.

Her companion, who had probably passed the night with her, was so short that he barely reached her breasts. He was dressed in a long black gown buttoned to his neck, and he wore a black straw hat that was pointed on top. His entire manner, his slack facial features, his unsteady, unclean gaze, continually leering at the rows of girls, testified to his identity as a man who had plunged to the depths. His head was quite small, his eyes set deep in their sockets, and his cheeks puffed. His face had that indeterminate color between that of one recovering from yellow fever and that of a drunken decadent. His hands were small, and of impeccable whiteness and fineness—certainly the most admirable feature of an otherwise despicable figure.

"Belvidere, Deidamia, Celestiella, Wales, Adelaide, Springet, Hannah, Gizard, Jane, Eliza, Diana, Adeline, Lydia, Penelope, Harry, and Semiramis still have to pay their arrears from last week," Madame Brulard's masculine voice sounded, taking an officious tone, which—by the way—did not suit her.

Those called each gave her larger or smaller amounts of money, according to their services, which slid nimbly into Parasina's open purse.

Pharis stood next to Elma, shaking; for this time the dark features of her mistress promised no forgiveness. She thought of Hyderilla's torments and feared something similar. Elma toyed with her black locks and seemed not to notice the short man, who stood in front of her and seemed about to devour her with his greedy eyes.

The girls all stared with great interest at Parasina's purse, as whole and half-eagles were marching in droves into her fund of sin.[21] There were still two more who needed to hand over their cash: Elma and Pharis, who were at the very end of the row.

"Now, my gold chickens," she began with repulsive overfriendliness, showing both rows of her teeth, "show yourselves worthy of your names—hurrah for my California diggin's!" The little man laughed dutifully at the bacchantic maenad's bad joke, sneering with sordid pleasure at both the girls. Pharis and Elma lowered their eyes, in keeping with the demands.

"You're shuddering, Pharis?" Parasina commanded, "Speak! I hope you're no dumb c—— like Hyderilla . . . you would fare even worse than she did . . ." As she spoke, she moved her hands over Pharis' shaking body, searching for money. Finding nothing, she commanded several girls to search the guilty party's bed with care. She herself rushed to lift the poor child's shift over her head to search, as Pharis covered her eyes with her hands. After this proved fruitless as well, poor Pharis's hands were tied behind her back with her own shift, and she was commanded to accompany Madame and the short man upstairs.

"Monsieur Dubreuil," Parasina turned to the short man, sounding each word incorrectly in the usual manner of Negro-French, "do you want to take care of this cheat's execution yourself? Go into this chamber with her; everything is ready: tongs, nails, hammers, brushes, and ropes—
and if this doesn't suffice, behind the tapestry of each chimney there is a universal tool *comme il faut.* I will leave you now to put my books in order. *À revoir,* Monsieur Dubreuil!"

"Madame!" Dubreuil called out to the woman, disappearing into the next room, after he had checked his watch, "'tis already eight—I have to preach at nine! I will put the punishment off until evening."

Parasina broke into thundering laughter at Dubreuil's words, holding her sides with both hands. "Please tell me what the theme of your sermon is today, Monsieur?"

"On the sixth commandment!" the little man responded, raising his eyes unctuously on high.

"It will have a poor start today," Parasina remarked, laughing away.

"Have no fear, Madame! The Holy Spirit will appear to me in the form of a glass of good cognac and enthuse me. I have been accustomed to it since youth. *À revoir,* Madame Brulard!"

"*Adieu,* Monsieur Dubreuil! The cheat will remain shut in the chamber until you return . . . depend on it!"

Dubreuil left the Negress's house and rushed to his room with lowered gaze, occasionally responding to the greetings of churchgoers he encountered on the way.

An Intermezzo and Further Events at Madame Brulard's

Just as is the case with Greek mythology, so also Catholicism once had its classical era. What were the crusades, after all, but an *Iliad*? The Christian peoples were bound together in flourishing life, filled with poetry, and their martyrs and saints were not yet hypocrites and charlatans. The immaculate Virgin was the ideal for women and obsessed youths, and many a believing soul died under the cross of the savior. A pilgrimage to Loretto was not yet a joke, a formal pose, or a deceitful speculation for the money of the masses. Enthused saints really believed in their visions, and so their deceptions were innocent. The charming elective affinity between Abelard and Héloïse could only germinate in such an age. A Raphaël of Urbino could only have created his delightful angelic heads and portraits of the Madonna under the warming rays of a Catholic sun. The great Dante Alighieri could rise "higher and higher" into heaven with his beloved; for his *Divine Comedy* was dictated by a believing heart.*

But cold skepticism crept in with Boccaccio's *Decamerone,* and the poet was transformed into a brooding scholastic. From this time on, classicism was at an end, not only in Catholicism, but in Christianity in general, and, with this, morally speaking, the whole pretension of an orthodox Christianity should have ended as well. The history of mankind would then have been saved the insult of three hundred years of hypocrisy. Christianity has used understanding only as an instrument for exploitation and shameful purposes. With Ignatius Loyola, demonic forces descended into churches sanctified by naive faith, driving rest and peace from the breast of the faithful. The holy bosom of the sole saving Church—a phrase in step with reality during the classical period of Catholicism—became a place of torment and execution where black broods and filthy fools dispute. The stink of corruption and corpses became a substitute for the scents of myrrh and incense.†

*This is an arabesque on the sermon mentioned in this chapter, whose content is not given to the reader, even though our omission will draw criticism for violating the journalistic standard that both sides be heard.

† Second arabesque on the aforementioned sermon.

How the reader manages to bring these reasonings into harmony with this chapter, how he is to discern even a spark of dialectic and logic in what has been said—those are simply the sort of things a reader of "Mysteries" has to be prepared to do.

The old French church on Rampart Street was crammed full of people today.[22] Many who could not get into its narrow interior stood outside on the steps or in the portal, balancing on tiptoes in order to hear the famous preacher's thundering speech. Up to a hundred cabs, *volantes,* and buggies rolled up only to depart because it was impossible to get through the crowd into the church.

Among those who had taken comfortable and advantageous seats near the chancel sat two ladies dressed in deep mourning, of whom the younger followed the preacher's unctious words with most anxious attention, often blushing and staring at the floor when she met his eyes. The older lady sat stiffly on a cushioned chair, her face turned to the altar. She held a black velvet prayer book decorated with a gold clasp set with precious gems. From time to time she was forced to look about in response to the noise and movement at the door, which disturbed her devotions. Her Scottish origin was evident from her long, full neck and her small, elliptical ears.

The facial lines of the preacher expressed a peculiar enthusiasm, with a forced eccentricity that would lead a connoisseur of humanity to doubt whether this man, who was proclaiming the Word of God, raising high his finger in blame, really had an unsullied heart and a pure, childlike faith. At least that was what one man who stood right by the chancel thought, as he looked up with restrained animosity, then examined the devotions of the listeners. He had not come here to hear the Word of God or to let himself be enthralled by an imaginative explication of the gospel—he was driven by a curiosity to see and hear the famous preacher, even in a place that was hateful to him. The angelic *Miss Dudley Evans,* who was here with her mother, the idol of the clergy of New Orleans, also happened to be the object of his love.

Whoever possesses a personality receptive to art and poetry will certainly never forget the impression that a Madonna by Raphael first made on him. Miss Dudley Evans was just such a Madonna, with all the allure of a fresh rosebud just opening, saturated with the sanctified aura of innocence. Even as a young child, growing up in the perilous magic circle of the Catholic garden of errors, she was imbued with an obsessive love for the Mother of God and an unlimited obedience to priests, something that was dangerous for a child but doubly so for a virgin. Often compelled by her mother to severe acts of penance and chastisement, her eyes had taken on a suffering and painful expression that contrasted with the rosy freshness of her face and exercised an endless charm on all who came near her. Miss Dudley was the perfect image of a saint, and if she had lived a hundred years earlier, she would certainly have been canonized by some addled pope—for her piety, surely, but even more for her ineffible beauty. Even the aloof King Solomon, the lusty singer of the *Song of Songs,* would have committed a sin or two on seeing her, despite his wisdom, and he would have held off saying "all is vanity" for a while.

The proclaimer of the divine—no, the desecrated—word stood on a prayer stool, since with his small stature he would otherwise hardly have reached the top of the pulpit. In his zeal, he often bent half his body over it, as if any moment he was about to fall into the crowd. He clenched his little hands together, his eyes rolled like fiery pinwheels in their deep sockets, and his body rose and fell above the rim of the chancel, so that at times he was not visible at all; he raised both arms in the air and let his eyes roll heavenward, then he became quite still and crossed his hands over his breast, muffling his shrill tone and sinking his eyes to the ground; then he popped up into the air as if possessed and howled like old Ahriman or raging Roland—all in the course of a few moments! And what enthused this holy man? What would enthuse any one of us under certain conditions and make him a Garrick in the pulpit?—*a neat shot of cognac.*

We will let him preach on, and we do not want to disturb the devotions of the worshippers. We will only note that the sermon took two hours, and that the enthused preacher closed with a powerful *anathema sit* against all heretics.[23]

On the evening of the same day, Monsieur Dubreuil mounted a cab near the Pontalba Building and headed for the Third Municipality.[24]

The dial on the cathedral showed eight o'clock.

The silver sickle of the moon swam cheerfully and happily in the star-studded heavens.

Monsieur Debreuil was dressed today in a long, brown paletot and wore a gray cap that was pulled over his ears. He frequently looked out of the carriage and then pulled himself back, putting his feet on the seat and pulling his legs up to his chest. "That damned moon again!" he mumbled in this cowering position. "This scoundrel always appears at the wrong time . . . a meddlesome fellow! . . . a troublesome observer! . . . *sacre nom de Dieu!* . . . I'll go back! . . . Hey boy, *garçon,* boy, hey!" he suddenly called to the young coachman, pushing back the window and leaning out of the coach: "Go back to Pontalba's!"

"What do you talk about? D'mned my bloody soul be d—— back

again?" the whisky-befogged Irishman argued, driving his horses even harder.

"Sacre nom de Dieu!" the other cursed again, "hey, hey *garçon,* boy, boy, *attendez un peu! . . . je vous donnerais deux Louis! . . . hé, hé garçon . . . sacre nom de Dieu . . .* I want to get out!"

But the coachman appeared not to pay any heed to the little man's raving curses. He traveled on, driving his horses, until they arrived at the place Monsieur Dubreuil had designated.

Now the cab had halted.

"And here is where the cleaning lady Boncoeur lives, gentleman," declared the suddenly courteous Patrick, pointing to a two-story frame house whose windows were all illuminated, "and over here lives Madame Brulard—or Hotchkiss, as you will . . . I should take you through the little door in the wall," he remarked with a roguish chuckle. "She has damned pretty girls, this Madame Brulard. Hey, gentleman, how would it be if you would be so good as to treat me such a black or brown angel . . . oh, and a little *mestiza* is there, the prettiest child in the whole parish of New Orleans anyhow . . . and that Semiramis! She is as black as the child of the Mother of God in Altötting . . . in all Ireland I have never seen such pretty black flesh . . . by Saint Patrick, gentleman, if I could buy Semiramis, I would give my holy patron saint for it . . ."

Monsieur Dubreuil bit his lip in anger, for the Irish coachman was talking so loudly that the residents of the cleaning lady's house had opened their windows to look for the troublemakers expressing their desires so openly. To avoid inconvenience and compromising têtes-à-têtes, he threw his wallet to the talkative Irishman and vanished into the nearby alley.

The overjoyed coachman wrapped his horses' bridle around an isolated fire rail and, with the full wallet, lurched into the aforementioned house, whose inhabitants greeted him with howling laughter and closed the door behind him.

We shall leave him in the company of these goddesses, who were not entirely unknown to him, and return to Monsieur Dubreuil, who had voluntarily surrendered his wallet with at least fifty dollars inside it.

The little man had hidden himself among the stacked boards of a lumberyard adjoining the alley, and he intended to wait there until the accursed Irishman and his cab had left the street. He listened carefully in the direction where the cab stood, but he continued to hear the impatient stamping and snorting of the horses. He would gladly have crossed from his hiding place to Madame Brulard's, but he was afraid of being seen and accosted. Besides, it was altogether too daring for a preacher respected and loved by the whole city to encounter many people in such a disreputable place, lest he be recognized. His attempt to sneak the length of the alley, in order to reach Madame Brulard's by a detour, failed at the very outset. The alley's exit was blocked by a board fence, and when he attempted to climb over it to reach his goal, several dogs began barking, causing him to retreat.

So he had to wait a full hour in nervous expectation until he heard repeated "good bye, good bye," followed by the rumble of a departing coach. At the same moment, the boisterous music of a wild bacchanalian dance sounded through the still night as he crept across the street, anxiously looking about. He was utterly astounded to discover that the music came from Parasina's house.

"What could be going on in there?" he mumbled. "She did not say a word about it this morning . . . and what could have happened to Pharis? Dancing and raving so that a person could go quite deaf . . . perhaps that rich fool from Buenos Aires has arrived, that windbag and gaucho. I can't stand these South Americans . . . a rude, miserable people."

Like a tomcat seeking his mate in heat, slinking then suddenly taking great leaps, so Monsieur Dubreuil crept along the building before springing with one leap up the step that led to the small door in the wall. Quickly but quietly he turned the key, opening and closing the door in an instant. He did not linger in the hallway, which led on the right to the great dormitory and on the left up the stairs to Madame Brulard's bedroom, as well as to the chamber where Pharis had been imprisoned since seven the previous morning. He was little interested in the swift flight of dancing couples or the intoxicating tune of a luxuriant saraband. He did not leave the key to the chamber resting in his pocket—he quickly rushed up the narrow, delapidated stairway and opened the door.

Pharis stood naked, with her hands bound behind her, just as he had left her, next to the open window. She bowed her head as Dubreuil entered.

There was no light in the chamber.

The moon lay like the ghost of a departed soul on the inclined roof of the great barracks of sin, and its chaste glow illuminated the unhappy girl. As Monsieur Dubreuil approached her, she closed her eyes and stammered a moving "Mercy! Mercy!". . . . . [25]

By the time the hour of ten sounded from the tower of the Catholic church, the dreadful crime had already been accomplished, and the moon was illuminating a *sin that cried to heaven.*

But the guardian angel of mankind wept and hid his face in sorrow.

We encounter Monsieur Dubreuil on the ground floor in the dormitory, now transformed into a dance hall. The occasion of the extraordinary festivities and intoxicating lust was Parasina's birthday, the 31st of January.

With stunning speed the enormous dormitory, where only this morning hundreds of matresses had rested on bare boards, had been transformed into an arena for the fairies, with golden mirrors, silk curtains, pallets for odalisques, lovers' sofas, special chairs, tapestries hung with satin, *contre-deux, joli-jolies.* Here the terpsichoreans with loosened garments, *Venus vulgativa,* wine-besotted Bacchus, indecent fauns and satyrs in modern form, blasé *flaneurs,* and fashionable knights of calomel fraternized with one another.

Dubreuil was relaxed and lusty. He played the guitar and tambourine like a virtuoso and was gifted with a splendid tenor; he often had the opportunity to display these talents between episodes, and he had earned the name of "troubadour," bestowed on him by his coterie.

Among other things, Parasina asked him to sing a vaudeville, whose verses of intermingled French and American idiom we render here. After a brief introduction, Elma accompanied him on the guitar, and a plump, fresh Negro girl rattled and drummed the tambourine:

New Orleans, on your porches
Sit the ladies white as chalk,
Not concerned about their make-up,
Calomel drives away their sweat.

Slender Negroes stand at attention,
With fans in their fat hands;
Here in this street
All the houses are for rent.

Summer is at the door
And the heat makes for concern,
Yet the old vice slips in
Surreptiously on dusty paths.

Instead of lovely blossoms,
Chewing tobacco grows in all gardens,
And the loveliest lady takes
Chewing tobacco as her companion.

When she wants to kiss her lover,
She kisses only chewing tobacco—

Whisky then, and julep drips
Off his black Yankee coat.

The tears are ice and soda
Which are wept for the dead
And the pocket book is the love
That unites a Yankee couple.

In the bar there is friendliness,
Handshaking and brotherly kiss
But they vanish with the treating
As everything must end!

Loveliest of cities! On your graves
I'll build my little house,
Quiet in the warm summer nights
Look on your empty streets.

I'll count the coaches
That follow the beloved dead—
Then tired out, from bar to bar
Pay out all my piddling money.

Until they take me from my cottage
To those graves
Where one must lie so still
And drink only stagnant water.

At the great bar where
Decay is the keeper
And whoever goes in
Never leaves that bar again.

The bacchanals and gross orgies lasted into early morning. The dancers, male and female, lay scattered about the carpets and ottomans, alone, intertwined, or joined together. Even Madame Brulard had forgotten her dignity in the general intermingling: stretched out on the floor in an indecent position, she snored like a locomotive in distress.

THE SOUTHERN CROSS

The Negro cannon, fired at eight o'clock during the winter months, signaling the white race's monopoly of the streets of New Orleans from this hour on, had always ordered home all slaves who did not have written permission from their master to remain away. Only occasionally was one seen rushing through the streets with rapid step, intending to make up for tardiness by creeping quietly, if late, into a master's home.

This evening closed a cheerless, sad day.

In a few minutes ceaseless torrents of rain had put streets and sidewalks of the lower portion of the city underwater. After the clouds parted in the afternoon and the water drained away near evening, the barrooms and cigar shops in the immediate vicinity of the St. Charles Hotel bustled with speculating loafers, shop salesmen, clerks of cotton brokers and money-changers, newly arrived foreigners, and the notorious dandies of New Orleans.

In those days the St. Charles Hotel still bore the splendid monopteros on its majestic cupola, which bestowed an extremely striking exterior on the building.[26] This is the crucible of speculation and politics of the American portion of our population. Here plans are spun to build railroads or dig canals, and often quite remarkable stock arrangements are made after several cocktails and brandies, confirmed at the bar with filled glasses. Never mind that the sources of these arrangements often change their minds by the time their throats are dry once more. The neighborhood of the nearby Veranda Hotel contributes to this process, being a place where there is always lively hustle and bustle even after the rest of the city has gone to sleep.[27] Right after eight o'clock, when the nearby streets, especially Camp Street, Magazine Street, and Carondelet Street, are almost empty, everyone with healthy legs and a fondness for good cheer is concentrated in the territory described. For a dandy, whether a loafer or one of the city's top ten, a cigar doesn't taste good unless smoked while leaning against a column of the St. Charles Hotel, inspecting the undulating crowd of people, where one can occasionally throw smouldering butts in the face of a cabdriver whipping his horse.

There is nothing here for the romantic, who must direct his steps to the streets of the French District, where people play *Domino à la poudre* and where the color line is not so strictly observed.

But now we are turning into nearby Magazine Street.

With the approach of darkness and the glimmer of gaslight, not just buildings of some importance but even run-down ruins take on a physiognomy of their own that is entirely at odds with what is to be seen in broad daylight. This is particularly the case if some sort of dark characteristic or historical reminiscence is tied to it.

Of all the buildings in New Orleans, with the sole exceptions of the old cloister of the Ursulines and the home of the free *Negresse* Parasina Abigail Brulard, none loomed in the night with such an ominous and mysterious exterior as the Atchafalaya Bank, opposite Bank's Arcade.[28]

Anyone who has dealt in any degree with the commercial relationships of New Orleans knows the story of the rise of this building, as well as the activities of its former directors.

At the time we present this building to the readers, it has already been empty and abandoned for some time, and the wind blows through the broken windowpanes, music for the rats and mice secure there.

The columns that decorate the façade had been so torn by wind and rain and their capitals so broken and dilapidated that even an architect would have been unable to tell what order they had been designed after.

The whims of storm had caused deep furrows in the gabled roof, which had long been formless but which on stormy nights suddenly acquired the form of a cross.

On the right of the main entrance is a stairway leading into the upper floor, and from there another stairway, heading without landings to a number of attic rooms. In the days when the bank still functioned, these attic rooms had been closed off from the upper story by a trapdoor, and it could be opened only by the keys of particular bank officials.

Now this trapdoor is open, and a heavy iron bar has been jammed in to keep it from falling. Several of the steps in the staircase have fallen through, and they have been repaired with old chair legs.

Before climbing half the staircase, one passes a window through which the rear building on the other side of the filthy back courtyard can easily be seen. For several months a Negro family has been living there, consisting of a gray-haired man, two women, and several children between six and twelve years of age. A booth, to which a long chain is fastened, its links half-buried in the dirt, shows that it was once thought necessary to keep a night watchman.

It was generally known that a Negro family lived in the structures in the courtyard, although it was not known precisely why they were there. Things were different with the room in the upper story. No one suspected that anyone was living there.

There is a dark blue satin tapestry over the two windows of this garret room, covering them completely so that not a ray of light can enter, requiring the use of artificial light even during the day. The originally raw walls are covered with the same material, embroidered with innumerable vignettes.

The floor of this room is covered with costly carpets. The room itself is divided into two, by screens set with doorways.

Cushions, ottomans, love seats, a tapestry of rose-red velvet, a divan of great width enclosed with the finest of curtains, a mirror held by two amoretti, and a silver candelabra with twelve arms, in rococo style, as well as many other luxurious objects, decorated one of the two chambers.

It is beyond imagination how these objects could have come here without the neighbors finding out. For it is certain that no one had even the slightest inkling that people were living in the main building, let alone that both splendor and comfort had taken their residence in the upper story.

Where everyone assumed there were rats and bats, the fairy-tale aura of sybaritic splendor prevailed.

Two persons were reclining on the soft pillows of the divan.

One is a young man, barely twenty-five, with beautiful long blond hair and large, heavenly blue eyes, half-veiled by long lashes. His glowing cheeks have attached themselves to another's bare neck, and with the fingers of his right hand he is fondling a luxurient forest of raven-dark hair.

He is naked except for a short blouse of white silk and a silver belt made up of innumerable fine rings.

At his side, with her right arm woven around his body, is the figure of a woman, her swelling breasts covered in ruby-red silk. She is looking into his blue eyes with such intensity and profound desire that it seemed she wanted to live in them and never depart.

"Five weeks have passed since the time I dressed up in your clothes on a whim? And yet it is as if only a few hours had passed—" she added to a conversation that had been interrupted for several minutes by fondling.

"We shall receive information today," the young man replied, "he promised us that."

"If he returns, we must ask him at once," she continued.

"Who would have thought!—When I let myself down from the window and was grasped by an arm!"

"Be still, my heart—I believe he is coming up the stairs right now—it is not yet time for him"

They remained intertwined as they listened.

They were not disappointed.

The rotting stairs of the narrow staircase groaned, and from the abandoned rooms on the lower story the one they longed for appeared through the opening of the trapdoor into the warmth of the luxurious chamber.

Both of them rose from their bed, expressing an attitude of veneration and love.

"May Venus Urania protect you!" they welcomed the one who entered, approached the two, and kissed their foreheads.

He was a gaunt, long-limbed figure, his torso somewhat bent and his snow-white hair hidden under a fur cap, which he had pulled down to his eyebrows.

His face was the portrait of unspeakable care and sorrow, and despite the goodness of his heart, expressed in his manner, at first glance he was horrifying.

Four generations had passed by his skull, and yet on earth he still bore with him a hope he would probably take to his grave.

His immense wealth dated from the year 1788. He had journeyed from Lake Itaska to the thundering waves of the Gulf, from the Atlantic to the Pacific, and he had returned to his native city as a savior.

He had opened the gold veins of California and Australia, years before the argonauts took their ship to rob the golden fleece there.

Now he stood in simpler clothing; more than a hundred years had beaten at his brow—and yet he still had not given up on fulfilling the dream that had accompanied him since his earliest youth.

Now he was making his last try, and if this failed, then his white hair would certainly draw him into the grave.

Lucy and Emil bowed involuntarily as he sat down between him. The old man began to speak.

Chapter 10

MANTIS RELIGIOSA

"Do not wonder why all the events of the last few weeks have vanished from your memory. If you want to accuse me as the cause of your forgetfulness, I cannot blame you. I cut off relationships that seemed beyond severing to you, and so you have been removed from the deceptive sphere of life that would soon have sucked dry the marrow of your souls."

Emil and Lucy hung on his every word as if under a spell.

The old man continued:

"You will find in these papers I'm giving you an account of everything that has happened since the night when your double masquerade led to a development you could never have imagined," the old man said as he handed Emil a red velvet valise containing several rolls of paper. "You may look at them only after I have departed. You will then leave these rooms and never return—I will leave with you half of my wealth, more than enough to support the lifestyle of an oriental potentate. With these treasures you shall return to the meanness and underhandedness of human beings, but you will no longer be compelled by need to sully the gleaming beauty of your bodies with dubious undertakings."

"But that night, when I let myself down and . . ." Emil did not say it, for Lucy threw him a warning glance.

"When you were grasped by the policeman's raw hands, I was nearby; I could not permit a policeman's coarse hands to injure the beauty which could only be prevented from spreading its warming glow everywhere by such mishandling," the old man joined in with enthusiasm. Then he spoke after breathing deeply:

"After you read through these papers, you will recall all the events that have escaped your memory." He turned to Emil, saying, "You will once more recognize the names of Jenny, Frida, Albert, and Karl as those of acquaintances."

On naming these names, Emil struck his forehead with his hand as if he had just awakened from a deep dream. It was at once as if all that had taken place had been only illusion and trickery—as if he needed only to awaken.

The old man understood this.

He grasped Emil's right hand and told him in a tone that communicated conviction and stilled all doubt:

"You are wrong if you think you were dreaming here, that you had fallen into the hands of a Cagliostro or some other black magician. I believe that the times are past in which people still believe in such conjuring and witchery. An enlightened century has cast all this dark nonsense away and understands only the laws and phenomena of nature. Man no longer needs to drink forgetfulness from Lethe's stream; we have in our grasp the means to lose our memories in happy dreams. It is not opium that weakens the nerves and numbs the power of human thought, and that brings death when used in excess. It is not incense, whose waving smoke makes one forget cares only for a moment, raising the most lurid images to the agitated senses and poisoning the organism in the same way as *Aqua toffana.* It is a modest plant at the source of the Red River that is not yet known to you nor to the entire civilized world:* It is the *Mantis religiosa.*

"A good twenty years before the first expedition under the first French consul,[29] I came to know the source of the Red River, and its discovery would have been announced to the scientific world if I had not found this plant in the mesa that surrounds this source like a yawning grave. The plant, hitherto known only to buffalo, panthers, and jaguar, contains the most valuable, but also most fearsome, gift of nature."

The old man released Emil's hand, which he had been holding, and he quickly passed through the opening of the trapdoor.

In a few seconds he stood once more before Emil and Lucy.

They looked at each other with astonishment. It was as if they were in the presence of a being of a higher nature, one who could steer their destiny.

The old man drew out a capsule, opened it, and displayed it to the amazed couple.

They saw, on closer examination, that it was filled with many small translucient grains, each one containing in its center a tiny black point.

"Is that the seed of the *Mantis religiosa*?" Lucy asked with a lowered voice, anxiously looking into the old man's face.

"The *Mantis religiosa*?" Emil seemed to want to ask, but his lips remained sealed, and he withdrew the question, keeping it in his heart.

"Yes," the old man interrupted the silence, "from this grain grows the rosy red bloom of the *Mantis religiosa,* whose aroma led you into the realm of forgetfulness. I myself tested its effect in my earlier years, but I am now too old; their perfumes are wasted on me—now all my memories, whose cares I had laid to rest, rise up from the depths of my brain without being summoned."

With these words, a tear formed in his eye. He then continued with a forced voice:

"Not only does this plant contain that analgesic property, but it also contains the germ of destruction—of a *dreadful plague.*"

"Of *yellow fever*?" Emil and Lucy responded as one.

"Yes! I use it as a means of revenge!" the old man raised his voice in solemnity and pathos, which caused both to shudder.

*At the time these words were spoken, Captain Marcy had not yet begun his expedition to find the source of the Red River. That source is still not known. All accounts of it, including that of Alexander von Humboldt and back to those of Lieutenant Pike and Colonel Long from 1803, 1806, and 1812, are unusable.

"It is yours to forestall a further visitation. I am leaving you today, and if you survive the trial by fire and keep your beauty from harm by using the wealth that I leave you, I shall reappear and lead you into a place where you will become immortal unto all generations. For know this: *there are chains to be broken here—and only beauty has the right to break them* and to place itself at the head of a movement, long desired by me, whose time has at last come. The motivation for cleansing our soil of the shame that has been committed against a portion of mankind should not be self-seeking, vanity, or mere profit. *You shall be the representatives of a breaking dawn!*"

The eyes of Lucy and Emil, which had been weighed down with petty interests and episodes of an ordinary life until a few weeks ago, now flamed like lightning for the high mission they were to fulfill for a portion of mankind.

The old man left them that evening.

Emil unrolled the pages he had left them, and Lucy snuggled next to him and listened intensely to a decoding of their most recent past.

Chapter 11

The Negro Family

Almost at the same moment that the old man sat down between Emil and Lucy to acquaint them with a mysterious plant, the members of the Negro family, which the reader knows lived in the courtyard of the Atchafalaya Bank, were engaged in a conversation that is all the more important because it sheds light on dark matters and will prove to be a thread of Ariadne through the labyrinth of later events and misfortunes.

The entire family was gathered about the fireplace in the kitchen, with the exception of a young girl who sat groaning in the corner, her right arm supported on a chair back.

The head of the family, a gray-headed Negro, had settled in an armchair and was warming his feet. Next to him on each side sat two women in their middle years, eating the remants of a frugal supper. Another woman, rather further along in years, held the wooly heads of two children under seven years of age in her lap as they quietly slept.

They were all simply but cleanly dressed. The women wore bright checkered cloths about their heads and snow-white long dresses without waists, in dramatic contrast to their black skin color.

"Thanks be to the noble stranger," the grayhead began, after lighting a short clay pipe, "who freed all of us from the grasp of our master. What would have become of all of us? You, Sarah, would probably have gone to the plantation at Derbigny and Breton, since you're a good washerwoman and seamstress. With you, Abigail," he turned to the other young woman, "they would have taken you to the St. Charles Hotel, where you would have had to work night and day. Old Master would have taken the two children to Mobile, so that all of us would have been separated from one another. And how did they treat you, Sarah and Abigail, in the auction halls? I have experienced much, and I've seen those situations, but never treatment such as you endured at Talbot's, even with—niggers," he added bitterly. "The blood ran to my old head when they stripped you so rudely and fondled you from top to bottom, and you had to put up with this not once or twice, but five or six times. Anyone who acted like he was ready to give a few thousand dollars for you grabbed and probed you. How many were there who didn't have a cent in their pockets, just came out of curiosity? Took the clothes off your body—if I had been ten years younger, I know what I would have done—but instead I am an old, worn-out, and tormented nigger, who hasn't a tooth in his head—ha, ha,—half I lost, half were beaten out of me—but that doesn't matter, I am and remain a nigger, a head of cattle! ha! ha! ha! . . ."

The grayhead argued on in this tone, letting his pipe go out time and again.

Cato—that was the name of the grayheaded chief of our Negro family—was all of sixty-five years of age, and that he was still strong and good for something was demonstrated by the fact that he had brought six hundred dollars under the hammer of the auctioneer a mere two years ago. He had already been the property of at least a dozen masters, each of whom had always sold him off to the highest bidder. He was as good a smith as he was a talented carpenter, and he knew how to keep a vegetable garden and even how to handle a hothouse. He could make trousers or jackets as well as any tailor, and he was much liked, or at least much used, on the plantation owing to his cotton-harvesting abilities. There was a time when Cato had the honor of commanding a price of twenty-five hundred dollars as a "black piece of human meat." In this way, Cato could be called a very wealthy man, despite his yoke of slavery; certainly richer than many a white gentleman, who would hardly have brought five dollars at auction. Cato was one of those extremely active slaves—obeying the slightest motion, sweating in the presence of master like a whipped dog—but when the time came to rest and the evening shadows passed over his eyes, his jaw clamped down as he sought ways and means to flee or to inflict harm, or at least difficulties, for his masters in secret.

He had sweated and bit down for sixty-five years, he had tormented himself and worked himself to exhaustion; he had filled the moneybags of his masters with thousands, but his price was too high to buy himself. How could he ever manage to get two thousand dollars, despite all his saving?

The eight hundred dollars he had saved over twenty-five years, which he offered his master to buy his freedom, was accepted; yet in exchange he got no emancipation papers but rather a better, more elegant fence for his cottage.

"Cato, I want to keep the eight hundred dollars safe," his master said then, "and when you've saved another eight hundred, you can go wherever you want."

Cato was a nigger; he had to bow his head and could only bite his lip.

Now Cato was free! A man he had never seen had bid a thousand dollars over five hundred, buying him and his family and setting them free. He gave them money and cared for their further maintenance in a noble fashion.

But the yoke of sixty-five years had so pressed on him and made consciousness of his present condition so inconceivable that he still held himself to be a slave, and on occasion he whimpered and apologized in situations in which free persons would do nothing. When he committed some lapse, when he broke a glass or cooking vessel, he cringed with fear and folded his hands as if he expected the whip.

When he wants to drink brandy, he carefully hides the bottle in some corner of the courtyard, then sneaks out during the night and takes a hefty pull on it before going back to bed, where he barely dares breathe out of fear that the smell of the liquor might betray him. So the poor man has lost his chains, but the marks they had left behind still hurt.

The two young women who sit beside the fireplace are the wives of his two sons, who had been taken away by the epidemic the previous year. The two sleeping youngsters are his grandchildren, and the older woman is the wife, or rather the concubine, of a free Negro who owns a cigar store in one of the northern states of the Union, but she happens to be in New Orleans at the time we encounter her.

The young maiden, or rather "woman"—for any Negress above eleven years of age is no maiden, so far as Americans are concerned—who supports herself in the corner on a chair back and has a yellow complexion, had been born free in New York and was taken in by the cigar-monger as his child.

"My husband has been gone a long time," the oldest of the women remarked.

"Father has not yet finished his business, and since he wants to return to the North next week, he will make good use of his time," the younger girl added in.

"Have you received much money from the old man?" the first went on in an indifferent tone, turning to the two younger woman.

"For the time being he gave us only a thousand dollars and paid the owner of this building the rent for our apartment for half a year," Abigail responded with a good nature and eyes beaming with joy.

The girl, who had been supporting herself on the chair back, now left it and approached the people gathered about the fire with a curious manner.

"After half a year has passed," Abigail continued, "we will get a house in the Rue d'Amour in the Third District, as a gift."

"So you don't want to go to the North with us?" the girl asked.

"Who said we were to go north with you?" Sarah responded.

"Yesterday Cato promised it to my husband," the cigar-monger's wife answered in an irritated voice. "He wanted to go into partnership with my Sulla . . ."

"Did you say that, Cato?" Abigail asked the grayhead in astonishment.

"Yes, I promised him," he responded, "but do what you wish." With that he nervously looked at the two women sitting next to him, as if he feared punishment.

"I don't understand at all, Cato, how you could promise that. You know perfectly well what our benefactor has planned to do for us," Sarah interjected.

The cigar-monger's wife and her adopted daughter threw a meaningful glance at each other.

At the same instant, the door opened and a tall, slender Negro in the finest clothing greeted them, removing his hat and holding it stylishly in one hand.

"I did a good bit of business!" he proclaimed. "I bought twenty thousand of the best Havanas, only eighteen dollars a thousand—the gentlemen in the Shakespeare Hotel will pay dearly when I return to New York . . . Now Cato, are you ready to go day after tomorrow?"

"The steamer leaves at four—Everything has been arranged! . . ."

"The people are staying here, Sulla," the cigar-monger's wife said, "Cato made his promise too hastily."

"But I have arranged everything for you down to the last detail, paid passage for all of you and made several purchases . . . When you you think about it, it's your fault and you'll have to compensate me for outlays I have made without any return . . . Here are the tickets, the captain won't take them back!"

He handed them the tickets and went to his wife's side, who silently poked him without the others observing.

"That is a total of eighty dollars, and we will repay you at once," Abigail responded, getting up and leaving the kitchen.

"Where is Abigail going?" Sulla asked Sarah.

"She's going to the bedroom to get you the money you spent on our behalf," she thoughtlessly replied, then she added: "If you need any further compensation, just say it and it will be yours. You should not be upset about that; you can stay here until your departure, and we shall part as good friends."

Abigail entered with the money in her hand.

It consisted of eight gold pieces of the newest minting.

The cigar-monger's wife looked at her husband, then at her adopted daughter.

"That is enough!" Sulla said, as Abigail handed him the money, "I will ask for no further remuneration from you, although I did spend some twenty more dollars and change for provisions which are now unnecessary. Since you refused to take money from me for board, I will ask for no more. I am only sorry that you won't be going north with us, but rather are compelled to remain here . . . But tell me, how did the old man come to buy you, free you, and then give you so much money?"

"We ourselves have no idea," the two women said almost in the same breath. "He was as much a stranger to us as you were, and he will probably remain as much a stranger in the future, since we saw him today for the last time."

"How so?" the cigar-monger's wife asked tensely, then she continued: "I would really like to see this strange man, who is so full of money through and through; if he is so generous, perhaps he is so for others as well . . ."

"You could see him yet today if you wait for him!" Sarah responded.

"If he is not too late, I would certainly like to meet him," Sulla said.

"If he is not too late?" his wife remarked, "Are you that tired?"

"Yes, I want to rest soon; you may remain awake until you have satisfied your curiosity."

"Do you want to go to bed right away?" Abigail asked attentively. "Then take this light. You don't need to close our doors; we will close them ourselves when we go to bed."

Sulla gave a studied yawn, and, after signaling with a look to his adopted daughter that she follow him in a little while, he left the kitchen with the light in his hand.

After Sulla was gone, one of the two little woolly-heads, who had been quietly sleeping, began to cry and look around in terror. The other child, a girl, awoke from her sleep and rubbed her drowsy eyes.

"Tom woke me up, and I was sleeping so well!" she cried.

"Tom must have had a bad dream," Sarah said, rushing up to the little one.

While the two women were busy with the youngsters, Sulla's adopted daughter also left the kitchen and joined her father.

The cigar-monger's wife did not seem to pay any attention to this. No more than the two other women did.

Let us look after Cato.

As soon as the cigar-monger had appeared, he had withdrawn from the fireplace and arranged his bed, which consisted of a few blankets and an old pad placed under a table on which several kitchen utensils lay.

The two women had repeatedly tried, with no success, to convince him to sleep in a comfortable bed that they had set up next to their own bedroom, which he had climbed into only once. Cato had been unable to shut his eyes that night, as he was in a continual state of anxiety that he might damage or endanger the bed through some movement.

Since then, he never got into a bed but instead slept on the floor every night.

As often as the women criticized him for it, he always answered, "A couple blankets are plenty for an old nigger like me," and so they left him with his illusions.

When everyone else was deep asleep, he would already be up putting the kitchen in order, setting the fire or cleaning the courtyard. When the Negro cannon fired, he always cringed and seemed to wonder whether he should be back at home with his master.

So the poor man had no peace, either by day or by night, and it was a serious question whether he would not have been happier had he never been freed.

Chapter 12

Sulla

The supposed cigar-monger, this veritable prototype of the fashionable Negro from the New England states, was about twenty-five. Despite his youth, he had already passed through the whole scale of trials and tribulations that a man of his years could encounter. Through this he had not become better, but worse.

He is, as it happens, a man with the most handsome form of face and a candid appearance, with burning eyes and impeccable lips, a rarity among those of his race, a slightly curved, fine nose, and a high forehead—one should say an intelligent forehead, if his black color did not preclude intelligence, according to our prejudices.

In spite of the peril that we might irritate the monopolists of the white race, his hair, piled up in wild curls, could be called handsome. At least it becomes him better than it does Monsieur Alexandre Dumas,[30] who is known to have made the acquaintance of some slave-breeders' fists in a New Orleans billiard salon because of his kinky hair.

There is a significant difference between a free Negro who lives in the southern states and a free Negro from the free states. Such a free person in the South will always be dominated by the New England Negro whenever they happen to meet.

Sulla exercised this power to a high degree over his southern compatriots, or rather his compatriots living in the South. After he left them, they discovered all too late that he had looted them, and then they cursed the damn'd Yankee nigger to the deepest cranny of hell, even to the calaboose.

This was the third time Sulla had visited New Orleans, and each time he had presented himself as the owner of a significant cigar business in the East, a situation that garnered him high profits.

Sulla was too smart and too experienced not to realize how dangerous it would be to let people suspect that he was lying about his profession.

He had met the Negro family we came to know in the previous chapter by pure accident. Encouraged by Cato's foolish talk, he had made himself known to the family, though he had been a stranger; he had visited them a few times, until, in their extreme friendliness, they had opened their home to him, his supposed wife, and his adopted daughter and let them stay until their departure.

He immediately dropped some of the intrigues he had been spinning with the help of his wife and child, because the inexperience and good nature of the new family appeared to make complex routines unnecessary.

He had to get their money, which he happened to have wildly overestimated in his imagination. That was a firm goal of his. He was now prepared for the most extreme acts if any unforeseen obstacles got in his way.

For him it was enough that they were in possession of a large sum of money. He must find the rest without delay.

He had not the slightest intention of taking the family with him to the East. That was only a means of swindling them of their money, eliminating his current shortages. He had chatted up Cato away from the two women until Cato had finally promised to go along and—as he said himself—go into partnership with him. He knew only too well that the women would not agree, so he had surprised them with the forged tickets and the irritated remark that he had already paid out so much money for other arrangements. The women were easily deceived by this maneuver; they did not consider that the tickets could be fakes, so they paid him eighty dollars.

With these funds, he intended to make his getaway if need be; since he was otherwise entirely out of money, he had to resort to such measures—besides, it was not unheard of for such a plan to fail.

A truly demonic, horrifying story is bound up with Sulla's origins.

We will briefly summarize here the principal data of his past, and also make the reader acquainted with his supposed wife and his adopted daughter.

Sulla's parents lived seven English miles west of Montréal, in Canada, in the little village of Marytown, where they owned a kind of tavern called a "traders' inn." The trade sign displayed a white rose on a black field, with large gold letters underneath proclaiming *hony soit, qui mal y pense!* How the owners of this bar came by these arms would be hard to say. One popular opinion was that it meant "Since the rose on this sign is white, but the owners are black, don't take it badly!" This was, however, a very dry explication, which required no Sphinx to compose it. Whatever was the case, the tavern was called "the White Rose," and the owners of the White Rose did a splendid business. Every stranger who visited Montréal had to have visited the White Rose at least once, and, moreover, he must have spent the night there.

When we speak of spending the night, this does not mean that a person actually slept there.

The thorns, which the artist had inexplicably left out of his sign painting, were all the more evident in the interior of the tavern.

A collector of insects was likely to find virtually anything there but sleep.

For starters, there was never enough room for visitors, so they often ended up in the ten-foot-wide marriage bed of the owners, who were naturally present themselves.

Victoria, the publican's wife, was honorable enough not to allow such excess guests to lie next to her, and she always used her fat husband, Sullivan, as an insurmountable barrier.

Although he had long since passed fifty years of age, Sullivan had a well-fed belly and small sparkling eyes, and fat was not lacking on his cheeks either. His pace was stately, and he knew how to keep his servants—most of them French—in excellent order. Many an Anglo who came over from New England forgot his ill humor when he heard Sullivan explain that he was descended from princes who had once ruled over twenty Negro realms and had founded cities and built forts on the Ivory Coast at a time when no Englishman knew that such things existed, let alone that ships might someday sail there from Baltimore harbor.

On such occasions, he would show a long dagger on whose blade there were several oval hollows, to be filled with the sap of a poison fruit only to be found on the Ivory Coast.

This dagger was the heirloom of a Negro prince, supposedly more than fifteen hundred years old. It was a valuable instrument, not just in practical terms but according to the worth of the metal of the handle. One Englishman who was a great enthusiast for curiosities once offered him five hundred pounds sterling for this weapon, but he had declined. He soon had occasion to regret this.

Victoria, who was twenty-five years younger than he, surprised him one day with the news that she thought she was pregnant. In her enthusiasm she went so far as to declare the names her child would have. A boy would be Sulla, and, if it pleased Providence that a girl see the light of day, she should receive her mother's name, Victoria.

Sullivan had no objection to the two children's names, but he could not quite understand how his Victoria could be feeling pregnant.

He appeared happy at the news and hid his suspicion.

But from then on he kept a sharp eye on his steady customers, as well as on all those who frequented his bar from month to month.

Until then, he had imputed the growth in numbers of his guests, and hence of his money, to his own charm and good service; now he realized all too well that his guests and all the wealthy foreigners who had found their way to his door had not been drawn by the *White* Rose but rather the *black* one.

Among those his sharp eye observed, a young mulatto particularly stood out. This young man had long been in the service of the governor, and he had a very pleasing appearance. He courted Victoria on every possible occasion, and it even appeared that he had some influence over the domestic arrangements, which Sullivan had failed to notice.

"Yes," thought Sullivan, "it appears I have been dividing my income with a third party."

Neither Victoria nor her lover suspected the storm gathering over their heads.

It would soon break.

Besides his tavern in Marytown, Sullivan owned a finely built summer tavern, in which the splendid ale and porter of Perkin's Brewery moistened the dry throats of the guests.

It was a beautiful, mild evening in Indian summer when the residents of Marytown went out in great crowds to enjoy themselves to the music of a German band from Montréal, which Sullivan had hired for the evening, and to do justice by the ale and London porter.

Despite his many workers, Sullivan was preoccupied fulfilling the wishes of his guests when he noticed that his wife was gone, which especially surprised him on a day when there was so much pressure and things to do.

The suspicion he had nursed for some time was further nourished and grew to such a degree that he put everything aside to find his Victoria.

After searching through the entire tavern and the bushes and thickets outside, he turned to go back to the White Rose, traveling so rapidly that he reached it in five minutes.

When he entered the barroom, he encountered two persons entirely unknown to him, sending up great clouds of bad tobacco smoke from corncob pipes. Since they did not appear to see him, he did not greet them and rushed instinctually to the cellar door, where he saw the faint glimmer of an oil lamp.

He had barely begun down the steep steps than he saw his wife embracing the young mulatto, begging him to join her plan before it was too late.

Sullivan held back just in time, though his feet trembled and his legs wavered. When he realized what was afoot, a cold shock ran through his body, and quiet reasoning and courage took the place of irritation and painful tension.

"We will have no guests in our bedroom tonight," he heard her say. "It will not be hard to get rid of him with his dagger while he is sleeping. He will come home drunk anyway, and so I'll have all that much easier a time.

You only need to wait in the next room and help me get him out of the way.—Since tomorrow is the day he is to go to Montréal for a week to purchase supplies, no one will miss him, and the rest will take care of itself—consider your child," she added, raising a finger.

Anyone can imagine the decision Sullivan made on hearing these words. He intended to sneak away as quietly as he had come, but he slipped on the trapdoor and fell headfirst into the cellar.

The next day they brought out the bodies of Sullivan and the young mulatto, both pierced by numerous dagger cuts.

Victoria of the White Rose vanished without a trace.

Two months after these events, a scene took place in Knoxville, a border town on American territory, the description of which causes the pen to dance the tarantella, as if it had been bitten by that poisonous spider. The pen itself turns against the hand and paralyzes it, a naked dagger wounding the hand that holds it.

Two murders took place in that little town, one right after the other, and the exquisite details of these crimes stoked popular rage to such an extent that a mob took the woman accused of the deeds, a very pregnant Negro woman, out of the hands of justice to exact the death penalty with their own hands.

For this purpose, she was barbarically paraded through the streets of Knoxville with a rope around her body and neck, to be hanged from a tree on the outskirts of town.

The main instigators of this dreadful people's justice were two Canadians and a young planter's son from Louisiana; the last of these was the bearer of a famous historic name and the son of a member of the House of Representatives, a Calhounist of the most rabid sort.

As the victim of this inhuman barbarism was about to be hoisted up, the noose around her neck, the mood of the once raging mob turned around and there appeared to be some effort to free her from the hands of her hangmen—then the aforementioned planter's son rushed on the poor Negro woman and snapped her into the air.

The clumsiness with which this was done prevented the noose from tightening quickly, which meant that the victim swung from the shaking limb in dreadful spasms.

Then the planter's son made himself a double hangman, climbing the tree, placing his foot on the shoulders of the half-hanged woman, and breaking her neck with his powerful fists.

At the same instant, a living being emerged from between the legs of the hanged woman, falling into the midst of the horrified mob.

So the hangman was the midwife of a poor Negro baby! The child was—Sulla. Victoria paid with her life for a crime she had not committed, while she had escaped unpunished for the atrocity she had executed in the cellar of her tavern in Marytown.

We will not deal with the subsequent complicated events in Sulla's life, since this brings us to a conclusion and we must take up the threads of our novel once more.

For the interim, let it be said that Sulla, once he had grown out of boyhood, became one of the most infamous and feared gamblers in Five Points, and he soon dedicated himself to swindles both great and small, from which he earned his keep.

The acquaintance of a Negress he met on a trip to Buffalo exercised such a dangerous influence over him that, at the age of twenty-one, he felt capable of every crime so long as it produced money.

A very young mulatto girl, who had run away from her parents at the age of six and possessed an acuteness without equal, became their inseparable companion and aide.

So we see that Sulla was determined to abuse the good nature and naiveté of Cato and the two women in the most shameful manner.

Chapter 13

The Manuscript

Emil unrolled the pages with a trembling hand. He began to read with a soft but understandable voice.

> When a sailor on the high seas encounters the lying image of the Fata Morgana, he drops his hands from the rim of his wheel and gapes in terror at the unknown form that appears to be advancing on his craft. In his mind he already sees his sails upset, his masts splintered, and his ship sinking into the depths of the sea—then all of a sudden, the mists lift from his eyes, a propitious breeze fills his sails, and he sets off for his goal with reinforced courage. The eerie Fata Morgana is soon forgotten; for him there is no more worry—he does not ask whither and why. How different it is with you!
>
> You, who have thus far run your ship of life right into the rocks of ordinary life, and instead of the Fata Morgana you have seen only the dreadful images of misery and despair. You had no reason to tremble before an un-

known peril, and even if you looked death in the face, you laughed it away with wine and kisses.

Lucy hung with flaming eyes on Emil's face, which never seemed so beautiful to her than at this moment.

Emil wrapped his arm more securely around Lucy and continued:

> But from the very moment you were so suddenly taken out of the sphere of your earlier life and effort, without any knowledge of the interconnections of the events that took place, you must often have been tempted to ask, "whither and why?" You already know the secret power of the *Mantis religiosa,* which I need not explain any further; but by reading these pages again, you will recover the memory it took from you. You will recall images long forgotten, which will emerge as if from afar, taunting your imagination. But beware of seeking to return to old relationships, or even to recall them in your minds. They will only hold you back from the high goal that I have set for you and toward which you must strive with a holy zeal. In the future, put aside the petty concerns of duty prescribed for less-gifted souls by law and tradition. Since poverty mutilates everything noble, drawing people down into the abyss of filth and vice, and wealth, when carefully earned over time, with great care and concern, only narrows a person and deadens any higher mission, I will leave to you all the millions you will find in the lower chambers of your present residence. I give it to you *unearned,* and without a drop of your own sweat, so that the concern, labor, and speculation needed to get it will not devour your beauty or the charm of your faces. *Only beauty, joined with the treasures of this earth, has the right to enter into the struggle for a higher idea and achieve it.* For ugliness, if rich, and beauty, if poor, will only be accompanied by ignoble motives in their actions and undertakings.

Like a confused wanderer who suddenly sees a light in the distance through the darkness of night, who cheers and runs toward the glittering star of hope with a quick step—that was how Emil and Lucy appeared now, as their darkness was pierced by such a bright beam streaming into their overjoyed and enthusiastic eyes. They understood all too well the tremendous truth of this splendid sentence—only a few moments before, the old man had said much the same to them in person—and they had heard him, but they had not *grasped* it!

"If you survive the trial by fire and keep your beauty from harm, when I return in five years, I shall introduce you to a place that will make you immortal unto all generations," Emil repeated the words the old man had said to them in solemn tones.

"For it is yours to shatter chains and free the South from its shame," Lucy repeated in holy enthusiasm.

After she had brushed a lock of her dark hair from her eyes, she began to read.

By the time Lucy had completed the following portion of the manuscript, it was already well after midnight.

What Emil learned from Lucy's lips clearly and solidly filled in the gap from that earlier night until their residence in the Atchafalaya Bank, and from that moment the *Mantis religiosa* had lost its power over them.

In the last line stood the name *Hiram.*

Emil and Lucy stared at this name wordlessly; it was as mysterious to them as a hieroglyph, and yet it seemed to them they had heard this name before.

(PREPARED FROM THE OLD MAN'S MANUSCRIPT)

1. The End of the Night of Masquerade

Even before Emil's feet had touched the ground, he was grasped from behind by the powerful arms of the sergeant of the night watch and ordered to accompany him without protest.

"You are known, señor, and whatever you intend to do in this masquerade you will be so good as to inform our esteemed recorder in the morning," he said in a courteous tone, quite at odds with his powerful fists. It was Luis Montes, the sergeant of the night watch in the Second District.

"You are known as well, Mister Luis, and I have as much of a right to ask you to accompany me," Emil responded testily. "If you don't let me go," he continued, raising his voice, "then tomorrow everyone in the city will know that Mister Luis, the mighty and strict sergeant of the night watch in the Second District, threw a young man having a joke by dressing in his girlfriend's clothes into the city privy,* out of jealousy . . ."

Mister Luis, who knew Emil quite well as a troublemaker, and who feared a personal conflict, reached under his cloak for his maritze† to call some privates‡ if need be.

Emil perceived this. With unbelievable agility he pulled his right arm from the sergeant's fists to prevent him from sounding his maritze—then,

* Calaboose.

† An instrument that gives a rattling sound, used by the night watch to call for help in emergencies. It is also used as a signal for fires.

‡ Ordinary members of the night watch.

before Emil's astounded eyes, Mister Luis fell to the ground as if struck by lightning. In the same instant, Emil saw an old, tall, gaunt figure looming over him, who signaled to him to drag the fallen man into the next alley and leave him to his fate.

Emil mechanically followed the stranger's directions.

Then, once he had recovered from the first shock, Emil asked his rescuer what had happened.

Instead of offering an answer, the figure took him by the hand and drew him forward.

Emil began to feel strange—for, after they had taken a few steps, the stranger ordered him to lay his own arm in his, and he covered Emil's face with a shawl.

Emil, who had apparently forgotten that he was in women's clothes, came to with a start. The conduct of the stranger appeared to him natural enough, if Emil was thought to be a lady. It occured to him for an instant that this old man might demand some recompense for his cavalier service, and he would have laughed out loud if he had not caught the stranger's eye, which looked into his face with bitter earnest.

"I know quite well what's going on with you," he said, interrupting the silence. "If you think I take you for a lady, you are much mistaken, and so I advise you to restrain your overheated imagination. Despite your masquerade, I knew you just as well as did Señor Luis, who now lies dead in the alley."

"Dead?" Emil repeated, pale with terror. "Whatever led you to kill him . . . ?"

"Yes, Señor Montes is dead," he interrupted soberly, "and I tell you, young man, he earned his death."

The old man said this in an earnest, harsh tone, inspecting Emil's face right through the veil.

"But dead—dead! Impossible—really dead, then? Consider, if they find him in the vicinity of Madame Wilson's house, if they've seen me—seen you—but no one knows you—but me—but what caused you to do that?"

Thus Emil maundered, failing to give his words the clarity appropriate for one of life's serious moments.

He was seized by an unspeakable anxiety. He attempted to get ahold of himself, in vain, to explain the episode as an ordinary fact of life—but he failed. Revulsion and terror gained the upper hand over his usual belittling frivolity.

He walked alongside the old man for a long time, always keeping an arm under his, saying not a word.

He did not even notice that he was already going along the levee of the Third Municipality, so that on their right side the masts and decks groaned and creaked, and the riverbank guards along the Mississippi sent their dark red glow up into the black coils of the clouds, which floated heavy and oppressive above their heads.

An intermittant sharp breeze shook the lanterns so violently that the gas flames only shed an uncertain glow, warning men to be careful of their hats.

Rousing song streamed from the barrooms, and with heedless cries the shoreboys and the sailors—who had only yesterday escaped the perils of the deep—wallowed in prayer to the American demigod, "Old Irish Whiskey," now and then throwing a significant glance at a tambourine girl, who raised the revelry yet another notch with her song and play. Many a picayune flew into her tambourine or her extended apron.

The watchmen beat their iron-bound billies on the sidewalks, making them echo a hundredfold throughout the city.

The old man stopped and let his arm part from Emil's.

"Now we are at the Hamburg Mill," he said. "Would you do me and yourself the pleasure of calling Lucy out—but—let's wait a moment, she's in the middle of a dance."

"Here, get up on this stoop and look through the gap in the curtain—you can see her—pay good attention to her—you see her in her frivolity for the last time."

Emil stepped onto the stoop and peered through the gap in the knitted curtain.

He saw Lucy in her masquerade, dancing joyously with a young Creole girl, seized in a saraband.*

The saraband was now at an end.

The old man signaled to Emil to go into the dance hall and return with Lucy.

While Emil pressed his way through the exhausted dancers, Lucy advanced toward Emil, dressed (we must recall) as a gentleman, hand in hand with the young Creole. She took one look at him and was shaken, then stared at him; then she fell into his arms as if she was insane, pushing back his bonnet and shawl, marveling at his coiffeur. Then she began to laugh, kissing him repeatedly without paying any attention to the people standing around, drawn by this strange show. They quickly formed into a circle around the couple.

*A flamboyant variation of the fandango, once a favorite dance of the Turks.

"Didn't I just tell you that this young, pretty gentleman was Madame Wilson?" a young French steersman said to his plump little Alsatian blonde, who hung on his arms half drunk.

"She is still the lusty Madame Wilson of the Mulatto's Settlement," he continued. "I'll be damned if there is as beautiful a woman in the whole Parish of New Orleans—look, look, honey— those splendid sparkling black eyes—damn, a man could go quite mad seeing her like that—look, look, how nicely those trousers fit her . . ."

Fortunately, the fat little Alsatian had such a heavy head from dancing, and perhaps also from drinking, that she didn't hear her beau's ungallant words.

Lucy's flamboyant behavior set Emil in considerable distress. How could he convince Lucy to leave the hall at the command of the stranger? Command? Yes indeed, it had been a command to him, for the man had such a lordly manner that Emil really believed he had to obey. An unexplainable intimation told him that he no longer belonged to himself, that he now had a master who would guide his steps and deeds from now on.

Emil was often a dreamer of the most extreme sort, and dreamers are inclined to superstition. The sudden appearance of the old man, in an instant, at the second when the situation with the sergeant was getting serious, had made him subservient to the stranger.

What was to be done now? The celebrants pressed ever closer to the two and appeared to be watching this strange scene with intense interest. He surely couldn't take Lucy's arm and head for the door, and even if he did, the entire swarm of the curious and the drunk would rush after them—and the old man? . . . These thoughts were crowding Emil's brain as the doors opened, the old man stepped to the threshold, and his awe-inspiring voice cut through murmur, laughter, and yelling. At the sound of this powerful voice, the guests scattered, turning away from Emil and Lucy to stare at the weird visitor. He called out into the crowd: "Lucy Wilson! I have a word to speak with you!"

Even before their overheated spirits could recover from their amazement, Emil and Lucy had vanished from the ballroom.

2. Another Home, and the Note

On the Rue d'Amour, in the Third District, next to weathered hovels of boards, stands a pretty, friendly little house in the middle of a garden filled with oleanders, magnolias, and lilacs. The little two-story house is pale yellow paint with bright green shutters. Out of the middle of the roof, covered with shingles, rises a belvedere with two little benches, from which one can watch the glimmer of the Southern Cross on a clear night in undisturbed peace.

Even at this late hour, a young man sits in one of the lower rooms in front of the fireplace, engaged in reading a note again and again.

His handsome features were sharply etched by the light of an intense coal fire, giving him and his immediate surroundings the appearance of a painting by Rembrandt.

Two wax candles that stood on either side of an inkstand on a round table with a white marble top had flickered out, and here and there on the wicks little sparks still glimmered on and off.

A high, unstable light flickered on the hearth as the fire rose and fell, flames flexing and licking the inner layer of coal.

The parts of the room beyond the periphery of the fire were wrapped in a magical darkness.

The young man is not alone.

Under the fine mosquito netting of a double bed, a young woman is kneeling as she drives the mosquitos out of the bedding with a peacock feather, carefully closing the curtains when she believes she has expelled them all.

True love has made her, a woman who had been supple and quick as a tiger and quick as a panther in the canebrake of Louisiana or Arkansas, as tame as a llama, cheerfully and patiently bearing her master's burden.

The young man, meanwhile, was enchanted by the young woman's fire and would happily let himself be ripped by the claws of this female panther.

It was Emil's first love.

They were passing their first night as bride and bridegroom.

The young man mused, shuddering over his happy possession. This was the third night he had passed with her.

The young woman was still kneeling beneath the curtains, looking at the spot by the fireplace with an intoxicated gaze.

The young man put the note he had been repeatedly reading on the mantel, supporting his handsome head in his flat hand.

The young woman watched his every move.

"I hope that my answer to these lines will separate me forever from my wife, and that it will cause Jenny not to concern herself with me in the future," the young man murmured to himself.

"Now I truly believe," he continued, "that I never felt any love for Jenny, and, beyond that, this relationship hinders me in carrying out the duties the old man has imposed on me; for Jenny would never tolerate what my Lucy gives me. So it would lead to ever more stupid disputes and petty quarrels, which would simply alienate me.

"I do not marvel that she has been able to find out where I live, since little Tiberius ran all over the city—and this note—hm! hm! Forgiven, everything forgotten—return to my hearth and home, hm! hm!—those are sheer stupidities which will no longer trap me. Sentimental nonsense—well, if he tells them about Lucy's presence, despite his promise not to—any answer is unnecessary, and Frida—she will not try to talk her into contacting me again.

"Since Tiberius, as I recall, saw Lucy weeping—oh, I hope that Tiberius will describe everything down to the last detail—I should not have forbidden him to—and how much Lucy has changed now that she loves me, no, more than that, she is madly in lo . . ." he was about to say "in love with me"—"No, that is a commonplace word, used, overused and used up—and who have I to thank! Who other than the mysterious stranger . . ."

Suddenly Emil listened.

Lucy was striking her tongue against her teeth, making the sound peculiar to her race when love was tormenting her.

Emil turned his face away from the coal fire, in which he had been engrossed, and focused his gaze on the magical darkness of the bed curtains.

"Emil my love," Lucy began, laying her right hand on her heart and turning the index finger of her left hand inward, "look at the movement of the pointer on the sundial of your love, how quickly it moves forward and begs that you do not allow the dark shadows of night to vanish in vain."

Emil shuddered sensuously at these words. It was the third time Lucy had spoken to him in that way; there was something supernatural about that marvelous conjuration.

"Emil, my love, look not so deeply into the dark glow, and let me clear the clouds away from your forehead . . . Don't you hear the raging music in my heart? . . . Come, lay your lovely head on my heart and listen how the love god plays the zaranda* there . . . Do you hear it? Now they are clapping their hands—the zaranda is still, and love has once again celebrated a new triumph . . . and you hesitate, my beloved?"

What Emil means when he sighs "Let me stand here a moment more, I am chilled," is a mystery that only love is capable of resolving.

"Emil, my love, how can you stare at the coals when you are cold? Don't

*A small stringed instrument that Cupid plays when he is certain of his victory.

you know that your Lucy's heart will warm you more? When the sun breaks through the lilacs and cypresses again, these coals will be extinguished, but not the glow of my heart . . ."

Emil responded, just as mysteriously, "It is still too early for me to lie next to your heart, my Lucy, sing me those songs you heard as a child on the plantation—sing me a Negro song!"

"Give me the melody," Lucy sighed.

Emil approached Lucy, wrapping his arm around her . . .

Outside the Southern Cross quietly glittered in the deep blue heaven.

3. A Key to Remembrance

Emil and Lucy had already lived several days in their lovely little house without receiving a visit from the old man. They had not forgotten him in their silent happiness—they longed for him with every passing hour.

Then, as Lucy was watering her newly planted orange tree, a letter fell at her feet. She turned around, but she saw no one. Without opening the seal or even reading the address, she rushed into the house and gave it to Emil, who was sitting, musing over a book lying open before him on a stand. Emil opened the letter. The hand was new to him, but he swiftly discovered the writer from its contents.

The letter said:

> Lucy's two old Negroes received their letters of emancipation yesterday, and they moved at once to her house in Orleans Street, which is now theirs. No one should now be able to say that Lucy Wilson owns slaves or that they will take their chains to the grave. They should live the few years that they still have free and without concern for their own support, not tossed away like used-up goods, as people do with mules that have become unfit for work.
>
> Lucy and Emil will leave their little house on this day and move to another home, where they will lose for a while all memories of their earlier lives and the distressing relationships that went with them. For the high purpose for which they are being prepared makes such a measure unavoidable.
>
> Later, after they have survived this interval, their memory of the past will no longer stand in the way. A healing gift of nature will take care of that.

The sense of the last words appeared to be an impenetrable riddle to Lucy and Emil. The notion that they were to leave the little house, which they had so come to love, disturbed them. But they complied with the old man's desires.

Two days later, in the darkness of night, the old man appeared to them in person and led them, after they had taken a farewell drink he had prepared for them, to the lofty apartment in the Atchafalaya Bank, where we met them so unexpectedly in the ninth chapter.

As Emil was rolling the manuscript up, a strip of parchment fell out, which told them the precise location of the treasure.

As the old man had commanded them, they left the Atchafalaya Bank with the treasure that very night, in order to find a residence of their own choice.

Book
II

Jenny and Frida

Among the thousands the Old World sends us every year, who soon learn the vanity of their longed-for desires and golden dreams, those most to be pitied are those who have ennobled their hearts and spirits with fine education and esthetic training, who have given a fine touch to even the most routine phases of their lives.

It is not proper for a man to wring his hands in despair and summon up his household gods, even if all of his hopes have been shattered on the stern rocks of pitiless egoism. He is, after all, in a land where the free development of his material and intellectual abilities are given the widest play, and even if he is poor and abandoned today, a lucky toss tomorrow could put him among persons who value his company and find him irreplaceable.

It is not so with a woman.

If a woman in a foreign land finds no replacement for the goodness and beauty she left behind, or if repellent conditions and the ordinary problems of prosaic life pull her out of her position of being adored and honored, a woman might easily let her tears flow, and look back on her home hearth with doubled intensity and longing. If the same woman commits an offense that sacrifices the paradise of her heart to secure her existence or that makes the decent conclusion of her life dependent on intelligent calculation, then it might be easier to cut the heartstrings that bind her to the fairy-tale dream of earlier days.

There is nothing more elevated and majestic than a woman's heart bleeding to death on foreign soil from unsatisfied longing. There is, on the other hand, nothing so contemptible and criminal as the heart of a woman who thinks of her homeland with bitter mockery and takes pride in her success at denying it.

Our stars in a blue field can encourage and even enthuse a man, for they remind him of the greatness of the nation called to spread its blessings to the entire globe. But a woman? The woman sees in the stars of our flag only the stars that once shone in the cloudless heavens of her homeland and enchanted her heart with endless longing. What does she care for the greatness of a nation? It is the greatness and richness of a heart that fills up, encourages, and steels life.

Jenny and her sister *Frida* are the passionflowers of an old noble family, once very rich and propertied. Their father was one of the first officials of the crown in a South German court, as well as a member of the assembly of estates.

The high nobility in the residence was then divided into two parties who constantly feuded over court offices, crown positions, and other important charges. One, the Protestant party, was the weaker, counting only a few favored by the ruling prince; the other, the Catholic, or court party, so called because it contained the former ministers of the electoral principality and hence, on the whole, was more propertied and richer than the Protestant, had precedent in all matters at court, and their members held virtually all important civil and military offices.[1]

The father of the two sisters was Protestant and thus a target for the intrigues and cabals of the Catholic party.

It was only through the efforts of the Duchess of Braganza, who then resided at court, together with the Duke of L*, that the intrigues of this party were stymied so that Jenny and Frida's father was able to keep his post for a few years. He owed this to his wife, who was an Italian from the famous house of the Barnardi Taron, related to Doña Maria da Gloria, if rather distantly. Enthusiastic for the principles and faith of her church, she had won the Duchess of Braganza, who held to her own church so intensely, as a close friend, and this explains her efforts to help him keep his status.

There were no important moments in the childhood years of the two sisters, except for their conversion to Catholicism at the age of six. This happened at the express wish of the ruling prince, who was interested in the two angelic children beyond the limits of his usual responsibility. The most that these children won by this act was that their hearts were brought closer to that of their mother.

Until the age of eleven they were under the control of a splendid governess, whose goodness of heart and pure goodwill had a positive influence on both the sisters.

After the sudden death of their guardian, they were brought to the noble residential school of the court town, where their hearts and spirits were developed and ennobled in the finest manner. Heaped with prizes, they left the school at sixteen and were introduced to the wider world.

Surrounded and treasured by cavaliers young and old, the two girls were queens of the balls whenever they were being staged. When Jenny and Frida appeared, a swarm of devotees gathered about them, warming themselves and basking in the glow of their youth. Yet no one was ever able to draw one of the two sisters to himself.

Their talkative amiability and unbounded naiveté never crossed the limits of being charming, enchanting, and exciting; but they also drove their sentimental devotees crazy.

High-level gossip designated first this man, then that, as the favored of the two graces; indeed, opinions were occasionally voiced which, had they gone unchecked, would have been dangerous to their continued liberty.

So, one fine day, people were surprised with the astonishing news that there were two more canonesses in the court, bearing the cross of the Order of St. Anna.[2]

With this unexpected news, all suitors and courtiers might as well have been struck by lightning, as they ran from one antechamber and boudoir to another spreading this dreadful news with the swiftness of the wind, giving free rein to the gushings of their hearts.

But when it became known, not long after, that the father of these new canonesses of the Order of St. Anna had fallen into disfavor with the old prince and would not receive any more subsidies for his finances, the disturbed moods were calmed and suitors sought their blossoms elsewhere.

Yet when Venus turns her eyes to the floor, Cupid takes the sharpest arrows out of his quiver and sends them truly and accurately, preferably into an immaculate lap.

Where Cupid is on the prowl, heaven and hell can do what they like—he will upend them both with the quiet whir of his little wings. He can build his nest as comfortably under the naked timbers of a peasant's hut as beneath the gilded vaults of a throne room. He ripens his rascality just as well under the bosom-kerchief of a seamstress as in the folds of a queen's purple gown. He flies with the same cheerfulness into the lap of a song-girl as into that of a Priestess of Vesta.

It was one of the most splendid galas the court had ever seen. In the court chapel, the high mass proper to such occasions was being celebrated. The archbishop himself in full regalia, buried in a gold-embroidered baldachin beset with diamonds, presided at the altar. His ministrants were two suffragan bishops, for the court assembled here, abounding with high nobles and the most elevated officers, would not have tolerated the lower clergy functioning before them.

Then—at the very instant the high priest of the sole salvific Church was raising the holy of holies to show it to the assembled, two sets of eyes, which had never before seen each other, met and blazed with devouring flames. One of the court pages, standing on the lowest steps of the altar with a wax candle in his hands, looked into the deep blue eyes of a young lady who was then a mere two steps away. Instead of rising to contemplate the holy of holies, her eyes had encountered the heavenly blue eyes of the young blond noble.

The young woman wore the black satin habit of a canoness. On the broad light-blue silk ribbon across her breasts, the Cross of the Order of St. Anna flickered in the purest enamel.

• • •

And so love entered Jenny's immaculate heart, to take her thousands of miles from her altars, to find a faithless spouse in Emil, the blond, passionate page.

Jenny stripped herself that day of her habit, as it was too tight for a throbbing, quivering heart.

For her father, it was the last day he would stand at his prince's side.

The bestowal of the Order of St. Anna on his two daughters, which had been tied to a considerable annual pension, had been his total compensation for the offices he had lost.

His property was insignificant, and he was barely able to cover the needs of a life at court.

One can then well imagine how distressing it was to him when a determined Jenny came to her father to tell him that she had ceased being a canoness, since the young Count Emil * was now the betrothed of her heart.

The old noble was at first distressed because Emil was without property and could only hope for rapid advancement in state service, and even that depended on him giving up his page's post and completing his academic studies. Still, he made his peace with his daughter's decision, for he knew her character only too well and perceived that nothing could be accomplished by force, since it would only alienate his child's heart.

So he gave in to the inevitable, and when Jenny informed him a year later of her wish to accompany her betrothed, Emil's brother, and Frida to settle in America, this double blow was particularly hard, but he gave his blessing. The considerable sum provided for them to buy property in the southern states was made even larger through her mother's unexpected contribution, so nothing more stood in the way of their journey across the wide ocean.

In most recent times, an uncanny voice sounds from our own shores toward the Old World, heard by its most wayward children. These listeners are often repelled and made sick by Columbia, and they soon long for their old household gods. But others regain their strength on the transatlantic soil and grow up like giants, in tireless striving. To them, the New World is the revenge of a repressed people; the New World takes them up with joy, happily showing them the paths they must take to forget their earlier humiliations.

• • •

I was there; I have never seen such a night.
There were no stars to be seen in the heavens, sir, it was gold-dust. The sea was so placid and lightly rippled that one could wish nothing additional to be in paradise.
That was not all. The ship seemed to set fire to the waves when it parted them.
There was nothing to do. The ship went forward with all sails up, topmast and side-sails in the wind, like a young maiden going to mass on a Sunday morning.
I stretched myself over the bulkhead and gazed into the water.
[Thousand and One Spirits]

The well-coppered three-master *Gutenberg* left its anchoring place. A favorable breeze soon drove it up the channel that divides the high-towering chalk cliffs of proud Albion from blooming Normandy.

By the time it swam on the roads of Lisbon, two whole days had not passed since weighing anchor.

The captain rubbed his hands with glee, for this was the *Gutenberg*'s first journey to New Orleans.

The crew was enjoying the fine day. Some of them lay in half-elevated positions in the lifeboats, weaving or tying cable; others were smoking short clay pipes filled with cut shag. Some chatted with pretty little peasant girls, dandling their long braids and inspecting the stiff linen and the silver chains beset with coins with which they were arrayed.

The son of the second mate, a boy of eight, sat on the neck of *Gutenberg* himself, well carved with book in hand, decorating the prow of the emigrant ship, his face turned to the west.

A colorful freebooter from the Schleswig-Holstein wars, wearing a blue blouse with a high collar of black, red, and gold, threw a hook as thick as his finger at the dolphins circling the ship. Several children, boys and girls, sat on the edge of the stern and clapped their hands whenever a flight of flying fish rose above the surface of the ocean only to vanish again in the glittering silver waves.

From the cables and lines hung the shirts and stockings of the steerage passengers, yellow from the saltwater, swinging in the splendid breeze. From a cloudless sky the sun burned down, melting the tar coatings on the tackle and the planks of the deck. But the rays did not injure anything, for the wind that filled the sails also cooled sunburned and tanned faces.

So it was for days, weeks. The trade winds had been blowing at the backs of the sailors stationed at the wheel for a long time—ever and ever still the right and proper direction.

Mysterious weeds, without a home, driven by wave and wind, swam on the surface of the Sargasso Sea . . .

The ship's fortune suddenly shifted when they entered the Windward Channel, as the wind ceased to blow into the sails and the air became motionless.

At Cape Henry, the keel of the boat stood still in the ocean.

In the same way, doldrums often prevail in the heart of people, after a period of haste and rushing forward on the flood of desires and hopes and before throwing down an anchor in the harbor of happiness.

When perverse winds forced a ship to tack, passengers share in a bad mood that banishes all high spirits and every good word. This is doubly the case with the doldrums. Whoever has been to sea before can recall the uncomfortable impression the dead silence, often lasting weeks, makes on those in the midst of doldrums.

When tacking, the movement of the ship still imparts a certain elasticity to our spirit. Stuck in the doldrums, a person is dead within a living body.

The deck passengers of the *Gutenberg* felt just such a distressingly bad mood. They lounged about and camped everywhere; they stood up only to sit down again; then they threw another disconsolate glance at the still sea, gaped at the sky, crept into their shelters, or cursed sailors who had taken some utensil or a bit of scarce food. There was only some life in these good people early in the morning, at midday, or evening, when they bustled about with their wooden platters and tin coffeepots in the galley, jostling one another.

The cabins afforded an entirely different vista.

Here accident had thrown together a company of the most select sort, a rarity worth some remark.

Save for the captain, the two mates, and the ship's steward, there were only six persons in the cabins. There was a Hungarian officer who had recently served with a regiment of hussars in Esseck, a German architect, a German cavalry officer, a student of law, and one without a profession but with no small knowledge and so pleasant that he had no problem making himself loved and irreplaceable by the entire company.

Besides these, there were also two ladies whose endearing, lovable manners poured out a certain charm over the entire company, just as the moon bestows a certain magic on a landscape without any special beauty.

They were Jenny and Frida, on their way to America three years ago.

Emil sat at Jenny's side. Frida was placed between his brother and their young cousin. The architect, who was called by his name of Albert in the frivolity, responded in brotherly revenge by addressing him as Karl.

We have encountered Karl in Algiers in later years, and we have already seen how tenderly the two sisters regarded this cheerful man, with his friendly eyes. He had decided to emigrate to the New World with his two cousins.

We already know what became of Albert, and what distresses his marital relationship with Claudine caused him.

Albert, who never left Jenny's side, and Karl, who never ignored Frida on the *Gutenberg,* brought their own motivations with them to America, and the unfolding of their stories, once they parted company, properly belongs to the telling of their future lives.

Frida did not hide her attraction to the young officer of hussars, although she was also being encouraged to intimacy by Emil's brother. The officer pressed for a commitment, which was actually brought to pass a few weeks after their arrival in the New World.

Here, in sight of the uncanny cliff formations of the isle of Haiti, Jenny had the fateful dream that has already been fulfilled in part in this story, if we call Hiram to mind, and part of which will perhaps yet receive its full significance in later years.

It was one of those windless nights aboard the *Gutenberg,* as Jenny awoke from sleep with a shock, reaching her hand out to her husband and suddenly embracing him in her arms. Emil, utterly surprised, sealed his wife's lips with a thousand kisses. Hot tears flowed from Jenny's eyes and down her cheeks, bringing him into painful distress until the terrified sleeper told him her dream.

Afterwards, when it had dawned and they could sit together on the deck, they both laughed over her childish terror and superstitious heart.

Emil did not yet have the slightest suspicion—a separation from his Jenny seemed utterly impossible. But Jenny thought often about it, and as time went on and she had moments to reflect, she ruminated over the strange dream.

We take the following moving portrayal from Jenny's diary:

> Now that a depraved woman has stolen my Emil, when I look back over the past days of love and peaceful life together, there continually arises from my soul that dream I had several years ago as our ship lay motionless among the

Antilles. It caused me great terror. Sailboat from beloved Germany, if only the storms had smashed you then! Oh, that you could have run on a sharp reef, and had the lightning written on our hearts: "They loved each other until death."

Emil! Emil! It is very late for me to write these lines. Frida has already been sleeping for an hour; perhaps she is dreaming of you as well, about our sunken love and our past happiness. Do you still think of the night when you pressed your terrified Jenny to tell you that dreadful dream? No—you've certainly forgotten long ago—are you lying in the arms of passion at this very moment? So look once more on this portentous dream, and if these pages ever come to you, may they gather your tears.

We remained on the cabin deck with each other until after midnight. Karl charmed us with his fresh humor and spun the plans he would carry out in the New World, plans which went years into the future. Castles were built in the air and torn down again only to be built anew in another place. Domestic happiness was described and relationships established. Emil's brother, the usually decorous cavalry officer, massacred thousands of Mexicans and saw his name shine among the heroes of the Republic. Albert, the architect, presented the finest projects for a cenotaph for Washington, and he heard his name mentioned in honor at the White House. The Hungarian raved for Frida, that is to say, he sat the whole night through beside her and said not one word. My Emil, who had studied law, chose the career of an attorney and saw himself rising to Senator or at least to the House of Representatives. Me? I participated heartily, but I quietly suppressed ambition and saw myself in the quiet idyll of a plantation. We left the deck with the captain's wishes that we sleep well and awaken fresh and cheerful in the morning.

Emil went to sleep right away. I remained wakeful for at least an hour. Then sleep descended on my eyelids to bestow on me the unspeakable happiness of glimpsing the dark shadows of the dream world, something I very much enjoyed.

I found myself alone on the ship. There was not a living soul. Black clouds hung in the sky, almost touching the masts. I ran about in my agitation, calling for Emil—but he did not hear me. My anxiety exceeded all bounds. I climbed the mast and called out the precious name of Emil to the broad ocean. But the old ocean appeared to mock me, I heard only its murmur, and I felt a heavy breathing. I saw no waves—it was so dark!—As I cried and climbed one mast after another, one rope ladder after another, I suddenly looked in the direction from which the isle of Haiti loomed out of the eternal flood. I perceived a gigantic figure with a pale, pale face, with gray, tousled hair and thin, wrinkled hands, first pressed cramped together and then spreading its fingers to fearsome length. Then the hands raised endless chains that lay at fingertip and dashed them against the rock of the cliffs. I heard them rattling—so loud that it seemed they were falling off of me. Descending from the cliffs I saw—oh, my senses still swim when I think of it today—Emil, *my* Emil, holding the hand of a beautiful young woman with long, black hair and great sparkling eyes. They approached the giant figure and bowed to it. He spread his hands over them in blessing and guided their heads together in a mutual kiss. It was so dark around me, and yet I could see everything. I saw the black, sparkling eyes of the woman and the sparkling heavenly blue eyes of my Emil, who hung joyfully on her mouth . . . then this painting vanished. A streak of fire swept across the island, illuminating millions of black men—they streamed in long columns, whose ends could not be seen, behind flowing, blood-red flags, rushing like spouts of fresh blood, and above these troops I saw that fatal woman along with Emil, and the gaunt giant figure strode before them, with an enormous balance in his bony hand—then once more I heard the rattling and grating of chains—then—oh, I really believed I could see for hundreds of miles, and that they were even drawing up on our coast—then loud screaming sounded, and I heard intoxicating, wild song, as if from the throats of the victors in a great battle. Then—oh the end of this dream is so distressing—my pen is weeping—Emil was separated from me forever! Is it really so? And yet it was but a dream! . . .

More pages from Jenny's diary lie scattered before us. Many have been lost, and we must sincerely regret that those lost are precisely the ones that come from her period of happiness and loving commitment.

Among those before us, we can find an incomplete sketch of the rest of the voyage until her arrival in New Orleans and the first efforts and accomplishments of the friends. We can find there that Jenny stayed with her spouse and Frida in the St. Charles Hotel for the first three months, and then she moved into a charming little house on Apollo Street that Emil had bought at auction for three thousand dollars.[3]

The friends from the *Gutenberg* sought to overcome the difficulty of alien conditions and new associations through mutual social visits and harmonious cooperation, and they became indispensable to one another. Frida, who had married the Hungarian hussar officer in a civil ceremony, over Jenny's and Karl's objections, remained almost every day with her sister, since her husband was usually occupied during the day in a cigar factory. At first Frida seemed happy and satisfied. But Jenny, who knew how to read Frida's eyes and who did not miss the slightest mood of her beloved sister, soon perceived that, for Frida, marriage was not a heavenly ladder upon which she could ascend to happiness.

Cousin Karl was able to get a position right away as clerk on a Mobile boat, partly due to his accidental acquaintance with the owner and partly due to his excellent English, already learned in Germany. He received the sum of a hundred dollars a month, a great deal for a novice in a foreign country. Whenever his boat was in town, he did not neglect Jenny and Frida, regularly visiting their houses in turn.

Albert, the young architect, had some initial difficulties but managed to win a position as a draftsman on the construction of an important building in New Orleans. Despite his restless activity, he still had enough time left over to taste forbidden fruit, and so it came about that on one of his romantic escapades he made the acquaintance of the lovable Claudine de Lesuire, who had been coddled and spoiled by her elderly aunt. Yet he never failed to make his regular visits to the cottage in Apollo Street.

So passed a year. Emil, who had been entrusted with the significant funds still at his disposal, with Jenny's concurrence and in keeping with plans made in Germany, was supposed to buy a small plantation. But after putting his wife off month after month, he proved untrue to his commitments and wasted much of the money through wild revelry with his brother and the Hungarian, who was already bankrupt. The good Jenny, who was not sheltered from her husband's conduct, tried everything possible to bring him back to the proper path. Whenever she corrected him, which she always did in the gentlest manner possible, it seemed for a time that Emil had indeed returned to his obligations. He swore it to her, indeed he wept whole nights on her shoulder.

But what was he weeping over? He was weeping because he could not love his wife as much as he once had; he wept because he did not have the strength to tell her.

It was already too late for him, and for Jenny.

Lucy Wilson had already caught him in her net.

So he soon sold the cottage in Apollo Street, since Lucy's expenses and the costs of the Mulattoes' Settlement were on the rise, and a house could be had in Algiers for less than half the price.

About this time, the Hungarian repaid Emil's generosity by suddenly vanishing from New Orleans, abandoning poor Frida to her fate.

Just as usually happens in life, where one misfortune is quickly followed by a second and a third, such is the case here.

During a gross orgy in the Mulattoes' Settlement, Emil's brother fell into a wild dispute with a Mexican desperado over a charming quadroon girl and was stabbed to death. For a brief while this episode brought Emil down from his usual excesses, and, after he received a letter from Germany informing him that his parents had decided to leave their homeland owing to repeated warnings of impending revolution, he seemed inclined to put his affairs with Jenny back in order and surrender his tie with Lucy.

He did not tell his wife about the letter.

But the glowing sensual intoxication with which Lucy held him captive was all too well calculated to make Emil a renegade against his own feelings and resolutions.

After much shifting back and forth, he finally avoided Jenny entirely, and he did not cross over to Algiers again.

But Jenny's loving heart would not give him up.

Who has ever listened to the secret heartbeat of a loving woman? Trivial public opinion accuses poor women who act as Jenny did of weakness and lack of character.

Yes, Jenny knew that Emil took his passion with him to bed, that he poured out his love to another woman's embrace, and yet she longed for him; she still loved him.

Was this weakness or a disgrace to her femininity?

Those who stand outside her heart cannot judge her!

What heroism, and also what endless love—in her abandonment to long for the lava-streams which singed the fancy pillows of her competitor's bed!

Jenny was ceaseless in her efforts to lead Emil back to her arms. She quickly discovered where he was living in New Orleans, and on the very day Emil dressed to go to Lucy's he had received a note from his wife that was so warm, so forgiving, so stormy and yet so committed and beseeching, that he gave a few lines to the messenger in which he promised that he would visit her in Algiers.

That is how to explain the words he directed at Lucy on the gallery of her house: "I still have one obligation to fulfill today!"

But as we know, Emil neglected to make his marital visit.

Was it his free will?

Let us recall Hiram.

Fate had intended another path for Emil than warming his feet on his home hearth.

Even Jenny's last attempt failed miserably. Nothing was to come of the letter little Tiberius took to the Rue d'Amour.

"Where is my Emil?" Jenny shouted into the dark night, once she had lost all track of him. What is happening in her soul now?

She weeps and thinks of her dream among the Antilles.

Chapter 2

Far Away

Things were already beginning to quicken at Mr. Watson's farm.

The reflection of the rising sun glittered on the terraces of St. Louis, opposite the farm, vanishing in the darkness of the heights running along Hyde Park to Colonel O'Fallon's properties.

Mr. Watson's farm was the most important on Bissell's Island,[4] and the vegetables he grew there were the most prized in the St. Louis markets. He raised the best melons, the finest and rarest vegetables; his small tree nursery was in the most excellent shape—due, by the way, to the efforts of a German gardener.

Though it was on unpromising terrain, the farm was frequently subject to floods, allowing the German gardener to produce the finest fruits. Even those that normally prospered only in stony soil grew here to the loveliest maturity. There were two rows of juicy gold-blotched apricots, besides sweet little Bredas and Alsaces. Next to them along the bayou ran Reine Hortense, bigarreau noir, and the early-ripening morello cherries.

One can even find here several varieties of plum which had only rarely prospered on the Kaskaskia River. Admiral Rigny and Prince of Wales plums decorated the table of a Lucas or a Chouteau in late autumn in St. Louis.[5] They were never to be seen at fruit wholesalers, for Mr. Watson knew only too well that his rarer fruits would bring substantial profit from the right customer.

The corn seen standing in various parts of the farm was only grown as fodder for the cows and horses, of which there were many. Mr. Watson had planted more than fifty acres of wheat this year, which had already begun to yellow.

Near the farmhouse, shadowed by two enormous sycamore trees, an effort was underway to raise twenty or thirty feet of castor beans.

There were twelve acres of potatoes and three of tomatoes, already red in some places, that reached in a narrow band all the way to the Mississippi, bordered by the thick forest.

Part of this forest had already fallen to the ax, and where the woodland was receding the standing stumps were in various states of being pulled up and removed. Hundreds of feet of the most splendid hickory board either lay on flatboats or still stood between the clearings of the decimated woods.

More than twenty or thirty workers had been occupied for several weeks. Some cut the trees, others stripped them down for lumbering, and others pulled up the stumps and cleared the fields of the stubborn mustang grapevines.

The reason for all this activity was that a company was planning to run a ferry to the Illinois bank.

This location was most suitable, so it had been chosen for development.

The path leading to the ferry landing had taken a part of Mr. Watson's farm, a part that one can imagine did not go for a low price.

As a result, he had to build his fences a bit closer, but his farm still remained the largest on Bissell's Island.

Mr. Watson had been a widower for some years, living in seclusion with his daughter, a maiden as pretty as a picture, and he left the place only when he took his vegetable wagon across the bayou bridge to the market in St. Louis, where he sold his produce in person.

He only took workers with him when he was hauling chickens, turkeys, and other fowl.

Sarah, the farmer's daughter, had not yet completed her fifteenth year. She was one of those beings who only enchant a fresh, green environment, one surrounded by flowers, trees, and bushes. She was a charm to look at as she slipped through the cornstalks, spreading her plump little hands to get through more quickly.

Towns and the environment of a more refined world left her cold.

Sarah was one of those light blondes tending to red. Yet she had a snow-white, pure, utterly faultless complexion. Her feet were not the smallest, and she was well-rounded and plump around the ankles. Her toes were like her fingers, short and fleshy, with the rare property of being able to pick up a corncob, a tomato, or any other round object from the ground.

It was always amazing to see her do this.

She would careen now one way, then another, fresh, lively, cheerful, without any artifice. If her father or one of the workers was busy in the fields or the vegetable garden performing some sort of task, she loved to sneak up unnoticed from behind and upset them with poke from a twig or a piece of wood, then turn tail or sneak behind a tree or bush.

The German workers on Mr. Watson's farm spoke of her among themselves as "our Gretchen in the bush."

Among her father's workers was a Hungarian who had appeared on the farm several weeks before in rather forlorn shape. Mr. Watson had given him work in the woods.

This man, who did not appear to be over thirty, had one of those mysterious faces that are the despair even of the greatest physiognomists. His heavy black eyebrows hung low over his dark eyes, giving him a sinister appearance.

His red woolen sailor's shirt and a large handkerchief of yellow silk, which usually fastened his trousers below the waist, gave him a storybook appearance.

A sensitive observer could not fail to notice any disturbance of his normal temperament, since it would be announced by a sudden uncanny flickering of his usually steady gaze and a mock turning-down of the corners of his mouth. He tried to hide his disturbance as much as possible, and he might appear calm if he thought no one was staring at him.

Such persons are no rarity.

A diabolical spark often flickers in the hearts of the strictest stoics, who seem the most peaceful, resigned persons in their symposia. This spark occasionally spreads to their entire beings like a flash of phosphorus, often bringing about something horrible—without our being able to account for it.

Little Sarah was not indifferent to Lajos—that was the Hungarian's name. She liked his long, black hair, his raven-black mustache and goatee. When he was engaged felling trees, she often rushed to him, bringing him a bit of ham or cornbread covered with syrup, sometimes along with a little flask of the good cognac her father served up only to rare visitors.

Little Sarah's bold, lovable attachment made no small impression on Lajos. The buxom little Yankee girl with the pale light-blonde hair and dimples on her hands had caught his attention from his first moment on the farm, and in his moments alone he had grieved that he could only take the role of a worker here; he would gladly have played that of a splendid lover.

The day on which Sarah would lose her heart grew ever closer.

It was on a Sunday when her father left at 4 A.M. with one of his workers and a fully-loaded wagon, crossing the bayou bridge and passing down the length of Broadway to the market in St. Louis.

Watson wanted to have breakfast in town, so Lajos and Sarah sat alone at the laden table.

"How do you like my father?" Sarah began the conversation.

"Mister Watson is a very active man and has a very good heart. If your father wants to retain me after the felling is over, I would have the greatest desire to learn gardening, and I would like also to take over the heavy work as well," Lajos replied, throwing a penetrating glance at the girl.

"Don't worry," Sarah replied, "if you wish to stay here, you will only be in agreement with my father's wishes."

"So Mr. Watson has already spoken of keeping me on?"

"We spoke yesterday evening of keeping you on the farm, in case you did not wish to seek your advancement elsewhere," the little one contributed pertly, then she continued: "I know very well that our neighbors Mr. Williams and Mr. Carr pay a few more dollars in salary than my father—but the workers are treated poorly. Beyond that, they have several niggers, and not everyone wants to work in such company. At least I can have no regard for any white man who works with niggers. When my mother was alive, my father had five slaves. At my request they were sold, and since then he only keeps white gentlemen on his farm."

"That is very nice of your father," Lajos said, without giving it a thought. But his eyes were constantly concentrated on the little mouth and the hearty eyes of the Yankee girl.

The first cup of coffee was finished.

Sarah rose from her chair and approached Lajos with the coffeepot to fill his empty cup.

The moment was right for the Hungarian.

As Sarah approached him, he grasped her tenderly on the arm, looked into her face with flaming eyes, and spoke to her in a decisive tone.

"Sarah, look at me!"

"Let me pour your coffee first, then I will look at you as much as you like," Sarah responded with childish openness.

"Look at me, Sarah!" Lajos repeated, turning aside the hand with the coffeepot.

"So I'll look at you, if you force me," Sarah laughed, putting the coffeepot down. "So, so—now I've looked at you—now let me pour some for you."

"You should look at me once more, my *dear* Sarah!" The *dear* was sounded so emphatically that a burning blush rose in Sarah's cheeks.

Her little hands and feet trembled.

The stamen of a blooming flower trembles in the same way when a butterfly first descends upon it.

Lajos was trembling as well, but with joy at winning the heart of an innocent maiden so easily.

Lajos knew perfectly well what he was doing.

As Sarah stood before him, unsteady and speechless, he checked the security of the location, threw a quick glance at the window and the open door, calculated the time of her father's absence with electric rapidity—in short, all his thoughts concentrated on making poor Sarah a martyr to her own feelings.

A shot from close by jolted Sarah back to her senses. Lajos turned about in irritation, and as Sarah bolted through the door he pretended to be doing something with the saddle tackle that hung on the wall beside the fireplace.

In his confusion he shortened the straps, then loosened them, shined the spurs with his shirtsleeve, blew on them, and polished them again.

When he thought he had held back long enough, he rushed to the door.

Sarah stood twelve paces away, before an elderly man in light farmer's clothes who leaned on a shotgun with a very long barrel.

"That was my General Taylor," Lajos heard him say to Sarah, "my finest turkey—I had always suspected it flew to your coop. It's not right of you not to have told me about it, since you know I've been looking for it for a week. I think William's nigger would have plucked his feathers—I would rather have had him alive. Well, in any case—we'll eat him here."

He lifted up the fat bird, its neck virtually torn off by buckshot.

"I can assure you in all truth," Sarah pleaded, "that we have never seen your bird within our fences, Mister Carr—you are really doing an injustice to my father when you think that of him. Besides, we have so many turkeys that we could hardly tell if twenty of yours came visiting."

"Well, everything is back as it should be. So far as turkeys are concerned, I don't want to dispute you. Even if yours are more numerous, mine are all five pounds heavier. You don't really understand how these things are done."

"We understand quite well, Mr. Carr. You look only at the thin ones and neglect to look into our coop, where they are fenced in and grow fat. Only today my father took fifty head to the market which were twice as heavy as your General Taylor, with whom you are so obsessed."

"Well, well, that's alright, then," the farmer calmed her. "But how's the ferry progressing? It's been abuilding forever—I cannot imagine what seized your father to make over this fine piece of woods to that bankrupt gang. At least they would have had to pay a bundle for it if it were mine—it isn't even a proper location for a ferry. The few Dutchmen who cross over from New Bremen[6]—that's their total freight!"

"'Dutchmen?'" Sarah repeated, "you would do better, Mr. Carr, to put aside your Yankee arrogance. To whom other than this hard-working, honest people you so contemptuously term 'Dutchmen' do we owe the current greatness of our state? Who else is responsible for the flourishing condition of our farms in Missouri? Mr. Carr, your niggers only hoe and plant the fields, but Germans must have cleared it and made it suitable for working. Note this once and for all, Mr. Carr, that I will tolerate no further abuse of the Germans, and that in the future you will say *Germans* and not *Dutchmen.*"

The old farmer stroked his chin and said with a smile: "Miss Sarah Watson surely has a beau among the Dutchm . . . Germans?"

"Stop it, Mr. Carr," Sarah gathered herself, "and if you want to eat your General Taylor right here, hand him over and I'll pluck him. Then you may wait in the front room until my father returns—don't forget to tell him that he had been keeping your turkey."

"I will leave that go," Mr. Carr responded, "your father is not to be trifled with."

"So you did not have the same regard for me?" Sarah asked naively.

The Hungarian, who had just stepped out of the doorway of the kitchen where he and Sarah had breakfasted, drew the farmer's full attention.

He turned to Sarah and asked her, "Who is this man?"

The sudden shift from their previous topic to the object of her love disconcerted Sarah.

The farmer commenced inspecting the Hungarian from head to foot, as Lajos turned his face half away, in the direction of St. Louis. Then he looked directly at Sarah. Sarah thought herself betrayed—it suddenly occurred to her that the old farmer had been listening to them. She blushed deeply and played with the leaves of a nearby branch of hazel.

"Do you know why I'm asking?" he asked.

"How should I know?" Sarah responded quietly but with irritation.

"He is a Hungarian, isn't he?"

"Yes, Mr. Carr."

"Does he work on your farm?"

"Yes, Mr. Carr."

"He's been with you for four weeks?"

"Yes, Mr. Carr."

"I believe I saw him in St. Louis once."

"So, Mr. Carr?"

"Pay attention to his movements, Miss, he might recognize me yet."

The farmer left Sarah and went to the kitchen, at whose threshold stood the Hungarian, who now turned his face toward him.

"How is the gentleman today?" the farmer greeted Lajos in a mocking voice.

Once Lajos got a closer look at the farmer, he turned pale and stuttered. He quickly recovered his composure.

"Do not bring me unhappiness, I ask you, sir!" the Hungarian begged, but in such a soft voice that only Mr. Carr, right next to him, could hear it.

Sarah remained exactly where the farmer had left her. She gazed calmly at the two.

When she saw Lajos turn pale and perceived how he beseeched the farmer with his eyes, her whole body started to tremble. Now she was certain that old Carr had been eavesdropping, and that for that reason he was interrogating Lajos.

"Then I will not bring you unhappiness, gentleman," old Carr responded once more in his mocking tone, "if I tell Sarah's father how you played the betrayer."

"I ask you, sir, do not bring me unhappiness!" the Hungarian begged once more.

"You want me to spare you, you who sent a poor soldier to ruin for a few measly dollars? Know that it was my nephew you betrayed—scoundrel!" the old farmer shouted in rage.

Sarah, who had heard old Carr's last words clearly, and who now saw that it concerned an entirely different matter than she had feared, ran toward the two when she saw the farmer approach Lajos with such a threatening manner.

Lajos gnashed his teeth and bit his lip bloody in his wrath as the farmer told Sarah: "You know, Miss, that the Justice of the Peace of the Second Ward is my good friend, and that I often sit in his office for hours. So I was with him one afternoon between three and four o'clock when this 'fine' gentleman entered and informed my friend that he knew of a deserter, whom he was willing to deliver to Uncle Sam for the standard reward of ten dollars—*ten dollars,* Miss! My friend asked for the details, and then he learned from the mouth of this fine gentleman that he had taken a voyage from Galveston to New Orleans and then from New Orleans to St. Louis, and that the soldier himself had told him in all confidence that he was a deserter from the Army of the United States.

"When the Justice of the Peace asked for the name of the soldier, I had to hear that it was my nephew, who had just deserted the dragoons in Texas. I make a significant nod to my friend. He gives him a harsh lecture for shameful betrayal and sends him on his way with the message that he did not mix with such business, but if he wanted his ten dollars he should go to Jefferson Barracks to get them."[7]

"Is that true, sir?" Sarah intervened, turning to Lajos.

"Miss Watson, I can say nothing more on the matter than that I believe this man is drunk—or . . ."

"Drunk?!" the farmer shouted, lunging at the Hungarian, who pressed his fist under the farmer's chin.

Sarah threw herself between the fighting men, who were trying to throw each other to the ground.

A wagon rolled over the bayou bridge.

Sarah ran crying to meet her father, who jumped from the wagon and rushed to the farmhouse together with his daughter.

He arrived too late.

Old Carr lay on the floor covered with blood, rattling his last. The Hungarian was already crossing the fence into the next farm.

Chapter 3

The Assault on Looking-Glass Prairie

"If you want to accompany me to Shellville, my other horse is at your service. You may also take one of these buffalo robes and tie it to the horse's body with this strap. This rope will do for a bridle, it's a quiet, gentle horse a five-year-old could ride. I would be happy to let you use my saddle, but see, I'm just used to it, and besides, I need it to haul my goods and keep them in balance while riding—as I said, if you want to accompany me, get Yellow Jack to bring you that horse from his stall. I have a friend in Shellville who can ride it back in the morning, since I'll not be back for several months. I've a notion to take a tour to New Orleans."

"I would rather have your Lydia be a wild and spirited beast; she would soon learn respect from my haunches!"

"I can see from your haunches that you're not mounting a horse for the first time—but I can assure you that my Lydia was not always so tame and quiet. Four months ago I fled a prairie-fire on Looking-Glass Prairie,[8] hoo! How the flames chased us. Just when we thought we'd made it, the wind suddenly turned and drove the lake of fire right into our faces, 'There!—now where and how?' thought I. My Lydia whinnied—no, it was no longer a whinny, she howled in fear and terror. Her mane stood on end, like the bristles of a cornered boar. She would have thrown me off if I had not pounded on her snout—she can't stand that. She stormed forward, me hanging on, and I lost more than two hundred dollars in merchandise. She did not let me rein up until the flames had chased us to Little Creek, where she plunged in and swam across without throwing me. We were saved. Since then she has been quiet and obedient, and she jumps at the sight of a trash fire. Look! That's the sort of beast she is. I wish you could have met her earlier, you'd never have wanted a better horse. So have them bring her to you. We leave in half an hour, since I want to get going tonight so I can be in Shellville at nine o'clock."

"First let's have a good cognac, Mr. Cleveland," remarked the other, a man with long black hair and a black mustache. "The night will be cool, and riding through the high, wet grass without warming the stomach would be bad for your health."

The peddler, for that's what Cleveland was, smiled at this splendid suggestion from the black-bearded stranger, since he knew quite well that the fellow didn't have a damned cent in his pocket.

So he would not insist on being treated.

The other had expected this.

They went to a forlorn little country grocery, such as one finds by the hundreds in Illinois. These are usually not far from riverbanks and always located so that the residents for miles around have no problem getting there.

This is where the gatherings for county and state elections take place. The area around these groceries is suited for the inevitable stump-speakers, who often stay for three or four days, naturally at the expense of their chosen candidates.

The country grocer always does his best business during these periods, often shoveling four hundred dollars out of his drawer and under the counter on a single day.

The grocer watches this mad bustle with pleasure, dropping a word here and there in favor of the speaker, who shouts his throat hoarse and repays the stormy applause of his listeners by hosting them at the bar.

Once whiskey and brandy have electioneered enough and people are supplied for their return, many a farmer buys colorful cottons or bonnets, fans, stockings, and so on for his lady, for these are all available in a country grocery. The grocer is cobbler, tailor, stocking-maker, dressmaker, blacksmith, all in one person. The enthused electors also do not forget their youngsters. For them they take home candy of all varieties and every color. Ginger cakes, molasses candy—in short, all the confections Yankees desire.

"Do good business, Cleveland, and if you do get to New Orleans, don't forget to bring me my cigars and greet my friends," the grocer called to the peddler as he rode off with his companion.

After a ride of two hours, they were on Looking-Glass Prairie, which extended as far as the eye could see.

The night was clear as the stars; only a few light clouds moved across the heavens, hiding the full disk of the moon for a moment.

Only someone who has taken a night ride through the endless prairies of the West can conceive of the splendid and silent majesty that reigns in such a place.

One believes himself to be listening to the breath of nature and forgets all those petty concerns and problems arising from people and the restless hustle of working life that so often disturb us and keep our natural sensibilities and desires in morbid tension.

One gives himself over utterly to his feelings, and at such moments the heart celebrates a festival, breaking the bonds with which rational understanding and conventional rules of social life bind it.

The banner of love gleams on the peaceful forehead of the youth thinking of his beloved far away. Whoever bears hatred and resentment in his heart forgives and forgets. Numbers vanish from the head of the speculator. Even the horse lowers his neck and follows his leader.

Listen! A scream sounds out of the darkness of high grasses, followed by a mournful gurgle.

A restless fluttering and flapping of wings rises above the dew drops.

It is a prairie hen and her chicks, roused from sleep by a passing pack of wild dogs.

You can't see the dogs; only the tops of the grass part for an instant and shake in the moonlight.

Then solemn silence reigns once more.

The breath of the horses rises from their nostrils and loses itself in the night-mist.

"Stay closer to my side," the peddler said, interrupting a silence of some hours, halting his horse, and looking around at his companion, who was a good fifteen paces back.

"The grass will soon be getting taller," he continued, "and it would be easy to lose sight of me—another half mile and it will be up to your neck."

"Yes, you're right, Mr. Cleveland. It is also much more pleasant to ride alongside you," the other responded, spurring his horse forward.

So they rode silently for a while next to each other, and soon they reached a place where the moist grass stroked their faces and made them wet.

"It is not always so chilly on the prairie," the peddler declared to his companion, "particularly at this time of year on such a lovely, clear night. Look over there, that last little cloud is just evaporating . . . look, look," he called out, "those large lightning bugs, how they sparkle, how they flash!"

The other man looked in all directions.

"You must have seen a shooting star, Mr. Cleveland, and you took it for a lightning bug."

"There, now there—now they're flying right in front of your eyes—there, didn't you see them? Look, look, they're still there—grab them!"

The other looked in all directions, high and low.

"Well, if you can't see them, I'll catch one for you," and with these words the peddler shot his hand straight out, but pulled it back in the next instant.

"What the devil! What are you doing? Are you insane? You could have put both my eyes out!" the other shouted.

"May heaven strike me," the peddler replied, "if your eyes did not look just like lightning bugs.

And so they did.

Since they were covered by the tall grass up to their temples, and the position of the moon joined their shadows together, they could see nothing of each other besides their eyes, which swam through the moist darkness of the prairie like glowworms.

Since the peddler's companion often faced him, this error was all the more understandable.

"I only wish," Cleveland mused after an interval, "that I had not left my buffalo shoes behind in St. Louis; they would have done good service here. My shoes are soaked through now."

"Mine too," his companion responded, "don't you have some blankets, an old undershirt or something else? I would like to wrap them around my feet."

"That's a good idea I'll use for myself as well," the peddler said as he turned to loosen the straps of his mantle.

The other rider broke down some of the high grass.

The peddler's horse suddenly stood on his rear feet and kicked so high that his hoofs flashed above the high grass in the moonlight.

"Psst, psst! John," the peddler cooed to his horse, leading her head to the ground with a practiced hand. "Psst, psst, John, what the devil—what's the matter with you?"

Two shots echoed through the silence of the endless prairie.

The horse sprang once more into the air and fell lifeless on the corpse of his master.

Lajos's eyes gloated at the booty he sought.

"Thunder and lightning," the murderer declared to himself, "if the horse had run away with the baggage, it would have been pointless to shoot its master—let me see, John, where did my bullet hit you? Look, look, what a lucky soul I am, another couple inches and the beast would have wanted to beat it."

While Lajos leaned over the horse, now kneeling, now standing while he ripped the peddler's baggage to pieces, Lydia came sniffing at the corpse of her former master, finally settling on the ground, her head on his breast.

Lajos was finished. Four thousand dollars, partly in gold, partly in Missouri bonds, was the fruit of his search.

And now?

"I can't ride to Shellville, since they know Cleveland's mare there," he thought to himself. To return without her would raise suspicion." It did not occur to Lajos that he could neither go to Shellville nor return from where he came, since he could find neither path by himself.

It was already an hour before midnight.

"Will you just get up, mad beast—I almost believe you're mourning for that old codger there—march!" Lajos cursed at the mare and kicked her in the withers to get her to rise. But the faithful beast would not budge from the spot.

The peddler's horse lay next to them.

Lajos suddenly sprang up with a cry of terror that reverberated through the still majesty of the night, his hand spasmodically shooting to his left cheek. This shriek even caused Lydia to raise her head and look around at her master's murderer.

Lajos roared as if a whole hell of furies and snakes were at work on his innards. His eyes sprang out of their hollows, as if they could thus more easily be witnesses to this dreadful scene. In all directions he saw the blood, which flowed from his cheek down to his lips.

Dreadful moaning and whistling arose from his breast, interrupted only by his fluent curses.

A pack of prairie wolves, led here by a mysterious instinct to descend upon the corpses, fell back over one another at the sight of this human fury who pounded the ground, howling, cursing, and whimpering.

The peddler's horse, in its last death-agony, had bitten the murderer's cheek.

The still of the night can pour out redeeming grace on a pure conscience and an innocent heart, causing them to forget sorrows and concerns. The evening glow of a star-strewn heaven can cause the poet to dream and can kiss his pounding fever. Disappointed love can wander along the wide arch of the milky way, to cry out its pain. But the murderer cursed the stars and moon, longing for the blinding sun.

Lajos stood next to Lydia, dispirited and exhausted.

He directed no more curses across the sea of grass—but all the more he continued to curse to himself.

"If only this beast were a person," he thought to himself, "I would leave behind a monument that would shame it even in death."

Lydia still seemed to have no desire to get up and bear the murderer's burden. Lajos did everything he could think of, but in vain. It was time to make a quick decision to get away from the place of his atrocity.

"To go on foot with this money, never having any idea which direction to go . . . ? Too bad I never bothered with astronomy—the stars would help me avoid the way I should not return. Should I wander for days, perhaps returning to this very place? The devil with it, does Lajos have so little spirit for improvisation?"

He stood for a few moments in indecision.

A thought flashed across the murderer's dark features.

"I will bring this stubborn beast to its feet," he said to himself, taking the peddler's useless baggage and setting fire to it.

He had calculated correctly.

No sooner did Lydia see the flame than she rose from the ground and got ready to run with a whinny. Lajos was prepared for this moment.

The Hungarian, this former officer of hussars, threw himself on the horse's back and grabbed the raised mane with a quick grasp.

"Thunder and lightning," he sounded through the silent night, "she's going like she's on her way to hell! Prairie fire, prairie fire," he laughed in the mare's ear, as the night heavens began to redden and the flames rushed after them with the swiftness of the wind.

"Prairie fire, prairie fire, Lydia! Forward, forward into hell!"

Chapter 4

Gretchen in the Bush

The forest greens and the heath reddens,
Winter with its feathery clothing flees,
The snow melts on the heath.
Where the wild birds once flapped enticingly
The farmer's child walks with quiet complaint!

Blue flowers, red clover,
Bloom not now, my heart hurts too much!
[Otto der Schütz]

Since the regrettable episode that had led to the death of old farmer Carr and Lajos's flight, Sarah had become an entirely different girl. She no longer snuck up behind her father to give him a pat on the back while he was engaged in his work. She no longer rolled about on the ground, and she spoke only a little or not at all with her neighbors. The guinea hens could now pass their nights in the open unmolested, for she no longer drove them into the hedgerows. The cheery redbird,* used to getting fresh offerings three times a day, had lost its good mood and bumped its black-feathered head against the sides of its cage with irritation and distress when another hand cared for it at noon. The cows showed their dissatisfaction over their lack of bran, which only Sarah could mix in the amount they craved. They trampled around unhappily, and at night, when they were closed in, they often raised as much of a ruckus as if a panther had attacked.

Watson shook his head in concern as he saw his daughter lose so suddenly her old high spirits and rosy freshness of life. He could not imagine that the episode with the old farmer could have made for such a total transformation of her old happiness. He thought he understood that much.

It often occurred to him that his child might have harbored a covert affection for Lajos, and so the episode tormented her heart. But when he weighed all the earlier conditions, he decided he had been incorrect. So passed the fall, making way for winter.

The limbs of the sycamore and cottonwoods groaned under the weight of snow, which covered the entire region far and wide.

The farmhouse was often so snowed in that it was all six hands could do to clear the snow immediately around the house. For several weeks the snow had prevented the farmer from going to the market in St. Louis, which put him a bad mood.

One evening, as it snowed and stormed quite heavily, the farmer sat alone with Sarah at a large table with a round marble top, which a lady friend from St. Louis had given her as a gift.

Both of them were concentrating on sorting flower and vegetable seeds into packets prepared ahead of time.

Watson's workers had already quit for the day. Outside the wind howled and shook the doors and windows of the farmhouse.

Next to the door lay a large hound that had been allowed into the warm room due to the stormy weather.

*The Virginia nightingale.

Sarah was very efficient at filling the packets with seeds. She had already placed several dozen in a basket that she now passed to her father to be sorted into their proper order.

No one spoke a word.

Watson, who was determined to discover the source of his daughter's change in mood, had remained silent so far this evening, wondering how he could move Sarah to some sort of confession. Since she had been avoiding his frequent questions, he now intended to get to his goal by an indirect path.

When Sarah passed him a second basket, he said: "If I had known that Lajos had such a touchy and heated temperament, I would never have taken him on. Then we would have been spared all the distress resulting from that act. Old Carr must have given him a lot of trouble for him to have fallen into such a rage."

"You would certainly not have taken such an insult with indifference yourself, father," Sarah responded without looking up.

"To be sure, my child. But when one has performed a dishonorable deed, one must tolerate being called to account for it."

"But father—you still believe that the Hungarian gentleman was capable of such an act?"

"Your own account of that fateful encounter gives me the right to wash my hands of him," the farmer remarked, observing his child carefully.

"You cannot do that, dear father—I believe for a fact that Mr. Carr mistook him for another, for one Hungarian looks like another. Didn't you yourself say to me that Lajos looked precisely like a young man who worked for us last year? Couldn't it just as well have been Marian? Marian was a nasty, evasive person whom I always feared when he approached me. But Lajos—it is not right to hold a person to be bad when you do not have proof," Sarah interrupted her own chain of thought, since she felt she had already said too much on Lajos's behalf.

The farmer, who perceived this interruption, continued: "Where on earth could poor Lajos have gone? Heaven grant that they don't catch him, since then you would have to appear in court as a witness—but that would be the least of it, since such a murderer, even if he did not do the deed as accused, must have a lamentable fate. In a case such as that, I would rather put an end to my life myself. Yes, yes, wherever he is wandering right now, his lot is certainly not enviable."

Sarah could no longer hold back her feelings. Hot tears coursed over her cheeks and dropped on the packet she had just filled with seeds of blue knightspur.

Joy beamed on the face of the farmer, joy that he had finally succeeded in discovering his dear child's situation. What more proof did he want? What could prove more than these tears that his child had loved Lajos, loved him even now? When he looked across at lovesick Sarah, who had dropped her little head and was trying to hold back the tears, it was no longer possible for him to torture his child or even to continue his interrogation.

He drew her to his lap and sought to soothe her to the best of his powers.

"Sarah, my dear child, why did you trust your father so little that you kept your concerns to yourself? Tell me, my child, has your love for Lajos buried itself so deeply in your heart that it has robbed you of all your personal peace, has robbed you of all your youthful cheer? Girl, girl, what changes you have undergone! If your dear mother were still living, she would hardly recognize her child."

"O Father," Sarah said in pained tones, "you are so good to your child—but Father, tell me, am I committing so great a crime when I love Lajos? You liked him, too, Father. You still remember the evening when all your other workers did not want to work any further since they had done their hours, and Lajos helped us dig the potatoes late into the night so you could take them to market the next day. What did you say then, father? Didn't you say how much you liked this Hungarian gentleman? He was so calm, so hard-working and solid?

Sarah opened her eyes and looked deeply into her father's face, as if she very badly needed a consoling answer from him.

"My child," the disturbed father responded after a pause, "there are certain norms and laws in human society that cannot be violated. The world does not pose questions of a young girl in love, it concerns itself not at all with the tears poured out by an unhappy love. With its hard hands it grasps only the naked facts. The sorrows of a love-filled heart cannot serve as the guideline for its procedures and measures. Believe me, my dear child, I would not place any barriers in the way of your love if Lajos had not removed himself from human society through his dreadful deed, which will always mark him no matter how splendid his heart and character."

"If the world rules in that way," Sarah responded earnestly, "then it is extremely unjust and without feeling."

"Lajos committed a deed that the law cannot ignore. His wrath, spurred by a severe assault on his personal dignity, is not placed on the scales of justice the Law holds in her hands. Take some advice from your father, who means well by you, shake off this unfortunate love and give your heart once more the peace you had."

In truth, Watson thought the Hungarian to be a splendid man, and in no way did he believe that Lajos had ever betrayed anyone. Lajos had long since been acquitted in his own court. He only held it necessary to keep his true conviction secret from his daughter in order not to strengthen her love. He understood quite well how easily a man's wrath could lead him to such a deed, and that Lajos was more sinned against than he was a sinner. The language he had used to lead Sarah to this subject had been calculated to discover the secret of his child's heart.

"It seemed to me that someone was at that window," Watson remarked as he raised his head and stared at the spot. Sarah followed his gaze automatically.

At the same moment the hound left his spot at the door and stretched his neck into the air.

"Look, Sarah, how alert Nero is!"

"You're mistaken, father—Nero, lie down, it's nothing."

"Close the curtains, my child," the farmer commanded, "that dumb animal really thinks he saw something."

Sarah left her place and went to the window in question.

She was in the process of releasing the cord that bound back the curtains when she suddenly dropped her hands and rushed to the arms of her amazed father, her face turned pale.

"Father, father, stay where you are!" Sarah beseeched him, holding him back.

"Father . . . Lajos!" those were the only words her father could get from her on repeated questioning.

"La—jos? . . ." trembled in extended sounds from the farmer's lips, and he, too, went pale as death.

From outside, the cry for help sounded ever more clearly and more urgently.

Nero's barks transformed into an uncanny howl that normally would be taken as the premonition of an impending death.

Sarah was not mistaken. It was indeed Lajos who had looked into her eyes while she had been standing in front of the window.

To explain the appearance of the Hungarian at this place, so unexpectedly, we will have to go back a bit.

When old Carr jumped on Lajos, the latter succeeded in escaping his fists through clever movement, only to throw himself at the old farmer with redoubled force. Lajos quickly threw him to the floor. In the first rush of his rage, the Hungarian pressed his hands so hard around the man's throat that in a few seconds old Carr had ceased to breathe.

Lajos had hardly noticed this until the dreadful results of his deed flashed before his eyes, and, without looking behind him, he rushed over the fence of the surrounding farms and did not stop until he fell to the ground on a limestone cliff near the bank of the Mississippi.

An impenetrable darkness surprised him. No stars were in the sky.

Here and there a steamer puffed by him, and the reddened faces of the stokers appeared to him in the glow of their fires.

He awaited the break of day with feverish agitation and anxious impatience.

He did not close his eyes for the entire night.

When the morning began to dawn, he noted with no small pleasure that he was on a landing where boats normally took on wood to stoke their fires.

He decided to take the next boat that would be coming up the Mississippi to load wood. He had no money whatsoever and also had no desire to pay for his passage by working as a deck hand, but, at the worst, he expected to be set ashore. Since the next landing was on the opposite shore in Illinois, he wanted nothing more than to be told to leave the boat.

That is precisely what happened.

About five in the morning, the *Amazonia* put in at the landing, having left St. Louis a half-hour before. It was in the habit of stopping here, since the wood was cheaper than in St. Louis or five miles further north.

Lajos boarded the boat and mixed with the considerable number of deck passengers.

The *Amazonia* had hardly gone twelve miles when the clerk of the boat made his usual inspection of the deck.

Several other passengers had boarded along with Lajos.

After the clerk had collected their fares, he approached Lajos, who sat at the end of the rear deck at a considerable distance from all the others. From afar, he seemed to be following the furrow the rudder was making in the water.

"I have no money," was his dry response when the clerk of the boat demanded his fare.

"If you've got no money," the clerk bellowed hoarsely, "then help load wood at the next landing, or we'll set you ashore."

When the *Amazonia* reached the next landing, Lajos left the boat and did not return.

The clerk and the mate searched the entire boat, looking for him to put him to work.

They sought him in vain.

The Hungarian visited farm after farm, offering his labor, but always hoping he would not be hired. On these occasions he did not have to be asked twice whether he might like something to eat.

So, after two days of wandering, he arrived at that country grocery where he made the acquaintance of Cleveland the peddler. He pressingly persuaded the man of his sad situation, how he had been looking for work for several days to no avail. Cleveland offered him a horse to ride with him to Shellville, where he could have a place with an acquaintance for good wages. We already know the rest, and now we have to join the story where we last saw him, riding madly forward, hanging with both hands onto the Lydia's mane for dear life.

The peddler Cleveland's effects, used as kindling, had started a fire in the rotting underbrush beneath the tall grass. A wind that began gently, then grew intense, turned a twelve-mile stretch of prairie into a lake of fire in a matter of minutes. The fire rolled in the direction of the wind with raging speed.

Since Lajos had the wind at his back, the crackling flames quickly reached him as well. They soon licked at the hooves of the racing horse—only a few more seconds and the man and horse would have found their graves there and then—but Lydia hurled herself into the floods of Little Creek, separating Looking-Glass Prairie from Rolling Prairie on the opposite bank. The flames leaped the gap time and again, strengthened by the intensifying firestorm, but they found no nourishment on the other side and spared that place.

Utterly soaked and shaking from the cold from head to foot, Lajos left the wet bed that had protected him so surprisingly from utter, unavoidable catastrophe.

He saw the racing lake of fire rolling toward him from afar, and it seemed to him that a mounting column of smoke marked the place where a farm or perhaps an entire village had gone up in flames.

Lydia appeared either to have drowned or to have run away. He could see nothing of her. But what outbreaks of wrath he let loose when he saw that he had lost all of the money he had robbed, that his four thousand dollars had vanished.

The straps of the money-belt that he had tied around himself must have loosened—he was sure of that. "Does the belt lie in the river, or is it on the scorched prairie? How many miles did I go, which way did Lydia take?" Those were questions whose answers were driving him to distraction.

It was only an hour after midnight.

"Thunder and lightning! Is the whole of hell conspiring to ruin me? Am I not Satan enough to command it to help me and join me? I believe that if a person has committed two murders in such rapid succession, he can justly claim the support of hell!"

His being was silent for a moment, then it broke loose with even greater fury.

"Money! Money! Honor, fame, good name—I would rather lose everything, but not my money! Satan, Satan—money, money!"

If the stars had been able to hear these words, they would have withdrawn back into their blue beds and quit glittering for one night. But they drew the sorrowing West along with them—far, far beyond the smoking prairie to the corpse of the murdered peddler.

The Hungarian rushed across the short grass of Rolling Prairie with long steps, after having looked about the banks of the creek for a quarter-hour. After some consideration, he thought it wiser to put the area behind him as quickly as possible.

Only now did he think about the dumb trick he had played by igniting the peddler's pack, starting a prairie fire. He saw only too late that it would have been smarter to have waited for daylight or to have departed in the most obvious direction. In neither of the two cases would he have risked as much as he had now actually lost. And weren't there other means as well?

As so often happens, even the cleverest loses sight of the right way and blindly blunders into ruin when confronted by difficult circumstances.

Lajos covered a considerable stretch in the remaining portion of the night. When he saw a farm in the morning, he was so exhausted that he would gladly have sat down to rest. His cheek also hurt him a great deal. He pulled loose his handkerchief and tied it about his face so that people could not see the dreadful wound, but he neglected to wash off the blood clinging to his entire face.

Keeping to his earlier tactics, he asked for work here as well, but only in order to get something to still his hunger.

The farmer, a Pennsylvania German, saw the blood-stained face of the approaching man, and he gaped in amazement as this pale man asked for work on his farm.

When the farmer remarked on Lajos's blood-stained face, he responded that he had tripped over a large stone during a night journey by foot and that the sharp edges of the stone had pierced his cheek.

The farmer, who was not entirely convinced by this story, invited him to breakfast, since the grain had already been harvested and he could do the rest with the aid of his fifteen-year-old son. Lajos's dreadful appearance also moved him to offer him a worn blue blanket coat with a broad black stripe up the back. Lajos took it with what appeared to be great thanks, and he put it on at once.

"Certainly you haven't been in the country long?" the farmer asked as the Hungarian departed, in a dialect peculiar to the peasants of Pennsylvania, made up of German and English words.

"No, not long," the Hungarian sighed in hypocritical tones. "We poor immigrants have a hard time until we become acquainted with the dominant style in your country. And even if a person has set a few dollars aside, if he gets sick, gets the ague or a fever, he is no further along than he was before, which is to say he again has nothing. You have no idea how bad it can be for one of us who does not know the morals and customs of your country. Whoever wants to earn something with his hands in honorable labor comes out the worst."

"Don't say that," the Pennsylvanian interrupted in a good-hearted voice. "You appear to me to have picked up the notion that one can only make his way here by swindling and conscienceless speculation. Believe me, even if you do find a man here and there who has gained his riches that way, this does not sully the character and solidity of our nation. Look around you, see all these flourishing farms with their beautiful, friendly cabins? They rose because of the labor of hands, and they cost a great deal of sweat. Visit my neighbors, and you will find nothing but hard-working, just men who can only bring honor to our glorious republic. I see by your distorted face that you have only seen the underside of our country. If you don't have a living right now, don't let that discourage you or lead you to the false notion that our republic is a bad country that does not know how to nourish its children. Come back to me, now, you look to be so sad and depressed to me that it would do you good not to reject the gift of a ten-dollar bill. I will not ask you the source of your distress—it doesn't concern me."

When the Hungarian left the farm, the farmer said to his son: "Sam, I don't know, but this man fills me with horror—I don't know what he's done . . . The bloodstains on his face and the bandaged cheeks do not please me—people just don't fall over stones and smash half a face. I wish him all possible luck on his trip—I have done my duty . . ."

Now Lajos began a period of truly Satanic striving that appeared to have as its goal the injury of his fellow man and the destruction of family ties. His path was laden with curses, and he did injury even to his benefactors when he was in the position to do so.

It is a grace to mankind that very few such as Lajos walk the earth. The world would become an open grave on whose edge the hyenas and vipers would hold their Sicilian Vespers.

Lajos was utterly filled with hatred for people, whom he believed existed only for him to exploit. He enjoyed encountering persons who had lost all the peace in their beings, or who once had been happy but now wallowed in the deepest misery. He saw all of them as allies who would stand at his side or at least be useful in some way, without his conceiving any obligation toward them. The same hand that was extended to help them would just as easily strike them to the ground. If Lajos had been a real human being, he might not have been grateful to the Pennsylvanian who pressed money into his hand, but he would not have imputed to him a bad motive, which was in fact what he did.

"That stupid codger," he said to himself, "he could just as easily given me a hundred-dollar bill. I hope Satan burns out his entire farm that means so much to him—that ramshackle peasant, who makes so much of this doghouse of a republic—cornbread, bacon, and molasses—molasses, bacon, and cornbread—those are the fine dishes this republic serves us on its great table. The White House treats ambassadors to corned beef and cabbage and hangs the temperance medal of Father Matthew around their dried-out throats. Bah, bah! If you served this people Tokay and Ruster, it would sweep both of them aside to make way for the syrup jug."

Winter had arrived, and Lajos was even worse off than he had been before that affair on Looking-Glass Prairie, despite many swindles and extortions of money. Since his flight from Bissell's Island, his exterior had undergone such major changes that he could only be recognized with considerable difficulty. A full, pitch-black beard covered his entire face, rendering him unrecognizable and hiding a good half of the scar on his cheek, which reached almost all the way to his lower eyelid. His manner no longer betrayed his criminal plans or a devilish decision, and nothing bothered him any more—the most amazing things could happen and not a line of his face would respond. Someone could step up to him and call him a murderer—he would have taken a slap in icy calmness without betraying his thoughts in the slightest.

The external person had changed—but his inner being was permanently active, though without having yet achieved anything great, even for evil. His crimes up to now appeared to be only so many links in a long chain of crimes he intended to forge that would make him great one day, if only in crime.

Trusting in his altered exterior, he had dared to return to St. Louis. In fact he was bold enough to visit the beer hall where the judge who had ejected him for his betrayal of the poor soldier was a steady customer and spent almost every evening.

Here, tormented by the bitterest need, thrown out of every boardinghouse, he finally decided to return to New Orleans in order to seek out Frida, who perhaps had some property and whom he had abandoned so shamefully the year before. He intended to extort money from Emil and start a free life at a greater distance.

But how to get to New Orleans? Without money? Perhaps he could decide to work for his passage. Or have himself set ashore time after time? That would require a useless journey of six to ten days, and it would conflict with his intention of getting there as quickly as possible.

How to get money in St. Louis, that was the important matter—for who would give him even a cent here? He would even have stooped to stealing. He was already so decadent and depraved that he would not hesitate to commit a common theft of a few dollars, although he would have preferred to arrange a murder from which he could make thousands.

He went across the street to the windows of the money-changers; he often stood musing there, several times deciding to seize a few hundred dollars through a bold grab and then flee.

That was such a dangerous game that it would only have been possible with the magical grasp of a practiced pickpocket.

Then one day his gaze dropped on Bissell's Island, which he utterly seemed to have forgotten, and where there was someone who was willing to do anything for him. "Shouldn't I go to Sarah and get some money? How would I, old Carr's murderer, be received by Sarah's father? Sarah's father has a good heart—should Lajos suddenly appear, wouldn't the man give him the means to go to another part of the Union? That deed was done only in a momentary seizure—Mr. Watson would be able to understand that—and he would not deny me his sympathy. I will settle the story of betrayal easily enough, in case Sarah has told her father about that—old Carr was either drunk or mistook me for another! Who has proof to the contrary? And where there is no certain proof, the scale of sympathy has to go my way. Today is perfect weather—deep snow, cold, raw wind—I, ragged and trembling with the cold—that will assure me of Watson's sympathy."

We already know he decided on that course.

He circled around the farmhouse for a long time, and he saw Sarah working with her father, putting the seeds in order and distributing them into packets.

So he turned his face to the window as Sarah came to close the curtains, to determine her reaction before making an appearance. He possessed this talent in the highest grade. His sharp eyes determined in an instant that he had not come in vain, and that if he did not have much to hope for, he at least had something.

Despite his long beard, Sarah recognized him at once—how could she have forgotten his eyes? Those glowing eyes that Cleveland the peddler had mistaken for lightning bugs buzzing through the high grass of the prairie. She recognized Lajos on the basis of these eyes, even though his face was extremely altered, unrecognizable.

Can a girl ever forget the eyes that first enchanted her with the dream of love?

As Sarah fell back from the window like a lovesick lily and rushed into her father's arms, the agitated hound leaped through the window, shards of which fell, tinkling. The animal landed on the Hungarian, throwing him to the ground with its momentum.

A dreadful cry of pain, mingled with the dog's howling, came to the ears of the farmer and his child.

"Father, father, stay where you are!" Sarah begged, when she saw him arise with the intention of rushing outside.

"Father . . . Lajos!"

"La—jos? . . ."

Sarah hung on her father's coat as he finally rushed to the door and called the hound by name.

The dog ceased to howl at once when he heard his master's voice, but he continued to pin the person's breast and neck on the ground with his paws, almost taking the breath out of him.

Watson was calm once more when he grabbed the hound by the collar and pulled him away from the Hungarian.

"What's this all about, Lajos? And at this late hour? Don't you know you should stay away from here?"

Sarah stood trembling beside her father, still holding onto his coat.

Lajos had already arisen, and he said with icy calm: "Mr. Watson, I am very sorry to have caused you unnecessary distress—if you had come a moment later, your Nero would have killed me—perhaps *he* wanted the duty of avenger—if I'm correct, that's the same spot where old Carr breathed his last."

"Quit that talk!" Watson declared in an earnest tone, as he helped the Hungarian to his feet.

"Come into our warm parlor and tell me what brought you here at this late hour—can I help you somehow? I will do for you whatever is in my powers—but first swear solemnly never to return here! If you ever dare set foot on this farm, I will hand you over to the courts without mercy . . ."

The Hungarian promised this, shaking the farmer's hand in a pathetic manner.

As they entered the parlor, the father and daughter remained standing in shock.

Lajos genuinely made for a hair-raising sight.

The hound had ripped wads of hair from his head, and they lay scattered over his shoulder and neck. Blood stood in thick, feverish drops on the scar, which the hound had reopened over his cheek, and the tip of his beard was tinged red. His clothes were ripped and ragged, and the skin on his frozen hands was torn in several places.

The farmer did not know at first how he should act.

Sarah sat in her father's rocking chair and hid her face in the folds of her dress.

It is surprising that Mr. Watson's workmen had not been roused from bed by the hound's howling. Probably, despite the deep snow and bitter cold, they had rushed to the daughters of neighboring farmers to tender their devotions.

There is no other way to explain it.

"You cannot go in this condition," Watson began again, "go into this cabinet here and wash the blood from your face. I'll give you a pair of trousers and a white blanket coat. If this clothing will not suffice, you can exchange it for something better when you get to St. Louis. If I had more money here I would give you more." He said this as he handed the Hungarian two bills, each worth twenty dollars—"Then lay yourself down to sleep and stay until I wake you."

The Hungarian had not expected such accommodation. He now saw that he had not misjudged the farmer's good nature.

That night Sarah did not close her eyes. The image of Lajos was continually in front of her soul.

Before day came, Watson woke the Hungarian and told him to leave the farm. When Lajos shook the farmer's hand in farewell, one question was on his lips, though no word was expressed.

"Where is Sarah?" he seemed to ask.

The very next day, a more decently clothed Lajos was lodged in a cabin of the *Sultana,* making its scheduled trip to New Orleans.

...

As winter turned to spring and the whole of nature once more sprouted and bloomed, Watson sent his little daughter to Russel's farm to gather herself far from the scene of the sad events, so that she could mend her heart in communication with Russel's happy, enthusiastic daughters.

The news he received about his daughter from time to time did not fill him with fresh hope.

Sarah also went about at Russel's farm in sorrow and silence, and her friends' games had no appeal for her.

She preferred to spend her time in the greenhouse, stroking the limp petals of the camellias and gardenias, or binding them to stakes. She concentrated particularly on two flowers, standing in bright-green glazed pots with narrow, brazen hoops. They were the cornflower, which grows wild in the Old World, and the goose-blossom, which is used as a decorative plant here and which no flower-garden or greenhouse can do without.

Why was Sarah so fascinated with these flowers?

In them wasn't she doing homage to the homeland of the man who still held her heart in thrall?

Chapter 5

UNEXPECTED

We find ourselves back in New Orleans.

On a corner of Chartres Street sat two men in one of the most elegant coffeehouses of the city, playing *domino à la poudre.*

This variation of traditional dominos is regularly played only in a few clubs whose premises a stranger may enter only under the strictest conditions. Three persons must participate in the play, one of them always being a *lady,* which makes up the characteristic difference of this variety of game. At the beginning of each round, the lady has the right to set the first piece. If it happens that the lady gets the double-white piece at the outset and plays it, then she forfeits playing any further, the others have to choose new pieces, and the game goes on with two players. The one who wins the game wins the exclusive favor of the lady—for a few hours anyway. This game is occasionally played without the presence of the lady; in this case the double-white will override an equal number of points and the losing party has to lead the other into the arms of an attractive lady. But the finer details of this gallant game do not belong here, since our *Mysteries* are also destined for the boudoir of the fair sex, which has always preferred to solve these riddles itself and not allow the cover of secrecy to be lifted by a stranger's hand. Coquettes and spinsters will have a hard time finding what they want in the *Mysteries,* nor will orientally lusty bloomers, since in New Orleans, as in all the parishes of Louisiana, the fair sex is forbidden to wear pants—except in the case of the wives of editors of German newspapers.[9]

Our two men were playing this time not for a lady but for money, which was basically a great deal wiser. The sum for which they were playing appears not to have been small, seen from the fact that the losing party bit his lip in rage as he demanded in a low voice opportunity to recoup, while the other gathered his winnings. But when the luckier of the two declined to comply with this request, in view of the fact that even if he won he could get no more—his opponent having lost everything he had—the loser pounded with his fist on the stone surface of the table so that domino pieces fell to the floor on both sides. He then abandoned himself to a torrent of rage.

Let's take a closer look around this coffeehouse, filled with people from the furthest lands.

In one corner sits a tall, gaunt man leafing absent-mindedly through the journals piled there. He sweeps his eye over the room only now and then, concentrating on the two players. He is clothed in an extremely strange manner. A long, narrow mantle of a dark color, closed to the chin by means of a high-standing collar, almost touches the ground and enshrouds the thin figure. Beneath the small collars, which bend a bit together at the neck, one can see a red lining. The sleeves reach halfway over the hands, almost covering them completely. On top of this, the mantle is buttoned in front down its entire length.

His narrow face, dominated by a disproportionately broad and high forehead, is yellow and pale, and his cheeks so fallen in that one could place a flat hand across them. His nose, which bends strongly outward in the middle, turns in so much at the end that it almost touches his fine, nearly invisible lips. Above his eyes, which are totally enclosed by green glasses with side-glass, there is a pair of bushy eyebrows of uncanny length. Above his forehead, from one ear to the other, runs the blue-red stripe of a scar, inadequately covered by gray hair combed across it. This head must once have fallen under an Indian's scalping knife, for this is the classic scalping line, rising upward from the temples. In any case, this man escaped this execution through some fortunate intervention. He had long attracted the attention of those around him. Curiosity drove many to try to start a conversation with him, all in vain. The most they could get out of him was "yes" or "no" in such a repellent tone that everyone lost the desire to bother him further with their words. So he sat two hours with his cup of mocha, like a silent senator who knows how to play his Trappist role to the hilt. If he had not answered his curious interrogators with "yes" or "no," it would have been easy to think that he was dumb or indeed a disciple of a Trappist order, which would have accounted for his strange garb.

Despite intervention by the host, one of the players had given himself over to the most dreadful curses. His opponent looked at him quite coldbloodedly and mockingly, only spurring him to more. The entire coffeehouse was enthralled by the progress of this scene, and bystanders encouraged the host to let the two continue so long as they did not endanger the other guests by physical demonstrations.

The old man in the black mantle suddenly pulled back his chair, which had hitherto seemed as if it had been nailed to the floor, drew a coonskin cap out of his pocket—the sort of cap Rocky Mountain hunters wear—placed it on his virtually bald head, rose, and advanced on the players with measured step.

All eyes were directed at him, the mysterious one, who had not participated in any way until now. All faces were tense, for the decision that was registered in his expression appeared to announce a new catastrophe for the two players.

As the *old man* neared the player who had lost, he spoke to him with an accented English that betrayed the Frenchman. "Permit me, sir, that I mix in your affairs and seek to encourage your opponent quickly to accept your request for the opportunity to recoup—and you, sir," he turned to the other, "will certainly not refuse me the fulfillment of the desire just expressed, since I am convinced that you are a 'gentleman' and well know the *point d'honneur* in gambling. It appears that you have completely plundered this man through the favor of Fortuna, and since you have probably set no time limit on your game, it is only just that you reopen it by risking what you have just won."

"Yes indeed, yes indeed, it is only just," was repeated by all mouths.

It is remarkable how much power some persons exercise over their environment. A single word spoken at the right moment, even their mere appearance, often leads to efforts, deeds, and decisions that otherwise would never have happened. And so it was here. The very persons who had been silent observers a short time ago or who had amused themselves over the two in feeble, fruitless small talk, now became partisans for the unlucky player and pressed to the table to support the modest and yet proud request of the mysterious man.

It is not surprising that, in a place where so many hundreds of persons enter and leave, a great sum of money is gambled despite a legal prohibition. Gambling in coffeehouses and inns is certainly forbidden, but no one pays any attention to it. How many laws are trodden underfoot here? How many police officers participate themselves! *Much is forbidden, but much is also tolerated.* This makes New Orleans the freest city in the United States. Though our gamblers avoid the use of noisy clinking coins by passing banknotes back and forth, no one would object if ringing gold coins were indeed tossed from one side to another. It is extremely rare for anyone to be stopped by the police. Exceptions are made only for notorious delinquents and vagabonds. Yet, despite this moral decadence, New Orleans possesses a decency that modulates the scale of the crime. It possesses a frivolity, a naivité, that disarms censoriousness. People do not even bother to operate behind closed doors because of the ban on gambling. They prefer to be found in the open. We do not wish to sing New Orleans' praises on this matter but simply to mention it against the straightlaced and the hypocritical sinners of eastern and western cities, to whom New Orleans is nothing less than the Sodom and Gomorrah of the United States, richly deserving of a nice brimstone shower.

The man who had earlier refused to play now took up the game again at the stated risk, cowed by the general applause of the bystanders and the decisive request, or rather demand, of the old man. Several guests pulled up their chairs and virtually besieged the table. A grandiose game at a green table could not have excited more interest than the one at this marble table where just two men sat opposite each other playing dominos. The old man stood close behind his man and appeared to watch him very closely. The game began. After only a few turns the game was won by the same player. "Domino!" cried the fortunate one, standing up from his chair and throwing out his breast, "I win again! And now, sir," he said after a pause, turning to the old man, "You have shown yourself quite helpful to my comrade—now *you* be so good as to help me get the money coming to me, for *he* doesn't have a cent in his pocket. There was not more than a hundred dollars in play! You see, sir," and he drew a handful of bills from his hat. "Everything in good Louisiana State Notes!" The bystanders were amazed, for they had had no idea the play had been for such high sums. Only the old man appeared unsurprised. He responded immediately:

"Do you trust your luck so little that you won't try it again? I will not impose a third time if Fortuna smiles on you once more. I am good for the demand you are making of your opponent."

The fortunate player was astonished at this repeated imposition by the old man—since he doubted the IOU for such a large sum from a man with such a wretched appearance. He responded, "Sir, whoever you might be, I beseech you to leave me alone with your impositions from now on, since I have proved to be patient up to now and have fulfilled your wishes—besides, you would have to possess unlimited riches to stand for every gambler with bad luck who has lost his money. To be sure, " he added mockingly, "you would have a considerable practice in New Orleans."

"If your doubt about the reality of my wallet is the hindrance," the old man responded with supreme calm, "it would be my pleasure to eliminate it." As he said this, he reached carefully into his mantle, bringing out a small, black, satin pocketbook with a peculiar silver clasp. He opened it and lay it before the eyes of the amazed guests, revealing ten times the amount won. A general murmur could be heard passing through the hall. "Who could that be?" they whispered to themselves. "It is a second McDonogh!" "The fellow has the devil in his body," whispered a short man, "just look under the mantle, you'll see horse's hooves." "I saw his tail when he came in," remarked a bigoted Spaniard. "And what long fingers he has! He lacks only claws!" These questions and remarks were exchanged so quietly that the old man could not have heard. He appeared concerned only with himself and the two players.

"A thousand dollars—a bagatelle!" the old man remarked. "Sit down now, my good man, and start over with good courage." The winner was easily dazzled by the sight of so much money, but he could not hide a certain amount of reluctance and anxiety.

The game began anew—then suddenly the old man thundered in the player's ears, *"Cheating!"* It caused the player to start and automatically withdraw his hands from the pieces.

It would have been impossible for the cheater to flee, since he was beset on all sides by an impenetrable wall. Everyone could see, so he made no effort to escape. He looked down, white as chalk, and let the words of criticism pour over him. Soon the call was found to be true.

The pieces had been cunningly marked in advance, which the old man had suspected from the start. Similar marks were found on five other sets the host produced when asked. People were amazed. The host avoided direct eye contact. The old man took the money he had laid down, replacing it in his pocketbook.

The cheat was arrested.

Searching for a Bride

A girl or little woman
Papageno wants for himself,
And such a tender pigeon
Is happiness for me—
Is hap-pi-ness for me!
[*The Magic Flute*]

Since his disastrous serenade in Toulouse Street, the Cocker had conceived a mortal hatred for all Frenchmen. When he heard French spoken on the street, he turned red with rage, like a boiled crab, and he swore—to himself—until they had passed out of sight.

As always, he held his usual internal monologue: "These Frenchmen think that they can make a person dance on his head just because they're Frenchmen. There is no decent life left in this town, they upset good morals and plunge many a guiltless maiden into the greatest misfortune. Still, I will say nothing about anything, so long as they leave my compatriot untouched. That good child could have been entirely corrupted by those god-d-d-damned Frenchmen!—If I had just not had my guitar in my hand, I would have taken care of them—yes, by God! If my compatriot knew of it, she would surely have scratched that Frenchman's eyes out, if he tried to keep me from giving her a serenade—yes, by jingo, whatever this French monster thought I was—yes, by God, to mishandle a man who heard lectures in aesthetics at Tübingen and almost passed the state examination—if I were to write that back to Germany, no one would believe it."

Today was to decide the Cocker's future: was he to kneel under the gentle yoke of marriage, or would he remain a bachelor forever?

In the first case it could only be Orleana, since only she caused him to feel what was proper to a married man.

For this purpose a special outfit was spread on his table.

Several days before he had washed and brushed the black frock coat that he had worn as a confirmand at the age of fifteen. It hung drying on the chair back.

From time to time he touched it and tried to determine when it would be completely dry. He appeared unconcerned that the arms were a bit short, since he considered that his lovely starched cuffs would be all the easier to see, and, besides, he had read in a book somewhere that women paid particular attention to a man's hands, so he believed this would light an unquenchable flame in Orleana's heart.

A letter he took to the Post Office had to convince Orleana all the more of his love.

The letter read:

Most Nobly Born Fräulein Orleana, resident in Toulouse Street, six Gschwärs from the Office of the "German Society"! Yes, in deed and without exaggeration, Most Nobly Born Fräulein!*

If I might be so bold, Fräulein, as to send you a few lines, that does not mean that I have determined in advance to make a claim on your love. I am a German, and that should be sufficient for you. I am not one of those pushy Frenchmen who seek to pull you down into the abyss of vice and moral ruin through underhanded narrative. As your compatriot, I hold it to be my obligation, even more my duty, to warn you against this scum, and if you would be inclined to bind my hands with the rosy chains of marriage, then say it without restraint, right out, as befits a compatriot. I possess to a significant degree all those qualities that a decent maiden can demand, and if you look back into your past in a few years then you will have to confess that you embraced a compatriot who always meant well by you. So that you cannot accuse me later of cheating you by keeping my lack of money quiet, let me tell you, from my very liver, that I have no money. I know in advance, however, that a compatriot maiden as decent as yourself would never demand money from me in advance. Since I have so much education, you will be satisfied with a good heart. So far as my personality goes, you will note that I am not as such a lightweight as those miserable Frenchmen, who have bad intentions at the outset. If you will permit me to visit you tomorrow at the dinner hour, you will see that you are dealing with a decent man. So tomorrow I shall be free to visit you and receive your good judgment. During the first period after the wedding, we could live in your own home, and I will need only a little cabinet for my shotguns, rifles and pistols, which I ordered so long ago and which I have to repair now and then. Still, we can talk about that later. Once again, expect me tomorrow precisely at the dinner hour.

Most humbly and respectfully,
Your deeply dedicated compatriot,
Kaspar Hahn

* Probably "squares."

As one could imagine, Orleana was deeply offended when she read this letter. If the letter was meant seriously, then it had flowed from the pen of a fool who had fallen in love with her. Or had someone dared to play a disgusting game with her? These questions set her virginal spirit into the most painful distress. After balancing these alternatives against each other, she thought it most prudent to wait until tomorrow, and, if the announced person did not appear, to take serious measures to chase down the author of this offensive letter. She hoped that her first assumption was true, since she felt competent to drive these ideas out of the head of a lovesick, blockheaded fool. She thought that a disgusting conspiracy against her feminine virtue was more than simply perilous, however. The very idea that her name might come in this way before the filthy tribunal of a mob was intolerable.

The Cocker applied all possible means his money was capable of supporting to make himself appear as much like a bridegroom as possible.

His beaten-in Hecker hat yielded to a silk hat, and his cotton sackcloth with red stripes yielded to white batiste set with the finest lace.

He had not purchased it: last Sunday he saw it lying in front of the Cathedral and took it.

As he concentrated on his dressing, he was interrupted by a man who walked into the room and approached him without knocking.

"*Comment s'en va,* Monsieur Kaspar?" were the first words.

"Speak German, Herr Weber—I don't understand French!" the Cocker responded with irritation.

"I only wanted to see if you had learned any French, Monsieur Kaspar—you have been in the *Saud** more than seven years. Look at the French children who already are speaking perfect French, and you are over thirty and don't speak a word."

"That is an entirely different thing, one who has been to university must think of more important things than learning French—you don't understand that, Herr Weber . . ."

"*À propos,*" the Lorrainer, a man still in his thirties, interrupted him, "how is it with your rent? It has been two months since I've seen any—I have no desire to wait any longer—'tis bad times, and I need my money."

"But my dear Herr Weber, I have told you that—if—that I have good prospects—no, no, don't look at me so dubiously, Herr Weber—no, no, you know I am about to marry a wealthy compatriot—and there will be an agreement from the outset how much pocket money I am to receive."

"Don't make yourself a laughingstock, Monsieur Kaspar—*sacre nom de*

* Probably "south."

dieu! You, you and the rich Creole married? What are you thinking about? There are others who are plotting for her—You? You? How could you object if I made a claim on her myself—I am a man worth at least twelve hundred dollars, and I have two lots besides in the *neuf Besen,** and what do you have? You can't even afford three dollars a month in rent. Don't make yourself a laughingstock, Monsieur Kaspar—I want my money and nothing else!"

"But my dear, esteemed Herr Weber, I am at your service, and that is enough said by a man who keeps his word of honor—it is all in order between us. Today I will have dinner with her—and she has already received a love letter from me."

"I'm telling you once more and for the last time, Monsieur Kaspar—I want my money. I want my six dollars—I want it now—then you can marry whomever and whenever you wish."

"How can you be so upset, Herr Weber, when you are at least half my compatriot, which means you have to overlook a few things? Give me your hand, Herr Weber, you will certainly never regret it. Look, today I promise you with a handshake—then you're 'set'—dear, finest Herr Weber, don't trouble yourself any further, or else I won't get to my dinner—and I have promised it with certainty."

The Lorrainer, who appeared not to be any great genius, half believed some of these assurances, feeling there might just be something in it, for now he sounded an entirely different tune: "*Eh bien,* Monsieur Kaspar! How long will it be before you get it all together?"

"That will be agreed upon between the two of us at the very outset today, so perhaps you can get your rent tomorrow, certainly the day after tomorrow—Herr Weber, you're not still mad at me, are you?"

"You funny man, why should I be mad at you—but you will certainly not have anything to do with me once you have married the rich Creole?"

"You don't know me if you think that of me, Herr Weber—I will not forget you—we will be quite faithful to each other, Herr Weber!"

"So adieu, I shall not trouble you any further, dress yourself nicely and do your duty well," the Lorrainer called out to the Cocker, as he held the latch in his hand on his way out.

"That damned Lorrainer shall not set his foot in my house once I'm married—he will be amazed—I shall pay him his six dollars rent—and that will be all. My compatriot would have a pretty reaction if I ever presented her with such a gross, coarse man—she would care little about his two lots

*Probably "New Basin."

on the New Basin. My compatriot is a decent, strong maiden and does not judge people by how many lots they have on the New Basin or anywhere else—she only asks for a loving heart, and I can offer her that from the outset when we get together. Kaspar, Kaspar, what will your friends say when they hear that the former rake, the old party, the Cocker, has married such an innocent, fine maiden—they will turn yellow and green from envy and distress."

As one can see, this had become a fixed idea with the Cocker: he believed that Orleana would sacrifice her youth, beauty, riches, and even further advantages without protest and that she would count herself lucky to be entitled "Frau Cocker Hahn."

A man seized by such hallucinations is not far from insane.

In the Cocker's case, this fantasy was the result of an excess of youthful sins committed with the female sex, which unfortunately would reach its culmination in a tangled combination of ideas and a malignant obsession with the wealthy, beautiful German Creole maiden.

We have already seen from his apotheosis of beautiful women that the Cocker was not without education.

It seemed impossible to him that Orleana would not be his life's companion—for, he still often said to himself when alone: "Even if I am not handsome, I am at least interesting, and how many examples are there that beautiful women choose ugly, interesting men over handsome and uninteresting ones?"

If he often gloated over his self-convinced good fortune, it often also happened that he felt pangs of conscience over his earlier way of life. Then he would fall victim to anxieties when he considered whether the Creole would see that his sighs of love had received a willing hearing in other places besides.

"I should not be concerned about that at all," he remarked to himself. "It is not possible that my compatriot would even think of that—oh, she will and must believe that she is my first love, when I swear to her high and low by all the saints in heaven, when I fall at her feet in the first storm of passion and beseech her with dreamy eyes focused on her heavenly face, oh, she will and must give the Cocker the trust he needs.

"Tomorrow, tomorrow, yes tomorrow, or the day after, at this very moment! What are the Lorrainer's two lots in the New Basin against two freshly covered bays in a marriage bed?"

At this point he interrupted himself laughing: "Cocker, by jingo, your good luck is making you witty—by God, how many authors of romances would envy this turn of phrase if it were printed in boldface, or in spread type—and this came to me out of nowhere, without my having to think much about it."

As he conversed with himself, the Cocker was searching for his moustache wax, which he discovered at last in an old boot.

He had a rather large mustache of reddish color that he now wanted to wax black; then he took a little tallow and melded the wayward hairs together so that their ends turned back toward his nose.

He placed his fine batiste handkerchief in the left pocket of his red satin vest, allowing the point to stick out.

His frock coat, which had dried completely, was a bit narrow over his back, and the two frock tails stood too widely apart, showing his bottom to disadvantage.

He cared not a whit about this, for he was convinced that his bride to be would only see the interior person and would not be bribed by external fripperies.

After he had inspected himself in his broken mirror twenty times over, front and back, never forgetting the interior person, he departed his apartment.

It was already nearly three in the afternoon, the hour when Orleana would be awaiting him.

As was the case the night he had given his disastrous serenade to Orleana, he once again went too far down Toulouse Street. He first realized his error when he passed Victor's Restaurant.

"Well, since I have already gone so far in vain, I can take a small one on the way—can't hurt—it goes all that much better from the heart, as Schiller says."

He was so preoccupied that he almost walked into Victor's, but he saw his error at the last moment and went right across the street to the Rheinpfalz.

The host of the Rheinpfalz, a tall, handsome man with a full beard and a truly military bearing, stood right by the door.

"Why so dressed up, Kaspar? Are you getting married?" he asked.

"Right on target, Herr Sch., and since you always have the best in stock, I want to take a small one along with me—I always like to come in here, and if all the hosts were as good as you, life in this damned New Orleans would be entirely different. There, Victor over there, he should remember me, if I have the time—alright—Barkeeper, there, there—I have to go right away—adieu, adieu, all of you!"

The host of the Rheinpfalz smiled as he watched the Cocker carefully strutting with wide steps on down Toulouse Street, his stretched-out frock tails behind him. He excited considerable curiosity from passers-by.

Let's see what Orleana is doing.

She was impatiently awaiting the appearance of the man who had so naively invited himself to dinner, and who intended to declare his limitless love and esteem.

In truth there were two place settings on the table, usually set for one.

She paced back and forth in her small but elegantly furnished reception room, now and then showing a slight smile on her face when she thought of the appearance of that lovesick, clumsy fool.

Orleana had never been so beautiful: never had her skin been so white and clear, never had the hygron* ever swum in purer water than in her marvelous eyes.

Her black hair, with bluish highlights, lay in warm fullness on the back of her neck, which, since it was more than half uncovered, would have been perilous to the virtue of the cherubim.

This neck, which had not yet felt the hand or the lips of any man, was Orleana's pride, and her fine classical sense had chosen clothing that would have allowed a worshiper of beauty and divinity in the female form, if he stood close to her, easily to immerse his eyes in the warmth of her entire back.

Far from all prudery, Orleana held it to be her duty not to hide from anyone the most beautiful gifts that nature had bestowed on her.

Betsy, Orleana's slave, announced a gentleman.

"His name, Betsy?"

"Cäshbär Jahn, if I understood him, milady."†

"That certainly must be Kaspar Hahn," Orleana thought to herself, then she commanded Betsy to lead the gentleman in.

She herself stepped before a large mirror, adjusting the garlands of evergreens hanging over it. She did this in order to use the mirror to measure the man entering without his knowing he was being observed.

Betsy pulled back the two wide doors, and the Cocker entered the reception room—or rather, he remained standing on the threshold.

After leaving the Rheinpfalz, the Cocker had rushed straightaway to Or-

* *Hygron* (Greek): the moist, happy swimming quality in the eyes of the Medici Venus and the ancient Artemis.

† It was Orleana's peculiar whim to be addressed as "milady." She demanded this not only of Betsy but of all who moved in her circle. One cannot put this down to vulgar pride.

leana's house, but, when he arrived, he suddenly lacked the courage to ring the bell, and he turned around.

After taking a small one in every barroom he encountered, he suddenly felt his piddling courage growing at last to such a size that he finally rang the bell and in pathetic tones asked Betsy, who opened the door, whether he could speak with milady.

But no sooner had Betsy returned with a positive answer than his courage fled a second time, and in such an astonishing manner that he felt totally sober, as if he had not had a single small one all day.

When Betsy finally opened the double door, and he saw Orleana busy at the mirror, at that moment he wished himself thousands of miles away, in fact he would have snuck away if he did not think that his slightest movement would be detected.

Orleana inspected the Cocker, frozen on the threshold, in the bright mirror.

He took his hat in his left, then in his right hand, then he pressed it so firmly under his arm that it snapped and crackled, then he took it from under his arm and held it in both hands in front of him—naturally assuming that Orleana had not seen this.

Once he finally believed that he had arranged himself sufficiently and brought himself into position, he wanted to take a step forward—when it suddenly occurred to him that he had not memorized a proper address to make him appear from the outset in a proper light.

What was he to do? Time pressed—Orleana could turn around any moment and see he was there.

Orleana, who had seen everything in the mirror, and who only appeared to be adjusting the evergreen garlands, quietly gloated over the embarrassment, clumsiness, and insecurity of this man. Finally her patience was at an end, and, before the Cocker's slow cogitations had reached the point of organizing a few words, Orleana turned about and approached the trembling Cocker with the entire grace of her being. The Cocker turned his eyes away from Orleana and sought someplace for his hat.

"Sir, do I have the pleasure of meeting the man who is to be my guest this midday?" Orleana addressed him charmingly, and when the man addressed moved his lips in response but made no sound, she bade him come into the adjoining dining room, set for two persons.

Nervously and with uncertain step, the Cocker followed her and seated himself on the chair Orleana offered him.

He continued to be silent; even his eyes did not dare to set themselves on Orleana.

"Sir," Orleana interrupted the silence, which was beginning to bother her, "your worthy lines that came to me in the mail yesterday still leave me in doubt as the reason for your being here, despite many attempts at decipherment."

With these words, all the Cocker's passion for Orleana returned.

"What?" he responded with a stormy emphasis, "You have no idea that I intend at the outset to—"

The Cocker did not complete this sentence, since his arm had struck a small crystal plate loaded with sweet potatoes, throwing it and its contents into Orleana's lap.

He grasped for them with hasty hands, and with such unrestrained confidence that Orleana stood up in shock and gave him no gentle slap.

This rather overhasty action against the Cocker should not alienate us from her.

Orleana, who had never been touched by any man, and whose own hands shook when she stroked her own body, was beside herself when the Cocker's coarse hands groped at the very spot where even Cupid had never dared to fly.

The Cocker simply thought that he had rescued some sweet potatoes with a quick grab; he had no idea that, in Orleana's eyes, he had committed a dreadful crime.

And what do my beautiful lady readers think the Cocker did when his cheeks were reddened by the slap of a tender lady's hand?

He did not stand up from his chair, did not even shift his weight to one side, but remained rooted to the same place with neck bent forward—he only allowed his hands to drop and grasp the edge of the table.

He looked as if he were awaiting a second chastisement.

"White hands do not hurt," he perhaps intended to say, as he moved his lips up and down.

But he made no sound.

How often thoughts and feelings can jump about in a second, making way for other notions, and so, as a result of a bizarre chain of thought, it seemed to the Cocker to be the proper moment to confess his love to Orleana and ask for her hand.

"Stay here, Betsy!" Orleana called to her departing slave girl, and she sat down in an armchair whose high back protected her from behind.

In keeping with custom, Betsy placed herself behind the chair.

The Cocker released his hands from the edge of the table and raised himself up.

A powerful movement seemed to arise from within him.

Orleana did not fail to observe this. After the first shock caused by the Cocker's clumsiness had passed, she had decided to wait for the next episode in this drama, which was why she ordered Betsy to stay in the room.

"*Fräulein,* most precious *Fräulein,*" the Cocker pulled himself together, "since I have made such a poor initial impression on you, and since I have brought your table setting into such disarray due to my lack of consideration, I am asking a thousand times for forgiveness that you had to use your hand to bring me such an inexpressible joy."

Orleana was amazed. She had never heard such a courtly and patient acceptance of a slap in her life. She almost felt sympathy for the Cocker.

"Dearest, most beautiful *Fräulein,*" he continued, "please at last have pity on me. I have not been able to close my eyes day or night out of fear that you would be taken from me. Oh, I know all about these malignant Frenchmen, who try every possible trick to lead me away from you—but I—I feel something in me like a father feels for his child, what the youngest boy feels for his first love—so I'll say it right out—I love you, I beseech you, I conjure you, not to keep me away any longer and not to deny me what your faithful compatriot's heart will pour out to me at the outset—Orleana, dearest, most beloved compatriot—"

"Herr Hahn," Orleana interrupted his speech, since the sentiments seemed to be growing too strong, "consider for a moment where you find yourself, and that I did not receive you that you should make some sort of scene here in my presence . . ."

The Cocker did not respond with a single word. He stared in despair at his plate, then at Betsy, who still stood at her mistress's chair back.

"You must harbor a rather high estimation of your own amiability, Herr Hahn, that you can write a love letter with so little restraint; beyond that, it is puzzling to me that you visit me with the joyful news that you have found in me your life's companion. A man of such education and appearance as you, sir, could enchant a thousand maidens in an instant. If you have decided that today is to be your wedding day, then I am obviously the first one to be visited on your rounds, and in this case you cannot be discouraged if Fortuna has not let you draw a winner from the urn at the first try. If I ask you not to darken my door again from this day forward or to send me any sort of message, as an educated young man with the world at his feet, you will know how to fulfill this my wish with the greatest proficiency."

Either the Cocker did not understand Orleana's words, or he did not wish to understand them.

Since he—as he said himself—had just gotten underway, he thought himself entitled to continue until he had gained victory over Orleana.

With the swiftness of a hickory nut falling from a tree, the Cocker fell on his knee and with an intense embrace grasped to his heart the leg—of the tall armchair, whose soft cushions no longer bore Orleana's sweet burden.

Only after a few moments did the Cocker note his considerable error. In shock he looked around the entire room.

He was alone.

He was about to marvel at how it could have been possible for him to make such an unpardonable error with the chair leg when Betsy appeared with her mistress's command to leave the house at once and never again dare to enter her presence again.

Without considering that he was in the company of a colored woman and that it was contrary to good tone to bow or give excessive compliments, he was unable to find the door due to his many declarations of courtesy and his apologies, and in this manner he soon pushed himself and Betsy against the wall or some piece of furniture or other.

Betsy, who did not understand a word of German, made every possible effort to explain to the Cocker what her mistress had commanded and how unwelcome he was at this place.

The Cocker threw another loving glance at the empty chair and bewailed the hardness of his fate as he departed.

...

"Claudine de Lesuire!" Betsy announced to Orleana a half-hour later, as she prepared to sit down at her piano.

Orleana stood up and met her friend halfway.

Chapter 7

Lesbian Love

——You are making me rage——I am going mad——
Speak, woman, what am I to give you?
You smile? Aha! Servants! Runners!
Strike off the Baptist's head!
[Queen Pomare]

She also sees on your shoulder——
As she covers them with kisses——
Three little scars, monuments of desire,
Which he once bit into you.
[Edith Schwanenhals]

"It is a real shame, my dear Claudine, that it did not occur to you to visit me an hour earlier.

My God, what a scene! What a cascade of offenses to the spirit, one after another! Don Juan with all his amiability, all his magic, penetrating play of the eye that could win the heart of any woman in an instant, the slim, blond Don Juan who rules in Madrid and Zaragoza, Seville and Santillana, on the Guadalquivir and Ebro as well as on the Ganges, stealing all of the god Amor's arrows from his quiver, this Don Juan, this seducer of maidens, terror of husbands—he stood before me, fell to his knees, and saw his power and connections go to naught on account of a chair leg, and all the laurels female adulation and love had wrapped about his brow were torn from his head in an instant. Don Juan has at last found his female conqueror. He will curse the hour, the minute, the second, in which he dared to try for the heart of a German Creole maiden! Don Juan has become a greenhorn in New Orleans."

Claudine stared at her friend with wide eyes. She was all the more amazed by the peculiar manner in which Orleana expressed herself, since she had never noticed any inclination on her behalf for Don Juans. On the contrary, she had always been determined to debunk them without mercy and only give them attention when she wished to show the failings and errors of the world of men. Orleana had always found an energetic opponent in Claudine, who always wished to soften with time her prejudice against men. She had never heard Orleana speak that way before. To speak of men in such a tone! To speak so lightly of Amor, quivers, arrows, hearts, pratfalls, without restraint—oh, oh—what had happened to Orleana?

"I don't understand you, my dear Orleana . . ." That was all Claudine had been able to respond to her dithyrambs. Orleana took a folded note out of a tiny drawer in her desk, upon which an address was written, or rather smeared, with large Gothic letters, and she handed it with a smile to Claudine, who stopped after reading a single line and stared at her friend with astonishment.

"What does this mean, Orleana, your statements and then this letter—I do not understand you—please, what happened? How did you get this shameful letter—who could have dared to write something like this? Orleana, please explain it to me—I cannot understand it."

Orleana, who did not want to test her friend's patience any further, now explained the entire business of the Cocker in detail. His rude conduct at the threshold of the receiving room, his clumsiness at table, the offense he committed when he fell to his knees—in short, everything that had taken place during the encounter, to the very end, was told to the astonished Claudine.

Orleana, who thought that recounting this droll love affair had provided the right atmosphere for the evening, was greatly moved when Claudine declared in a mournful tone suited to touch the heart, "My dear Orleana, I believe you were right; men are incapable of valuing a woman's love—men are all raw in matters of love."

"How am I to understand that? What made you so reflective all of a sudden?"

When Claudine fell silent, a tear in her eye, Orleana continued:

"Your silence disturbs me, my dear friend. How does it happen that you, who were so happy only a short time ago, have suddenly abandoned marveling at and beseeching men and now can level such a harsh condemnation against them? But I will no longer press you or storm your soul with troublesome questions, my good Claudine—for your silence and the tears in your eyes tell me that I must be silent if my friend has decided to harbor care in her heart and not reveal it even to her Orleana."

"Am I that to you?" Claudine now interjected vigorously. "And this at the very moment when my heart tells me that I must cut myself off from the entire world and live only for my Orleana—Orleana, Orleana, if you only knew what I still felt for you when I stood at the altar with Albert and you handed me the bridal crown! Orleana, perhaps it is heaven's revenge for a crime that I took then only as an innocent child's game, and only now that I have separated from my husband do I think of this cri . . . oh no, no—Orleana, it could not have been a crime that I love you—no, no, no, Orleana—"

"Claudine, Claudine!" Orleana interrupted with a blush, "Do you really love me? Oh, so I did not err after all—how often I trembled when I was near to you—and when once you draped your arm around my neck. Oh Claudine! If it had been a man, I would have remained as cold as marble—Orleana has never trembled in the presence of a man—and she will tremble in the presence of none in the future. Orleana loves her femininity too much to give it to any other than a female friend, to her Claudine—wait a moment," Orleana interrupted herself with a thought, "Didn't you say you have separated from your husband—or did I hear incorrectly?"

Claudine blushed and paled by turns as she placed her hands in Orleana's and described the events of that evening, when Albert had damaged her dignity as spouse so thoroughly through a flippant phrase that he'd caused a break no man on this earth could heal.

As we already know, Claudine did not appear at breakfast on the morning after that fateful night, so Albert had to eat alone. On the same morning, as Albert was rushing to Algiers to visit the two sisters, Claudine's maid took her note on the way to the market and delivered it punctually to her aunt on Bourbon Street. The elderly Baroness Alma de St. Marie-Église rushed at once to her niece, finding her still in bed.

Claudine's lines so astounded the old lady and so piqued her curiosity that she could not wait until Claudine came by at the appointed hour but decided to rush there herself. She could not even wait at home while the horses were harnessed. She, who had not set foot on the street in several years except to mount a carriage, rushed like a young girl to the street where her niece lived. She found her still in bed, as mentioned, half awake, in the deepest negligée, her hair loose, tangled, and tossed across her naked upper body.

The maid, who had eagerly been following the development of this drama, was sent away by Claudine, who did not want an observer who might not be trustworthy or who, in any case, would learn too much at once.

One can well imagine the distress the elderly lady felt when Claudine told her in short, decisive words the cause for her note. The old baroness applied all her arts of persuasion to convince her niece to forgive her loveless husband and take him in her arms again.

"'Marriage is the grave of love!'—What was he trying to say with that? Nothing at all, my dear child—your Albert loves you as much now as he ever did, and he had no purpose at all when he pronounced this fatuity to you. Albert is one of those young, thoughtless fools—there are thousands of them. They want to know everything, perceive everything, try everything, and in the end they know nothing at all. He got this silly saying from some writer, or perhaps he heard it from some oversmart moneyman, and he thought to impress you the other night. Albert? What does your Albert know about marriage? The two of you know nothing of the troubles and stresses that come in married life. What does Albert, what do you yourself know about marriage? You have only been married a few months!

I lived thirty-five years with Monsieur de Saint-Marie—I can assure you, my dear, unsophisticated child, that it is not all that fatal for a husband not to love you as much as a girl would like. And yet Monsieur de Saint-Marie was not a man who one could say neglected his spouse. Live with each other five or ten years and you will not become upset over some thoughtless, frivolous saying. You do not yet know men, my unsophisticated little Claudine—the more they complain, the more they love. A man who is always carrying you around by your hands, praying to you like a god, speaking courteously to you night and day, constantly seeking to pander to your vanity and your heart, is not worth much in marriage. Such a man should never be trusted. He would only be doing it to mislead you for some purpose or to do things behind your back, so that when you find it out, your lot would be anything but enviable.

"Look, dumb, silly little Claudine, see how pointlessly you martyr yourself. If Albert didn't love you, he would never have said something of that sort; he certainly wanted to put your love to the test. Oh, I could give you enough other examples of this! How dreadfully Monsieur de Saint-Marie, my late husband, treated me oftentimes! And did he love me any less? No, my child, to the last moment he bore his Alma in his heart. So calm down and let me hear no more of your unhappy decision. You would certainly deeply regret it in the future if you sacrificed your heart's peace due to a mere whim or rudeness on the part of your husband. Make up and love each other as emphatically as before, and don't bother me over such a silly matter—will you promise me that, little Claudine?"

These and other efforts by her aunt could not shake Claudine's decision. In the end the half-disgusted Baroness gave her consent to a separation of the two spouses, but with the condition that she be able to speak with Albert about it.

Several days later Albert paid the old lady a visit that ended so badly she poured out all her wrath on him, and she now insisted that the divorce take place as soon as possible.

Once the necessary preparations for this had been made and the legal act of divorce obtained, Claudine moved in with her aunt, and Albert lived alone in the same home where he had once passed such fine, sweet hours in the arms of his spouse.

Orleana, who was living at the time in Ocean Springs, on the high bluffs overlooking the Gulf of Mexico, had not received any news at all from her friend on this matter. It would be difficult to discover the motive for Claudine's neglecting to do this. Perhaps she thought it more proper to tell Orleana of her troubles on her return.

And so we find the poor sufferer today with her Orleana.

. . .

Softly, softly! Quiet, quiet now! Trust not the night—close the curtains as tightly as possible; don't talk so openly, for the walls have ears.

Softly, softly! Quietly, quietly, so the evil world cannot hear!

Rubens, Rembrandt, Raphael Santio of Urbino, lend me your brushes; Beethoven, let a fugue vibrate with the force of a rocket through my veins and seethe my blood; you, land of the Nibelungs, send me your fiery wines; Canova, give me the mallet you used to make your Paris—or better—Paris, give me your apple, that I may lay it between Orleana and Claudine. You, Pallas Athena, step aside for a moment, for your armor weighs down your bosom too much. Priapus may leave, too—for here you will find no man at all!

Yet, if it pleases you, my hermaphrodite Ganymede,* come and serve your ambrosia to Orleana and Claudine!

"Do you really love me, Claudine?"

"How beautiful you are, Orleana!"

"How beautiful is your dark blonde hair, your blue eyes!"

"How splendid your raven black hair and the midnight of your eyes!"

"How sweet and supple your waist is!"

"How proud and majestic your stature!"

"How small your white hands are!"

"How heavenly pure your arm is, that no man has ever touched!"

"Claudine, this delicate paleness of your face!"

"Orleana, the beautiful blush on your fresh cheeks!"

"Claudine, how harmonious, how moving your voice is!"

"Orleana, how inspiring your words are!"

"Do you really love me, Claudine?"

A believable writer from ancient Greek times tells us that on the isle of Lesbos there once lived women who did not allow themselves to be touched by any man, since a whim of nature had given them the gift of being sufficient unto themselves.

If any maid in the broad region of Greece was blessed with this gift, she rushed to this island to seek a companion for life. When the Romans became lords of Hellas, they transported these women to the City of the

*Ganymede's masculinity was certainly not the reason Zeus loved him. As a god, Zeus could also see him anytime he wished in his Titianesque nightshirt.

Seven Hills and exploited them as slaves, compelling them to assist in the baths.

They only lived free in a few places in Greater Greece, enjoying there the same rights no one had disputed on their island.

Later, when the Romans were subjected by the Germans, many reached Lombardy, Switzerland, and southern Germany.

In Switzerland they gathered and found a place for their secretive activities, most of all in Meran.[10]

Both the Cabots brought along many of them to America, and Sir Walter Raleigh transplanted them to Virginia, where Queen Elizabeth extended them her full favor, protecting them to a surprising degree.

There are many fables about Elizabeth and Raleigh, and the *Chronique Scandaleuse* has sought, in vain until now, to plumb the motives that led the Virgin Queen to show disfavor to Sir Walter.

Until now no one has discovered—or no one has dared to confess—that the cause was her jealousy of Raleigh due to his relationship with a lesbian lady.

In the Cabinet of Beauties of the new royal palace in Munich is a portrait of this competitor,[11] and her surprising resemblance to Orleana can only be the result of an elective affinity, for Lesbos "produces no children."

So much for the closer understanding of the mysterious stirring of feeling on the part of our beautiful Orleana.

Bedchambers where a man seldom or only briefly appears—bedchambers that are not touched even by male servants—bedchambers on whose soft carpet only a woman's foot ever steps—bedchambers whose beds, sofas, and hangings only the satin of a woman's robe whispers by: such bedchambers are a hell of torments and pains for a man, as Amor breaks his arrow and throws it at his feet in disgust as he departs. Whoever enters whole departs sick of heart and soul. Drunk in his senses, he thinks of the satin robe that rustles at his knee; he presses his hand on his hot brow, and his senses collapse as his fantasy contemplates what the heavy satin rustles against. It is the veiled image of Isis, the Cathedral of Love, Sensuality itself that is impressed on the whole of nature.

It is certainly no crime to lift the veil from this image; certainly it is no sin against the holy of holies of femininity to contemplate it; it is certainly no sin against the Holy Spirit to enter this cathedral of love with covered head. Nature herself is responsible for having wandered from the path when she creates flowers whose pistils will not accept masculine pollen, whose pistils in fact leave their flower cups in order to join one with another.

Quietly, quietly; softly, softly now; close the curtains as tightly as you can; do not speak so loudly, for the walls have ears, too.

Quietly, quietly; softly, softly, so that the evil world does not hear!

"Do you really love me, Claudine?"

"Oh, how the fresh warmth of your proud neck drives me wild!"

"How your breasts make my blood boil!"

"Orleana, Orleana, how excitingly loose your clothes are!"

"Claudine, Claudine, how tightly you are corseted!"

"Orleana, Orleana, how easily your clothes fall away!"

"Claudine, Claudine, how difficult it is for me to get these things off of you!"

"Orleana, how pure and white your shoulders are!"

"Claudine, where did you get the scars on yours?"

"Orleana, Orleana—Albert did that."

"And you really love me, Claudine?"

Claudine began:

I sowed Measured Love[12]
In my garden,
A whole bed full
I could hardly wait
Until they came, until they bloomed,
So I could pluck them
For my love.

And when they came
Sprouting up
I generously
Sprinkled them with water.

Orleana responded:

Buds hung
In fullness, soon ready
Your watering
Did them good.

Claudine continued:

But when I came
Out one morning

What did I see—good heavens!
Oh terror, oh horror!
The buds lay broken
Bent on the ground
I mourned mightily
For the dear departed.

Orleana finished:

Now to your beloved
You cannot give Measured Love.
I mourn much for that,
For her young life.

As I said, the hermaphrodite Ganymede may enter without hesitation; his presence does not disturb, and it is high time his divine drink moistened their burning lips.

Come closer, my Ganymede, don't turn your little nose so high! Almighty Jupiter is long since dead, Olympus is abandoned and empty, the whole race of the gods died out—you must reconcile yourself to serving mortals.

Come in—you'll find an old friend; see how loose Cupid flits from one lap to another in his confusion and cannot figure out quite where to begin. You can tell that such visits are a rarity for him!

Quietly, quietly, softly, softly now, so the evil world does not hear.

Close the curtains as tight as you can!

Don't speak so loudly, for the walls have ears.

"Do you really love me, Claudine?"

"Orleana, Orleana, how embarrassed I am!"

"Claudine, Claudine, how happy *I* am!"

"Orleana, my angel, where are you taking me?"

"Claudine, my little woman, how I want to kiss you!"

"Orleana, Orleana, I'm really embarrassed."

"No, no, my dear little woman, I am only *kissing* you!"

"Orleana, oh leave me alone, I ask you so much!"

"Little Claudine, my little woman, then tremble no more!"

...

Wherever the law claps love in permanent manacles, where the Church proclaims sensual denial, where false modesty and inherited morality keeps us from giving nature its rights, then we lie down at the warm breasts of

Mother Nature, listening to her secrets and surveying with burning eyes the great mechanism in which every gear moans the word *Love.*

There is rejoicing in all the spheres, the fanfares of the universe resound, wherever love celebrates its triumph. But lightning bolts flash from dark clouds whenever tyrannical law and usurped morality seek to compel the children of earth to smother their vitality and entomb their feelings.

How small and pitiful the nattering of parties seems, how petty the drama even of our own revolution, against the titanic struggle of sensuality against law and morality.

"Revolution!" the nun cries out in her sleep, throwing her rosary in the face of the Madonna.

"Revolution!" the priest of the sole-salvific Church mutters as he rips his scapular into shreds.

"Revolution!" thunders the proletarian when he beholds the fair daughter of Pharaoh.

"Revolution!" the slave rattles, when he sees the white child of the planter walking through the dark passageway of cypresses.

"Revolution!" the horse whinnies, mutilated by greed.

"Revolution!" the steer roars, cursing its tormentors under the yoke on its shoulders.

"Revolution!" the women of Lesbos would storm, if we were to rebuke their love.

• • •

New Orleans is the Meran of the United States for lesbian ladies, where they hold their mysterious gatherings, unhindered and unseen by the Argus-eyes of morality until now. Strangely enough, as everywhere else, they reside only alongside bodies of water, since their norms hold that they cannot do without the nearness of water. So we find them in clubs of twelve to fifteen on the Hercules Quay, along the Pensacola Landing, and all along the entire left side of the New Basin.

They have lost their earlier location on Lake Pontchartrain. They were driven out, in part by the efforts of F∗, in part through the efforts of old McDonogh.*

My esteemed lady readers will visit one of these settlements in the third volume and be convinced that lesbian ladies are not as bad as most, and

*We could not determine whether they have resumed their previous location now that McDonogh has been dead for several years.

that they are as decent and well mannered as the rest of the world of women, after their fashion.

It was three o'clock when Cupid fluttered through the shutters, through which a cooling west wind blew over the slumbering women-friends.

The moon smiled knavishly and the stars glittered with delight as they spotted Cupid flying down Toulouse Street, blushing red from head to foot, with flaccid bow and empty quiver.

Albert

Albert took on an entirely different way of life after separating from Claudine. If he had once been active and tireless in his efforts to secure their keep, now his temperament veered in the utterly opposite direction: whereas he had previously applied his powers to fulfilling his duties and perfecting his talents, he now set out on the uncertain course of a roué and wallowed in intoxication of the senses, only interrupted when compelled to rehabilitate himself and go back "into production." He had lost his financially remunerative position as a draftsman with the large construction project on Customhouse Street, since the architect in charge was persuaded by his frequent absences to engage another young man with as pleasant an appearance and as considerable a talent. So Albert resorted to earning his money from irregular work with various architectural and surveying offices: one week he drew in Bank's Arcade, the other at Reynold's, and often he worked under Captain Lafarell at A. Knell and Keathing, for an amount that was a stark contrast with what he had earned earlier.

He had rejected Claudine's offer to have her aunt grant him a yearly payment of seven hundred dollars, for despite his excesses he was still sensitive enough not to take money from a woman who had decided to separate from him. Claudine had tried time and again to offer him some of her aunt's money, which would not simply save him from temporary embarrassment but also secure him a carefree existence for several years—but Albert always declined.

This would be the proper moment to describe an occupation eminently suited to an educated man lacking a trade or any other means to make money without hard labor. With good luck and opportunity, it can even lead to a respectable income. I mean what is called plan-making, which is to present buildings and properties the owners want to sell to the public on sheets of paper, decorated with considerable coloration. New Orleans has two central markets for this occupation in the Second District, the first in the St. Louis Exchange Alley, which is so crammed with lithographers, bookbinders, booksellers, book peddlers, book printers, job printers, architects, civil engineers, surveyors, and "working" or "stout" draftsmen, stuffed into every last corner, that the few remaining traders in canaries and birdseed, hatters, lawyers, "quatre-colonnes," and such can hardly breathe. The plans of lots and houses that are prepared here have their showplace or gallery in the rotunda of the St. Louis Hotel, where they are described as "à la french."[13]

The general emporium for these plans, however, remains Bank's Arcade, where some of them cover the walls of the great barrooms and others are displayed on green-colored stands at floor level or on platforms four feet high.

Yet the grand barroom of Bank's Arcade Hotel is a mere vestibule to the true shrine of art and good taste, unfolding in the most beautiful and fitting way. That residence of the muses is none other than the office of the auctioneers Beard and May, where one enters into a veritable garden of house and lot plans, whose avatars have either already been sold or long for their imminent auctioning. The massive expansion of Beard's business, as the best-known and most widely famed auctioneer, not just in New Orleans but in the whole South—perhaps in the entire United States—means that the efforts of architects and draftsmen are concentrated here. Here an entire trade is dedicated to selling houses and lots by means of these plans, a craft found nowhere else in the United States, save for Leffingwell and Elliott in St. Louis.[14] It works this way: When the owner of a property or a house wants to sell his property as soon as possible, he goes to the office of the auctioneers Beard and May and orders a plan that will represent as precisely as possible the area and outline of his house and the situation of the lot for sale. Mr. Beard immediately walks upstairs and orders the desired plan from an architect. Once this is completed, his house nigger and personal marshal, Jim, takes it and hangs it either on the walls or on green display stands in the barroom of the Arcade. Here the plans are checked by those seeking to buy, who often discover all too late their error in buying a house based on a painting.

Here one can often find gatherings of the Nestors of draftsmanship, reviewing with great zeal achievements and advancements in the realm of architecture, surveying, and so on. Dr. Engelhardt, Hübner, Walther, Niemayer, and Neumayer already have generations of drawing behind them, so that they enjoy precedence over their colleagues in art and criticism. In the painting of landscapes, the ideal is Keathing's full, juicy burst of color from his drumming-brush.*

This describes Albert's present occupation.

He was living in the very same apartment in which he had spent that traumatic night after the honeymoon, which had caused the decisive split for both of them.

Other than a few necessary feminine properties and utensils that Claudine had taken with her to her aunt, everything remained in the same order as before. Nothing indicated that a woman was lacking, for one could see the same organization and punctuality that had prevailed before.

The porcelain figurines and various other knickknacks still stood on the shelves, arranged just as Claudine had left them.

The young maid, whom Albert had kept, made sure that nothing gathered dust. Every day she carefully took up the knickknacks, dusted every porcelain figurine, every dish and flower basket, and placed everything back in the same sequence.

She did this as a result of Albert's specific order.

Bridget, which was the maid's name, had an easy time of it, and she had nothing else to do but to cook for herself, for Albert rarely came home at all. It was seldom that he slept in his own bed even once in any particular week.

Although he saw that he would have had to be a capitalist to afford the expenditures that his irregular, disorderly way of life demanded, besides maintaining an unused apartment with a servant he still insisted on not renting the rooms his wife had occupied to anyone else.

For this purpose he made a very peculiar contract with the Irishman who owned the house, a contract that no Yankee would ever have accepted.

We will come back to that later.

On the evening in which Claudine lay in Orleana's arms, Albert was attending the opening of the "Louisiana Ball," which had never been as brilliantly arranged as it was now.

The merry company entered the temple of Terpsichore already somewhat heated, for they had passed through several barrooms, oyster shops, billiard parlors, and cafés, and whenever one of them assured the other that it was high time to visit the ball, the reply was that it was better to have a few more drinks, since the night was long enough and no one wanted to grind shoe leather for six or seven hours.

*A short, full brush used with stencils. *Drumming* is the technical term for stenciling.

Thus they finally arrived at the stairs leading to the ballroom, not because of a specific decision but because the scarlet thread that had led them through innumerable barrooms had its end there. It would never occur to a determined roué to appear at the Louisiana Ball in a ball-costume. Light, modest clothing and a few eagles in the wallet—that was all he needed. As a precaution, one also kept a small dagger ready and well hidden, since sailors, mates, and river boys could be dangerous rivals for the pretty dancers.

"Gentlemen, come back if you will—I have the strictest order to search everyone who enters to make sure they are not carrying weapons," the porter called after the merry company as they stormed up the stairway to the ballroom.

"You're being absolutely pedantic again today, Monsieur Dufleur," Albert replied, as he halted his friends and had them submit to the usual frisking.

"Submit quietly," the Frenchman whispered to them, "I am not being all that thorough; besides, you Germans are not all that dangerous. You only bring weapons to impress the girls—if there is trouble, you're always smart enough to give in or beat it in time. You know I just have to act as if I'm doing my job, since that fellow over there"—he motioned at the head porter with his little lynx-eyes—"is very serious about it."

After Dufleur's frank explanation, only a boor would have objected to being searched from top to bottom.

"I felt your little stiletto," the porter whispered to Albert, "but it doesn't matter—I'm just telling you so you don't think I'm too dumb to detect it. But I'll give you a piece of advice, don't stick it in your shoe in the future. It could happen that I wouldn't be here, and that fellow over there would never give it back—'t'would just be too bad for your little knife, which must have cost twenty piasters."

"Twenty?" Albert replied with a low voice, "what are you thinking, Dufleur? You couldn't get it for fifty."

After the porter had done the same honors with Albert's colleagues, the troop stormed up the broad staircase.

The last notes of an egregiously awful polka were sounding in the ballroom. The band members, consisting entirely of Germans, were laying away their instruments, and each was hosting the first girl who fell into his hands.

The break was being filled by a "sevens' dance," which the sailors of the *Isaac Newton* had hastily arranged. The second mate had commandeered a violin from one of the musicians and began playing a dance, with less than imposing virtuosity.

Three cute little levee-ladies inserted themselves as swiftly as arrows between each two dancers, and when they changed partners they were tossed and caught by the dancer opposite.

"Halloo, hey, Mary! Up and down! Now you, then me, now to me, then to you! Halloo, hey girls! Now up, then down! Now to me and then to you!" And so the dance went on in this way, tirelessly; it was truly amazing how these drunken heroes of the sea and the levee-ladies could keep it up so long.

"Come on, fatty," one of the sailors protested, taking hold of a rather plump man wearing a black frock coat, with more than half of his white batiste-handkerchief hanging out of the left pocket of his red satin vest. "Do you want to risk a dance? You damned landlubbers don't have any fire in your bodies—here, try it with Mary—halloo, Mary, hey, fatso, now up, now down! Now to me, then to you!"

The Cocker—for the fat man with the black frock coat and the fine batiste-handkerchief was no other—glared at the son of the sea with large eyes, despite the fat bearing down on his eyelids, and mused over a suitable answer. He had rushed straight from Orleana's dining room to the Louisiana Ball, in order to revive his spirits and to free himself—at least for this evening—from the silly melancholy into which his compatriot had dumped him.

"Well, you damned landlubber, get going!" the sailor roared when he saw that the Cocker was not joining the sevens' dance by tossing black-eyed Mary into the air.

It was the Cocker's misfortune that this son of the sea was a German, for, since the Cocker spoke only German, he could understand him. He could not ignore the man's words, delivered as they were in a true sailor's style.

"Sailor," the Cocker finally replied, carefully taking his long coattails under his arm for protection, "Dance with Shellroad Mary yourself—sailor, I have foresworn dancing for tonight."

If the Cocker ever told a lie in his life, he did it this time, for he had come to the Ball to dance, to drown his love-pangs in the arms of the daughters of Terpsichore.

"Damned landlubber, you will renounce nothing here!" the sailor roared even louder, kicking the Cocker into the middle of the sevens' dance with his knee. "You're not going to waste time here, fatso! Halloo, hey, fatso, now to me and then to you, now to you and then to me!"

"But sailor," stammered the shaken Cocker, "haven't you considered that I cannot do your worthy dance without having practiced a bit at home?"

"Oh, it's you, Gasper!" Shellroad Mary shrieked, finally recognizing the old acquaintance from earlier days—naturally only as a bystander, since the Cocker had played a non-speaking role when he met her on expeditions with friends to Cassidy's, knowing not a word of English, and, despite seven years in New Orleans, not a word of French either.

"You're here, my sweetheart Gasper?"

"Virgin Mary, you see that I am not prepared . . ."

Now he received a push from the sailor which made both his ears ring. "But sailor, you're a compatriot . . ."

"Halloo, hey, fatso," the sailor interrupted him once more as he attempted to hoist the Cocker into the air.

"Lout, thief, scoundrel!—*Sacre nom de dieu,* thieving lout, where did you get this handkerchief?" a foreign voice suddenly thundered out of the confusion that engulfed the Cocker. At the same instant a hand groped in his vest-pocket, seizing the handkerchief with the lovely lace. "Thief, thief, gallows-bait! Where did you steal this handkerchief?"

Once the Cocker got a better look at the man whose lips poured out this flood of abuse, he recognized to his dread the same Frenchman who had dealt with him so violently during his serenade and had driven him away from Orleana's house.

The Frenchman had noted the Cocker from the moment he entered the ball and had not let him out of his sight, and he did not fail to see the lacy handkerchief. When he stood directly by the Cocker, he could see the name Orleana embellished on the end of the handkerchief, precisely as his sister had embroidered for Orleana. Even without the least interest in the fashion of "the Moor of Venice" (though the beautiful Creole was not his Desdemona), the Frenchman was still profoundly offended that this priceless valuable had somehow ended up in the Cocker's possession. He had oft considered speaking with the unfortunate serenader on this matter, but the proper moment had never presented itself.

Now, when he saw the poor Cocker so beset by the sailor from the *Isaac Newton* and the dancers, he suddenly let loose, bestowing the insults already listed, delivering them with blind fury.

The sailor's attention suddenly shifted from the Cocker to the cursing Frenchman. Through a strange chain of thought, the drunken seaman now decided to make the Frenchman the object of his brutality and raw humor. He not only forced the Frenchman to return the batiste handkerchief, but he also ordered him to fall on his knees and beg forgiveness. The Frenchman thought that was asking too much, so he drew a derringer from his coat sleeve and advanced on his tormenter in a martial stance. The bouncers, who wanted to step in to pacify the situation, were not heeded but instead were harassed and mistreated to an extreme by several sailors and high-skirted ladies.

The Cocker seized the opportunity to rush to the stairs and shriek "Watch! Watch!" at the top of his lungs. Then he lunged down the stairs and into the street without paying attention to Dufleur, who was advancing on him.

If he had remained in the Ballroom for a few more minutes, he would have seen that he had no need to call for help. The night watch had been there in the Ballroom all evening, four men strong who were mingling with the dancers.*

The Frenchman, who had been brought into high indignation by an excess of alcohol, defended himself against the watchmen, who descended on him with the rage of a beast. After vain struggling and bumping, he finally had to submit to overwhelming force. The sailors and girls surrounded him on all sides, ripping out his hair and kicking him in the shins—even kicking him in his belly, which (among others) Shellroad Mary herself did, until the night watch put an end to their game. Two of the watch finally took the Frenchman between them to Golgotha, the calaboose, where, as fate would have it, he was thrown on the same horse blanket where a short time before the Cocker had embraced his broken guitar.

The merry company led by Albert had joined the fandango, which was supposed to close out the Ball's evening's program.

A kingdom for a fandango! You've already danced yourself half-mad, your eyes are dim, your feet are asleep, you are hanging on the breast of a pretty, young dancing girl, and, without recalling that there is a dancing girl there, you grope, grope—in my case you grope for thin air—without a thought left, you mechanically grope in your vest and pants' pockets to see if there

*In more recent times, under the management of A. Cambre, the Louisiana Ballroom—at the corner of Esplanade and Victory Streets, of course—is no longer under such a strict police control, since a more select public has come to occupy its halls. They no longer admit sailors and shoreboys in red shirts and broad workers' trousers. Those are restricted to the Hamburg Mill and Old Jack. Despite that, one cannot always prevent the sons of Neptune from smuggling themselves in, and their rowdiness with them. This restriction to the elite does not, however, apply to the ladies. And properly so, for our lovely women of Orleans are welcome everywhere, whether they are prostitutes or pastors' daughters. The most brilliant of the current fancy-dress balls is the "Masquerade Quadroon Ball," but it is at the same time the most scandalous. Madame P * 's balls on the Bayou Road are an analogue to these Masquerade Quadroon Balls, where the *grand feminine world of New Orleans,* otherwise presented only at the balls in the St. Charles Hotel, clandestinely bathes in the lustful lake of *Venus Vulgivaga.*

is still any money there. The musicians stare indifferently, gathered at the bar and with no desire to do another round. Your eyes are swimming, your nose bobs, and your tongue lolls, but your feet and hands no longer work—you let your dancing partner do things in front of everyone, as if you were not a man at all, but rather a milkmaid or a midwife. You lurch, your slack thighs flail, your back wouldn't hurt if a hundred fists were to bounce off it—you don't care whether the woman next to you raises her dress above her knee to look for the bruise she got from falling during the last dance. Then the god of music and his disciples mount the platform for the last time—an overture! Listen, the fandango is calling, wake up! wake up! Before the finale surprises you and you've been had.

Albert was certainly not a practiced dancer—he didn't even know quite when to enter the dance and when to cross over—but when the notes of the fandango sounded in his ears, he rose up, bowed, and moved about just like a full-blooded Castillian, he snarled and snorted like a gaucho, and he pressed and rubbed like the sphinx Atropos, who grew as thin and sinuous as a water-nymph in the throes of love.

That's what a fandango will do!

Look, just look at Albert, how changed he is! How he throws a green net over Shellroad Mary's shoulders, how he goes back, how she goes forward to him, how they both come together! These rounded elbows, these eyes—this bacchantic everything!

Bestow your lyre on Albert at this moment, my dear convalescent in the Rue Amsterdam,[15] you would get it back right away:

All the gods of love rejoice
In my heart, and fanfares
They blow and call out: "Hail!
Hail to Queen Pomare!"

She dances. How her little body moves!
How every member bends so supinely!
There is a fluttering and a swinging
Which seems to want to leap right out of her skin.

She dances. When she turns about
On one foot, and stands still
At the end with extended arms,
May God pity my reason!

So she dances—and blow
The gods of love a fanfare
In my heart, calling: Hail!
Hail Queen Pomare!

The fandango was at an end.

Some of the band members had packed their instruments away in cases, others had tucked theirs in their coats. They yawned, shrugged, and looked at one another with sleepy eyes.

All the dancing girls except Shellroad Mary had left the ballroom.

The manager's helpers had enough to do getting the sailors who were lying about on their feet and on their way. So they kicked many a backside, clubbing them on the head mercilessly with their billies, wherever they happened to be lying.

Albert's merry company was still here. They had sobered up a bit and appeared not even to be tired anymore.

Albert mounted the bandstand with Shellroad Mary, who drove him crazy, and from there he preached a sermon concerning the importance and meaning of a ball.

Shellroad Mary stood right behind him, resting her head on his shoulder.

She was a large woman with a marvelously long, extended waist and full, soft hips—with the feet of a Bettina von Arnim and hands such as no god could make for an angel.[16]

Despite her bacchantic looseness, if a special occasion called for it, her features could express a sensual earnestness that attracted all the more, since the contrast of earnestness and sensuality so often serves to cover virtue and innocence.

It was this combination which drew Napoleon to Mademoiselle von Teba. It was that earnestness which earned her the imperial diadem.

If fate had made Shellroad Mary the child of a prince, had she been born on the shore of the Seine instead of that of the Mississippi, she would have done as much grace to lilies and purple as to the golden bees of the Merovingians. She would not have been an embarrassment to any Bourbon, Orléans or Napoleonic. But instead of Your Imperial Majesty, she was just Shellroad Mary. Wasn't Mary Stuart, in her own way, when her husband Francis II addressed her, nothing but Shellroad Mary? Brantone, who preserves her depressing farewell song for us,* would certainly have been

*It begins with the following famous lines: En mon triste et doux chant, / D'un ton fort lamentable, / Je jette un oeil tranchant / De perte irreparable; / Et un soupirs cuisans /

able to sing similar verses for Shellroad Mary, had he laid eyes on her. No estate or office protects a person from this dilemma.

It is characteristic of the cretinous prudishness of the Cocker that he was not infatuated with her.

With his more elevated sensitivities, Albert was enthralled by Shellroad Mary's "eternal feminine" aura.

To protect herself from a chill, immediately after the fandango she had clothed herself in what is called a "monkey jacket" of dark green silk, with three rows of yellow buttons. Her light chestnut hair lay loose on her neck and bosom, and she had pinned a decoration, a bright green crown of fine metal leaves woven with freshwater pearls, forward in her hair, where her widow's peak met her forehead.

She had placed her head on Albert's shoulder as if musing, and she half-listened to the words he addressed in French to the merry company and the few remaining guests.

Albert was heard saying the following: "Messieurs, and you my dear dancing girl"—he gave Shellroad Mary a pat—"before you depart for home, allow me to direct to you a few words of encouragement and consideration. All of you now present have had to earn a few dollars during the week, with great effort and with unspeakable torment and martyrdom, which you have now sacrificed in a single night. Will you regret this? Will you become irritated when you reach into your pockets and find them empty? After such dissipation, has such a repressed idea ever occurred to you, so that you make a sour face instead of smiling at the transitoriness of the joys of this world? I tell you now that you are committing a serious injustice if you allow such nonsense to arise. The charm of gold, messieurs, does not consist in picking it up and putting it down again, but in paying it out. Whoever does not pay out has no money, even if he is as rich as Croesus. The worker who sacrifices a few dollars to have some fun is richer than McDonogh or Judah Touro,[17] who invest their sums in cotton and building lots. I certainly would not want to deny these gentlemen any possible enjoyment, but they would be upset if they thought of possible and probable use for the same money in speculation. But in order that my assertions can have a semblance of truth, it is absolutely necessary for one to be unmarried, since the crying and whimpering of babies robs one of enjoyment as completely as the rustling and squeaking of drays and the study

---

Passent mes meillieurs ans. [Ed.: In my sad and soft song, / Of a tone quite sad, / I throw a cutting eye / of irreparable loss; / And in poignant sighs / My best years pass.]

of a boat manifest. *Messieurs,* if you here present are not married, take my advice and avoid this farce and remain bachelors for life. Don't let yourselves be misled by the abusive term *dried up,* for I can assure you that this phrase is only a revenge on the part of professional married men. Jaundiced married men invented this phrase to impart irritation and distress into the butterfly life of a bachelor. Since a heavy mountain lies on their hearts, they insist that everyone be visited with the same curse. Since they are unable to accomplish this in the ordinary course of events, they have their revenge by smuggling such a title into human society."

Thunderous applause told Albert that he had not spoken in vain. Certainly the merry company made the most noise, but even the married employees of the manager beat their billies on the planks of the dancing floor to show their undivided approval.

Albert and his merry company were the only stragglers capable of making their way home with reasonably steady steps. They had passed their crisis of exhaustion after the fandango, and they felt as sober in the fresh air as if they had never had anything to drink. Only now and then did one of them place a hand on his forehead or moisten lips with a tongue.

Shellroad Mary parted from them a couple blocks from the Louisiana Ballroom, since she had promised to spend the night with a woman friend in this area.

Kisses flew back and forth—and Shellroad Mary finally tore herself from Albert's embrace. As a sign of her unlimited attachment she took with her a couple of hairs bitten from his black moustache.

Once they arrived on Royal Street, the merry company scattered to the various quarters of the city, and Albert went on alone until he turned onto St. Louis Street in order to go straight home, to sleep for once in his own bed.

When Albert passed the Rue des Ramparts, he noted two men a short distance away, one trying to dispute by coarsely gesticulating at the other, who held a watchman's billy in his hand. When the second man grabbed the other's arm, Albert heard the following words, which caused him to smile:

"But watchman, I can assure you that I was not the one who smashed in Victor's shopwindow, although he has thoroughly earned it from me, but I am not about to settle my accounts with him right now—for I am forgetting nothing. I have never been a friend of public scandal, least of all of kicking in windows or wrecking shops. Let me go, watchman, I have had such a lousy day, my compatriot, the Frenchman in the Louisiana Ballroom—oh, if you only knew, you would give me some sympathy rather than be so mean as to stick me back in the calaboose, and beyond that you are my compatriot—another German, watchman—consider what that means!"

"Stick you in the calaboose again? If you have already been in the hole, then you're not too good to try it again," the nightwatch responded, laughing. "Compatriot or not doesn't concern me, old loafer—march, march with me to the hole!"

Albert, who knew the "old boy" as well as one of his own merry company, went up to the two and whispered a few words into the watchman's ear. The watchman then released his hand from the arm of the Cocker, who, without thanking his benefactor, ran away.

"Charley, whatever caused you to seize the poor man so that his few remaining cents would have been taken in front of the recorder tomorrow? There are enough rich loafers in the city who have earned being locked up a hundred times over—you do it like everybody else, those fellows remain unmolested because they can put a few eagles in your hand. This poor fellow can't do that, so he has to rot, and only because he is supposed to have kicked in somebody's shopwindow—here—there are five dollars for you—that's all I have."

"Not bad," the watchman responded, sticking the money into his pocket with pleasure as he pounded his weighted billy three times on the sidewalk with such official dignity, as if he had done no injury to his duty as a savior of his country.

Albert made the rest of his way home in thought. When he passed a graveyard near Claiborne Street, he paused a few moments, took off his hat, and let the Gulf breeze cool his heated brow. It was a night similar to that on which he had walked with Claudine near this graveyard, when his mounting dissatisfaction had forced him to fight with her. As bright as it had been then, the silver crescent of the moon steered its way through the deep blue ocean of the sky, the gold-embroidered mantle gleaming over the City of the Gulf. Had Albert felt happiness then? Did he feel it now? "You remain a puzzle to people," he whispered to himself, placing his right hand on his heart, "Who is able to understand you—you human heart?—If you are heaven, why did you expel your most beloved angel, who climbed up to you on a ladder of desire and love? If you are a hell, why do you praise innocence, love, and fidelity in your heart? If you are a lamb, why were you cruel as a hyena when you tore up the grave of unhappy love in order to drench yourself with heart-blood? If you are a tiger, why don't you take refuge in a virgin's bosom before she suspects that there is such a thing as love? You are giving me no answers, my words are echoing in vain; you are so calm, my heart, so gentle—who knows whether you will not breed snakes in a few hours? Heart, my heart, you are the creation of a cruel divinity, who cannot bear to have other beings happy—or you are this cruel, perverse divinity itself, who gives something only to tear it away, who soothes pain only to call it down all the more throbbingly? In any case, whoever and whatever you are, we are all damned to carry you around for life, and we cannot do without you, unless we pay for it with our lives . . ."

"There will come a time when you will say something different," sounded a voice behind him, coming from a man who was riding past, spurring his horse.

"Was that intended for me?" Albert thought to himself, as he turned about and looked after the rider.

Book
III

Dedicated to the Creole Marie Lolette Bloodword

I see you, in your place, wringing hands
On the heights of the Appalachians standing
The image prophetic of our time, *Cassandra,*
Foretelling misfortune.
from "Cassandra" by L. Reizenstein

Marie Lolette! More than nine years have passed since I first saw you beneath the deep-blue sky of Italy. It was near the Bay of Spezia, not far from the place where the flood bore away young Shelley, the beloved of Lord Byron. You had just come from Genoa, wishing to have an outing with your friend Taron among the groves of olive and orange belonging to the *cavaliere* Pittore. It was on a marble bench, decorated with the arms of two famed families of doges, that you met a young student with a tanned face, not yet paled by the kiss of women—you encountered him in the midst of his daydreaming, as he was tracing the verses of "Orlando furioso" on the narrow neck of his snow-white greyhound.

"You are from Genoa, Signor?"

"Would that I could say yes, Signora—but, sadly enough, I have come directly from Germany."

"Your accent has not betrayed you—but you were certainly not born in Germany?"

"Not born there, no! But I am regarded as a German, though I was still playing with the tassels of a cardinal's hat in Rome when I was six."

"Then you are really an Italian?"

"Yes, from my mother's side."[1]

"Then I shall take back the question I directed at you, Signor; I had already determined your origin from your reading matter, since a German would never be reading 'Orlando furioso' here in Spezia, so few miles from Genoa, but rather the 'Frühling' of Kleist."

"Could I pose to you the question you posed to me, Signora?"

"I was born in Louisiana, and the waves of the Mississippi sang me to sleep in my cradle."

"From Louisiana? That was ever the land of my dreams, to rest under palms and to muse in the shadow of the forest primeval, that must be a divine pleasure!"

Marie Lolette! What you answered me with has turned true. Two years after that meeting I left Italy to find in your birthplace crippled palmettos instead of stately, feathered palms, and sick giants of a lost time instead of a forest primeval.

It drove me from your place of birth, for it bore no interest for me when you were lacking.

Those words you called to me nine years ago, "Seek, but you will seek in vain," have accompanied me on all my fruitless wanderings. The Niagra thundered it at me when I clambered its rocks and stared into its depths. I saw the Indian carving this with his tomahawk on a thousand-year-old giant in the forest. I rode through the grasses of the prairies, and I heard them whisper: "Seek, but you will seek in vain!" I saw a ship weigh anchor and longed to board it, and the masts groaned, "Remain here, for you are seeking in vain!"

In vain, in vain! So many, many years! Finally you have shown me the way I have to go in order to *find!* I have launched myself on this promised path, and I do not need to stop my ears with wax or have myself bound to the mast, as did Ulysses, my companion in destiny. It would not have taken much for Circe to bewitch me and turn me into a pig. But a divine cowherd called "Husband" rescued me from this momentous metamorphosis in the nick of time.

Chapter 1

One Year Later

At the time the following events occurred, the portion of our city now known as the Fourth District had not yet been annexed. The Fourth District once had its own administration and bore the proud name of Lafayette. This denomination has continued despite the new classification, and no true resident of New Orleans who has any consideration for this prodigal son of a barfly queen-mother would ever use such a flat engineer's expression as "Fourth District." Proud Lafayette not only had its own municipal administration, but it even had an independent German newspaper. This paper was known as the *Courier* and the *Lafayette Zeitung.* It, too, had to surrender to annexation and renounce a monopoly over its area. The millionairess Madame Delachaise was supposed to have had some influence over the advance of our municipal boundaries. Her vast plantations, where Negro houses once stood and cotton once burst from billions of bolls, are now the faubourg or suburb of Plaisance and Delachaise, and where nigger-drivers once drove their massa's black dogs to work, German enterprise and German patience has created independent property, each owner working his vegetable gardens and planting his magnolias and China elms by his own hand. Where once one rode through swampy plantation land, often slipping into mud up to the knee, now the finest roads have arisen and locomotives cross the land, signaling the active speculative energy and entrepreneurship of our contemporaries. Jefferson City, Greenville, Hurstville, Rickerville, Bouligny, all the way to Carrollton—who knows if in ten or twelve years they will not form a single city of New Orleans, whose area and number of inhabitants will exceed that of London and New York? And what then? What will then become of that fatal mark of Cain the South has burned into its own forehead?

Let us look in on one family in Washington Avenue, living in an old, broken-down frame cottage. They are involved in a conversation that obviously must have grown out of a disagreement. Their faces are agitated and inflamed with excitement, and irritated displeasure can even be found in the expression of a newborn child stranded between two mattresses in a hatbox, once the repository for the hat of an officer of general staff.

The other members of the family are all sitting around a large chest, some seated on overturned wash-basins, some on bundles of dirty laundry.

A small girl of about five is standing next to her mother, her head in her mother's lap.

The mother is a woman of forty-nine, with a noble and impressive allure, a face that is earnest and inspiring of trust. She is dressed in a blindingly white, embroidered dressing gown, and she looks anxiously from time to time at a girl of seven sitting to her left, whose syrup-smeared hands have somehow to be kept away from her own fresh clothing.

About her throat, white as marble, is a broad, black velvet ribbon joined in the front by a clasp of two doves. Her hair is black as ebony and covered in the back with a black net, a coiffure that makes her hair appear thicker and fuller than it is.

Her dark eyes have a soulful expression and are seldom entirely open. Her nose has a slight bend in the middle, making a charming impression, particularly in profile.

Save for some fading of her freshness of color, she has lost nothing of her earlier beauty. She is one of those rare women who are dangerous to young men even in her older years.

She is *Melanie,* which is what her husband, former adjutant general of the King of B*, calls her.

He is only five years older than Melanie and of a powerful, impressive build. His gray mustache and beard, his high forehead, the two deep creases between his eyebrows, his pursed lips, his short-cropped hair—everything reminds one of Wallenstein's profile. His face, even if creased by deep wrinkles, has a fresh and cheerful appearance. The bright blue eyes are large and have an intense glow.

He is wearing a long, blue coat with two rows of silver buttons bearing a lion in relief, a standing collar now creased over, on which one can see white threads where there once was gold braid.

The old man was smoking his pipe, whose wooden bowl skillfully portrayed a boar-hunt in bas-relief. The silver fittings, half rococo, half modern, betrayed attempts to pry them off in order to sell them during a shortage of money.

Hugo, a young man of eighteen, is playing with his father's tobacco pouch, looking around and seeming bored and dissatisfied. He bears his right arm in a sling.

His hair is light blond. His face is handsome, and it could almost be called pretty. His normally clear, expressive eyes had dimmed much today because of his depressed and dissatisfied mood.

One could easily take him for a sailor or deckhand owing to his red wool shirt and his leather belt with a knife holster at his hip. He also has the swinging, unsteady gait of a sailor.

Other than the inhabitants, the little room in which the family finds itself holds little worth remark besides the strange furniture already mentioned.

On the mantel is a picture of a young, pretty man in a page costume, surrounded by a wide, golden frame.

He has a striking resemblance to Melanie—the same wonderful eyes, only they are blue instead of black.

Looking at Melanie next to the picture, no one could doubt that the young man in the page costume, which was richly embroidered in silver and had epaulettes, was her son.

"Amelie has fallen asleep in my lap," Melanie declared with concern. "The poor child didn't close her eyes all night. How glad I am that she's sleeping now, poor child!"

"I wasn't able to sleep either, you were constantly pulling the blankets away, mother—father keeps telling you not to do that," Gertrude whispered impertinently in a whiny tone. "I don't want to lie next to you any more . . ."

"Me neither!" murmured eldest daughter Constanze, a girl of sixteen. "I will just not come to bed anymore unless I get a decent cover—it is truly a scandal that a count's daughter has to lie about on planks like riffraff. I will take my gold bracelet to the pawnshop tomorrow and buy a good featherbed, for myself alone—then no one will lie with me again."

"But Amelie, really?" Hugo asked ironically.

"*She* least of all!" Constanze replied. "She should sleep with Mother by herself. Why did she lose my pretty ring in the street?"

"I'll never go to bed again," Hugo interjected with irritation.

"Why did Mother ever have to sell the featherbeds!" Constanze added in a languid tone. "We got nothing from that money at all."

"Father, you don't need to buy any more tobacco," Hugo remarked.

"I would rather you had bought us sugar for our coffee," another sniveled, "I cannot go on drinking it bitter like this, and we haven't had butter in the house for five whole days."

"If my arm were only better I would go back on the boat as a stoker," Hugo added with boredom, "then at least I would have something good to eat and drink—lying about on a bearskin with nothing to eat or drink is becoming intolerable."

"The emperor has lost all his rights when there is nothing left," remarked an elderly lady sitting on a suitcase. She was known in the family as "Aunty Celestine." She was intensely engaged in stitching a collar, now and then turning to ward off a little Bolognese dog that jumped up and snapped at her needle, the focus of all his attentions.

When he became too bold, he received a stout slap from Aunty's thin hand.

As a hostile world might put it, Aunty Celestine was not entirely right in the head.

The old gentleman, his wife Melanie, Hugo, Constanze, Gertrude, Amelie, Suzie (only two weeks old), and Aunty Celestine—this entire family had been living for a month in one room in a tenement on Washington Avenue. One would expect that these sorts of conflicts and tensions would arise, and that such shortages often brought the children into opposition with their parents, whose noble style of thought and love for their children caused them to respond either with silence or consolation.

The eldest daughter, Constanze, was quite a pretty girl. She did not have regular features, but they were piquant, seductive, and charming enough. The slightest movement of her slim body was magical, and when she slept she was Pasithea herself* who retains all her beauty even in repose and when caught unawares, and who never is to be discovered without her charms.

When in bed, Constanze lay like a sculpted goddess.

* Pasithea, the Grace of Sleep in Homer and Anacreon.

The sole fault she possessed was shared with all her sex—she was, on occasion, more or less moody.

She argued long and hard with her siblings until her mind escaped to that undiscovered world whose bright colors reflect the dreams of young, innocent girls.

Aunty Celestine, who had been working intensely at her collar, now stood up suddenly, took a map from the wall, and rushed with it to Constanze. As she held it in front of her face, she moved her bony finger unsurely along the rivers of central Germany, finally halting at the Elbe, following the river's course from Magdeburg to the North Sea.

As was Aunt Celestine's way, she lolled her head on her left shoulder as she hummed an old tune about a count's daughter who had lived in splendor, was seduced, and ended her unhappy life in the deep.

"I would rather you sat down again and worked!" Constanze growled, grabbing the map of Germany from her hands so that it flew toward Melanie and little Gertrude. "If the Irishwoman comes this evening for his collar and finds it unfinished, we will have nothing to eat again!"

Aunty Celestine stepped back from Constanze and, waving her arms in the air in her usual manner, declared, "Little Constanze, I always knew you disliked me." Then she turned to the other members of the family: "But I tell all of you, it is an utter lie that Aunty Celestine murdered her husband . . . but I did predict that misfortune . . . yes, I know, you dislike me . . . that's why you torment me so!"

"Celestine, I ask you for heaven's sake, please be quiet, or don't speak so. No one has done anything to hurt you," Melanie turned to her, lowering the awakened Amelie to the floor. "We respect your misfortune and have happily received you. Now it is up to you to endure the misfortune which has come upon all of us unearned . . ."

"Yes, I predicted it," Aunty Celestine continued pressingly, "but don't dislike me! . . . I was a beautiful, good girl, as young and pretty as Little Constanze—but it is an utter, utter lie that Aunty Celestine killed her husband."

"Would you please be quiet!" Hugo called out with irritation. "All day these crazy words. It is enough to drive anyone mad!"

"Once you liked me a great deal, and you liked to read my songs—they were mad songs, weren't they, my boy?"

With these words, Aunty Celestine began a weird giggle that she produced almost every day in such conflicts. Then she would always fall into a remarkable ecstasy such as was attributed to the Korybantes, the servants of Cybele in ancient times.

"Isn't it true, your Aunty made mad songs, boy? I composed another one just yesterday, do you want to hear it?"

Like a cat purring when it is in a good mood, Aunty Celestine began to hum a melody to a song, whose last verses are preserved here:

So you are separated
O faith, hope and love,
So were stolen from me years
Of youth's finest forces.

I sang on the banks of the Elbe
There I joked and laughed,
Now bad persons say
I killed my husband.

So we are separated
My German fatherland,
You great city on the Elbe River,
You lovely North Sea coast!

There was a certain charm in the manner in which Aunty Celestine presented these verses, a charm that cannot be denied in the song itself, even if it does not strictly follow the rules of meter. In any case, this song of the deranged aunty had more poetic worth than all the lyrics of all our living poetasters, taken together.

"Ha, ha!" she suddenly burst out, "ha, ha, ha . . . Where am I? . . . We're back in our Germany, on the Elbe, in our dear Magdeburg . . . ho, ho, ho! He is there among the prisoners, one arm yellow, one arm black! . . . ho, ho, ho! . . . Come as you are, come, come, but come fast! . . . Merciful God, help me . . . the prisoner is trying to free himself from his chains . . . Do you want to stay where you are . . . oh, oh, leave me alone, don't kill me . . . I have never done you any harm—hurrah, hurrah, all you little folk, come as you are . . . tomorrow we're going to America! . . . ho, ho, ho! . . . Did you pack my wedding dress and the great white veil with the Brabant lace! . . . Farewell, Germany, farewell . . . We're going to America! . . . Come, come, just come! . . . There! There you have it . . . the yawl has already set out from land—look, look, now they are climbing out of the yawl and into the great ship—there, there!"

Aunty's confused monologue had no visible effect on the family. They let her continue her strange noises and talk without interruption.

After several minutes, she returned quietly to her original place, sitting on the large suitcase and resuming her sewing.

The Bolognese dog jumped up to her, wagging its tail, and started snapping at the needle again.

The newborn child in the hatbox began to cry, raising her little hands.

Melanie rose from her hard seat, lifted Suzie from her strange bed, and sought to quiet her by clicking her tongue.

At the same moment, Hugo arose and went to his mother, taking Suzie from her hands and kissing the baby so intensely several times that Suzie only cried louder than before until she was finally returned to Melanie's arms and quieted down.

The father continued to smoke his pipe without saying a word, looking to Constanze from time to time, who sat depressed and with lowered eyes, holding her gold bracelet in her hands, opening and closing it, examining it from every angle.

Amelie gnawed on her nails to pass the time and seemed to be brooding as Mother held Suzie in her arms and calmed her.

Gertrude whittled at a silver medallion with her father's penknife, bouncing it on the chest and causing it to ring. She then picked the peeling leather off her shoe soles and threw it in the fireplace.

"You don't want to go into service with Mistress Evans, Constanze?" Father interrupted his silence, after pounding out his pipe and placing it on the chest.

"Constanze will be reasonable," Melanie interjected with concern.

"I am sure that a *Mistress* Evans could be quite pleased with the service of a *countess,*" Constanze remarked in a clipped tone, laying her index finger aside her short nose. Then she continued, "If this Mistress sets conditions for me, she might well consider whether they would be acceptable to me. She will not be able to use me for ironing or washing, for she has black domestics aplenty who are more practiced in this work than I am. I would be capable of cooking, but these Scots do not like French cuisine. As a chambermaid, helping her with dressing and hair, I could perhaps agree to serve most suitably—at the most I could agree to take such an engagement if Mistress Evans needs a companion. The companion of Princess Alexandra of B∗ would certainly not be too poor for a *Mistress*!

"Constanze, Constanze—don't stick your nose so high in the air—consider that circumstances compel us to leave aside our usual etiquette, and that it is no shame to serve in this country . . ."

"No shame to serve? It's supposed to be no shame for a white girl to serve in the South, in a slave state? It is all very nice as it's described in the emigrant guides—but the reality is something else. A servant remains a servant, whether in a republic or a monarchy. Whoever serves might be sought-after, used, well cared-for, if he does his duty—but he is never respected or regarded as the equal of his master. That might do for a man, however it is, he can more easily set himself above it, but I hold it to be downright dishonorable for a girl . . ."

"You frighten me, Constanze," Melanie interrupted in shock, "I cannot understand where you got such a dangerous philosophy—one is dishonorable only when one has committed a dishonorable act that besmirches our conscience and places us in a dubious relationship to human society. But I do not find anything dishonorable in giving in to necessity and forgetting an earlier station in life in order to earn one's bread by serving others."

"Paul de Cock taught her that for sure," Hugo remarked languidly.

"I have received instruction from no one in situations where my own understanding tells me what I am to do and what I am to avoid," Constanze said.

Melanie stated, "Then your understanding has certainly not told you to avoid making your fortune with the wealthy Scotswoman. Mistress Evans has spoken of you in most positive terms with the prince of Württemberg, and it is your obligation to earn her favor, that she might later find in you a friend. If the prince only knew what has happened to us in his absence and how poor our situation is, he would encourage you to take Mistress Evans's engagement, for children always heed others more than their own parents."

"The prince of Württemberg will not be able to move me to do something I don't want to do," Constanze responded stubbornly.

"If I only knew where His Royal Majesty currently was, I would make him aware of our dreadful circumstances. Is he back in the city?"

"If His Royal Majesty were here, he would certainly have sought us out," Melanie remarked thoughtfully. "Oh who would have thought a year ago that we could sink so low!"

"If only we knew where our dear brothers were, Mother," Gertrude sighed.

"If only we could find Jenny and Frida," Constanze said.

"But Mother, you said that Emil was in America. Aren't we in America now?" Amelie remarked.

"America is very large, my dear child," Melanie answered, stroking her child's cheek with her hand.

"It is inconceivable to me," Melanie's husband declared, "that despite our searching and advertising in the newspapers, we have yet to hear anything from our children or from Jenny and Frida."

"And that even Prince Paul knows nothing of them, though he said that he had frequently visited them some time ago," Melanie responded.

"I really don't know what I am to think. When we mentioned them, he seemed to speak of them with reticence and move the conversation to another matter. It would be dreadful if we remained without any information about their location. I cannot bear this thought."

Melanie's eyes dampened as her husband spoke these words.

"If they were no longer alive," she said, "if they had died here, we would have heard—to pass our days without any hope of reunion is just too dreadful."

"You should go to the consul tomorrow, shouldn't you, Father?" Hugo asked.

"I don't expect much from my visit to the consul. He assured me a week ago that he would do everything in his power to find out where they are. But as is the case with many businessmen, he easily forgets to pursue another's interests when they are not exactly in his area of work. But I will be certain to go to the consulate tomorrow, and I will ask again at the German Society."

"The German Society will care even less for our sorrows and concerns," Hugo declared in a distressed tone, glancing down at his bad arm, "When I think how they snubbed me when I pressingly asked them for some sort of job, it makes me want to do them some harm if I could."

Melanie responded, "Fi, Hugo, soften your words—such rawness does not befit a young man of education. The good people cannot store up jobs or supply support for the thousands who ask their help. That would be asking too much. The German Society does what it can even if it is only possible to find positions for a few out of the many. You must not place your expectations too high or demand the impossible. Considering the immense claims made on the German Society, you cannot blame them for often being touchy or irritable with those who make great demands.

"Such corporations are always in an uncomfortable situation in the face of those needing help and advice. One should not continually stress the downside of this association without recalling its accomplishments and efforts. How broad is the area it covers? Where are limits set to its work? Where does it cease to be a supporter and advisor? And in what situations can one expect it to grant us support and participate in family interests? Hugo, if the German Society could offer you nothing at that time other than to advise you to take work as a deckhand, it has already done its duty so far as I'm concerned. It is too bad that you scalded your hand on this occasion, but it would be very unjust to blame the German Society for that and to deprecate its accomplishments."

Melanie fell silent and laid Suzie, now asleep, back in the hatbox, kissing her youngest on her closed eyelids.

Hugo was still fuming about the German Society, but he did not dare to contradict his mother. Perhaps he feared a severe rebuke from his father.

Constanze, who had been thinking about a good bed, now turned to Hugo and said: "You know, brother, I have just had a fine idea. Guess what?"

"How can I guess what you've thought up? You girls think too much anyway, and one could spend his whole life guessing what it is. Just tell me what you've come up with—it's too boring to take the time to guess what it is. I am not in the mood to do riddles or charades. Tell me what's on your mind!"

"I'm not going to tell you, Hugo—you have to guess!"

"Have you perhaps decided to accept Mistress Evans's engagement?"

"No. Now you can guess again, and if you don't guess correctly you won't learn."

"Do you want to take your gold bracelet to the pawnshop in order to buy a good bed?"

"You almost guessed it this time—you are almost there—so, for the last time! Get yourself together, Hugo!"

"Yes, what should I say—let me think a moment."

"No, no, that doesn't work, then it would not be an art."

"Is it perhaps . . . is it?"

"Hurry up. By the time I count twenty-five . . ."

"Would you give me a kiss, Little Constanze?"

"Not correct, Brother, but if you give me a kiss, I'll tell you what I thought."

The parents smiled and waited to hear what their daughter's secret might be.

Only Amelie seemed to have something against it, for when Hugo went to his sister to compensate for his failed guess with a kiss, she rushed to Constanze and whined: "You should give me a kiss first. Hugo doesn't need one. He was so mean, too, wasn't he Father? Wasn't he, Mother?"

As Constanze leaned down to kiss her little sister, Hugo approached and gave Constanze three kisses, one right after another—one on the mouth, one on the forehead, and the third in midair between the lips of Constanze and little Amelie. Amelie was quite upset with her brother, and she pulled her sister down to the floor and held her tight.

"Now I'll tell you," Constanze laughed after shaking loose from Amelie. "Do you know what, Brother? You could just go over to Live Oak Square and ask Mr. Anderson to let you take some moss from his huge trees so that we could have a good night's rest."

"So we all will have good beds, Constanze?" Gertrude enthused.

"That's a smart child, our Gertrude," Melanie quietly said to her husband, "if only we could get her to school soon. She's learning nothing at home no matter how hard we try."

"You'll have a bed, Gertrude," Constanze consoled her.

"What about Amelie, too, Sister?" Hugo remarked, looking at his sister.

"Amelie? I would rather she found my ring," Constanze responded.

"But Constanze! Don't make such trouble with Amelie—look at the poor child, how she's crying," the good mother admonished. Now Amelie really began to weep, holding both hands over her eyes and heading for the corner.

"But who will help me gather the moss, if we get permission from Mr. Anderson? I cannot do it alone, as you see, Constanze. Also, I have to be careful not to make my arm worse."

"Nothing simpler!" Constanze responded. "I will accompany you over there. You climb up the tree and throw the moss down to me—then we'll haul it here together. Aunty can stuff the mattresses."

"Let Gertrude do it," Aunty Celestine objected, "I have to finish this collar—you'll do it, Gertrude, won't you?"

Gertrude nodded positively.

Hugo left the room with his sister and went across the street to Live Oak Square.

Chapter 2

UNDER THE LIVE OAKS

For several years an effort has been under way to change French street names, either by translating them into English or completely renaming them in English, or by shifting the names from one street to another. In this way, the earlier *Rue Douaine* is now Customhouse Street; *Quatrième* Barracks, the earlier *Place d'Armes*—bordered by the *Maisons de Pontalba,* the cathedral, the courthouse and the levee—is now Jackson Square, so that the *Place d'Armes* had to migrate to Rampart Street, where General

Jackson was earlier to be found. Often this exchange of French terms for English ones has robbed the streets of their original character and given rise to an entirely false picture of the original quarters. This is particularly the case with Frenchmen Street in the Third Municipality. What is there about the name "Frenchmen Street" to recall the old *Rue des Français,* where five grenadiers of Emperor Napoleon Bonaparte built their houses next to one another, bestowing on the pompous club of houses the title of "Emperor's City" in honor of their leader? Two of these houses still stand, today quite weathered and deteriorated, but Frenchmen Street will tolerate no false pride and has become utterly American. Anyone may look into these houses, with their long, gabled roofs, at the rooms where the remnant of the guard once lounged, smoking their short pipes and talking of Austerlitz and Marengo. A tailor lives in one of them, and he thinks neither about the Old Guard nor of the Prometheus of St. Helena. A German cobbler has been living in the other for a good ten years, and on his greasy walls hang neither Napoleon nor Josephine, neither the king of Rome nor that of Monthalon, but rather Hecker, Bassermann, Kinkel, and Kossuth, the girls on the barricades, and Jenny Lind—these are the heroes and darlings he displays. How times change!

Thankfully, the banal Presbyterianism of our present-day Anglo-Saxons has still not quite had its way with the Third Municipality, so it has not been able to rob us of the lovely name *Rue d'Amour.* But what does the future hold? Perhaps our children will know nothing of the *Rue d'Amour,* and in its place the council will have put some heathen name like "Yankee-Doodle-Dandy Street." This drive to Americanize everything could easily degenerate to vandalism in any city other than New Orleans. We certainly recognize changes when they contribute to the glory, prosperity, and greatness of a city. We applaud all the creations of this latter day, but at the same time we have so much respect for historical memory and tradition that we are extremely uncomfortable when a change that is not an improvement is made. When this happens, we must condemn such alterations as a vain nationalist farce.

As is well known, New Orleans was only divided into three corporations, called municipalities, in 1836.* These municipalities are now united into

*Our city was first divided into four wards in 1792 by the governor of the province, Baron de Carondelet, who was responsible for several "improvements" in the city at that time. Thus there was the first street lighting in 1793 (gas lighting did not arrive until 1834, the same time as the water works). That same year, our watchmen were mobilized. Baron de Carondelet also had two forts built in 1793, one at the foot of Canal Street and the other at the place where the mint now stands, as well as many other innovations.

one corporation, together with the city previously known as Lafayette.[2] The amalgamation of the municipalities into a city corporation produced the term *districts,* which are not truly analogous to municipalities.

The word *municipality* has something so characteristic of the French quarters that the present designation simply doesn't fit.

One obsession of Americans that cannot be criticized is that they name not only cities but also streets after famous men, great writers, war heroes, and the like. To be sure, this baptism often takes place in an odd manner, since the names are given before the places themselves are actually in existence. Many streets owe their names to mere chance.

This is the case with Washington Avenue.

This street received its name because a former horseback peddler pitched his booth here and sold people nothing but pictures of George Washington.

Climb onto a Magazine Street omnibus on Canal Street and tell the driver you want to stop at Washington Avenue. If the driver is not an ass and has nothing else on his mind, he will stop his horse at the designated place, and, once you've paid your picayune or presented a ticket, depending on the situation, you will dismount, turn to the right, and come to Live Oak Square, which owes its name to the imposing live oak trees on Mr. Anderson's property.

Live Oak Tree! Called *Moosbaum* by the sons of Arminius, you are the sole poetry here, other than the beautiful daughters of Louisiana! Your palms, Louisiana, where are they to be found? Your palmettos are not good enough for us; they are the grubby orphan of the fern family under which dromedaries kneel and the Bedouin embrace their girls. Louisiana, was your architect so stupid as not to allow your skies to be borne by the slim, tall columns of the palm? Didn't he know better than to supply only crippled palmettos, which feed on mud their entire lives? Dear Louisiana, you have misled us in the Old World with the tales of how slim and tall your palms are, and how majestic their crowns! But we forgive you the lie, for your live oaks are even prettier than the palms of Guyana!

Live Oak Tree! You are not the lime tree about which the children of a village dance. No Philistine dares to linger in your vicinity, for your poetry would scare him away and leave him unsettled for the rest of his life. He would realize that you are nothing like an oak in the Teutoburger Forest. He would jump back when your long beard blows in his face! Live Oak Tree, what splendid poetry to sit in your shadow with the daughters of Sodom!

Live Oak Tree! If only our Grabbe[3] had known you, he would not have fooled with the Drachenfels near Düsseldorf—he would certainly have completed his "Don Juan and Faust" in your company. Old giant live oak, you look ill and your long hair has paled. Are you perhaps mourning for your departed brethren, who have been cut down by the sons of civilization and stacked into lumber parks? You look so confused, my live oak, come, let us comb your long hair!

As with everything else, so must the live oak serve the Yankee in his speculation. Do not believe that he has the least regard for this tree, that he loves it only half as much as his wife and children. The live oak is no more and no less to him than another tree, and he would be perfectly capable of sawing down one limb after another if each branch would earn him the worth of a lot or a hundredth of a lot. Are you friends of beautiful gardens, fine trees, lovely oleanders, good lilacs, and fairlylike cinchonas? Just don't let us know—we won't believe it. And should there be one among you who is moved even a little bit by the blooming of a hydrangea, you may rest assured that this rose will bestow a fine basketful on you, for she wants nothing to do with the heroes of business.

So it is a common routine for speculators to set at a higher price for a lot if a live oak tree stands on it. Naturally this is the case only with properties on which the homes of our businesspeople stand.

Therefore the great live oaks on Mr. Anderson's property bestow on it no small value.

The home of Mr. Anderson, born a Swede and once a sailor, consists of a narrow two-story frame house with dirty, peeling window frames, boards raw and gray with age, and a small built-on kitchen. Above his roof hang yards of moss from a live oak, whose thick trunk stands far away within the fence. When the east wind blows or a breeze from the Gulf wafts through the hanging tangles and garlands of this moss, they tap on the house windows or flit like the gray hair of an old man in the wind, without leaving the place nature has anchored them.

Anderson owned a large milk business, and he had had a stall built next door for this purpose that took up nearly the full depth of the lot. It contained his kitchen and the horses and milk-carts necessary for his business. To the left of this stall was a boiler of considerable size, set on a ring wall of bricks, to cook his animals' feed—made from a mixture of bran, beans, and pea pods. A great number of fowl are always flocking around this boiler, finding the spilled and dried feed splendid nourishment. Two large dogs press their bodies against the warmth of this wall when the weather is wet and cool. The area between the house and the stall contains several shanties, where Anderson's workers live.

The entry to these buildings is a large gate, always blocked with heavy timbers that must be removed before one can come in.

The garden in front of the house is poorly maintained, and the owner has even neglected to fill all the muddy space with gardening soil.

This was the place Constanze now strolled on her brother's arm.

Although the day has been wet and cold, the sun is now shining again like a giant blast furnace, driving spring growth out of the muddy earth to the rejuvenating light in a matter of hours. All those trees that had put aside their coats of leaves in the winter months now gaze from a thousand eyes and suck eagerly, drunkenly from the fiery breasts of the Louisiana sun. Magnolias, orange trees, cinchonas, and all the other evergreens shoot out new needles, shaming their dark green winter garb with their fresh splendor. The spireas, junipers, denzias, and hollies shake old pollen away and put on their spring dress with gusto. The small red cerculio ventures once more onto the platters of red cedar, sticking his trunk into the fragrant nectar. *Lourier amandier* is proud as a peacock, tearing away the cobwebs, which now yield to the pressure of his vital force. The evergreen thorn tree drops his old spines and presses out new ones. Among the evergreen bushes, the *Mahonia aquifolia* lustily spreads her wide branches against the neighboring myrtle, and the "bright rosy purple" gives way to the "queen of the prairies," which brings forth fresh kernels.

There is life and action, kissing and pressing, stressing and pushing under Louisiana's glowing heaven—and all in a matter of a few hours.

Only the live oak is dark and dismal.

Its black-green leaves are hidden under hanging moss, and, while it might have its own springtime secret, the live oak gives no inkling of it. He gazes at us like a giant of primeval times, shaking his long hair when we ask him how old he is.

Where are the slim, feathered palms?

Look about. The palmetto is good enough for the clumsy alligator.

It was already 2:30, precisely the hour merchants, lawyers, and brokers in our city leave their offices to take dinner with their families. The omnibuses are filled at this hour, and a person can wait from two until five o'-clock without finding a place. This is particularly true on the Magazine and Apollo route, where the top businessmen live. The horsecar crosses Nayades Street and drops its hungry passengers here, particularly at Tivoli Circle. The second group of elites live around Dryades Market, at Withe and Thalia Streets, and the Dryades omnibus lets them out here—although, as is the case with almost all buses, the chief stop is in Canal Street.

The brother and sister stood in front of Anderson's property.

Hugo knocked on the large gate with a rock while Constanze peeked through the wide gaps in the fence.

"There's no one in there, Sister," Hugo said with an irritated air after knocking several times in vain.

"Is that so, Hugo? Just look through here—they must not have heard you," Constanze replied, pushing her brother over to the gap in the fence.

"Somebody is coming—do you want to ask for Mr. Anderson?"

"I think it would be better if you asked, Brother."

A worker in shirtsleeves and reddish-brown trousers opened the gate and asked Hugo what he wanted.

"We would like to speak with Mr. Anderson—is he not at home?" Hugo asked in an accent that showed that he was German.

"You speak German?" asked the worker. He told the siblings that Mr. Anderson must have gone into his house, since it was midday.

"You can wait here until he comes back," he added after Constanze stated her concern that they might be disturbing Mr. Anderson.

"Just look up there," Constanze excitedly called to her brother, who had climbed over the low fence with her to step over to Anderson's house. "Look up there, that splendid moss. No, no, it is just too fine—you can see it all from here—oh, oh, and back there, dear Brother, no, it's splendid, a fortune . . ."

"That would be enough to stuff the mattresses of an entire regiment of soldiers," Hugo joined in, phlegmatically.

"Oh, I cannot believe we will be allowed to pull that down—it is all just too pretty!"

"Anderson will not care what tree we pull moss from if he gives us permission."

"What will you say when he comes, Brother?"

"I'll just ask him for permission to take down moss."

"But what if he asks you what you want it for?"

"Such a businessman has no time to ask about that. He will either permit us or deny it straightaway."

"But what if he does ask?"

"He won't!"

"No, dear brother, what if he does ask you? What would you tell him? You couldn't tell him that we have no beds—that would just not do!"

"But he won't ask, Constanze."

"No, no, understand me correctly, hypothetically, if he were to ask you—I am only supposing."

Anderson's arrival interrupted this little dispute.

Hugo approached him with his sister.

"Mr. Anderson, would you be so good as to permit us to take down a few armfuls of moss from your live oaks?"

"What for?" he asked.

If Anderson had been an American, he would not have asked, but Swedes are very curious, they must know everything.

One could see that Hugo's knowledge of the ways of businessmen did not rest on a sound foundation, as it did not allow for nationality. Constanze was not so far off.

"For our henhouse," Hugo quickly responded to the Swede's question.

"For your henhouse?" Anderson repeated in astonishment. "Do your hens need moss to sleep on?"

Constanze would just as happily have dropped through a hole in the ground. Her embarrassment was without limits. She turned away from the two and looked at the long moss that enclosed Anderson's home in a dark frame. She soon chirped and hopped on her feet, silently thanking her lucky stars that the conversation quickly moved to another subject after they received permission to take down as much moss as they wished.

Anderson, who was a great devotee of fowl of all kinds, still found it worthwhile to ask the young man what sort of hens they kept in their chicken coop.

"Various sorts," declared Hugo, "a creole hen is there, I believe, but, as with most fowl, you can't really keep them in perfect order. Soon one runs away, the rooster sneaks out of the yard, then a brood-hen, and there is always plenty to do—I could not even guess how many we have at home."

"Then you must not pay much attention to your animals," Anderson remarked. "I know precisely how many hens I have, and if one is missing I know where to go to find it. For instance, I know a man not far from here who loves my creole hens so much that he cannot let two weeks go by without taking one of them."

Anderson smiled roguishly when he spoke these words.

"Is that your wife?" he asked.

"No, it's my sister—she has only accompanied me here to help me to take moss back, in case we could receive permission, Mr. Anderson," Hugo responded, presenting his sister Constanze to the wholesale milkman.

He greeted her, making a little bow with his head and pushing his hat back so that his whole forehead was visible.

"'Tis most ungallant of this man that he did not give us a worker to help," Constanze said to her brother as she approached the loveliest of the live oaks in the square.

"Yes—one should hold it against him, but perhaps he does not know any better," Hugo consoled her. He had only now realized that Anderson had shown too little cooperation and gallantry.

It was characteristic of Anderson not to have much to do with the fair sex. Since his earlier career as a sailor had rarely brought him together with *ladies,* he had adopted a patriarchal tone toward them, which was quickly broken off when anyone tried to join him to one. Then it was all he could do to hide his clumsiness in their presence.

Although he had considerable property and was years beyond being a young man, he remained a confirmed bachelor. He had never been able to decide to marry, for reasons easy to derive from what has been said.

Yet he liked Constanze the moment he saw her, and, if he did not act gallantly toward her, that was due to his distrust of himself. He was afraid of acting badly in her presence, and so he preferred to avoid doing anything at all that might show he was even aware of her.

The results will confirm that our interpretation has a foundation.

"Brother, I have no idea how it will be possible for me to go up, the live oak is too broad—if only your arm were better you could climb up yourself . . ."

"This way, Constanze?"

"No, not yet, bring your shoulder closer to the trunk and somewhat lower to the left."

"Yes—now you're not helping me at all, Hugo—I cannot keep doing this—try it and raise yourself a bit—so—so—now it's right, now just a little—just a very little further if possible . . ."

Now Constanze was sitting in the place where the enormous main trunk of the live oak divided into two great branches, each with a circumference of fifteen feet.

"This is not easy as I thought, Hugo—the things don't want to come off," Constanze called to her brother down below.

"Be careful, Constanze. If you don't keep your leg around the branch, you could lose your balance and fall."

"I won't do that, Brother. This dumb bark scratches me so—I am sitting solidly enough. If only I didn't have to stretch so far to pull down the moss, it is so solidly attached—has it grown to it, Hugo?"

"Constanze, you can see that from there better than I can."

"So—there are a few bushels' worth, there, catch them!"

"Just let them fall, Constanze, they won't hurt you," Hugo laughed aloud.

"This dumb bark scratched me again, Brother—I don't want to do any more—I would rather climb down . . ."

"That would be silly, Constanze, you were only too happy to get up there—be reasonable and think of your bed tonight."

"You can talk, you're down there and look up at me so comfortably!"

"You're not demanding that I climb up with my bad arm?"

"But Hugo, now it scratched me again—I won't put up with this dumb live oak any more."

"Let it scratch, Little Constanze, scratch it back!"

"But Hugo, it is really nasty of you to keep making fun of me."

Constanze finally managed to get several bushels of hair from the old live oak; the more she saw the pile on the ground grow, the more she was spurred to continue. The bark of the nasty live oak had already hurt her several times, but she no longer paid much attention to it. If you had seen her delicate little hands, you would have noticed they were bleeding.

"That's enough, Little Constanze, that's moss for at least five battalions—now climb down, we will take our treasure home together. Aunty Celestine can help us haul the rest over when we come back a second time. One trip won't do it."

"Just this one last bit up there, Hugo. Oh, this long, beautiful moss, when I have that I'll be finished!"

"Little Constanze—look out and don't be so careless! It is much too high for you—you could lose your balance and fall."

Despite her brother's well-meant advice, Constanze climbed higher and higher, so nimbly that one might have thought she had been trained for that purpose. Then she finally reached a spot where she could grasp her last plunder. With her knee wedged against one branch, she held fast to another branch with her left hand and was about to grab the superb moss when the branch under her knee gave way—confusion caused her to reach behind her instead of in front of her. She briefly lost consciousness and hung for a moment between heaven and earth; only her left hand clung to the little branch, which threatened to break at any instant.

Hugo, who had looked away at this crucial moment, his attention on a cow grazing nearby, no sooner heard his sister's cry of fear than he forgot his bad arm, ripping it out of its sling, climbing up the tree with marvelous agility, and taking her in his arms.

Constanze was saved. But then something happened which could have had even worse consequences than falling from the live oak tree.

A bull that had been pleasantly browsing among the blossoms and his harem was roused into such a nasty mood by poor Constanze's cry that he began to roar and charged with great strides toward the tree, just as the brother and sister were getting ready to come down. At the same time, the cows were making such a dreadful noise that Constanze became concerned and asked her brother to climb a bit higher and stay with her until someone arrived to liberate them.

The bull stormed about the trunk of the live oak like a bedeviled Uriel, boring his short horns into the tree in his blind rage. He plowed the soil all around, then threw his rear legs in the air, then charged at the trunk, giving it solid blows, then rushed about in wide circles, roaring and stamping.

The cows, who saw their esteemed gentleman consort carrying on in such a hair-raising manner, all joined him in the same manner, making crazy forward and sideways jumps.

Anderson's workers, who were cleaning out the cow stall, removing unnecessary decorations and contributions in the cows' absence, watched the dreadful dance with amazement. They stuck their heads over the fence and appeared at a loss over what to do.

"Put your dogs in here!" Hugo cried to them from his place of exile. "They will bring the dumb cattle back to order!"

This had the expected effect.

Whether it was customary obedience or fear of the dogs—it is always hard to tell, since to this day the psychology of cattle has been little studied—the bacchantic cow-maenads, with their roaring satyr in the lead, restrained their madness and soon passed through the open gate of the cow stall in splendid order, returning to their reserved places. The bull did make an attempt now and then to pose as a sultan, but even he finally quit acting up and ambled to his fodder trough.

Who could be happier than Hugo and Constanze? The brother and sister embraced and kissed as soon as they touched solid ground.

"How does it happen that your arm has so quickly recovered, Hugo?" Constanze asked her brother with a roguish laugh.

"On your account, Sister, it was healed in an instant," Hugo responded, replacing his arm in the sling, for it hurt him twice as much now that the excitement had passed.

"You certainly hurt yourself, Hugo—does your arm hurt again?" Constanze asked with concern.

"Oh, that's nothing, Sister—it is better. Now come and let's gather the moss the mad cattle scattered all over."

"You shouldn't carry anything, Brother—stay here a bit, I'll go and ask Aunty to help me."

Without waiting for Hugo's objection, Constanze flew across the street and entered their tenement.

The Irish woman was in the room paying two dollars for the work she had ordered. Then she ordered two more collars for the end of the week.

"Constanze and I will complete them, Aunty," Melanie said as Aunty reached for her needles to start anew. "Relax or knit little Amelie's shirt."

"Mother, permit me to impose for a moment on Aunty's good nature. I cannot bring all that moss across the street by myself, and Hugo's arm hurts so badly," Constanze explained.

"I don't know if Aunty is willing to do it," Melanie responded, "I cannot decide for her."

Aunty Celestine did not have to be asked twice, since the prospect of a good bed gave her old legs wings. Together with Constanze, she rushed across to the live oaks.

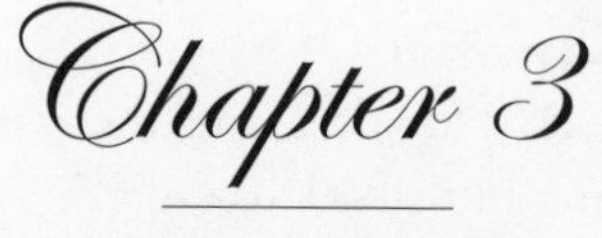

Chapter 3

THE COFFEE PICKERS

It had been a long time since Constanze had slept as well as she had in the night just past. After she had brought the dearly bought moss back with Aunty Celestine's aid, she changed her previous resolution by stuffing her father's mattress first of all rather than her own. Father slept together with Hugo. She stuffed and smoothed their bed with a mastery that would have made a Venetian carpenter proud. She did this in order to make up for the many pains her brother must have suffered in his bad arm.

Although Constanze continually fought with her brother, she still had the greatest affection for him. She lovingly bandaged up his arm with the greatest care before they went to bed, reinforcing the sling with a new knot and instructing him on how to lay in such a way as not to endanger it. Then she urged her father to take great care not to nudge Hugo's arm in his sleep and cause him more pain.

Little Amelie had cried half the night on her mother's neck, so she was consoled with a good moss bed on the following day.

Gertrude didn't sleep well after she laid herself down, either. She had her index finger in her mouth and seemed to be thinking about something.

Aunty Celestine, who was also looking forward to a new bed the next day, likewise couldn't sleep. She jumped up at least twenty times during the night and ran about among the mattresses lying on the floor. Once she bumped into Hugo's head during her wanderings, causing him to awaken in terror and give her a severe rebuke. Now and then she ran to the window and tapped on the panes, humming her melody of the unhappy, seduced daughter of a count. Then she gathered herself and laid her head on the suitcase, only to spring up and dance around the room again. She kept this up the entire night.

Is there anything more important to a girl than a good bed? What girl would begrudge Constanze the fact that all her thoughts and wishes were concentrated on a better place to rest? One can read a girl's character from the greater or lesser care with which she makes her bed. A girl who is never excited about her bedcover, even if it is of silk and eiderdown, is either not quite well or is given to reading boring novels. A good, spirited girl knows every stitch of her bed, whether it's a side-stitch, a front-stitch, a hind-stitch, or a baste-stitch. Such a girl is also involved with her mosquito netting. She pulls it back so that it does not look baggy but rather has beautifully equal folds. A good, spirited girl in New Orleans will never kill a mosquito in her bed after it has fed on her, since that would leave a mess. She will only try to shoo the mosquito away, and if this doesn't work, she will keep it safe—and all so as not to dirty a fresh bed, even if it is only a modest ticking filled with moss.

A marriage bed is something entirely different. A girl's bed thinks, "Oh, how much the little one loves me!" A marriage bed thinks, "Never mind, they'll fix it."

It is a sad mark of the times that our Epicureans have so little bed philosophy. Even Daniel Webster, one of the greatest and most thoughtful Epicureans of this century, has neglected to lay an amendment for a decent bed compromise on the Senate table.

Just such an "internal improvement" should long since have earned the attention of our statesmen. It is a sad sign of the times that so much is still rotten in the state of Denmark.

New Orleans has been summoned by a wise Providence to take the initiative in this matter.

New Orleans has always been the leader in the United States in everything that heightens enjoyment of life and makes the dullest people into Epicureans. Not just in leisure but in so many ways of making a living.

New Orleans is the one city in the United States where one is almost never thrown out of a boardinghouse. Nowhere are there more decent, noble, or generous boardinghouse landlords than in New Orleans.

The landlord of a boardinghouse in our city would rather lose everything he owned than consider throwing out a boarder just because he wouldn't or couldn't pay, whether he was a political refugee, a degraded aristocrat, a literary vagabond, or a journalistic adventurer. If there is ever a

Last Judgment, as mythology tells us, the Lord in the Vale of Josephat will not place the boardinghouse landlords of New Orleans among the goats but rather among the sheep.

That is not all.

New Orleans feeds its man. Whoever hungers in this town is either too lazy to open his mouth or has an abnormal stomach lining. Every boardinghouse landlord allows the most miserable passenger, even if he is not a regular boarder, to participate in the wedding at Cana. And if he cannot appear in his wedding slippers, the landlord will walk with him to the old shoemaker and go security for him. If he has no coat to put on, the landlord will accompany the unfortunate to the auction sale. If he is thirsty and there is nothing at home, the merciful Samaritan will take him to a bar. If the penniless man is an impassioned smoker, he will not be given the poorest cigar; he will be sent to Hermann Schlüter on Common Street to be supplied[4]: "A fine recommendation from Mr. NN, and he desires that you should supply me with a pair of your best regalios." If the poor object of charity is used to good wine, he will be sent to John Fischer in Royal Street to drink a bottle of Rüdesheimer in good cheer.

But if one is so perverse as not to be on a good footing with his boardinghouse landlord, he can still go into any "dime house" at lunch—but for his stomach's sake not to a "picayune house." Have such a good brunch that a lack of dinner can be tolerated. When that time comes, don't go to the bar but stroke your belly happily, shake your neighbor's hand, and depart with dignity.

That is not all.

If New Orleans feeds its man, it also does the same with whole families.

Those who represent this branch of the population are divided into four categories:

1. *Levee Rats.* This category includes that hopeful youth of both sexes who have made it their métier to bore into whole hogsheads of sugar and molasses, collecting the contents into baskets or bottles. If they do this too visibly, they have to watch out for the wharf police.

2. *Cotton Retailers.* This category is the most dangerous, since they are concerned in subverting the primary source of our greatness and power. In doing this they have often managed to cause important deficits among our cotton brokers. They maneuver in the vicinity of the cotton presses, particularly on Tchoupitoulas Street and the corner of Claiborne and Canal Streets. The great shadowy trees in Claiborne Street protect them from the prying eyes of the night watch.

3. Rag Pickers. In all innocence they enter houses, looking for rags and taking what they can find.

4. Coffee Pickers. This is the best class. They consist of the most modest poor of our city.

This is an orientation for what follows.

Several days before the affair of the moss and the live oaks, Gertrude stood in front of the door listening to several children chatting.

They were telling one another about their winnings in coffee, which they had brought home to their parents. Among them was a cute little girl, poorly dressed but with cheerful little eyes.

Gertrude, who felt herself drawn to this girl, spoke to her and learned that her father, an Ohio raftsman, had been dead for more than three months and that her mother, who worked taking in laundry, was very ill. Her neighbors had supported them a bit so far, but they appeared to be growing tired of it. She herself was too small and weak to be able to earn anything in any sort of service. Since her mother loved to drink coffee and there had been none in the house for days, she had decided to go coffee picking with her playmates so her mother would have some to drink again. At first she had been ashamed to do this, but when she thought of her mother she changed her mind.

Children form friendships very rapidly, particularly girls. They also pick up things so quickly from one another, whether good or bad. What we call naughtiness, which appears so attractive in children, has its origins in mutual friendship and affection. If they are girls, they will play mother and child with their dolls. If a girl and a boy, they will play the roles of man and wife.

Gertrude's curiosity was so aroused by all the talk about coffee picking that she asked the little one to tell her the next time she went hunting for beans. As a child, Gertrude naturally thought only about how she could most easily get away from her parents' house without their knowing. The thought of how she would return, or the terror that would strike her parents and siblings if they discovered her missing, never occurred to her.

The two girlfriends parted after making promises to each other to go on the next coffee-picking trip.

After Constanze was so praised by her parents for bringing in the moss with Aunty, Gertrude suddenly decided to do something to better their lot as well, so she, too, could get a "Good little child!" from her parents.

That was what had kept her thinking all the previous night.

She thought of the little coffee pickers, her girlfriend and her girlfriend's sick mother. She made a quick decision, not stopping to consider any complications.

Gertrude was a bit over seven, a lovely child. The forget-me-not blue of her eyes gazed out at the world so true-heartedly, looked in your face so peacefully, that in moments you wanted to gobble up the little dove in a gulp.

Her little mouth, which hid a full row of glistening, elegant pearls, was as red as the half-bloomed blossom of a Lilliput oleander.

Her neck, as mobile as that of a turtledove, was of blinding whiteness and impeccable purity. Such turtledove necks are proper to girls who ripen young and are fashioned by nature to make themselves and their husband happy by becoming a mother.

Today Gertrude was wearing a dark purple barège dress with little white flowers edged in black. It was no longer very new, but still she was neatly and cleanly dressed. Her thick blond hair was tied in two long Louisa braids that reached down to her waist.[5] Her stockings were white, to be sure, but had been darned and repaired in many places, alterations that Gertrude owed to her tireless Aunty. Only shoe repair was beyond Aunty Celestine's talents.

For the sixth time, Gertrude stood in front of the door waiting for her girlfriend to pass by with her little basket on her arm.

Finally she got what she'd been waiting for.

She joined arms with the raftman's daughter and walked away.

"How far do we go to get coffee, Lorie?" Gertrude asked her friend after they had gone several blocks down Magazine Street.

"Oh it isn't very far, Gertrude. I think it would be best to do it this way, like all the children in this area do when they go coffee picking—an omnibus is about to come, we can jump up in back on the step, which costs nothing, Trudy."

"That bothers me, Lorie, we could easily get hurt!"

"I don't like doing it when the omnibus is underway either, so I always wait for the moment when the gentlemen and ladies are climbing in and out."

"You are much smarter than I am, Lorie, I would not have thought of that," Gertrude responded, looking at her friend. "But if no one climbs in or out, do you know how to get on anyway? I wouldn't risk doing that while it's moving."

"Look at me, Trudy, now we go to that corner where people are always standing to get on—that's how I figured it," Lorie responded calmly.

"How smart you are, Lorie," Gertrude declared in her astonishment.

Lorie turned about suddenly, and, spotting an omnibus in the distance, she grabbed her friend by the arm and pulled her along to the designated place.

As Lorie had predicted, several persons were awaiting the arrival of the omnibus.

When it halted and Gertrude bolted forward to take her modest place, Lorie stopped her and signaled that she had to wait until everyone had entered.

As the omnibus departed, Gertrude and Lorie were standing on the back step, holding each other with one arm and wrapping the other around the frame of a window of the door to keep their balance.

Before we bring the two friends to their goal, we must describe something more precisely for our lady readers: Between Julia and Notre Dame Streets, fronting on Commerce Street, stand three vast warehouses known to the merchants of New Orleans by the names *Pelican, Star,* and *Eagle.* The wealth of Mr. Touro is stored in them.[6] The warehouses themselves do not belong to him, they belong to the wealthy Samuel Cohn; Touro rents them for his enormous deposits. Samuel Cohn is known in the business world as Paris Cohn, and he is one of the richest and most respected men of our city, one of the few who combines his wealth with unbribable honesty, untiring efficiency, and iron patience in matters of business. He is called Paris Cohn to distinguish him from the many Cohns in New Orleans, almost all of whom are merchants and are more or less devoted to Mammon. They amount virtually to a single family, tracing their business routine and mercantile dominance from the free city of Hamburg. Many of them live in this city now, and here they are held in great respect.

The Pelican and the Star normally only contain plaster, cable, and sailcloth, while the main product in the Eagle Warehouse is coffee. Thousands of sacks, most containing Rio and Domingo coffee, fill the huge rooms of this warehouse, testifying to the enormous traffic between our city and foreign harbors.

What Venice was in its days of glory, New Orleans would long since have become—the queen of the seas, the monopolist of world trade. The merchant of Venice would be just as much at home here as he once was in the city on the lagoons. There is also no lack of Shylocks, with the sole difference being that the Shylocks here are not Jews but orthodox Christians who thirst not just for their pound of flesh but for whole shiploads. Yes, New Orleans would long since have become a Venice if an invisible hand had not punished it in many a year for a crime that meanness and selfishness has held to be a necessary evil.

The scales of world history often oscillate over centuries until they finally allow one pan to sink under the weight of its guilt.

Now let us return to our friends.

Gertrude, who lay with her head to the opening of a sliding window, had attracted the attention of an elderly man who was sitting in the back corner of an omnibus. He continued to observe her with the greatest interest. Often it even seemed as if he had made a sudden decision. His restless movements and his intense stare, which seemed precisely to follow every action of the girl, in turn drew the attention of a younger man, who now followed the older man's gaze with the same curiosity.

The elderly man was aware of this.

"You appear to be disturbed that I pay so much attention to you," the younger man said to the elderly man, lifting his hat slightly with his right hand, as if he intended to show respect through that gesture.

"That is anyone's right," the man addressed replied. "You would not hold me to have violated the etiquette of omnibuses if I had fixed you with the same stare."

"You are watching one of the two little girls who are standing out there—if you are so interested in that blonde little head with the forget-me-not eyes, I can only be amazed that it has not yet occurred to you to ask the pretty child to take a place next to you," the young man said.

"If I thought this was a good idea, your urging would have been superfluous, sir."

"Then if I am permitted to approach that blonde child as I please, I shall try to get her to take a place next to me," the young man responded with rascality as he rose to carry out his intention.

The elderly man, who seemed displeased by this, stepped into his way and pulled on the reins so the omnibus driver halted.

"Do you wish to get out, sir? All the better for me and the two poor girls—then there will be room enough for both of them, and a third will find a place somewhere or other."

"Good evening, gentleman," the elderly man called to the other, as he seized the hands of the two girls, who had hopped off the steps. He asked their permission to accompany them for a bit.

The other man, who had also dismounted the omnibus, did not want to concede at all. He grabbed the elderly man's arms so clumsily from behind that the old man turned about in shock to remonstrate with his accoster.

In the meantime, Gertrude and Lorie mounted a different omnibus that passed at that instant; they looked back anxiously at the two men, who appeared no longer to be aware of them in their own agitation.

Before the omnibus had passed out of sight of this place, Gertrude was able to see one of the two men throw the other to the ground. Then it seemed to her that the other one rose up and made a new attack. Finally she could see nothing further.

After that, the journey went rather quickly.

The friends had no further problems after leaving the place were the two gentlemen fought.

Oddly enough, not a single additional person entered along the entire route to Julia Street.

"When I tug your dress, Trudy, jump right off," Lorie declared. "We will be on Julia Street very soon, and from there we just have to cross one street to reach our goal."

"But Lorie, I certainly can't do that?"

"Why not, Trudy? It is much easier and safer to jump off than to clamber aboard. Just get off quickly when I tug . . ."

Now the omnibus passed by Julia Street, and Lorie gave her friend the tug, calling, "Come, Trudy, come now . . ." as she sprang from the step. But Gertrude not only didn't follow her courageous friend, she hung even closer to the window frame.

When Lorie saw this, she cried out to the driver with her full voice to halt.

The omnibus driver thought someone wanted to get on, so he stopped.

Gertrude jumped down and ran to her worried Lorie, who embraced the shocked Trudy and kissed her tenderly.

The omnibus driver, who was not sure what to make of this display, cursed at the "damned Dutch girls" as he departed.

There is certainly not a street in New Orleans where one is in more danger of being run over than Tchoupitoulas Street. It requires the talents of a true gymnast to get across without being trod on by horses and mules or flattened by a mass of drays. One should be able to do knee-bends, toe-touching, sit-ups, jumping-jacks, and all the exercises on the parallel bars, at the master's level. Only after this has been accomplished should anyone dare to cross this street between eight in the morning and four in the afternoon.

Gertrude and Lorie had to wait at least a quarter of an hour before they managed to get to the opposite sidewalk.

As they turned onto Commerce Street, they spied the entire company of coffee pickers restlessly at work in front of the Eagle Warehouse: girls and boys, men and women, young and old—all colorfully intermixed as if they were at a bookseller's fair in Leipzig.

Lorie recognized many in this troop who were mere novices in the business. They were mistreated, pushed away, and rejected in the most godless manner by the long-term guests of the Eagle Warehouse, and some of them who thought they would be able to march home with rich booty saw their hard-won gains pitilessly taken by the experienced workers before they were chased away.

Since these beginners still sought time and again to resume their collecting, there was no end to the dispute and abuse. A small red-headed Irish boy took an old woman's apronful of beans and emptied them into his gray hat. The old woman chased after him for a ways until the little boy, Patrick, threw back her empty apron as he circled and mocked her. The old woman returned to the scene of her activities and began picking beans anew. Little Patrick sat opposite the Eagle on an empty lime barrel, holding his hatful of beans on high and singing ceaselessly:

Little Patrick Horner
Sat in the corner,
Eating a Christmas pie;
He stuck in his thumb,
And pulled out a crumb,
Crying "What a nice boy am I!"

Now and then he rushed across the street to the coffee pickers and hit the tireless old woman in her stiff neck or knocked the beans out of her apron. She finally grew so upset with him that she lifted a stone and almost hit Patrick in the head. He finally ran away and sang again.

I come from Alabama
With the shovel and the hoe . . .

Little Patrick Horner
Sat in the corner . . .

When Lorie and Gertrude approached the coffee pickers, hand in hand, some of the girls greeted them in the most surprising manner. They extended their arms to them and modestly yielded the place where the greatest harvest was to be gathered. Gertrude, who thought that the little coffee pickers' deference to Lorie was amazing enough, was utterly astounded when they offered her several baskets full of the finest beans. On Gertrude's protest that she was being offered too much, since she was incapable of carrying all of it, two boys and a grown girl offered to help her. Even the same old woman whose work had so often been interrupted by the irritating

Patrick, so that her treasures were less than the others, dropped a few handfuls of beans into Gertrude's basket. Lorie always nodded her thanks in response to these gifts, and one could see from her cheerful face that she was not indifferent to the positive reception her friend was receiving.

The entire troop of coffee pickers now advanced as a body toward the next-to-last gate of the Eagle Warehouse, the part of the building closest to Notre Dame. The alert coffee pickers had not been slow in perceiving that the large scale had been rolled under the arch of one of the many gates. Being experts, these freebooters knew full well that the sacks with frayed stitching would be emptied and the emptied coffee would be shoveled into new sacks then brought to the scale and weighed. On this occasion one could always hope for big winnings, for no matter how carefully the shoveling was done, so many beans were kicked down by the workers' feet that a bystander would need twenty hands to catch all the beans jumping and bouncing about.

Lorie saw at once that these were not gray-green Rio beans but Java pouring out its cornucopia, and like the wind she was after the yellow-brown things that rained down on her head then bounced into the gutter or beyond.

Sacks of Java or Domingo were normally only opened in the upper rooms of the warehouse. It was an epoch-making event among the coffee pickers when such an aristocrat among coffee bags lost its way and ended up downstairs.

One must remember that it was not poetry that drove these men, women, and children, old and young, to dive at these lovely Java beans. Rather, it was solely the splendid expectation of earning a few dollars.

After all, many groceries of the third rank in New Orleans draw their imported goods from these coffee pickers, supporting this transitory trade to the best of their ability.

Coffee pickers of such dubious qualification are more dangerous than the sweet-water pirates of Bayou Barataria and Bayou Lafourche. While the latter can be kept at bay with a well-disciplined deck watch, it is virtually impossible to keep the coffee pickers off your heels when they come into the vicinity of a sack of Domingo or Java. They do not do this with Rio coffee, since little is to be earned from it. Who is capable of watching or catching these coffee pickers? What watchman wants to be told to look behind every sack to see whether a coffee picker has dropped anchor there? Besides, this dangerous variety of picker has such sharp teeth that half the watch of the quarter in question would have to patrol night and day without hands. Just imagine properly guarding these thousands of sacks, piled from the floorboards to the rafters! There were efforts three years ago to set traps in the Pelican Warehouse, but a Negro of Mr. Touro's was caught in one, at a loss of two thousand dollars—the Negro lost a leg as a result of this misunderstanding—so that was the end of these fateful machines. Since that accident, the warehouse pirates have been pursuing their craft more actively than ever, but if one figures the losses, it still has not equaled the expense of amputating the Negro's leg.

More recently, the pirates have utterly vanished from the Pelican, as they have no taste for the lime barrels stored there. Thus the Eagle Warehouse has become the scene of harvesting and capering.

Gertrude and Lorie have now brought their own harvest to a happy conclusion.

Suddenly the first recalled that she had left the house without telling her family.

"What will my parents and siblings think, Lorie, when they cannot find me?" a concerned Gertrude anxiously said to her friend.

"It was not that long ago that we left, Trudy. Your parents have probably not even discovered you were gone—and if they have, they will not be mad at you when they see the lovely coffee. I thought once just as you did—my father was alive then. Lindsey's children enticed me out into the city, Father and Mother searched the entire house from top to bottom, asked through the neighborhood, sent to all acquaintances or went themselves to spy me out—but naturally they could not find me. Oh, and how my heart pounded as I headed home—how afraid I was—since my father was very strict, Trudy. Then, when my parents saw me coming from far away, they ran to me, Mother with a joyful face, Father earnest and reproving—then I showed them my coffee, and all was forgiven at once. See, Trudy, it will be no different for you, don't you think?"

But Gertrude was not pacified with these words. Besides, she was a bit ashamed to have advertised the miserable situation of her family so publicly by visiting the coffee pickers.

Lorie, who could not ignore her friend's sudden depression, naturally could not figure out the real reason. She believed that Gertrude had a troubled face simply because she feared rebukes awaiting her at home.

On their return to Tchoupitoulas Street, they had to wait again for several minutes, as the drays storming back and forth blocked the entire street.

Gertrude grew ever more restless, and she urged Lorie whenever an opportunity appeared to rush across the street.

Finally the right moment seemed to have come.

A space formed between two rushing drays which had to be exploited in an instant if the girls were to cross. Otherwise they would end up under the cart's wheels or the legs of the horses.

Lorie bolted like lightning and ducked under the head of the horse at precisely the right moment—any later and she would have gone to the ground.

Gertrude, who followed right on Lorie's heels, came too late—there was a dreadful cry! She touched the wheel of a cart loaded with cotton—then she felt herself embraced by a powerful arm, which brought her out of the chaos to the secure sidewalk. Wheels and hooves passed over her little basket—in a few moments nothing more was seen but a few bits of wicker and some scattered beans.

Gertrude, her temples pounding feverishly, was so shocked by the episode that she had not even looked her savior in the face. Now, when she looked up and met his eyes, she stormily embraced his neck, laughing and weeping as she sobbed: "Thank God! You're here, Prince?"

"Countess Gertrude," her rescuer joyfully called out in a tone which clearly said, "so it *was* you—I did not err after all."

"Prince, you're here?" Gertrude repeated, "Oh what happiness, Prince!"

"Come here, Countess, let us take a cab to the St. Charles Hotel—wherever something unusual takes place a curious crowd always forms," the prince of Württemberg whispered in Gertrude's ear, with a glance at those standing around.

On their way to the St. Charles Hotel, the prince spoke not a word as he led Gertrude by the hand. Gertrude was silent as well. The prince was exquisitely embarrassed as to how to understand Gertrude's curious situation—Gertrude, her eyes lowered, awaited a word from her rescuer with great anxiety. In this manner they reached a cab stand.

The prince was the first to break the silence by asking Gertrude, "Countess Gertrude, may I escort you to your home?"

"Prince, we live on Washington Avenue, opposite Live Oak Square," Gertrude responded, meeting this considerable gallantry with a reply that brought the prince out of his embarrassment.

"To Washington Avenue," the prince called to the cabdriver, "halt opposite Live Oak Square."

When they had gone about five blocks, Gertrude saw Lorie weeping as she ran back and forth with her little basket on her arm.

"Lorie!" Gertrude called from the carriage, without really intending to. She simply gave in to the pressure of her heart.

Lorie, hearing her friend's familiar voice, looked in all directions, but since she could not imagine Trudy in a cab, she looked everywhere among the pedestrians.

"Whom are you calling, Countess?" the prince of Württemberg asked his little lady—then he added, "Forgive me that I ask you."

"It was Lorie, the raftman's little daughter, Prince—" Gertrude replied.

"How a person can lose all presence of mind when dealing with a child!" the prince thought, since Gertrude's quick answer told him what he had not dared to ask.

Chapter 4

THE PRINCE OF WÜRTTEMBERG

Many might be surprised by Gertrude's conduct. Gertrude, who had been raised in a princely court, who had been kissed and caressed by the beautiful daughters of the House of Wittelsbach and idolized by the male camarilla of the court although she was still a child, suddenly recovered her earlier training on unexpectedly encountering the prince. She only resumed being a child when she called out to her friend Lorie from the carriage. Despite the dreadful problems that had befallen her family, although she had been altered in habit and matters of the heart and had become a child of nature, still the prince's noble face sent the warming rays of spirit and heart that changed a child into a lady, imparting a charm that only those who have been truly elevated in spirit are in a position to enjoy. This mixture of childishness and maturity made Gertrude one of the world's most lovable creatures. Her parents judged correctly when they quietly whispered to each other, "Our Gertrude is certainly a mature child!"

Gertrude had been gone from her parents no more than half an hour by the time her absence was noticed.

Since she had never been gone even for a few moments without obtaining permission, her parents were in a state of disturbance and anxiety that would only vanish with the reappearance of their beloved child.

Constanze and Hugo were of the opinion that Gertrude had rushed to the live oaks to satisfy her curiosity in the shadow of these giants. We already know that they were incorrect.

As Melanie set out with Amelie in hand to seek her little daughter, Aunty

Celestine shook her head and launched repeatedly her cycle of corybantic grimaces and ravings.

"Have I not always prophesied the coming of a great misfortune? But no one wants to believe Aunty Celestine—they spurn her—yes, yes, just go, you will regret having come to America? What are you doing now? Away from me, I have done you no harm—have I not always prophesied that a great misfortune will soon come to pass?"

And so she continued for a long while. Hugo, whose bad mood always returned on such occasions, seized Aunty Celestine by the arm and forced her to sit down on the suitcase.

"Dumb old thing, you," he growled, "it is intolerable—jabbering such nonsense just because things aren't in the best shape, when one has enough to do just doing something to lessen problems and accidents. So stop all this nonsense and strange talk—it's enough to make someone want to take a cold bath or press a gun against his forehead . . ."

"Don't let me ever hear that again, Hugo," Father interjected earnestly, "it bespeaks a reprehensible frivolity to release your displeasure in such a manner—such speech is the most unworthy a young man of your age could ever utter. To express such a wish, which one would never even conceive in spirit except to torment and injure the morale of his relatives, does not lead me to pronounce a good sentence over your heart, son . . ."

"It was not meant that way, Father," Hugo responded.

"That is what everyone says who does not find a good reception for a repellent speech. I hope to God that your unnaturally bad mood will depart once your arm has healed."

Melanie entered the room with Amelie. She had searched in vain. Unending concern and anxiety were painted on her heated features.

"I walked through the entire neighborhood, and I could not find the naughty child anywhere," the good mother began almost breathlessly. "The sick mother of the dead raftsman thought it was possible that Gertrude had gone into the city with her Lorie, since she had often said that she would take her. That was also was Lindsey's thought— I was there as well. The dear, bad child, how could she have gone out without permission?"

"Calm down, Melanie," her husband consoled her, "Gertrude has certainly gone off on a walk with Lorie, and she will soon reappear—but you may give her a little scolding when she returns, so that she will take care not to give us such distress in the future."

Hugo, who stood with his little sister at the window that opened on

Washington Avenue, aimed his attention in the direction from which he expected Gertrude to come.

At that moment a cab that had been rushing up Magazine Street turned into Washington Avenue, rolling more slowly over the planks laid there.

"Here comes Gertrude," Hugo remarked in jest, lightly nudging his sister with his arm.

"If we had a carriage, I would almost believe it myself," Constanze responded as she looked after the cab, which now halted a couple paces from the tenement.

"Mother! Father! The prince with Gertrude!" both Hugo and Constanze cried out at the same instant as they stepped back from the window and turned to their parents.

"The prince with Gertrude?" they responded with astonishment as they rose and rushed to the window.

Whose pen could describe the amazement that seized Melanie and her husband when they saw the prince of Württemberg standing in front of the carriage door and offering Gertrude his hand to help her down? They looked at each other, speechless, and remained standing at the open window until the prince and Gertrude were close enough to shake hands with them.

"Your Royal Highness! You do us the honor . . ."

"Royal Highness? Pah, pah—always these empty titles," the prince responded in a cheerful tone, half irritated. "When will you start calling me simply Citizen Paul, my gracious countess?"

"Citizen Paul," Melanie responded with a bounce, "now it is my turn to correct you on account of your 'gracious countess.'"

"Not at all, Your Grace," the prince responded precisely, "the titles have an entirely different function with ladies—a woman might be proud of her dignity in her own right, but it just as well befits a woman also to be proud of an inherited noble name. It would be silly for a man in a republic to insist on a noble title that could only have been given to him in a monarchy. Here a title is only honored when it is tied to great wealth, which is what Americans respect. But you are depriving a woman of a part of her dignity if you take away any part of the standing they have worked to assume since childhood, that of a lovable spirit keeping the vestal fires of majesty and virtue."

"Enough, enough, Your Royal Highness," Melanie commanded, folding her white hands with grace and looking the prince in the face with disapproval.

Suddenly Melanie appeared to recall that she was addressing the prince from her window and realized she had committed an irresponsible act of discourtesy in not having invited him into their room. The exact thing occurred to her husband at the same moment. After welcoming the prince with a deep bow, he had stepped behind Melanie. When his wife turned and her eyes met his, they quickly understood the impropriety of their conduct and rushed to the door, whose latch the prince already held as he escorted Gertrude with traditional courtesy.

The prince of Württemberg was one of those beings who draws our interest at first sight and keeps our curiosity in thrall.[7] Although he was far beyond his years of being a Don Juan flitting among a thousand blossoms, he still preserved that tender, careful conduct in the presence of ladies which marks out a man ready to marry. He could boast of the fact that, despite his advanced age, he still received many a rose from the hands of fair ladies in reward for his charm and chivalric gallantry. His face radiated that noble quality found in all the Hohenstaufen that will never totally vanish if they survive for hundreds of generations to come. His handsome forehead continually proclaimed the proud motto: "Behold the Guelfs, behold the Ghibellines." When he turned his conversation to the desperate state of German princely courts, his eyes danced with an uncanny fire that sparked out at his listeners. If his spirit were not bound by some important undertaking, his face would take on a less attractive appearance, and his eyes would be covered by that mysterious veil, lifted only when Cupid whispered to him, "You have loved and been loved!" Since love plays a large role in all the efforts and activities of princes, we cannot pass over it in silence. Love had taken the prince far from his assigned place, causing him to breathe a purer and fresher air on the soil of a republic. Love had led him to the canyons of Mexico and to climb the Ori Saba. Love had brought him down the Humboldt River and allowed him to see the Rocky Mountains. Love was the oar of his Indian canoe. Love stuffed his peace-pipe among the Blackfoot and the Flathead Nation. Love brought him to the wigwam of a Sioux chief, whose beautiful daughter bestowed on him a necklace of alligator teeth. Love led him to anchor at the Cape of Good Hope. Love brought him to the *saalah* of the Queen of Madagascar, and almost every year love led him back to New Orleans.

Only when love has played such a great role in the active life of a man can one say to him with confidence, "You are one of those fortunate ones who has not lived in vain."

Our esteemed lady readers already know from an earlier chapter that the prince of Württemberg was a passionate entomologist and that the two sisters in Algiers always thought of him when they found a beautiful butterfly or a rare beetle.

His extensive collection, particularly from the realm of insects, offered everything that any researcher of nature could hope for. Coleoptera, orthoptera, hemiptera, neuroptera, hymenoptera, lepidoptera, diptera—in short, all of the known orders were found represented in the greatest detail in his collection of insects. Cheloniera, saurians, ophidians, and batrachians were either preserved in alcohol jars or, if their size did not permit that, stuffed and made pleasing to the eye by the skilled hand of a taxidermist.

He had brought an enviable selection of cephalopods and pterapods, and he owed several rare casteropods and annelids to the collecting zeal of his countryman, Professor Finke.

Similarly, on his birthday he had received the rare Paris and Priamus butterflies from the charming hands of Mistress Evans's angelic daughter.

As the prince entered this more than humble room, he saw at once the circumstances in which this family he so treasured found itself. In an instant he determined to remedy the family's difficult situation.

He had left the family in quite prosperous conditions before his last absence from New Orleans, half a year earlier, and he had left with the certainty that they would profit from his own experiences and his well-meant advice in America.

When the prince returned again after half a year, he had tried at once to find the count's family to be sure that they had been able to thrive in their new environs.

Since it was likely that they still lived in the house they had been renting the year before, he had gone there at once. But he'd learned, to his amazement, that the count's family had left several weeks earlier, and someone mentioned that they might have left New Orleans entirely for some reason or other. His zealous research among the neighbors and those acquainted with the family were to no avail, and he was forced to rely on chance.

Chance brought the prince success this time.

That elderly man on the omnibus today who could not take his eyes off Gertrude as she rode on the back step, that man was none other than Prince Paul.

When he first looked out and saw the little blonde head, he had no doubt whatsoever that it was the young Countess Gertrude. But when he looked at her little companion, who also had a basket on her arm and who obscured Gertrude's body from behind, he thought he had made a great mistake. Yet, after repeating his inspection with care, he became convinced that he had not been wrong. She had to be the count's daughter Gertrude—this mobile dove-neck, this beautiful blond hair plaited into two long braids in the manner of Queen Louisa, the assured bearing despite her poor clothing. The family must have fallen on evil days—but in such a brief period of time? And yet—it could not be any other—this beautiful child is and remains forever Countess Gertrude!

This is how the prince cogitated until he finally fell into that astounding conflict with the man who had been enthralled by Gertrude's charm and attractiveness. As the fight began, Gertrude managed to escape to another omnibus.

We already know the rest of what happened.

We will soon determine who the young, or rather younger, man was, and from the mouth of the prince himself.

When the prince brought Gertrude to her parents, he felt toward the child as if she had been his own daughter.

Indeed, to look at them casually, there was in fact a certain similarity between them when their eyes met, a similarity that no one would dare to mention if they knew the loving and loyal attachment between Melanie and her husband.

Guiltless misery, significant material want in private life and the life of a family embarrass us only in the presence of those who have seen and envied us in our time of prosperity and honor. Such persons come under our groaning roof only to gloat over our misfortune and maliciously play on the contrast between their present happiness and our misery. We never have to be ashamed in the presence of balanced and truly educated persons, even if our misery is in the starkest contrast to their prosperity.

The old count and his wife Melanie had barely received the prince and Gertrude into their humble room before they proceeded to tell him the reason for their unfortunate situation, so far as was possible and decent, without any hesitation or unnecessary excuses. Even more, since they knew this man of the world would be delicate and perceptive, they believed their openness would help open the way to placing their eldest daughter in service to the lady mentioned.

So they sought to fulfill their obligations and pay the proper tribute of thanks to the saving genius of the treasures of this earth.

With such a perception in mind, it was necessary for the first approach to be in a joking tone, which could only be changed over to seriousness once earnestness and smiles had won out.

"Your Royal Highness . . ." Melanie began.

"But Countess . . ." the prince interrupted.

"But Citizen Paul, you seem to forget."

"Your Grace, we are competing even before we take the time to be happy about seeing one another again—please, above everything, say Citizen Paul, or, if this is too hard to say, say simply *prince.*"

"Prince—please, could you call me Mistress Clifford?"

"A prize makes you more contentious, if that's possible, my dear countess; Mistress Clifford will have a hard time contending with such spirit." Then the prince bowed to Melanie, seating himself between her and the count. "You know well how to win a turn. Clifford! Clifford is a pretty name, and you are now exchanging that High Tory for their noble German name . . ."

"My wife has managed to revenge herself against you, Prince!" the count remarked, looking at Melanie in the most lovable manner in the world.

"Mister Clifford," she said to her husband in a half-smiling, half-serious manner, "if you believe that I have ever conceived the slightest idea of revenging myself against Citizen Paul, I am ready to receive any response from him or from you with the greatest thanks."

"Now listen, my Melanie, I must decline 'Mister Clifford'—Mister Ernst would work if you are horrified by my aristocratic name, and your own," the count remarked with half-veiled irony.

"Beloved, you win!" the prince conceded. Then he turned to Hugo, who sat on a mattress next to Constanze, plucking moss out of an open seam.

"New Orleans air seems to agree with you, Hugo. You look stronger and healthier than when I saw you last—but you're wearing your arm in a sling?"

"This arm would have made me a citizen," Hugo intoned in a powerful voice, "if I had been able to blame this on the Mexicans. Uncle Sam is a splendid shepherd of the purses of wounded soldiers—but he doesn't concern himself at all with how many deck hands or sailors scald an arm or a foot in a year."

The prince took a closer look at Hugo, dressed in a red wool shirt with a knife holster, who in fact looked much more like a deck hand than a former officer of light cavalry.

"You were on a boat and scalded your arm? Is that really so?" the prince asked with sympathy. "It's dreadful for a young, educated man to serve such a hard apprenticeship, to work with a spade when once he commanded. But there was no other job to be had? I thought it would be easy for you to pursue another, less perilous profession."

Hugo sat silently while his sister Constanze looked first at one parent, then the other.

She thought it was high time to dare to reveal to their benefactor, the prince of Württemberg, the whole series of misfortunes and troubles that had befallen them.

Melanie spoke on behalf of her husband, who was not good with words.

"The fact that you have greeted us as an old friend, finding us here in dreadful circumstances, and that we have been this way for some time, gives me the right to try your patience for a while, Prince. I will retell to you our unfortunate situation, which arose from our failure to observe the wise advice you gave us with such good intentions. But first I would like you to explain your mysterious encounter with Gertrude, and once you have been so good as to fill this gap, I will ask you to lend me your ear."

The prince turned to the protégée standing next to him, grasped Gertrude's hand, and brought her to his side. Since he saw that Gertrude had been disturbed by her mother's words, he turned to the parents and said: "Before I tell you, permit me to come to Gertrude's defense if she has been somewhat unconventional or has done something not in tune with her obedience as a good daughter."

"With the greatest pleasure, Prince," Melanie and the count both responded, turning to their daughter with the purest curiosity.

Gertrude's whole face turned bright red, so that the ruby of her young blood shone through the snow white of her turtle-dove neck.

"Prince—not everything!" she whispered, so softly and pleadingly that the prince's cheeks glowed.

"But Gertrude, your parents will not be upset."

The prince continued: "This is the third day since our ship reached the wharf here. The journey here from Rio was tiring and exhausting in every sense. Dead tired as I was, I could not neglect to seek out this family so precious to me"—with this he gave a light bow to Melanie and the count. "When I came to your old apartment, I was given an answer that was not just unsatisfactory but also brought me unparalleled distress. Certainty of the most tragic sort is nowhere near as terrifying as such uncertain groping and investigating. The most dreadful images came to mind, tormenting me for two days, until at last an accident or a grace of God—whatever you want to call it—finally took satisfactory form . . ."

"You are making much more of this than we deserve," Melanie interrupted.

"Your Grace, if these hyperboles arise from my heart, they are more equal to our friendship than when the truth is clothed in coarse words," the prince responded in earnest, loving tones.

A light blush, like the rising sun reddening the pale face of Adonis, shone on Melanie's cheeks.

Her silence told the prince that Melanie would take the rest without protest.

"Today I was once again engaged in the expedition I have taken as my duty. For this purpose I was on my way to Bouligny, where a friend lives—a hearty, faithful soul to whom I entrust everything that distresses or torments me. I wanted to get his advice and ask his help. But as so often is the case, one leaves a friend in the best of health, shakes hands for another day—and tomorrow you come and find him in a coffin."

The prince spoke the last words in a soft voice. Then he continued.

"I left his family, who had found themselves in an unenviable situation because of his unexpected death, with the promise to visit soon to put their affairs in order.

"In him I bore another hope to the grave.

"Since the real reason I had traveled to Bouligny had been for naught, I started my journey back to the city.

"I had no desire to wait a few minutes for the steam car, so I mounted the old line on Magazine Street and changed to a second omnibus that would bring me directly home.

"Several streets further, two girls climbed on in back and took their places by the step. Each of them had a little basket on their arm."

Gertrude looked at the prince in confusion.

Hugo said to Constanze, half-aloud, "Pay attention, Sister—that was none other than Gertrude and Lorie."

"One of the girls drew my attention so intensely that I watched her without interruption. I thought I recognized her, but to see her in this place and in such company caused some doubt to appear. And yet I thought again that it had to be her—it could not be anyone other than . . ."

"Than Gertrude!" Hugo supplied with unseemly haste.

"With Lorie!" Constanze joined her brother in haste.

Gertrude sat uncomfortably, as if she were on hot coals.

"Pardon me, Prince, if I interrupt you for a moment," the count said, "Gertrude will make her own confession as to the purpose for this trip around the world."

Then he bent forward and said to his little daughter, who sat next to the prince on a barrel-top chest: "Gertrude, we have nothing whatsoever against your taking a little walk with your neighbor Lorie, but to go into the city you should first get permission from your parents, whom you deeply upset through your long absence."

Melanie, who wanted to cut her husband's untimely pedantry short, freed Gertrude from this painful confession by asking the prince to be judge in her case.

The prince continued: "Since you all know that this blonde child was Countess Gertrude, I will assume that in what follows. As I looked so intensely at Gertrude, recalling to mind what had been such a lively experience a few months before, a man seated across from me in the omnibus began to look at me in the strangest way. He seemed upset that I had given my entire attention to little Gertrude, and he asked me in a malicious tone whether I wanted to invite the blonde child in with me."

Gertrude happened to hit her elbow on the prince's right thigh, but with a purpose.

"Fräulein Gertrude," he said, "you will certainly be unhappy with me that I let you stand outside and did not have the decency to invite you in with your little friend. When I think of that now, it is inconceivable even to me. As so often happens, one neglects obligations of decency or simple charity through having too many interests. But my charming rival is to be criticized because he blamed me without giving youth and beauty its due."

Gertrude thanked him with her forget-me-not eyes and looked playfully at Constanze, who put her hand on her bosom to suppress a giggle.

"You are making Gertrude too proud, Prince," Melanie said.

"Soon she will be called 'The Rose of New Orleans,' Constanze," Hugo whispered.

"If it weren't *me,*" Constanze responded, flashing him the fine rose of her cheeks. Then she fluffed the skirt of her dress so that her little feet were visible, to make her brother aware of these beautiful gifts of nature.

He looked upon his beloved sister with flaming eyes.

"My neighbor," the prince continued, "must have just stepped out of a barbershop, and if one recalls how rejuvenated one feels when he leaves such a place, then you cannot blame someone if he believes himself to be young and handsome. I will not call him young, but at least he was younger than his rival, despite graying hair."

"Gray hair and a receptive spirit often serve as a better guarantee of continued interest than the full hair of a young man, who uses vanity and fancy to play on our very soul," Melanie declared, dividing her charm between the prince and the count.

"My rival would have been saved by that, my dear!"

"That has not yet been said, Prince."

He shrugged his shoulders.

"A comic scene followed, which I can hardly keep a straight face while describing," the prince continued. "When I got out in order to make a closer acquaintance with my blonde mystery, my rival followed on my heels and threatened—for what reason is a riddle to me to the present moment—to beat me up."

"Prince, you're joking!"

"I saw it myself," Gertrude remarked.

"You were whisked away from me by the other omnibus, so you never did see this marvelous event to its conclusion."

"How easily a person can innocently fall into such a distressing situation!" Melanie said with regret.

"'Do you know who I am?' my rival asked me in a proud tone, closing one eye and looking sternly with the other over his eyeglasses. 'How am I to know?' I responded, filled with astonishment. 'Do you know with whom you are dealing and that I am not to be trifled with?'—I, naturally, was in great suspense and could not do justice to his pretensions, since I had never seen him before. 'You have no idea, then,' he continued. 'I am no greenhorn anymore. I will tell you so that you will be able to regulate your conduct toward me in the future—I am—'"

All of them listened with close attention.

"'*I am the Deputy Surveyor of the Second Municipality and certified Plan Inspector!*'

"'What do you have to say to that, sir?'

"'I was expecting some sort of marvel.'

"'What sort of comment is that?'

"'I have never heard of the office!'"

"It is in fact laughable."

"Prince, are you joking?"

"If only he had said, 'I am the President of the United States.'"

"Or even better, 'I am the mysterious husband of Madame de Pontalba.'"[8]

"Or he should have said, 'I am the richest planter in Louisiana. My plantations extend for hundreds of miles—I am a man, look at me, am I not richer than a prince? Do I not bear the destiny of the entire South in my hands? Is not Bayou Sarah in my power, and do not all the cotton bales there bear my arms?'"

"That would have been something!"

"Then one could have kept a straight face."

"Then he would have found envy rather than ridicule."

The prince, the count, Melanie, Hugo, and Constanze traded comments for several minutes, until they had exhausted the subject and the prince took up the story again.

"We only separated," the prince of Württemberg completed his portrayal of this comic episode, "after we had each made a physical test of our strength."

"Until you won, Prince?" Melanie asked naively.

"There was no question of victory here, my dear—that is obvious—although the plan inspector is probably drumming about all over town, 'I came, I saw, I conquered.'"

Now the prince continued the story of his little adventure with his little blonde to its conclusion, including the baskets with the beans, Lorie, the rescue, and the journey hither; nothing was left out.

But Gertrude carried on a secret conversation with her heart in which she confessed to herself that her feelings for her rescuer were more than gratitude.

Despite her youth, Gertrude was already a thinking girl, with more than coffee picking on her mind.

In keeping with their agreement, the narrative now passed to Melanie.

She began in her gentle and endearing manner: "In truth, one cannot be upset at the turn of fate which has ruined our carefully tended resources and threatens to loosen and even tear apart the bonds of our family, in view of the fact that we did not follow to the last point the well-meant advice of our benevolent friend. I can confess to you, Prince, without any hesitation, and my children will make no protests to their mother on that account. The fact that Constanze shows such contrariness that her pride has prevented her from taking service offered for months by Mistress Evans has had a negative effect on all my children. Our poor situation led Hugo to use language against his parents yesterday that he had never dared use in less difficult conditions. What will become of our family in the future will be left at your disposal, my Prince."

"Countess Melanie," the prince picked up the conversation, "how relieved I am now that you offer your hand so trustingly, so I may bind us together all the more closely in friendship by helping lessen your distress."

"If you interpret my words in this manner, Prince, I ask you to be merciful to me in your evaluation of what I am to tell you."

"When the sun sinks beneath the peaks of the Sierra Nevada, the stars bow and send a farewell to the Queen of Heaven," the prince responded with fantastic gallantry, blinded by the brilliance of Melanie's fine spirit. He rose from his place, and, after Melanie's permission, with her husband's approval, he kissed her hand before seating himself again.

At his father's nod, Hugo left his place at his sister's side and filled the old count's pipe.

Then he sat down again at Constanze's side.

The old count seemed to think more than he spoke, and he conceded the entire conversation to the prince and his wife.

Constanze and Hugo listened, nudging each other now and then or teasing back and forth when their mother was too frank to the prince.

Suzie sucked on her little hand, keeping her eyes closed like a newborn kitten. Time and again Aunty Celestine rushed up to Suzie and put her hatbox back into a secure position.

Celestine otherwise did nothing, she simply stared straight ahead. The Bolognese dog played with Hugo's silver scabbard, a remnant from better days.

The prince appeared not to pay any attention to Aunty.

Amelie ran in and out, hauling oyster shells from the street to build a little house.

"About two weeks after your departure, Prince," Melanie resumed, "we decided to go to Wisconsin and buy property in that young, blossoming state. We committed the thoughtless error of withdrawing our small capital, which you know consisted of fifteen thousand dollars, from Finley and Matthews. To make matters worse, my husband has a peculiar dislike of keeping money in a bank, so he preferred to turn this entire amount into notes and lock it up in a desk. Part of this sum was supposed to purchase a farm and the utensils and tools necessary for it, and part was to take care of our other living expenses. But our fate willed otherwise."

Melanie was silent for a moment.

The prince made use of this pause to say, "I have no notion what is coming, my dear Countess, but allow me to anticipate you a bit. How did it happen that you did not enter the firm we had discussed earlier, which would have been to your advantage in a few years with the proper leadership? As far as I recall, you could have purchased that firm for fifteen thousand dollars."

"I lost my two thousand dollars too!" Aunty Celestine suddenly cried out during the pause.

"Calm down, Aunty, the prince will learn this too, soon," Melanie requested.

"Man thinks and God leads, my Prince—our plans often fall through even when the controls for carrying them out have been set with great care," Melanie said as she turned to the prince.

"You certainly aren't a fatalist, are you, my dear Countess? In this country you have to do your thinking and guiding for yourself, and you should not trust Providence at all or leave anything to it so long as you are able to act on your own," he responded.

"Even storming heaven, Prince?"

"Yes—taking power from fate and placing it in your own hands!"

"We are moving away from the subject, my Prince—allow me to complete my sad story."

"Pardon me, my Countess, for interrupting you."

"On the day the catastrophe I am about to describe took place, Hugo went out to get a really good look at the city, since we had decided to leave New Orleans in a few days. We knew from the newspapers that the western waters were not navigable yet, due to ice, so we wanted to make a stop in St. Louis. There we would pass the winter, until the ice was no longer a hindrance to our entry into the Promised Land—as we called Wisconsin. You will accuse me in silence for my slowness, my Prince, and perhaps blame me for hesitating to tell the whole story. That is the way it is with us women, as it is hard for us to give away cheaply what had such a dreadful result for our family's life."

"It would hurt me, my dear, if you had the slightest doubt as to my understanding of women's ways of thinking. Women love preliminaries, and they are more conscientious in these than philosophers of the modern school, whose logic consists of proving what is obvious."

"I see, my Prince, that we belong in the age of the Medici," Melanie responded with a smile.

"And I would join Franz von Sickingen," the count declared in pathos, looking at his wife and expecting some acknowledgment of the sharpness of his comment.

"Continue your story, Mother —what Hugo saw and how it happened," Gertrude asked. She was still sitting at the prince's side.

"One day, while we were basking in sweet dreams of the future, Hugo stormed up the steps and told us that the splendid St. Charles Hotel was in flames and that the Methodist church on Poydras Street had also been consumed by fire. He gave us such a dreadful description of the fire, how the monopteros in the cupola of the hotel fell down into the entry and how one of the great columns fell right across the street, crushing two children, and much more. This upset me to a degree such as I had never experienced as evening fell. Once some people's imaginations are stimulated, they can be uncontrollable, creating images and phantoms that belong to a world for which we cannot account. That was how it was for me that night. In my spirit I saw nothing but rising flames, fire hoses, temples turned to ashes, columns falling down, and thick clouds of smoke. Often it seemed to me that I saw myself in the midst of a lake of fire—I screamed for help, calling for my husband, my children, then I saw myself alone, separated from and bereft of all my beloved."

Melanie spoke these words with such intensity that her entire face reddened and her eyes sparked with a liveliness the prince had never seen before.

"Countess, I begin to suspect—it was prophetic," the prince said with quiet seriousness.

"The closer the hour approached in which we would normally go to bed, the more my anxiety and tension rose. I said this to my husband, and he attributed my anxious condition to the description of the fire, predicting peace and improvement for me on the following day."

"I thought it silly to believe in prophecy, but when I think back over that terror, it mocks the practical explanations I had once given for such things," the count added.

"We went to bed. But I was unable to rest and could not get to sleep. I went to the next room and asked Constanze to lie down with me and talk a bit, to pass the time until gentle slumber could descend on my eyes. Constanze was still making trouble over her unwillingness to take a position with the old Scotswoman. This evening she seemed literally dedicated to tormenting me with her views. But I let her ramble, since it was only to pass the time. We even spoke of you that evening, my Prince . . ."

If the prince and Melanie had looked at the count at this instant, they would have seen that these last words had not pleased him, for he made a sour face and snapped the cover on his pipe bowl several times—which he normally never did.

He was like all men who have beautiful, attractive, spirited wives. They love to see their better halves make an impression due to beauty and allure, they like to hear them praised on account of the size and richness of their thought, the blinding beauty of spirit, the splendor of heart, for love of children, tender devotion to their spouses. What they don't like is being called the most enviable of mortals—no husband can accept that, even if he was born on the icecap of Greenland.

But the count's displeasure was short-lived.

"Constanze," Melanie continued, "could not understand why we had encouraged her to enter service, since she could rightly claim a servant for herself. She did not want to see that we only wanted this in order to bring her into an intimate relationship with the influential Scotswoman. Mistress Evans liked her, as you told us yourself, Prince, and she longed to have

Constanze with her. If Constanze had just gone there, the rest would have followed. We all knew that there was no other way we could gain entry, for other than yourself, Prince, she has not received anyone in years."

"Other than monsieur Dubreuil, the confessor for both her and her daughter," the prince interjected. "And if Mistress Evans had known that I'd visited her only in order to get around the disgusting plotting of that clergyman, she would certainly have shown me the door—for, since she holds that priest to be a particularly pious and honorable man, even the slightest mistrust concerning the holiness of his person would appear to her a great crime."

The prince then said the following words quietly to Melanie and turned and said the same to the count.

"Constanze was to have been a guardian angel for the mother and the daughter, since their confessor forbade any male presence in the house whatsoever. He did not even permit a female friend to enter, so I bestowed the office of rescuing angel on the serving maid."

Husband and wife stared at the prince without being able completely to decipher the meaning of his words.

Aunty raised her head at the mention of the name of Dubreuil. Then she folded her hands and returned to staring into space like she was catatonic.

"You must explain that to us once more, Prince, when we are alone," Melanie said while looking at her spouse, pressing toward the prince.

"I will be pleased to do so," the prince assured her.

"Why did you only start complaining yesterday when I was unable to make up my mind to go to Mistress Evans? Earlier it was not a matter of money, and now that we are impoverished, it turns out I am to investigate some sort of conspiracy," Constanze remarked. Despite the fact that she had seemed indifferent to her mother's conversation with the prince, she had followed everything, even the softly spoken words.

"Earlier it would have been proper and nice of you to conform to our wishes, but after our misfortune sheer necessity cried out for you to silence all contradiction," Melanie responded to her daughter in a punitive manner.

"Mother, if you had said that before, I would have gone into service with Mistress Evans without protest," Constanze grumbled.

"Constanze!" the count retorted in a severe tone.

"The prince would be so good as to use me as a tool to cross some sort of intrigue or destroy a conspiracy," Constanze said softly to her brother.

Melanie took up the threads of her narrative: "If you are determined to sleep, then you can just about figure that you will remain awake. On the other hand, when one tries to prevent slumber, it comes all the more certainly. That was how it happened on that fateful night. First of all, Constanze fell asleep at my side. Then it was my turn in a matter of minutes. It was a peaceful, still night, not disturbed by the slightest sound in the street. I only heard the low breathing of my other children from the next room.

"You usually dream at night about those things that have most occupied you during the day.

"My senses were occupied in the world of dreams with flames reaching to the sky, collapsing houses, giant columns of smoke rising on all sides, leaving me no way out—then I suddenly jolted out of my sleep, and as my eyes opened I saw yellow light glittering in front of the windows, and the mirror that hung opposite the bed was bathed in flames. I rubbed my eyes, opened and closed them, to be sure I was awake. Then I heard the noise of the watchmen's rattles and the uncanny fire cry. I shook Constanze, who fell back on her pillow still asleep, babbling incomprehensible words. I jumped out of bed, woke my husband, my children, Aunty—it was just in time, Prince! The panes of one window blew in and flames poured through the opening. Prince, it was a dreadful moment."

Melanie was silent for a moment, pressing her hands against her breasts. The prince watched her face with the greatest attention.

"I drove my husband, my children, and Aunty through the door, barely half-dressed, and I did not relent until they had all rushed down the stairs. As I later learned, Aunty Celestine returned and threw some featherbeds into the courtyard below. I had already gone halfway down the stairs myself when I thought of the money my husband had locked in the desk next to my bedroom. There was not a moment to lose. I flew rather than ran to the room, when my eyes fell on that picture, Prince, that hangs on the chimney, which shows my Emil in his costume as page."

Hot tears formed in Melanie's eyes at these words, and fell on her beautiful hands.

"'Mother, Mother,' my Emil seemed to be saying, 'do you want me to perish here? Mother, Mother! Protect your child!' Prince, my son's face shone as if transformed in the flames licking the windowsills. I reached at once for a chair, easily took the heavy picture down, and, with this treasure in my arms, I intended to rescue the money from the desk, our entire fortune."

Melanie placed her right hand on her forehead as she seemed to take thought.

"It will always seem strange to me, Prince, whenever I think about what happened next. I have tried with all my spirit to give a clear picture—I already had the money in my hands when a figure as pale as death clutched me with one hand on my arm, while he took the money with the other, like a bolt of lightning. I fell down, a troop of firemen emerged at the top of the stairs—I could no longer see the figure. Prince, in an instant we were poor people—only my maternal heart had preserved one treasure, the souvenir of a lost son, whose image hangs there on the gray wall."

Melanie left her seat, went to the chimney, and stared into her son's blue eyes for a long, long time.

The prince was moved to tears.

The old count let his pipe fall from his mouth as he looked at his wife with concern.

Hugo and Constanze ceased teasing and whispering to each other. Gertrude lay her little blonde head in the prince's lap and sighed.

Little Amelie let the miniature house that she had constructed with such care from oyster shells fall down. She rushed to her mother, weeping.

Only Aunty Celestine remained cold, toying with the Bolognese dog, whose ears she pinched until it crawled under her skirt, whimpering.

The prince lifted Gertrude's head from his lap and went to Melanie. "Leave the sorrows and pains in the past, Countess, and hope for the joys of the future," he consoled her.

"Prince, I am a rich woman, and my sorrows will be transformed into joys the moment I see my son with my own eyes. The artist who made this portrait never imagined that there would come a time when a mother's heart would find her son there."

"Your heart will find the original, Countess, trust in me and in the future. I will not part from your side until I know you are all safe and happy."

"Your Royal Majesty, how you warm my heart—how good it is to find such support in a land that does not know compassion for the sorrows and problems of others," the count said.

"And you can still recall the form and face, Countess?" the prince asked Melanie, as he recovered his equilibrium enough to return to the conversation.

"It was only a moment, Prince, and yet his entire exterior so impressed itself on me that I could choose him from thousands. That face is unforgettable to me, Prince—I have never seen such an evil, truly satanic gaze. The figure wore long hair, black as pitch, a dark beard and—strange how it often happens that one sees everything in a single instant—I saw a wide scar on his cheek . . ."

"You had never seen this person before?"

"No, Prince, which makes it all the more inconceivable to me that he knew of the money."

"He perhaps did not know of its existence until he saw it. He was certainly one of the professional thieves who swarm by the thousands in New Orleans, and, wherever a fire breaks out, they are always the first to enter the houses and steal from the beset people, often with the greatest boldness, under the pretext of offering to help. When he entered the room, you had already taken the money from the desk, and he saw at once with his thief's eyes that it was good booty, so he took it, Countess. You see, this robbery can be explained quite naturally. This thief also might not have looked so dreadful—the pale, satanic quality was probably a product of your overheated imagination. The worst, most depraved scoundrels often have the most guiltless faces."

"Oh no, Prince, my imagination did not cause me to see anything other than what I actually saw. When I think of it, I still feel the horror that dreadful face inspired in me."

"Countess, allow me to interrupt your chain of thought to pose a question whose answer will clarify me concerning something."

"Do as you please, Prince."

"How did it happen that the people in whose house you lived then responded to my question whether you were still around in an ambiguous manner, shrugging their shoulders and doubting whether you were still in New Orleans? Was it the house where the fire broke out?"

"I will be able to satisfy you on that, Prince. As soon as the fire was extinguished—it demolished only the top floor, which was soon rebuilt—my husband had to tell the owners that we were now unable to pay the rent, since we had lost all his money in the fire."

"Their action was still not necessary," the prince remarked, turning to the count.

"But they were still very upset about it—yes, when we left the landlord had words with us which caused me great upset. He remarked, in short, that it seemed strange that the fire had broken out specifically on our floor, and that there were people who were wont to have convenient fires which gave them an excuse when they were too closely beset by their creditors."

"That is disgusting!" the prince cried out.

At the same instant there was a knock on the door, and in stepped a small, slight man who bowed with courtesy and greeted the prince in French.

Aunty Celestine had hardly glanced at the new arrival before she leaped into the air and began howling like a person possessed.

AUNTY CELESTINE

> who gives up his old intention
> And falls into confusion over his new plan
> Until he begins to despair of everything
> [Dante][9]

In order to understand Aunty Celestine's mad ravings, which exploded the instant she laid eyes on the small man, we must go back to the time of her girlhood.

The noble proprietor von Nesebeck was known in Magdeburg as one of the richest of cavaliers. He normally passed the winters in town with his family, and he lived otherwise only on his property near Huxburg Castle. The Huxburg is well known to tourists, since a church with a convent lies near it on the heights, surrounded by thick forest. There is a splendid inn nearby, which was frequented by students from Jena and Leipzig, particularly during vacation seasons. Concerts and balls alternated with drinking sessions and pranks, and many a young nun must have suffered heart-pangs when she looked over the convent walls to see the sons of the muses singing fraternity songs, lustily brandishing rapiers in the air, or practicing a new dance step. Herr von Nesebeck, who was a man of the world and a practiced drinker who owed the finest years of his life to passionate fraternity days, often came from his estate to the Huxburg in the company of his two daughters. It was his habit to take his daughters to the esteemed abbess, who showered the sisters with little packets filled with the finest *Nonnenfürzchen.*[10] (The *Nonnenfürzchen* of the nuns on the Huxburg had originally been made for Count Görz's truffle-hounds, who developed a sure instinct for that mystery of the soil after eating these delicacies. Whoever has eaten truffles at Count Görz's table knows how to tell the difference between these and those found elsewhere.) Herr von Nesebeck would only retrieve his daughters from the cloister after he had become soused and caroused sufficiently with the peasants and the fraternity boys. Whenever he brought a new hunting cap with him to the Huxburg, it was soon so ill-used that it would be a shame not to buy a new one.

But Herr von Nesebeck had so much money that his purse would not be emptied even if he had to buy a new hunting cap every second.

Of course a hunting cap does not cost as much as a real Panama straw hat, and a Prussian thaler is a measly thing when compared with a dollar bearing the motto *e pluribus unum.*

Herr von Nesebeck had been married three times, and yet he seemed like anything but a married man. Whoever encountered him, in his short hunting habit with its white embroidered collar, loosely draped with a green silk scarf, whoever noted the care with which he trimmed and trained his moustache, whoever found him in the company of women, whoever saw him drinking at the student drinking contests, would never have believed that he had ever entered the constraints of a marriage bed. Rather, he would be seen as a confirmed bachelor who prefers to run through his fortune by himself rather than be forced to take a wife in order to share the joys and sorrows of his peculiar life on this earth.

There are men who seem literally to be selected by fate to marry several times. Once restricted by the bonds of matrimony, they long for the status of widower. Yet when they are freed once more by the death of their better half, they take the plunge a third time and make another acquaintance with Hymen. Such men might have the misfortune to lose their wives twenty times, and they would still marry a twenty-first time.

The relationship of such men to women was entirely different from the husbands who are said to be "true till death."

While the latter sort have to court the woman of their heart, the former are beset by women courting them. In one case the lady falls in love with the man and seduces him, in the other case the man loves and seduces the woman.

We find the same to be true with some species of carnations.

Herr von Nesebeck was thirty-five when he took his third wife. She was the youngest child of a count in the Arco Valley, a true angel for lovability and goodness of heart. He brought a little daughter into the marriage, a souvenir from his first wife, who had also been from a rich and propertied family. The daughter was called Celestine, a name she had exchanged for her original name of Henrietta. There could have been no more proper name for the child, as it happened. One could hardly believe that Celestine belonged to this vale of tears at all. She seemed to be a true child of heaven, a star fallen to earth. So light, so sunny, so pure, so heavenly, no child around could compare, far and wide.

Herr von Nesebeck always called her the treasure of his heart, and when he gave parties there was no end to the admiration and flattery. When the father drew friends and acquaintances to the table, he placed Celestine at the center and let the cavaliers shower his little daughter with incense.

Whoever received a thrown kiss from Celestine on such occasions boasted as if he had received grace from a goddess.

Such were the days of Celestine as a child.

His third wife gave him another daughter, who was given the name of his mother, Melanie. On the day Melanie was born, Celestine celebrated her tenth birthday.

The next day, the mother died, and for a while this darkened the joy over the birth of a new member of the von Nesebeck house.

A year after the death of his third wife, Herr von Nesebeck tired of being a widower. But this time he did not look for his bride in the districts of Prussia or Old Bavaria. Rather, he turned to the land of the Nibelungen and sought the hand of the daughter of a Hungarian magnate from the famed and once mighty house of the Counts Esterhazy von Galantha.

While this tireless vagabond had lived happily with all his earlier wives, this marriage was a hell of torments and sorrows.

The result was that the tormented husband undertook ever madder extravaganzas, and he found compensation for the troubles he endured at home only in the bars with his old friends—none of whom had ever left him, since he was in gold up to his ears.

The *Junker* could still not forget his lusty student days,[11] so he was most often seen among the young men given over to hunting and fraternity life. He bore the colors of one group, then another, and the old boy loved them all.

His extremely noble way with money led many hopeful young students to go over the limit and take on habits that their slim budget did not allow.

The honeymoon was barely over by the time Herr von Nesebeck began entertaining thoughts of becoming a widower as soon as possible.

But this time his wish was not heard, and, still not a widower after the passage of thirteen years, he gave up all hope of ever becoming one again.

From then on he dedicated all his attention to his two daughters. Celestine had already reached her twenty-fourth birthday without deciding to follow her father's wishes and make an advantageous alliance.

Celestine was one of those enviable girls who only begin to show their true beauty at the moment when others start to wilt, becoming more beautiful with every passing year.

The education she had received since her sixteenth year made her even more irresistible.

"A person could go mad, Herr von Nesebeck, when he views your daughter without the slightest expectation of ever receiving even the smallest favor from her. From this day forward I shall not set foot in your house if you do not clearly grant me the expectation of not being treated by her in the future with such deadly indifference," said the Prussian government minister von Sch*, one of her many suitors.

"Your excellency assumes too much of me if he thinks I am in the position to dispose of my daughter's heart," the father of the beautiful Celestine responded.

The Prussian minister made his peace.

He kept his word and never again set foot in the house of Herr von Nesebeck.

He would soon learn how the minister would revenge himself against his daughter.

At this time a Creole was residing in Magdeburg who was making a sensation due to his fluency in all the romance languages as well as his general learning. Abbé Dubreuil—for that was the Creole's name—was the lion of the hour in all circles, watched by all the ladies with no small interest, despite his diminutive stature. He had just come from Louisiana, and he was on a papal mission. Since certain responsibilities bestowed on him by the Holy See bound him to Magdeburg for a period of years, he had received approval from the archdiocesan court for his request to act as father confessor of the nuns on the Huxburg.

One day the abbé received the following letter:

Your Grace,

M. Dominique Dubreuil!

Several extraordinary messages reaching me concerning your splendid personality have led me to dare approach you to make an offer that easily would bring you a large sum of money, one that would make the salary for your papal mission look like small change. As soon as I am assured that you are carrying out the demands I give you, I will see that you receive the sum of ten thousand thalers, half of what has been set aside for you. You will receive the balance when your efforts have been crowned with success. Have no fear of compromising yourself in any way by accepting my assignment, for the means for carrying out my plan will prove to you that any mistrust is out of place. You will not be shocked or in any way distressed when I tell you that I hold you to be a man ready to do anything for money. My openness should move you to trust me utterly. If you hold me to be a scoundrel or rascal for having said this, it would not concern me. I would even prefer this response, so we would have nothing to fear from each other in the future. But to business: You know the beautiful Fräulein Celestine von Nesebeck, and you have certainly seen her often among the canonesses on the Huxburg, since you serve as father confessor there. Celestine von Nesebeck is a good Catholic and, as such, a splendid prospective victim for the acquisitiveness of a priest of the Sole Salvific Church. I put that in only to make you aware of the correct means, since I well know that such a practiced servant of St. Ignatius of Loyola will need no training from a layman; I just wanted to indicate what you should try first. I have learned from dependable sources that Fräulein von Nesebeck has granted her heart, free until now, to a young student from Jena, and she is probably trying even now to convince her father to aid the association by moving the family council to support it. This alliance must either be delayed by years or, even better, destroyed at once. If the alliance described meets with the stubborn opposition of the family council—which is likely, since the happy suitor is of bourgeois origins—you should not be prevented from separating the lovers in such a way that they can never come back together.

I shall await your response with impatience, under the code name A. Sch., Berlin, *poste restante.*[12]

p.s. You may fear my influence should you dare to set further conditions for me.

It was an easy matter for the decadent priest to come into possession of the promised sum, since he had never shrunk back from such a problem before. The first thing he did was make a detailed investigation of the familial relations of Herr von Nesebeck. He had himself introduced to the noble proprietor and his family by a person of high status and respect. In a short time be had made himself so beloved and irreplaceable that the old Herr von Nesebeck entrusted him with exclusive religious guidance over both his daughters. The abbé gave them instruction in foreign languages and the dogmas of the Catholic Church, and soon he had won so much trust from Fräulein Celestine that she sought the privilege of having him as her father confessor.

At about the same time, there was a horrifying murder of a young noble student who had been traveling on horseback back to university with a fat wallet. Despite all efforts on the part of the authorities, the culprit could not be found. Then the rumor suddenly surfaced that the student marked as the Fräulein von Nesebeck's future bridegroom had been party to the deed. Yes, some witnesses even appeared to verify this, so the young man was arrested. After he had been locked up for several weeks, he was condemned to life imprisonment at hard labor in irons. Who had harbored such hostility against the life of this active young man? It was a priest of the very Church that continually has the slogan "love thy neighbor" in its mouth yet in fact falls like a predator on its own children, robbing them of repose and peace.

That was not enough for the Creole.

Not satisfied with the payment that he'd received, as promised, he sought also to exploit the passions of the unhappy Celestine, who was now permanently separated from the object of her love. He did this in a way not even Satan would not have dared conceive.

The Abbé Dominique Dubreuil had won some influence over the heart of despairing Celestine through false sympathy with her sorrows, but to no avail. Now he resorted to a method that he hoped would achieve his shameful goal with greater certainty. He offered the release of her lover from the hands of justice if she would grant him certain favors.

Poor Celestine, would that death had called you away from life before you had to experience your locks being crowned with the belladonna of violation instead of the fragrant myrtle of marriage!

...

That dreadful night of madness descended on the senses of the unhappy girl as soon as she awoke from the priest's embrace. The radiant beauty of her spirit became the silent demon of Holy Scripture.

Poor Celestine passed a full fifteen years in the private asylum of Doctor Blanche on the Montmartre. Her madness spread ever wider, so that her spirit was soon entirely in the grip of dark confusion. Her father, now well along in years, applied almost his entire fortune to healing his daughter, whose madness remained a riddle until his death. Celestine was also sent to be treated by several other physicians of the famed asylum of Bicêtre, but none could bring about her recovery. After another fifteen years had passed, it appeared at last that the famous Dr. Falret had succeeded in freeing Celestine, now fifty-five years old, from the dark night of madness. An unexpected accident suddenly brought her illness to an end. Dr. Falret happened to send her back to some malicious madmen whose happiness consisted of tormenting her. One of these creatures gave her the idea that she had been sent there to be killed and that whoever remained there would be robbed of life at the first opportunity. This statement put the unhappy woman into the greatest possible anxiety of death, so that she begged her overseer to get her out.

Melanie was now her only living relative. The last years of Herr von Nesebeck had been an unbroken chain of sorrows and troubles of all kinds. Other than the fact that the dreadful situation of his beloved Celestine had poisoned all his joys of life, his wife's extravagant conduct often brought him to despair. He lost her two years before his own death; she died of a fall from a horse during a steeplechase at Pückler-Muskau's.[13] The prince had her buried in his own plot, with a monument of a Carrara marble swan, ridden by Cupid.

Old Nesebeck could hardly endure it when, after her death, he learned of the vast burden of debts his wife had heaped upon his shoulders.

He died separated from his children and abandoned by his old drinking companions.

Melanie, who married the Bavarian count of *, already had five children, of which the oldest two, Emil and Ernst, had emigrated to America, Emil with a wife and her sister.

At this time Melanie's half-sister, the unhappy Celestine, came into the count's family.

It was true that episodes of madness occasionally appeared, and she was often paralyzed by benign ecstasies. Frequently she still had the fixed idea that she was married and had killed her husband. She fantasized about Magdeburg and the Elbe, she dreamed of a prisoner who wanted to do something bad to her, and, since the family had arrived in America, she often took the role of a prophetess of misfortune.

They had brought her across the ocean with them.

That was Aunty Celestine.

Chapter 6

Corybantic Fits

O lovely childhood in the old Fatherland! O marvelous life and weft of your maidens, O Germany! In the woodland and on the meadow—in the thicket and in the bower, in the barn and behind the oven, in the church and on the dancing floor, in the cheese-hut and in the valley, on the arm and in the lap, milking cows and gathering straw—O maiden, how magical and enchanting you were in your Germany! Maidens, you were beyond the years when one might call you children, and yet you still had fun with wood shavings, tying them around your head like curls. You still placed a couple cherries behind your ear and convinced yourself that you could fool a hummingbird. How your heart beat, you German maidens, when you cracked an egg and found two yolks! Where did all this sparkling and shaking, that blooming and loving, that weeping and longing come from? It came because you had heard nothing of the Almighty Dollar and you would allow no one to pour molasses on your salad. Because you did not yet know the phrase *How much?* and it never occurred to you to discover whether your neighbor had a "vacant" or an "improved" lot. Because you cared more for your flowers than your fashionable dress. Because you would rather have sewn stockings than woven ones. Because people called you *deutsch* rather than *Dutch*. In short, because you still did not know that the golden apple of Hesperides had a rotten core. You maidens and women all, why did you ever leave Germany? And you maidens whose slender, tender bodies were clothed in the splendid mantle of aristocracy in the old homeland? Well, you will either become Messalinas, or—what is worse—you will burn your feelings at the stake of your heart.

The prince of Württemberg rose in shock from his seat when Aunty Celestine began to howl with obsessive terror at the entrance of the slight little man. Gertrude reached for his hand and pressed her blonde head on the prince's right thigh. He had acknowledged the greeting of the arrival with obvious decorum, nodding slightly, and he was trying to present the man to the count's family when Celestine's conduct became so dreadful that the entire family rose at once and pulled together into a tight knot.

The little man, who looked quickly back and forth between the prince and Aunty Celestine, stood as if nailed to the spot.

Melanie, who noted this, called to him in an anxious tone that demonstrated all too clearly her suffering: "Do not blame us on account of this unexpected encounter, sir—it will soon pass . . ."

"Gracious lady, His Royal Majesty wanted to do me the honor of presenting me as the preacher at the *Rue des Ramparts* and as the father confessor of Mistress Evans."

"How is His Grace . . ." the prince began, just as Celestine turned on the stranger with a rage that caused him to pale like a corpse.

"Mother, Father! Mother! Mother!" the children screamed, shrinking back.

"Are you insane, my lady? Leave my poor head in peace—God keep you, what do you want, what are you about? So let loose of me at last—Prince, get me out of the hands of my persecutor!" Dubreuil cried—for our esteemed lady readers will already have recognized him—in confused pathos as Celestine grabbed him by the hair and threatened to throw him down.

"Aunt, leave him alone or I'll poke you with my knife handle, you dumb old thing, you!" Hugo screamed, grabbing the weapon he had named.

"Hugo!" the count sternly corrected him, "You seem to enjoy being coarse, put the knife back!"

As Hugo avoided his father's gaze, he encountered his mother's eyes, which seemed to beseech him not to irritate his father. Then she pulled herself free of Gertrude and Amelie, who had held her back with their embraces, and rushed to Suzie, who been brought into an exposed position in her hat-box.

"No, I will not let go of you," Celestine cried out, as she pressed Dubreuil's arms so close together that his elbows touched each other. "No, no, I shall not let you—just look at me, look, look, don't you recognize me any more—ha, ha! I have not forgotten you—those are your eyes, that is your nose, those are your unctuous lips—Dominique Dubreuil, don't you know me any more? Look, just look how you are trembling, look into my eyes, holy man, if your memory has vanished, then I ask your God and your saints, and they will tell you the story once again—Abbé Dominique Dubreuil, don't you know me any more?"

This was not just madness.

Among these words flitted a light blush of conscious thought.

"The lady is insane! Free me . . . !" the abbé gurgled with uncertain accent, since Celestine lay with her breast on his face, overwhelming him.

The prince of Württemberg and the count went to the two and attempted to pull Aunty Celestine from the preacher.

"No, I will not release you," she cried repeatedly, wrapping her hands ever tighter around Dubreuil's thin arms.

"I will not release you, Dominique Dubreuil, until you recognize me again—no, no, no, I will not release you!"

The wind coming in through the window played with the ribbons of the preacher's black straw hat, which the observant Amelie had rescued from the floor and placed on the table, making the ribbons flap up and down.

The preacher's long, thin hair stood out at his temples like the wings of a gray-black bird of death on a poisonous tree in Borneo.

"Madame, if you do not release my arms, and if you, Royal Highness, do not liberate me, I will scream, which will bring the whole neighborhood and raise a scandal!" Dubreuil said in such a determined tone that one could see that he intended to carry out his threat at once.

And he did just that.

"For God's sake, sir—consider—Aunty, Aunty, listen to us—Gertrude, there—take my shawl and hang it over the window. Amelie, stay with me, and don't open the door again. Sir, consider how this looks—" commanding and begging in turns, Melanie ran nervously about the room and really had no idea what to do.

Dubreuil screamed with his full might.

Suddenly Aunty Celestine let him loose and ran away from him, then toward him, then away, then back, until she finally was able to express her inner pressures with the following words: "Priest of love, how cowardly you are—powerful man of God, you are screaming like a child at the hands of a weak woman. O Dominique Dubreuil, you are smiling because you hold me to be insane—ha, ha! Dominique Dubreuil, how do you look to me? . . . Do I look so old that you can't recognize me—I was as young and pretty as Little Constanze—are my cheeks no longer red, my lips so pale? You look so fatherly and pious now—Dubreuil, Dubreuil, should I fall at your feet again in the confessional? Dominique Dubreuil, you have grown so old, so ugly, and yet I still recognize you—and you didn't recognize me any more? Priest of love, protector of innocence, have you never heard of the beautiful Fräulein Celestine von Nesebeck?"

The count, who had stationed himself with his back against the closed door, and Melanie, who stood beside him, had hoped in vain for a quick end to Aunty's excesses. These episodes, which had already occurred so often, usually lasted only a few moments, and then Aunty Celestine would quietly sit back down on her travel bag. They now wanted to wait quietly for this moment, and they told the prince not to do anything but to let her go ahead. There would then be plenty of time to explain their situation to monsieur Dubreuil and make amends for his distress through a strong show of sympathy.

They were wrong this time. Even more, they found Aunty's words this time to have a rare clarity and conscious intonation. At Celestine's last words, Dubreuil visibly trembled, despite the restraint that he sought to display. His pale, sweaty face seemed to grow longer, his knees knocked and his eyes were bolted desperately on Celestine's face.

"Let me go before you experience a yet greater scandal—your mad lady seems to want to go to extremes," Dubreuil said, turning to the count and Melanie and moving to the door.

The count opened the door.

"Do not speak of this episode, my good abbé—it is not our fault," the count said quietly to Dubreuil, who rushed out without hearing him.

Celestine did not hinder him.

She had set herself before the fireplace and appeared to be calm.

Melanie's shawl, which Gertrude had hung over the window to keep passersby from getting a glimpse of this dreadful scene, fell to the ground as a result of the count's heavy footsteps, opening up a vista for everyone to view with the greatest awe.

The setting sun cast a bright red into the mean room, illuminating the entire family. A light red spot that the oblong hat-box broke into ellipses swam over Suzie's head, giving her the appearance of a baby Jesus.

Behind the hanging limbs of live oak lay the blood-red head of the setting sun, and the moss of the live oak swaying in the light west wind seemed as if the breeze were parting the sun's hair.

"Mother, look how pretty Aunty is!" Gertrude called to Melanie. She, along with all the rest, obeyed this call.

The last ruby of the evening sun was leaving Celestine's face, swaying for an instant on her forehead like a small meteorite, until the family's eye caught her.

Celestine turned her back on the fireplace, which she had earlier been studying, and now stood like a mourning Niobe at the grave of the evening sun.

"Mother, see how strange Aunty looks—she does not seem as crazy any more," Gertrude said once more to her mother, tugging her dress.

"Madame Countess," the prince whispered in Melanie's ear, "Your sister must have once been a stunningly beautiful woman!"

"That is a strange remark, Prince," Melanie responded with shock.

"Just look, Countess!"

"Prince, pardon me—that is very strange talk."

"But Mother, what is happening with Aunty?" Gertrude interrupted in a rather loud voice.

"Look, Countess, and you, too, Fräulein Gertrude—"

"What, Fräulein Gertrude?" Melanie interrupted the prince, "what are you talking about?"

An amazing change was indeed taking place in Celestine. Although she had earlier always been bowed and kept her head to one side, she now stood erect with head held high. She seemed to have become taller in an instant, and her hands rested calmly on her bosom.

Was it the unexpected appearance of her seducer that so transformed her in posture, dignity, and speech? Or had the light shadows of madness that had crossed her brain now and then since her release from the asylum simply slipped away all at once? Would she be able to look back on her dreadful past with a steady gaze in her old age? Would the matron be able to weep over what the girl could not, since her brain had been oppressed by the evil demon of madness? Did the Celestine of twenty-six years of age still harbor the feelings of a girl? Perhaps the blooming heart of the virgin had slumbered thirty-two years only to awake in its full beauty and fullness one day? Would the bosom of this matron begin to heave once more, after so many years, like a pair of wilted leaves hanging on a dry stick? Would Cupid flutter about her gray hair, having been so long banned from these luxuriant locks?

Why not? Doesn't the flower spread itself to the world once more for a few moments before its end?

Celestine was no longer insane. At her first glimpse of the priest she had looked back to her youth with dreadful clarity. The departing spirits of her long night of madness only danced here and there on the wildly coiling clouds of her thought.

The prince, Melanie, the count, Hugo, and Constanze quietly recollected the words Celestine had directed at the priest.

But only the prince interpreted these awful hieroglyphs correctly and detected the abbé's dreadful deed. "A madwoman," the prince thought to himself, "does not speak that way—how did Celestine know the priest, who was being presented to the family for the first time, and only the count had met him once before? Other than the count, the rest of the family knows of him only by hearsay. 'Dubreuil, Dubreuil, should I fall at your feet again in the confessional?'—didn't she say that? And Dubreuil was involved in some sort of mission in Germany in his youth, as he told me himself! 'Don't you recognize the beautiful Fräulein von Nesebeck?' Didn't Aunty ask him in that way? When she was still beautiful, young, sought-after—that monster of a priest violated her in the confessional, and she went mad as a result! Now it is all clear before my eyes—the devil himself shudders before the servant of God. And you intend the same with that angel of a girl, the daughter of Mistress Evans—you are preparing the same fate for Miss Dudley Evans? So that is why you are so close to her, for that very reason you became her father confessor?"

So it went on in the prince's interior as he reviewed all of Aunty's words, and his swift mind quickly brought order out of chaos.

He looked closely at Aunty Celestine.

Her face shone, transfigured, when she turned from the window and sought Melanie with her eyes. Melanie stood for a moment dumb with amazement and wonder. Celestine spoke not a word at first, but her eyes said with greater clarity what her lips still had to keep silent. They were no longer the beset eyes of a matron but the stars of a young, hopeful girl. Her face was pale, but this paleness had a purity and transparency without equal.

She rushed toward Melanie, who went to meet her, and they embraced. Then she did the same with each other member of the family.

They were deeply moved by Aunty's tenderness.

Even the prince received her attentions.

For several seconds she stood before him, hesitating, pulling back then advancing again—then she grasped his hand and kissed it. With a long look she regarded the prince, who was utterly confounded by Celestine's extraordinary beauty and majestic presence, and he returned her tender greeting with a soft press of his hand.

Hugo and Constanze hardly dared breathe—they were so taken by this elevated, solemn moment.

Celestine's gaze now moved to Emil's portrait over the fireplace.

"How beautiful, how beautiful!" she suddenly cried out in enthusiasm, "that is your god, Melanie! Isn't that correct, Sister?"

"Yes, dear Sister," she replied in a woeful tone, "he is the god of my heart, my son—but what has happened in your soul, Celestine? How your eyes hang intoxicated on that picture!"

"Aunty was in love with Emil!" Hugo said to Constanze, no longer in mockery but in sympathy. "Did she ever meet Emil in person, Constanze?"

"I don't know, Brother—but you are as pretty. Emil always seemed more like a girl or a young woman. I don't like it when men are *too* beautiful—they normally don't have much spirit," Constanze answered.

"You might be right," Hugo agreed, creasing his forehead as if he wanted to appear thoughtful and at the same time give his sister proof of the correctness of her remark.

"You are vain, Hugo," Constanze said, who had not missed her brother's forced game.

"Vanity is not my smallest virtue," he remarked dryly, "if I weren't a little vain, I would already be rid of all my civilization."

"I saw an Indian at the market whom you would not call a civilized man, and he still seemed rather vain."

"That is not a just comparison, Constanze—you don't understand me at all."

Now Aunty's conduct called for their attention once more. She hung sobbing on her half-sister's neck and seemed almost suffocated by her tears.

"Celestine, my dear good sister, what is the matter with you now? You seemed so friendly and happy before." Melanie asked.

"For that very reason, Sister," Celestine responded as she sobbed. "What was I? What am I now?"

"It is a dreadful revenge of nature to break madness so that understanding can torment and torture the soul," the prince said quietly to the count, looking in his eyes with a question.

"Now I can only marvel, Royal Highness, but perhaps the future will provide some guidance," the count said slowly, moving somewhat closer to Celestine and Melanie, his arms crossed.

Gertrude would not move from the prince's side. Now and then she looked up at him as if she wanted to ask a question.

Amelie moved anxiously between her mother and Aunty Celestine, trying to get them apart, since she believed Celestine might do her mother some harm. They did not part, so she began to weep.

When ominous events and unexpected episodes so rapidly storm past one another in this family, so visited by trouble, one wishes we could place a pen in the hand of a higher power so that it could better register the horrors on paper.

Celestine hung with the full weight of her body on her sister's neck, which made it hard for Melanie to keep her feet. Celestine's face had turned to the picture over the fireplace.

Celestine's features were beautiful, as pure and pale as alabaster—and as cold.

"Merciful God! Aunty is dead!" Melanie screamed in terror, looking for her husband.

"Dead?" they all cried almost at the same time, except the prince, who went to Melanie to free her from the embrace of her departed sister.

"I was prepared for it, it couldn't have gone any other way—this sudden transfiguration of her face—that picture—my dear Countess, there was no other way," the prince said quietly, with an element of solemnity in the intonation of his words.

"Her recovery was her death, Prince," Melanie responded with a shaking voice.

"Awakened fire had to kill the heart—it came too quickly."

Hugo, who had rushed out of the room on his father's signal to get a physician, was lucky enough to run into one a few steps from the house, and he came right back through the door accompanied by the doctor.

"Doctor, is it true that Aunty is dead? Isn't she just asleep?" Amelie chattered and kissed the dead woman on the lips. After several vain attempts to find life, the physician finally held a mirror before her half-open mouth and said: "No breath fogs the surface—she is dead."

The superficial verdict of the coroner read: death of stroke.

...

The prince of Württemberg remained with the family the entire night and helped keep watch at Aunty's bed, which had been made into a daybed as best as could be done hastily with the available material by heaping up mattresses.

Hugo went into the city and fetched at the prince's behest several lights and wax candles, together with various other utensils and objects needed for the present situation. By this means it was possible for the prince to realize a peculiar but proper wake in this poor apartment. It would not have been at all difficult to move the count's family to a decent apartment this very evening—since all the furnishings other than the picture could be abandoned—but the prince was certain that this haste would hit upon the couple's opposition, and it would also disturb the quiet dignity of this moment with an improper, fancy exterior.

"Brother, I never expected that when we pulled the moss down from the live oaks we were preparing a deathbed. Poor Aunty, she dragged it over so quickly and happily, so that you and I could have a good bed," Constanze said to Hugo with a sorrowful manner. She had pushed two chests together to make a bed for the night and now sat on a bundle of washing, laying her head in her brother's arms.

"I could slap myself," Hugo said, "when I think that I was so rude to her a few moments before her death—but you know yourself, Constanze, that I meant no harm by it."

Gertrude had fallen asleep with her head in the lap of the prince, who sat next to the count and his spouse beside the improvised daybed. Little Amelie lay next to her on the floor, her back next to Gertrude's little legs, breathing in a soft, sweet slumber. Her reddened eyelids showed that sleep had crept up on her while she was weeping for the dead, cold Aunty.

As the sun was reddening the dark moss on the highest branches of the live oaks, the prince left the house on Washington Avenue for a while, so that he could weave flowered wreathes for the future of his beloved friends.

Chapter 7

In the Hamburg Mill

For connoisseurs of mankind and portraitists of morals, it is of no small interest to seek out the sources of names of places where crime and shame have triumphed, where painstaking maneuvering and unrelenting strictness of criminal plotting have prospered despite the Argus eyes of the police and even continue to flourish long after public opinion has condemned them.

The Hamburg Mill had once been a boardinghouse for sailors, with a Spaniard named Viala as its owner. Viala himself had been a sailor until his fifty-fourth year, but in all this time he'd never managed to advance further than second mate. On a voyage from Marseilles to New Orleans, he had fallen from the highest crow's-nest on the mainmast during a severe storm, smashing both arms and his right shin. In those days the brig *Dolores* still was a credit to our wharf, and its captain, Antoine Du Ponteil, gave second mate Viala every possible assistance. He had such a generous manner that he entrusted the man, disabled for sea duty, to the care of a capable physician at his own expense, and he helped him establish a boardinghouse in the Third Municipality. Since the unfortunate man had lost both arms and his left leg, this kindness saved his life.

Unfortunately, poor Viala was one of those good-natured tipplers who could never take a drink alone but always had to have a select company about him. Even that would not have dumped the former second mate into perdition, but the fact that his inseparable drinking buddies had such large holes in their pockets did lead to his ruin. His more than ordinary inclination to the fair sex also helped draw pennies from his exchequer. He was particularly fixated on Indian Creoles, and he always fell into a fit when his cashbox would not permit him to satisfy the just claims of these overenthusiastic entertainers. When Viala had sunk so low that he had sold off his candy jars, empty ale bottles, and mugs, it was his fortune to become acquainted with a woman from Hamburg who moved him to sell her the boardinghouse with all equipment for a modest price.

Once it was in the possession of this lovable lady—who, it should be said, had once brought all Hamburg to its feet through her amiability—this seaman's boardinghouse took on an entirely different appearance. Under her control, the old Seaman's Exchange received the name *Hamburg Mill,* in the following way: A lady such as Mrs. V∗—as she called herself—soon became the goal of all the desires and silliness of lovesick roués and vagabond lovers. The uninhibited sons of Neptune were soon replaced by dandies of the Third Municipality, recruited mostly from swindlers of every sort, rampaging unemployed clerks, ill-starred sons of wealthy parents, and all sorts of rich and poor layabouts par excellence. Although Mrs. V∗ well knew the loose conduct of her guests, this did not distress her. On the contrary, she saw that these loose and frivolous birds were providing her with a decent living. "There's nothing better than our Hamburg girl," German gentlemen both high and low whispered to themselves if they had just treated Mrs. V* to some of their prickly wit. So "Our Hamburg" remained the matins, noonday prayer, and vespers, while Berg, Ahrens (Müller), Locke on the Armory Market and Ältermann Haase's Little Crispin were the beads of the rosary one would devotedly chant. Mrs. V* was one of the pertest, liveliest, and most infamous brunettes—to be sure, no longer pretty enough to promenade successfully on the new levee, but pretty enough to make a private boardinghouse a great success. At this time the "Hamburg Mill" was still simply "Private Boardinghouse, Mrs. V*," and, at the beginning, it adhered strictly to the norms and expectations of such a place. She only varied from her sisters in the profession by having no daughter. It could never be determined quite why. This does not prevent us from mentioning the origins of the term *Hamburg Mill,* although we know that we are telling nothing new to a true child of New Orleans.

As is the case with all women from Hamburg, Mrs. V* often had the most baroque and original ideas, and when she threw all her good nature into a task she was without equal. So one evening—it was near the culmination of Mardi Gras—she served her boarders a brilliant supper, lacking nothing the palate of the most habituated glutton and gourmand could covet.

Before the guests were seated, Mrs. V* rang her bell three times and informed them: "You will already have noted, sirs, that there are napkins on your plates, and you will find them there every evening at supper from now on. Do not unfold them too quickly. Open the napkin carefully, so your neighbor cannot see, and be on the lookout for a bright red stripe found only on one of the napkins. Whoever has this stripe should follow the directions on the enclosed note precisely."

Three days passed before the secret was discovered, since only the fortunate ones who discovered a red stripe on their napkin could understand it.

It finally became common knowledge on the fourth day. When the bell rang for supper, they asked one another in a mysterious manner:

"Which of us will get the stripe this evening and go 'into the mill' with our lovely Hamburg lady?"

From this moment forward the private boardinghouse became known as the "Hamburg Mill," or, more correctly, "The Mill of the Woman from Hamburg."

This is what is found written in the annals of the old Hamburg Mill for the years 1838–42.

Then important changes befell this establishment, so that only three years later it would hardly have been recognized by its earlier habitués.

Mrs. V∗, the spritely, bold, much-tested courtesan and playmate, was stricken by the pox so dreadfully a week after Mardis Gras that when she showed herself among her guests they could only offer her the courtesy demanded by decency. When a nun's face is consumed by pox, it is of little importance, since pockmarks are not a hindrance for one who wishes to commune with cherubim and seraphim. But when the face of a feminine roué is disfigured by any sort of illness, such as smallpox, she has no choice but to devote the rest of her life to a solid, decent profession. For what beauty clothes cannot likewise be veiled with ugliness. Even though the *beautiful* Mrs. V∗ loved to be a little loose and frivolous—from her own point of view—her situation now that she was *marred by the pocks* would not have been enviable if she had tried to continue to depend on male generosity. Mrs. V∗ knew what she had to do, for she was a woman of spirit, which is the same as saying she was from Hamburg.

She left the Hamburg Mill, in which she had so often celebrated the nocturnal rites of Venus, gathered a half-dozen of the greenest, juiciest girls, and renamed herself Boncoeur the milliner.

Since she thought her extraordinary reputation made it impossible to find a place among the noblesse of her craft, she took her regiment of girls, who could all wield a mean needle, to that stretch of streets in the shadow of the *negresse* Parasina Abigail Brulard's residence.

But since her newly established millinery shop did not exactly flourish, despite its seductive shingle proclaiming *Boncoeur* (which means "a good heart"), she took away the notice for "Milliner and Dressmaker" and nailed up a simple board advertising "Ironing and Washing" in its place. That worked. After two weeks she was able to put the old shingle in place, a witness to greater prosperity.

But let us return to the Hamburg Mill.

If the Hamburg Mill under the aegis of Mrs. V∗, alias Boncoeur, was merely an innocently disreputable nest that never harmed anyone but itself, it became a hell of the most shameful vice and crime under her successor, the free *zambo negresse Héloise Merlina Dufresne.** Arsonists, murder-

*A zambo Negro is the offspring of a Negro and a female mulatto. A *zambo negresse* is the *non plus ultra,* a ragingly insatiable sensual being. Owing to the crossing of the colored blood, one can call a *zambo negresse* "man-crazy" with emphasis. The other shadings vary in sensuality according to the following sequence: *zambo,* resulting from the impregnation of an Indian woman by a Negro; *mulatto,* the child of a white man and a Negro woman; *dark mulatto,* the child of a Negro and a mestiza; *mestizo,* the child of a white and an Indian woman (also possible with a colored quinteroon—otherwise a pale mestizo); *chino,* the child of an Indian and a Negro woman; *copperchino,* through colored inheri-

ers, and thieves drank here together with the most debased creations of the colored race, from whose female portion Merlina drew most of her income. That son of civilization, the white man, stood dark and silent at the bar, just released from the deadly embrace of a *chino zambo.* He drank to forget what boiling sensuality had not allowed him to forget only moments before. Other than one free Negro from New England, Merlina did not tolerate black men in the mill. She did this partly out of consideration for the Caucasians, but also—and this was the main reason—to avoid the conflicts of heated bestiality that would otherwise have arisen.

Like most *zambo negresses,* Merlina had a short waist and a long lower torso. On the other hand, she was tall, and her round head displayed a tiger's forehead, bobbing and weaving on her short, full neck. She wore her lightly kinked hair wrapped cunningly around her head against its natural wave, and in the evening she would drape it in a white turban, leaving her dark, cinnamon face bare to the temples, enclosed in a white frame.

Her ordinary clothing consisted of a waistless dress reaching all the way to the floor, the opening of which allowed a glimpse of the first crease of her breasts. A dress so loose was the special privilege of a *zambo negresse,* given as they are to nonchalance.

Merlina, by the way, was no longer young, although she was only sixteen. For women of this type flourish between their seventh and eleventh years. A *zambo negresse* is already wilting by the age of eighteen, and her glistening white teeth have already begun to acquire that dark blue sheen that is the certain signal of a loss of freshness. Merlina was *already* sixteen! This age fills a white man with horror, and he sinks into depressed complaining and dawdling. Place a *zambo negresse* of eight alongside a Pompadour or Du Barry,[14] and you will see the difference. Make a *zambo* girl cry and you will learn what tears are. Make her laugh and you will have to concede that you have never before seen what laughter is. Stimulate her jealousy and you will have to confess that the woman falls into the same category with tigers and panthers, even exceeding them in some cases. Drink with a *zambo* and you will glimpse the god Bacchus in all his majesty and glory. Have her put a dagger in your hand, and you will act

---

tance on the male side; *quadroon,* the child of a white man and a female mulatto; *zambo chino,* the child of a Negro and a chino woman; *pale chino zambo,* unnatural coloration of the dominant shade; Creole (in its colored variety), the child of a white man and a mestiza; *black mulatto,* the child of a Negro and a quinteroon; *dark chino,* produced by the impregnation of a mulatto woman by an Indian of good race; *dark zamba,* the child of a mulatto woman and a zamba; *chino chola,* child of an Indian and a chino; and *pale chino zambo chola,* a colored creation with a dreadful confusion of species (a pitiful race).

better than Garrick and Iffland.[15] Have her cut your nails, and you will discover the magnetic fluid of the universe at its very source. Merlina was *already* sixteen! And you, paleface, are *merely* thirty or forty! It is a secret of chemistry which neither Liebig nor Boussinggault can explain.[16] Their knowledge of molecules is of no avail here.

The Hamburg Mill had received an organization under Merlina's command that was utterly different from earlier times. The two oyster shops that had adjoined it before were now joined to the mill, which gained not only space but—what was more important from the point of view of this enterprise—also security. The one oyster shop, when combined with its rear buildings, consisting of a coffee room and the spacious bowling alley of an Italian man, Lombardi, covered the rear of the mill, providing it with a rear guard which protected a passage to the rear alley and could be very important in any encounter with the police. While the front elevation of the Hamburg Mill took up only thirty feet of the levee, the annexation of the oyster shops tripled its size. The deepening of the property dwarfed its earlier restrictiveness. Merlina spent a good thousand dollars melding these parcels together into a whole, and she paid another eight hundred for other improvements. After selling his oyster shop, the Italian Lombardi worked exclusively for Merlina. He turned a portion of the mill where the Hamburg lady's dining room had once been into what appeared to be a miserable fruit store. Besides the usual varieties of fruit, he sold the worst brands of cigars, clay pipes, chewing tobacco of the poorest quality, firecrackers, and the like, and he pumped soda and mead. On the right side of the fruit store were little stools, such as are normally found only in oyster stops of the third rank, those patronized by vagabonds and petty thieves. The door to the inner sanctum of the Hamburg Mill nightclub was hidden by a closet six feet high, crowned with fruit baskets, raisin boxes, and round bags of figs. In front of this closet was a counter topped with the pump for the soda and mead. The leaden pipes of the pump attested to the fact that the beverages being served to thirsty sailors and levee workers were half-poisoned owing to the underuse of the equipment. Lombardi's very negligence in managing his fruit store and soda fountain told any intelligent observer that the mill was not a legitimate enterprise.

Although he was only thirty-five, Lombardi was an utterly ruined man with dreadful habits, disgusting, oozing eyes, and an uncleanness without limit. He had been thrown into the state prison at Baton Rouge when he was only twenty. Although he had been sentenced to life imprisonment, he was pardoned by the governor after eight years. For two years he earned a dishonorable living in New Orleans and its environs, until fortune led him to an immigrants' ship, where he came to know a German country girl whose parents had died at sea, leaving her a considerable sum in cash. Thanks to his minimal knowledge of German, he soon was so involved with the naive girl that she offered him all her money in exchange for a promise to marry, which is how he obtained the oyster shop that he later sold to Merlina. After he had maintained the poor girl with mere promises for a full year, giving her barely enough to eat, she suddenly died—he said it was climate fever. Those who knew him better thought otherwise. But since there was no proof, everyone had to hold their peace. Beyond that, Lombardi was so feared as a nasty character that no one was about to bring the matter into a public court. It was generally known that the ugly, filthy Italian was in touch with every rascal in town, despite his apparently hermitlike existence, and that because of his connections he had nothing to fear from mere suspicions and speculations. People who lived in the area and knew him held him to be the German girl's murderer.

The greatest crimes were imputed to him—even the captain of the guard once said to him on leaving the fruit store one day, "Look out, Lombardi, it is well known that this fruit store is not your only source of income—my people are watching!" And yet the Italian was utterly secure. "Keep your people off my neck, Captain," he had responded boldly, "If they were not so ready to crawl in here and drink my cognac, I would be concerned, Captain! Yes, just wait, you won't take this bird back to Baton Rouge in any cage—one or the other will help me!" he mumbled to himself after the captain had slammed the door in his face.

To the left of Lombardi's fruit store, on a piece of black tin affixed to the doorpost, were the uncertain words, "Furnish'd Rooms to Let." Below the tin sign was posted a strip of paper with a message in French. After the usual *Chambres garnies à louer* was appended *pour garçons.* This part of the building belonged to the Hamburg Mill. The privilege of overseeing the rentals had been bestowed on a person with a good reputation. The renters themselves, with a few exceptions, had no idea that they were under Merlina's roof and that the sword of Damocles hung perpetually above their heads.

The actual whereabouts of Merlina's cohorts and her satellite Lombardi were in the middle of the rented building and the fruit store, hidden in such a way that one had to be well acquainted with the place in order to have any notion of how to get there. The alley running to the Italian's old oyster shop only led to the mill's back rooms, from which one could access the remnant only by crossing the yard all the way to the fruit store's back door, lifting the cover to the double door by means of a switch, and thus going up into the salon of the Hamburg Mill itself.

On the right side of the salon, a carpet-covered door led to two smaller rooms, separated only by a light tapestry barrier hardly two feet high. Here slept the female employees of the *zambo negresse,* in rather decent beds with sulphur-yellow mosquito netting. In the middle of this dormitory was a simple enclosure in which the overseer of subordinate personnel had her bed. One could observe everything that went on here from the security of this enclosure. Merlina had commissioned a *pale chino zambo chola* as overseer: choosing someone with this combination of blood guaranteed the strictest control of order due to her complete absence of humane sympathies. If Merlina wanted to go to her own room, she had to pass through this dormitory, which was illuminated with a camphene light the whole night through.

On the left of the salon was a little chamber that opened to the right for the kitchen and wood bin, and, beyond that, diverged in another direction, ending in a door to a narrow, covered passageway leading to four larger rooms, numbered 97, 98, 99 and 100, each with their own lock. These rooms all would have provided a view of the levee if anyone had opened the shutters. This had not happened since Merlina moved in.

The mill's salon, which sat parallel to all the rooms mentioned, was the gathering place for Merlina's guests. The uninitiated were not permitted to enter here; before anyone could pass through the double door, in response to "Who's there?" he had to say the password, *Death or Merlina!* Then the person entering had to knock twice with his left knuckles on the back of his head and receive a small card from Merlina* These cards had a narrow red border that seemed to be an unbroken line but actually consisted of innumerable hearts, each barely a twentieth the size of the head of a pin. Right at the edge of this line, at each corner, was the initial letter of a code word. This card had to be returned when the guest departed. He could only keep the card if he was a member of the 99th or 100th degree. The walls of the salon were decorated with four mirrors, about eight feet tall, whose richly decorated gold frames were hung with black crepe, probably to keep their surfaces from being tarnished by the thick tobacco smoke.

*You will recall that in 1851, when a mob destroyed the Spaniards' cigar stores, cards of this description were discovered behind a smashed compositor's chest in the office of the Spanish newspaper *La Patria,* which had such a baleful role in the Cuba affair. These cards were thought to belong to a royalist club. They actually belonged to a compositor of the *Patria,* also an engraver, who was supplying Merlina through a go-between. [Ed.: This riot is described in the last book of Emil Klauprecht's novel, *Cincinnati* (1854–55); see the edition translated by Steven Rowan, edited by Don Heinrich Tolzmann (New York: Lang, 1996), 573.]

All around the room by the wall were little tables with matching comfortable easy chairs. In the middle was a great round table with a white marble top, usually only occupied when *domino à la poudre* was being played. Merlina had once participated when the establishment was reopened, but she now abstained from it because her presence often provoked coarse excesses. Everything remained quiet when a game of *domino à la poudre* was being played. The attention of the players was only likely to be disturbed occasionally by momentary noises.

That is how things were in the upper parts of the mill. Balls were not staged here. During Mardi Gras, Merlina had Lombardi's fruit store cleared, and she gave picnics and so-called cow-tails, to which everyone was admitted free. This hospitality was covered by doubling the price of the drinks. In the same way, the barroom Merlina opened a few months later, next to the fruit store, was open to all. This barroom was supposed to draw the public's eyes away from the real goings-on. She gave it over to an old Irishman, who put a young German man behind the bar and proceeded to neglect management day and night—for this unreformed child of St. Patrick sat drunk all day in his easy-chair, with his feet on a table, cursing and joking with the passersby or spitting at their backs to pass the time of day. When he was somewhat sober, he would go behind the bar, open the cash drawer, and count the money taken in. If the income seemed too small, he would cuss out the poor barkeeper, threatening to chase him out. When these gross accountings occurred too often, the mistreated barkeeper revenged himself by taking a few dollars from the old man on a regular basis. "That drunken swine," he thought to himself, "curses every time he checks, and he is never satisfied, even when he knows no more could have come in. I see no reason to be cussed out for nothing."

This barroom, together with the furnished rooms above it, was what was known as the Hamburg Mill to the uninitiated. This designation was correct only insofar as the barroom and the other rooms were *part* of the infamous Mill.

At about the same moment those in the little house on Washington Avenue were gathered lovingly and compassionately together holding their wake at the bed of the deceased Celestine, a man in his middle years sat at one of the small tables in the grand salon of the Hamburg Mill. Quietly and without showing any distress, this man had just finished bandaging a significant wound on his foot. Now he supported himself on the table with his left arm, propping his cheek on his palm. His face, framed by pitch-black hair, had been turned into a veritable marble bust by the glare of a camphene lamp, which set his skin against the darkness of his hair and beard, as well as his large, wide-open eyes. He had taken off his coat and vest, even untied and put aside his light cravat. His long but full neck, as well as his hairy chest, were just as pale as his face. He was starting to get up to light a cigar when he heard someone mounting the hidden staircase. He let the hand holding the cigar sink and called out in a shrill tone, "Who's there?"

"Death and Merlina!" replied an anxious voice, coming from a man of middling height who was entering the salon.

"Hell and the devil, Gabor! Death *or* Merlina! If you say it wrong once more, I'll break your neck!"

"Calm down, Lajos, I tell you, it will still do," the new arrival responded shyly.

"Calm, Gabor? One does not get disturbed by such a dog—I just tell you that so you will be prepared if Merlina continues to permit you to visit us."

"How so, Lajos? Did you tell her stories about me?"

"Shut up, Gabor!"

"Sure, sure, Lajos—give me the card."

"You don't need one."

"Why not, Lajos?"

"You'll see."

Gabor took a couple steps back and bowed almost to the floor.

Merlina, who always entered the salon to present the card after the password had been given, had made her appearance. Today, as always, she wore her long, waistless dress of blinding white, and she had combed her long, black, woolly hair straight back, set in the middle with a golden claw. Her solid, projecting forehead lay rumbling like that of an irked tiger-cat above her eyes, and she displayed what Lajos, in his demonic obsession, had called her "nice nasty stare." Agitation had colored her pure cinnamon skin dark violet, a change of coloration apparent on her forehead, her whole neck, and all the way down to her loose breasts. Her lurking eyes spat like a Roman candle, sending sparks and stars in every direction. Despite the animalistic formation of her face, this female *zambo negresse* could still be called beautiful. It is not just symmetry of members, or pure harmony of facial features, but also the violent bestiality of a predator which is beautiful—even if only animalistically beautiful, or devilishly beautiful! Even cold, emotionless Lajos's feet trembled when she settled on his lap to stroke his luxuriant forest of hair away from his face. Lajos was the only one whose wishes and orders she followed. She had become the custodian of his most secret thoughts. No plan was carried out without him, no crime set in motion—in short, he was the factotum of the Hamburg Mill. And how Merlina guarded herself in his presence! She may have sat on his lap, combed and stroked his hair, but at the least sign of flirtation, she sprang up and with one jump was out of the salon and shut up in her room. She knew that if Lajos ever won favors from her, he would leave her, and in doing so he would not hesitate to stick a dagger in the heart where he had sought comfort only moments before.

She turned to Gabor, speaking in French, bearing him down with her tiger-eyes.

"Sir, you will have no card today, for you have become redundant to the mill. We cannot trust you—you are ready enough to join every undertaking, but you are too cowardly to carry it out, and you abandon your friends when you should protect them or at least lend them a hand. Don't let us see you in the mill again, and beware of spying or betraying us."

"Gabor will not do that," Lajos joined in, "he knows I will kill him—Death or Merlina!"

At these words, Gabor trembled like an ash leaf.

Lajos approached nearer to him, turned up one leg of his trousers to the knee, and said sarcastically as he pulled back a bandage and displayed a large burn: "There, you dog, look! I got that from the fire on Julia Street because you ran away even before the fire hoses got there. Look here, dog! I had to fend for myself, and I could have died in the flames. 'Death or Merlina!' Do you know the motto? Do you understand its meaning? Merlina for valor and unshrinking action—and death? Death for the dogs who are unfaithful to their masters. Now, unfaithful dog, do you understand the motto now?"

"You cannot kill me, Lajos—such a poor man who doesn't even know where he will rest his head come evening—I will certainly follow your lead in the future and be a good little doggy," Gabor groveled and pleaded, wishing he were anywhere else but here.

"Out of the mill, dog!" Lajos thundered at him with a look that caused the shocked man to flee.

As Gabor hurtled down the stairs, he jostled past an old man coming up who seemed not to notice in his own haste.

Lajos's shrill voice sounded from the salon: "Who's there?"

"Death or Merlina!" the new arrival panted as he went to Merlina and Lajos, pressing Lajos's hand.

"Wasn't that Gabor running away? Did he have something pressing to do?"

"There was something he should have done," Lajos responded, "and the future will tell us whether we will ever have anything to do with him again."

"If he plays informant against us . . ." Merlina said, seating herself at the large round table with the marble top.

"How so?" the new arrival asked. "Did Gabor pull some sort of trick? I would hardly be surprised. I never really trusted the boy."

"He didn't pull any tricks," Lajos responded, "and that's why we've dumped him. But the dog did do me a bad turn."

"What did he do?" the other asked with concern.

"He abandoned me at a fire."

"So you set a fire for nothing?"

"No—Merlina has the money—but I got a bad leg out of this affair," Lajos responded.

"As you did that time before?" the other asked.

"You mean like that one half a year ago, when I took the fifteen thousand dollars from the woman with the big picture in her arms? Well, that was my fault then. That stupid old wound still hurts as much as the one I got today, especially when the weather changes."

"You're a true bad-luck bird, selected by heaven to pour out your blood for a sinful humanity, poor, poor lamb of God! But the Lord shall bestow grace on His children when the hour of accounting arrives, and you, Lajos, will earn at least the crown of the seraphim. Two burns, one on each leg, and a monstrous scar on your cheek—ha, ha, first-rate marks of Cain—Cain, Cain! Lajos, Lajos! 'Where is your brother Abel? The blood of thy smitten brother cries unto me for vengeance!' Ha, ha, ha!"

"Cain? Yes! As you like it—it doesn't really matter whether one kills a brother or a usurious Jew," Lajos responded in a tone of bitter coldness, lighting his cigar on one of the camphene lamps, lifting the cylinder with a sure hand.

"Smoking makes the head heavy and stimulates sin," the new arrival remarked.

"You are wrong, abbé—I think easier and quicker with a cigar in my mouth. On top of that, it is something you can put between the teeth to work off your rage when this dog of a world drives you mad and there are no human victims to be had. And if smoking stimulates one to sin, then please acquaint me with this sin, abbé. If it is a sin that pleases me, I will never again be without a cigar in my mouth, save while I am committing that sin."

"Now Lajos, you are already well practiced with this fine sin. By St. Anthony of Padua, what splendid sarcasm! Ha! Ha! Lajos, it is a shame that you cannot love!" the abbé proclaimed. By now my lady readers have surely already recognized Monsieur Dubreuil.

"Do you mean that, abbé?" Lajos asked harshly, as if it irritated him that the abbé would launch such a hypothesis in Merlina's presence.

"I wash my hands clean of the blood my disciple has spilled," Dubreuil responded in an arrogant tone to Lajos, who figured the abbé had beaten him this time.

"You are in good form today, abbé," Lajos commented to Dubreuil indifferently.

"I have no cause to be so today—everything is going wrong—Death or Merlina!"

"Death or Merlina," Merlina called out to the abbé as she leafed through a valise, appearing to do accounts.

The motto also found an echo with Lajos.

He then asked the abbé: "Did you suffer a setback with Mistress Evans's beautiful daughter?"

"There can be no setback yet, since I have not even tried my luck."

"If you are able to bring the girl down, Merlina will pay you . . ."

"How much?" the abbé interrupted, looking rakishly at Merlina.

"How much, abbé? What entitles you to ask how much? As for me, with what?"

"Well then, with what?"

"With nothing!" Merlina responded curtly, rising from her chair, "When sin has its own reward, it would be silly to give further rewards. But you seem to be avoiding your obligation, abbé—Death or Merlina!—what is your plan?"

"Lady Merlina—until now I have done what was within my powers. In a few weeks you will be able to claim the result for the Hamburg Mill fund," Dubreuil responded.

"You are certain that the old Scotswoman will grant you that much money following her daughter's death?"

"I am absolutely certain, Lady Merlina—you know that she long ago promised me the sum of fifty thousand dollars for the supposed construction of a Catholic church among the heathens of Africa, restrained only by the thought that she would be doing an injustice to her daughter, her only child. She told me that Mistress Dudley might accuse her after her death if her fortunes are not as fine as she would have liked. So I have developed a very clever plan: I will bring that mooncalf saint Mistress Dudley Evans to the confessional in the church on *Rue des Ramparts,* at a time when no one else is there. I will paint the joys awaiting her in heaven with such splendors that she will be utterly charmed and fall into my arms of her own accord. Oh, it will be an easy matter, believe me, Lady Merlina; believe me, Lajos!"

"I certainly envy your bringing the angel down, abbé, but the rest makes no sense," the Hungarian remarked. "But to the devil with it!" he cried out. "Even though you've brought the angel down, she is far from being dead, abbé. You'll not get away with a simpleminded allegory—where is 'Death or Merlina' in this matter?"

"I will not permit you to scold me, Lajos. Listen a bit more: Once I have brought the angel down—which is not strictly necessary, but I am of course doing it because I want to enjoy something a little better than oysters and turtle soup for once—as I said, once I have made the moonstruck lamb into a fallen angel, I will strangle her with little trouble."

"Hell and the devil, abbé," Lajos interrupted, "You are a greater Satan than I had thought you to be—but ask yourself whether this isn't a bad idea. What point is there for you, and in the end for the mill as well, that you have strangled the angel? Her mother knows that you went with her to the church—on whom will suspicion fall other than yourself? And if you should see the sacristan, the custodian, or some other person? A church is not such a secure place. What do you think of that, abbé Dubreuil?"

"You do me a great honor to place my bagatelle higher than Satan himself, and yet you do not have confidence that Satan can also get out of tight places. I tell you, Lajos, that you are a much greater Satan than I am. Otherwise you would not have commented so cunningly, since you certainly have an idea what has to be done to turn the tragedy of the House of Evans into a comedy for the Hamburg Mill."

"So tell me, get started and bring the matter to a conclusion—you can see, Lady Merlina and I are waiting in the greatest suspense," Lajos pressed.

Dubreuil continued: "As I said, I strangle her, leave her lying, and depart the church. When I do this, there is not a soul in the church—that will be between three and four o'clock. At about 4:30 a Negro comes into the church to clean it for the following Sunday. The Negro has hardly set foot in the church—I am of course biding my time in a place where no one can see me—and I enter right after the Negro. There is the Negro, the seduced and throttled Dudley Evans, and who other than the nigger could have done it? Or do you really believe that the slightest suspicion would ever fall on me? God forbid! Even if someone caught abbé Dubreuil committing the act, no one would believe it. Look, my Lady Merlina, look, my Satan Lajos—a priest has an advantage. The nigger will be lynched, of course—and even if he isn't, how could a nigger dare even open his mouth against such a pious man? You see, you see! Then the result and lesson of the whole fable: the unhappy mother will grant me all my wishes in her first moments of sorrow over the dead lamb. She will transfer fifty thousand dollars, she will make over her entire fortune to charitable foundations for building churches for the heathens and camels in the Sahara—oh, it will all turn out for the best—they will need a mess of masses as well."

"I shall be on your heels from this day on, abbé, so that when you've really finished her off, you will not be tempted to give the mill too little of the treasures you have harvested—abbé Dubreuil, you know the motto?"

"Death or Merlina!" he answered to the Hungarian's weighty question.

But to himself he said, "These louts are all ill at ease and distrusting. Oh well, I shall see."

Merlina's face, which had been covered with purple at Gabor's cowardice, had begun to recover its natural coloration, and she swung in lusty turns from the Hungarian's death's-head to the sickly pallor of the abbé. She lifted her long, waistless white dress to her thighs, as was her practice when she was in a good mood, jumping on Lajos and pressing her tiger's forehead like a bacchante on his naked, hairy chest.

The Hungarian at first took no heed of her, but a flame suddenly flashed in his eyes, only to vanish just as quickly behind his dark lashes.

"Death or Merlina?" Merlina called out questioningly, rubbing her forehead on the Hungarian's hairy chest.

"Death or Merlina!" he replied, blowing a thick cloud from his cigar down Merlina's back, so deep that it reappeared out the skirt of her dress. It looked for an instant as if she were floating on a cloud. A second, sharper puff made the illusion perfect.

"Semele and Jupiter!" the abbé called out as he rubbed his nose on his coat-sleeve.

"An unfortunate attempt to be witty, Dubreuil—you would have done better to say, 'The devil and his cat'—to hell with Jupiter and Ma'm'sell Semele—Death or Merlina!"

"Death or Merlina!" the abbé repeated, taking a respectable pose once more.

Merlina parted from the Hungarian and resumed her seat at the large round table. The golden claw that held her long, woolly hair in the middle had been pushed aside by her embrace with the Hungarian and threatened to fall off.

Lajos, who noticed this, approached Merlina and arranged her disturbed coiffeur, carefully placing the golden claw to run against the natural wave.

Then he sat down opposite Merlina in an armchair and said to the abbé: "What did you mean, Monsieur Dubreuil, when you said that everything was going wrong for you—did you try some other infamy elsewhere?"

"I will tell you right out, Lajos, if it pleases you and does not bore Lady Merlina—but first I want to collect laurels for my well-planned devilry concerning the moonstruck girl."

"Laurels, Dubreuil? Before you have earned them? If you had a less ugly nose, abbé, I would bite it off to compensate Lady Merlina for your premature pretensions."

"I would do even more, abbé, if you were not so old and ugly," Merlina declared, extending the tip of her tongue and showing both rows of her teeth.

Dubreuil remarked, "The laurels would have been earned already, as soon as I rejected your first plan. You see that my new plan is superior to poisoning, a method that always has unpleasant results. My own maneuver is also better than martyring the angel to death though fasts, penances, and hair shirts—saints of that sort are astonishingly tough."

"As tough as you are, abbé." the Hungarian said coldly. "If you committed any offence against your duties as a member of the mill, your toughness would not help you."

"Lajos, I do not deserve such distrust—I appeal to Lady Merlina's sense of justice," Dubreuil responded, drawing nearer to the round table.

"Monsieur Dubreuil, receive your card. You are henceforth a member of the 99th degree," Merlina said to the abbé as she presented him with the identification proper to his new rank.

Dubreuil now sat down in an armchair at the large table, a station that had never been allowed him in his earlier rank as a member of the 98th degree. Now he was even permitted to sit right next to the *zambo negresse* and look at her directly, should a friendly glance from Lady Merlina invite him to do so.

"You have not yet explained your reversal, Dubreuil. You certainly are in a strange mood today," the Hungarian remarked, sending a long cloud of smoke in the abbé's direction.

Smiling, he waved the cigar smoke from his eyes with his hands and turned his scrawny neck in Merlina's direction: "You have already heard something from the prince of Württemberg, Lady Merlina?"

"I have not only heard from him, I have seen him many times," she responded.

"Where and when did you have that pleasure?" abbé Dubreuil asked with a bold gaze, inspecting the *zambo negresse* carefully.

She did not notice the ambiguous leer and seemed to be studying the copies in her valise.

"Where and when, Lady Merlina, if it is permitted to me to ask?" the abbé repeated with a somewhat less rude gaze.

"You are making rather too quick a use of your freedom as a member of the 99th degree," Merlina commented, drawing in her neck even more and looking down the loose opening of her dress.

"No more than you have permitted me, Lady Merlina," Dubreuil responded, looking at the Hungarian sitting silent and cold in a negligent pose in his armchair, puffing his cigar with long breaths.

"The prince of Württemberg?" Merlina declared in a questioning tone, as if she had only just thought of it and was dredging something out of her memory. "The German prince? Yes, I know him—on sight—when I worked at a coffee stand, I served him more than once. He came regularly at three in the morning to the French market—arrived in a hurry, downed two or three cups of chocolate, one after another, and rushed away as quickly as he had come."

"But how did you know who he was?" Dubreuil asked with an insistent tone.

It was really a marvel that Merlina was so patient as to comply with the abbé's curiosity.

That was not her usual way.

"How did I know the German prince, abbé? I only know him on sight—as I recall, I have only dealt with him personally once."

"Yes, but how?"

"Damned inquisitorial procedure—the priest can be identified in every word! The Jesuits have branded your very tongue," the Hungarian cried out with a cutting tone as he pulled his armchair away from the table and crossed his feet on the marble top.

"It is the abbé's right to be shameless," Merlina responded on Dubreuil's behalf.

"Merlina, you were premature with your club cards," the Hungarian remarked, turning a look of mockery at Abbé Dubreuil.

Dubreuil appeared little concerned by this intermezzo, for he continued in his searching tone: "Yes, but in what way, Lady Merlina?"

"Damned Jesuit!" the Hungarian interjected without excusing his manner in the least.

"Give the Jesuit his rights, Lajos, Tartuffe was a Jesuit, after all, and . . ."

"You do not offend me, abbé," the Hungarian interrupted Dubreuil, "but I will slap you if you dare to make improper comparisons."

"One crow does not peck out the other's eyes—wherever there is a millstone, then the miller and the miller's wife are not far away," the abbé responded dryly.

"Not always," Merlina interrupted, drawing her hand across her tiger's brow.

"Not always, Merlina?" the Hungarian asked, tossing his dead cigar butt between the abbé's legs.

"Not always, my millstone Lajos."

"Not always, my miller's wife," said the Hungarian, turning the allegory of Merlina around.

"So, about the German prince . . ." Dubreuil pressed.

Lajos stared at the abbé, but this time he said not a word.

Without waiting for a new petition from the abbé, Merlina replied, "I saw the German prince for the first time—and spoke to him—when I was still on the plantation near Derbigny and Breton. He stayed there for about a week, walking the whole day in the swamps with an old Negro, looking for snakes and bullfrogs."

"Aha!" the abbé declaimed.

"Aha? Why aha, huh?" the Hungarian asked.

"Well, well—I just mean that, ha!" the abbé said in jest.

"Don't be so mysterious, Dubreuil—no one believes you," the Hungarian remarked, then turning to Merlina, he asked: "Does the prince eat snakes and bullfrogs?"

"He probably does eat them," Merlina responded. "We often ate them on the plantation."

"The bullfrogs I can believe, but the snakes?" the Hungarian asked.

"The snakes especially!" Merlina answered.

"But of the snakes, you let the green snakes in particular go?"

"Particularly not *them,*" Merlina responded, "they are the best of all—with a dozen green snakes under your belt, you could drive ideas out of the devil's head."

"How so, Merlina?" the abbé asked out of curiosity.

"If the devil wants to embrace a female panther and sees that she has eaten green snakes, he runs away to hide in his hole in hell."

"Then the devil is a big idiot, with more than a damned close resemblance to an angel," the Hungarian said.

"Lajos, what would you do if you knew I had green snakes in my body, if you sensed devilishness rising in yourself?"

"For a panthress?" the Hungarian responded, clapping his teeth together.

"Sure, what else?" Merlina responded.

"If I felt a bit of the devil . . ."

"A bit of love . . ." the abbé supplied a word for the Hungarian.

"Dubreuil, be quiet or you will get a slap—now, if I felt a bit of the devil coming on, and I knew or you told me you had green snakes in your body, I would make the beast dance, Merlina."

"Infamous!" the abbé proclaimed.

"My Lajos, you're bigger than the devil!" Merlina shouted, drunk with high spirit. She rushed to the Hungarian, who defended himself with his hands, dropping his feet from the table and standing in order to fetch a fresh cigar from his coat pocket.

Merlina returned to her place, murmuring and purring, scratching her woolly hair in all directions.

This appeared to irritate the abbé. He was perfectly happy to see Satan playing with the tiger-cat, as she opened his cold lips to warm life with her burning tongue. In this way Dubreuil was like an old bawd who likes to watch a couple making love. We have already seen him at Parasina Brulard's, where he had the same command that appeared to belong to the Hungarian in the mill. One can understand how Parasina could be interested in the wretched little body of the preacher only by contemplating the peculiarities and strange whims of female sexuality from a darker side.

Today the woman is everything, and tomorrow she will be nothing. The sexual relationship forces her to take the veil, and the same relationship drives her into the arms of the goddess Libido. Black or white—it is all the same!

"Lady Merlina," Dubreuil grasped the line of conversation once more and moved closer to the *zambo negresse,* "then you came to know the German prince in this way?"

The Hungarian had returned to the place where he had been sitting when he had finished bandaging his burn.

"Not precisely in this manner," Merlina responded after a rather long pause. "Before he left our plantation, he came to me—perhaps it was simply by chance—and asked me whether I knew of congo snakes. I said yes, and he promised me a good reward if I could catch one before our next meeting and keep it for him."

"Aha!" Dubreuil responded.

"You have no idea what sort of animal that is, abbé," Lajos remarked.

"The congo snake is the most poisonous beast in Louisiana, it is wider than it is long and has two fleshy things on its belly which almost look like feet," Merlina declared.

"And you were supposed to catch and keep this ugly, poisonous beast for the prince, Lady Merlina?" Dubreuil asked once more. He glanced at the Hungarian, who was staring at Merlina's shadow on the wall.

"Yes!" the *zambo negresse* responded.

The Hungarian had finally completed his study of the shadow; he stood up and slouched back down in the chair at the round table.

"Now abbé," he began, "it is high time you bring your 'reversal' to an end for Lady Merlina and me. We have wandered completely away from our original subject due to your silly curiosity and fruitless chatter. Put an end to your interconnections and leave the rest to idle talk."

"Oh well," Dubreuil tossed off languidly, and then he began.

"A vile episode happened to me this evening. So vile that even a novelist could use it to some effect. I have to go back at least thirty-five years if I am to develop this nonsense suitably. Oh well! I will make it quick, so I can be free of my tormenters as quickly as possible. It is known to you as well as the entire mill that Mistress Evans is entirely under my holy slippers, despite her tremendous wealth. The fact that my influence is so great that she permits herself to be locked up like a nun along with her daughter is almost too odd to be believable. I have forbidden them on pain of the most dreadful pains of hell to receive any male other than the prince of Württemberg. The reason for this should be obvious to anyone in the mill. I have also ordered the strictest *clausura* for Miss Dudley, pious as a lamb, and I have promised the sweetest reward that heaven provides. I have even demanded that she break completely with her female friends. She has done it, and she will follow my commands in the future . . ."

"Until she has been throttled, and her blood has been transformed into gold for us," the Hungarian interrupted the abbé for an instant.

Dubreuil continued, "Mother and daughter are so unbelievably blind that it would take a trained oculist to break their stare. I can do what I want with them. They dance the way I whistle. When I weep with emotion over their sins, they cry along with me. If I say to Miss Dudley, 'Miss, the Lord wishes that you make a general confession, for your sins cry unto heaven,' the dumb little goose really thinks she has sins, and she throws her naked knees on crude wooden steps and calls on God's mercy, for the intercession of the Mother of God and all the saints from A to Z—and all of this for nothing and less than nothing. The little goose is that stupid! The mother, of course, is not much better—but her torments of soul are not as interesting, having spent her better years having babies. Ha, ha! This playing angel and manipulating longing for the Savior and his boob of a foster-father, the carpenter Joseph—it is inconceivable to me how people can still be so dumb and allow themselves to be ruled by us priests. Ha, ha, the stupid people will never shake off this pious bunch of feelings and superstitions. Oh well, we priests do quite well in exploiting this stupidity—where there are sheep, there must be a shepherd! And if there is a God in heaven, He cannot begrudge us priests any more than the devil is upset with us, whom we have so splendidly, magnificently represented."

"You're getting disgusting, abbé, with your eternal preaching tone," the Hungarian remarked. "Even if all you priests are atheists, the old filth still clings to your tonsure. Get to the heart of the matter!"

Now Dubreuil recounted that he happened to pass through Live Oak Square, and he saw the prince helping a young girl from a cab and talking for a while at the window of an old tenement. Since he suspected there was an adventure afoot, he passed by the building several times after the prince and the girl had entered and threw several glances into the poor chamber within. When he saw the count, he had to conclude that the count's family, of which the prince had spoken positively, lived there. A second quick glance through the window revealed to him the beautiful girl of whom Mistress Evans had often spoken. Finally he saw the prince settle in so intimately with this family that his limitless curiosity caused him to knock on the door and enter.

Then Dubreuil told of the corybantic fit of the unhappy Celestine, hiding nothing of his earlier shameful deeds from them. A sprinkle of sarcasm and ironic comments managed to spice up the dreadful crimes of this monster in priest's clothing, and soon Lajos and then Merlina were rapt with marvel.

"You have made little progress since you seduced that angel and bankrupted her mind, abbé—you must have been barely out of diapers—really fabulous, very mythological. That is better than the tale of Hercules, who strangled snakes while still in his cradle," Lajos declared to Abbé Dubreuil, in cutting sentences, now that the latter's narrative was at an end.

"Well," he responded, turning his mouth into a repellent smile, "I was only twenty-two then—not very young for us Creoles."

"I envy your great knowledge, abbé. Being a papal attaché at twenty-two is always enviable," the Hungarian remarked in a tone that left open whether it was irony or admiration.

"You must have come down in the world, Monsieur Dubreuil, not to have gone any further than preacher in a chapel and father confessor to an old woman," Merlina commented.

"It was owing to Father Rothaan's work that my advancement was held up," Dubreuil responded.[17]

"What sort of being is Father Rothaan?" Merlina asked languidly.

"That is the general of the Jesuits, Lady Merlina."

"Did he fear the little giant?" Lajos added in mockery.

"In matters of the petticoat, yes," Dubreuil declared weightily.

"The petticoat?" the Hungarian repeated.

"What else? The general spat poison and flames when he discovered I had seduced his mistress," Dubreuil answered.

"You're a dreadful person, abbé. What foolishness, seducing the mistress of the Jesuit general!" the Hungarian declaimed, with a touch of fun.

"Isn't that so?" the abbé intoned.

"You are always dealing with mistresses, abbé."

"Excuse me," Dubreuil countered, "think of Miss Dudley Evans."

"She's a mistress, too, abbé—heaven with all its angels and saints make use of her . . ." the Hungarian said.

"Splendid, Lajos! You outstrip Rabelais and Aristophanes!" the abbé proclaimed.

"So that justifies you in your lament, 'Everything went wrong'—that you recognized the madwoman to be a seduced former parishioner?" Merlina returned to the old theme.

"Well, yes. I had wanted to make a new acquaintance and refresh an old one," Dubreuil responded.

"Now you will leave that alone," Merlina said.

"Yes, I now find myself in a very uncomfortable situation. The prince, who had always held me to be a very pious and respectable man, will now have an entirely different attitude toward the life and work of Abbé Dubreuil," the Creole remarked with gentle irony.

One could see that the abbé had previously believed that the prince had respected him and held him to be a man of honor. He did not have the slightest notion that the prince was pursuing him, and that he had only visited the house of Mistress Evans to confirm the truth of a letter he had received ten months before from a friend in Texas. The letter said:

> Dear friend,
>
> I have learned by accident that the Creole Abbé Dominique Dubreuil resides in New Orleans, and that he has already acquired a considerable reputation as a preacher. If this is the same scoundrel who was active a few years ago under the name "Gonzales," and who precipitated so many families into misfortune, I beseech you to use all your powers to thwart the plans of this dreadful priest, who gains entry into a family circle, where he is most respected and sought after. I draw special attention to the pretentions which this scoundrel has as a father confessor for young girls. In Mexico he

committed the greatest acts of shame under this cover. Be careful of yourself, for this snake is capable of any deed. Many greetings from my family. If your researches in nature bring you back to our vicinity, do not hesitate to do us the honor of a visit.

Respectfully,
J. S.

San Antonio, 21 May 18—

"Washing yourself white is no magic," the Hungarian remarked. "You are so inventive in every other matter, abbé, and yet you see problems here?"

"What good is it to present the matter differently once distrust has descended on the prince?"

"You had a brother, abbé—he looked precisely like you—and thirty-two years have passed since then, as you admitted yourself."

"Aha!" Dubreuil cried out.

"At last your 'aha!' has a reason," the Hungarian responded.

This discourse was interrupted by the appearance of a man, whose torso was already emerging from the secret entry into what we know as the actual center of the Hamburg Mill, the salon.

Merlina turned about and called, "Who's there?"

"Death or Merlina," the new arrival responded, adding, "When New Orleans sleeps, the mill is awake—the members of the 99th and 100th degree bring death and destruction."

Dubreuil, a member of the 99th degree, answered, "From the north comes smoke, and no one is alone in his tent."

"Howl gate, scream city! All of Philistia cowers! The waters of Dimon are filled with blood—in the night cometh destruction over Ar in Moab, it is gone!" said Lajos, the member of the 100th degree.

The man who had just arrived stood and shook hands with Lajos and Dubreuil.

Merlina stood from her easy chair and spoke, raising both arms in the air: "This is the burden of Damascus. Behold, Damascus, there will no longer be a city, but only a tumbled pile of stones!"

These words were exchanged as often as one of Merlina's gang advanced to the 99th degree.

Lajos, despite having spoken his lines in a solemn tone, thought to himself: "Such nonsense is used for the most prosaic undertakings. If anyone overheard us, he would marvel at the dreadful curses binding the members and what sort of majesty and dignity they conjure up. You will have to console yourself, Prophet Isaiah, that your verses have found a refuge in the mouths of the arsonists of the Hamburg Mill."

Dubreuil probably thought the same. But no one dared reveal his contempt to the others.

Lajos, with his cold, deadly skepticism, a murderer and robber by habit; *Dubreuil,* the posthumous son of Sodom and Gomorrah; *Lombardi* (for he was the one who had just entered), who hid the heart of a hyena and the poison of a rattler behind his disgusting cynicism—all three of them lied to one another about their exclusive dedication to the mill, although they clung together and punctually gathered as members of the 99th and 100th degree. Lombardi thought he had influence over Lajos, as Lajos did over Dubreuil, and yet the priest's slyness dominated both of them. If Lajos often treated the abbé in a casual and disrespectful manner, he committed the error of not seeing why the abbé permitted this, and why he submitted to this protectorate. The same was the case with Lombardi. Without suspecting it, he had stepped behind Lajos, and, though he was the Pontifex Maximus of the mill, he had become the obedient servant of both the Hungarian and Merlina.

So despite their rivalry and self-deception, these men had entered into a close fraternity, and for all too long they had been disposing of the lives and properties of the residents of New Orleans with horrifying energy.

Lombardi, the filthy, slimy one, who had been exploited by Merlina from the outset of her new arrangement, had ceased to be the soul of the mill since the Hungarian had joined. But since he was irreplaceable for many things, Lajos was smart enough not to make him feel that he had a secondary role.

Dubreuil saw right through the Hungarian's prudent attitude toward the former Pontifex Maximus of the Hamburg Mill, and, in doing so, he understood the tendencies of both with utter clarity.

Lombardi's appearance at this moment leads us to a more detailed description of his personality.

There is a particular sort of traveling merchant in the larger towns of Italy, particularly in Florence and the States of the Church, who might put in at an inn for the night and decide to take a perfectly innocent promenade when the stars are blazing, freed from the burdens of their travel and jostle for sales. These merchants, nursed at the breasts of song-girls and raised in brothels, are called *gli pipi* in courtesans' jargon, one of those coterie terms that the Italians mint by the thousands and are to be found in no dictionary. Such expressions eventually get citizenship and become stereotypes of the locality where they originated. The *pipi* appear to fall in the category of *lazeroni,* though they always have money despite their filthy and dubious appearance. A *lazerone* will hate *pipi* and will often even persecute them with the greatest bitterness. They know perfectly well that *pipi* always have money in their stocking and that they only wander about with such freedom because they enjoy the privileges of a *lazarone.* Despite the freebooting they themselves do when they are abroad, they feel themselves to be secure. Hardly a week passes without one of the *pipi* being pulled dead from the sewers, and the police know perfectly well why they have to search for the culprit among the *lazaroni.* These *pipi* took over the positions once held by court jesters at some of the earlier Italian courts, and they have precipitated the most astonishing scandals.* They usually soon depart from the place of their activity and earning and then play the great men in provincial towns. In place of their earlier cynicism comes elegance and fashionable clothing, so far as the treasure they have gathered permits. Lombardi was such a *pipo* in his homeland. From his fourteenth to his nineteenth year, he had loyally followed this way of life, but then, tirelessly pursued by *lazeroni,* he decided to leave Italy. After only half a year in New Orleans, a serious misdeed on his part sent him to Baton Rouge with a sentence for life. We have already mentioned his pardon from the governor, as well as his partnership in the Hamburg Mill.

Lombardi, who was a bit over thirty-five years of age, was less than average height. His originally compact physique had developed tremendous muscular power, which even the dubious life of a *pipo* could not weaken, but his continuous excesses in all sorts of debauchery managed to give him that paunchy, yellowed appearance that elicits no admiration and fills any healthy, strong man with contempt and disgust. Such persons are perfectly at peace with being half-corpses, yet they also seek to revenge themselves on nature by sapping any signs of vitality and turning other people's cup of life into a drink of poison. The Italian's back displayed tabes dorsalis, and whoever looked into his dripping eyes was shocked at their lack of human spirit. Those eyes—well—those eyes! If a person describes them, he is risking sullying his own hand by using the pen to do it.

*One has only to think of the two *pipi* from Sinigaglia who took the present Emperor of the French, Louis Napoleon, along with them to New York, and who, because they had not been treated with respect, wove that shameful plot of revenge against a brothel which nearly landed Bonaparte in the Tombs. [Ed.: "The Tombs" is the popular name for the municipal holdover prison of New York City.]

Whoever ate fruit from Lombardi's fruit store or was able to drink its mead and soda was either a superficial observer of human distress or a hungry, thirsty nigger. The Italian's sole foot cover consisted of a pair of sandals that he had fished out of the road, half-flattened from being trod on and which he had not removed from his feet for several months. He had not done this out of miserliness but simply because he had a peculiar hostility toward any sort of fresh new object touching him. For that reason, he also wore the same coarse red undershirt summer and winter, over which he never put any white shirt. He took it off only to turn the greasy, dirty side to the inside, until the addition of more dirt made it necessary to repeat the maneuver. He had not been able to tolerate smoking for a long time, and, since he routinely vomited when he tried, he restricted himself to taking snuff and chewing. The latter had so much become his habit that he did not even cease it in his sleep. On top of that, he loved keeping the brown juice of chewing tobacco in the corner of his mouth, letting it run down into his black chin whiskers. Whoever came by his fruit store and saw the man early in the morning could lose his appetite for the whole day. Such were the charms of Lombardi the fruitmonger.

The Hungarian, the abbé, and Merlina pulled their armchairs several feet away from him as he sat down among them.

Lombardi, who always thought this was a sign of the respect they harbored for him, made no attempt to approach them; he was accustomed to the situation and appeared quite satisfied with it.

He declined a cigar the Hungarian courteously offered to him, since—as he said—he had completely given up smoking.

"Lombardi, now you don't smoke at all, and yet you did it with a passion before?" the abbé asked.

"Smoking just costs money—it is otherwise of no use," the Italian responded, pushing a chunk of chewing tobacco to the other side of his mouth with his tongue.

"You are right, Lombardi," the abbé declared, "the money one pays out for cigars could be spent for something better, and it is injurious to the health—it lodges in the chest if one does not watch out."

"And stimulates one to sin, abbé," the Hungarian said with irony.

"That too," Dubreuil responded, "but the chest is more important."

The Hungarian pulled his shirt even further back from his naked chest, pounding it two strong blows with his fists, and said, "Look, abbé, how smoking attacks the chest!"

"There is no rule without an exception," he answered.

"Two exceptions out of four!" Merlina cried out, opening the top of her dress to the side. "I smoke too!" Then she asked for one of the cigars the Hungarian had offered and proceeded to puff away.

"You certainly have made this a holiday, Lombardi—I wanted to bring you some notices—but I couldn't find you in your fruit store the entire day." the Hungarian said, turning to the Italian.

"I was nailed to the posts at the Metairie Race Course," he answered.

"To the devil with the Metairie Race Course and the whole of Metairie Ridge," the Hungarian responded, "if a person wants to waste his time, he can always go there. Horse racing doesn't interest me anymore—I prefer to see men racing."

"You have to prefer animals when there are no people to be seen," the Italian said, pressing his index finger to the right corner of his mouth.

"Was there a big purse?" the Hungarian asked indifferently.

"The first race drew little, the second took two thousand dollars—two-mile heats!" the Italian responded.

"Two-mile heats!" Lajos repeated, "the beasts must have sweated mightily!"

"And bled as well," Lombardi added, "the Jockey Club has sharp spurs."

"Only children need spurs," the Hungarian remarked. "Thighs are what tell a horse to fly."

"Yes, if they have thighs like you Hungarians," the abbé contributed.

"No—if one has been an officer of hussars," Lajos intoned, taking the stance of a rider without difficulty.

"One cannot find an officer of hussars in the current Jockey Club—they prefer horse-traders," the Italian responded as he bit into a new piece of chewing tobacco, having spit the previous piece into a red and blue checkered handkerchief.

"What were the beasts' names?" the Hungarian asked.

"Atalia Taylor, Mary Bourbonet, Conrad the Corsair, and Lydia Prairiefire," the Italian answered.

As Lombardi recited the racehorses' names, the Hungarian's pupils seemed to enlarge and seek a focus on the opposite wall. He drew his cigar halfway into his mouth and bit into it.

He seemed to brood over it.

"Which was the most successful among these beasts?" he asked, without letting on that this question was motivated by more than simple curiosity.

"Lydia Prairiefire—rider's dress, red, white, and green," the Italian answered, adding the colors like a professional.

"Red, white, and green!" the Hungarian repeated. "Fortune has brought together the Hungarian national colors—a malicious coincidence if it is a

Hungarian horse.* Then we would have to seek the *fines regni* on Metairie Ridge.†

"Those are our colors, too," the Italian protested.

"In more recent times, to be sure," the Hungarian said, "the difference is only in how they are put together."

"That's quite possible," the Italian remarked, not having noticed the ambiguous meaning of the words.

"And who was the winner?" Lajos asked in a drawn-out tone, as if he were not much interested in the response.

"So far as I know, Lydia Prairiefire, who belongs to Mister Cleveland, a farmer from Illinois," Lombardi the Italian answered.

"Has he been here a long time?" the Hungarian asked—with bated breath, holding his hand in front of his face and coughing.

"Well, as I heard—several weeks. The fellow is, by the way, a big humbugger and knows how to make himself interesting."

"How so?" the Hungarian commented.

"He claims to have been assaulted once and lain for three days in the middle of the prairie. The prairie had been set ablaze, and the flames had passed over him, but without touching his body in the slightest." Large drops of sweat formed on the Hungarian, running over his face down to his hairy chest. He threw his head back on the back of the chair and stared at the ceiling with a ghastly look.

Lombardi and Merlina looked at him in amazement.

The abbé moved his armchair away from the table, as if he was afraid.

The Hungarian spread his arms wide, as if he were trying to ward off something. Then he seemed to return to himself, calling out in fearful mockery: "Thunder and lightning—if that ruined carrion is back on his feet, it is not certain whether I am a dead man myself." And without pressing for any further description from the Italian, he sprang from his armchair and shouted like a madman: *"While New Orleans sleeps, the Mill is awake—the members of the 99th and 100th degree bring death and destruction!"*

Then he turned to the Italian and said: "Lombardi, let's go into number

*This is a reference to a paragraph in the *Vorpœezy Tripartitum.*

†The arsonist is playing on article 2, paragraph 5 of the *corpus Juris Hungariæ,* which speaks of the famous *juramentum,* the oath of the king: *Fines regni nostri Hungariæ et quæ ad illud quanque juro et titulo pertinet, non abalienabimus nec minuemus, etc.* [Ed.: We shall neither alienate nor diminish the limits of our kingdom of Hungary nor whatever pertains to its rights and titles.]

100—the abbé may accompany us." Then he turned his distorted face to the *zambo negresse* and whispered, "Merlina, my panther, I shall see you tonight."

She stared at the Hungarian.

"Death or Merlina!" Merlina's triumvirate thundered as they rushed to the club room.

At the same instant, a man of very dark coloration left his post on the outside of the salon door and slipped into the wood bin that adjoined the clubrooms in various directions. Once the club members had closed the door behind themselves, he left his hiding place as carefully as before, went to the double dormitory where, as we know, a pale *chino zambo chola* was in control, and knocked at Merlina's room.

"Be careful, Sulla!" someone said to him, "the Hungarian would kill you if he saw you."

Chapter 8

Clubmen of the 99th and 100th Degree

> Behold! You richest and most esteemed of your citizens tremble before me, great city! They hold the highest offices and compete in great dignity for the favor of the people, and yet they are scoundrels as great as we are—for they shake our hands in friendship in the darkness—and on the street they do not even know us. Thus Don Luis, *el gran desperado,* sends down his anathema on you, o great city!
>
> [Old Spanish Drama]

Le Sage's limping devil understood the rare art of lifting the roofs from houses,[18] revealing things to his favorites that gave them more experience and wisdom in a matter of minutes than Doctor Faustus and his guide learned through deep contemplation on the Logos and the homunculus. The limping devil then flew from Paris to the Pyrenees. After he had washed his sinful member clean once more in the baths there, he flew to Gibraltar. From there, expelled by the English, he swept over the pillars of Hercules and landed on the highest peak of the Atlas. Then he tapped the tops of the palms of Bileduldgerib and sank to his knees in Liberia. There he fell in love with a beautiful daughter of *Nigritia,* to whom he made proposals. After having courted her for several weeks and not advanced an inch beyond his starting point, he turned to the slave sale as a means to reach his goal more easily. When he was told that no black human flesh was being offered for sale, he became so weary of Liberia that he quickly flew away, not stopping until he had reached the Southwest Pass and cleared his throat and sneezed at the sight of New Orleans.

The limping devil no longer gave a damn about his former beloved in Liberia, since he now had plenty in New Orleans. It also gave him great pleasure to teach moral philosophy, since in this way he raised both roofs and petticoats. He did so once at the Hamburg Mill, where he encountered the wildcat Merlina.

Although all the clubrooms of the Hamburg Mill were locked, the Pontifex Maximus, the Italian Lombardi, had received the prerogative, unlike all the other clubmen, to enter any one of them to check their contents.

The rooms marked with the numbers 97 and 98 were occupied by subordinate members, who had the same rights as members of the higher grades but a reduced claim on profits. These subordinates received more a stipend than a solid portion of the booty. Whoever stood out in prowess by performing various crimes would advance to the next higher number. We have already seen, with Dominique Dubreuil, the sort of ordeal one had to survive to win this sort of advantageous advancement. The clubmen of the 97th and 98th degree were the tools and obedient servants of the mill, and they were as necessary to it as wheels to a wagon. They were placed in the most difficult positions and told to carry out the boldest of deeds. Their pasts were enclosed, as if by a more or less imposing frame whose gilding became progressively worn and soiled by their time in service, until they were fit for nothing but being tossed into storage. While trappers are recruited from the most loathed of human society, notorious criminals, convicts, and the like, in contrast, the clubmen of the mill were able to mingle with the great, and they were all the more dangerous because they were able to harvest the greatest respect from their fellow citizens because of their apparent prosperity and respectability.

The clubrooms of the 97th and 98th degree were rather spacious, with simple but comfortable furnishings.

Here members awaited the commands of the 99th and 100th degree as they discussed ways and means of carrying out their crimes.

We shall soon see what these consisted of.

If there was nothing to do, or if an enterprise was too perilous, they simply drank the whole night through and drowned their fantasies in the embrace of the pale mestizas or wild zambas.

That was the tax by which these subordinate clubmen's income was siphoned to Merlina's advantage.

Merlina, who visited this part of the club seldom or never, still kept it under the strictest control.

This was easy for her to do, since Lajos had given direction and spirit to the Italian's management through his touch of genius.

But let us return to the chamber of the 99th and 100th degree, whither Lombardi, Lajos, and Dubreuil have rushed from the mill's salon.

These club chambers, despite having separate doors outside, were divided only by a light curtain, which could be moved to make entrance and exit from one of the chambers an easy matter.

The Spaniard Viala had left the tapestry curtains to the pretty lady from Hamburg, who had used them for many a maneuver in her bedroom.

On her departure from the mill, Mrs. V*, later known as the laundress Boncoeur, had left the curtains behind, and they fell into the hands of the clubmen, who were smart enough to use them at this precise place.

It was now after eleven o'clock.

Abbé Dubreuil and Lombardi, who could not understand the Hungarian's strange conduct, followed his commands mechanically. If the Italian had never before understood that he was being dominated by the Hungarian's coarse character, he could sense it now, since Lajos revealed his full force without stint on this night.

The news that the peddler from Illinois, with whom he had taken his tour through the tall grass of Looking-Glass Prairie about a year before, was not dead after all had worked such a transformation on Lajos's usually deceptive treatment of the filthy Italian that he threw off his usual care like so much irritating ballast. For the first time he revealed himself to the Italian as a dictator.

He did not consider the risks—he *desired,* and that was enough.

The abbé coughed for a good spell, while Lajos leafed through the Book of the Mill several times, then shut it in distress.

"Lombardi!" he interrupted the silence, looking at the Italian with a gaze cold as marble.

"You are acting strangely, Lajos—" Lombardi responded, reaching for the book.

"Lombardi!" the Hungarian called out once again, "I am sick and tired of treating you courteously, as you have grown accustomed to being treated by me. You can shriek and howl like a hungry wolf—but I shall command and you shall obey!"

"Obey whom?" the Italian asked, browbeaten and uncertain how he should act in response to such conduct from the Hungarian.

"The Pontifex Maximus of the Hamburg Mill!" Lajos intoned with a sharp accent.

"Then I would have to obey myself," the Italian said in confusion, sensing the tremendous force the Hungarian was unleashing on him.

The abbé continued to cough, appearing neutral in this conflict.

"You obey and I shall command! You, the abbé, and all of you in the mill! What are you cheats and sneaks, thieves and arsonists compared to Lajos, clubman of the 100th degree, who must arm himself against the asp that has poisoned our very air? Which of you has ever raised a dead man? Which of you has gone into competition with a corpse? Which of you would not have fainted when you heard that someone you had murdered was racing for a purse? Which of you has ever seen a corpse riding a horse, and who has seen a drowned, charred horse win a prize? You marvel at me, Lombardi? You saw that silly ass Cleveland but not the peddler's corpse! Don't look at me with so much pity, Lombardi. Don't you understand me? I left Mr. Cleveland from Illinois lying dead in the middle of a prairie fire a year ago, and now he comes here and joins his mare with the racehorses."

The abbé unbuttoned his cravat and rocked his chair on its legs.

"That's amazing enough," he said.

"I will obey," Lombardi responded, adding quietly, "if it is true that the dead have returned."

"Lombardi! Even if that wasn't true, I will command, period!"

"Well, then I'll obey," the Italian said in utter confusion.

"And when you are ready, I will take your gun," the abbé remarked, still skeptical about the resurrection story.

"A gun is too good for you, abbé—rosaries for nooses, those are the weapons of a priest!"

This sudden transformation of the Hungarian passed just as quickly as the dissatisfaction, the amazement, and the pure disgust broke against his stubborn, cold heart. The roaring hurricane had to give way to stillness, and the vessel that had been pitched back and forth, whose pilot had wanted to command the winds, once more rode over the yawning grave of the ocean, that implacable strangler. Once the stillness came, no star illuminated the night; only lightning bugs whirred about the mast and sails, decorating the majestic, eternal darkness without illuminating it. These lightning bugs had stirred a corpse back to life once upon a time, and they had set him on the path that would lead him to his ruin.

The Hungarian had not been overcome by fear when he listened to Lombardi telling his fatal story—the large, cold drops of sweat that rose on his forehead and breast were not the offsprings of an anxious spirit, and his haunted eyes did not look away because his inner voice had told him that the dead would have their revenge. No—he already sensed that he had to get the peddler and Lydia out of his way before he could leave New Orleans untouched.

Deadly peril caused him to boil with a desire to hunt, leading him to gnash his teeth like a predator until he forced his rage down under his bloodthirsty tongue with the instinct of a hyena.

The Hungarian took up the great Book of the Mill once more, turning the pages with a calm and certain hand to the notes he sought.

This book, called *The Club Book of the Hamburg Mill,* was approximately in the format of a ledger, with a heavy binding trimmed and clasped in silver. It was dark red, with the notorious motto "Death or Merlina!" printed in every important place, in full, dark letters. The notes of the book, together with the entire narrative, were composed in French and made incomprehensible in spots through a special jargon used in the club, further degenerating in places to impenetrable hieroglyphs that only the sphinx Merlina or the clubmen of the 99th and 100th degree could explain.

The short, stubby key that opened the lock of this book normally hung on a red silk cord shot with black, which was wound about the book in a threefold tie and bound with a special knot after the settlement of business. The noose created by this knot resembled the initials of the Lady Merlina.

Opening and closing this book demanded no small talent.

Until this time, Lombardi had had first access to the book, and he had always handled it in a manner that did not please the Hungarian at all.

As Lajos grasped the book, paying no attention to the prerogative of the former Pontifex Maximus, Dubreuil shot a sideways glance at the Italian, whose momentary subordination he had noted, even sensing a similar reticence in himself. He could still not explain how and when such conduct could be peacefully justified when conflict broke out among the very directors of the mill.

Lombardi was shocked.

The abbé no less.

Lombardi perhaps quietly hoped for Merlina, and the abbé constructed strategies of defense, coordinating them with what he had already seen.

Dubreuil could see only too well that the strange episode with Cleveland the peddler had only been the occasion for the Hungarian's declaration of independence, and that Lajos had long been harboring the desire to free himself from the irritating restrictions of some of the club's norms. He wanted to enjoy the advantages without paying any attention to the duties connected with them.

"Death or Merlina!" the Hungarian cried, taking up the Book of the Mill.

"Death or Merlina!" Dubreuil and Lombardi responded at the same instant.

Lajos began: "A balance of five hundred dollars is due from the St. Charles Hotel—if the rascals do not pay up tomorrow, take the usual measures. Dubreuil, take that to Mr. A*, of the 97th degree."

The abbé departed his present club chamber in an instant to fulfill his duty in room 97.

A pair of pale *mestizas* who rustled past him as the door to 97 was opened delayed his return longer than usual.

"In the future, the arson money will be collected before the fire is set."

"Good," said Lombardi and Dubreuil.

"Here is the application, letters A. F. H. P.—he wishes to have his two houses on Tchoupitoulas Street, which are in poor condition but heavily insured, burned down. For its services he is paying the mill twenty-five hundred dollars—further, we can claim from him the sum of a thousand dollars for that house in Algiers that belongs to the broker. We do not know why that is to be burned down."

"Good," Lombardi and Dubreuil responded.

"Received from Julia Street, first payment six hundred dollars, second payment fifteen hundred dollars, then third the balance of nine hundred dollars due.

"Received from Camp Street, seventeen hundred dollars for entry and theft, letter Z.

"Received $575 from St. Louis for a local trading house—the commissioner will pay double."

"The percentages are included," Lombardi remarked.

"Naturally," the Hungarian said, "we will proceed as usual. For the Christmas term, seven hundred dollars from the cotton press—the agent pays nine hundred dollars to the company."

"It is better to reduce his take by two hundred—the scoundrel can't be trusted."

"Keep it as it is—if Gabor doesn't meddle in an improper manner, nothing is to be feared."

"It's impossible to know," remarked the abbé.

"If anything is missing, we can make the cotton press pay a second time and drive them into a corner with threat of a suit."

"Yes, they will have to give in," Lombardi agreed.

"Here's a little job . . . the lumberyard office in Magazine Street is to be broken into and the large iron money chest broken open—Mill gets forty dollars."

"The rascal is an infamous cheapskate, he could pay double. We will skip it unless he pays at least eighty," Lombardi interjected.

"And the money the clubman finds there . . . ?" Dubreuil began, questioning sarcastically.

"Five hundred dollars are supposed to have been stolen, but it will not be in the box. The fellow at the lumberyard probably wants to cheat his partner with a fake robbery."

"Leave it be, then," Lombardi said, "forty is enough for a mere five hundred dollars."

Lajos now signed a slip with six corners, pressed a yellow seal on it, and handed it to Dubreuil with the words:

"Take this to Mr. A*, clubman of the 97th degree. He is supposed to collect half of the forty dollars the day before the break-in."

The abbé left chambers 99 and 100 and went to 97.

When he returned, he asked for a brief intermission.

The Hungarian conceded it. Lombardi nodded his approval as well.

"Mr. A*," the abbé began, "asked the clubmen of the 99th and 100th degree to pay special attention to him in the next distribution of tasks—he has heaps of debts and a wife with twelve living children."

"It is not our fault that he has so many brats. No one ordered him to bring such a regiment of weeds into the world," Lajos remarked.

Then he added: "Tell the clubman of the 97th degree that from now on he should not be indifferent to our lady's *zambo cholas* twice a week. Then his productivity would make us a profit rather than eat into his capital."

"Only five *zambo cholas* are left in the mill, and three of them are already in an interesting condition,"[19] the Italian Lombardi remarked. "It would be hard for him to win the same interest from the remaining two—but the clubman could favor that dark mulatto, Hyderilla, or Pharis and Elma."

"It is probably too early for Pharis—she is still suffering from her time with Parasina Brulard," Dubreuil responded.

"You still have the tongs, brushes, and chin-nails with you, abbé?" Lajos asked.

"For what purpose?" the abbé declared, "if we are concerned with raising a new generation at the mill?"

"Before you come to the mill tomorrow, go to Madame Brulard and fetch these tools—just so we can have an *argumentum ad hominem* with you once in a while," the Hungarian responded.

"Good!" the abbé said.

"Red Rubric—the empty warehouse on Religious Street is safest before twelve o'clock—one may enter from the alley into the annex. It will be most easily burned down if the carpenter's shop is done first——that would be today." The Hungarian gazed at his watch and turned to Dubreuil: "Which clubman has it?"

The Hungarian had barely posed this question to the abbé when they heard the pounding of the fire bell, which sounded all the louder in their ears because the wind propelled the full tones to the windows of the mill. At the same instant the night watch shouted out loud their "Fire! Fire!" and sounded their rattles. The rattle and jingle of the engines, mingled with the cries and tumult of the firemen told of great peril.

"The clubman is punctual," the Hungarian interrupted the momentary silence, "'tis just five minutes before twelve o'clock."

"Religious Street—right?" Dubreuil asked.

"That's to be expected, abbé—if you haven't just drifted off to sleep," the Hungarian said in a malicious tone. "One can see that you are still a neophyte in the 99th and 100th degree. I expect more precise orientation from now on!"

"Good!" the abbé said, coughing harshly and pinching his thin lips.

Lajos now opened the mill book at the beginning, marked a number of places with red ink, and read the general balance after taking a precise review.

"Money paid in: the mill's gross for the half-year, $75,000; carried over, $16,000; transferred to the clubmen's fund, $14,300; remaining to the mill, $45,000—of which $25,000 goes for the grant in Texas—leaves a net sum in cash of $20,000 for the mill."

"This half-year is pretty thin," Lombardi groaned, who was hard put to endure the orders of the usurper.

"The Scotswoman will fatten our thin goose again," the abbé remarked, but he suppressed a smirk of triumph.

"We'll see," the Italian said.

"*Cuban Matters,*" Lajos continued: "Gabor's report of the 25th—two thousand dollars received from the Spanish ambassador . . ."

"For what?" asked the abbé, who had not learned everything as a clubman of the 98th degree.

"It's good you reminded me of that, abbé, it is our responsibility to tell you about everything you did not need to know when you were still in the lower ranks."

"Very nice of you," the abbé responded, "I am proud of all this attention."

Lajos responded, "Gabor received that sum from Washington on the pretext that he had been initiated into the secrets of the invasion of Cuba."

"That lout makes money with his genius at swindling—but let's drop him, he's fired."

"Extremely unwise," the Italian grumbled into his greasy beard, which had just received a plug of chewing tobacco.

"The *Pampero* left New Orleans on the second of August, with General Lopez on board.[20] The Royalist junta offered a very noble reward if we could agree to place two clubmen aboard as spies. They were to report to Governor-General Concha as soon as they landed. Just so that their lives would not be at risk in some disastrous landing by the filibusters, each was to carry a gold cross on their breasts with a portrait of Queen Isabella.[21] They would be able to prove they were good royalists with this sign—it is the sign of the Royalist junta of New Orleans and its branches in Louisiana. They were also to carry their club cards with them."

"Quite good," Lombardi and Dubreuil remarked, almost at the same instant.

"I believe we are choosing Campo and the Dutchman from Galveston."

"Agreed!"

"Both of them are trained blacklegs—they're the best there is," the Hungarian intoned.

Now Lajos closed the book and wove the key around it.

"Death or Merlina!" he called out. Lombardi and Dubreuil repeated the motto.

The clubmen were distracted by a second fire alarm. They clearly heard a watchman in the street, who called to another: "Over at Parasina Brulard's—the fire broke out at the laundress's, Boncoeur."

When Dubreuil heard this, he began to get up to leave.

"Abbé," the Hungarian called to him in a commanding voice, "you are forgetting your rank!"

Dubreuil sat down at his place again, disgruntled.

The Hungarian's arrogance irritated the Italian even more than before. But he said nothing.

"Then go," Lajos said to the abbé, having made him aware of his plenitude of power by holding him back for a moment.

Perhaps Lajos wanted to test the abbé's patience.

As the abbé left the club chamber and passed through the grand salon of the mill in order to take the passageway down, a long shadow followed on his heels, vanishing only when the abbé left the lighted area.

He rushed toward the place that was burning.

Once Dubreuil had left the chamber, Lajos turned to the Italian with a calm and sure voice: "Admit something, Lombardi."

"What, then?"

"The priest," Lajos continued, "is a scoundrel—what do you say to that?"

"I think so too—he is perhaps as big of one as I and you."

"You should say, 'as you and I,'" the Hungarian responded.

"Nonsense!" the Italian said.

"A matter of indifference!" the Hungarian retorted, "You should be glad that I took the dictatorship away from you."

"If I had cared about it, your attempt to take it would have been in vain. I let it happen in order not to cause an abrupt break among the clubmen—by the way, I am quite happy that no one did me any significant harm."

"Lombardi, did you think it a great injury when I took away your office of Pontifex Maximus—or did you give it to me voluntarily?"

"Yes—but it was an injury I am always able to make good."

"I have no idea how you would be in the position to do this—or are you spinning some sort of plan?"

"I know what you are trying to say, Lajos—but you're dead wrong—that would injure me as well," the Italian interrupted the Hungarian.

"You are really to be feared, Lombardi—you are so capable of reading the innermost thoughts of your fellow man—I envy you that advantage."

Lombardi fell silent, appearing irritated.

"Look, Lombardi," the Hungarian continued, "I was forced to take command here."

"Who compelled you?—Certainly not I," the Italian responded, forming his mouth into a forced smile.

"The situation compelled me to do something I would never have done otherwise, or only with great reluctance. It is the situation of the mill: its income is dropping day by day, and its payments are rising—the two watch officers are demanding all of twelve hundred dollars more for their silence and occasional assistance."

"I know," Lombardi responded. "The rascals are starting to make extreme demands of us. If it continues like this, we will hardly have enough next half-year to cover living expenses."

"Your needs are easy to satisfy, Lombardi, but I have five times the obligations."

"I don't understand."

"Yes indeed. First of all, I have to take care of myself, and that is always the most important thing—you concede that, don't you, Lombardi?"

"And secondly?"

"The mill."

"You don't have to concern yourself with the mill. If nothing comes in, it gets nothing."

"Quite correct," the Hungarian remarked, "but that isn't the way a good clubman talks!"

"Thirdly for your wife, isn't that right?" the Italian asked.

"Yes, for my blonde cat Frida," Lajos answered, almost smiling.

"Fourthly?"

"Fourthly, for my sister-in-law, Jenny the green widow."

It was part of the Hungarian's commonness that he named these persons by their first names in such a locale. By doing this, he put them in the same category with the Lady Merlina's courtesans.

"Fifthly," he continued, "for my child."

"A new offspring of the House of the Counts of Est . . . ?"

The Italian did not pronounce the name, for the Hungarian's glance caused him to hold his tongue. Then the Hungarian spoke: "I forbid you, Lombardi, to give my family name again—think what you will of it—but the tobacco chew in your mouth shall not soil it."

The Italian grimaced, flaring his nostrils.

The Hungarian added, "The watch officers are not to receive that twelve hundred dollars extra—they are to be satisfied with the two thousand dollars they receive already."

"Such a thing is not advisable, the scoundrels are possessed of the devil," Lombardi responded.

"Even if every hair on their bodies is a devil, they shall not receive any more! That Spanish ruffian will drop his demand to five hundred if I press him hard. The other watch officer knows why he should keep his mouth shut. I once helped him drown his mistress's child in the canal—and since he has a wife and three children, he, too, would stay in service with us for five hundred. On top of that, the beast drinks like a broom-maker, and his crummy salary as a watchman does not cover the half of it."

"Hm! hm! If that's so—on my account, if you could make an arrangement to the mill's advantage, we will be satisfied," the Italian responded with a thoughtful shrug of the shoulders.

"Now on another matter," the Hungarian said. "Do you happen to know where the peddler Cleveland is staying, and where his mare is?"

"I rode into town with him after the races—he sat on his racehorse and chattered away. The Irishman who keeps the grogshop outside accompanied us part of the way, then he left us, as he said, to pull the wool over the eyes of some damn'd Yankee, since he had been cheated while purchasing some land."

"Beside the point, Lombardi—I'm asking you whether you know where Cleveland is living and in which stall he is keeping his animal?"

"I have no idea where he's living, but his animal is fed and curried right there where I keep my own."

"I have no idea where you keep yours."

"In Oliver Dubois's boarding place."

"That's the livery stable across from the Liverpool and London Insurance Company on St. Charles Street?"

"The very same," the Italian responded.

The Hungarian thought for a moment, then he asked Lombardi: "Do you know the animal precisely?"

"Of course. One always pays attention to a racehorse, particularly when it has won a prize."

"But have you studied it closely? There are marks that are common to many horses, and it's easy to make a mistake."

"The most certain marking that Lydia Prairiefire has is that her left ear is an inch shorter than the right."

"Quite correct," the Hungarian remarked, adding, "and she has a divided mane, half combed to the left, half to the right."

"And the nostrils are filled with mucus, with a healthy overgrowth."

"Quite correct."

"A mare like that will not permit herself to be mounted by any stud."

"Horse doctor!" the Hungarian jested, "Lydia Prairiefire will soon be treated by you."

"I am no veterinarian, Lajos—I cure them with my elbows."

The Italian made a certain movement.

The Hungarian stepped on his foot.

"All right, horse doctor, this time you will try your art on Lydia Prairie-fire. May Aesculapius and his hosts protect you!"

"I told you before that I cure mares with my elbow—if it comes to that, I can settle our peddler's miss with a powder. I've got nothing against that."

"Lombardi, where did you learn to prepare this powder?"

"The horse-trainer of Count Quaglio taught me this in Florence—I was barely a youth, all of ten, and I already understood as well as anyone how to treat dogs and horses. There were three horses belonging to Count Farnese, three sisters—splendid, fine Isabelles. The assistant trainer only had to put the reins in my hands and show me their belly-bands—and there was the little imp Lombardi behind them whipping away. Old Farnese once found a pill in my cap and scolded me for it. I, a true *pipo,* gave him a gallant reply, so gallant indeed, that he winked and gave the little Lombardi a tip. The *lazaroni* would have tried to beat me to death if they had heard that."

"You would be perfectly ready to pass the whole night informing me of the high points of your youth," the Hungarian interrupted the Italian, whose memories of early years caused him to shake off the filth acquired in the gutters of New Orleans, if even for a few moments. Even Lombardi the *pipo* was a fine fellow after all when compared to Lombardi the fruit merchant.

Since we fear that those of our lovely lady readers who are not devotees of horseflesh or passionate riders will have no interest in this jockey talk, we will omit what followed, all the more so since the delicate passion for horses threatened to degenerate into the poetry of grooms in the mouths of these two clubmen. So don't pelt me with gauntlets, ye amazons of New Orleans! The falcon was blind.

The grudge the former hussar harbored for the mare of Cleveland the peddler was entirely in keeping with his character. A man such as Lajos, who loved horses much more than people, had to turn the full measure of his wrath against any horse that had done him a bad turn or had failed to submit to his command. He would have been perfectly ready to sacrifice his best friend for a good horse. Although he would have been happy to have put Lydia out of his way himself, he decided not to, for reasons known only to him. Instead, he gave Lombardi instructions. He also wanted the death of the peddler at any price, for he understood that the man would be very dangerous to him one day if allowed to live.

Before the clubmen separated for the night, they summoned three more members of the 98th degree and ordered them not to let Gabor out of their sight, to note his every move, and to report everything faithfully to the college of those of the 99th and 100th degree.

The reward for thorough compliance would be a payment of no small amount. In the same way, they were also instructed to keep a watchful eye on the prince of Württemberg, a dangerous opponent of Abbé Dubreuil, a clubman of the 99th degree.

Lajos took on himself the task of keeping tabs on the abbé. The abbé's plans to murder Miss Dudley Evans had raised his distrust and signaled him not to trust the priest's word. His plan for murder seemed too gross even for such a degenerate Jesuit, and Lajos would have been happier if the priest had taken a less perilous path.

Chapter 9

Under the Bed

Suddenly the canebreak rustles; with a roar
The lion springs. What a steed! Did a finer mount
Ever languish in the stables of a royal palace
Than the pelt of the racer the King of Beasts now mounts?

He strikes his teeth into the muscles of the neck
The dark mane waves about the great horse's stern.
With the choked cry of pain it jumps and flies in torment.
Look how swiftly a camel joins with the hide of the leopard.
["Löwenritt"]

When we allowed the Negro family to disappear so utterly from the view of our esteemed lady readers, it was only to prevent too rapid an unravelling of the knot so carefully tied by that mysterious man during his time in the upper chambers of the Atchafalaya Bank. Here we will only remark that Sulla was prevented from carrying out the robbery he had planned together with his adopted daughter and that he left his supposed wife and adopted daughter after many trials and tribulations, finally finding a sure refuge only in the Hamburg Mill. Here we cannot assert with any certainty how he came here, but it is likely that Lajos met him in one of the many Negro cafés and brought him here as a useful tool. We have already noted that

Sulla was the only black man in the mill, but we believe it is important to stress the fact that he was the only one would have significance.

His duties in the mill were of various sorts, but they were so arranged that he was able to do what he wanted for half the day. Since the clubmen who did not actually spend the night in the mill only began arriving in the evening, the Negro normally only had to stand behind the bar in the grand salon near the door leading to the two dormitories from seven o'clock until ten or twelve o'clock. One should not assume that the bar of the Hamburg Mill's salon was an ordinary one, where one doggedly sat or crowded about until one threw down his dime or picayune and then departed—no, the bar of the mill consisted of a complex of T⁎ chairs and loveseats, in whose midst a display of the rarest and finest wines, arrak, and so on, arose. The center of this cascade was the black barkeeper himself, who distributed his blessings from there. When Lajos was in the mill, Lady Merlina herself ordered two dark mulattos to serve him his favorite drink, true Tokay.* On such evenings, the run-down Lombardi would knock back several quarts of peppermint brandy, which still rarely lifted him out of his malicious cynicism into the higher spheres. After he had had enough, he usually collapsed, quiet and dumb, to be hauled off to bed by some of the girls of the mill, holding his head and feet. Whenever the abbé was present, he would sing disgusting vaudevilles and allow himself to be moved to give a sermon on the Seven Deadly Sins for the instruction of all.

When Merlina had had a few glasses of the Hungarian's Tokay, she was no longer recognizable. Her pulse raged, and the fire in her eyes seemed to singe her lashes and widen the hollows in which they sat. Her long, white dress grew too tight for her about the shoulders and bosom, and it peeled back to cling to her short waist. Then she seemed like a dark wolf, bedazzled by a rapid series of northern lights. When she was in such a rapture, she would reach for the Hungarian's black hair, turning it in curls and placing her golden claw on his head. He simply sat next to her, cold and pale, smiling only when she kissed the scar on his cheek. No one ever saw him drunk: in fact, with every new glass he seemed to chill and petrify more.

* It is well known that Merlina Dufresne got her wines directly from French ships and that her champagne was not just sparkling Franconian and her Bordeaux not faked with Brazil wood. Her varietal wines, such as Port, Madeira, and the like, were from pure sources. But once the Hungarian surprised her with the first bottle of Tokay, she put all the others aside. One can only speculate how much money the Hungarian paid to get this noble drink, since true Tokay is drunk only in the Viennese Hofburg. What is sold in Austria and Hungary under the name *Tokay* is nothing but a more or less fine example of "Ruster Ausbruch" [Ed.: rotgut].

His eye only fixed now and then on the Negro Sulla, who often stole glances at Merlina. Sulla, who had developed a raging passion for Merlina, had sought to dampen the heated elements in his being through superhuman efforts, and he believed he had succeeded well enough to look Merlina in the face without betraying himself in the least.

Merlina was certainly aware of Sulla's passion, but instead of trying to reduce it she seemed to do her best to stoke it. She loved only the Hungarian, with a depth almost beyond explaining to a white person. Still, it gave her great pleasure to attract Sulla and then repel him, to appear to consent to what she punished him for a minute later. In fact, she often went so far as to order him to bring her something at night as she lay in bed, where she lounged half-dressed. When the Negro came, making the greatest effort to open the door as softly as possible, she would draw a pistol from under her pillow and threaten to gun him down if he did not withdraw immediately. At first Sulla did not know how to interpret the conduct of his esteemed mistress. And yet he fell into the trap a second and a third time, every time withdrawing as terrified and hopeless as before.

Today he hoped and feared in equal measures.

Sulla could hardly wait for the clubmen of the 99th and 100th degree to depart. Once they had withdrawn into their club chamber, he slipped quickly through the salon and through the dormitory to the door of Lady Merlina's first room. When he opened the door, Merlina quietly called to him: "Look out, Sulla! The Hungarian would kill him if he saw you."

This time Sulla did not withdraw.

He walked boldly in.

Merlina left her room and rushed to the overseer in the bedroom, telling her to keep a sharp watch for when the clubmen left. She was to warn Merlina with three knocks on the door. She then closed the outer doors leading from the salon to the bedroom and from there went into her own apartment.

Whoever thinks this strange should recall the words that the Hungarian had whispered to Merlina when he left the salon together with Lombardi and Dubreuil.

The clubmen usually left their chamber around one o'clock, and it was only a few minutes after eleven when Sulla entered Merlina's room.

"Merlina, you are not frightening me this time, even with a pistol in your hand," the Negro responded to his mistress's warning, barring the door behind him.

Merlina gave no protest, and she did not make the slightest hostile movement.

She removed the golden claw from her coiffure, sticking it in a fat velvet pincushion. Then she loosened her long, woolly hair, allowing it to fall halfway down her broad forehead.

The room in which Sulla now found himself with Merlina, besides containing two chaises longues of red velvet covered by sparkling white covers, was furnished with a so-called master bed, with tall legs as thick as an arm and a wide, elaborate base. The bed's columns were of the finest, most refined construction, each ending in a broad snake's head, whose eyes constituted the rings through which the frame for the mosquito-netting passed. About the top of this master bed ran marvelous decorations in the form of figures and leafwork such as was once encountered in the swan beds of the Incas. A long, green silk rope descending from the top to the bed level served as a bell-pull. This was one of Merlina's inventions, and she had already driven several clubmen half-mad or left them half-dead with it. For when the nervous clubman believed his luck was at last assured, and that he was about to dip his burning member into the dark moistness of the zambo—without penalty!—Merlina would suddenly rise on high, cross her legs like a Chinese figurine, and yank on that fateful rope. The aroused Tantalus was always utterly unprepared for that maneuver, and he had no time for complaint or lamentation.

But woe to the clubman who dared to protest or to tell anyone about the trickery of lady Merlina after departing the site of his torment. She would have revenged herself terribly. She would not have threatened him with a dagger or a pistol, no—in her arms he would have suffered the dreadful torment of having the whole organism destroyed and burned away before he was ready. A dreadful death indeed, when love shoots its arrows at the wrong target! A terrible torment when they are shot before love's light wing can cool the burning cheek and glowing lips. Then, instead of the lovable cherubs of the wedding night, furies dance in the temple of Venus, and, in the place of cascading locks of hair, the snaky head of Medusa adorns the pillow of love, turning it into a deadly geyser.

It would have been a lovely night—lovely, because the fire-bell had ushered in the nocturnal celebrations of Venus.

The Negro placed himself sideways against the doorway, and, although he had already barred it, he even attempted to pull the chaise longue against it as well.

This maneuver did not hinder Merlina.

She let the Negro go on with what he was doing.

After he had brought the chaise longue against the door, he still did not seem satisfied.

He thought the best thing of all for his purposes would be the large, heavy washstand with a dark marble top that he had seen in the other room.

He pulled the chaise longue back from the door and pushed the washstand against it. When he had brought it up to the door, he sat on the marble top and for a long time looked at Merlina, who had watched quietly throughout all his exertions at barricading.

"Sulla, be careful! I will send a Hotooh after you," the *zambo negresse* cried at him, as she settled in a half-reclining position on the bed.*

"The Hotoohs should be glad I don't attack them," the Negro responded, his burning eyes fixed on Merlina.

"The Hotoohs have sharp knives and broad claws—don't come too near me, Sulla, or you will be out of the mill tomorrow."

The Negro set one foot on the carpet, the other was still raised.

The *zambo negresse* did not move, but she kept all the closer a watch on his every move.

The Negro did the same.

When he set the other foot on the floor, Merlina called out repeatedly: "Be careful, Sulla, or I'll put a bullet through your brain," she reached under her pillow, drew out a pistol, and directed the barrel at the Negro.

"Go ahead and shoot, Merlina, the bullet will just bounce off my hard head."

"If that's the way it is, Sulla, then I won't shoot," the *zambo negresse* responded, putting the weapon back in its place.

Sulla made a light movement and gradually let himself down from the marble top of the washstand.

Now he was standing erect. His arms hung down insecurely, but his hands reached inquiringly for the master bed on which Merlina sat, three steps away.

* *Hotooh* is a word of dread for all those colored people of New Orleans who are not actually members of this association. The grossest mistreatment and blows they have to endure from overseers and nigger-drivers do not frighten them as much as what happens when a Hotooh from New Orleans is set on them. In the same way, Negro women silence their children with the word *Hotooh,* in the same way that the threat of "Schwarze Peter" or, more recently, "Hecker," stills children in Germany. The secret association of the Hotoohs, composed for the most part of pale mestizos and colored quinteroons, originally had a less dangerous purpose. One often hears from their lips phrases such as *black nigger* and *yellow Creole pony,* and, in their circle, one will discover a disdain toward darker shadings. A colored aristocracy has arisen among them which is no worse than the aristocracy of birth or money when it comes to snobbishness.

"Stay where you are, Sulla—but if you reach me with your arms, I will take this needle."

"Merlina, I will not remain here, even if I go to hell," the aroused Sulla declared in a decisive tone.

"Look, Sulla—I only have this needle, but if you come near me, I will poke out your eyes."

"I will not remain here, Merlina," the Negro repeated, pulling his body back as if he feared to advance despite his declaration.

His attention was drawn by a soft knock on the outside of the door.

He looked behind himself.

Merlina left the bed and went up to Sulla. He moved involuntarily to one side.

"I'll be right back, Sulla," she said, opening the door.

The Negro grasped her hand, which was just turning the key, and stared in her eyes.

"I will be right back, Sulla," she repeated emphatically. "Sit down for a moment on that chaise longue. There are some cigars in that humidor."

"I don't want to smoke. But if you are tormenting me in vain once more—who was that who knocked? When will you return?"

"In a few minutes, Sulla, I did not remember this when I let you in."

"What didn't you think about?"

"For a moment I didn't think that anyone needed me at this hour."

"Why are you taking the key, Merlina? Leave it in—that would be better."

"No, Sulla, it is better for me to lock the door from outside—it is possible that the Hungarian will come while I'm gone, and if he found you here . . ."

"Yes, and what if he did find me here?"

"He would kill you, Sulla."

"I will kill him," the Negro responded with such a terrifying look that Merlina looked away from him and tried to rush out the door.

"Leave the key here, Merlina, I can bar the door myself. When you come back, you only need to knock—I will open at once."

"If you don't let me take the key, Sulla, I'm not coming back."

Sulla looked searchingly at the *zambo negresse,* and he tried to press a kiss on her forehead. But she put her fist against his mouth and said with furious scorn: "If you intend to be pressing, then you have no business being here!"

"Then shut me in, Merlina, but I beseech you to come back quickly," the Negro added.

Merlina drew the key from its hole and went out the door, which she then locked from outside by turning it twice and withdrawing it.

When Sulla saw that he was alone, he looked around and carefully inspected his locale for the first time.

As he looked at the door through which Merlina had departed, it seemed to him that someone was looking through the keyhole and then withdrawing, since a bright ray of light would shine in and then it would be entirely dark.

He paid closer attention, and he continued to see the alternation of light and darkness.

"Merlina is in front of the keyhole and is observing me," he thought to himself. He approached the door from the side and hung his handkerchief over the lock so that the keyhole was completely covered. Then he remained still for a few moments and looked around the room.

When he approached the bed, always with his face turned to the door, he noticed that the handkerchief had fallen from the lock. He went back, picked it up, and replaced it. He put his ear to the lock and thought he heard a soft breathing.

He listened with tense attention. Then his handkerchief fell a second time, this time onto his face, covering it completely rather than settling on the floor.

He took it off with irritation and looked through the keyhole.

An eye was looking in, but it vanished quickly.

He did not move. His eye remained glued to the keyhole. He saw nothing more, and when he turned back the light through the opening remained.

One will recall that the clubmen were still in their chamber at this hour and that they did not leave it until at least an hour after midnight.

Sulla went to the stand where the pincushion holding Merlina's golden claw lay, and he took it. Then he rushed to the door, hung his handkerchief over the lock for the third time, and secured it this time with the claw so that it could not fall.

Now he crept around the room and approached the bed. His curiosity drove him to lift the pillow. Under this, jammed against the bolster, he saw the pistol Merlina had pointed at him. Next to the pistol was a black dagger sheath with silver fittings. The dagger itself lay beside its sheath, the blade turned outward. When he tried to cover this with the pillow again, the movement of air caused a narrow strip of paper to drift through the air. He hastily grabbed at it. It had a few lines, which had been illegibly scrawled with cheap, pale blue ink:

I have not been pleased with the abbé's conduct for a long time. In the same way I find the presence of Lombardi to be irritating. The priest may very well get the Scotswoman's money through his trickery—but it is another question whether the mill shall have any of it. If Gabor does any more wrong, then the mill owes him its boot, for, since he is no better than a dog, he must be treated as one. I think it would be best to stop him right away, once he has the two thousand dollars from Washington. He will not be happy with his portion, and so it would be easy for him to leave us and do us harm in some manner. I will decide later what I will do with him once I get back from Mobile. Is Lombardi even needed any more? How long will he be? Above everything else, try to get ahold of Sulla's papers, for if he has no proof in hand that he is free, he will have no time to get new proof. It is not a matter of the five hundred dollars I can sell him for but simply in order to get him out of the mill. He will not revenge himself on us, since he will not know who stole his papers or who sold him. He will be sure to fall into the trap if we send him across the lake next week. Bartlett thinks he would easily be able to get $2500 for him.

Lajos

One can see that these lines had been written at a time before the Hungarian had dared to stage a coup d'état against the Pontifex Maximus. Likewise, Gabor had still been an active member of the gang.

The Negro stared in amazement at these lines, which told him just in time of a conspiracy against his freedom.* He put the bed in order with the greatest care and stuck his lucky find in his vest pocket.

When he had turned around and faced the door, he saw a flame at the lock; in an instant his handkerchief turned to ashes on the floor.

It appeared to him that someone was again looking through the keyhole.

Clothing is one of the characteristic signs of a person. One can accept with certainty that men who leave the lower portion of their vests unbuttoned are endowed with stormy sensuality, a quality promising women the greatest happiness. Men who routinely button the entire vest, not omitting a single button, are either too straightlaced or harbor fears about their belly or abdomen, an anxiety that women never forgive, even with the best substantial evidence. Congenital elegance leads many to wear nothing but black frock coats, which cannot be dispensed with even in dubious professions. A man who courts the lady of his heart with a white cravat and a

*Recall from the first volume that Sulla was from New England. The legal status of free blacks could be abused in the South. That was the case with a black man named Bacon from New Hampshire, who was sold to Alexandria on the Red River in 1851.

white piqué vest can be certain of victory, while a colored tie will repel and discourage even the most willing woman. Whoever wears a coat buttoned up is either a clergyman or a wholesale grocer, an organ player or a piano teacher of young ladies. Whoever wears a dark vest in the summer either has none of a lighter color or is a journalist or drama critic. Because of the absence of white piqué vests among these latter persons, the life of the salon is closed to them. No lady will consider permitting even the slightest liberty to such a dark-vested journalist or drama critic. In the same manner, any lady maintaining good tone will, with just dudgeon, show the door to any courting man wearing underpants in the summer.

This is particularly the case in New Orleans. In no town does the cream of chivalry count for more.

The Negro Sulla wore a black frock coat both summer and winter, with white cravat and a white piqué vest, displaying an elegance that he did not put aside at the bar. Why he still had no success would be hard to determine.

Sulla was feverishly agitated, and in his heart he cursed the hardness of his fate. Besides the distress that the letter was causing him, he understood that the strange episode with his handkerchief was not calculated to cool him down and slow the rush of his blood. He saw only too well that Merlina was leading him about on a fool's leash and making fun of him. He passed an hour in the greatest upset, without the *zambo negresse* making an appearance.

He sat down on the bed and stared at the door. After some consideration, he dropped his original decision to ask Merlina for an explanation of the note. He thought it was better to be silent on the matter for a while, in order to avoid too much premature conflict. Yes, even his dismay over such a shameful conspiracy could fade into the background of his overheated imagination.

Another hour passed, and Sulla still sat on the bed in most anxious expectation.

Finally his patience broke. He left the bed with a desperate glance and was about to rush to the door—then, with the footsteps upon the floorboards, he became aware of a person, and immediately Merlina opened the door and hurriedly asked him to hide himself because the Hungarian would be right there.

The request was so pressing and appeared so well meant that Sulla turned at once to find a suitable place to hide.

"Here, Sulla," Merlina pressed, pointing under the bed, "lie down quickly there, and I will pull down the blanket so he cannot see you—quick, quick, Sulla—I hear him coming now."

Sulla lay under the bed, and Merlina pulled the covers back and to the floor.

So Sulla seemed to be completely hidden.

After Lajos had escorted Lombardi, clubman of the 99th and 100th degree, to the opening in the floor of the salon, he had rushed to the two dormitories, recalling the words he had whispered to Merlina. He found the outer doors closed. The pale *chino zambo chola,* who let him knock at least six times, finally opened the door, saying she had been in a deep sleep.

"Is Lady Merlina in her room?" he quietly asked the guardian as he entered.

She answered affirmatively.

In fact, Merlina was rushing to her room even as the pale *chino zambo chola* was neglecting the Hungarian's command to open the outer door.

When Merlina had left the Negro, she had lingered a long time at the door, often looking through the keyhole, as he had been correct in observing. When Sulla had hung his handkerchief over the lock, she had taken a curved hair needle and pushed the handkerchief off. She repeated this a second time, and, when Sulla affixed it with her golden claw, she lit it with a match and burned it in an instant.

Was it mere curiosity that drove her to such conduct, or was there another reason?

Merlina's strange extravagances and baroque ideas about feeding on the anxieties and embarrassment of her victims were so innumerable, even when she was in a good mood, that one has to pause for a moment to pay attention to her every action and attitude.

During the two hours she left Sulla alone, she roused the girls of the mill for a night conference, awakening several of them for that purpose. There she specified the places some of them would take for the remainder of the night.

The dark mulatta Hyderilla was assigned to a clubman of the 98th degree, as were Pharis and Elma, who had already drifted off to sleep. They were ordered to comply with any of the clubman's desires.

The two girls did this very reluctantly, since they knew the clubman of the 98th degree to be a raw fellow who would subject them to the most brutal treatment without regard for their sex. Yet they had to obey.

As Hyderilla was leaving the dormitory together with Pharis and Elma, Merlina rushed to the beds of the pale mestizas.

These unhappy creatures were permitted to sleep the night away untouched.

As it was said in the mill, they were having "after night."

Some of them lay uncovered on their mattresses, tightly hugging their pillows in their arms—a pose that the world of dreams often bestows on these fallen angels.

The pale mestiza Semiramis, Merlina's favorite and (unbeknownst to her) that of the Hungarian as well, had taken a particularly touching position. She had fallen asleep in a crouching posture, with her face pressed against the pillow and the arched portion of her anatomy held high.

In this way she displayed the "double curve," a form so highly valued by the ancient Greeks and which played such a great role with Thorwaldsen and won so much patronage for that sculptor.[22]

Alongside this double curve, revealed in bright light, the warm shadows fell at an angle of forty-five degrees along the inside of her thighs, making a bright red belt that reached halfway along her body.

At each of the sleeper's breaths, this red belt loosened a bit.

Merlina raised the mosquito netting and stroked Semiramis's body three times in rapid succession.

At this touch, the pale mestiza sank down on her knees and turned on her back.

Merlina repeated her manipulation with a sureness of touch only possessed by one of the colored race.

A white would have to resort to animal magnetism in such a situation.

Semiramis rubbed her eyes and looked about, still drunk with sleep.

When the girl had come to, the *zambo negresse* sat next to her on the bed and made a swift examination, whose whole process we cannot repeat here. It is not that we fear that excessive frankness would injure the tender feelings of our esteemed lady readers but rather because we are wont to keep such things secret, by their very nature.

Merlina asked, among other things:

"Semiramis, who stole your red belt yesterday?"

"The clubman of the 97th degree, the Dutchman from Galveston."

"How are the clubmen of the 99th and 100th degree doing?"

"I had to obey."

"Did you see Gabor yesterday?"

"Unfortunately. My pretty diamond brooch was gone when he left me."

"The cad! He will have to disgorge it when Lajos speaks to him."

"Lajos is angry with me. He will be happy when he hears of this theft."

"Did you see Lajos? That is not the clubman's way."

"Yes. He warned me against Sulla. He even threatened to tear my heart out if I paid the slightest attention to Sulla."

"Watch out for yourself if you're lying."

"I am not lying, but I beg that you tell Lajos nothing about it."

"Lajos is not indifferent to you, Semiramis."

"What good would it do me if Lajos weren't indifferent to me—Lajos warms another bosom."

"Semiramis, you're a spirited little cat, but don't pull in your claws when Lajos licks your paws."

"I do everything to please the queen of the night—but no, we must obey, and we love to obey."

Merlina now moved closer to the mestiza and allowed Semiramis to scratch her back with her long fingernails.

That was one of the *zambo negresse's* weaknesses. Only Semiramis was capable of satisfying her totally.

The others either scratched her back too hard, or they were so soft with their fingers that Merlina was not satisfied.

When the scratching was at an end, the Hungarian began his repeated knocking on the outer door, as we have mentioned, without it being opened to him.

We have already described his arrival in Merlina's room.

He sat on the soft upholstery of the chaise longue that stood directly across from the bed, under which Sulla lay hidden. Merlina had settled on the floor with her head in his lap. She cast a glance at the bed, perhaps to see how secure the hiding place was. Merlina's unforgivable nonchalance had actually put the Negro in a very perilous position. Only the best of luck could prevent his being discovered and exposed to dangerous conflict.

The Hungarian sat in shirtsleeves, with his black cravat tied like a sash across his chest.

Merlina stroked her long, full hair behind her ears, displacing her small white cap.

Her eyes sparkled like those of a cat in the darkness, and on her broad tiger's brow burned the repressed glow of the most majestic sensual intoxication. That was always how it was when they were together.

At first he did not say a word, and neither did she, until Cupid finally spoke. The *zambo negresse* now stood up and threw herself back on the bed, holding her arms up and seeming to count on her fingers. On this occasion the blanket hiding Sulla moved a bit. Merlina did not note this. She seemed to have forgotten that she had to be concerned with anyone else.

"Merlina, my panther," the Hungarian declared tenderly, moving his right hand across his breast.

"One, two, three, four . . ." Merlina counted on her fingers.

"What are you figuring?" the Hungarian asked in a detached tone.

"I just wanted to count up the number of times you left this room disappointed," the *zambo negresse* responded, and she continued: "Four, five, six, seven—seven times!"

"What the devil, Merlina, leave off this childishness—people decide whether to make love or not, and that is enough!" the Hungarian said, pressing his lips together, since he had made his own decision and was determined to carry it out at any price.

"People decide whether to make love, Lajos, and *I* have decided today *not* to make love—to each his own will!"

"Do you still have a couple of rats-tails, Merlina?"

Rats-tails was the malicious name the Hungarian had given to the cigars from the Italian Lombardi's fruit store.

"You don't need to smoke now, my Lajos—your panther has something better for you than cigars."

"I demand no more than rats-tails. If Sulla is not yet asleep, he could get me a cherry cobbler."

"There are no straws and no seasonings left in the mill, my Lajos."

"I don't need a straw to drink a cherry cobbler—I will sip it."

"But no seasonings?"

"Not necessary," with these words he raised Merlina's head from his lap with both his hands, getting ready to go.

Merlina pressed herself to him and asked him not to leave her, saying that Sulla was probably already asleep.

"I shall drive that lazy black dog out of bed . . . Do you have his papers?" he interrupted himself.

"It will be taken care of at the right time, my Lajos," Merlina responded, not very happy at the question since Sulla was lying right under the bed.

"It will be taken care of at the right time, my Lajos," she repeated to calm him, and, in order to mislead Sulla, she added, "Sulla will put the papers concerning the bar in order tomorrow morning."

Even if Sulla had not read the narrow slip of paper, he would still have found this extenuated answer a matter of concern.

Despite his compromising position beneath the bed, a light smile appeared on his lips when he heard these words.

Lajos probably accepted this incomplete response to his question because he believed Merlina just wanted to irritate him. So he curtly responded: "Make sure you settle the matter at the latest the day after tomorrow."

"That will be done, my Lajos," Merlina responded, just happy that the Hungarian made no more of it.

It is an indubitable mathematical truth, established according to the reasoning of a human erotic, that wherever the highest moral decadence has marked the character, there the spirit also has its greatest triumph; if an infamous coven of amoretti and maenads cavort in the seat of sensuality, the emperor spirit still can take its throne in the brain and send down thunder and lightning in a truly Caesarean manner.

Whoever is not capable of quaffing a whole Vesuvius of sensual scandal at one gulp without injuring his moral consciousness or his heart's peace has little to fear from the imperial splendor of the spirit. Whoever ties his spirit in the boots of morality, driving Priapus and Venus from the temple of love, overturning in blind fanaticism the tables of the money-changers in the foyer, might be called a solid man—but for this fame he must accept the fact that Cupid will show him his back at every opportunity.

For that reason, Voltaire and Rousseau are more powerful spirits than Montesquieu or Diderot. For that reason, Shakespeare and Lord Byron are greater than Milton, More, and Shaftesbury. For that reason, Goethe and Heinrich Heine are greater than Schiller and Ludwig Börne. For that reason, Boccaccio and Casanova are greater than Dante and Torquato Tasso. For that reason Calderon de la Barca is greater than the entire Spanish cycle of the aesthetes. In short, it bespeaks great poverty of the spirit when the moral man begins to weep before he has yet finished laughing.*

How much good could Lajos and Merlina Dufresne have done for the world! The one, if her skin color had not condemned her to a fixed relationship with the Caucasian race, the other, if he had turned his excess of hyena instinct against the enemies of the common good! The Hungarian Count Lajos Est***, once a chivalric, polished hussar officer and son of one of the oldest magnate houses—here on the soil of a republic became a habitual murderer and arsonist. Even more, for ten dollars he betrayed a

*It is one of the maladjustments of our time that lyricism has been allowed to alter the character of the novel. People have felt themselves compelled to this because a truly objective conception appears to be the monopoly of genius, and the innumerable proletariat of the spirit need a precise commentary in order to understand anything. *Hannibal is at the gates!*

poor soldier who had fled the compulsion of Uncle Sam and trusted him with the story of his desertion.*

The scenes that now follow should be taken in the sense indicated above by the feminine elite of my respected circle of readers, and we will not be accused of overstressing the complexity of their spirits or of besmirching the purity of their character.

It is still a great good fortune that, even when a man is dressed like a Philistine, the genius of woman offers her arm as that of the falconer, and she gives him a sure lead.

"For the last time, Merlina! Tell me, do you want to or not? I have no desire to pass days or months in pining or wallowing in sentimentality like a boy in his fledgling years. The devil with your love, then, if I have to quibble for it. Do you want to or not, Merlina? You know I have no time to waste."

"No time?" Merlina asked, raising her head out of the Hungarian's lap. She did not turn her head to face his but cast a hair-raising glance at the place where Sulla was hidden.

"You know that Tiberius will only wait in the rowboat until three to take me across to Algiers. If I come later, he will leave the bank without me, and you know that I have to be with my wife before the night is over—rather, you don't know it—but I *have* to be there at three, for special reasons."

"And for special reasons I have to ask you to leave me alone now," the *zambo negresse* responded in an intensified tone.

At this instant several powerful sneezes emanated from under the bed. It was too close, too clear, to think that it came from outside the room.

*We do not dare to publish the hierarchy of misdemeanors and crimes Lajos had behind him when he first stepped onto the hospitable American soil. This is because it would then be easy to trace his family name, and we have a close friend of this family still in Debreczin. From his own account, we will take one citation that is telling enough to show that he did not suddenly become what we see here. In 1848, when Herr Schell still had his beerhouse and Mr. —pape entertained the merry company with his singing, enchanting people here and there in his black velvet jacket and long golden locks, Herr Viereck would show up to declaim every evening and grimace at the company. It was around then that the host held his lotteries, offering both Yankee notions and German cockades as prizes. It was then and there, when Mr. A. J. still performed, when he whacked Mr. —pape on the head with his hollow seal ring, when everything was spirited and happy, a pale, quiet man in the most dignified cavalier clothes drew everyone's attention. When the merry company there got him very drunk, he told the story of how, as a child of only five or six, he had snuck into the bedroom of his sisters, set nettles on their eyelids, stuck them with needles, and cut them in the clitoris with a penknife. This man was Lajos, who then owned a cigar store. After he went bankrupt, he suddenly abandoned both New Orleans and his wife. What was his name then? He bore a German name then, a perfect translation of his Hungarian one.

As if shocked by a galvanic battery, the Hungarian leaped into the air and landed so hard with his knee on the head of the *zambo negresse* that her upper body lost its balance and fell forward.

In the same instant a figure slipped out from under the bed, slick as an eel, remaining hidden by the mosquito netting as he reached behind the pillow and drew out both the dagger and the pistol.

Since these weapons were in the light, the Hungarian saw the flash of the dagger and the metallic shine of the pistol barrel.

Merlina lay with her head on the floor and crept toward the bed, her hands advanced and fingers spread.

The Hungarian reached into his right trousers pocket to be sure that he still had the room key.

He backed up a few steps and looked at the *zambo negresse,* then at the bed from which the sneeze had come.

The figure had planted itself directly behind the mosquito netting, and the camphene lamp hanging in the middle of the room threw the shadow of this figure three times larger behind it.

With a glance the Hungarian was able to recognize the shadow of a Negro head, with its woolly hair.

The *zambo negresse* also saw the shadow in the same instant. Quick as a tiger-cat, she rose from the floor, sprang to the top of the bed, and instinctively reached under the pillow.

But the dagger and the pistol were already in other hands.

"Hell and damnation! Are there wild boars in the bushes here? A black buck and a brown sow! A fatal pleasure indeed, going hunting for boar without weapons!" the Hungarian remarked in a bitterly cold, harsh tone as he advanced decisively on the bed.

The *zambo negresse* had stationed herself with her back to the part of the wall where the head of the bed extended. Her eyes flew left and right. With her right hand she held the five-sided column of the master bed. Her left hand seemed undecided.

Sulla alone knew his true situation. Since fortune had put that fatal note into his hands, he knew what the Hungarian and Merlina intended with him. Merlina, who did not have the faintest notion that Sulla knew of the conspiracy against him, and Lajos, who saw only a competitor before him —both were in the dark as to the meaning of their encounter. Instead of the two of them joining against the Negro, since they were coconspirators against him, Lajos thought of both Merlina and Sulla as opponents, seeing not only a competitor but also the falseness of the *zambo negresse.* Sulla, meanwhile, directed all his wrath against both Lajos and Merlina.

The Hungarian did not know whom to turn against first. Contrary to his usual practice, he was carrying no weapons today. He knew about the dagger and the pistol under the pillow—but he had already seen them in the hands of the other man. The key, which he now took from his trouser pocket, was his sole weapon.

There was a fearful pause.

The Hungarian stood solid and sure, the key in his clenched fist, barely a step away from Merlina, who was shaking with rage. Her right hand was still wrapped about the bedpost.

The Negro stood as before, so that neither Merlina nor Lajos could see him, since the mosquito netting gathered on the left side of the bed threw a shadow that covered him.

The Hungarian, who had lost sight of the shadow the Negro threw on the wall as he advanced on the bed, leaned forward and saw the shadow of a raised arm with a drawn dagger, together with a pistol, which rose and fell along with the other arm.

He had made his decision in a flash, a decision that would have to be carried out just as quickly if he was at least to save his life, now in the balance. The rapid carrying out of his plan might win him the means to revenge himself properly, perhaps purchasing the life of one person through the death of the other.

He leaped with a single bound onto the bed, tearing through the mosquito netting and falling on the surprised Sulla, knocking him to the floor with the weight of his body and the power of his attack.

He fell to the floor with the Negro, ending up atop him.

The Negro almost managed, with Herculean effort, to turn the Hungarian to the side. But as he mangled the Hungarian, biting him on his cheek, the raging pain inflicted on the now thrice-bitten cheek caused the Hungarian's muscles to exert superhuman force. He assaulted the Negro by turning his arm and pounding him in the mouth with an elbow, so that Sulla turned up his eyes in agony, groaning faintly.

When Merlina saw this, she wrapped her legs around the column of the bed, climbed to the top, and struck the laths of the uppermost board of the thin wall, pulling the board itself out and slipping through into the neighboring dormitory.

Here she roused all the girls from their beds, and, bringing an ax from the wood bin, she called to them.

"Death or Merlina! Cats, follow me!"

This will not be the first place to remark that Lady Merlina's cats were not able to get themselves properly dressed all that quickly. The whole troop of pale mestizas and dark mulattos was on its feet immediately after the first call. Even the two cholas who were in an advanced interesting condition joined up. They wore knitted night-jackets over their abdomens, in keeping with their hopeful situation, so that they were less exposed to a chill than the others, whose entire uniform consisted of a white shirt with a tie at the top that could be widened or narrowed according to wish.

"Cats, follow me!" Lady Merlina's familiar voice sounded time and again, as some of those still overcome with sleep rubbed their eyes and tried to burrow under the covers. The details of what they were doing is superfluous here, since those initiated into relations between the races know full well that in the fruitful body of a chola things happen that only a god is in a position to explain.

The haste in which the girls were roused by their mistress hindered them in choosing even the most minimal clothing. For that reason there were neither stockings nor shoes, and the few who practiced the evil custom of sleeping without a nightshirt were lacking even that covering. Those who wore the aformentioned knit jackets constituted the dress circle in this dark, naked chaos, where colors competed with one another in all possible variations. This wild nakedness now advanced, with the Lady Merlina and the pale mestiza Semiramis in the vanguard, toward the door of the bedroom.

Just a few blows with the ax, and entry was gained despite the locked door.

Merlina's cats followed their mistress automatically, only discovering what was afoot when they spied Lajos and the Negro.

The Hungarian had meanwhile raised himself from the floor, and he stood on the Negro's breast, which no longer showed the slightest sign of life. His face was as pale as death, for Negroes become pale, too, when life has flown. But this paleness is similar to that of old oil paintings that have lost their varnish and whose dulled pigments allow the naked canvas to shine through. That is how the dark, shiny surface had changed.

Lajos held the pistol in his right hand, ready to shoot. His index finger lay on the trigger, and it was only owing to the Hungarian's utter calm and coldness that the cocked hammer did not fire. With the slightest vibration of the finger, the person in front of the barrel would have been dead. The Hungarian's left hand held the dagger. The handle had been bent back on both sides and wrenched loose from the guard. The tip had been broken. But the sharpness of the double-blade would still permit him to strike it in to the hilt.

Merlina was stunned. She looked first at the Hungarian, then at the Negro.

Lajos looked at her calmly. Then his lips curled back into an ice-cold smile.

Thick, black drops of blood stood on his cheek. The Negro's teeth had torn deeply into the old scar and stripped away the epidermis even across the bridge of the nose.

Most of the cats appeared indifferent and untouched by this dreadful drama in front of their eyes. Only a few shrank back in fear. Among the latter were the pregnant cholas.

The pale mestiza Semiramis leaned down and looked carefully in the Negro's face. She glanced questioningly at Merlina, as if she expected some sort of order.

"You killed Sulla, Lajos? Sulla was innocent!" the *zambo negresse* said in a wild cry. She placed the ax on her shoulder.

The cholas, who had pulled back, now drew nearer.

"Whether innocent or guilty, it's all the same—the black dog is finished and that's it!" the Hungarian replied.

"I made a fool of Sulla and enticed him here—I wanted to extract his papers—he carried them in his left vest pocket."

"The black dog was ready for a wedding. With that black frock coat and his white vest, he will make his bride happy."

The Hungarian noted a slight movement beneath his feet. Had the Negro's breast moved, or was Lajos getting giddy from standing on this body? He looked down and stepped more firmly on his breast. His position was uncertain. The breast did seem to heave.

He looked more carefully at the Negro's face. The wide-open eyes were without sparkle or life. No breath came from the blue lips. And yet the breast did move.

The Hungarian became irritated. He stepped on the Negro's neck with his right foot, while his left remained where it had been before.

This light motion was the result of a crass illusion.

The Hungarian turned the Negro's face to the floor.

His manners did not betray the least hesitation.

"Drive the cats back to their nests—we will celebrate our honeymoon, my panthress!" the Hungarian now said in a cheerful voice, and his face took on a certain liveliness. He let his arms drop, and he pointed the barrel of the pistol at the floor. He threw the dagger on the top of the master bed.

These words wrought a wonderful change in Merlina. A dark red passed across her face, all the way to the Cupid's fold of her lip. Her whole body appeared to be bathed in flames, and in her pupils gleamed the golden shaft of a panther-driven chariot, like a comet passing through the dark ocean of the evening sky. The teamsters were the Lady Venus and Cupid.

The *zambo negresse,* who burned for Lajos in a truly demonic manner and was perfectly capable of surrendering utterly to her sensuality if it were released at the right moment—Merlina, the sixteen-year-old wildcat, whom Lajos so fittingly called his panther—Merlina, who had only teased her victims heretofore, often letting them bleed to death unattended—Merlina, who despite her amorality had not loosened her belt for any man, who was cold and thoughtful when others flamed and burned for her—Merlina, who could only be moved by an extraordinary and terrible episode to give away what she had guarded like the golden fleece despite her murderlust and cruelty, that which she often had struggled to preserve by might and main—this same wildcat, that very panther, panted and glowed to surrender to the man she had so often fooled and cruelly rejected.

The Hungarian had only a mild tremor as he turned from the Negro's body in order to claim in the arms of the *zambo negresse* what her eyes foretold would come to him.

If Merlina had been able to read his thoughts, she would have pushed him away in dread and rage. The very arms that sought to embrace him would have been transformed into serpents.

Merlina's cats departed the bedroom at Lajos's nod, after the pale Mestiza Semiramis received the order to stand watch at the door, to be relieved by a chola if necessary.

"Leave Sulla where he is, my Lajos!" the *zambo negresse* told the Hungarian as he lifted the Negro's corpse in order to drag it out.

"Leave him there, my Lajos," she repeated, "Sulla, though dead, has earned the right to observe our happiness—look, look how he shows his teeth and glares at us so intensely!"

"Help me prop him up against the wall—he will be sensible enough to stay up and not fall down. How nice his black frock-coat looks—come, Sulla, let's loosen your cravat so you may breathe better, silly fellow! Why did you have to die before I could sell you? Mr. Bartlett will mourn for the lovely nigger who ran away from him into hell. There, there, my esteemed barkeeper of the mill, stay here and watch us carefully. Dumb bumpkin, why did you have to bite my poor cheek and soil your lovely white cravat? Look here, there are blood spots on your lovely white vest. Don't show your teeth so boldly, my poor little nigger—you have no idea how dumb it looks when a dead beast still puts on a show—there, there, just keep quiet and don't run away!"

Merlina greedily lapped up these words, quietly marveling at the Hungarian's good mood.

They helped each other set the Negro against the wall. But each time they thought he would stand up, his legs slipped away and he slid back down to the floor.

They tried several times, but always in vain.

"If I had my rifle here, I would stick it into his mouth and jam it through to his stomach—he would have been happy to stand up then."

Another attempt to get the corpse to stand up failed.

Whenever they believed that they had succeeded, he always fell back to the floor. His head continued to be held high and a bit bent back. His fists were still tight.

The Hungarian, who held the Negro's body for one last try to place him erect against the wall, happened to reach into the vest pocket and detect a piece of paper.

He let the troublesome corpse fall and reached for the vest pocket.

It was the Negro's celebrated papers, which Merlina had promised to steal.

As he took these papers out, a narrow note fell, open, to the floor.

Merlina had climbed onto the bed to bring the mosquito netting into order.

She was just emerging. Only her head and shoulders were still hidden under the cover as she arranged the pillows and covers, thinking only of the Hungarian's love.

Only a glance was needed for the Hungarian to see that it was the note he had sent Merlina from Mobile. It brought him suddenly out of his Satanic calm.

His forehead burned like a blast furnace, and his hairy chest rose in wild heaves.

"Betrayed again!" he cried out in a terrified tone, leaping at the *zambo negresse.*

He grabbed her by the arms, bringing his face close to hers, staring directly into her eyes.

"What is the matter with you, my Lajos? My Lajos, my Lajos!" She screamed.

"Yes, infamous serpent—your Lajos is here—he will embrace you with his love, and you will receive as a corpse what you had promised him alive. I would have liked to embrace you trustingly, properly, tenderly, and humanly, my panther, but I cannot trust you alive, so it will be as a corpse."

The Hungarian's face transformed itself into a dreadful mask as he spoke these words. His eyes were bloodshot and had taken on the fell blue shimmer a hyena displays when it falls upon corpses from an opened grave.

It must be recalled that Sulla had found that note as he was searching through Merlina's bed.

On glimpsing this note, the Hungarian inevitably thought that he had been betrayed. Who but Merlina could have given the Negro the note, making him aware of the conspiracy that threatened his freedom? Then had Sulla been initiated into all the secrets? So he, the head of the mill, had stood under the control of a black barkeeper without even suspecting it? And what could Merlina and Sulla have been planning against him? Were they even laying plans to get rid of him? Did they fear him at all? Or had they used him to carry out innumerable crimes and atrocities whose harvest had once flowed into the coffers of the Mill?

Merlina's conduct at Sulla's death? And now? So different! Hadn't Merlina turned to him because she saw that no more deals could be made with the dead Negro?

These thoughts coursed through the Hungarian's brain with the rapidity of a lightning-bolt.

. . . . [23]

Merlina no longer knew what was happening to her when the Hungarian's long black hair fell about her neck, and he gazed down on her with half-closed eyes.

Semiramis, who had been delegated to stand guard outside the door of the bedroom, had been watching this hair-raising episode from beginning the end with the curiosity peculiar to her race, and she was barely able to suppress a cry of terror. She turned her back on the tragedy whose course she had followed up to this point and stared at the floor, moaning to herself.

She had seen everything, but she had not understood everything.

Despite strict orders, she left her assigned place at the door and crept into bed, pulling the covers over her head.

A cold sweat ran down her forehead. She wanted to rise again and rush back to the bedroom to see whether she had dreamed it all. Yet something unexplainable prevented her from carrying this out.

With uncertain step, the Hungarian left the place where he had committed his double crime against Merlina.

Was there a greater monster on earth at this instant? Had the two hemispheres ever harbored a worse criminal?

The Hungarian wandered several times about the bedroom, like a ghost, throwing a glance into the dormitory.

The cats of the mill had all sunk into the deepest slumber. A few breathed softly, others cried out in their sleep and tossed about. The overseer was snoring like a man, or rather like a member of some sexless race.

The Hungarian paused and leaned on the splintered door. He was probably the only being in the mill who was awake at this moment.

Merlina dead—Sulla dead! Everything quiet, observed by no one! Should he abandon this secure position without drawing any advantage from it? Didn't he know the place where the whole wealth of the mill was to be found? Why not become a wealthy man with one blow? What value did the lives of all these people in the mill have, anyway? And wasn't it better to ruin it all, leaving no one behind?

The pale murderer reasoned in this manner, taking steps at once to carry out the decision he had just made.

To get to the mill's money, he had to creep under the bed and raise a plank.

On one side of the bed the legs of the *zambo negresse* hung down to the floor, cold and stiff. Her torso lay in a grotesque state under the mosquito netting. He grasped the legs and threw them up on the bed. He did this so quickly that the corpse fell off the other side, striking the Negro on his forehead as he lay with his face pressed against the foot of the bedpost.

The Hungarian ducked down and crept on all fours under the broad master bed.

The plank was not as easy to raise as he had imagined. After several failed attempts, which left his fingertips torn and bloody, he crept on all fours out from under the bed and fetched the ax Merlina had left beside Sulla's body. He returned with it to the place where the money lay hidden.

After much effort he finally managed to raise the plank.

Underneath it there was a hollow about two feet wide and the same distance in depth, entirely filled by a book. He took out the book, crept out from under the bed with it, and laid it on the top of the washstand Sulla had shoved against the door such a short time before. He opened it, and his expectations were not disappointed. With each page he turned, his eyes fell on a valuable banknote, none less than a hundred dollars in value. By the time he had leafed through the book from start to finish, he was in the possession of a hundred and twenty thousand dollars.

He folded the banknotes together with a calm and practiced hand, sticking them into his trouser pockets.

"Money! money!" he chortled to himself, and his eyes were revived again.

He looked at his watch. It was 2:00 A.M.

High time to get to work quickly.

He went quietly through the two dormitories and entered the club chamber of the 99th and 100th degrees. Here he opened a drawer under one of the tables, at which he had sat an hour before with the other clubmen, discussing the affairs of the club and giving orders to the subordinate members of the gang.

Beneath the Book of the Mill, which was wrapped in waxcloth, lay the dreadful murder instrument of the college of clubmen of the Hamburg Mill. Merlina had taught them how to use it. Since the origin of the *zambo negresse's* gang, it had been used more than twelve times. Seven times it had been used against clubmen, when it was determined to be necessary to neutralize them. It was a *tar mask,** which was pressed over the face of its selected victims until they suffocated.

Lajos took the tar mask from a waxed bag and hid it in his shirt, across his breast. Then he went through the salon of the mill as quietly as he had first entered the club chamber, exiting through the passage in the floor.

Before we follow his footsteps, we should remark that the Italian Lombardi slept next to his fruit store, separated from it by a thin carpet partition. He slept upstairs only on rare occasions, such as when he longed for one of Merlina's cats or when he was too drunk to get downstairs.

Lombardi had gone to bed right after taking his leave of the Hungarian, who had himself rushed from the club chamber to Merlina.

But he had been unable to sleep, for the Hungarian's attitude to his own office as Pontifex Maximus of the mill lay on his breast like a mountain. He had not even undressed.

To pass the time, he bit off a large piece of chewing tobacco.

Lombardi's bedroom was totally in agreement with his exterior and competed with it in dirtyness and disorder. There was no window, and the little air that entered came through a very narrow, barred hole above the door.

This person could have lived like a lord, but his filthy soul rejected every comfort. The grimiest and most down-at-the-heels ragpicker would not have deigned to lie in his cot, which had been fouled and pigmented in the most repellent manner by the results of his frequent drunkenness. Used, torn pieces of clothing, tallow candle-ends, cigar stumps, used chewing tobacco wads, orange-peels, lemon-peels, and empty matchboxes lay every-

*It should be recalled that a tar mask was found in the possession of the infamous schoolmaster Dyson when he was arrested last summer (1853). Its purpose was never explained. How did Dyson come into possession of such a mask? Who taught him how to use it? The Hotoohs, who have already been mentioned, are supposed to use this dreadful instrument of murder.

where; a tin pot that served him, besides in its original purpose, as both a drinking vessel and as a washing pot, did not help mark his setting with the scent of *milles fleurs.*

The best object to be found in the Italian's bedroom was a Venetian lamp, whose light passed through glass colored dark blue and ruby red, formed in an octahedron. This lamp, which had been brought over from Italy and which had once given him great aide in his work as a *pipo,* could be turned in any direction, and it would keep the position given it. Today the red lights of the lamp head were turned toward his cot. On the ceiling the reflection from the octahedron swayed, lengthening and narrowing in keeping with the air currents passing through the narrow hole over the door. The Italian sat staring emptily at this play of light as he tried to master his distress over the events in the club chamber.

The Hungarian stood at the back door of the fruit store, from which he could survey the entire yard all the way to the alley. This view was interrupted by the hanging laundry, which flapped with the movement of air through the courtyard.

The moon, which had a large halo tonight, beamed down a weak and uncertain light.

A mockingbird screamed as if its throat would burst, copying first the meow of a cat, then the cawing of a crow, then the crowing of a cock, whistling charming bastard songs or trilling like a mad opera singer in between.

Hardly two steps from the back door of the fruit store was the entrance to Lombardi's bedroom.

The Hungarian looked in through the barred hole over the door. It was no surprise to him that he saw light, for he knew that the Italian never slept in total darkness.

He drew the tar mask out of his shirt, but in such a way that he could replace it quickly. Then he placed his ear against the door and listened. He heard the Italian coughing, and he heard the straining of the cot's straps.

He knocked, first softly, then a bit stronger.

"Who's there?" the Italian's voice sounded from inside, in such a dubious tone that one could easily imagine that he had just been brought to consciousness.

"Death or Merlina!" the Hungarian sounded his password.

The Italian left his groaning cot and pulled back the double bar on the door.

"I thought you were already asleep," Lajos told Lombardi the fruitmonger, affecting a waggish smile.

"If you were of the opinion that I was asleep, why did you wake me, then? . . . Does the mill have a new order?"

The Italian ushered the Hungarian into his bedroom, stretching out once more on his filthy cot.

"Your bed is worm-eaten, Lombardi, and it creaks and groans like an old nun," the Hungarian remarked, looking for a place he could sit without soiling his trousers. He removed the black silk handkerchief that he had draped across his breast like a sash, and he carefully spread it on an old chair that had only half a back. Then he moved closer to the Italian's bed, leaving a small space still open.

"The Lady Merlina sends me down to you, Lombardi, to discover how you're doing, since she thinks that you have not really been well for several days."

"Thanks, thanks!" the Italian smirked, very flattered over the *zambo negresse's* tender attentions.

"Lady Merlina concerns herself with you like a mother," Lajos continued, pressing his left arm against the mask under his shirt.

"Tell the Lady Merlina that I am quite well since dosing with calomel—only a bit of back pain and an ache in my gums, but that means nothing since I am used to it," the Italian responded, spitting a considerable quantity of chewing tobacco onto his greasy bedspread and biting off another plug.

"Then I can withdraw and assure the Lady Merlina that you feel excellent," the Hungarian said.

"You do not exactly need to use the word *excellent,* but you could tell her that it goes passably well with me," the Italian responded.

The Hungarian now looked across the Italian's bed, leaning a bit forward.

"You are looking for a particular thing, Lajos? It is here on your right, you don't need to fuss," Lombardi commented, bending his back, which suddenly hurt him again.

"Not that," the Hungarian responded, "I saw a rat so shameless it was gnawing on your shoe, and it did not let our presence interrupt his feeding. You spoil your rats, Lombardi, and you train them to be real gourmands. That's not right."

As the Italian leaned to the other side of the bed in order to see the gnawing rat, the Hungarian swiftly drew the tar mask from his shirt and fell upon him.

Before Lombardi could defend himself, the Hungarian threw the mask over his face and pressed it on with both hands.

The Italian reached for his face and tore at the mask in vain. He leaped into the air, but he fell back at once. Then his hands and feet twitched for a few more moments until he lay back and gave up his spirit.

Then across the tar mask scrambled the cold body of a rat.

"So there was a rat after all!" the Hungarian laughed, "If you paint the devil on the wall, he comes to call.

"I want to take along one souvenir of you, my greasy *pipo*—the lamp is just too pretty. My blonde Frida will be glad to be able to sleep by its light—she loves colorful lamps and lusters. But, you hard-luck fool, just so your soul in hell does not lodge a complaint with Lord Satan and his Lady, saying that I stole something from you, I will pay royally for it. If you leave the money, that's your own problem." The Hungarian looked at the Italian as he spoke these words, and then turned to look away, throwing a hundred-dollar bill on the table on which the lamp stood. He then unscrewed the small lamp head from the lamp and put it in his pocket. He threw the oil lamp itself on the fruitmonger's bed, causing the rat, which had returned and was already gnawing a hole in the throttled man's throat, to bolt away.

Unbeknownst to him, however, there was another person present besides the Hungarian and the suffocated man.

Hastily but silently as a Hotooh, the Hungarian streaked up the stairway into the Hamburg salon.

He heard the loud rattling of the clubman of the 98th degree, who had been granted Pharis and Elma for the night.

"You dogs and cats will not laugh for much longer," Lajos thought to himself. "The shutters are nailed shut and I will close the escape and even block the lower doors to make sure—but just a minute! I could wake Semiramis—no, that won't do, it would spoil the whole joke."

The Hungarian went to the bar, whose shelves held not only wines but also several vessels filled with spirits. He took their glass stoppers out and poured their contents on the carpet. Then he tore a strip from a newspaper and lit it on a camphene lamp. He held this burning fuse to the alcohol-soaked carpet.

Then he went swiftly to the exit in the salon and pulled the trapdoor after him as he was halfway through. When he came to the foot of the stairway, he locked the door leading up and threw the key into a trough in the yard.

When he came out to the street, there was no one to be seen in the vicinity of the mill.

He could hear the clinking of coffee spoons and the clattering of cups and plates from the direction of the market. The butchers were already drinking their coffee.

The Hungarian proceeded at an easy pace to the place where he had commanded Tiberius to wait with a rowboat until 3 A.M.

The waves on the Mississippi from the wake of a newly arrived steamer were lapping against the posts of the wharf. A cannon salvo and its reply indicated that the steamer had just come from overseas. The torches on the riverbank sent their glow toward the fortunate arrival, illuminating the red stripe above the cabin portholes. One could hear the monotonous refrain of the sailors and the captain's commands through the rattle of the anchor chains.

"The *Georgia*!" a man could be heard to say, "Coming from San Francisco—a golden cargo and a merry mob!"

The Hungarian turned about and met the eyes of the harbor watchman. They greeted him and asked him if he knew anyone on board.

"If it's the *Georgia,*" Lajos responded, "then I came down here in vain. The steamer with my friend has nothing to do with this one."

"That's a bother," the watchman commented, leaving the Hungarian, who turned left and went along the wharf, descending to the level of the river.

There he found his boat, tilting up and down in the agitated water. It was tied to a post with a cable. Little Tiberius lay on the bottom of the boat, sleeping. The oars lay crossed above his head.

Lajos stepped onto the boat's seat, shaking the Negro from his sleep. He sat up in shock, but once he recognized his master he calmed down. He stepped out of the boat, loosed the cable from the post, and threw it into the box over the keel. The Hungarian sat forward on the seat and looked back idly in the direction from which he had come.

Tiberius pushed against the riverbank with one of the oars, ably maneuvering away from the shore.

The moon's halo had unwound into a long, narrow strip of mist, leaving the disk of the moon free.

Tiberius was a capable ferryman. The oars rose out of the waves like two long, black arms, then plunged immediately back in.

They had already made half of the passage when a snow-white seagull settled down so close to the Hungarian that he could have grasped it with his hands.

"How did seagulls get here, Tiberius?" he asked the small Negro, who always knew much more about such things than his master.

"The *Georgia* brought them," Tiberius declared. "Sea birds often hang on the masts and travel as far as the city."

"Bad-luck birds!"* the Hungarian thought. "The nest is not burning yet." He looked back at the place were the mill stood.

He pulled out his watch. The hands stood at five minutes before two. "That's impossible," he said to himself, putting the watch to his ear.

The watch had stopped—at the moment when he had placed the tar mask over the Italian's face.

The strokes of the oars quickly brought the boat to the opposite shore. Tiberius pulled the oars in, laying them next to the gunwales on the sitting boards. Then he jumped out, grabbed the cable, and bound it to a hook with a true sailor's knot.

The Hungarian stepped slowly out of the boat, and, as soon as he was on the soil of Algiers, he stood with folded arms looking toward New Orleans.

The last silver beams of the moon shone over the Gulf City. Then thick clouds of smoke, which the wind drove in snaky streams, hid the moon completely.

The Hungarian's eyes flamed in devilish joy as he saw this.

"From the north comes smoke, and no one is alone in his tent—howl gate, scream city, all of Philistia cowers!" he proclaimed in a dramatic tone as if he were in the midst of his clubmen of the 99th and 100th degree.

Little Tiberius looked curiously at his master, who had said the words to himself, half-aloud.

Now they left the riverbank and proceeded with rapid steps.

The Negro followed the Hungarian at a short distance. The Hungarian often looked behind himself.

The fire spread rapidly, appearing to set the whole of heaven aflame. The dynamic breezes drove millions of sparks into the dizzying heights, spreading so that it appeared the heavens had lost all their stars or the stars themselves were all showering down into the bosom of the marvelous city.

When the Hungarian turned his back on New Orleans again, he heard the dull report of a building collapsing.

...

On the same day, the evening edition of one of the English-language newspapers published the following passage:

* Seamen predict misfortune when a seagull shows itself in sweet water. The same is true of the silver sprick. This bird is snow-white with standing pink feathers at the base of the beak. When breeding, they make a cry like that of a peacock. This excites a particularly eerie feeling when heard late at night. These are often encountered at Cape St. Henry, in Haiti, where they hang their nests on the side of Coabore.

> It is truly horrifying, justifying the opinion that our city stands under the influence of an evil demon who takes his pleasure in keeping our hard-tested New Orleans in terror. Yesterday an entire row of buildings, most of them brick houses, as well as the left wing of that great warehouse that once belonged to messrs. Albin and McPherson, and on which the infamous Parasina Brulard had bestowed such a bad reputation, burned to the ground. Today, between two and three in the morning, a second fire alarm set the residents of the same quarter in the greatest distress. The fire was said to have started in the notorious strangers' inn called the "Hamburg Mill." We have not yet heard anything about loss of life.

The reporter of a French-language journal was somewhat more precise, eschewing the fatalistic tone of the English-language paper.

He said: "One can think what he wishes, but this much is true, that these fires following in such a rapid succession are not the result of simple negligence or any other accident. One can assume the opposite, which is that it is the work of a well-organized arsonists' gang who has already pursued its criminal trade for several years in this city. It is to be hoped that the police will finally do their duty and not be so negligent in pursuing such criminals."

After the journal described the two fires, it expressed the fear that several lives had probably been lost. A separate editorial promised to report in greater detail the following day.

At the close, the French-language journal added: "We cannot deny the most profound sympathy for our bold, brave fire companies, whose strength and health have been so abused and tested. These brave young men believe they are sacrificing themselves for the preservation of the property of our fellow citizens, and they do not realize that they stand under the criminal control of certain persons."

A German newspaper in the French Quarter, which has an educated and sophisticated readership due to its location, went a little further in an article under the headline "City News":

> We owe a debt of gratitude to our esteemed colleagues in the French-language press for responding to the dubious theory of the English-language papers that the recent frequent fires are the result of chance by asserting that the fires are the issue of a criminal conspiracy. Yet we must protest that they remain silent about something that is on the tip of their tongues, which is that those arsonists are largely the tools of persons who cannot bear to see a house stand for long once the insurance exceeds its value. The Spanish-language press approaches our own opinion, but it is premature in asserting that these accidents and crimes are the fruits of our republican freedoms.

The Machiavelli of the Spanish press continues to hide in the purple folds of His Catholic Majesty's cloak. Haven't demonstrations by our Cuban patriots made them any wiser?

PARALIPOMENA

Pensacola Landing, New Canal
Headquarters of the Lesbian Women

Sir!

In a grail held by the lesbian women on 18 March,[24] it was moved and adopted to seek in writing to convince the author of *The Mysteries of New Orleans* not to fulfill the promise he makes to his esteemed lady readers in the seventh chapter of the second volume, namely to publicize our assemblies and to reveal their intimate nature. We do this because we would be exposed to danger of being attacked by raw intruders and a curious moral proletariat. But since we realize how sacred such promises are that an author makes to such a respected and educated readership, and since we are not so foolish as to demand such a strained delicacy, we shall try to satisfy the public ourselves by touching several points while leaving the most dangerous matters out. Please permit us the following assertions:

There are very many maidens in New Orleans who could not be moved to take a man at any price, even if he were an Adonis in appearance and a Croesus in wealth. These maidens possess such a hostility against anything that is called a man that they fall into a swoon at the slightest contact. Others abandon themselves to outbreaks of righteous wrath on such occasions. Their conduct is, of course, in keeping with their temperaments, and they know no bounds whenever their dignity is injured. The assumption that we live in clubs of several members is true only insofar as we have several gatherings in isolated places lasting several nights. Otherwise we live in pairs, keeping our households just as the majority of society live together as man and wife. In the eyes of the world, when one of us has chosen a life-companion, we are just good friends, sisters, or simply persons who deeply esteem each other's qualities.

The majority of us are of German extraction, but we came into the world on the soil of Louisiana. These German Creole maidens are much honored among us, since they express the peculiar type we represent to the highest degree. They flame with particular intensity for the charms of pretty, young married women, since they see them as a satisfying substitute for the ability to reproduce.

When such a combination comes about, it is inevitable that children will enter the community, children whose beauty and composure would shame the gods. We are solidly convinced of this, and these presumptions make up a major part of the tradition of our Holy Grail. King Arthur of the Round Table is our ancestor and the Grand Master of our association. Sir Walter Raleigh and the Cabot brothers receive the next level of our adoration and esteem, since they are the ones who transplanted us to the New World and won us entry into the mysterious palmetto boudoir of Louisiana.

Sir! You are the first and only person who has dared to mention our secretive existence in New Orleans, and this in a work that has charmed the souls of women of spirit and heart. You have touched on the fact that has never before been dealt with in detail, since they had not yet realized that the majority of men are unworthy to unfasten their garters.

Sir! Please do not say anything further about our occasional gatherings, and we will seek to honor your restraint by serving you the chalice of the Holy Grail and placing you at the same table with Arthur. In the blood that the chalice contains, you will read the tale of woe of that sex which has abandoned the gods.

Lesbia
New Orleans, April 1854.

Book
IV

Prologue

THE FATA MORGANA OF THE SOUTH

I

The bank of the Red River where it receives Cache Creek presented a lively, picturesque scene in April 1852.[1] Toward evening, part of a company stationed at Fort Belknap on the Brazos in Texas had pitched tents barely five feet from the edge of the riverbed, and the soldiers were making all possible efforts to settle in comfortably and well. A U.S. flag the size of the ensign carried by a lancers' regiment fluttered at the entrance of each tent. The tents were of sailcloth, stretched on four poles set crosswise. The humidity of the evening had forced the soldiers to shed their jackets, which were scattered on the wool blankets spread under the tents. Two Delaware Indians, hired as interpreters and guides, were engaged in gathering the dried buffalo excrement within a radius of fifty to a hundred feet of the camp. Once they had filled their bags, they returned to the bivouac and emptied their carefully gathered burden into the great fire they had started as soon as they halted. Then they sat down among the soldiers, passing the pipe from one mouth to another. In return for this service, which the campers did not seem to value very highly, they each were treated to several pulls on a demijohn filled with the best gin Texas had ever produced.

One of the Delawares had shot a buffalo the day before, skillfully skinned it, and packed the best cuts in the wagon after rubbing the flesh with the salt and spices available. The buffalo meat was now brought out, and pieces were cut and fried over the fire on a long, wide pewter pan with a narrow rim. Several birds that had been shot were also prepared for eating. A hard ride of five days had given the soldiers such an appetite that they snatched the meat out of the pan half-cooked, bolting it down greedily. They did not forget to take gin in substantial quantities, however. The small birds, feather-stubs still sticking out, were left to the leader of this detachment, who seemed to prefer them to the tough buffalo steaks. This gourmand was Captain Marcy,[2] who had received an order barely a month before from the War Department in Washington to pursue the course of the Red River from the confluence of Cache Creek, known to rise in the Wichita Mountains, all the way to its source. This expedition up the Red

River was not the first; forty-five years earlier, after the First Consul of France had ceded the vast Louisiana territory to the United States, Captain Sparks had undertaken to follow this American Niger to its source. Even before he could reach the villages of the Pawnee Pigua Indians, he and his men were forced back by a troop of Spanish soldiers, and he was compelled to turn around and regard the expedition as an utter loss. A second expedition, headed by the famous Lieutenant Pike, was sent out the same year by the U.S. government, with no better results. This was in 1806. In 1819 and 1820, another attempt was made to reach the source of the Red River, this time by Colonel Long of the United States Corps of Engineers. He described the situation in his extremely interesting account:*

> We reached a creek flowing in a westerly direction, which we took to be a tributary of the Red River. Accordingly, we followed its course several hundred miles until we found to our distressed surprise that we had explored the Canadian Arm of the Arkansas instead of the Red River. Since our horses had been almost ruined and it was already too late in the season to consider returning to seek the Red River before winter came, we decided to continue our route to the settlements on the Arkansas. We had depended entirely on Pike's map, which shows the Red River as the source of the Canadian River.

We see, then, that none of the expeditions sent to explore the Red River had managed to reach its source.

The Mexicans and the Indians living in the neighboring region have the habit of calling any river whose water has a red appearance the Rio Colorado, or Red River, and it is no wonder in a region covered with red clay how the Canadian River, tinted red, should also have been called Rio Colorado. This explains Alexander von Humboldt's error in saying that the Red River rises at Natchitoches, about fifty miles east of Santa Fe. There is no doubt that he received this information from the Mexicans. This also explains the misunderstandings of Colonel Long and Lieutenant Pike.

This was the extent of achievement so far as the search for the Red River's source was concerned, up to the moment when Captain Marcy and his companions arrived to pitch camp at the confluence of Cache Creek and the Red River.

*The following words are from Captain Marcy's account to the Geographic Society of New York on 22 March 1853. [Ed.: Reizenstein probably refers to the American Geographical and Statistical Society of New York, established in 1852. See Arthur A. Brooks, *Index to the Bulletin of the American Geographical Society, 1852–1915* (New York: American Geographical Society, 1918).]

Outside a large tent, its entrance covered with double curtains, sat a small, slight man on a simple chair in front of a small table. He had the same sort of oddly marked features one finds among Texas Rangers: he was deeply tanned, with cheekbones so prominent that they threw small shadows on his cheeks. This man's eyes were light gray but shadowed by dark, full lashes.

These eyes did not make a soulful impression. No signs of life, heart, and spirit were apparent in these eyes—but they shone like the eagle-eyes of a hunter, displaying the wild nature of a trapper combined with a ruthless routine of applying knowledge and practical understanding in matters of business. In short, this was the true archtype of an Anglo-Saxon raised on the Rio Grande, who participated in wagon-trains such as those Americans and Mexicans use to bring goods from Santa Fe, and who had had a dispute or two with the Tonquewas Tribes.

The vertical crease that divided both eyebrows and ran toward the center of his large forehead indicated the mathematician, the eclectic researcher of nature, and the surveyor. His whole being reminded one of Colonel Frémont, the pathfinder who crossed the Rockies.

This man is *Captain Marcy.*

On the small table in front of him lay Pike's old map, the sole authority that this man had to complete his honorable quest for the source of the Red River. In his right hand he held a radial compass, which he often compared with the scale placed at the bottom of the map. He marked off several orientation points and now and then shook his head in dismay.

The stars in the cloudless sky twinkled like diamonds in the dark purple robes of Ptolemaic kings, appearing all the more numerous because the moon had not yet risen.

The light of his lantern dimmed, for there was a breeze. The flame only sputtered when one of the Delaware Indians rushed by to retrieve the horses and mules, who dared to wander toward the bluffs as they fed on the splendid vegetation of the soft, fruitful bottomland.

Two persons sat on a small munitions chest of strong hickory near the table. They had joined the expedition after speaking briefly with Captain Marcy.

The one had beautiful, rich blond hair and large eyes of heavenly blue, while the other had eyes that competed in blackness with the night. Each was clothed in light summer garb and carried a small straw hat with black ribbons that fell over the rim in back.

They looked first at the captain, then at his troop of soldiers sitting around the large fire, devouring their buffalo steaks with genuine hunger.

Captain Marcy left his place and sat next to the two on the munitions chest.

"I believe it is the same mysterious man who stood before the Inquisition of Louisiana in Baron de Carondelet's time, and when they were about to pronounce sentence, he suddenly vanished," the captain began. "It is necessary to reach the source—if we found the *Mantis religiosa,* whose existence you describe, the South would be freed of a great burden. Even if this plant covered thousands of acres, it could be eradicated in a short time." Those he addressed remained silent, seeming to brood over something at the same time.

The captain continued: "Your old man's power does not appear to reach so far as to be able to hinder our undertaking, and if you have reason to believe, as you say, that he is no longer alive, then we can reach our goal with all the greater certainty." Turning to the person with the light blond hair and sky-blue eyes, he said, "You will yet be a credit to our army, and perhaps a German hero will soon join the pantheon of our great republic, between Washington and Lafayette."

"I will never be that!" was the shy response.

"Why not? The corps of cadets at West Point will train you to be a fine soldier in the course of two years—have no doubt of your military ability. Believe me, you have taken the wrong path of life up until now, and you have not recognized the true mission Providence has marked out for you."

"Captain Marcy, I and my companion are bound by a fearsome oath—even if we have wasted in frivolity the millions the old man gave us instead of supporting propaganda to free the helots from their bonds, I cannot understand how I could enter the service of a government that persecutes that propaganda on all sides and pursues it to death."

"And the *Mantis religiosa* was the means of revenge for your propagandists, and their dreadful influence would not be suppressed until they had won their victory—and yet you told us of this marvelous plant? Wasn't your silence on this included in the oath?"

"No!" was the answer.

"Yes!" came an uncanny sound from the banks of the Red River.

The two fell into each other's arms with a cry of terror.

The captain stood up in shock and advanced toward them.

II

Like a priestess of Vesta, earnest and chaste, the evening approached the hour when it traffics most happily with spirits, communing with them for joy or sorrow and preparing for the coming morning. On the highest plateau of a mesa stood the burning sickle of the waxing moon, spreading its light on the endless ocean of prairie, from whose bosom rises the mysterious source of the Red River.[3]

Panthers and jaguars emerged from hiding and gazed, intoxicated, at the moonlit plains. Softly and thoughtfully they stepped, as if they feared to tear the innumerable blossoms under their claws. Colorful butterflies flew, their wings heavy and cumbersome, through quiet air, finally sinking, exhausted, in the grass. They had already plunged their snouts into the blossoms and greedily sucked their narcotic nectar. Tiny emerald-green snakes rose up and hissed at the lightning bugs circling their heads, as if mocking them.

Only the murmur of the Red River's source, springing out of the prairie-ocean then emerging once more in the midst of a canyon, interrupted the solemn, majestic silence of the night.

A man and a woman stepped out of the darkness of the canyon.

They crossed the moon-silvered area, often stooping to look at the pinkish-red blossoms that had only opened today.

"Mantis religiosa!" the man called out in a solemn tone, plucking a blossom.

"You die this year without seeds, in order to carry them a millionfold the following year."

"Hiram, I honor your noble wrath, but please do not visit the unhappy city once more with this dreadful disease," the woman said, wringing her hands in supplication. "Think, many of our people die along with the whites, and they would curse you if they knew their murderer."

"Diana Robert, it is my will, and you know that it will not be altered by any woman's voice. How you have disappointed me! Just as have Emil and Lucy, on whom I set all my hopes. The throttling angel will massacre all he can, and he will not spare your own blood. Leave here this very moment and go to the lower rooms of the Atchafalaya Bank in New Orleans, where your relatives and friends are now living. Tell them that when Hiram visits and they see his yellow mask, the city will tremble and weep. You know the way we took, and nothing must keep you, since the slightest delay could cost you your life."

"But Hiram! The whole, long way on foot?"

"You may ride my other pony, Diana Robert, it will take you home safe and secure through the canebrakes and palmetto swamps."

Diana Robert returned to the canyon, downhearted.

Hiram looked after the departing woman for a long time. Then he turned his gaunt face, paled by troubles, toward the mesa, from whose highest level the waxing crescent of the moon was rising.

He spread out his arms horizontally, like a cross that had defied storm and weather to somehow retain its shape.

"Waxing moon! Symbol of the Crescent City!" he cried out, so loud that he seemed to want to be heard by the stars themselves. "How long will you continue to shine on the colorful hustle and bustle in the streets of New Orleans? You will kiss the gravedigger's hungry hands, and your glimmering light will hang on the spokes of the hearses. O Moon, you always remain the same, whether your light bathes a corpse or the thriving children of pure nature. You alone are happy, Moon, for your face is always cheerful and peaceful, and you are never depressed by the crimes and atrocities of people. Enviable vassal of the great spirit of worlds, loveliest diamond in the diadem of heaven! Moon, if only I could change places with you and have your cheer and your smile forever! If Hiram, the Circling Cross of the South, could win you as an ally in his holy struggle, your sickle would harvest the heads of his enemies and sever the chains of the helots!"

Then it suddenly appeared as if the moon understood him, for dark shadows spread rapidly on its surface, gradually appearing to form numbers.

Hiram stood starkly, watching this miraculous game on the silver sickle. Now the numbers formed up one after another, throwing shadows on either side. They stood, black but glittering.

"You have joined my struggle, symbol of the Crescent City!" Hiram cried out in holy enthusiasm, and in his eyes burned the fire of noble revenge.

"What do I read on your shining face? That will be the summer of terror: *Eighteen Fifty-Three!*"

Chapter 1

ANGEL AND GENIUS

That is of the god Amor
A holy cathedral, a temple of love;
In its tabernacle, like a lamp, burns
A heart without falseness or fault.

One of the most frequented churches in New Orleans is the *Protestant Episcopal Church*—usually called Christ's Church—on Canal and Dauphine Streets. On certain holidays it successfully competes with the Cathedral and St. Patrick's Church near the Odd Fellows' Hall, not to mention St.

Joseph's Church on Common Street, the heavenly refuge of Green Ireland.[4] The Episcopal Church's popularity is due not to a high number of parishioners, since its flock is relatively small in comparison with those of the other religious sects in New Orleans, but rather to the nobility of our pious population. In most recent times, it has become a matter of good tone among the cream of the Creoles to pass through the portal of this church at least every other Sunday. All of the clubs of higher society are represented here, whether their members are believers in the papal or episcopal church. They have particular pews and pay substantial rents for them; the old Pelican Club has two rows, for instance, and for their use it must pay twenty-five hundred dollars a year. This church has always had the most educated and liberal clerics, insofar as a particular confessional coloration permits liberalism at all. McNeal and Ogden are major decorations of the salon, and they throw a rare and enviable aura upon the circle within which they move. The former is a poet, and his Highland verses are to be found in all the boudoirs of our clime. Ogden still held a chair at the *Jardin des plantes* in Paris ten years ago, where he taught botany and carried out the Jussieu reforms together with those of Serres.[5] Both of these priests live now in the Dauphiné, which is what the Creoles call the extension of Dauphine Street starting at Bienville. Their gallantry, barely exceeded by those chivalric abbés in the days of the Kings Louis, goes so far that there is barely an album in which they have not penned a tender remark for its pretty owner or that does not harbor a significant amulet of some sort from them. Strict and conscientious within the limits of their duties, they are the most lovable company outside them. The most respected families of New Orleans trust their daughters' education and training to them, and their success has been so astonishing that any young lady seeking to be regarded as educated must have received their basic tuition or their more advanced education.

A high holiday had once more led the *haute volée* of New Orleans, particularly that of the Second District, to Christ's Church in great numbers. Since it was just around noon, and the hot sun bore down upon the church, the ladies' fans were in continuous movement, disturbing the devotions of many a cavalier. Instead of the air freshening a bit with this movement, the crowd was so large that the oppressive heat forced many to leave the church and begin the journey home. Among the many vehicles that stood before the church, there was a splendid carriage whose body rested on the finest, most delicate springs, suspended barely two feet above the ground. The door was decorated with a simple, dark red heraldic shield crossed from right to left by a silver bar. In the divided field there was a black star with a chalice beside it, over which levitated a host. Above the shield was a crown set with nine pearls.[6] These arms were repeated several times in the silver bridles of the horses, whose legs and heads attested to their fine breeding. On the high driver's box sat a Negro in the finest black habit and snow-white gloves; he had shed only the right one in order to remove a knot his whip had developed from use. Another Negro, in the same clothing, was standing at the side of the open door, raising the doorstep, which was covered with soft carpeting.

"Who might own this splendid vehicle?" asked a young German man who, like so many others, was standing in front of the church to admire the beauties coming from the service. He said this to another bystander who recognized him at first glance.

"I don't know myself—probably some French viscount or marquis. These Frenchmen are crazy to put heraldic arms on a coach door in a republic. If I had my way that would come down at once! I cannot understand Americans for putting up with such nonsense. That sort of thing is an offense to our simple republican ways . . ."

"Simple republican ways?" the other interrupted him, laughing aloud. "One can see that you're very green here despite having lived here for seven years, Kaspar. Otherwise you wouldn't talk such nonsense. Simple republican ways? Who told you that? Where did anyone tell you such silliness? You will still find simplicity in the backwoods of the Far West, and seldom enough there. Their women cannot survive anymore without powder and perfume."

"You don't understand me—I am only talking about the old aristocratic nonsense, those infamous coats of arms—if I had known that they'd be everywhere here, I might as well not have left Germany. By God, my heart turns when I see something like that. I never would have imagined it in a republic."

"Let the people paint as many coats of arms on their coaches as they want, that doesn't concern us at all. But what upsets me is this: you're one of those hotheads who thinks he has found an aristocrat when he sees a fine shirt and cannot imagine a good republican in any way except with wild, uncombed hair and dirty clothes. This refugee mentality doesn't work here, Kaspar, especially not in New Orleans. Still, I would be curious to find out who owns this splendid equipment. Let's ask the nigger up there on the seat."

He approached the horse and spoke to the black coachman in the driver's seat.

"Please, who owns this wagon?"

"I don't know."

"Who has hired this lovely carriage?"

"I don't know."

"Please, don't you know your master's name, damn'd nigger?"

"Damn'd ——" was the coachman's response.

Irritated, the German ceased questioning the Negro, for the simple reason that he did not want to embarrass himself any more in front of the bystanders. The black coachman actually appeared to have enjoyed goading the German.

"How arrogant these niggers are—the fellows are prouder under their yoke of slavery than we Germans are," the disgusted young man moaned, taking his friend's arm to get away from there as quickly as possible. The Negro's nonchalance was truly hard to bear.

The eyes of the vagabonds standing in front of the church suddenly turned to two ladies coming down the broad stone steps. They went quickly toward the carriage, which had moved right up to the sidewalk.

The Negro at the door stepped back with a bow as he pulled back the silver handle with his right hand.

The ladies assisted each other into the coach with mutual gallantry.

"The most beautiful girls in New Orleans!" declared a Frenchman who looked after the coach as it departed, striking his walking stick several times on the sidewalk.

"It is just too bad that they are so seldom seen," another remarked.

"It is no wonder, since they never go to the theater, to a concert or a fair—they might as well be the T——s. Such jewels should be shown more often," a third remarked.

"The one is worth a million, with as many lots as others have hairs on their heads," an American said.

The young ladies sat opposite each other in the coach.

They were of the same age, barely past their seventeenth year. One of them, sitting in the depths of the coach, had light blonde hair, almost golden, which was unfashionably worked into broad braids put back over the ears, enclosing the classic oval of her pale, sorrowing face. These were the lines of a *mater dolorosa,* only purer and still touched by the rays of youth. In her splendid eyes heaven itself seemed to take its seat, they were of such brilliant, divine blue. But tears hung among the stars of this heaven, which went away only when her soft lashes covered them. The sparkling white of her neck, her tiny, fine hands and feet, her calm and sure posture, everything vouched for her origin in the high aristocracy, declaring that this pearl had been conceived in silk and gold. Her pale yellow barège dress, whose flounces were bordered with satin bands of the palest pink, only went to make this enchanting blonde almost transparent, contrasting dramatically with her mild, spiritual face.

The young lady who sat opposite her was a striking but refreshing contrast.

The rich, chestnut-brown hair, whose broad, full waves set off the most charming red of her cheeks, pressed her small crepe hat even further back on her neck, allowing her whole face to radiate its lively magic. Her eyes were the same color as her hair, hiding a rare fire in their pupils that evoked veneration, but as soon as one drew near, the fire would vanish into the distance like a mirage. The features of this warm brunette were not regular, and an artist would never have used them for his model—her face was not beautiful, not in the way that the blonde's was, but it had plenty to charm and interest. It was modern, interesting, cute. She wore a carmine-red dress of thick gauze with three rows of flounces, the uppermost of which were hardly a hand's breadth from the indentation of the bodice. This had a narrow belt of chrysoloid green watered silk.

After they had passed down the full length of Canal Street, the carriage turned into Tchoupitoulas Street.

The two young ladies had spent their time from the church to the named street sunk in contemplation, as chaste and pure souls are always wont to do after they emerge from a house of God.

"How I thank you, my good Constanze," the blonde said, turning to the other lady, who had just restored her gilded marquise comb, which had fallen out of her hair, to its proper place, "that gracious Providence has led you to our house and led you, a guardian angel, to me."

"Your thanks are owed to His Royal Highness, Prince Paul of Württemberg—not to me, my dear Dudley! The prince was the protecting spirit who watched you and freed you from the unhappy bonds in which the unworthy abbé held you."

"You must have thought me a child, my dear Constanze, when you considered how little I thought for myself."

"You had been forbidden to think, dear Dudley—that is not your fault," Constanze responded in a pained tone.

They were silent for a few moments, then Constanze said: "Learning to think is always combined with a danger, unfortunately—your head has gained, my friend, but the still quiet of your heart has been disturbed."

"See what a child I still am—your words flow clearly and unmistakably, and yet I cannot understand their sense."

"It is perhaps just as well if you do not understand, friend of my soul."

"I have only thought twice in my entire life. The first time was when heaven took my father, and the second time was when I lost my trust in the abbé."

"The first time was to the advantage of your heart; with the second time you lost your heart."

"You frighten me, Constanze—I lost, but I bear this loss happily, since heaven returned double to me by giving me your heart."

Constanze left her seat and settled next to her friend.

"You are so good, Dudley, and I have to weep over the betrayal that was made against your pure soul. Come, kiss me!"

The Negro who had stood by the door of the carriage in front of the church and who had taken his post at the rear as soon as the two women entered, peeked through the little window to observe how the two friends kissed one another by turns on the forehead and the mouth. He smiled and quickly withdrew, so as not to be observed satisfying his curiosity.

"My dear friend," Miss Dudley Evans began once more, placing her right hand in Constanze's left, "when I think of that hour when the prince of Württemberg brought you to our house and you were received so lovingly by my mother, I always feel a pang, since I can hardly forgive His Royal Majesty for not having had the stroke of genius sooner to make your lovely family known to us. Warm sympathy and certain interest would have chased away my unhappiness."

"The sympathy was there, even if it was late. Who knows what would have become of me, my parents, and my siblings, if the prince had been traveling a few months more, or if he had not accidentally met Gertrude?"

Miss Dudley wore a pleased smile as Constanze spoke these last words.

"You're smiling, my Dudley, oh how glad I am to see that! You are thinking about that droll business about the coffee-picking that the prince once told you of in his charming manner?"

"It's a good guess, my dear Constanze—I was just thinking of your little sister and what she was doing when we came home."

"As well as of her genius at coffee-picking," the old count's daughter said, smiling puckishly.

"Yes, I never forgot that. I have heard it told twenty times already, even more thoroughly and more precisely than by His Royal Highness. At first your little sister cast her eyes to the ground when I touched on this theme—now she often raises the matter herself."

"Gertrude has never been happier and more lovable than she is now, Dudley. She prays to you as if you were a saint. Yesterday she showed me a garter and asked me who owned it. When I mentioned you, she embraced me and acted utterly foolish."

"Because she had found one of my garters?"

"Yes. She said that you lost it by the large agave in the bower. She saw it right away, but she said nothing, and when you left she picked it up and hid it in a box. She decided that if you asked about it, she would not give it back to you."

"But what did your little sister do with the garter?"

"She kept it as a memento."

"A memento of me? Then I must give her something better, Constanze."

"It depends on whether another memento would please her as much. For her the charm is the fact that you know nothing about it."

"But I know now."

"But she thinks that you don't know."

Dudley Evans was silent for a moment and looked at the count's daughter with tender eyes. She extended her hand to her friend again.

"Do you know, Constanze," Dudley said with a lively accent, "when we get home I shall act as if I'm searching for something."

"That's good, Dudley. Gertrude will offer her assistance, and when you say you are looking for the garter, her troubled conscience will soon betray her."

"I am curious how she will act."

"Certainly in an original manner, as ever."

"I will demand the garter from her if she confesses taking it."

"She will confess her error, but she will not give it back to you."

"Do you think so?"

"Yes, I know her all too well—she would die if you insisted on it."

"Why so?"

"To be sure, she is just that remarkable a child."

"Oh, how sweet you both are! I could never do without you both. The very thought that we could ever be separated really makes me sad."

"I feel the same way, my dear friend, a separation from you seems impossible to me."

"I have to be upset with His Royal Highness whenever he takes Gertrude away from me in order to show her a pretty butterfly or a glittering bug, even though I am a bit jealous about the fact that he lets her keep the insects she finds."

"Isn't it true that the house on the Bayou Road where the prince resides once belonged to your mother?"

"Yes, my father had it built four years ago. For that reason she would sell it to no one other than the prince, which seems entirely natural to me."

"But what if he sells it again?"

"He cannot and will not, for he received it only with the promise that he would either live there himself or return it to mother. I would not entrust it to anyone else, least of all to an American, who would have no idea what to do with the lovely magnolias and cypresses."

"Dear Constanze," the blonde said jokingly, raising her index finger, "I was born on this soil as well."

"That's an entirely different matter, since your mother and father were both born in Scotland, so you are not precisely an American, thank God."

"You say 'thank God,' Constanze? Is it something bad to be an American?"

"Yes, since they lack heart and character."

"I never noticed."

"Because you never thought about it."

"You are cruel, Constanze."

"I did not want to offend you, Dudley, pardon me."

Dudley Evans knocked to signal the driver, giving the coachman a sign to travel faster. He immediately drove his horses forward.

"This is an ugly street," she said, "and the sun is unbearable. Your parents and siblings will love it across the lake—the air that blows there is healthier and cooler. We have to stay here another fourteen days. They will be all the more surprised when we bring Frida and Jenny. How your parents will rejoice to be able to embrace them again, after longing for them for such a while."

"If only the prince could manage to find my brother Emil as well. Poor Jenny is sometimes entirely disconsolate."

"Dear God will bring us these joys, too," Dudley responded with a hopeful look in her eyes.

"How do you like Frida's husband, my friend?"

"Quite a bit. He has an interesting, noble appearance."

"And a handsome face, although it is marred by a broad scar."

"I had not noticed."

"You hadn't? You just said that he had an interesting, noble appearance."

"Yes, his attitude and manners please me. You can tell by looking at him that he has enjoyed an excellent education."

"All of the Hungarian magnates' sons have that—though they are somewhat too proud and domineering. They are seldom able to bear contradiction, and so they often fall into the most uncomfortable situations."

"That is not the way I find him, Constanze. I am convinced that Hungarian officers must be that way and no other. Lajos is exactly as one reads of this nation in books."

"It is perhaps as well that he received a good lesson from a desperado's dagger."

"Is that why he has the scar on his face?"

"As he tells it, he had a duel about a year ago with a half-mad Mexican in Matamoros. It went well, in that neither was able to wound the other. But as they parted the Mexican jumped on Lajos, threw him to the ground, and cut his cheek with the point of a dagger."

"That's just too shameful!"

Lajos is of the opinion that his opponent was half-mad, since otherwise he would have ended the conflict honorably and not added such a shameful wound."

"That is possible—no one in their right mind is that raw and vicious."

"I would believe anything of a Mexican. Just look at them, they are a nasty people. I cannot think of a Spaniard or a Mexican without a dagger. When people speak of Mexico, I think at once of the pile of daggers and stilettos they constantly carry around with them."

"I didn't know that, Constanze. When I hear Mexico spoken of, I always think of fine feathery palms and splendid cactus and bounteous garlands of lianas. Now and then I think of Santa Anna with his wooden leg."

"You have the tales of the prince of Württemberg to thank for this association."

"That is quite possible, Constanze. The prince is utterly enthused and flames when he speaks of Mexico and his Parangas."

The carriage now went more slowly.

Dudley Evans rose a bit from her seat and looked out.

They were already in Annunciation Square. On the right-hand side, diverging from the church, surrounded by cypresses, oleanders, magnolias, and Weymouth's pines, stood the residence of Lady Evans-Stuart, Dudley's mother. From the outside, this house seemed to be only a simple, uncomplicated frame structure produced according to the ordinary American stereotype. But once you set your foot inside, the glimpse of a double ceiling with its accompanying niches revealed a purified taste. Luxury ruled in the furnishings, which did not display the coarse tastes of a moneyed aristocrat but rather the harmonious and sensual culture of an inherited élite who has been handed down her qualities in the purest manner. In short, this was the luxury that unfolds in every direction and does not injure.

A rather elderly man walked across the green grass of Annunciation Square with a pretty blonde girl on his right hand. They took rapid steps, their eyes turned to the approaching carriage.

"The prince and Gertrude!" Dudley calls out joyfully, and a pretty pink suffuses the tender, transparent paleness of her cheeks.

She has the Negro halt the carriage, and she and Constanze get out.

"Angel and Genius!" the prince of Württemberg declares as he stands before the two friends together with Gertrude.

"And you, Royal Highness, lead us on to Psyche," Constanze responded curtly, looking at her little sister, who was holding a small argus butterfly between her soft fingers.

"Mythology and Christianity," the prince of Württemberg entoned. They went to *déjeuner à la fourchette*.[7]

Chapter 2

On the Flight to Nineveh

It is sad but all too true that a guardian demon stands more steadfastly at the side of a bad person, guiding the way through vice and crime, than does any guardian angel in helping and protecting a good person. Anyone who knows people will have to confess this time and again, and in a thousand cases there will hardly be one instance in which sin is its own punishment or in which it exacts its own revenge. Whoever relies on these axioms is in no position to do anything good, since this assertion of inevitable recompense preaches indifference to the good and assures security to the evil. Disappointment over the failure of morality to win out is what confuses and obscures the concepts of right and truth. The greatest criminals are certainly those who have never been reached by the arm of Themis,[8] since they have always managed to exploit the virtues or vices of those who could harm them. Since they properly believe that they have nothing to fear from the existence of conscience, they capitalize on conscience and press it like an amulet to their cold hearts. While a hasty misdeed delivers many a good person to justice, thousands of crimes will not manage to endanger the freedom and security of such a true criminal. Is it happenstance, or is it a demon protecting them over the course of their lives?

A year after Lajos had left Watson's farm and boarded the *Sultana* to begin his journey to New Orleans, we saw him as a clubman of the 99th and 100th degree. The subject of this chapter and the following will be the events that happened to him during this time, as well as his activities from this return to the Gulf City until the moment when we hear him being discussed with such esteem by the two women-friends.

Without hesitating to fill in this gap, we are still tempted to remain silent about a particular serious matter, since divulging it would probably have serious consequences in intimate family circles. But someday a gust of wind from somewhere will lift the veil of its own accord, freeing us of the accusation that we have injured the hearts of the innocent, striking their eyes with blindness.

When Lajos left the Watson home, deep snow with deep wind-driven drifts, some three to five feet deep, covered the ground, threatening to swallow him up. Along the bayou, from the farmhouse to the bridge leading to St. Louis, there were several hollows that could prove fatal to anyone who did not thoroughly know the lay of the land. Lajos, who knew precisely every nook and cranny of the farm, even all of Bissell's Island—such a sense for detail of place is instinctual in such characters—avoided these sinkholes with care. He thought he had passed all of them when he jumped the fence and turned in the direction of the bridge. Then he stood and looked back on the farmhouse, as if he were remembering something he had missed on his departure.

"That dumb little goose would have loved me if I had had enough money," he mumbled to himself, "but so . . ."

He had extended his right foot, and it sank into a ditch the snow had hidden and leveled. The ditch had just been dug, so he had not known about it. He sought in vain to get out, to at least raise his head above the snow so he could cry for help. He flailed through the snow in both directions. A labor of Tantalus! The sinkhole was too broad for him to reach the side and climb up. Death appeared inevitable. He would gladly have sent a curse up to the open air, but the snow pressed on his pale lips, seemingly repaying him for his evil deeds. Then he suddenly felt a hard object on his shoulder that extended all the way down his back. Instinctually he reached back, and his hands grasped a picket barely two inches thick. With the weight of his body he pushed it down several feet, but it also raised him enough for him to taste the cutting air of winter morning.

A worker employed at the lumbermill barely two paces from the bayou bridge had seen the Hungarian sink into the ground, and he had rushed to the sinkhole with a picket in order to help him. As we have seen, this deus ex machina came just in time, or rather at the wrong time, since it would have been better for this satanic monster to have vanished from the earth in precisely this manner.

"Now I can breathe adequately—I certainly owe you a drink, since I cannot offer you anything better," the Hungarian said to his rescuer, who was taken aback by the man's chilliness.

"I have no idea how you got here, sir, but I can assure you that you do not need to be concerned about any demonstration of your thanks. I saw your life in peril, and I saved it. That is reward enough," the lumbermill worker declared.

"Never mind, I do not have the slightest scruples on this—I owe you a drink, then each will go his own way," the Hungarian remarked.

"I can tell from your pronunciation that you are no Yankee—you are certainly a German—then I am all the happier for rescuing a compatriot," the worker said, looking into the Hungarian's pale face, half in marvel, half in dread, for the Hungarian's eyes burned with offense.

"No German!" Lajos spit, still in English but bitterly cold, "but not far from it."

"Then you are certainly Swiss?"

"Swiss? Pah! Must a person always be Swiss if he is not a German? I will not respond to that—Swiss and Germans are the scapegoats among the nations."

"I cannot understand what you're trying to say, but it is as if you are trying to irritate me," the worker declared in a dignified tone.

"Pah! Let's leave it at that! I owe you a favor, and that's that!"

The German worker, a man still in his best years, shook his head in misgiving over the Hungarian's strange conduct. He walked alongside of him, wading into the deep snow, for it was early in the day—the walkways had not been cleared and the roads had not been traveled on enough to be used with ease.

"Here is Farmer's Home," the Hungarian said, pointing at an old frame building, "there we can have a drink. Do you know this bar?"

"Not much, I don't visit it more than three times a month. The boss doesn't like us to."

"I wouldn't care a damn about my boss," Lajos declared. "If you offer those scoundrels a finger they take the whole hand."

"You'll not get very far so long as you're compelled to work."

"Who told you I work?"

"Your arms are strong enough, and that coat is more suitable for a farmer than for a do-nothing."

"Isn't your boss a do-nothing who makes you work like a dog so that he can lie about on a bearskin? You're the ox on his treadmill, and if you don't measure up, he shows you the rod."

"It isn't that bad, sir. If you don't have the freedom to quit working, there is nothing you can do; even if my boss is a do-nothing, I couldn't care less, so long as he pays me decently."

They entered the barroom of Farmer's Home.

The bar called Farmer's Home was an old two-storied frame building belonging to a former official of the Elector of Hesse who had left Germany in the thirties and, after good and bad experiences in various parts of the Union, had settled down to earn a living in St. Louis. What he tried did not turn out well, and he soon sank so low that he had only twenty dollars left. One day he wandered, disconsolate, through the streets of St. Louis, playing with the thought of leaving town with the money he still had and taking a boat up the river, when he was suddenly drawn to signs of the Missouri Lottery displayed from an office, inviting him to come in and try his luck. He bought several half-shares and full-shares up to the amount of fifteen dollars, since it seemed too extreme to put his whole fortune on a single share. He passed the rest of the day with the greatest impatience. What was he to do if he won nothing? Hadn't he robbed himself of what he needed to travel on? These thoughts tormented but did not destroy him. In fact, the closer the time of the drawing came, the more enthusiastically he built castles in the air. They burst at once like soap bubbles, then he built new ones, painted in the brightest colors. At last came the moment when his luck was to be decided. He did not dare to be present at the fatal drawing. When the board with the new winning numbers was put out, he approached it several times without having the heart to look and see if he'd won Fortuna's gift. Finally he had to do it, and a quick glance at the large red numbers of the winners caused him to stagger back several steps. The joy of what he had seen transformed his face into that of the most fortunate of men. He had won the solid sum of nine thousand dollars! Nine thousand dollars, so suddenly received, is not to be sniffed at, particularly when one is in such a critical position as to have seen one's purse of twenty dollars decimated, as was the case with our Hessian official. On top of that, it is very hard for anyone in the ordinary course of things to come into possession of this sum, especially a German bureaucrat in America!

The first decision our lucky man made was not to leave St. Louis, and the second was to realize a long-treasured idea to marry. The object of his most intense desires was the daughter of a starch manufacturer in St. Louis who had an important operation on South Second Street, across from the convent. The hard-hearted father, who had been unwilling to release his daughter under the earlier conditions, now had nothing against it whatsoever, particularly once the happy suitor provided two thousand dollars in cash for his business. The starch manufacturer did his best to make his son-in-law into a settled citizen of St. Louis, trying to convince him to establish a solid household. But our former Hessian official had no desire to go into partnership. Perhaps he thought he was weak in starch. The social situation of his wife somewhat resembled that of his previous wife, who had been a linen supplier to a princely court and had died in Germany. Since he had loved his first wife with all the fire of an inflamed lawyer, the best prospects existed for the second match. For several months it went quite well. They loved each other, and they both were interested in the income at their confectionery on Franklin Avenue. Ice cream, soda, mead, pineapple sherbet, candies, and pies sold well, and it seemed there was little else needed to provide the foundation for a substantial fortune. But the gods willed it otherwise.

Either they envied the fine couple in their busy happiness, or they wanted to put the Hessian official through some sort of ordeal. But their lives were to be disrupted by an entirely innocent book, *Introduction to Swimming, Particularly on the Back and Treading Water.* One day, when the shop lacked paper for wrapping sweets, the young woman encountered this book in her husband's book locker as she was ripping out pages for this purpose. Her eyes fell on several woodcut illustrations showing male and female swimmers. This drew her into reading, and soon this pastry baker fell into the obsession that she should become an excellent swimmer. She wanted her husband, who she knew was a good swimmer in his own right, to support her in her efforts. Since he loved her, he agreed at once. Our bureaucrat took her to the water and taught her the art of swimming as best he knew how. After six weeks she had made such progress, particularly in the back float, that she already excelled her teacher. Who was more pleased than our bureaucrat? Whereas he had once been bored swimming by himself, now he had the loveliest companion in the world. All of his dreams of naiads and sirens were now literally fulfilled. The mania for swimming that had swept up his Little Obsessive, as he always called his wife in all tenderness, soon drew other followers, who made a lot of work for him. And the confectionery? It suffered from this madness for bathing. Whereas she had once taken care of everything herself, now she passed the work to other hands. The young woman wanted nothing so much as to talk about swimming, while the husband, who saw the business approaching ruin with every passing day, said not a word to his Little Obsessive. If he ever said anything, it was a gentle hint. More than a year passed. She had become a champion swimmer, but the confectionery had suffered a great deal. The hopes that our bureaucrat had harbored for the winter season were washed away. Since his Little Obsessive was no longer able to bathe in the river, she sought a replacement at home.

The first thing the Little Obsessive did to develop her nautical power was order a monster tub. This measured ten feet, three inches long, four feet, seven inches wide, and a disproportionate seven feet deep. Since the Little Obsessive measured all of four feet and a bit more in height, she had to pull over a table in order to climb into and out of the immense tub. The water was three feet above her head when she stood on the bottom, so handholds of gutta-percha had been made and placed about so she could pull herself above the surface and climb out. Two faucets above the tub provided hot and cold water. Under these conditions, the Little Obsessive had pursued her passion with great success for two months, and she had never appeared so beautiful, healthy or more at her best. The Hessian bureaucrat, however, experienced bad days and worse nights. Often she jumped up in the middle of the night, waking her husband, the pastry chef, his sister the counter clerk, the cook, and even the drowsy young man who had to sleep in the shop to guard at night. She would drive them all to arrange her bath, or (to use an Americanism) to "fix" it. What good were her husband's protests against these midnight uproars? He was preaching to deaf ears. Little Obsessive had it in her head to mobilize the entire house whenever she desired to bathe in the middle of the night. Since all complaints, even threats, produced nothing, her tormented husband was compelled to resign himself to his fate with all the patience of a true Christian. But he did not cease trying to figure out escapes and ways to put an end to this nonsense. Little Obsessive was no longer of any use in the shop, for her lack of attention led to the worst stupidities. If anyone came and bought a cake and she received, say, a five dollar bill, the buyer would wait in vain for the proper change. It often led to a real scandal. The uproar would draw a crowd that would eagerly follow the course of events or take sides. Little Obsessive would declare that she had determined to give no change because she was collecting to create a swimming school on the Meramec River next year, where anyone who came could swim for free. Of course, no one was satisfied with this.

She was cited, and, since she continued to be adamant in court, she was held to be insane, so her husband had to pay the money out of his own pocket, together with substantial court costs. It is remarkable that it never occurred to our bureaucrat to separate from his Little Obsessive. At least he was never heard to consider it aloud. Why the father-in-law, the starch manufacturer on South Second Street, closed his eyes to what was going on remains a mystery. So Little Obsessive found herself in a nautical mood on Christmas Eve, when the shop was filled with customers. For a change she wanted to prepare her bath by herself. After she had filled the tub with cold water so that about two feet of water filled the bottom, she turned it off and jumped in. Then she pulled herself up on the gutta-percha and opened the other faucet, which let in boiling hot water. In order not to scald herself, she stationed herself at the opposite side of the tub and watched the water stream in. After a few minutes she found it necessary to raise herself in order to turn off the faucet and turn on the other one. But when she gave it her best try, the handhold broke and she fell back into the tub. The hot water now rose to the level of her breasts. In desperation, she tried to get up to the faucets, but to no avail. She always fell back down. She screamed with all her strength, but no one seemed to hear her. Hence she met a dreadful death, and help came only after the water ran over the edge of the tub and flooded into the confectionery next door. Only then did they drag the unfortunate woman out of the monster tub, terribly scalded.

His Little Obsessive's death had a bad influence on the hitherto orderly life of our bureaucrat. In his grief, he utterly neglected his business, and in a calm moment he used his remaining money to buy the old frame house near Broadway and establish the bar, Farmer's Home. Our bureaucrat had told this story to the worker at the lumbermill.

After the Hungarian had settled down at the bar with his savior, a man entered and went to a spirit lamp to light up his cigar. The Hungarian stood in such a way that his back was turned to the man, while the German worker from the lumbermill was about to join his glass with the Hungarian's in order to give the customary toast.

"Don't clink glasses," Lajos declared rather harshly, bringing his glass to his mouth. "It is possible to put down booze without ceremony or ancestral customs. You are and shall remain Philistines, all of you—you don't even understand boozing as you should. I pray to hell if you could ever show me a Hungarian who would have been pleased by such a foolish comment and would not use his glass to shove the teeth down the throat of anyone who dared such pretension."

The German worker stared at the Hungarian with large eyes, and he was at a loss as to what he should do, as is the case with all good-humored persons in the presence of such characters.

"So you are a Hungarian?" was the sole question his distress permitted. Then, when the Hungarian did not respond, he asked again, in order to cover his embarrassment.

"If you are a Hungarian, then you are certainly one of many who had to flee to our hospitable shores, pursued by Austrian bloodhounds?"

"On the contrary," Lajos declaimed in his bitterly cold and cutting tone, "if I had not had to leave my homeland due to a dumb stunt, Görgey would have found in me a good friend."[9]

"Görgey? The scoundrel Görgey?" the worker asked in an agitated tone, seeming to wake from his repose, for he puffed out his breast and pounded on the table with a clenched fist.

"Scoundrel? How was he a scoundrel? More courage is required for grandiose betrayal such as Arthur Görgey committed than to run away to the Turks. Scoundrel? Only a coward is a scoundrel! But that's stupid stuff—drop it—I am no friend of arguing at a bar. Let's drink one more, then we will go our own ways—but have you heard of Rosza Sandor?"[10]

"Why?" the other declared, his face red with the agitation the Hungarian had caused him.

"Why? Because I hope he lives! He was the only one of the entire bunch who still has courage in his body. Such a fellow is worth more than a thousand Kossuths, of whom I unfortunately carry the Christian name."[11]

"If I did not have a wife and children," the worker said with all the dignity of an offended hero of freedom, "you would not leave this place alive. You deserve to be run through by every Hungarian who still wishes well to his fatherland."

"Hm! Hm! That sounds pathetic, and it would lead to a suitable response if my spittle glands were in better condition and I had not lost too much of that noble juice through abusing calomel."

On speaking these words, the Hungarian turned about and showed his face to the man who had just entered and lit his cigar on the spirit lamp.

"By the devil, Karl—how did you come here, not from New Orleans?" the Hungarian said to him, with a tremor of displeasure despite his coolness and composure.

"Lajos!" the man he addressed responded with astonishment, inspecting the Hungarian from top to toe with a slow gaze. Then he approached and extended his hand.

The Hungarian responded to the handshake of the cousin of his New Orleans wife with feigned friendliness.

"Goodbye!" he said to the worker from the lumbermill with an irritated nonchalance, slapping the money for the two rounds on the counter. Without Lajos's seeing it, the worker pushed back the part for his own drinks and paid them himself.

When they were back on the street, Lajos held Karl by the arm; Karl did not appear very charmed by this friendliness. He was still thinking about the exchange he had just overheard, not to mention the shameful abandonment of Frida. He was too distressed to be able to speak right away.

"Karl, What do you think of this fellow I wound up so much? The fellow was ready to box me or fire a slingshot at my head—if he didn't have a wife and child," Lajos added, looking at Karl with repellent warmth.

"You were certainly not serious," the cousin of the two sisters declared with a touch of light irony, putting both his hands into the broad sleeves of his paletôt. It was a bitterly cold morning.

"I would take it badly, Karl, if you harbored the least doubt. You know already from New Orleans that I like to make jokes, and that it gives me unending pleasure to lead dumb, stupid people around by the nose. I cannot resist this vice. It is a true passion of mine."

"Lajos, it was a very bad trick when you abandoned your dear wife, and it brands you a man without feeling," Karl said earnestly, pulling his arm back from the Hungarian.

"I beseech you not to not preach morality to me now. It was a bad trick on my part, I admit, but please do not confuse frivolity with lack of feeling. Even before we met, I had decided to rush to New Orleans and beg her forgiveness. It will certainly be a tough knot to untie, but I am determined, and I flatter myself that I can win her heart, which I have so dreadfully injured, once more."

"You might be deceived, Lajos. I know your wife's character too well."

"You are surely a great devotee of her amiability, Karl?"

"It would do you better to avoid any ambiguous references and inform yourself of your wife's current situation. Your decision to go to New Orleans appears very dubious, in fact, and is probably a ruse to put me off, to avoid just punishment from me. Do not expect me to try to talk you into returning or offer myself as an intermediary between you and your honorable wife. On the contrary, I would advise her against it, should you ever presume to enter into an intimate relationship with her."

The Hungarian stepped back a bit when he heard this, sounding so loud a roar of laughter that several persons passing on the other side of Broadway stopped and stared at the two of them, surprised and curious.

Karl, who saw full well that the Hungarian was not going to part so quickly, sought to control his raw outbreaks on the open street, preferring instead to draw him to his hotel, where they could reach an understanding in private, unobserved by others—if there was anything about which to reach an understanding.

"If love does not speak through these words, may all my friends go to the hangman. You, Karl, peacemaker, matchmaker, protector and advisor to tearless straw widows, venerator of the domestic hearth—you want to stand in the way as I pour out the remorse of my heart and call out the voice of my conscience to abandoned household gods? Karl, you are in love with my wife? Confess it, poor sinner!"

"If you would accompany me to my hotel, you will learn further details. The street is not the place to have this sort of discussion," responded the cousin of the two sisters in a decisive tone; he was deeply offended by the Hungarian's rudeness.

"Wouldn't it be the same if I besought you to accompany me to *my* hotel? The initiative rests above all with me, cousin Karl, or do you not understand that?"

"I really don't care, so long as it does not take place in another world," Karl declared. He could tell from the Hungarian's appearance that he was not staying at any hotel where appearance or elegance was insisted upon.

"You certainly believe," Lajos responded mockingly, "that I am not staying at any hotel, or at least at one which is quite miserable, such as an ordinary boardinghouse. That is easy to excuse, Cousin Karl, since you judge my situation from the shabby farmer's rags I am wearing, and so you believe you are justified in placing my nobility in question."

As he said this, the Hungarian reached into the side-pocket of his blanket cloak which he had received from Farmer Watson, and he drew out the two twenty-dollar bills, holding them up close to Karl's face.

"What do you mean by that?" Karl said, pushing the Hungarian's hand away.

"A proof that the greatest bum can still have money," the Hungarian declared.

"That doesn't concern me, and when you call yourself a bum, you are accusing yourself. Now I would like to ask you to follow me to *my* hotel."

"Good!" Lajos answered, pushing the paper money back into his pocket. They then walked more rapidly, laying a great stretch of road behind them without exchanging a word.

Each of them seemed to be brooding about something. Only their thoughts were worlds away from each other.

They turned onto Franklin Avenue and arrived at the corner of the first block, at Fourth Street. Here the sidewalks and pavements had been completely cleared by the store people or homeowners who swept the snow into the gutters. The vegetable market on Third Street was poorly supplied due to the deep snow, and on Fourth Street there were no lurkers: even the eighty-seven-year-old Dutch Mary, also called the Tomatoes Lady, with her quavering chant of *Eier und Butter zu stah'n,* had been kept away by the stormy weather. There was only one hen-man present, and his plucked geese and cackling hens cried out. Across the way, in Louis Bach's beer-house,[12] the German element of St. Louis held forth in its full consciousness, proclaiming over eternally full glasses the approaching springtime of the people and a dreadful defeat for the natives at the next municipal election. Further down, a news carrier for the *Demokratische Presse* was in over his head—he was trying to give his paper to a man and decry the *Anzeiger des Westens,* and he was being severely beaten for it.[13] A bit further along, a rabid horse-trader was leading four ponies of similar coloration toward the courthouse,[14] where a considerable market for these animals was held on certain days. This is a trade that is carried on by a type of person who always has a stud ready and also makes a lot of money breaking mules. These business heroes in such an occupation are people of the most dangerous character, both here and elsewhere in the Union, and they often dominate the voters at the ballot boxes with their ingenious rudeness.

They had now arrived at the Planters' House.[15]

Planters' House takes the first rank among the hotels of St. Louis, and it is, so far as comfort goes, better arranged than our St. Charles, Verandah, St. Louis, and City Hotels, although it is far behind what these have to offer in splendor and external appearance.

"So this is your hotel, Cousin Karl?" the Hungarian asked his wife's cousin as he entered with him. He said this in a tone entirely different from that which he had used earlier. He also buttoned his farmer's coat up to the throat, probably to hide a shirt of dubious whiteness. Karl was silent and went quickly up the broad stairs. Here he stepped to the side for a moment, taking his key from the blackboard. Then he sped up the narrow steps along the main hall to the third floor, opening room 135. Perhaps without meaning to, the Hungarian removed his crushed hat and arranged his tousled, long, black hair with his right hand. Then he straightened his cravat and entered after Karl.

"You live quite grandly here, Cousin Karl. What are you paying?" Lajos asked, looking in every direction.

"Two dollars fifty a day," he answered dryly.

"That's not much," the Hungarian responded with relief. "When you figure everything together, as well as the comfort that is offered here, you are always better in a house of the first rank than with the loafer mob in the Virginia Hotel.[16] What you pay there for the comfort is lost through the poor company and bad atmosphere."

"I don't think so," Karl responded, offering Lajos a place at his side on the sofa. “If I were paying for it myself, I would not be such a fool as to pay two dollars fifty every day for lodging and food, even if I had a hundred thousand dollars.”

“If you did not pay for it, then I am free enough to ask you who has been so good to you? I have never had the good fortune, though I have often had more need of it than you.”

“That could very well be,” Karl declared, “and concerning payment, it goes to the account of a firm in New Orleans that entrusts me with the delivery of western products.”

“Then you are no longer involved selling slaves? That was always a profitable business, and you understood it from the ground up. One must concede that.”

“I gave that business up when my first problems of survival had been overcome. It had disgusted me from the start, and I have always been glad to be free of it.”

“That would be a matter of indifference to me if I could make money doing it. Whether you lead people or oxen to the market, it’s all the same thing. Could you fix me up with a position of that sort, Cousin Karl? I would do my duty scrupulously. The sale of slaves remains the most noble of enterprises. And then there is the splendid thrill in your own skin when you’ve unloaded the colored blokes! You see, Cousin Karl, I am a man with southern principles, a passionate champion of National Democracy!”

“Let us speak of other matters,” Karl took the initiative again, after he’d sat quietly for a few moments.

“About what, for example?” the Hungarian asked, who was half-aware of why Cousin Karl wanted to speak with him in his room.

“We will have a duel!” Karl responded, standing up.

“I’m happy with that, only I want to know the grounds in advance.”

“You know what you said when we turned onto Broadway?”

“God damn it, I don’t remember anymore.”

“Just think about it!”

The Hungarian acted as if he were thinking, then he hastily asked: “Perhaps it’s because I said you were in love with my Frida?”

“Yes. That’s why we will have a duel.”

“But all joking aside, Cousin Karl, that is childish. Men such as ourselves would not put a bullet in another’s brain over a woman. Nonsense, Karl—stupid business, a game for kids!”

“I will accept it if you will. I find sufficient ground to be my own second. Will you accept?”

“Yes indeed, if you are set on it. We will shoot at each other on a sackcloth, that would be the most reasonable. Right now, here in the room, I'm ready. The bullet will be the arbitrator, Satan will sit on the pistol barrel."

"I did not bring you here to make jokes. I hope that you will duel with me in a manner proper to a gentleman."

"Well all right. With pistols, not cannons, obviously—you have two pieces available, since you are so hot to fight?"

"If you agree, say it and spare me your frivolous jokes."

"Yes, I want to! You could give me a pistol, since I have no weapon save this Bowie knife."

Karl stepped to a bureau and drew a six-shot Colt revolver from the drawer.

"I only have this one weapon, but I will give it to you and buy one for myself, if that will satisfy you."

"I don't want your revolver, but I want to go buy one myself, if you will give a few dollars based on my honest face, since the money I have is already committed elsewhere."

"That should not create any problems for you—here are ten dollars."

"I would throw these ten dollars back in the face of anyone but you—when is the duel?"

"Tomorrow morning between six and seven."

"Good—where?"

"Behind Weizenecker's vineyard, in New Bremen, if you know the place."

"To be sure, not far from Hyde Park."[17]

"We'll meet again, then," Karl said, making a movement with his hand which told the Hungarian to get up and leave the room.

Once the Hungarian had left, Karl reached into his travel bag and took out a small sheet of paper edged with a narrow gold band and laid an elegant, carefully pressed envelope next to it. After some consideration he reached for his pen and wrote the following lines:

Dear Cousin,

If I do not arrive in New Orleans after the passage of four weeks, I ask you to pass the enclosed papers through Tiberius or some other reliable person to the firm of K. & W. Do not delay the delivery any longer than the period I have indicated, since it is possible that the business of that firm could suffer if there is delay. What moves me to request your assistance is—please have enough presence of mind not to be shocked—I am going to have a duel tomorrow morning with an acquaintance I have met here in St. Louis who has badly offended me. Pardon my laconic proceedings, and do not accuse me of lack of feeling or tenderness. Many greetings to your sister

Jenny, and if my luck is good, we will be able to spend a couple fine, happy days with the lovely family of Doctor Austin in Ocean Spring. How much it would please me if I could move Jenny to leave New Orleans for good. For her thoughts of Emil find all the more nourishment in this odious city. Live well, dear cousin, and find nothing amiss in the apparent contradiction that one can think lovingly of a woman friend far away and thus write something of this sort.

With friendship, your cousin
Karl

Karl had hardly written half the letter before a remarkable episode took place one floor below him, on the second floor of the Planters' House. When the Hungarian descended, his attention was seized by a lady he glimpsed through a half-opened door, swaying in a rocking chair. The lady had her back turned to him and appeared sunk in thought, with her head on her chest. Through the wicker webbing of the chair back he could clearly see the form of her head, with thick blonde curls cascading down over the upper portion of her dress. A shawl laying half on the floor, half on her left chair arm, shocked him out of his usual coldness and indifference.

"Perhaps the woman is sleeping," he thought to himself. "The devil take me if that is not my wife, and the shawl is the one Karl gave her in New Orleans." He pursed his lips together and reached for his Bowie knife. As his gaze moved momentarily from its original target and moved about the room, he noted that on the little table inlaid with mother-of-pearl there was an album of chrysaloid green that banished all doubt. Now looking at the lady, then at the album, he quietly advanced to the small table, softly putting his hand to the album and opening it. He could not be mistaken. He saw his own drawing, his own handwriting. He drew his Bowie knife from its sheath and held its grip with a tight fist.

"It is she! It's Frida—hell and damnation—Karl has her with him," he thought. Suddenly, as if he thought better of it, he returned the knife to its sheath and hid it in the side pocket of his farmer's cloak. Then he nudged the little table with the tip of his boot, so that it made a little dance and then fell over. The lady awoke with a shock, with her first glance falling on the Hungarian, who stood there as if rooted, looking at her with cutting intensity.

"Only the window is open to you, my faithful Frida, the door is blocked," the Hungarian said, pulling down the corner of his mouth in mockery.

"What do you want here, sir?" the lady responded, looking questioningly in his face.

"Am I drunk, or are you my faithful Frida?"

"I demand again, sir, that you leave my room. Your mad words permit me to suppose that you are in a dubious state."

"Hell and damnation—such unexampled boldness!"

The young lady rushed to the bell-pull, but before she was able to grasp the ring the Hungarian pulled her away, holding her arms fast.

"Don't cry out, Frida, I advise you, you could force me to extremes—hmm, what a serpent, aren't you perhaps ashamed of me?—a person would have to be crazy not to offer a hand to such a pitiful-appearing robber."

The lady's terror at these words and the person who said them can hardly be described. The lady could not be Frida, since such dissimulation would have exceeded all the boldness any actress in this genre could ever have presented. And just recall gentle, calm, and clear-thinking Frida. How could she have presented such a false mania, acting as if she hated him from her very soul? As we shall later see, Frida herself in no way hated him at that time. Had the Hungarian been deceived? This could be no spook of an overheated imagination. The magic lantern of jealousy cannot project false forms, for jealousy knows its objects down to the last hair on the back of the neck—even pronunciation and tone of words, which betray a German despite every effort, reproduced Frida in every way. It was Frida, it had to be Frida!

"Hell and damnation, Frida, look at me, my dear—you could drive even the most certain man mad—unheard-of! How am I to begin? Look at me—quit this foolery! Look at me—or do you believe you can turn my head through your conduct, so that I end up believing it's not you? Well, by God, Frida, Frida, don't push it too far!"

The lady was no longer able to hear the last words; she collapsed into unconsciousness, so that her tormentor had to release her hands and catch her around her waist to prevent a hard fall. He did not do this out of consideration but merely from instinct, shared even by the rawest man. For she was a beautiful woman, and who could allow a beauty to fall to the floor without easing her situation as much as possible? Even centaurs will do that.

Once the Hungarian was convinced that the lady was not pretending but was in a genuine swoon, he stood several moments with his arms akimbo in the presence of this woman he believed to be his wife. What was he to do? Should he rush out, block the doors, and storm up to Karl to exact a dreadful revenge? Should he remain silent? Apologize? Leave her unattended—without revenging himself on her?

These thoughts raced through his brain, each struggling for the upper hand.

"What if she weren't?" he said to himself, "But by the devil, it must be her!"

Then he suddenly thought of the birthmark on his wife's upper left arm, in the form of a split heart, which he had first spied through a blouse sleeve of white gauze aboard the *Gutenberg*.

His wife had told him in a tender moment that Jenny had a birthmark in the same form, also of glossy black velvet, only somewhat closer to the elbow.

The Hungarian ducked down to the floor and grasped the lowest fasteners on her blouse sleeve to open it. It did not open as easily as he had expected. After several attempts, he became impatient, drew out his Bowie knife, and slit the blouse sleeve with one motion. Her arm was so situated that, had the birthmark been there, he would have seen it as soon as the sleeve was cut away.

If the Hungarian had been able to look into his own eyes at this moment, he would have seen reflected a fine naked arm on which was burned an anchor, of the sort sailors receive when they are initiated.[18]

The Hungarian, whose total imagination was concentrated on finding the split heart, did not even see the anchor, since it was not the birthmark. That is the way it often is with ordinary episodes of life. When a person is expected, for example, and someone stares continuously at one spot in expectation, he only has eyes for that one object. As a result, he does not see objects that would never have been missed if he had been observing less intensely.

The Hungarian made an ugly face when he did not find the birthmark.

"If it is not her, all the better in some ways," he said to himself, turning an indescribable look at the unconscious woman.

"But what about the album!" he thought, suddenly. "Wasn't that my own handwriting? It would be all too amusing if that was her album, if it were also my writing—this time Mr. Satan has bagged a big one! The fellow must be feeling very witty!"

Before he picked up the album, which had fallen from the little table onto the floor, he carefully closed the door.

He did not restore the little table to its treacherous legs, but rather he simply lifted the chrysaloid green album and opened it with so much haste that it almost fell out of his hands.

"Thunder and lightning! The thing is entirely different! Different pictures, different mementos. But my things, my handwriting? He leafed through at random, finally finding the fatal page.

He saw, read, and read some more.

"Similar autographs! Nothing more! How did that scoundrel come to America? Did he escape from the lead mines of Venice? And such a scoundrel still found a nest in the souvenir book of such a lovely lady? We will investigate this when we get to New Orleans, where he is now, as this proves. Wonderful, excellent! A vein of California gold in this city of dross—with that scoundrel in the situation, there is money to be made!"

With the closest attention, he had read the following several times:

> From the instant when you, Miss, took pity on a condemned, innocent man, and gave him your hand to escape from the killing air of prison, the star of my happiness, which had seemed to have set forever, is once again arisen, fine and sparkling, appearing to me in fabulous splendor in the still of the night, when love tolls the beating of my heart. My profession compels me to pursue my duties as a physician in New Orleans, and I will particularly dedicate my efforts to that illness which has carried away so many unfortunates through many a year. I have followed your counsel to take a different name to avoid problems. I shall not see you again. Keep these lines in remembrance of a man who could never possess you because the prejudice of the Old World has branded him a common criminal. My happiness consists in bearing you forever in my heart and to permit no other wish to arise but to know you are happy. You will find in your journey to Milwaukee the leisure which will do your restless spirit such good.
>
> Your thankful
> Gabor von Rokavar

"Infamous hypocrite and moral bum!" the Hungarian ejaculated. "The scoundrel is still the same—the lead mines of Venice have not weakened this toad's poison—yet I might have some use of this paper, or at least make a fool of the thankful Gabor, or, if that scoundrel possesses anything, perhaps I could squeeze money from him."

He tore the paper from the album and stuck it in the jacket of his farmer's coat.

In the hotel, the signal had been given for lunch. At that moment the Hungarian heard several doors open and slam shut. He rushed out the door and down the stairs with a degree of composure.

As he reached the lowest steps, he encountered two young ladies, elegantly dressed, and he heard one of them speak the words: "Our dear Frida appears still to be sleeping, we shall surprise her in bed."

"It is silly of her," the other responded, "since she knows that Lajos is returning at eleven." The Hungarian stood stunned for a moment, then he rushed out of the Planters' House, murmuring to himself as he crossed to the courthouse.

"All of St. Louis is a nest of witches—now there is even another Lajos!"

The first thing the Hungarian did was go to the nearest coffeehouse, order a whiskey punch, and then check in the *Missouri Republican* under "steamboats" for the next boat departing for New Orleans. He discovered that the *Sultana* was leaving the next morning at ten for the Crescent City. He quickly decided to take this steamer to New Orleans, since he was determined to leave the scene of his bold atrocities and crimes. Having made such a decision, there was no more thought of the duel. This was how he trifled with the trust of his cousin Karl. The ten dollars he'd received for the purchase of a weapon was instead taken to a hatter, where he bought a fine castor hat for nine dollars. Then he picked up a pair of silver-gray kid gloves and paid for them with the other dollar. He paid ten of the forty dollars Farmer Watson had given him for a coat that was good and fashionable if not fine, and five for trousers. He bought a simple black alpaca vest for two dollars and a half-dozen store-bought shirts with nine dollars. From the remaining fourteen dollars, he bought a pair of fine shoes and a travel bag, all for ten dollars.

His total fortune, which had amounted to fifty dollars including the ten he had from Cousin Karl, had melted down to four dollars.

Then he sought a private boardinghouse where he could be sure he was not known, and, having found one, he put his things in order and made ready for the next morning. He stuffed all the clothing he had worn before, as well as his torn shoes and ragged hat, into his travel bag, so that it acquired a stately bulge that could only do honor to the person carrying it. He put on his new clothes straightaway. He looked so transformed in these that his landlady almost did not recognize him when he appeared at the dinner table. After the midday meal, he went out again and took care of several sundries, further decimating his purse. He had to get a cigar case, cigars, a comb, and a toothbrush. As he figured it, he had only a dollar and a half left. The boardinghouse would cost at least a half-dollar until the next day. He drank up fifty cents of the remaining dollar and only possessed a last half- dollar on the next morning when he boarded the boat.

He allowed himself to be treated to a drink by the captain of the *Sultana,* in order to make the man's acquaintance, which is vital for any passenger without means desiring passage to New Orleans. It often happens that sharpies are more favored by luck than are modest, honest men, and that was the case here as well. Immediately after the first drink, the captain of the *Sultana* discovered that the Hungarian was a nice, entertaining man "of high education," as he said it, and this splendid gentleman was not at all backward about announcing that he was unable to pay for cabin passage right now, which ran twenty-five dollars. When he arrived in New Orleans, he would have no problem covering the debt on the spot. The boat clerk made a doubtful face when the captain informed him of his decision in this matter. But that did not matter, since Lajos appeared well covered and splendidly cared for. A captain is a patron not to be passed up if one is an insolvent passenger.

As soon as they passed Cairo, the Hungarian felt intolerably bored. He even appeared to avoid the captain's company, perhaps because his attempt to win a pecuniary advance had failed utterly. He also avoided the sole attractive lady in the ladies' cabin, with whom he had made a passing acquaintance on a lovely, moonlit night, because all she could talk about was her baby, who had died in St. Louis of cholera, and her husband, who had asked her to come to New Orleans, where he had opened a dry goods store and made "plenty money." Lajos went around the entire boat, sitting sometimes by the paddlewheel, sometimes on the steps to the top deck, where he would smoke, then throw his cigar into the river and light another. During the day he would lie for hours in his cabin, only driven out by the sounding of the bell for dinner and supper. This is how he passed the time as far as Donaldsonville. There he would discover some variation in the monotony of his existence. While he was turning one evening to cross the aft area of the cabin deck, he heard a splendid song from the 'tween decks. It was a woman's voice that drew him with all intensity. They were well-known songs that conjured up many a memory of the Old World. They sang the beautiful duet in *Alessandro Stradella*.[19] What a beautiful voice sang Stradella in the 'tween decks!

Italy my Fatherland,
How beautiful to look upon
Walled in by blue clouds,
Crowned with flowers.
My mouth praises you—my song is for you,
My heart beats in hot passion for you.

Venezia bella—bride of the sea,
You are praised to me by all,
Where of evenings with soft, enticing lute,
The barcaroles sound.
Before the high balconies, up and down move
The gondolas of lovers,

And roses fall as friendly reward
To the singers of these songs.

The Hungarian paced back and forth on the deck as the Leonora took up her part. Could such song work its magic on the heart of a murderer?

I praise Rome's holy walls,
The powerful construction of high domes.
It fills my breast with a pious shudder,
In my heart it says: trust in God!

"Damn'd!" the Hungarian cried out, loud enough for one of the deck passengers to look out, and then he repeated the curse. The singer did not allow herself to be disturbed:

And the clouds over Campagna,
How splendid, when Aurora shines,
The lark raises a light wing
And chirps the morning song.

"Let them go to the devil!" Lajos cried out between verses. "This gang would be able to turn a fellow soft!"

"Quiet up there!" the voices rose to him, and he saw some had risen from their seat, which consisted of a board set on the railing, and moved to get a look at the disturber of the peace.

Barbarino's song rose above the roar of the *Great Missouri,* which the *Sultana* was just passing in a betting race. Malvoglio continued:

I praise Naples,
Under the burning sun,
I rest in a stack
And yawn on the beach,
And gobble macaroni
Without an end
With you bums
With *dolce far niente.*
I sleep *alla stella*
Covered by heaven
And dance the tarantella
When my dear wakes me up!

Had it all finally reached the Hungarian, or was it simply out of a desire to make himself heard that, as soon as Malvoglio's part was finished, he joined in to sing the penultimate verse of the "Romanze" with a full, powerful voice?

> *Jo sono pittore*
> Quite quick with my hand,
> Called Salvatore
> *Il rosa.*
> In chasm
> And crypt
> And horror
> At home!

"Encore! Encore!" sounded from all the mouths on the lower deck, as they made every effort to see their unknown partner on the gangway. When the Hungarian saw this, he pulled back from the railing, over which he had been leaning half his body. Then he brushed the satin dress of a lady and felt a hand on his shoulder. He turned around in amazement. It was the same lady who had lamented so about her baby and had so bored him that he had been neglecting her for days.

"How sweetly and movingly you sing, sir!" the lady declared in a lively voice, adding rather more quietly, "That's a very nice song, sir—Hungarian songs are right behind our Yankee songs as the prettiest."

"That was not Hungarian but German!" the Hungarian responded with irritation, for the woman irritated him.

"My God, that was German, sir? I would not have believed that songs in German could sound so sweet, very sweet, mighty pretty, indeed!"

"To be sure!" the Hungarian responded mockingly, to revenge himself for her classic "indeed."

"Certainly," the lady said, without having noted the Hungarian's sarcasm in the slightest. "How sweet you must have felt, sir, when you sang this song!"

"I cannot really say, ma'am, a little tremor of feeling, that is all."

"Oh, that reminded me so painfully of my baby."

"What, my tremor of feeling?"

"Oh, do not mock me, sir! Every song reminds me of my baby, since I always sang to it before it went to sleep."

"Then you are a singer as well, ma'am?" the Hungarian declared, bowing.

"Certainly, sir!"

"Then you will certainly not deny me a modest request?"

"To sing a song?"

"The loveliest America has to offer."

"The most lovely? Why yes!"

The lady pressed her hands against her bosom with her best grace, and she began:

Miss Lucy has a baby,
Lucy, Lucy la
She rocks the baby Lucy
And put it in the grass . . .

The noble songstress was interrupted in midtune by hellish laughter from the lower deck. She rushed away, mortified, since she saw that the Hungarian appeared to enjoy this interruption.

The Hungarian never learned who the singers were, or the Leonora. They were no longer to be heard. He himself quietly conceded that he had only been listening, and that they had almost managed to put him in a sentimental mood.

When the boat arrived in New Orleans, he had the pleasure shortly before embarkation of overhearing the lady tell the first mate the same tale about her baby that he had heard at their first encounter.

Chapter 3

Interludes

We now lead those of our lady readers who are so inclined back to Algiers, to the lovable cottage in which the sisters live.

Frida's wise, placid sense appears to have had a pacifying influence on Jenny's unruly and passionate feelings for her absent husband. The nights when she complained about her hard lot, hanging on her sister's shoulder for hours, grew less frequent. In fact, Frida sometimes thought Jenny's longing for Emil was receding, or at least taking on a milder form.

Since the time we first became acquainted with Jenny and Frida, since that day when Jenny embraced Cousin Karl, important changes had taken place in their little household. It is not as if they had altered the way of life they had chosen—no, things went on much as they always had—but they had accepted occupations that gave some hope of a better future, if not a glittering one. Whereas once they had simply lived off the interest of the little capital that remained after Emil's spendthrift ways, now they were able to put money away for emergencies and to gather more interest, while they earned enough to support a modest existence.

The two sisters were perfectly aware that a person who did not know English and French was doomed to a subordinate position, so they had concentrated great patience and effort on learning these languages, and their efforts paid off all the more because of their mastery of German philology. So far as English went, Frida had some advantage on Jenny, just as Jenny outdid her sister in French. The difference in their accomplishments arose from their characters. The more passionate and emotional Jenny was naturally more inclined to French, while the reflective Frida had an easier time with English. So it happened that when Frida applied for a position at Boursier's Institution (*Rue Toulouse* 184, between Rampart and Burgundy),[20] she was hired immediately after taking an examination, though for the modest salary of thirty-five dollars a month.

In a mere two months as a piano teacher, Jenny had won entrée to several wealthy French families and acquired no small reputation. Her pupils loved and respected her, and they invested so much enthusiasm that Jenny enjoyed her hours of teaching. The rapid progress of her female students drew others who had already begun with other teachers but whose parents decided to submit them to Jenny's greater talent.

The two sisters' leisure time was occupied with caring for the little flower garden in front of the house, with raising rare, good vegetables, with improving the household utensils, and—especially on Sundays—with reading good books. Frida had chosen Goethe as her darling, and she began studying him systematically, rather than making only the quick survey that most of her sex would. As a chief result, she gained a peaceful, secure view on life due to his poetry. If Frida had thought of her husband, she would certainly have had reason to complain over her fate, but her pain evaporated in the light, silver clouds of an Italian sky, and she found a safe haven with the two Leonors. Jenny, on the other hand, preferred to press the lyre of Karl Egon Ebert and Lenau to her heart, or she looked for her Emil in Kinkel's *Otto der Schütz.*[21] She was afraid of reading novels.

They had very little time during the week, since their teaching hours, which they kept conscientiously, used up the entire day, so they had taken into their service a German maid who had only arrived on the Bremen ship a few months before. She was a very young thing, but despite her years she was a capable and practiced cook. She had served in student inns since the age of twelve, and she had taken turns overseeing the kitchen. In everything else the good little one was a spirited, stupid little fool. As soon as she stepped away from the kitchen stove, she might as well have been in a

Spanish village. This is all the more amazing, since a students' maid is experienced in *everything,* whether on the dueling field or in the seraglio. But this is the wrong place to hold her past against her, since touching the virgin soil of America washes away all sins. Every girl becomes a virgin again if she doesn't bring a man with her. The maiden was named *Urschl.*

Meanwhile, the sisters had constant trouble with little Tiberius, who never wanted to mind. Instead of staying at home when his mistresses were gone, he wandered about in the bushes or hung around with the young black men on the neighboring plantation. That alone would have been fine, but when the Don Juan in him began emerging, that was too much—also a bit too early, since Tiberius had just turned ten a few months before. Even this would not have been too bad if his thoughts had remained with the daughters of Ethiopia, but his imagination avoided this fruitful field and turned to a white woman—a daughter of *Germania.* The moment Urschl, the saucy cook, entered the house, Tiberius believed he was destined to take a place in her heart from which no master or missus would ever dislodge him. Miss Urschl, who was still quite green and who had barely escaped the claws of the Immigrants' Intelligence Bureau with a whole hide, was quite pleased at Tiberius's courting, particularly after the crafty fellow made it clear to her that, after the two ladies, he was the first in the house and that they had bestowed on him command over her conduct both in and outside of the kitchen. The saucy cook from the Lüneburger Heath—where her uncle still held sway over several fields of buckwheat—had naturally not acquired the southern outlook on the relations between black and white, so she subordinated herself without complaint to the commands of the "moor," as she called a black person.

Tiberius was smart enough not to command the cook in the presence of the sisters. His communication with Miss Urschl was also elevated by the fact that Tiberius knew enough German to be able to make his erotic feelings known. When the girl from the Lüneburg Heath comprehended that her Tiberius was serious, she began to play coy and cause her black shadow to sigh and boil. The following episode demonstrates, however, that Miss Urschl was a pretty dumb little goose: The sisters had left Algiers by ferryboat at eight in the morning, as was their habit, to pursue their professions in New Orleans. Tiberius was alone with Urschl in the kitchen. He had functioned as cook earlier, and he had an excellent understanding of how to prepare some dishes, thanks to Frida's careful tutoring. The sisters could not do a thing with American cooking. *Bouillon à la reine, ragout en coquilles,* roast veal with *sauce remoulade, flameris, blancmangés* and *crèmes,*

Bettelmann, armer Ritter, Magdeburg sausages, even Bavarian *Dampfnudel, Rahmstrudel* and *Mehlspatzen* were all rare dishes in America. Urschl knew how to fix all of them, so Tiberius could bow out of the kitchen entirely. Despite that, he snuck back to Urschl's atelier as often as he could; the saucy cook was truly astounded at his knowledge of cooking and assured him that she would never have expected such knowledge from a moor. But Urschl was all the more astonished when Tiberius assured her that he had figured it all out himself with no one's advice. Another reason he had been banished from the kitchen was that he could not resist nibbling, and he even had the dreadful habit of taking whole handfuls of raisins or pimentos to give to his friends. Once the ladies had caught him exchanging a whole pot of sugar for a paper kite. Naturally, the sugar and the kite were returned to their previous owners. As punishment, Tiberius was put in the cooling hole under the cistern for four hours, including dinnertime, where he was shameless enough to devour a whole jar of canned peaches the ladies had stored. No sooner had the ladies set off for the ferry that morning than he rushed back to the kitchen and sat on the floor next to Urschl, who was busy washing cups. Since, in his tenderness, he had even begun pinching the bare legs of his beloved, Urschl had had the foresight to gather her dress between her legs and press them firmly together.

"My sweetheart," the little black Don Juan began.

"What do you want?" Urschl asked, turning a bit to the side where her black beau sat.

"I wish we were masters in the house, or that I would be massa and you my lady."

"I'd like that, too," the saucy cook declared.

"I wish we could just get married."

"I'd like that, too, but that wouldn't work, since we have no money."

"We'll save the money. We already have twenty dollars and a picayune—five times more, then we'll go to the justice of the peace."

"Tomorrow my month is over, then we'll have another eight dollars. Keep the money carefully, Tiberius, so no one steals it."

"Don't worry, my sweetheart, it is in a good place. When you get your eight dollars, take care that the ladies do not see that you give it to me to keep for you."

"It's obvious that I'll be careful," Urschl declared.

"Come sit with me, my sweet Urschl."

"No, not now, Tiberius—I have no time—yesterday I was almost late with the meal."

"*Never mind* if the ladies have to wait for their meal a few minutes."

Tiberius was pressing her more, when she heard someone upstairs going back and forth.

"Devil!" the little scoundrel cried out. "There is someone in the upper room."

"Go up right away, Tiberius, and see who it is. You left the door open again," Urschl said anxiously, turning to do something at the stove.

"Devil, hell!" Tiberius cursed, pressing another heartfelt kiss on Urschl's shoulder. Then he left the kitchen in a hurry.

"Is anyone there?" he called out as he entered the hallway and looked around.

"Anybody there?" he repeated, jumping up the stairs all the way to the upper story.

When Tiberius opened the doors of the drawing room, he discovered a young man in the dark blue, white-bordered uniform of the American No. 2 Fire Company sitting languidly in the deep armchair beside the piano, with one leg laid on the other.

He had placed his heavy hat next to himself on the floor, its bottom turned up. He held a notebook, which he quickly opened and closed. His eyes stared at a picture opposite him, that of a young, beautiful lady. She was wearing a dress of black velvet, and across her breasts was spread a broad, bright blue sash from which hung the enameled cross of an order, half hidden in silver fringes. Anyone seeing this young man for the first time would take him for a Creole. The clear, tan color of his skin, his handsome black moustache, and the full, dark hair justified this assumption.

Tiberius did not recognize the young man at first, since his fireman's uniform rendered him unrecognizable for some moments.

"The ladies have gone over to the city?" the young man asked the Negro boy, who looked at him in puzzlement. He was an unaccustomed sight in his uniform.

"The ladies will be back home at midday," Tiberius responded, still astounded. He went back toward the door.

"Tell the ladies that I was here and will return after the firemen's parade."

"Yes, sir."

"The young man made a sign with his hand that Tiberius was to withdraw. He remained sitting in the armchair for a brief time and brooded over the picture hanging opposite him. Then he quickly left the cottage and boarded the ferryboat that had just crossed over from the opposite bank.

Once he arrived on the soil of New Orleans, he saw that the procession of the fire companies had already begun moving along Canal Street. The engines, decorated with ribbons, rosettes, and garlands of flowers, the fluttering banners, the fresh, youthful faces and strong bodies of the firemen in their various uniforms, the happy music of the bands, including splendidly outfitted Negroes with drum and fife—all of it offered a fantastic and enjoyable sight. The chivalry of all New Orleans was on the march, and the *petits-maîtres* of the French District hung on the gaze of the hundreds and hundreds of ladies who stood on the verandahs and balconies, occasionally sending sharp arrows at the firemen's hearts. In return, they gazed boldly, wantonly into the raven-black eyes of the best ladies of the Crescent City. Everyone was overjoyed and cheerful. Only the brokers of money, real estate, cotton, provisions, and so on displayed dumb, ash-gray faces. In return, they were graced with not one glance from the made-up ladies.

The young man we met only a moment ago in the two sisters' charming cottage now joined the ranks of his company and took hold of the hose engine.

Let us look back at the cottage in Algiers.

Tiberius, after having waited patiently until the handsome fireman had left, rushed at once to the kitchen to dedicate his attentions once more to Urschl exclusively. He found the cook hard at work slicing eggplant to lay in a pan already crackling on the stove over a rather intense charcoal fire. Fried eggplant was the two sisters' favorite dish, and it had to appear on their table at least every other day. This was probably the only American food they had come to like. Tiberius fell once more into his old wicked ways, sitting on the floor and pinching the saucy cook on her naked legs. He did not just leave it at that. He groaned and sighed like a love-sick Adonis, even though he had barely passed his tenth year. Urschl was in a hard situation. She knew quite well that it was not easy to serve two masters. Either the midday meal would be ready at the proper time and Tiberius had to stop his gallantry, or the former would be delayed so that she could give her black Adonis a hearing. Which to prefer? Urschl, who did not want to give her employers occasion to be upset with her, but who did not want to be too harsh to Tiberius, either, resorted to a trick.

"What time is it, Tiberius?" she suddenly asked the black scoundrel, who continued his pressing without letup.

"I don't know," he responded, "it couldn't be much before ten."

"Oh, get up and look at the clock in the dining room."

"That's unnecessary, my dear, sweet Urschl. It must be about the same time it was yesterday."

"Go and look at the clock, Tiberius, or I will be in trouble when the ladies come."

"Why, then?"

"Shortly before they left, the ladies told me to tell you to take the small carpet downstairs and beat it until they got back. You were also supposed to catch the rabbits that are making so much trouble in the flower garden."

"I will pound the carpet, and I'll have time to catch the rabbits tomorrow or the next day."

"No, Tiberius, that won't do. The ladies commanded me expressly to have you catch them before midday and stick them back in their little brass hutch."

"Never mind, Urschl, there is time for that later. I could say that I looked for the damned rabbits but could not catch them."

"If you don't want to upset me, Tiberius, do it."

"But when I have pounded the carpet and caught the rabbits, I'll return to you, my sweet, dear Urschl."

The saucy cook rewarded the obedience of little Tiberius with a couple of juicy kisses. He left the kitchen and rushed to complete his assigned duties.

Tiberius was occupied a good two hours with pounding and cleaning the carpet, so it was already past twelve when he went into the flower garden to look for the fugitive bunnies, without success. He searched through everything, even throwing a glance now and then over the neighbor's fence to try to spy them out on alien territory. In vain! The bunnies had either burrowed under the ground in order to make a safe attack on the young, fresh plants or utterly vanished from the premises. Or, more likely, they had been caught by a covetous hand.

He was contemplating leaving the garden in order to search under the woodpile and sugarcane pile in the adjoining yard when he happened to glance at the north side of the house. To his amazement, he saw the two bunnies on the wooden hatch of the cistern. One of them, a cute, snow-white beast, was acting out its role as a male, while the other, also white but with a black stripe on its velvety belly, was hopping away. It was acting out the role of a female.

Tiberius had enough zoological wisdom, or at least enough experience, to know that bunnies do not climb onto cisterns but rather remain on the ground. At first he thought that Urschl had played a joke on him so he would have to search a long time. But on closer examination, he discovered that both the bunnies had reached the cistern in the ordinary way. The cistern was the same height as the very deep window that adjoined the little room in which the bunnies had been shut up by Frida shortly before the sisters left. She had forgotten to close the window completely, and the bunnies had found their escape through this opening that led nowhere but to the cistern. When Tiberius saw this, he could hardly wait to get the little beasts into his hands. They could not escape him, for sure, even if they went back through the window into their room, where they could be all the more easily grabbed.

Tiberius flew more than he walked up the stairs to the room from which the rabbits had dared their stroll to the top of the cistern. He entered softly but swiftly. The bunnies were still in the same place, the one still demonstrating his maleness, the other her femaleness.

"Bissy, bissy, bissy!" the pleased rascal purred, rubbing thumb and forefinger against each other.

Whether it is true that love is blind, or whether they were simply terrified by the sudden appearance of the Negro boy—the bunnies did not watch their footing and fell through the slats of the hatch and into the cistern's deep belly.

"Tuff!" the Negro cried in shock, sticking his head into the cistern in curiosity. It held two thousand gallons of water when filled to the top. At the moment, however, the water stood only three feet above the bottom, although there had been a big rain two days earlier. This paucity was due to Urschl's negligence: when she had drained off the water for the next day, she had not turned the faucet tightly enough. As a result, the faucet had opened while everyone was sleeping, wasting much of that vital element. It will soon be seen that a benign spirit must have caused the faucet to open, thus saving two persons from an otherwise inevitable death.

"Tuff! Tuff! Bissy! Bissy! Bissy!" Tiberius called out into the depths of the cistern in an almost tender tone, where the two bunnies splashed about, hanging onto the ladle. How was the dear couple to be rescued without the aid of a second person?

"Urschl! Urschl!" the little one howled from the cistern.

Shocked and shaking all over, the cook ran out of the kitchen and discovered her Tiberius with widely spread legs, as Negroes are wont to do, standing on the hatch of the cistern. At that instant, she had no idea whether he was making a joke or whether his howling had some foundation. But since he did not cease his howling for Urschl, she ran up the steps to the room and flew through the window that Tiberius had opened before going out on the cistern.

"Urschl, Urschl! See how the rabbits are drowning—Tuff, Tuff—Bissy, Bissy, Bissy!"

"Jesus Christ, Tiber—did you throw them in?"

The saucy cook turned to Tiberius so suddenly when she said this that he slipped and, as he tried to steady himself by grabbing Urschl's dress, he pulled her into the cistern along with him. The fall was sudden, but no less suspicious even if one overlooks the results. Tiberius, who landed on his feet, pulled the saucy cook, who had landed head first, out of the hostile element. In thanks she sprayed his face with the water she had swallowed.

"No matter, Urschl—the water isn't deep."

"But the bissies, Tiber? Jesus Christ, if the ladies come!"

"Never mind—they could have landed as well as we did."

"But Tiber—the bissies, the bissies?"

"No matter, they're quite dead anyhow."

And so they were. The good little animals had already lost their lives. The cook sought in vain to awaken their vanished spirits by warming them on her bosom. But Charon's boat had already rowed them beyond the warmth of life.

Only then did she wonder about how they were to get out.

They hung silently together for a long time while they inspected their prison on all sides and recognized the impossibility of getting to the light of day. Tiberius was the first to break the silence. Standing up to his waist in water, he warded off mosquitos here and there, for the hatch had fallen completely off, making their entry easier. His eyes were filled with the image of Urschl, then water, then fire. Tiberius, stamping like a young bull that has been taken from a rich pasture and tied to a post—who would dare, in the presence of such a tableau, to continue to doubt of the existence of romanticism in America?

Romance is there, but no one sees it, since the virgin Columbia has not yet produced a Tieck or a Stollberge.[22]

Chapter 4

A Parrot in Cupid's Service

When the sisters returned home, they were not a little astounded to find the garden gate, the yard gate, and the front door open. Their astonishment turned to distress when they found two cows trampling their flower beds and borders, greedily stripping away the fresh leaves of the mulberries they themselves had planted. When they saw that both the beds they had planted on either side of the shadowy path, in the form of a heart, had been robbed of all their decoration, tears came to their eyes.

"It is dreadful of Tiberius to pay so little attention to our property," Frida said to her sister.

"We have let him get away with too much up until now, my dear Frida, we should have kept a closer watch on him and punished him more," Jenny responded, gazing at the ruin about her.

"I think it would be best to sell him before he causes new injuries from his limitless carelessness," Frida remarked.

"I would have suggested that to you long ago if Tiberius had not been a remembrance of Emil, who gave him to me on my first birthday in the New World. Tiberius seemed to be an entirely subservient boy—only later did I discover that he had a sneaky character that could not be altered by the best, most careful handling."

"That's the way all Negroes are, Jenny. Only a truly military discipline will keep them within limits. You have seen that he did not dare to utter a sound, and that he was as obedient as a dog when Karl was around."

"But Cousin Karl is often too strict with him. You can punish a person with fasts and work, for a time, when others wish—but to beat him, even with a light belt—I don't like that, Frida. I could not see my worst enemy beaten, even if he displeased me greatly."

"Cousin Karl hates that too, dear Jenny—but he knows how to make exceptions, and you have to admit that they always came at the right moment."

During this conversation, the sisters had drawn near to the cistern.

Frida, who first noted that the hatch had fallen away, said: "Yet another proof of Tiberius' negligence. He only had to go into the room and replace the hatch from the window—that certainly takes no great effort. Still, he leaves the cistern open, and the dust and dirt that flies about makes the water undrinkable and unhealthy, particularly at this time of year."

Frida stood together with her sister.

The former, having taken a look, continued: "It is also inconceivable, by the way, how boards could fall down at all without having been moved on purpose. Tiberius probably committed some foolish stunt while we were away."

"Didn't you close that window, dear sister? See, it is completely open. Perhaps Tiberius saw the bunnies and had some fun with them," Jenny contributed.

"This boy finds that irresistible; we've forbidden it more than twenty times. If he could be gentle with them, then of course he could play with them. But he nicks them in the ears or the legs, or he ties them together."

"Urschl lied to me, missus—Urschl is guilty of all the trouble!" sounded from the interior of the cistern.

The two sisters looked about in wonder, and when they did not see Tiberius, whose voice sounded once more in their immediate vicinity, they thought the rascal was hidden in the cooling hole under the cistern, eating the preserves.

"Missus! It wasn't me, Urschl is guilty!" sounded for the third time from the belly of the cistern.

That was just too strange to the ladies, for the door of the cooling hole had been closed from outside, and when they opened it they found everything in good order and Tiberius was not there.

Inside the cistern, the saucy cook used both hands to hold the mouth of her betrayer, to whom she had sworn eternal faith only a short time before, and she admitted to him in a soft voice that cleaning the carpet and catching the rabbits had been a pretext. The ladies had not told her this; it was only a trick to get him away in the easiest manner possible, so she could go ahead and finish the midday meal. Tiberius appreciated this confession. That made him all the readier to pass all the guilt to Urschl. The little rascal did not think that she would revenge herself by revealing his own improper conduct toward her in the kitchen. At least he did not believe that Miss Urschl would do that, since she would be compromising herself as well. And the new episode in the cistern? One can see that this black, untrue beau depended on the wayward cook's modesty. Such an attitude would have befitted any grown man.

It is easy to imagine the astonishment of the two sisters when they discovered the hiding place of Urschl and Tiberius. Things got rather rough in a confrontation in the parlor afterward. Tiberius adamantly denied the accusations made by Urschl, who described everything in exquisite detail. After the cross-examination that Frida undertook with the little blighter, he was declared guilty. His sentence was delayed until Cousin Karl, who was then in St. Louis as an agent of K. & W. returned. Urschl, who had been blindly foolish enough to give Tiberius all her money, was to receive her money back from him. He had clearly intended to swindle her of it. She also received notice that she would have to leave their service at the end of a month. The sisters gave her a day off so she could seek new masters at the German Society or some other place.

The two sisters were now sitting at the midday meal, and Tiberius, now transformed into an enthusiastic waiter, came down the stairs with a half-emptied terrine. As he turned to go to the cookhouse, the young man with a dark blue, white-bordered fireman's uniform stepped into his way and asked if he had performed his mission. Tiberius was nonplussed, quavering out a simple "No, sir!"

"No?" the young man responded. "You did not tell them anything about my being here?"

"Pardon me, sir—I forgot," Tiberius stammered.

"All the better," the young man murmured to himself as he entered the house, as naturally and securely as a practiced member of the household.

He could tell from the terrine Tiberius was carrying that the ladies were in the midst of eating. Without further ado he knocked at the half-closed door of the dining room. When he entered, the two sisters rose from their chairs almost at the same instant, and Jenny cried out: "You already have your fireman's uniform, Albert? I would not have believed that you would honor my wishes so quickly. Splendid, fine, my friend."

"And I congratulate you for your fine choice among the companies. American No. 2 has the most handsome and best educated men," the blonde Frida added in.

"Ladies," Albert declaimed with a diplomatic bow suited to a salon, "words from such lips are the best blessing for my estate." Then he turned to Jenny and said: "And you, my dear, may regard me as your vassal henceforth."

"And I am proud that a man has so completely overcome his prejudice to please a friend," Jenny responded, as the prettiest pink advanced across her lovely cheeks.

"My friend," Albert responded somewhat more dryly, "my prejudice against fire companies was more powerful than my will. But the will of a beautiful woman cast it all overboard."

"Now you see what woman can accomplish," Jenny declared.

"If we want to," Frida opined.

In order to explain the friendly reception Albert was receiving from the two sisters, we will have to return to something in our friend's recent past, namely that nocturnal incident that had its most important moment in the Louisiana Ballroom.

"There will come a time when you will say something different." These words from that mysterious rider had sounded in his ears the entire night. Several times he attempted to sleep, but in vain.

He woke little Bridget, who had gone to bed as soon as her master had arrived and was sound asleep, and he had her prattle on to him about silly things just in order to give his thoughts a new direction. She told him about her parents, her homeland, her trip to America, the sorrows and troubles she had endured on the transatlantic passage, and her arrival on

American soil. And after long wanderings her account arrived at the time when Claudine hired her as a serving maid. Bridget's talkativeness was in fact an excellent remedy for her master's sleeplessness. By means of her narrative, he fell asleep, his left hand on his forehead. Bridget, who had not noticed this, since Albert was turned with his face to the wall, as was his habit, talked on for some time, until her own eyelids fell from exhaustion and she let her upper body sink from her chair onto her master's bed.

Albert slept until the sunlight warmed the bed. Sleep had not refreshed him. He felt weak all over his body, to an even greater degree than when he had gone to bed. He stood up, discontented, put on his morning clothes, and went into the side chamber. Bridget was already waiting for him with coffee. He wished her a good morning, which he had never done before, and even permitted her to drink her coffee with him at the table. He poured himself nearly half a cup of cognac, smoked a very strong Figaro, and read some of Heinzen's *Janus,*[23] then he sampled a few editorials in the Boston *Investigator.* Today he did not touch the New Orleans newspapers. The politics disgusted him, and their serial columns offered nothing interesting. He was about to start Heinzen's presentation in the Columbus *Revolution* when there was a knock at the door. The landlord entered with true Irish amiability. Only Bridget, who had a great respect for Green Ireland, stood up from her chair to greet Mr. Fitzpatrick. He sat down at once without saying much. The conversation soon turned to the fatal issue of rent. They arrived at the agreement that a certain contract that Albert had made with Mr. Fitzpatrick orally should be fixed in writing. The contract declared that a third of the rent owed, coming to one hundred and ninety-five dollars, should be paid in half a year, and that the balance and interest should be paid once the construction of the new customs house had been completed. The modification concerning the customs house had been made by Albert in a momentary flight of good spirits, and he had no idea that Fitzpatrick would take it seriously and accept it. The balance had been owed for some time, and, since the young architect was convinced that he would not live to see the customs house completed, he was not bothered about it. All the less so because he expected to make the first payment without difficulty.

No sooner had the cheerful Fitzpatrick withdrawn than our friend received a second visitor.

This was a Spaniard, one of the richest cavaliers in the Third District, whose real property had a value nigh unto a half-million. He wanted Albert, who was known as a talented surveyor, to measure a tract of land bordering Metairie Ridge and prepare a map, for which the Spaniard was ready to pay the sum of four-hundred and fifty dollars. This offer came just at the right moment for our friend. He had given his last bit of money, as we know, to free the Cocker from the watchman. A small advance was not rejected. That same day, Albert carefully examined his long-dormant equipment and hired two persons to carry his theodolite, surveying table, standards, and the like and to help with the surveying itself. For Albert, it was a time of activity and practical accomplishment. Since he did not wish to carry out his tasks negligently, he had to put all disturbing thoughts to one side and commit himself totally, which is precisely what he did. It had been his habit in the past to leap from utter sensuality to practical work whenever there was money in it. It was thus easy for him to carry out his assignment with the most assured care and scrupulously to bring it to completion.

On the seventh day after the start of his commission, Albert's wallet experienced the most important phrase of Genesis, "Let there be light." The Spirit of Worlds, when He created his ichthyosaurus, plesiosaurus, mesosaurus, megalosaurus, and the other monsters of the primitive world, could not have been more pleased than the young architect when he received four hundred dollars at one blow. But the bottle had its revenge on him, in old roué fashion, and the refreshing tide was soon followed by a sterile ebb. Our friend's first heroic stunt was to camp on alien terrain for several nights in a row instead of regularly flying back to his own hedge, which would have suited a young man with orderly, solid thinking, preserving his married man's virtues even as a widower.

Shellroad Mary? Yes, if he could find her while he still had some money. He had not seen her since the evening she'd bitten a couple hairs out of his black moustache. It never occurred to him, even in his wildest dreams, to spend money in the presence of men. A girl should enjoy it with him, and, among all the girls of New Orleans who enjoy a bad reputation, it had to be Shellroad Mary. Her limitless decadence, joined with a marvelous waist and an inexpressible, serious yet beautiful face, was what he longed for, the only thing that could hold him in thrall. Now his highest desire was to have *Attic Nights* with her, true *symposia.*[24] Shellroad Mary had been living until recently over the tollgate where the New Orleans and Banking Canal Company controlled access to the Shell Road. One fine day Albert rode out to search for his classical playmate, whom he called his living Musarion, to lead her in triumph to ***. But he could neither find Shellroad Mary nor trace her down. Some said she had gone across the river, some said across the lake—destinations so imprecise as to give no guidance at all. Albert was furious. As he turned to go home, his horse fell over near the tollgate, and the impact injured his ribs. He was brought into the tollbooth, where he lay until a physician appeared and brought him into town in a wagon. Albert recovered quickly, and, since it was his principle always to pay a physician half of the fee demanded, his purse was not much lighter than before. On the day he recovered, one of his best friends had a similar accident with the same horse, falling and breaking his arm.

Now a new era began for our friend. Yet only the radius of the circle of his life changed, the periphery remained the same. With a person such as Albert, whose entire being was occupied in satisfying sensual desires, to whom it was intolerable to concentrate on material survival except when absolutely necessary, and who did nothing to be loved nor disappointed, it was an ominous event that he had fallen in love. This time it sounds like something out of *A Thousand and One Nights,* for the god Cupid used a parrot to revive an inclination long since buried in the heart of our friend. When Albert had recovered enough to take short strolls and excursions, he suddenly had the idea of going across to Algiers to portray New Orleans in a manner that would exceed all his previous efforts.

For this purpose, he chose a point on the opposite bank that was almost directly across from the Odd Fellows' Hall,[25] so he could center his picture there. In this way, that portion of our city between St. Patrick's Church and the Cathedral, on the one side, and that between St. Patrick's Church and Annunciation Square, on the other, would appear in the main field, the smokestacks of the steamboats would be partially obscured in the foreground, and the Third Municipality and Lafayette on either side would be hidden in the forest of masts. The idea was fortunate, and in fact the heavens themselves seemed to be trying to aid the artist's work. With nothing but a small sketchbook, Albert boarded the ferryboat at the Canal Street landing. Once he arrived on the opposite shore, the young architect turned to the right and went about fifty paces along the top of the levee before sitting down at the place he had designated. A tree trunk lying across the dam suited him perfectly as a place to lay his sketchbook. He planted an umbrella behind him in the soft ground to shield him from the rays of the sun, and thus he sat, like a silhouette-portrait of an artist from the Old Country.

It was a splendid morning. The steeds of the sun-god whinnied for joy as a Gulf breeze kissed their shimmering flanks. They stamped their ruby-red hooves on the gates of the young morning, scattering the high cirrus clouds in all directions. O splendid spectacle, when Helios sheds his first rays on the hands of an artist! The dome of the Odd Fellows' Hall was bathed in a fairy-tale glow, while further down from St. Charles Street shimmers the Eye of God, with square and compass. This shimmer comes from the Freemasons' Hall,[26] whose façade breaks through the narrows of Commercial Alley every morning but vanishes once more when the sun rushes westward. The god Cupid prefers to haunt at such moments.

"*Señor caballero,* ho, ho, ho—no understand," our friend suddenly heard a voice that seemed to come from so close by that he could not avoid looking around for the odious killjoy.

"*Señor caballero,* ho, ho, ho—how are Frida and Jenny?" the stranger continued, with a voice swinging from masculine to feminine and back. One could just as well swear it was that of a man as they could it was that of a woman.

"*Señor caballero,* ho, ho, ho. Have you forgotten Jenny so utterly—ho, ho, ho, *señor caballero,* your Jenny loves you from the heart, and it hurts . . ."

"Scoundrel!" the young architect cried out in irritation, throwing all his artist's tools to the ground. He looked in all directions, but he could see no one. He did not notice a small something moving in the dark shadows of a cypress not far away.

"*Señor caballero,* ho, ho, ho. Your Jenny loves you from the heart, and it hurts . . ."

"It's enough to drive one mad!" Albert raged, his eyes almost popping out.

Our lovely lady readers have already recognized the jester on the cypress tree. It was, in fact, none other than that talkative Papchen from the lovable cottage. He had made use of the sisters' absence to abuse their trust in leaving him free to roam by wandering into forbidden territory. Papchen had sat quite happily through the whole warm night in the deepest shadows of the cypress branches, cheerfully snapping at the beetles and the occasional grub. He probably had recognized the young architect as soon as the young man approached the place where he settled. When he began to draw, Papchen figured it was the proper time to pose a few questions and make a few remarks to disturb him, using phrases Jenny had taught him in her obsession with Emil. It was quite irresponsible for the bird to undertake such plagiarism and so drive our friend mad with it.

It can be seen that Papchen was no small-scale jester.

"Señor caballero," the colorfully feathered rascal began from the top. But Albert spied him in that moment, and he stepped quickly to the cypress, catching him with a quick grab. Papchen was not pleased at such a swift arrest. He beat with his wings, pecked with his beak at our friend's hands, and made every conceivable effort to make his dissatisfaction known. But it was to no avail, and the delinquent had to obey. He grumbled with his thick tongue, but he spoke not a word.

Albert, who had not shown himself in Algiers since he'd met Cousin Karl at the sisters' place, now determined to return the captured Papchen, so as to restore the once-close relationship his own ungrounded and senseless bad humor had since clouded.

This must have been foremost on his mind, since otherwise he would not have left behind his sketchbook and paraphernalia, along with his umbrella, in his confusion. Let us rush toward the two sisters' residential sanctuary along with Papchen, and we will see what is happening there. Jenny and Frida had quickly discovered the parrot's disappearance and dared to take a rather distant walk of the area to find him. A few moments after Albert had left, they arrived at the place where he had left his things. Frida, who was curious by nature, could not leave the artist's materials lying undisturbed on the ground with only an indifferent glance. Once she had determined that absolutely no one but her sister was nearby, and after repeated examination of the area, she dared at last to put her pretty hand on the sketchbook. She then pulled back, extremely surprised, turned to Jenny, and declared: "My God, sister, guess whose trail we are following here?"

"Little sister, don't frighten me. Just who would we be tracking? Don't touch someone else's things, for heaven's sake—what if the owner should see you?" Jenny snapped out of her reverie, for she had been thinking of something other than Papchen the whole time, and she had only pretended to be looking—so as not to upset Frida.

"The person this belongs to," the sensible blonde replied, "will not protest—look here, little sister, what name is here under the corner of the cover—look, look, 'Albert R*.'"

"Albert? My God, that is strange!" Jenny declared.

"Let's take the things home—he can get them there," Frida suggested.

"Yes, let's do that," Jenny agreed.

"Well, who knows if we won't find him there when we go home? I have a feeling."

"Then all the better, Frida, we will hold the things until he explains why he has not visited us in so long. He can reclaim them when he apologizes and promises not to neglect his lady friends any more."

"Yes, let's do it."

Frida pulled the umbrella out of the muddy soil, Jenny took the sketchbook and instruments under her arm, and so they proceeded, looking about now and then, to their happy home. They seemed utterly to have forgotten Papchen.

This was not the case with Papchen. When the sisters opened the garden gate they saw from the crushed shells that someone had entered, then they heard with amazement the familiar phrases from the magnolia tree.

"Ho, ho, ho—no understand. How are Jenny and Frida?" Papchen had managed to get out of Albert's hands as he'd arrived at the front steps. Failing, after many tries, to catch him, Albert sought Tiberius to help and learned that the ladies were away looking for Papchen. He was just now coming out with Tiberius. Albert stood stunned when he saw the ladies with his sketchbook and umbrella sitting under the magnolia tree with Papchen. Jenny no sooner spied him than she called out.

"Look, what a strange find we made! We went out to find our Papchen, and instead we found an umbrella and an artist's sketchbook."

"And I," Albert declared as he approached calmly, his hat in his hand, "I went away an artist and returned with a parrot—I caught your dear Papchen, but he got away from me again."

"Were you really the lucky finder, Herr R*?" Frida responded.

"And on account of Papchen, you forgot umbrella and sketchbook?" Jenny asked in a tone that cheered up the young architect.

With this sort of exchange they all went into the delightful cottage: Frida, Jenny, Albert, Papchen—little Tiberius had caught him in no time—sketchbook, and umbrella. Our friend, who was severely lectured for absenting himself for so long, was relieved to find that the sisters then quickly left behind all reference to his long avoidance and moved onto a conversation that was as serious as it was practical and well intended. Frida spoke of life in the western states as superior to that in any of the slave states, and she finally declared that many a young, capable man whose activities eventually decline in the exhausting climate of the South would make tremendous progress as a useful member of society in the splendid states of Illinois, Iowa, or Wisconsin. Jenny had nothing in particular to oppose her sister's assertions, but she believed that things were the same throughout the United States, whether in the South or the West. People were the same everywhere, and money and the shopkeeper's spirit had general precedence over spiritual qualities, the beauties of the soul and heart. In her view, anyone unable to reach his goals in the South would also strive in vain in the West.

Albert smiled comfortably at Jenny's definition, since he knew he was the obvious target. He was not going to be untrue to the South so long as he whiled away his time in the shadow of their magnolias and lilacs with his friends from the lovable cottage.

Albert paid attention to both opinions, so as not to give either preference. In response to a further, mild opposition on Jenny's part, Frida referred to a letter they had just received from the West, which deserved to be cited because it came from a man she respected and who even had some impact in the eyes of her sister, Jenny. Here is the letter.

Chapter 5

A Letter from the West, or, The Voice of a Friend from Highland

My gracious Countesses!

When we had the honor of being presented to you by His Royal Highness Prince Paul of Württemberg, I recognized at once in you the friendly, noble sensibility that you have so often shown to me ever since. How often have I torn up letters I wrote with the greatest care, entirely because I feared to bore you and thus not merit being answered. Yet, on the contrary, I have always encountered tender attention, and until now I have always had the joy of seeing all my lines carefully read and faithfully answered by you, gracious countesses.

You have permitted me to tell you much about St. Louis and its beautiful surroundings. This time let me entertain you with the account of a small country town in Illinois, where I now live. My dears, particularly Countess Jenny, do not expect any look back at the Old Country, with which I have broken once and for all. A look at Europe, so desolate and overpopulated, is so sorrowful that it is good to turn away from it. What is more pleasant and consoling than the beautiful picture of our great painter Kaulback, who can show the destruction of Jerusalem in the background and the flight of the Holy Family, the hope of the world, in the foreground? How swiftly has Germany become mere background for me! Yes, that demonstrates once again the infinity of nature and the mighty predominance of the drive for creation over destruction. Germany, like all of Europe, rushes to its doom, but young America rises to its future ten times as rapidly.

What particularly pleases me, and what awakens in me such a high faith in the future of this country, is the comment that in the foundation of these settlements there is nothing mythic, not even anything romantic. Here they know nothing about the childhood of a state. Organizations, even the smallest, start out at the age of maturity, with practical consciousness and masculine energy. There are never any miraculous foundations or obscure connections. Everything is owed to men with axes, teams, and plows. No devil has ever raised a bridge and demanded the first hen that crosses as a reward. No, a Mr. So and So put it up two weeks ago. There a church does not owe its existence to the intervention of Mary, or, when it goes well, to the mysterious arts and powers of Freemasonry, but rather it is built like any house. In one word, there is no romanticism here. Here youth is the workforce, and, if it continues as it has, it will seem that the land was once inhabited by giants. Are the cows and horses here as intelligent as the peasants were in Pomerania and Brandenburg? Is it any wonder that here a *simple* person with his primitive capacities takes his place alongside the experienced, learned, and hard-tried German farmer, judge, or foreman? Here in Highland, for example, perfect justice is dispensed, and yet Esquire Suppiger has not drunk and gorged away five years at a university, nor has it occurred to the government to require that he practice five years before he can take up his office. My God, how simple it can all be if one has no interest, no profit in the matter.

Now I come to my Highland—*nomen est omen.*[27] May it continue to be a savior to many oppressed German families! Our Highland thrives in physical as well as moral matters. The capital grows almost every day with the arrival of well-to-do families and the value of energetic hands, and if cholera had not made such a severe visitation, instead of a dozen there would be a hundred houses in the town. The value of the soil increases, since the immediate surroundings are settled more with every passing day, and the Anglo-Saxon tribe does not deny its child-producing power. In the last year a significant French population has settled here. It consists partly of workers, but also partly of persons from the more educated, prosperous class that has turned to agriculture. All that we are lacking at this point is a pair of factories managed with care and supplied with capital, so that a closer market could be provided than that in St. Louis.

Native-born Americans prefer large towns with such businesses, but an arriving European, particularly a German, is so exhausted from the torpor of European commerce that he prefers to turn to less-productive agriculture than to invest his capital and effort in industrial undertakings. If he knew how much easier, how much less perilous, how much more profitable commerce is here than it is in Germany, he would abandon the deceptive peace of farming life and exchange it for the creative joys of industry, to the benefit of himself and his country. Yet here lessons are to no purpose. It is only a question of time.

But our population grows in moral matters as well. First of all, a reading circle has been formed and is open to every citizen of good reputation. We subscribe to eighteen German, French, English, and American journals—some scholarly, some political papers—and we have laid the foundations for a town library. With the growth of the town, this young institution will unfold, hopefully spreading finer fruits of social grouping rather than those of religious sect-making. Unfortunately, in Highland we have *not a single decent school,* although there are two or more churches seething with internal disputes. Unfortunately they have built three churches to entice superstitious peasants from the Odenwald, so we have to worry whether the spirited inhabitants of our place will get an opportunity to teach their children to read and write. Unfortunately they seem to prefer inviting yet another thievish killjoy of Christian charity as a preacher of the Word of God than to try to hire a good teacher for children . . .

We will avoid giving the end of the letter, since it has nothing further interesting to a sympathetic reader. In the place of the full name stood only the initials E. B. B. and under them, on the left: "Highland, Madison County, Ill., April 1852."

Frida had finished the letter. She turned to Albert: "Well, how did you like this letter?"

Albert seemed to hesitate, or to be holding back an honest answer. Frida saw this.

"Say it right out and openly," she said, "how do you like this letter? How do you like the views of our friend in the West?"

Instead of an answer, Albert redirected the question to the two sisters, though it actually appeared aimed at Jenny: "Please, ladies, how did you like the letter?"

"I liked it a great deal," Frida said at once. "I find in it an expression of healthy practicality, and I recognize in its style the man the prince presented to us a year and a half ago."

"I respect and treasure everyone's views when they arise from genuine conviction," Jenny responded. "Our friend may be able to justify the way he portrays things in the New World, and I have nothing against that. But the fact that he has pushed our Germany so much into the background, and that he subjects his own homeland to so much satire and bitter irony cannot please me. He is happy that there is no romanticism in this land, and he is literally overjoyed that only practical understanding and raw workforce dominates and sets the tone. He does not even want to permit the farmer to enjoy his idyllic peace, and he encourages him to turn to a more profitable business—manufacturing. Such encouragement, while spoken rather softly, is theft in the heart of each who sees his personal equanimity rather than some filthy factory as his fortune. Those raised in the dust of the counting house and the storeroom or those estranged from higher education might be drawn to factories. Those who have no idea that there are other regions on this earth in which heart and soul are warmed and made happy. The blossoms of art and scholarship grow in the romanticism of folk life, and a land whose woods, pastures, and mountains do not possess the gentle thread of romanticism might be good for a big meal, but the heart will starve and the soul will languish."

Jenny was silent as she awaited a reply. Frida, who was of an entirely different opinion than her sister, now turned to Albert, who had listened to Jenny's words with close attention:

"Well now it's up to you, my friend, to give your opinion of the letter. Well, tell us how it pleases you."

"If I am to confess openly without fear of being expelled by you—I can only respond negatively to your wishes that I speak my opinion," Albert declared.

"Look at me!" Frida cried out.

"Albert!" Jenny raised her forefinger.

Frida looked at her sister, then at Albert. Albert looked at both at the same moment.

Had Jenny betrayed herself? This threatening movement with the cry, "Albert!" Why not "My friend" or "Herr R.," as custom would demand? Would the portrait of Emil that had been the idol of her heart yield to another? Or did some other play of nature reveal a similarity in Albert?

That is at least probable.

Albert, who was seized by the same sympathetic magic, hid his embarrassment in the funereal answer: "The letter would be something for your esteemed cousin, my ladies. Utterly my own point of view!"

"You are right, my friend," Frida said. I read it aloud to him before he left for St. Louis."

"Then your dear cousin has departed?" Albert asked with astonishment and secret joy.

"Didn't you know that, Herr R.? You did know it—don't prevaricate," the two sisters said at once.

"Of course I had no idea," Albert responded, "I haven't seen you in a long time."

"And we haven't seen you either," Frida responded rather acidly, since she understood that the young man would not have mentioned Cousin Karl without a purpose.

"And did your cousin express the same views on the letter from the West as you, dear friend?" Albert began again, turning to Frida.

"Our concepts of America agree almost completely," the blonde answered.

"As well as I can recall, you had entirely different views earlier. Your old homeland was supremely important and you loved romanticism like a mother loves its child."

"Earlier, yes."

"That was Cousin Karl's influence," remarked Jenny, who had taken up some needlework. "Cousin Karl is a very good and upright man, always friendly and involved in good things. I love and respect him with my entire heart—but he is too egoistic about any decision once he has made it. I cannot say that he hates romanticism or that he throws rocks at poetry, but he does not talk about these matters as much as is proper for a man of feeling. He does not dwell on such things."

"Let's change the topic, dear Jenny," said Frida. "We would like to recall a promise our friend made about a year ago and has not yet fulfilled."

The young architect started. Jenny seemed to recall something.

"Well, dear little sister, don't you know any more?" the blonde asked.

"I cannot remember any more."

"And you cannot either, friend?"

"I had no idea I had made a promise I had not kept."

"Do you recall what a bad mood plagued you in those days? And can't you recall the remedy my sister Jenny and I prescribed for it?"

"I think I recall it now," Albert responded, "but I thought it was a joke, since you know the hostility I harbor against all associations."

"Oh that!" Jenny cried out lustily. "Oh right, that's it!"

"And now, my friend, how is your promise doing?" the blonde continued.

"I just told you that I took your good advice for a joke, and I weighed my promise on that basis," the architect assured them.

"That would be a pretty picture if you kept your promises out of a sense of fun and for the sake of your friends, even if you did not think they were not meant seriously."

"Well, I will say nothing of that," Jenny responded to her sister's words, "but would our friend keep his promise if we asked him *in all seriousness* to join a fire company?"

"I will!" the young architect cried out, only too glad that Jenny was not quite correct in her inference. "Yes, I will," he repeated again, though a bit more softly. "But I hope that my old sin is forgiven me."

"It will be forgiven when you fulfill the promise you made," Frida said, extending a tender hand to our friend. Jenny did the same, but with more warmth and a pressure reserved only for Albert.

"So the next time we greet you it will be as a fireman," Jenny said to her friend as she accompanied him into the corridor to bid him farewell. "The fire companies are the sole societies I respect, since they are not dedicated to mere ostentation, as is the case with certain societies in our city. This is because the firemen's association has a high, noble goal in mind, the preservation of the life and property of their fellows against certain doom. Because the *deed* is primary when they show personal courage and steadfastness in moments of mortal peril. Certain other societies exhaust themselves in speeches, display, and marching, and, when action is called for, they fall over one another, for they have words but no individual courage. They are good with the pen, but they are too cowardly to cock a pistol."

Chapter 6

THE CONFESSION

We now move on to the moment when we saw the two sisters enthused as the young architect entered the house, wearing the uniform of the fire company. We have already mentioned their surprise, as well as the joyful reception, given their earlier conversation with him.

The midday table had been cleared, and they proceeded into a small room at one side of the drawing room, which had been used as a study, or more properly a siesta room, when Frida's husband had still been there. As small as this room was, its window still had a splendid view of the nearby plantations and it was anything but simply furnished. Genuine Italian carpets of a silver-gray sea color crossed with purplish-red velvet covered the floor and window cove, presenting a simple but extremely dignified ensemble. Around the walls were portraits of famous horses; the one of a steed called Black Prince particularly caught the eye. It was set in a heavy gold frame on whose upper edge was a feathery riding whip bound in gold. On the fireplace mantel were two horse busts, one of which was certainly Lady Wilmington. While he was still an officer of hussars, the Hungarian had obtained these from a traveling Englishman, exchanging a Newfoundland dog for the items. Next to a bookshelf, whose glass doors were draped with green silk, hung a holster covered by a bag made of deerskin. The sofa, which was entirely black, decorated with small silver pins, stood in front of the window. This, as well as the overall aura, reminded one at once of the furnishings of Hungarian noble families. Now Jenny and Frida sat on the sofa together. They had the architect sit between them, despite his protests. He had wanted to sit opposite the two sisters in a rocking chair, since he knew from experience that it was better for his peace of mind to sit opposite ladies rather than next to them. And sitting vis-à-vis them often provides a prettier view than sitting next to them. Abbé Chaulieu would have approved.

Frida, who did not wish to miss her teaching hours without good reason, left our friend alone with Jenny. Earlier she had recounted the crime of Tiberius and the saucy cook as best she could, and everyone had laughed heartily over it. The cistern affair particularly helped lighten our serious friend's mood. Urschl's confession concerning little Tiberius's continuous pressure could of course not be mentioned.

Jenny was silently upset with her sister, who had left her alone with the young man without a thought rather than urging her to do her piano practice. Probably the blonde thought it good that her sister could at last pour out her heart to a friend, for she had no doubt that they were friends. That was assured by the love and enthusiasm Jenny had for firemen—*her Emil* had once been a member of a company. It is often hard to understand the moods of a woman's heart. It is impossible when this mood appears in the garb of love.

After Frida had gone, Jenny rose from her seat and went to the bookshelf.

Jenny carefully drew the architect out of the minor embarrassment that would otherwise be unavoidable despite his expected moves, slippery as an eel, responding to her moving from his side. He directed a long, tender gaze at his friend, who stood with her back to him in front of the open bookcase.

"You are certainly going to surprise me with something rare to read, my dear friend?" he asked.

"No, rather with a rare collection of steel engravings," she responded, drawing a long, narrow folio from behind a bookend where it had been wedged.

The young architect stood up from the sofa and stepped toward Jenny, receiving the folio from her hand with a splendid grace, almost too graceful for a man, and took it back to his original seat.

Jenny took her seat beside her friend with a practiced turn, and, as he was about to open the folio, she placed her hand over it to stop him.

Jenny looked mysteriously at the architect.

"Is this folio a Pandora's box?" he asked.

"And what if it were one? Would you be terrified by it?"

"No more and no less than you, my dear friend."

"Well—let's dare it, then," Jenny said in all seriousness. But she had barely drawn out the first steel engraving and passed it to her curious friend than she broke out in pleasant laughter, joined by that of the young man.

"A collection of wagons! Truly splendid, marvelous! A remarkable obsession, that! No, I have never seen a collection of this sort so perfect! And here are the details—a strange passion indeed!"

Whoever has ever seen or actually owned such a collection can vouch for the pure astonishment of the architect. In the finest of engravings were tilburies, rockaways, Jersey wagons, barrouches, sulkies, buggies, cabs, gigs, Prince Alberts, landaus, coaches, phaetons, volantes, and many more, all of them ordered according to the form of their hitches and placed under their assigned rubrics.

They reviewed the steel engravings thoroughly, and Albert replaced them, one by one, in the proper subdivisions of the folio. Jenny had held the folio open with both her hands in order to make it easier for her friend to look through it. Now she tossed the folio onto the rocking chair across from the sofa, causing it to rock back and forth.

"The wagons are throwing the rocking chair off balance," Albert joked.

"Not for long. Soon it will stand as quietly as if it had never been touched," Jenny responded, indubitably imparting a symbolic meaning to her words.

"So it often is with the human heart, when it is touched by some object and oscillates for a time . . ."

"Until it once again is at rest," Jenny completed her friend's thought.

"You are right, my dear Jen . . . friend," he interrupted himself swiftly. "The human heart is like a rocking chair—whoever occupies it . . ."

"Leave off," Jenny begged, "do not carry the jest any further, my friend."

"Who inspired it, my friend? I was serious and shall remain serious until I leave you—if you had not introduced a joking mood with your collection of wagons," the eyes of the young architect flamed, with a fire that flowed in the form of words from his lips.

"You know why. Behind the airy garlands of jesting are often hidden the pale roses of earnestness. One jests because one cannot dare to be serious."

Albert said nothing. He leaned his head back and looked dreamily through the open window at the cloudless sky above.

"Since we are now talking seriously," Jenny continued, "I will tell you a story my sister Frida and I heard while we were having a little stroll to Mr. Logan's plantation several weeks ago in the company of Madame Delachaise. The story is so serious that you will not dare to smile even once, unless you believe that we were the victims of a bold fraud."

"You make me curious, dear friend. I only ask you not to tell me this story if it is likely to cause me to fall from this heaven in which I am now suspended."

The brunette with the beautiful dark blue eyes, the nineteen-year-old widow, Jenny, looked into the face of the fascinating widower Albert as he said these words, a bit agitated but pleased. "If you let yourself fall from your heaven, my friend, that is your own fault—I shall not try to cause that," she said with such sincerity that one could see she was ready for whatever came from these words.

But Albert said nothing. Once again he leaned his head back and looked dreamily through the open window at the cloudless sky above.

Jenny moved back and forth on the sofa restlessly.

"Well, do you want to hear the story, friend?" she asked. "It shouldn't cause you to fall out of your heaven. It is something that only touches my sister's heart and over which we have no power, either for good or evil."

"So tell me, dear friend," Albert said, taking care to preserve a friendly, harmless manner.

Jenny began: "My friend, you know the path that runs along the Opelousas Railroad on the way to Mr. Logan's planting. Before you arrive there, there is a place where everyone has to dismount to take a detour on foot because the drainage has created deep mud. Soon, once the Opelousas track is finished, it will be unnecessary to pass this place. But this detour does have its compensations. There is a splendid cottage worthy of a prince, half hidden in high evergreen bushes, from which the occasional live oak emerges; its massive branches, their tops beset with moss, cast a gigantic shadow, enveloping the cedars, magnolias, and cypresses in darkness. Smaller villas are surrounded by enchanting gardens in which the finest roses in the world—Queen of the Bourbons, Souvenir de la Malmaison, Triomphe de la Guillotière, Pourpre de Tyre and Nemesis—squander their magical perfumes. Still, I don't want to bore you with an enumeration of all these beauties of nature, my precious friend. You know all the ways and climbs that run through that paradise better than anyone in all of Algiers. Forgive me that I have the bad habit of repeating things long since known and felt."

"No, no—please go on, dear friend, from your red lips this stream of eloquence flows so splendidly, so fresh with youth, that one could believe he sat with you at the spring of Castalia."[28]

"You are a lovable flatterer, my friend. If you had said this to Frida, you would not have escaped some rebuke."

"How more welcome it would be to me to get a little rebuke from you.

But you would be silent in this matter, since you know that to earn a rebuke I would have to have said something that was untrue."

"Flatteries are untruths of their own sort, my friend . . . and thus I too would have the right . . ."

"Good, some sort of penalty, or . . ."

"That you listen to me quietly until I have told my story to the end."

"That is hard, but I shall submit completely to this penance."

Jenny played with some loose threads of the bright green kerchief on her bosom as she continued: "It was about five weeks ago when Monsieur de Delachaise picked us up in his comfortable coach to take us to Mr. Logan's plantation, where we had been invited to a tea dance. We departed from here between five and six o'clock. When we came to that difficult place, Monsieur de Delachaise, who was driving the coach, dismounted in order to help us get out. Frida refused to leave her seat, and she seemed determined to risk the dangerous passage that she had often avoided before. Despite all of Monsieur de Delachaise's arguments, she remained adamant. I found myself compelled to take the detour alone. You know that little clearing in Ranney's Timber, where the majestic boughs of the sycamore rustle and from which the eye can sweep unhindered all the way to Logan's Plantation?

"In this clearing, barely twenty paces away, I was astonished to see my sister Frida, who I knew to be in the coach with Monsieur de Delachaise at that very moment, and she was on the arm of a man—what man?

"You marvel, my friend, but do not argue that it was an error or a hallucination—I saw her on the arm of her husband, as he lived and breathed. I stood for a few moments as if rooted to the spot. My Frida then left her companion's hand and rushed out of the clearing into the thick woods.

"'Frida!' I heard the man call, 'Why are you running so? Come back—we must be in New Orleans by seven o'clock.'

"'Leave me here, Lajos! It is just too beautiful here!' she responded. What could have been more certain proof that this was my sister, Frida, and her husband, Lajos? But imagine my astonishment when I heard my sister's voice behind me, calling me by name. When I turned around, I could not trust my eyes. It was Frida, who had come by the same trail I had just used. When I looked back into the clearing, that man also was vanishing into the woods, with that Frida—which Frida?—still well ahead of him."

"That Frida—which Frida?" Albert repeated mechanically.

"To this day I have no idea, my friend. Frida could not explain this episode either. An even less agitated soul than hers would see this to be a portent of an approaching misfortune. But she thinks it is nothing but a Doppelgänger."

"And the Lajos you saw at that Frida's side?" the young architect pressed Jenny with curiosity.

"Frida does not concede that at all. She thinks I must have been in error. She is not to be convinced."

"And how did your dear sister come to be on the same path with you, since you say she felt better staying with Monsieur de Delachaise in the coach?"

"The coach had slid halfway across and sunk into the mud up to the axle. Monsieur de Delachaise, wading in the mud up to his knee, brought Frida to dry land without injury. Then he walked to the next plantation to ask for a Negro to help pull the wagon out. While Monsieur de Delachaise was fetching a Negro, Frida went her own way, which greatly disturbed her escort when he returned with his helper."

"That is more than remarkable!" Albert declared.

"You mean the appearance of the two Fridas?" Jenny asked.

"Yes of course, that's all," our friend responded, somewhat confused, for he saw that Jenny was observing him with a strange, indescribable gaze.

"You are not paying attention to what I'm telling you," Jenny said.

"Of course I am—I was!" the young architect assured her.

"What is going on? Confess it! Be totally honest!"

"Oh, tell me, dearest friend, what god has bestowed on you such enchanting eyes?"

"What concern are my eyes to you, my friend? Do my eyes tell you more than they tell others? But Albert, my Albert!"—Jenny suddenly rose from her seat as if transformed—"Who gave you *your* eyes?" Then she sank into the architect's arms as if exhausted.

"My God! Jenny, you love me! You love me, Jenny?" Albert cried, stormily wrapping his friend in his arms.

Jenny lay this way at her friend's heart for several minutes.

Albert's temples pounded as if he were in a fever. In his eyes flickered a fire so pure and chaste, as he had never before experienced.

For the very first time, he was in love.

And Jenny? Did she love him back? Could she forget the idol of her heart, her Emil, on his behalf? Albert was aware of her unbounded obsession with her faithless husband. And now? Wouldn't all his senses fail if he harbored the mere thought, the mere possibility, that she loved him too?

"My Emil!" he heard Jenny moan.

Albert started at the sound of this name. "My Jenny!" he whispered, lowering his head to hers.

"My Emil!" Jenny now cried out, as if tormented by intense dreams.

The hands and feet of the architect trembled.

For a moment, Jenny's overheated imagination had taken hold of him and sought in him her Emil.

"Emil, Emil!" she sounded again, so pitifully and painfully that it cut deep into the architect's soul.

"My God!" Albert thought to himself, "such dreadful self-deception. Poor Jenny! And I, poor devil that I am, to have taken such liberties with an angel unawares!"

"My Jenny!" he called out, pressing a hot kiss on her shoulder. "My Jenny!" he proclaimed even louder.

He repeatedly dared to plant a kiss on the alabaster shoulder of Jenny, who lay with her head in his lap, her eyes covered by both her hands. When he began to rise up to take a look around the chamber and seek a way out of his uncontrollable situation, he suddenly felt a tender hand slip under his belt, where the name of his fire company was displayed in white letters, and then he felt his belt being yanked back and forth. When the young fireman looked down, he saw his friend with her eyes fixed on the belt, as if she was trying to decipher the full name of the company, which was unevenly displayed on the surface of the belt. Then Jenny suddenly turned her eyes to him and cried out: "My Emil, you entered a new company and told me nothing about it? Be honest, Emil, why did you keep it from me?"

Then she sank back into his lap, covering her face with both hands.

We know quite well that it was warm outside, and that it hadn't rained in a long time. Louisiana's sun does not play games when it has really made up its mind to make the earth thirst. The cisterns were utterly empty, and their staves were springing apart in places, despite their iron bindings. The water of "The Father of Waters" is not for drinking, since it is as warm and unhealthy as the saliva of a dying horse. Ice? Oh yes. Stafford & Co. have *plenty* of ice, and they supply four parishes with it. But that is only for people. Cattle and the soil itself also want water. They thirst just as much as we do. Water lilies dried up and the irises have long since passed away. Palmettos sought out the ancient mud in vain, finding only dried-out, cracked gullies. Don't anyone tell me that New Orleans is a filthy swamp-hole. Outside the river, where is there even the slightest sign of moisture? You expected a swamp-hole, and instead you find a Sahara, a Sahara of dried-up people and numbed spirits. Run down to the *Canal Carondelet* and don't let this journey bother you. Once you've walked its length back and forth several times in a day, you will return home a sweating mummy. But your wife and babies will rejoice in the restoring liquid, and they will praise the creator of all the worlds, who conceived Louisiana among the various paradises.

We know full well that it is this way many a summer.

Yet this was not summer but winter.

We know full well how the winter is in Louisiana. They call it spring *sanspareil*—and spring *sanspareil* was having its most beautiful day. It was a bit warm, but a delightful breeze wafted through the open window, where Jenny lay in the lap of the handsome fireman, dreaming of her love for Emil.

Albert sat there as pale as a corpse. One elbow was supported on the sill, his handsome face pressed into his flat hand. Where was his flaming gaze now? Where was the red that had burned on his cheeks only a few moments ago? Why did his tousled hair hang about his pale face like fluttering leaves? Why aren't his dark locks still combed smooth? Why is he letting his friend lie in his lap so coldly without pressing her to his heart?

Look, now something strikes him on the ear, giving him a gentle blow.

It cannot be Jenny, for she was done with teasing him. Further, she was holding onto his neck with her hands with such intensity that he was only able to support himself on his elbow with some effort.

He carefully turned around and saw in an instant what he wanted to know.

It was nothing but a paper kite that little Tiberius had been trying to fly on the large field outside the fence of the two sisters' property. The kite did not want to fly today. The air did not cooperate, either. So the window was as far as it got, jolting our friend for a moment out of his daze before floating slowly down into the garden below.

"You're not flying very high today, poor kite!" Albert called to it with a soft, drawn-out voice.

He pressed his head into his hand once more and again looked as stiff as a corpse in a painting.

If his belt, which had bound him only a few moments before, had not been lying on the sofa, it would have considerably restricted his breathing.

Spring *sanspareil* sends down blossoms and flowers like hazelnuts. While Boreas storms through the broad prairies of the West in a snowy garb of white, and the iron horses sleep in solid ice, spring *sanspareil* is kissing its golden fruits and admiring itself in the metallic mirror of its evergreen leaves. Spring *sanspareil* is the darling of beautiful women, since it pours out the flowering buds of honeysuckle, whose enchanting fragrance wafts through their bedrooms. One bough of honeysuckle, covered with a thousand blossoms, reaches through the window, waving up and down. Albert doesn't notice, but Jenny drinks in its fragrance with great intensity. She is still lying with her head on her friend's shoulder, half dead and utterly ravished by the fragrance of the honeysuckle. It would be better for her to remain ever thus, for when she opens her eyes, she will see to her horror that it is Albert and not Emil.

Albert now sought to extricate himself from Jenny's embrace without hurting her. But she was already coming to her senses at the same instant, and she released her hands from about Albert's neck, raising her head and looking sadly into his face.

Albert was in the most dreadful situation any lover can find himself. He, who had never shied away from the fire of a feminine eye, now closed his eyes like a person who did not have the courage to look into the abyss that lay before him.

"Albert, Albert! For heaven's sake! What have I done? Evil man, why do you have to look so much like my Emil? Open your eyes and let me see my Emil in you for the last time. Yes, yes, the eyes are black as my nun's habit, and my Emil's are as blue as the ribbon of my order's cross—but isn't your gaze the same? Your hair is so dark, and my Emil is blond—but isn't it just as soft, doesn't it flow with the same rich fullness about your neck? Doesn't your belt surround the same waist, although it is still not that of my Emil? Tell me, tell me, evil man, why you go through my dreams arm in arm with Emil? Tell me, Albert, what would the world say if it knew of this? Would it be able to understand this? Wouldn't it cry out, 'Look, she is an adulteress who tries to veil her shame by telling us that her confusion is not culpable'? Oh, the world would only judge the deed and not the imperious commands of nature! So, my Albert, if your Jenny is still dear and precious to you, flee! Flee far away into the world, or, if you don't feel strong enough to remain close by, never cross over to Algiers again. If your path ever leads you by here, turn your eyes away from the cottage where your friend lives, your friend who will bear your memory to the grave."

Albert, who had fallen into a terrifying stupor since his strange catastrophe with Jenny, wept bright tears which ran down his pale cheeks. He stood up and threw himself on his knees at her feet, and she began to rise. He grasped her two hands with stormy haste, leading them to his lips.

"God forgive me," he said, "if I received love that belonged to another. Forgive me, my dearest Jenny, for not being strong enough to tear you from your delusion—but it is too sweet to be loved, even if it is at the expense of another heart. Dearest Jenny, I shall fulfill your wishes—today I see you for the last time—but grant me one more kiss on your divine lips before I depart. Splendid woman! Did I ever know love without you?"

"Albert! Albert!" Jenny replied, the liveliest red on her cheeks, as lively as the blush of a virgin standing before her marriage bed. "Go from this house and no longer tear at the smarting wound of my heart—and if you should ever encounter my Emil on your life's pilgrimage, you will look without shyness into his beautiful eyes. You will see your own image in him, and—you will forgive your Jenny."

"Splendid woman!" Albert cried out in joy. "You are reconciled with the god Cupid—another god might try to impose guilt on you, but he will not be heeded. And now, fare thee well—your splendid image will never vanish from my soul, and if I should ever meet your Emil, I will put my arm around his slender body and whisper to him, 'You were with your Jenny without even knowing it . . .'"

"Albert, before you leave me forever, one more word: Down below in the garden at the side of the balsam bed is a banana tree. If you search its trunk, you will find the letter *E* carved under a brief verse. Cut an additional *A* into it, but in such a way that the *E* and *A* are joined together—now fare thee well, and here is this kiss—and this—and this!"

When Albert went down to the garden, leaving his fireman's belt behind in the chamber in his confusion, he found the banana tree. On its trunk, about a foot from the ground, half-hidden in the thicket of dark blue foliage, he discovered the following verse: "I know not what inborn charm leads them both / And does not permit them to forget."

He found the *E* under this verse. "Emil, I don't know how to tell you anything about the magical compulsion that your native soil still has over you," the young architect whispered to himself. "You have Jenny to thank that your homeland still thinks of you at all. Poor Emil!"

When Albert finally turned his back on the lovable cottage, *A* and *E* stood indivisibly entwined.

Chapter 7

Complications and Revelations

That was how matters stood when the Hungarian arrived in New Orleans on board the *Sultana.* He eschewed surprise and thought it more fitting to prepare his spouse for his appearance with a few lines directed to her. Frida's reception of him after his two-year absence was heartier than one would have expected in view of her character. The Hungarian played the penitent so perfectly that Frida forgot all her hostility and forgave the cad completely. Since his hopes about his wife's pecuniary situation had been fulfilled to a degree, which had been his motive for returning in the first place, he found it good to place himself voluntarily under his wife's auspices so long as there was nothing better. This was in order to stifle all distrust his wife might harbor. His calculation achieved complete victory, and he had to admit that he had been correct as ever—he was by no means tossing his hook into an empty pond. Poor Frida! She gave him her undivided trust once more and even engaged in private reveries about happy days to come. There were only two matters she could never settle, and they tormented and irritated her. The first was why Jenny was so closed and silent to her and why she permitted not a glimpse of what was in her heart—something that had never happened before. She thought for a while that Albert had some part in the secret cares of her dear sister, particularly since she had happened upon the banana tree, with its *A* and *E* joined together. But then, when the conversation touched on Emil and she noted Jenny's moist eyes, she assumed the source of Jenny's limitless melancholy was her longing for her faithless husband, who had not sent a word.

The other point that saddened her and often stimulated her anxiety was the fact that Lajos had experienced the same mysterious encounter with her Doppelgänger. The episode in one of the staterooms at the Planters House in St. Louis, which the Hungarian had related to her—though with significant alterations—had been just the thing to confuse her practical and placid senses and to draw her into eerie speculations. Cousin Karl's letter, which had reached its addressee shortly after the Hungarian had arrived in New Orleans, completely failed in its purpose and even detracted from the reputation of the man who had previously stood so high in Frida's estimation, whose solid and reasonable suggestions had always been received with unlimited veneration. Furthermore, her husband's intimations and seemingly well-founded assertions about the dueling affair were calculated to chase every inclination toward Cousin Karl from her heart. After Lajos's prevarications, she could not believe that a man such as Karl, who could write such a heartless letter and challenge her husband to a duel on a whim, could ever have been her friend.

The Hungarian, who had reason to fear a visit from Karl after his return from St. Louis, mustered all his slyness to avoid a meeting. Little Tiberius received the strictest order to send Cousin Karl away any time he came to visit. Although obedience was not one of the black scoundrel's greatest virtues, in this case he followed the Hungarian's commands to the letter by showing the door to Master Karl, who had often punished him harshly.

During this period, the lovable cottage was so enclosed and guarded from all angles that one would suppose that its beautiful occupants were being held in close confinement. This was true for Jenny in a certain sense, since her frequent indisposition led her to cease her piano instruction and stay at home. Frida only came home during the midday hours, after which she went back to her duties and returned only after five in the evening. Tiberius had to escort her over. On one of these passages to her school, she encountered Cousin Karl. Karl greeted her warmly, with all the friendliness he could muster. Frida did not respond with a greeting, instead acting as if she had not seen him. Tiberius was then able to grant a malicious smile to his former persecutor, keeping his cap solidly on his head. Karl, who had experienced more than one such encounter by now, and who had become irritated by repeated rejection, could not misinterpret this episode. He was correct in seeing Lajos as the source of the disturbance, and he believed he had been slandered to a grand degree. Karl was a decisive man, and once he undertook to do something he did not rest until he had succeeded. Yet he was somehow too reserved a man of the world to raise a scandal to get what he wanted. Since he always chose the straight and honorable path, he always lost. In keeping with his nature, he wrote his cousin Frida a letter in which he asked in the friendliest manner the reason for her sudden estrangement and hostility to him, and he requested that she not leave him any longer in an uncertainty that tormented him day and night. The letter was so well composed, so truly and decently written, that it could not have failed in its mission if Frida had seen it. But Tiberius, who was given the letter, betrayed its author. Tiberius passed the letter to the Hungarian, who did not hesitate to do what the situation demanded. As requested, Karl received a response in two days. But what sort of response? He wept bright tears as he read it. Tiberius had brought it to his office and vanished without giving any answer or greeting. Karl was so distressed that he went to his superior at once and asked to be relieved. The letter had been dictated to Frida by her husband, and it was intended to bring about a definitive break.

After three months in Algiers, the Hungarian suddenly abandoned his orderly way of life and began spending his time in the Third District, where he often passed the hours until late into the night. He told his wife that he had become foreman at a soda factory and that he had an obligation to keep the night watch at the factory at least three nights a week. Since he had stopped asking his wife for money and began making a regular contribution of no small amount, Frida did not have the slightest doubt about his story. She was quietly pleased over her husband's sense of enterprise, and she only wished from the bottom of her heart that Emil would return and push away the dark clouds resting on Jenny's brow. But before we go any further, we have to unroll a small moral panorama of New Orleans before the attentive reader. We shall step carefully so as not to break any shells.

Just as New Orleans has an entirely different physiognomy from all the other cities in the Union, it also contains within itself several distinct types. There are three of these types, clearly distinguished according to district. Whoever crosses Felicity Road from Lafayette will remark at once that the modern Anglo-Saxon is in charge, that is, that he is in the First District. To convince oneself of this, one does not even need to look up. All one needs to do is to observe the long shadows on the ground—long legs and thin, stretched necks with protruding Adam's apples are to be found in abundance. It is no marvel that the moral condition of this district is better than is the case in the Second and Third Districts, for wherever long legs and cadaverous necks are to be found, Lady Venus is not inclined to stay.

Once a person has Julia Street behind him, he is in a region where every cross-street sees an increase in long-leggedness, until the long legs reach such a degree, particularly on Tchoupitoulas Street, that one flees head over heels across Canal Street. But he would not be completely safe yet, and if he has the misfortune of wandering into the Gem, across from the post office, the long legs and scrawny necks would reappear in force—but for the last time, since the Gem is the last outpost of this type. There are only two streets in the First District that suffer bad reputations. They are Gravier Street and Perdido Street ("street of the lost"). Long-leggedness only appears on these streets when those afflicted with it are in the process of collecting rent from fallen angels. Whole blocks were constructed for this ambiguous speculation. Whether the speculation by our nabobs and Croesuses on the surplus value of prostitutes improves the moral climate of the district is an open question.

In the Second District, the First Municipality of happy memory, the skin color grows browner, the hair shinier, the eyes darker and more curious, the necks shorter and fuller, the noses shorter, and (since elegance and gallantry have brought chewing tobacco into discredit) the teeth whiter. They laugh, joke, and play literary games more often, and their vests and trousers have burn-holes from paper cigars or cigarilos. Moustaches are in finest flower there, as for a long time the male residents have been ashamed to show themselves with naked faces among the beautiful, dark-eyed tulips. It would be unheard of for a man without a moustache to win a hearing from the lady of his heart here. For in this district only moustaches descend into the laps of the fair. The thermometers of morality are Chartres, Royal, Toulouse, Orleans and Dauphine Streets. If the mercury rises here, it also rises on the other streets. If they are doing poorly, then all languish. Bienville Street is the most guiltless of them all, for there are many Teutons on this street who remain loyal to their little wives and educate their children with rural values and morality, insofar as they do not allow themselves to be ruined and seduced by the French. The lion of this district is *domino à la poudre.*

In earlier times, the Third District possessed two free ports, one for ships and one for dancing girls. The first has vanished, and only the second survives. Parasina Brulard Hotchkiss's palace, with its subsidiaries running back and forth across the entire district, is still fondly recalled, as is the colorful Mulattoes' Settlement and Creole *Mulatressages.* Here the infamous Hotoohs hold their illicit gatherings, their "naked balls" and shocking orgies. In this district live most of the pale chino cholas, whose deadly qualities are well known to any denizen of New Orleans. Most women of this coloration are free, since they are useless to their masters as slaves and they have a dreadful effect on children entrusted to their care. Their inns are concentrated in the interior of the district, and only the Hamburg Mill stood (stands?) directly on the levee.

Fortune led the Hungarian directly to the mill without his having known a thing about the institution. He happened on Gabor von Rokavar at Lombardi's fruit store as he was engaged in a heated discussion with Lombardi. Gabor and Lajos, who had known each other previously, quickly declared themselves inseparable comrades, and Lombardi immediately made the acquaintance of the Hungarian officer of hussars. He decided there was no risk in introducing Lajos to the Lady Merlina Dufresne. Lajos soon joined the mill as a clubman, which was his status at the time we first encountered him on his departure from Bissell's Island. The reader has already learned the character of the clubmen of the Hamburg Mill from an earlier volume of *The Mysteries of New Orleans,* as well as the Hungarian's efforts as an arsonist. The two gangs of arsonists that operated out of the Lady Merlina's establishment were entirely dissolved through clever maneuvers, and then the clubmen of the Hamburg Mill had a complete monopoly in their hands. One might object that the manner we have presented this gang of arsonists to the reader lacks enough practicality and precision to be believable in all its ramifications. We believe that we can dispel this doubt by pointing out that it would be dangerous for us to give naked facts without the garb of a novel. Further, we do not feel our chosen genre demands that we compare our bemused imagination to criminal statistics. This attitude was necessary so as not to degenerate into bizarre fantasy or to spur criticism to no avail. Among the innumerable fires the clubmen of the Hamburger Mill started, the one that reduced the splendid St. Charles Hotel to ashes was by far the most important and that which was realized in the most criminal and bold manner.

Sure enough, this matter is still covered by an impenetrable veil of secrecy, and not one of the scoundrels caught setting other fires has ever confessed anything about it. Incidentally, the flames that destroyed the St. Charles Hotel also devoured a Unitarian church at the corner of Union and St. Charles Street, leaving it in ashes.*

This was almost the same time the Hungarian committed the crime against a family just arrived from Germany, taking them from prosperity to desperation. If help had not come to them at the right moment, they would have descended forever into an abyss of misery and need. While Lajos had been wandering the streets of the First District one day, fortune led him to the exchange office of the bankers Mathews and Finley, at the corner of Camp Street and Commercial Place. There he noted a rather elderly man at the payment table receiving a quantity of banknotes. For the Hungarian, it was a single thought to see the money and to decide to take it. He followed the man at a short distance as he went on his way harmlessly and slowly. It was too early in the day for Lajos to attack and rob him on the street. Then a marvelous accident showed him the way to come into possession of this very significant amount of money. After he had followed his selected victim a few blocks, a small blonde girl came out of a large, dignified house and ran straight to the man.

"Mama and the children are visiting the old miss over there—she told me to wait for you until you returned from the banker. Then I was to tell you to put the money in the large desk in the big room and keep the key, in case you have to go out, for we probably won't be back until after eight."

*On the same spot, Judah Touro had a splendid structure built that occupies the entire front of the block along St. Charles Street, universally known as Touro's Row. It might interest many of our readers to know the rents Mr. Touro draws from this building, which are guaranteed for some years. Messrs. Bullitt, Miller, & Co. pay $3,500 a year (running until 31 July 1857); J. H. Ashbridge & Co. pay $2,500 (until 31 August 1857); Mr. Gregor & Co. pay $2,500 (until 31 July 185–); Schmidt & Co. pay $2,500 (until 30 September 1857); Messrs. Chin and Bolton pay $2,500 (until 31 August 1857); and W. Simpson pays $4,500 (until 30 September 1858). None of the other shops in the building rents for less than $1,500, so Mr. Touro receives an annual income of $25,000 from a single building. And what did the Unitarian church get? The prayer stools and choir stalls? We really don't know.

"You mean preparations for travel have already been completed, as we said at breakfast, and Mama and your siblings have already been gone for some time?"

"Mama only left two hours ago—I waited for you the entire time, Papa—as far as the other matter goes, everything is the way you wanted it."

"Give Mama and your siblings my greetings, Gertrude, and tell them they should not stay out too long."

"Adieu, Papa!"

"Adieu, my child."

One will already have recognized the elderly man as the count, Melanie's husband. This brief conversation, which was carried out in a rather loud voice by both parties, attracted Lajos's attention to a very high degree. The first decision he made was to follow the count to his apartment, gain entrance under the pretext of a visit, murder him, and take the money. He could not carry out his plan, however, for at the very moment he began mounting the steps, he heard people behind him. Three men passed by and stopped before the count's door. One of them pulled the bell, and the count appeared immediately and admitted them. They were business associates who had matters to settle with the count before his departure. The Hungarian walked dejectedly down the steps and awaited the men's departure in the lower hallway for two hours. In the end, bored with waiting and fearing that the entire family would return, he spun another criminal plan, that which led to the impoverishment of the entire family and which Melanie later described to the enthralled prince of Württemberg.

Everything the Hungarian dared in this situation was a success, all the more marvelous because he did not invest a great deal of effort or intelligence in it. The theft from the count's family was a success simply because of his quickness and physical dexterity. He seemed to be the darling of his special demon, which blinded the eyes of the police and saved him from the revenging arms of Themis.

The reader has long been waiting to be told more about the arrival of the count's family in New Orleans, as well as their efforts to find Emil and the two sisters. But before we fulfill these tasks, we must look at the lovable cottage several months earlier.

Frida, who naturally had no notion of the Hungarian's shameful profession, bestowed on him all of her earlier love and respect, and she was overjoyed to find that she was carrying something under her heart that she could not conceal from her husband. He came home late one night from the mill to find Frida, dressed in a sparkling white negligée, sitting on the front porch in a rocking chair. It had been quite humid during the day, and there had been a small thunderstorm that had cooled the air somewhat. Jenny was sad and completely out of sorts. Her sister had pressed in vain to discover the source of her care, despite all tender efforts.

Jenny would admit nothing, but she declared she had a physical complaint that, as she described it, must have been caused by her upset nerves. So they sat together for three entire hours, without Jenny's depression lightening for a moment and without Frida's being able to move her sister to a confession of her problem. Jenny finally wished her sister good night in a pained tone, returned her tender kiss, and went back to her room, where she laid down at once. Frida found herself utterly alone on the porch. The lightning had grown stronger, and distant thunder echoed from the vast mass of black clouds that rose in an instant to mountainous heights in the south, announcing an approaching storm. The agitated air felt as cool as the breast of a seagull on the lightly clad body of the unhappy blessed one. She laid her hands in her lap and studied the opposite shore in hopes of seeing her husband in the flashes of lightning as Tiberius brought him to the Algiers shore. Whether it was because the flashes of lightning were so bright or because the thunder that followed was so loud that it distracted her from her task, she did not see her husband until he stood behind her and gave her a tender, "Good evening, my Frida."

She started a bit when she suddenly felt his hand on her shoulder, followed in the next moment by a stormy embrace.

"Still up so late, my child?" he asked in a gentle tone, helping her out of the rocking chair, as was his habit, and sitting in it himself to provide her a place on his lap.

"'So late,' my Lajos? It would be better to say 'so early,' for midnight has long since passed, and if there were not so many black clouds, you would surely see the first glimmer of daylight," she responded, touching her blonde head to his strong, broad chest.

"Then we should go to bed, my dear child. I am very tired and exhausted."

"You torment yourself so much on my behalf, my Lajos—you should give your job to another so you could have your night's rest."

"It is not yet time, my Frida, I have to keep working at this—then, if God wills that my health holds, I will start my own business."

"If God wills it, Lajos? Heaven has blessed me, and in the future it will spare us all trouble."

At these words a hellish fire began burning in the Hungarian's eyes.

"Heaven has blessed her?" he asked himself. But with feigned joy he asked his wife, "Heaven has blessed you, you say? Did I hear correctly? Are you . . ."

"It is just as you think, Lajos, in several months we will be the happiest couple on earth."

One must not forget that this scene takes place a long time before the fire at the Hamburg Mill, and no doubt it helped lead the Hungarian to set the fire.

Jenny's condition grew more hopeless with every passing day, and Frida lost all expectation of things improving, especially since her sister refused to see a physician. Then a man who could bring light into this dark situation appeared, in the form of the prince of Württemberg. He came one day to the charming cottage to visit the two sisters and collect the butterflies and beetles they had been gathering for him. He was received as a good friend, as was always the case when he appeared. The joy over his sudden, unexpected appearance was so great that even Jenny's mask of suffering lightened a bit, and her eyes—blank since that scene with the handsome fireman—glittered with life again. But all too soon her good spirit retreated and the quiet demon of her sorrow recovered the upper hand. The prince was too much a connoisseur of women for the cause of her distress to be hidden from him long. When they went for a stroll in the garden after dinner, the prince between the two sisters, Jenny suddenly broke away and left the prince alone with Frida, making excuses of feeling unwell, then went to the opposite side of the garden. The prince looked at the blonde in confusion and stated his concerns for her sister.

"My dear Countess Frida," he said, going to the bower on the right side of the sheltered path, "shall we be seated here for a few moments?"

"As you wish, Prince, but I ask you not to be disturbed if I leave you soon, for I cannot leave Jenny out of my sight for long. She could easily harm herself."

"But my God, are things so poorly with Countess Jenny that you have something to fear?"

"I cannot say for sure, Prince, since I could deceive myself in this matter, but prudence requires that one always be prepared."

"How should I interpret your words, dear Countess? You are talking in riddles."

"Prince, you know that I have never kept secrets from you, so long as they did not deal with the inner sanctum of women's matters."

"I know that, dear Countess, but I beg that you do not misinterpret my words."

"Utterly not, Prince—you always speak honestly, and so it is my duty to give you what you always demand from yourself." Frida laid her index finger on her mouth and then continued: "Since my husband has returned, Jenny sleeps alone once more. You know, Prince, that hitherto we two sisters slept in one bed and were as happy together as a young married couple. I always came to bed earlier than Jenny, who often stayed up until one or two hours after midnight, reading her romantic poets or writing little essays that she would read out at breakfast. By the time Jenny was done with her studies, I was already in the deepest sleep. So she would strip down to her stockings and her minimal negligée, then she would climb into bed and awaken me. Then I had to remove her stockings with my own hands, and formally cover her up and get her to sleep like a little child. I was so used to that, and we were so happy and pleased to do that, so it was only with pain that I separated myself from her side when my husband returned. Jenny asked repeatedly that I spend the night with her, and my husband had nothing against it, since he knew how dependent we were on each other. So we began sleeping together again—my husband was often gone the entire night anyway. I half slept, half wakened, and, when I did sleep, I dreamed the dumbest stuff, about fires, dead horses, or murderers and robbers, so that I was always happier when I was awake. My sister lay right across the bed, taking practically all the room. Since I did not want to wake her to get into a more comfortable position, I rolled up as tightly as possible against the top of the bed. I now believe that my bad dreams came from this uncomfortable position. One night I carefully stretched myself further across the bed, and, since I found no opposition, I reclaimed half of it. Only then did I realize that Jenny must have moved to the other side. I probed about, looked around, and arose—my sister was not with me. Then a shadow stroked the mosquito nets, spreading itself against the columns at the foot of the bed. In the next moment the room became quite dark. 'Are you in front of a light, Jenny?' I called out, lifting the curtains and sticking my head out toward the fireplace, on whose mantel the night lamp stood. Jenny was indeed standing in front of the lamp. Her left hand was on its glass top, her right near the flame, so that one could see the fine, rosy blood shimmering through her hand. 'What are you doing, dear sister?' I called out time after time. 'Lie down.' No answer. I have to confess that I felt an uncanny shiver. I rose from the bed, but no sooner had I placed a foot on the carpet than Jenny rushed from the lamp to the window, open because of the heat."

"I suspect, Countess Frida, that your sister is a sleepwa—" the prince did not finish the word, since Frida placed her hand over his mouth.

"Please, Prince," she continued, "don't frighten me. Hear what I have to say first."

The prince nodded.

"Jenny rushed to the window and leaned her whole upper body out of the window—I ran to her in shock, grabbed her around her middle, and insisted that she tell me what was the problem. Instead of answering me, she wriggled out of my grasp and climbed onto the windowsill, acting as if she wanted to jump out. 'For heaven's sake, Jenny, what are you doing?' I asked her, clinging to her neck. She audibly exhaled and turned to me and repeated several times . . ."

Frida was silent for a moment.

"Do not torment me any longer, Countess, what did she say?" the prince declared hastily.

"Spare me, Prince, it is almost impossible—and yet—as a trusted friend, perhaps you see better, my senses are so confused when I think about it. Perhaps it was only the language of the world of dreams—in sleep we often say things of which the heart does not know. My good Jenny repeated, 'Albert, Albert, if you love me even a little bit—Emil, forgive me, my Albert, my Emil—Albert, aren't you my Emil?'"

Frida appeared to be exhausted. She folded her hands in her lap and looked thoughtfully at the prince's face. He passed his right hand repeatedly across his forehead and asked: "Countess, why were you so disturbed by your sister's words? What are you looking for in them? What significance do they have for you?"

"Prince," the splendid blonde responded, "my sister loves Emil to distraction, despite his faithless conduct. She is also not indifferent to the young architect, since he has Emil's mannerisms and even the same look—which Jenny assured me, though I could never see it. The young architect is obsessed with Jenny, as a person raves for a beautiful flower or an appealing bouquet. I have no notion how much further it goes—it would be a betrayal of my good sister—or is it already betrayal if I have told her secret?"

"My dear Countess," the prince of Württemberg interrupted her, "the well-being of your sister depends on your telling me honestly your fears for her. Don't consider it mere curiosity, and do not believe that you are committing some sort of crime against your sister's heart if you entrust a secret to an old family friend whose highest mission is to ease pain and settle distress."

"Prince, Prince—you are going too far in your praiseworthy zeal, no, no, Prince, a secret such as this, what we women . . ." Frida closed her eyes and blushed, turning her face toward her lap.

The prince laid his right hand on his friend's shoulder, gently inclining his head forward and saying carefully, "I believe I have detected your sister's problem—haven't you noticed her strange posture?"

"Prince!" the blonde sounded in a deeply moving tone. "Could my own sister have forgotten herself so utterly?"

"Quiet, divine woman!" the prince soothed her. "You should sympathize with your sister, not condemn her."

"Condemn my sister? No, no, Prince, I will kiss her again and again. Oh Jenny, Jenny, if I had even suspected!"

"My dear," the prince of Württemberg finished, "think of Goethe's *Elective Affinities,*[29] only in reverse, and your sister is free of all guilt."

After such a fortunate analysis, the prince of Württemberg held it to be his first duty to speak with Countess Jenny. Even if he had some misgivings about trying to relieve her depression with an honest approach, still he felt himself obligated to save at least outward appearances and protect his friend from a bad reputation she did not deserve. So he determined to persuade Jenny, through Frida's mediation, to leave Algiers and spend her confinement far away from New Orleans and its environs. Further, since Jenny's compromising condition coincided with that of her sister Frida, it was also helpful for the latter to enjoy herself as much as possible in relaxing surroundings, exchanging a shared depression for a fragrant springtime of the heart. Pass Christian was the perfect place for this purpose. The prince had access to a roomy, pleasantly located villa there that belonged to his friend Baron von Seckendorf, who was usually in San Antonio, Texas. During its owner's absence, this villa was reserved for a select family circle who visited during the regatta. This suggestion pleased no one more than it did the Hungarian. At first he heaped false tenderness on Frida, even pressing her to delay her departure by a month on the pretext that he would be able to take leave of his business and join his wife and sister-in-law for a time. But after a few days, he declared that he feared he would not be able to get away for months, so he thought it better for them to hurry up and leave while the clear, splendid skies seemed to favor traveling.

Who was happier about this than the prince of Württemberg? He made the necessary purchases for a long residence in Pass Christian, along with several hanging screens, porter chairs, chaises longues with enclosures—in short, everything the prince could imagine useful for the convenience of his countesses. He also did not hesitate to help pack the chests, bags, and palmetto baskets, sneaking in many a present for the countesses to discover after their arrival.

There would be adequate service in Pass Christian, for there were two older mulatto women and three young, healthy cholas used to working, all of them the property of Herr von Seckendorf. But the sisters also wanted a German maid along with them, since they thought such a servant would be more comfortable and discreet for the time of their confinement than any colored person. Urschl, who had been unable to find a place, though she had walked her feet raw going to the German Society, was hired back by the prince and accepted by the sisters after a brief debate.

In the end they felt pity for their saucy cook, although she had recently been condemned *in contumaciam* for her scandalous conduct—unable to find a new situation, she had been kept in the house. The reward for the sisters' kindness toward her was that they did not have to waste their time seeking and training a new domestic. Tiberius was to take charge of the kitchen once more, winning new laurels frying eggplants and making banana-tomato salads. When the sisters, accompanied by the prince and the Hungarian, departed from the lovable cottage to board the boat awaiting them, the saucy cook waddled after them, covered with boxes and bags, wearing an expression as satisfied as that of a mother whose baby has used the toilet for the first time. She was truly glad to get going, since Tiberius had made her life hard since their encounter. He had even insulted her a few moments before their departure, sticking out his tongue and thumbing his nose.

That was when the count's family, Emil's parents, arrived from Germany. The prince, who was informed of their arrival the day after, did not neglect to visit them right away, since he was an old friend. The reader already knows of the trials and tribulations of the count's family, and will now understand why the prince of Württemberg was so secretive when he came to speak of Emil and the two sisters. He thought it best to await Jenny's full recovery from her confinement before leading her and Frida to the arms of her parents-in-law. He wrote a very convincing letter to the two sisters in Pass Christian, and they adopted his suggestions to every detail. The old count was unable to obtain any information about his son or his daughter-in-law because Emil was known there under an entirely different name. The count's family learned of Frida's marriage only at the very last, when the prince was about to reunite them.

Jenny's child, a splendid creature with large, bright blue eyes and dark hair, was taken by the prince to his mansion on Bayou Road. There the baby was cared for as a precious jewel and raised in expectation of the time when conditions would permit returning it to its mother's arms. Frida, who became a mother almost in the same hour, had to get through sad, hard times in the first few weeks. Her child, a boy, came into the world quite sickly, and his prospects were not thought to be good. He was certainly a remarkable child. He did not have the uncertain, fluid features of almost all newborns, rather they were pronounced, or better, sharply marked. The eyes, the brow, the thin lips, the chin—everything declared the Hungarian, his father. His head showed a thick, dark head of hair, and he also brought five little teeth into the world. At the place on the cheek where his father bore his dreadful scar, there was a gray mark which ran to the corner of his mouth. Frida was overjoyed with the child, precisely because of his striking similarity to his father. She watched this sickly creature day and night with the greatest anxiety, renouncing every comfort for herself. The extent to which the Hungarian loved his child after his spouse had returned to the lovable cottage, however, can be deduced from his conversation in the Hamburg Mill, where he prostituted his wife in the most dreadful terms with his partners in crime. We might add that when he approached his child for the first time, something within him swore and flailed about. Perhaps he was terrified by the gray mark on the innocent child's cheek, reminding him directly of the murderous scene on Looking-Glass Prairie? Certainly no husband had surer proof of his wife's fidelity than did Lajos when he beheld his child. Such fidelity!

That is how far matters had come in the lovable cottage when the prince of Württemberg and Countess Gertrude surprised her oppressed parents and then passed the night watching at Aunty Celestine's bed. As we already know, the Hamburg Mill fell victim to flames the same night. We will rejoin the story as the monster looked back with crossed arms at the fire from the Algiers shore before passing by Thompson's Foundry on his way to the lovable cottage,[30] little Tiberius at his side.

Chapter 8

One Night in the Life of a Young Woman

After their return from Pass Christian, the two sisters at first lived a rather sheltered life. This was partly because they needed to recover from their residence away and partly because they were trying to buy a lot just on the northern border of their garden. With this expansion of their property, they wished to create a proper place for the prospering fowl they had been raising. Frida had resigned her position at the college as soon as she arrived in New Orleans and turned all her attention to her child, since her husband told her he was earning twice as much as before. Jenny's situation had changed in that she no longer gave piano lessons in the city, but she had a few selected pupils come to her house. That was much better for the good-natured Jenny. The time she had wasted traveling to and from the city could now be applied to her favorite occupations. She only left the lovable cottage twice a week to travel to Bayou Road and the mansion of the prince of Württemberg, to see her child. That was where she first met Gertrude and Constanze, even before their parents had learned of her own and Frida's presence from the prince. He had brought Gertrude and Constanze to Mistress Evans after the death of Aunty Celestine, and the other members of the family had been taken across the lake.

Jenny passed many of her free hours when not in Bayou Road sitting next to her sister under the banana tree, where a small bench had been placed. She herself called this place "Jenny's Rest." And indeed it did give her heart a great deal of peace to be near the intertwined initials. No one disturbed her here. Once the prince came as she was wrapping her bosom kerchief about the trunk of the banana tree, covering the *A* and *E*. She jumped up in confusion and fled like the wind into the cottage. The prince stood speechless for a few moments, unable to make sense of Jenny's strange conduct. After he'd checked several times whether he was being observed from the residence, he knelt down and unwrapped the kerchief from the tree. When he saw the *A* and *E*, Jenny's distress became clear to him.

"I should be upset with you, banana tree," the prince whispered to himself. "Until now I thought that Countess Jenny had told only me and her sister her deepest secret, but now I see that she has initiated you as well."

The prince opened his shirt and tucked the betraying scarf into it. Then he left through the garden door without speaking to the sisters.

Jenny was aflame when she came to her sister and told her that the prince had found her at the banana tree.

"It was good that that happened, dear little sister. Why were you hiding your secret from our old friend? It was often on the tip of my tongue, but I always believed that you would tell him yourself."

"You are right, sister," Jenny responded in a confidential tone. "It was a mistake that I kept it from him."

"The prince is the best father-confessor in the world," Frida said, "he forgives all sins."

"He becomes more cherished with every day," Jenny said, "I love and treasure him like my own father."

"Who knows?" Frida said jokingly.

"Frida!" her sister commanded, shaking her finger threateningly.

"I have no idea," Frida responded, "but the prince is not nearly as boring as other men of his age."

"La Rochefoucauld once said, 'There are few men who understand how to be old.'" Jenny recited meaningfully.

"The prince is one of those few," Frida contributed, with as much meaning as her sister.

The sisters conversed in this manner quite often.

Today Jenny and Frida sat with each other late into the night. Between them stood a little cradle, which they took turns rocking. The little one in the cradle appeared to sleep quite peacefully. Frida placed her right hand over the surface of the little bed, carefully, so that no opening was made in the mosquito netting, since with the least opportunity the mosquitos could flit in and bite the child, awakening him. Both of them wore long, snow-white shirts trimmed as blouses. They had each combed their hair back and fixed it with a simple needle. As always, before they went to bed they had thickly powdered their faces, necks, and bosoms. The climate of Louisiana demands this, and women who ignore it soon see damage to their skin. The sisters never failed to powder themselves or do anything else that had to do with cleanliness when they got ready for bed. Their small, narrow feet were a marvelously alabaster white, and their elegant toenails were tinted with the prettiest pink.

"Your husband is out quite late tonight, dear sister," Jenny remarked as she looked through the mosquito netting at the sleeping child.

"I was just thinking about that," Frida responded. "Tiberius has been gone an hour and a half."

"So long as there has been no accident," Jenny worried. "Tiberius so often makes mistakes when he rows."

"Oh, I am not concerned about that, for my husband is an excellent swimmer."

"That is true, Frida—but tell me, what did your husband tell you last night in bed that made you laugh so loud?"

"Just a moment, Jenny, didn't you hear what he said?"

"If I had heard it, I would not have asked, dear little sister. It must have been something extraordinary, since you laughed so hard. Isn't that so?"

"It was, Jenny, and I have to start laughing again when I think about it."

"So tell me, what was it?"

Instead of answering, Frida was silent, acting in a mysterious manner in order to arouse her sister's curiosity.

"So tell me, little sister, what was it?"

"I will tell you sometime, Jenny—it is already too late tonight, and my husband could arrive any moment."

"Then he cannot know?"

"Of course he knows."

"Then why won't you tell me?"

"I want to, Jenny—just not tonight."

"That is pure spite on your part, Frida—it cannot matter to you whether you tell me today or tomorrow. It would be better for you to do it right now, or I will assume you will find some other excuse tomorrow."

The two sisters suddenly heard something. Frida released her hand from the cradle and looked questioningly at her sister.

"There must be a fire, Frida." Jenny said.

"Not very close? Come, sister, let's look out."

The two sisters left the room arm in arm, but only after they looked in at the child to make sure he was still sleeping.

The wind carried the sound of the fire bells across from New Orleans, so it sounded like they were very close.

When Jenny and Frida reached the porch of the cottage, they looked across to the opposite bank and saw high flames leaping to the heavens.

"That is a big fire!" Jenny cried out. "Look how it spreads, Frida."

"These continual fires in New Orleans are dreadful. There is hardly a day when one is not jolted out of peaceful sleep once or twice. It is almost as if it were planned that way. It is downright unnatural."

"That could well be so, Frida—there are enough evil people in New Orleans."

Beyond the fence that enclosed the garden they saw two men running. They halted at the nearby docks and talked in loud voices.

"I think that's Johnson's big warehouse," the sisters heard one of them say.

"It can't be that—Johnson's warehouse is another block further back. If I'm not wrong, that's the Hamburg Mill," the other responded.

"It's no loss if that's ruined. One hears so much, and if the half is true, then it deserves to go up in flames. 'Tis just a band of loafers that lives there."

"If only the band of loafers burns up with it, the neighborhood could be happy—but decent people have to suffer as well," the first responded.

"You could be right," the other said. "Look at the long lick of blue flames. That's alcohol burning."

"Now do you think it's the big warehouse?"

"Yes. That much alcohol and liquor could never have been in the Hamburg Mill—look, look, the blue flames get longer and more numerous every moment. There, they rise behind as well—and yet it's got to be the mill. Look over there, where the wind carries the smoke away, you can see the neighboring buildings quite clearly. I can imagine they are quite close to the mill—look, look, it's even clearer now."

"That could well be, I never paid that much attention."

The men left the dock and walked further down along the riverbank.

Jenny, who, like her sister, had distinctly heard every word the men had said, said: "Didn't the men say that the . . . what did they call that thing?"

"Hamburg Mill, I believe."

"That must be a dreadful nest, according to what the men said about it. You will have to ask your husband, Frida, when he comes back. The name sounds mysterious—I would be curious to learn more about it."

"It depends on whether my husband knows anything about it, or if he has even heard the name."

"It is quite possible he knows, for I have never met a man who knows so much of the place—he is a living directory."

What is going on in Jenny's head at this moment? Are those not the dulled eyes of a quiet madwoman? Frida, Frida, wrap your arm around your sister's slender body so she doesn't fall over the balustrade in her fit of joy! I beg you on my knees, Frida, pull the arrows out of Cupid's quiver before he shoots all of them into your poor sister's heart. For the one she loves is too far away to form his lips into a kiss; he is over there, over there across the wide river, standing in the middle of the flames, mocking the destructive fire. Isn't that a vision? Is your imagination simply following an enticing but misleading beacon? Could that handsome man with the singed hair and the glowing face who stands on the highest gable of the Hamburg Mill to fulfill his duty as a fireman, could he really be your Albert? And you are sure that you recognize him, Jenny? It is a long way from Algiers across to New Orleans, but I believe you, for I know that the eye of love sees a long way.

The cool breeze played with the curled hair of a goddess.

Blue-eyed Frida embraced her sister as she leaned over the balustrade of the porch, reaching her arms out in tempestuous desire at the raging firestorm.

"Frida, good, good sister, don't you see my Albert?" Jenny cried out, as loud as if she were alone on this earth with her sister.

"Jenny, dear good little sister, be reasonable, what is the matter with you? I beg you, for heaven's sake, little sister—O God, my God, those eyes—little sister, you terrify me—what is the matter with you, then?"

"Don't you see my Albert? There, there, don't you see him, standing in the midst of the flames—O God, let them do him no harm. Look, look, now he is going higher up—O God—will the ladder hold him? Oh, look at him, just like Emil!"

They actually saw the slender figure of a fireman on a roof timber that had been spared from the flames. He was directing a hose with a practiced hand on the flames beneath him. He stood securely, as if he were not in the slightest peril but on solid ground. His profile rose out of the glowing coals, and it was only erased when the thick smoke rose and covered the roof.

It was high time for the fireman to leave his perilous post. Indeed, at the same instant he darted down his ladder, the cross-timber fell down into the smoking ruins and glowing coals.

Jenny saw the fireman retreat, and she waved her handkerchief in his direction, as if she were convinced he could see her.

Was it really Albert?

Frida did not want to concede this to her sister at first, but in the end she believed it, since that was what Jenny wanted.

A merry jingle at the garden gate told the sisters that someone was entering.

"That is your husband, Frida," Jenny said. "I am going to my bedroom; I am in no condition to see him. Wish him good night in my name, and do not forget to ask him about the Hamburg Mill."

The two sisters gave each other their usual goodnight kiss, and Frida whispered in her sister's ear, "But don't eavesdrop again, dear little sister!"

"Quit that, Frida!" Jenny responded quickly, rushing away.

Jenny was right. It was Lajos who came down the garden path. He was followed by little Tiberius, who was whistling to himself his old song, "Susannah don't you cry."

Frida left the porch and went to meet her husband halfway.

He barely raised his eyes from the ground as she gave him her hand in greeting. He thanked her curtly and did not even offer her his arm, which he had never failed to do before. In silence, he helped her carry the cradle into the bedroom. "I am tired" was all Frida could get out of him when they arrived in the bedroom, which, as we know, adjoined Jenny's little room. The door that connected them was only lightly closed during the night. That was Jenny's wish; she did not want to feel she was alone.

Jenny was already in bed when Frida and Lajos entered. She had just snuffed out her light.

Without saying anything, Lajos went to the door and turned the key twice in the lock.

Frida looked at her husband's maneuver with astonishment, for she could not understand his conduct.

"Why did you shut the door, Lajos? Jenny will pass the night in distress."

"My sister-in-law is not a child anymore. Being when a door is locked—it is really ludicrous!"

"Don't speak so loud, Lajos, she can hear you," Frida begged.

"So what if she does hear it? One has to learn to do without this childishness—if she would just think about it, she would be ashamed of herself. It's really very boring, this eternal fooling around . . ."

"What's the matter today? Did something unpleasant happen? Come, Lajos, tell me . . . don't be such a growling bear."

"It is no marvel a man is upset when he has to go begging."

"Tell me, what's the matter?" Frida asked nervously, becoming extremely tense.

"All my efforts gone to hell!"

"You don't need to swear, Lajos—did you lose your job? Are you in a dispute with your employer? That would not be such a great disaster that you need to be rude. A man such as you can always find something—and even if this were not the case, I could teach in the college every day. They would be glad to have me, I'm sure, Lajos . . ."

It would be superfluous to remind ourselves that, at the very instant Lajos was complaining to his wife about losing his job, he was carrying in his pockets the large sum of money he had found under the bed in Merlina's bedchamber. But one consideration must be stressed at this point, since it enlightens us about the Hungarian's conduct toward his wife. Why had he always shown such delicate self-denial and care around his wife, despite his repellent character and crudeness in his other relationships? At his arrival in New Orleans, as well as during the first months after his return to his wife, it was obviously money that had compelled him to this. He had no profession, but Frida had some property and was teaching—though it was often a burden, why should he not play the complete charade, since his support depended on it? But by the time he became a clubman of the Hamburg Mill, he was making so much money that he could afford to import the finest and costliest wines, such as had never come to New Orleans before. Despite that, he voluntarily continued to wear the straitjacket of a solid married man and tender father. And even now, when he had the entire treasure of the mill in his possession, he kept up this tender and yet perverse reserve. This might seem unbelievable to many, since they have no way to see it from the Hungarian's point of view.

The facts were this:

Jenny and Frida had not written to their parents in Germany since the disappearance of their husbands. This was either due to shame at admitting that they had been wrong in their choice of spouses or—more likely—because they wanted to wait until their relationships could become clarified and ordered enough for them to return to their parents' bosom. Three letters had arrived from Germany. The first, which Emil had kept from his wife, came from Emil's parents, as we learned in the second volume. This letter reported that they had decided to emigrate with the entire family, owing to the threat of revolution. They indicated that they did not appear entirely satisfied with Frida's marriage, since it had been completed without the parents' consent, and they mourned over the unhappy death of Emil's brother.

The second letter came from the sisters' parents, yet it was not addressed to them but to the prince of Württemberg. They begged him to let them know something about the situation of their beloved daughters, Jenny and Frida, with all the honesty of an old and trusted friend. In the very last lines of this letter they specifically said that, even if their situation was not exactly splendid, they were not incapable of sending some money if he felt it necessary. This letter, which had come into the prince's hands before the Hungarian had returned to Algiers, was forwarded to the two sisters. The prince also committed the error of taking counsel when he should have given it. Jenny and Frida would not consider authorizing a response on the prince's part, nor would they write anything themselves. If they were frank, their dear parents would be devastated and suffer great sorrows—and they did not want the burden on their conscience that would result if they described their circumstances other than they were. They would rather give no answer whatsoever than lie: that was the sum total of their decision after several meetings on this matter with the prince.

The third and as yet last letter had been addressed by the sisters' parents to Emil. Since he had given them an address in English, the letter was announced in the list of an English-language newspaper.[31] The prince of Württemberg, meanwhile, was spending several days in Adayes, an old Spanish town on the Red River, to look for a rare beetle, the *Scarabaeus Theophilus,* which has violet-blue wing covers and copper-colored stripes and bears a dramatically curved horn on its broad neck-plate. It had only recently been discovered. The sisters seldom looked at an English-language newspaper, so the announcement was unknown to them. As it happened, however, the Hungarian always read the letter lists and saw the notice. This was eight days after his acceptance into the club of the Hamburg Mill. He went straightaway to the post office and received the letter, then he went to the nearest coffeehouse to read it carefully. His face lightened visibly as he turned the first page and began reading the second. It was concerned with no less a matter than that an uncle who, long lost from view, had returned from India a wealthy man. He had visited the sisters' father as soon as he arrived in the capital, and he was quite upset when he did not find his *Friderle*—this is what he called Frida—the gold-topped little girl he had once bounced in his lap and kissed. When he heard—the letter went on—that Friderle had gone to America with her sister, the old uncle had been in despair, and had he not been ill he would have made the journey to a foreign land at once to see his Friderle, whom he worshiped like an archangel. The uncle—it said at the end of the letter—lay ill for months, and he never ceased fantasizing about seeing his Friderle. He was always about to send this or that splendid gift to her, but he hesitated to do so until he got well. Although the uncle had no doubt that he would eventually recover, he had recently composed his will, declaring Friderle as his universal heiress—the uncle's estate was supposed to be worth between ten and twelve million dollars.

The Hungarian destroyed the letter on the spot, for several reasons. The destruction had no effect on Frida's inheritance, of course, which would come to her sooner or later. Frida would be one of the richest heiresses in the world, without having the slightest notion of her impending great wealth.

One would think that the Hungarian would have avoided placing himself in peril as a murderer and arsonist, considering his future fortune. That did not occur to him. His life as a clubman of the Hamburg Mill pleased him so much at the outset that he seemed willing to risk everything. In the end, however, sated by all possible enjoyments, he set about winning the treasury of the Hamburg Mill and burning down the mill itself. But whenever he was about to set this plan in motion, some insurmountable hindrance always appeared. Yes, there was even a time when he let the plan go completely, as the Lady Merlina and the pale mestiza held him tight. Yet what he had earlier not been able to accomplish with his slyness now fell to him as a result of accident, in a remarkable series of astonishing scenes. Think simply of the chapter "Under the Bed." This deed was to be the capstone of his crimes, and then he could live solidly, take up an apparently honest occupation, and quietly await his wife's inheritance. To be everything to his wife, to appear literally to carry her in his hands, was part of his current plan.

Since Frida as yet knew nothing about her expectant wealth, she could not have the least suspicion that he was kind and helpful only because of the money. During the crossing on the boat, he'd decided to display irritation over the loss of his supposed employment, something he intended to be a transition to a life that would exceed his wife's fondest dreams. His unpleasantness about his sister-in-law's fears was also nothing but part of this planned feint.

Let us return to that night.

"Look, Lajos," Frida continued, "if it is nothing more than your losing your job, I am really distressed with you for upsetting me so much."

"No, it's nothing more, Frida, but that is enough to upset me. The thought of unemployment, even for a short time, is unbearable to me. I am so used to action, to producing like a machine, that I already feel very unhappy."

"But Lajos," Frida responded in an almost motherly tone, "you complain about my sister Jenny because she is so childish and is afraid when a door is closed to her—tell me, isn't it just as childish of you to be so upset about being unemployed for a little while? And then, Lajos, there are so many things you could do—in our garden, in our yard, even in the house—or, if you prefer, music and reading. You see, there is no danger of you having nothing to do."

It was a characteristic of Frida's trusting character that she never penetrated this monumental guise for a moment. Even though the unfortunate woman was intelligent and clear-thinking in many regards, she was easy to mislead once she had granted someone her trust. And although Lajos had so grossly abused her trust once before, she still allowed herself to be cheated again, blinded by his penitence along with his seemingly unshakable dependence and love. In addition, she was unable to deny her husband tolerance when he returned so late, usually at one or two o'clock in the morning, exhausted from supposed labor in a factory. If it had ever occurred to her to look at his hands or check his cleanliness, she would have learned otherwise. And yet, with all her good will, Frida still would not have thought much about it. The little scolding she gave him demonstrated the purity of her character and goodness of her heart.

"We shall see what there is to do here—perhaps it will go better than we think," Lajos said with affected placidity, unconsciously touching the pocket where the mill's treasure was hidden.

"As *you* think, Lajos," Frida responded.

Lajos went to the cradle and lifted the mosquito netting enough to look in. Then he closed it and said: "The child looks strikingly like me, doesn't he?"

"He is the spitting image of his father's face," Frida said happily. "Even that!" she continued, stroking Lajos's scar.

"The Mexican desperado who gave me this wound certainly had no idea that it would be used to recognize the father in the son," the Hungarian remarked so quietly and comfortably, as if he was happy with his whole heart over his similarity to his child.

"Say instead," Frida said softly and confidentially, "that God loves your wife so much that he granted her a second husband in a son." Then she clung to his neck so intensely that he had to lean over, causing something to fall out which made a sound when it hit the floor.

Frida heard it fall.

The Hungarian felt it.

Frida searched for a long time around the floor while Lajos watched with a smile on his lips.

"It is nothing, Frida, we were imagining things." he said. He had already seen that it was lying under the cradle, close to the rear rocker.

"I see it, Frida," the Hungarian said with affectedly childish enthusiasm, but a Satanic smile was on his face.

"Tell me, Lajos, where is it, what was it?" Frida begged, gathering her long nightgown up in front in order to kneel more easily.

The Hungarian ducked down and raised up what she sought.

Frida saw it the instant Lajos reached for it. Now that he held it high, where she could examine it, she raised herself on his outstretched arm and cried out: "Oh how pretty these splendid colored lenses! Did you bring me that, Lajos? Oh, I have wanted a pretty night lamp for a long time! Ours looks so sad and ugly."

It was the lamp-head he had stolen from the Italian Lombardi after suffocating him with the Hotoohs' tar mask.

Lombardi didn't need it any more. Now the Hungarian could let it shine in his own house without any hesitation.

The *pipo* Lombardi is dead, but Lajos, the officer of hussars, lives. The living have always enjoyed what the dead leave behind—it is ancient custom.

"My dear husband," Frida said with a tone of voice that cannot be reproduced by words, "tonight we shall sleep by the light of the pretty, pretty little lamp—look how perfectly it fits in the base—we should throw the old thing here right out the window, it's no good any more."

Frida took the old lamp-head and threw it out the window.

Lajos had taken a seat at the cradle. He looked dreadfully pale. This was not unusual for him, but when Frida looked at his face this evening, it seemed to her that she had never seen him quite so pale. At first she thought it was due to the colored lamp, since the green lens was pointed at him. She turned the top so that the pure white lens, between two ruby-red ones, was pointed at him, in an attempt to give a truer illumination—but to no avail. Her husband's face remained as dreadfully pale as before, almost gray-green. Was it because of that hair-raising episode in the *zambo negresse's* bedroom? It must have been, for when Frida said, "tonight we shall sleep by the light of the pretty, pretty little lamp," he thought it best to declare he felt unwell and ask permission to spend a few hours in the garden, in the open, in the cool. Frida gave in reluctantly, and after her husband had departed the bedroom with a buffalo robe under his arm, she unlocked the door into Jenny's little chamber and let her sister in until her husband came back.

Let us leave the two sisters alone with the baby in its cradle, as we follow the Hungarian.

He went to that side of the porch that surrounded the façade of the cottage, then spread out the buffalo robe and stretched his whole length out on it. He turned his face in the direction where the smoke still rose from the fire, sometimes stronger, sometimes weaker. The firemen had withdrawn a quarter hour before, and here and there crowds of people could be seen curiously observing the gutted Hamburg Mill, gawking at the ashes and ruin. The moon beamed bright light down on the site, so that it could easily be seen from the lovable cottage.

After the Hungarian had lain down for a good while, he suddenly sat up, reached in his pocket, and took out the banknotes that he had carefully bundled. He folded them in half and fingered them as if he were trying to count them. He did this not once but several times in succession, like someone who could not believe he was in possession of such a vast sum. He weighed the notes on his flat hand, and made several other maneuvers with them. Then he heard a squeaking, like the sound of new shoes. He looked quickly about and saw Gabor von Rokavar, who greeted him with the sort of bow peculiar to ordinary members of the Hamburg Mill. The Hungarian, who was usually so aloof at surprises, started at this. For the appearance of this person, banned by the Hamburg Mill, was all too unwanted at this moment. But in the next instant he regained his full presence of mind. He rose quickly and turned to Gabor, growling in a contemptuous tone: "You dog, why are you disturbing the peace of your former master?"

"The doggy would like a bit of the pretty banknotes his master has in his hands," Gabor responded with a sweet smile but still rather bravely.

"Damned soul, I'll cut your throat if you don't tell me what brings you here and why you were spying on me!" Lajos said in a bitterly cold voice.

"Go ahead and talk, Lajos," Gabor urged. "I think it would be better for us to make an agreement, and you give me half of your itty-bitty profits."

"Itty-bitty profits? What itty-bitty profits? damned Hungarian *Scandonicz!*"

"Why are you cursing about Hungarians, Lajos, aren't you a Hungarian yourself?"

"But I am no *Scandonicz*—tell me, what do you mean with itty-bitty profits? Do it quick, or I'll slit your throat." Lajos drew his long Bowie knife on saying this.

"Don't speak so loudly, Lajos, the ladies will not be able to sleep, and they might disturb us before we have come to an agreement," Gabor responded, without showing the least disturbance over Lajos's manipulation of the Bowie knife.

"Death or Merlina, damned Scandonicz, what is your nonsense all about?"

"It doesn't mean a thing, Lajos. Your doggy only wants half of the pretty banknotes you were just counting out—nothing more, Lajos—such a poor, rejected doggy as myself is satisfied with very little . . ."

The Hungarian would have jumped at Gabor and run him through with his long Bowie knife, but he understood quite well that such a violent act on an open porch would be dangerous for him. And who could guarantee that this cunning Jew Rokavar—his grandfather, a banker to the court, had bought a patent of nobility from the Habsburgs—did not have several persons hiding and ready to charge in if anything happened to Gabor? Wasn't his current brave attitude, which he had never displayed a hint of before, proof enough of this? He was sure that the Jew had seen him leaving the Hamburg Mill, and, if so, then he must know that he was the cause of the fire that immediately followed. Obviously Gabor wanted to learn from him precisely how it had happened.

Rokavar was made fully aware of Lajos's hesitation from his handling of the Bowie knife. He saw Lajos throw a cutting, distrustful eye over the garden, as if he feared that Gabor had allies hidden away. That was to Gabor's advantage. Indeed, he tried to reinforce Lajos's insecurity by throwing a few sideways glances about the garden himself, particularly where the shadowy, tree-lined walk vanished into overgrown bushes. But this sudden change of conduct only demonstrated that Gabor von Rokavar had no help hidden away. The Jew, who was trying to act important, had caught himself in his own trap, showing the Hungarian his real situation.

"Good, Gabor," Lajos now said, "you saw me with a bundle of banknotes?"

"Yes, worth over a hundred thousand dollars," the Jew responded dryly.

"You were spying on me—you stood behind me as I was counting, right?"

"I admit spying on you, Lajos, but heaven knows, not here—it was not here that I saw where you got those pretty banknotes."

"'Not here,'" the Hungarian thought. "Obviously the Jew saw me counting the notes—but 'not here'? What does he mean with 'not here'? perhaps he—but no, that is utterly impossible—no, hell and the devil, that would simply be impossible!"

"Not here?" the Hungarian now casually asked the Jew.

"Here as well—but here is not where I saw you get your pretty banknotes, those pretty little things!" the Jew smirked.

"Speak more clearly, Gabor," the Hungarian said in a measured tone, as if he wanted to reach some sort of understanding.

"Where else could I have spied you than in our pretty little mill itself?"

The Hungarian's arm that held the Bowie knife started a bit. Yet Gabor's last words did not come unexpectedly.

Gabor von Rokavar continued.

"God's marvel, Lajos, you did well with our Lady Merlina. God's marvel, I would not have believed you could be so in love—and how nicely you polished off that little nigger! And the little banknotes you brought out from under the bed—that was the sweetest . . ."

The Jew spoke in broken sentences, searching the Hungarian's face to measure the impact his words were having. Lajos did not look at him at all but rather leaned against a pillar of the porch and ran his eyes over the garden, from which even the last shimmer of moonlight had vanished.

What was the Hungarian brooding over, while still not missing a word of what the Jew was saying?

Let's look into the yard that adjoined the garden, connected to it by a small gate.

The Hungarian's eye swept toward this yard and remained for a long time fixed on a particular spot. This yard, which now belonged to the two sisters, had earlier been used by a barrel-maker as a cooperage. There was nothing left to indicate this earlier use but a pond, ten feet long and five feet wide, whose murky water, covered with slime, was enclosed by a brick wall. It could not even be seen by those who did not know it was there, since it was entirely surrounded and covered by nets of weedy vines.

It had been a hoop-pond—that is, a pond coopers put their binders in to soften them until they had the proper elasticity. This pond stood right by the tall garden fence and was so located that whoever approached it could be seen neither from the cottage nor from any other place but only by one who passed through the gate between the garden and the yard.

The Hungarian was thinking about this pond.

"I see," he turned to Gabor von Rokavar, "you hid somewhere in the mill and saw everything. Although I cannot conceive how you did it, I don't want to quiz you any further—you can give me a complete account some other time. Here, Gabor, you may have the half of the treasure you asked for—but I will destroy you if you ever attempt to damage me with your foolishness. Mark my words! Here, I will count out the bills."

At these words the Hungarian took the bundle of notes out of his pocket, held the lower half fast and fingered through the upper half. When he was ready, he took the half and handed it to Gabor, who grasped at the bills hastily but did not put them away. Instead, he held the notes in his free hand, as if he didn't know what to do with them.

Lajos, who was surprised by this, asked him, "Well, perhaps you believe you didn't get the right number, or that I cheated you? I will give you time to count, as much as you want."

Gabor von Rokavar thought about it. Not because he doubted the correct division of the money but because the Hungarian had advised him to count it. Would he use this opportunity to send him into the next world with a thrust of his Bowie knife? Perhaps the Hungarian only seemed to trust Gabor because he thought someone was hiding to see if anything happened to him. Who knows? One can never be too careful, particularly with such a person as Lajos. The Jew weighed all this as the Hungarian advised him to count the notes himself.

Gabor von Rokavar, who could see at a glance that he had enough money, stepped back a bit and said: "I will review the notes if you throw away your long knife."

"I will keep it," the Hungarian responded. "The Bowie knife cost me three hundred and twenty dollars—gold grip, real steel—hm, hm, you're truly crazy, aren't you Gabor?"

"You could throw it somewhere you could find it when I'm gone," declared the Jew, who was only now getting nervous.

"Fearful asp of a *Scandonicz*!" the Hungarian hissed, throwing his knife away in a broad arc. The Jew's eyes followed the flight of the knife with joy, seeing it fall on a nearby empty lot beset with half-sprouted grain, wild hemp, and blackberry bushes.

Gabor did not suspect that the Hungarian was preparing a fate other than death by a Bowie knife. So he permitted himself to believe that the Hungarian would willingly divide everything with him. Despite his cleverness, it did not occur to him that the Hungarian would try to recover the notes, the entire treasure of the mill, from him before he had departed. Once the perilous knife was gone, Gabor trusted the Hungarian—that is, he believed that Lajos would want to use him in the future, since he knew that, other than Abbé Dubreuil (who was not in the mill at the time of the fire), no other clubman was still alive. For what other reason would the Hungarian settle so quickly, if the he did not have something to gain? Only his momentary joy over getting the money could have made the Jew so blind. With much less, or with no money at all, he would have been better prepared. Gabor was reinforced in his misplaced trust when the Hungarian began speaking about Abbé Dubreuil's plans to take over the property of Mistress Evans. Lajos presented the Jew with advantages they could gain from this, using such glowing terms that Gabor dropped all his suspicions. In the course of conversation, they had walked all the way down the porch steps and were now standing in the garden.

A pale strip of light was glimmering on the horizon, which still became lost in the dark shadows of the night sky. The thousands of cicadas, frogs, owls, ahingas, and bitterns that present their concerts every night under Louisiana's sky had hushed, and only a locust performed a duet with a red-striped prairie cricket.

In the garden itself it was still very dark, since the thickly planted trees and bushes did not allow the thin morning light to peek through. Despite that, it was possible to feel the dawn even in the midst of darkness, whether it was the fresher air or human understanding that betrayed it. Only the white paint on the trunks of some trees, which had been painted to protect them from certain insects, glowed in the fresh, green darkness. Otherwise one could barely see the garden path.

Gabor became ever more animated in his speech, earning a gentle reproof from the Hungarian, who had to remind him that everyone in the house was asleep.

"We'll meet tomorrow at the Hotoohs'," the Hungarian said with a determined voice, as he brought the Jew to the gate that led into the yard with the pond.

"Do I get to the road this way? I have to hurry, I need to get home. I was staying with my old landlord behind Thayer's plantation. I can't go over to New Orleans yet, and it's too risky with a rowboat, even if I could find a rowing boy, since I'm carrying such a sweet little nut! The ferry boat is always safer—do I get to the road this way?" the Jew repeated, stretching his neck through the fence gate, into the yard.

The Hungarian stood behind him.

"Of course," he responded, "you'll cut at least three hundred paces off the walk to Thayer's plantation."

The Jew stepped into the yard.

The Hungarian was right behind him and to his right.

He grasped the Jew's hand, supposedly in farewell, and said again, "Then it is certain, Gabor? Tomorrow at the Hotoohs' for sure . . ."

"I'll see you," the Jew assured him.

The Hungarian released the Jew's hand and acted as if he were stumbling. "Those damned cows," he cursed. "There is always one in the way." Then he led the Jew along the fence, warning him to be careful not to fall over a cow.

"God's marvel," Gabor responded, "what are cows doing among honest people?" He carefully tested the ground with his feet before he stepped. "God's marvel, I thought I was about to step on a cow," he called out again, taking a few more steps.

They were only a few paces away from the hoop-pond.

Just before he'd supposedly stumbled over a cow, the Hungarian had taken off his coat and held it by both sides, at the bottom.

Now, as Gabor went a little way from the fence to avoid the vines that entangled his feet, Lajos threw the coat over Gabor's head with lightning speed and pressed him against the fence.

After a few moments, the feet of Gabor von Rokavar ceased twitching.

The Hungarian had throttled him with all the force of his sinewy hands.

"That was as good as the Hotoohs' tar mask," he said to himself as he unwrapped the coat from the strangled man's head and put it back on.

He took the money, as well as a wallet he found,* so he could examine

*A letter that the Hungarian found in Gabor's wallet from Frida's Doppelgänger, whom we know from the Planters House in St. Louis and from Jenny's story, can be added here in a note, since it does not shed any light on this mysterious marital association. Who was the Lajos she mentions in the following lines? Who was she? What relationship did she have with Gabor? Could the cowardly, cunning Jew have written the lines the Hungarian found in the Doppelgänger's album? Perhaps we shall be able to shed some light on it in the future, but for now we have no way of doing so.

The letter in question read:

Herr von Rokavar!

Since my arrival in Milwaukee at least three weeks have passed, and Lajos has yet to appear. I can explain his inconstancy all the less since he promised me in St. Louis by all that's holy to come in a few days. As a result, I find myself in the most dreadful situation imaginable, since I left him my jewels, my money—my everything. I will tell you at the first opportunity of the awful thing that happened to me in my

the contents in daylight. Then he seemed to hear a piercing shriek from the cottage. He turned and listened, but everything fell silent and he assumed it was some nocturnal beast that had been taken by a predatory bird.

He lowered the body into the pond and restored the order of the bushes and mustang grass that had been disturbed.

When the Hungarian returned to the cottage and entered his wife's room through the drawing room, he stumbled upon a dreadful scene. Jenny rushed to him at the sound of his footsteps, terrified and pale. She pulled the Hungarian into the bedroom, where the new lamp shed its peaceful colored light from the mantel of the fireplace.

The Hungarian was slightly irritated, as he thought that Frida and her sister had seen or heard something. He perceived at once that he was wrong.

It was something utterly different that caused them to look so terrified and distressed.

After the Hungarian had left and Frida had ushered her sister into the bedroom, they had remained awake for a while awaiting the Hungarian's return. When he did not come back, Frida assumed he was going to remain on the porch until the break of day, which he often did, despite his wife's efforts to dissuade him.

Jenny had lain down with her sister, and they quickly went to sleep.

They might have been slumbering no longer than half an hour before they were awakened by an unusual cry from the baby. When they looked into the cradle, they saw that the child had pulled aside the mosquito netting and wrapped himself in it. In an instant, Frida leaped from her bed to the child. Jenny had half her body out of the bed. But who could describe their terror when they touched the wet, cold body of a rat, stretched out on her child's neck, which would not move despite all their beating and shrieking?

A dreadful cry escaped from the breast of the unhappy mother.

With the wrath of a lioness whose young are in danger, she ripped the ruined mosquito netting to bits and grabbed for the rat.

---

hotel in St. Louis, since I am presently too distressed and depressed. I will tell you only so much for now, that a Doppelgänger of my Lajos, a true devil in human form, attacked me in the most terrible way. I cannot tell you how I am suffering when I imagine the evil results that can come from the visit of this Doppelgänger. I tremble at the mere thought, and it makes me as cold as if I were touching a corpse. Advise me, Herr von Rokavar, of what I should do if Lajos does not appear, but also purge from yourself every hope of ever being mine again.

Your well-meaning friend Frida

But new, indescribable terror!

The teeth of the rat were fastened in her child's neck.

Jenny also came to the cradle, but she fainted at once.

Frida could not pull the rat away, since that would only worsen her child's situation.

Her whole body shaking with rage, the usually calm Frida gnashed her teeth and displayed the eyes of a Fury—despite her pretty blue eyes, her golden hair.

She had once heard that rats feared Greek fire, and that they fled at the sight of it, never to return.

It occurred to her, couldn't the colored lenses of the lamp attachment do the same service?

A flash of thought. In an instant—it was done.

When Frida held the lamp up to the rat's eyes, it left its victim and scurried across the cradle onto the floor.

Frida let the lamp fall and threw herself on her child, showering it with a thousand kisses.

When she arose, she saw Jenny before her, pale as the idol of death. She could not speak, but she had seen everything.

The lamp stood quietly and discreetly on the mantel of the fireplace, as if it had not the slightest guilt.

Neither Jenny nor Frida had picked it up from the floor and put it back in its place.

The child slept forever.

Then the two sisters had rushed out to find the Hungarian, and that is how he found things.

The cold scoundrel's knees buckled as he stood before the dead child. Perhaps, for the first time in his life, something moved in his heart which could be called decent human feeling. He could not weep—as ever. Nature had denied him this since birth. The murderer had never wept as a child.

...

On the evening of the very day we accompanied Countess Constanze and Miss Dudley from Christ's Church to their home, Lady Evans-Stuart and the prince of Württemberg were in a conversation that has much to offer us and that also tells us something of the present situation of Abbé Dubreuil. We will join the last moments of this conversation, which will be very interesting for our lady readers.

The old Scotswoman was just closing a rather large letter that she had been reading through with close attention. On the envelope that lay in her lap, one could see the broken seal of a count, and the address read: "To his Royal Highness, Prince Paul of Wuertemberg, New Orleans, Louisiana, U. St."

Lady Evans-Stuart shoved the letter back in the envelope after folding and laid it on the alabaster bureau standing next to her.

"It appears that you are right, Prince," Lady Evans-Stuart told Prince Paul of Württemberg in French. "It is indeed the same Abbé Dubreuil who committed the infamous crime against Aunt Celestine. His papal mission to Magdeburg took place in the same precise time." The old Scotswoman continued with great agitation, "Oh, that I should have to endure such from a priest in these last days of my life, a priest who belongs to a church to which I have given all my honor and veneration since childhood!"

"Calm yourself, Madame," the prince responded in a warm, sympathetic tone. "We are proud of having saved the life—the life and the innocence of your angelic child."

"And I had suspected nothing, utterly nothing!" Lady Evans declared in long, drawn-out words.

"And on the day the abbé was to go to confession with your child—you were irritated with me when I asked that it be prevented," the prince commented calmly.

"Do you really believe that the abbé would have done the same with my child? . . . It is dreadful to think of."

"Madame, it would have happened—he made the same preparations with Aunty Celestine—you have read the letter . . ."

"I am writing to Rio de Janeiro today . . . he is supposed to have fled there with some money entrusted to him by the bishop."

"Are you sure, Prince?"

"He was seen on a ship sailing for Rio."

"May the revenge of heaven, which he has so offended, pursue him," the old Scotswoman said with all the fire of her religious feelings.

Both were silent for a few moments.

Lady Evans-Stuart took up the conversation first.

"But Prince, to come back to the count's family again—as good a heart as you have and as charitable a sensibility, it was still mean of you to keep Jenny out of the arms of her parents-in-law for so long."

"I have adequate grounds for this," the prince said secretively.

"You are always bearing mysteries, Prince," the old Scotswoman said.

"Secrets—no mysteries!" the prince cried out in a lively manner.

"But tell me, Prince, Lady Evans-Stuart continued, "how did it happen that Count Lajos * is in such bad graces with his wife's cousin?"

"I cannot really give you a satisfying answer on this, Madame. Count Lajos * is a very respectable, solid man—I have nothing against him. He pleases me through and through, and, like all Hungarian nobles, he has something very attractive about him. Unfortunately, I meet him very seldom, for he is busy every day and often late into the night."

Lady Evans-Stuart leaned a bit toward the prince and whispered softly: "Wasn't Count Lajos * untrue to his wife once? Such is told in certain circles."

"Not that I know," the prince responded.

"More mysteries, or secrets—as you prefer, Prince," the old Scotswoman remarked.

Then, when the prince made no response, she continued.

"Didn't the count abandon his wife for two years? Confess it, Prince, you know, you know, you must know—"

"Yes, so far as I know, he was gone for two years. Some circumstances unknown to me might have compelled him—in any case, I can assure you, Madame, that there is no more loyal or solid man anywhere."

"As they say," the Scotswoman continued, "he was supposed to have been engaged for a long time in a factory. That amazes me—a Hungarian nobleman, from such an old house . . ."

"Madame," the prince responded, "Count Lajos * is far above such scruples."

"Perhaps he is playing the role of a Cincinnatus," Lady Evans opined, "waiting until someone calls him from his factory, as from a plow, to take the dictatorship. His fatherland has not yet played its hand."

"Madame, you could be right," the prince declared, laughing maliciously, "but I would not risk my health in a factory on such a hope."

"So in fourteen days, Prince, you will accompany us across the lake. You and Count Lajos * will be able to perform your offices as cavaliers among the ladies."

"It is still unclear whether Count Lajos * will come," the prince said. "Since the death of his first and only son he is very depressed."

"The trip across the Lake can only help his mood, then," the old Scotswoman responded.

"I will do my best to convince him to join the expedition," the prince said.

"Since he does not yet know the parents-in-law of his wife's sister, Count Lajos * would have all the more reason to come along."

"That would be the only thing that would move him to go," the prince said earnestly. "I shall try."

As the prince took leave of the old Scotswoman, he said to her with concern: "Madame, do not delay your departure any longer than you have already planned. There could be serious consequences."

"How do you mean that, Prince?" Lady Evans-Stuart asked in amazement.

"There have already been some deaths from yellow fever, and many believe that it will grow to an epidemic of unique proportions.

"The summer of *Eighteen-Fifty-Three* was prophesied by Lakanal in one of his writings as a summer of terror."

Book
V

Prologue

The Criminals' Dock on the Mesa

A year had passed since the night when Hiram had imparted to Diana Robert the strict command that she go to New Orleans and announce to her relatives at the Atchafalaya Bank that when Hiram came to the Tropic of the Southern Cross, when they saw his yellow mask, the city would weep and shudder. This was in 1852, after the conclusion of five summers, the last summers that the *Mantis religiosa* would bloom without bearing seeds. The *Mantis religiosa* blooms every year, but it only bears seeds on particular years. A mysterious numerical symbolism runs through the whole of nature, as yet unstudied and likely to remain incomprehensible until the end of time. Just as was the case with the year 1847, so also the year 1853 was inscribed in the South's great ledger of debts. Roses on the cheeks of blossoming women, do not blame Hiram if you must pale and die; a pitiless destiny drives him. And isn't it really your own fault if they have to take you to the grave so soon? Didn't you know that those times would always return, those times of misery, need, and violent obliteration? And didn't you still teach your children those cursed principles that shame your republic and will yet murder it in the future?

A year had also passed since Emil and Lucy had sought the source of the Red River with Captain Marcy and tried to find the *Mantis religiosa* for him. Only at the last moment did Hiram appear and remind them of their oath with a thundering "Yes!" After the terror that Hiram's sudden appearance caused them, Emil and Lucy parted from the captain, who continued on without their help to search for the mysterious source of the Red River with his expedition. But an invisible hand led the captain astray and took him a hundred miles away from the home of the *Mantis religiosa.* The captain later reported to Washington that he'd found the source of the Red River, but the fact that he had not discovered the mysterious plant proved that he had made a great, if excusable, error. The branches and tributaries of the river in question are innumerable, and they had already misled Alexander von Humboldt as well as the well-informed Lieutenant Pike.

And a year had passed since that night Hiram had read the number 1853 in the gleaming sickle of the waxing moon.

This triad of moments had taken place in 1852, and the year that stood prophetically in the gleaming sickle of the moon, 1853, had already begun.

We are at the source of the Red River. And that hour has returned in which the light of the moon combs the black pelt of the panther and covers the dark scales of the cobra with shimmering emeralds. Outside the corridor of rocks stands a pair of long-necked flamingos. The fresh water bubbles in glittering droplets cover their pink feathers and sprays the soft down on their warm, living breasts. They are having a marvelous game at this moment. As soon as their game is finished, they will sail away from here, hundreds of miles away, to where the bed of the river is deep and wide. There they will have their midnight meal; in the vicinity outside the canyon, there is no more food for them. Here they are merely swarming and meditating.

From the cleft of the highest peak of that massif of rock that stares southward with its dark gray spikes, Bald Eagle arises, *our eagle,* with its pale skull and long, gaunt legs. It is the same eagle that tried to take the traitor Arnold from his prison and that used its freedom to become a traitor itself. Bald Eagle is not satisfied with dawdling in the moonlight, with fish and little worms—his favorite dish now is the flesh of black people. He hunts down and torments this black prey unto death. Although this lord of the air possesses an immense hunting region—the area of fifteen states—he is still not satisfied with that; he flies far, far beyond the frontiers of his realm to fetch back the black prey that has fled from him.

Over there, right under the nose of a coal-black panther, arises a weird, ghostly black head. It is a true comrade of the night. Its eyes are shy, as if veiled in a dense mist. It is *Nebraska Owl,* the bride of Bald Eagle, who nuzzles with him in the unsteady moonlight as if this addled blockhead had any notion of love and tender desire.

From a different region, flying in from the south, sailing on heavy but sure pinions over the majestic plain of the mesa, comes the bird of Louisiana—the *Bleeding Pelican.* What is this bird doing in the solemn stillness of the midnight hour? And so many hundreds and hundreds of miles from his swampy home? Now it strikes its wings on the outer arch of the stony canyon, from whose bosom rises ominous bubbling and splashing. Does Louisiana's bird have a rendezvous with the eagle and the owl?

Today the moon is on the wane, no longer reminding us of that great city in the South called the Crescent City. Just like the waxing moon, the reversed sickle lies above the terrace of stone, on its uppermost plate. The sickle flickers blood-red for an instant, and that mysterious wind that is wont to come during an eclipse of the moon blows.

It might be that there has been a partial eclipse of the moon—but if you look at the calendar, you would see that that cannot be, for the moon is clearly in its fourth quarter.

But now? Where has the moon gone all of a sudden?

It is really nothing more than that the three large birds have taken their places in front of it, covering it until it can rise a bit more.

These three birds are Bald Eagle, Nebraska Owl, and Louisiana's Pelican. What are they doing here together? Do they await someone? Are they perhaps holding a court over their brothers and sisters on the rocks of the mesa? Doesn't Bald Eagle sit there like the judge in a secretive lynch-mob court? Doesn't Nebraska Owl, with its shadowy, thick head, look precisely like the assessor of such a court, his face covered by a mask? Why does Louisiana's bird lower her head, gazing downward with moist eyes at her breast, from which heavy drops of blood drip down?

The judicial appearance of the eagle and the owl is deceiving.

Both of them, together with the pelican, are in fact sitting in the *Criminals' Dock on the Mesa.*

Two figures emerge into the illuminated night from out of the canyon. Innumerable drops of water glisten on their naked bodies. They had been depressed and tired from the singeing heat of the day just past, and so they have taken a cooling bath. They immersed themselves in the spring that is the source of the Red River, and now they are walking arm in arm over the broad plain of the mesa. The coal-black panther they arouse does them no harm. After he becomes aware of the two figures, he continues to stand tranquilly, observing them with an intoxicated gaze. Who are they, these two figures? If all the gods had not been chased away long ago, one would be ready to swear that they were Endymion and Artemis. The stars of the Centaur or the Southern Cross do not shine as brightly. The belt of Orion would pale if it were bound about the shimmering loins of these figures, who could enchant even the wildest son of the mesa, the coal-black panther.

"More than a year has passed since He took us from the captain's party and brought us to the mesa—the time of testing is nearing an end, and we can once again return to the beautiful gardens and homes of people—we will say farewell to the *Mantis religiosa,* forever."

"Your heart is happy and serene, my love, and you dream of the golden days of the future—but an inner voice tells me that these months lived in the mesa will not be the least happy of our lives. My beloved, you are looking forward to our return to New Orleans—would to God that no cloud covers the sun of your glittering hopes. Look at your feet. The seed pods of the *Mantis religiosa* are bursting, and they foretell another great disaster for the good city of New Orleans. We will be there when the visitation is at its most fearsome—to be sure, we will be spared, for the *Mantis religiosa* is an antidote, but who wants to live in the midst of the dead, with heaped bodies and corpse-wagons rattling about day and night? Who can be happy when one sees everything about dying or wilting? And we shall see things worse than death in New Orleans—my innermost being foretells me that, and he told us himself . . ."

"It is better for us to enjoy ourselves, for we are compelled to go back to that city—and why are you so sad and depressed? Look at yourself, look at me, lover. The year we have spent in this lonely, ominous mesa has poured out a cornucopia upon us. The roses that had vanished from your cheeks have returned, and now they bloom more beautifully and fresher than ever. Your curls are richer and more golden, and they fall in a fullness I have never before seen upon your full, alabaster-white shoulders. You were beautiful, my lover, when you put on my clothes that time, but now, when I behold you, you are even more beautiful, and I shudder at the thought—but no, jealousy and distrust have been banned forever from my heart, and I grasp the warm marble of your divine body with trust and never-conquered warmth . . ."

Lucy sank into Emil's arms. He did not push her away until the stern, deeply bowed head of Hiram rose before them and they heard from his mouth the solemn words: *"Your child shall be called Toussaint L'Ouverture!"*

"Our child?" Emil and Lucy cried out at the same instant, looking at Hiram questioningly.

"Have no doubt!" he answered in a strict, spiritual tone.

"Today is the twenty-first of April, 1853. In this year, in this month, and on this day, a Caucasian and an Ethiopian shall bathe in the source of the Red River. They shall walk across the mesa and fall lovingly into each other's arms. They shall then conceive a son, who shall be the liberator of the black race: thus it is written in the book of Hiram II, the Freemason."

Hiram was silent for a few moments, then he continued.

"But you shouldn't shout and rejoice over this news. Remember for a moment how enthusiastic you were when I told you of the mission you were to fulfill? How joyfully your eyes flamed when I told you that you would be the representatives of a new dawn? That you would have millions to support a proper propaganda, and you would have had to work at it with all your might? But what did you do when you left the Atchafalaya Bank? Your enthusiasm vanished once you had possession of the riches, and you traveled about in the world like a royal couple, such as people always like to see and celebrate with incense. It was only a short time before your treasures had all fallen victim to your profligacy. Impoverished, you returned to the soil of America, and fortune brought you into the hands of Captain Marcy—you discovered from him the purpose of his expedition, and what did you do? You betrayed the *Mantis religiosa* for mere profit. Your criminal vanity took the compliments that the captain gave you as truth, when the captain placed you," the old man turned to Emil, "on a level with Washington and Lafayette. And you took this apotheosis quite seriously, Emil; you were really of the opinion that you were a great man—but a single word that I shouted into his camp to him from the Red River caused you to come to your senses. I took you and Lucy to the mesa, in hopes the prophecy would be fulfilled—and it has now been realized in you. Although she has been barren until now, Lucy will bear a son, who will be the liberator of her race. This son will fulfill his mission, no matter how many obstacles are placed in his way. On the day of liberation, when the chains fall to the ground everywhere with a great jangling, the *Mantis religiosa* will disappear forever, and New Orleans will be free from that plague of fever that now falls on the town with an intensity never known before."

Lucy and Emil stood with downcast eyes as the old man spoke these words.

From the stone terrace they heard a mournful whimpering. Then it sounded again, like cries for help from a mother whose children are being snatched away. Then everything grew very still, save the occasional cracking and splitting of the seed capsules of the *Mantis religiosa,* whose feathered kernels were blown on a soft wind in the direction of the Crescent City, New Orleans.

The mournful whimpering began again, and at the end it grew so loud that Lucy and Emil raised their heads and turned their eyes in its direction.

"That is the bird of Louisiana, the Bleeding Pelican," the old man said, as he raised his right hand in warning. "She weeps and mourns her children, who have been snatched away too soon by death. As often as the seed capsules of the *mantis religiosa* burst, the pelican appears here and bemoans her unhappy fate. What she has borne, cared for, and protected over many years is taken from her in a single summer, and she tears open her own breast in her pain, so that innumerable drops flow onto the stone terrace . . ."

"The poor bird!" Emil and Lucy quietly sighed at the same time.

"Do not mourn for the bird of Louisiana," the old man declared in an earnest tone, "for you are the ones who are the cause of her despair."

Once more it was quiet on the broad, uncanny mesa. No further complaint came from the breast of the unhappy bird. She hid her head in her wings and wept still tears. But Bald Eagle and Nebraska Owl moved restlessly back and forth, striking the cliffs with their wings as they watched the old man approaching with Lucy and Emil. Bald Eagle raised his white head alertly. "Bald Eagle!" Hiram called up to the stony terrace where the three birds sat with one another. "Don't raise your pale head so proudly! It would be better if you hid your head in your wings with shame, as Louisiana's bird is doing out of grief and sadness of heart. Where is your high-flying now, Eagle? Do you no longer recall the deeds of your forefathers? Don't you think any more of Bunker Hill—of the fathers of your republic? Bald Eagle, you have become a filthy predator, stuffing your belly with the flesh of the children of another climate, whom you have dragged into your country to be manacled and beaten. Miserable hunter of human beings, may the time soon come when they recognize the traitor and judge."

Screaming, Bald Eagle raised himself from his perch, attempting to fly to the heights. But he immediately sank back down, exhausted and heavy.

"The stars no longer want you!" Hiram called to him. "They fear your filthy venom!"

Bald Eagle tried to fly into the heights once more—but once more in vain! The stars rejected their unclean visitor. He now raised a shrill cry and departed in a low glide across the endless mesa.

Did it have to come to this point, that our eagle, who once led us to victory in battle and before whose defiant eyes the enemy fled and trembled, now creeps away and flees like a poor sinner?

"What sort of an ugly bird is that, with the broad, thick head and the shy gaze?" Emil finally dared to say; he had been observing solemn silence with Lucy until now. He pointed up to the stony terrace as he spoke.

"That is Nebraska Owl," the old man declaimed earnestly, his eyes burning with an inexpressible glow. "Great misery will come over our republic out of Nebraska," he prophesied. "A man, who is now called the young giant of the West, will soon be branded a traitor for his companionship with this owl;[1] Bald Eagle will take Nebraska Owl under his wings, and together they will dominate the Capitol. I will not see what will come from that, for my gray hairs will draw me to the grave before the completion of this summer of terror—as my destiny desires!

"Many a generation has passed over my skull, and I should be satisfied to have wandered the earth for this time—and yet I leave reluctantly. I would like to be able to greet the day when your son is born, he who shall free the helots and redeem beauty from the filthiness, torment, and misery of the world."

Even as Hiram directed these words to Emil and Lucy, Nebraska Owl had left its perch on the terrace and flown off in the same direction that the Potomac languidly and reluctantly directs its flood. The Owl often turned in flight; even at a great distance one could see here and there the glitter of two green points of light.

From the spot where the three birds had perched together only a moment before, a marvelous image arose, framed by the glistening, gleaming sickle of the moon.

With a glance at the image, Emil sank to the ground, pale as a star in the milky way.

He had seen a dreadful picture.

He saw the old count, his father, Melanie, his mother, his sisters, Constanze, Gertrude, Amelie, and his brother, Hugo. All were laid out next to one another in coffins, and over them grinned the disgusting visage of the Hungarian, as cold and pale as their corpses.

Yet the picture showed more, images much more terrifying—but everything had vanished by the time Emil opened his eyes once more.

That was the last *Fata Morgana* on the mesa.

Six days after these events, on 27 April, *Hiram the Freemason* was on his way to the Atchafalaya Bank in New Orleans. Emil and Lucy had preceded him to the town by two days.

Chapter 1

Red Today, Dead Tomorrow

The curse of yellow fever had already lain on New Orleans for several weeks.[2] Those who could flee had already fled, and those who remained behind either lacked the means to travel or were held here by some sort of responsibility. Perhaps there were also those for whom ambition and filthy greed dictated that they risk their little lives despite all arguments to the contrary. There were many in the last category, and, amazingly enough, they were the ones whose ranks were least winnowed by the dreadful disease. Ambition and greed offered their bold faces to death in this dark, sad time, and death rarely dared touch its finger to these already pale, cold children of Mammon. Death can be bribed, too, after all. There were hundreds and hundreds of stories from this time of terror to witness.

Would that we could rip the nails from the coffins of misery and despair and have them appear as accusers in the courts. And if these silent witnesses could speak? What would they say? Wouldn't they yell out at that physician who now passes through the streets of our town in comfort and dignity in his elegant coach: "Hold your horses, murderer and robber! Climb out of your coach and walk, as you did before! Should you glitter and carouse simply because you pulled the last cent out of the pockets of hundreds of poor sick persons, and then killed them?" And what would that quack, a robber and murderer, reply if they could hear those voices?

He would laugh maliciously and give this dry answer: "What concern is your howling and whimpering to me about the dead? What concern are the dead in the moist earth? I have only had one purpose, and I accomplished it—I wanted to make money." That is only a single image of them, but doctors are still the most striking actors in that dismal setting, which is called the palmetto boudoir of Louisiana, with its poisonous miasma. These actors have sated themselves the most, have killed the most, and are the greatest of thieves: can anyone blame us if we place them at the very head of the column of robbers and murderers, they who exceeded even the plague itself in cruelty and insatiability? There is no contradiction to such an accusation; any opposition in favor of such quacks, or even in favor of real physicians, will not be listened to. The people have seen it themselves, felt it themselves, and complained over the manifold losses; there is nothing libelous in such an accusation, and it is not seen as injurious once public opinion has accepted and registered it. The wounds that they inflicted on us are still to be felt, then, and many families who were plundered and robbed then by these scoundrels are even now perishing! Yet revenge raises its finger threateningly—and no one knows what the future holds for that physician, robber and murderer.

Certainly there are exceptions, where are there none? But there are only a few of this profession who remain in honorable memory. Among a hundred demons there is an angel now and then, someone who works to lessen the misery of his suffering fellow human beings with noble dedication and selfless sacrifice. Hail to them, for they bear an awareness in their breasts, rare among physicians, that they are neither thieves nor murderers.

"Go away! Go away! You'll find no heart here—if you have no money, you seek in vain."

"Go away! Go away! That one was only a quack, but he demanded money, even more than the other, for he has been well paid for the murders of his patients. No one is murdered for nothing—Money! Money! You have none? Then get out, get out, just go! You're still trying here? Still nothing there? Go away, go away—go back to your loved ones and tell them that they must die!" Hounded by this voice, whose source remains unknown, a poor, beautiful girl goes from house to house; she has sought a physician for three hours, in vain. She is about to collapse from exhaustion, but her anxiety spurs her steps ever anew. Everyone at home is ill with the yellow fever—father, mother, and siblings. A sympathetic soul, who sees the beautiful girl weeping as she runs through the street, determines the reason for her tears and directs her to a house on * Street, in the Third District, where a *** physician lived who would be sure to help and whom it would not be a waste of time to visit. The poor child betook herself there—and now she enters the house, where doctor *** lives. The child trembles from joy and inexpressible excitement when she learns from an old woman that the doctor is at home and will appear right away.

Let us take a closer look at this beautiful poor child.

It is a girl of noble and gentle face, who has barely reached her ninth year. The blue of her usually bright forget-me-not eyes has been clouded by the many bitter tears they have poured. The intelligent little face, which appears already to have seen things beyond the ken of children, has to capture the heart at the first glance, and when you see the child pale and suffering, you are driven to ask from the innermost part of your being: "Child, what's the matter? And if I can help you, will you trust me?"

The girl wore no covering on her head, and her long, blonde hair hung down, half plaited in braids and half loosely spread down her neck, far over the indent of her delicate waist. One could see that she had no time to adorn herself or give her makeup the slightest attention. And how could she? She had kept watch the entire previous night at the beds of her sick parents and siblings, and, by morning, sleep had overcome her—yet she could not even enjoy that for very long, since the doctor again failed to show up, having determined the day before that there was no more money to be had. That was how the girl had come to her wandering and finally to the door of this doctor in the Third District.

The doctor did not leave her waiting for long. Accompanied by the old woman, he soared like a hawk into the room, where the girl awaited him with a pounding heart.

"Someone is ill? Probably yellow fever?" the doctor asked hastily.

There was something repellent in his face as he asked this. Out of these gray eyes there gazed not the slightest bit of good will; a certain incontinence had singed his lashes, leaving a red rim in their place.

When he spoke, his mouth displayed an ugly white line on the lower lip, such as one finds on many varieties of shellfish if one jabs them with a finger. Despite his appearance, this person had once married a maiden who was pretty as a picture. Now he had only a rather elderly and immeasurably ugly woman as housekeeper.

The beautiful girl pulled back shyly and hardly seemed to have the courage to answer this repellent specimen's questioning.

"Someone is ill? Yellow fever, huh?" he snorted at the girl.

She stepped forward, rather more courageously.

"Well, yellow fever, or something else?"

"Yes," the girl answered, as tears brightened in her eyes. She directed an unspeakably distressed gaze at the doctor.

"Is your father, your mother sick?" the doctor continued.

"Everyone at home is sick, all the way down to my little sister."

"When did the illness befall your relations?"

"Three days ago by now."

"And they have lain all that time without a physician?"

"Oh no, we called a physician at once, but he did not come today—probably because we were unable to give him the money he was demanding," the girl added softly and hesitantly.

"Do you have money now?" the doctor asked in a superior tone, half turning on his heels.

"Oh no—where could we get money all of a sudden? We have barely enough to buy ice for the packs."

"Yes, then I cannot help you," the doctor declared, turning his back on the poor girl in order to pass through the door.

"There you have it—another beggar," remarked the woman, who had returned with the doctor and who now inspected the girl from head to foot. Then she added acidly, "I thought so right away, that begging was afoot—people think that one should slave away for nothing and risk one's health to boot—"

"Doctor, doctor!" the poor child cried, seized by the deepest pain, rushing after the cold man of money. "Even if we cannot pay you right away, we will pay you double and triple later; oh do come, come home with me!"

The doctor, who already had the door-latch in his hand, turned to the girl and said: "Why didn't you come to me at once when your parents and siblings were attacked by the fever? The physician you had at the start certainly was not willing to visit you for nothing."

"Oh no," the girl sobbed, "he would not have taken a step into our house if we had not given him twenty-five dollars."

"There you see: now, when you have nothing left, I am supposed to come . . . Well, as I said . . . if you bring me money, I'm ready to come, and otherwise not. But still, I'll give you some good advice. Take your whole family to the hospital, or have the Howard Association send a doctor . . . they are readier to do that than one of us."

"They told me of the Howard Association, too," the tormented girl declared, "but if only I knew where to go—"

At that very instant, the door opened so quickly that the doctor, who still held the latch in his hand, was roughly shoved aside.

A young, quite elegantly clad man entered and, without ceremony, went to the shaken doctor and aggressively ordered him to come with him.

"Did you bring a cab? My horses need a rest, they have been greatly strained today," the doctor responded sullenly.

"Just come quickly, doctor, my wife has suddenly become unwell, and all symptoms point to yellow fever. Hurry, it is a good distance from here, and I have already visited four physicians and found not a one at home—"

"To devil with it, my friend, I asked you if you had brought a cab! I will not go a step from this house on foot," the doctor responded in a phlegmatic tone, in rudest contrast to the agitation of his new visitor.

"No," the young man responded with a stormy tone, "'tisn't necessary—we can mount at the next carriage stop—hurry, hurry, 'tis not a minute to be lost."

At these last words, the excited young man grasped the doctor's arm to pull him along.

"Not so fast, my good man, I am not to be led about in this manner. Either you bring a cab to the house, or you give me the proper assurance, in case—in case we cannot find a cab at the halting place."

"Gladly—you are to have everything I have, but just come right away, I need you at once."

As the young man spoke these words, he released the doctor's arm and rushed to the large round table that stood in the middle of the room. There he emptied out the entire contents of his wallet on the marble surface of the table, adding several smaller coins he had pulled from his vest pockets.

The doctor placidly raised his eyeglasses in the air, pressing them on the bridge of his nose with his right index finger.

The old woman went immediately to the table, her eyes glittering as she inspected the money.

"Thirty dollars!" the doctor called out. "What are you thinking of, my good man! I will not take a step beyond my threshold for any thirty dollars—ha, ha—a remarkable imputation, that, sir. In these times, the most pitiful quack will not accompany you for this bagatelle."

"You are cruel, doctor," the young man cried out in despair, "you shall receive another fifty dollars when you arrive at my home—hurry, hurry—demand of me what you want . . ."

The old woman quietly nudged the doctor with her elbow and whispered to him:

"You can go with him, old boy—the man has money."

Then she went back to the table and gathered the thirty dollars.

"Well, come along," the doctor said to the young man, "but this is the last time I leave my home under these circumstances."

They both rushed to the street. But where is our good child?

The poor, pretty girl had withdrawn shyly when the elegant young man stormed in so rudely, and she had watched the whole procedure with a pale face and pounding heart. By the time the young man departed the room with the doctor, she had already left the house of this most despicable of all physicians in despair and stood for a few moments, as quiet and stiff as a column on a street corner. Many people passed her by, poor as well as rich, men, women, and children—still no one paid any heed to the pale child, pretty as a picture, with the long, loose hair and the suffering, forget-me-not eyes. Why should they be concerned with her? Everyone already had plenty to do, and most of them worried that they might be walking the streets for the last time and would be lying in the swampy, wet ground the next morning. The curse of yellow fever often strikes so unexpectedly that no one can contemplate the next hour cheerfully or with a light heart. The phrase "Red today, dead tomorrow" dropped from every mouth that opened. So enjoy yourself, my friend, and give a kiss to this and that person, for who knows whether you shall ever meet again.

At such a time of tribulation and dreadful destruction, one constantly heard whispers from persons who never spoke on peaceful, fine days. Everyone spoke to you, everyone wept, sighed, and feared along with you. And even though they did so, you still had no friends, and only your money was always good to you, stroking your troubled cheeks and telling you: be not concerned, my friend, you have always carried me with such love in your heart in peaceful times, now I shall requite your love and tenderness. That is what money says; the unfortunate believes this slick, false serpent, and tomorrow he is dead.

The girl, although still half a child, felt the total seriousness of this dreadful time. Pain pays no respect to age. It can gnaw just as well on the heart of a child as it can on that of a maid or a mother. Her parents and siblings were lying helpless at home, without custody or care, and yet the girl stood like a column on the street corner, and she would surely have stood that way for even longer if a man had not knocked her aside to place a ladder against the post of a street lamp. The pale girl—where could her thoughts be?—was profoundly shaken, only now giving a thought for her sick parents and siblings at home. She walked a ways, then looked one way and the other—should she try again and ask where a doctor lived? But who knows what was happening at home?—so run, run back home, child; you'll not find any doctor, you'll not find any heart, for you have no money. Run to your home, as poor and careworn as you left it—for you will at least be with those who love you, even if they will soon be dead, too!

Driven by these inner voices, the girl ran as if she were being pursued by the evil spirit of the dreadful illness itself, on and on, until she turned at last onto the street where her family lay sick and helpless. She remained standing at the corner of the street. There were only four more blocks to go and she would be home. But she had to rest here at the street corner for a few moments—the good child could not go any further without taking a breath of fresh air.

She pressed herself into the depths of a shop doorway and repeatedly reached for her heart with her little hand. But in the next moment her hand dropped from her heart and moved to her forehead, near her temples. The gaslight, burning not far away, held this in its full shimmer and illuminated her strange look. Now the girl was no longer leaning on the shop door, she had dropped to the stone doorstep and was pressing her two little hands on her forehead.

Drunks rushed past, wild young men disturbing the nighttime peace. They were wandering from coffeehouse to coffeehouse, offering their libations to the goddess of death. They were joking and laughing as they bustled past, calling out a stormy "to your health!" at the dead-carts creaking and groaning over the uneven pavement stones. A watchman making his rounds thought it odd that a child was sitting here on the stone doorstep, holding her forehead in her hand. He gently touched the child with his staff. The girl started and tried to rise, but she had to set herself down again. "Take me home, I live right around the corner, I think I am ill," she sighed as she rose to meet the watchman. Her temples throbbed and her forehead burned. The watchman, who had already seen hundreds of such cases on the open streets, knew at once what was the matter with the child. He took his staff under his left arm in order to help the child up to take her home. Then another child's head suddenly slipped under the watchman's arm, and two thin arms clinged to the neck of the sick girl who was on her way home.

"Gertrude!"

"Lorie!" sounded in reply, as poor, sick Gertrude, the daughter of the old count, draped herself on the neck of her little friend, whom she had not seen since their adventure with the coffee pickers. The watchman observed this drama with amazement and patiently let it take its course. Had the watchman been a German, able to understand the language of the two friends, hot tears would have been running down his cheeks.

The joyful agitation with which Gertrude had been seized at the sudden appearance of her Lorie appeared to put her deceitful enemy to flight momentarily, but only so it could later descend on its poor victim all the more greedily. The unexpected improvement Gertrude now believed she was feeling was one of those dreadful mirages that those attacked by yellow fever often experience in that terrible time.

The count's daughter would soon learn this.

"How did you come to be here, Gertrude? What does the watchman want with you?" Lorie asked.

"Nothing, dear Lorie," she replied, "I just asked him to bring me home since I could not walk any more."

"What's the matter, Gertrude? Are you sick?"

"I was earlier—but now I think I was just imagining it. All you can see are dead-carts and coffins, and in the end one becomes convinced one must die."

"Aren't you afraid of yellow fever, Gertrude? You shouldn't be afraid, or you could really get it—that's what the people I live with say."

"You don't live anymore with your mother and—"

"I have no mother anymore, Gertrude—she is dead," Lorie said, her voice shaking as she shed hot tears.

"Dead, Lorie?" the count's daughter sighed, leaning her little head on her friend's shoulder.

"Yes, Gertrude. We brought Mother to the Charity Hospital, and whoever goes in with no money only comes out in a coffin. There are ugly, disgusting people in that hospital—they put her in with the worst persons sick of fever, and so she had to die, nothing else could have happened. Then they took the few things she had, and they did not want to give them back to me, even though I am her child and should have what was hers.*

*It would be easy to give in to temptation and make a complete portrayal of the economy of the Charity Hospital during the epidemic if it would not somewhat distract from the course of our work. Although certain facts that are at our disposal to publish would challenge belief, they would still not be exaggerated. It appears that people were happy to neglect in the most shameful way those with no means. In a few rare cases, a sense of decency alone led to better treatment of the sick. The meticulous care that was expended on the sick poor is shown by the complaints of so many of those who had the good fortune

And now I am serving some strangers—I was taking them a piece of ice right now—"

"Lorie, my legs are growing as heavy again as they were before," Gertrude said suddenly, clinging so tightly to little Lorie that she almost pulled her to the ground.

The watchman, who had been standing quietly observing, now approached the two children, leaning down to Gertrude to say: "It would be best if I took you home—you are not feeling well."

"Yes, Gertrude, the watchman and I will take you to your parents—where do you live?" Lorie asked anxiously, looking her friend in the fase questioningly.

"The third house around the corner—oh take me, take me home . . ." Gertrude asked, trying to stay on her feet. But she lacked the strength. The watchman took her in his arms without further ado. Lorie walked alongside, hauling her large ice block, bound with a rope, behind her only with difficulty.

"This is the third house from the corner," the watchman said, "is this it?"

"Yes," Gertrude answered, barely audibly.

The watchman set the child on the ground after he had opened the door leading to the mean apartment. Then he returned to his appointed rounds.

---

to survive and leave the institution. We will risk posing the question indirectly: perhaps so much property disappeared so that the deficit would be as small as possible at the final accounting? This question seems rather out of turn, and if anyone could be found who could answer with "yes," he studiously observes the silence of a Trappist. Being pressing would only make the matter worse. A poor German brought to the hospital had his bag broken into as he lay in his sickbed, and he was robbed of his possessions down to his last cent. It happened that he recovered his health despite his poor treatment, and the unfortunate left the hospital as thoroughly depleted as if he had fallen into the hands of highway robbers rather than into the hands of an institution of public welfare. There are even some who use acts of violence, offensive to every noble instinct, to extort bribes. Such acts of exploitation are the source for the many recurrences those unfortunates experience, since they lack all means to obtain the further care so needed by those recovering from an illness. It is true that there are three asylums for poor convalescents, but their facilities are so poor and the conditions of entry so tyrannically high that they are of no use. If one considers the enormous sums collected for the "sufferers" from all parts of the Union that have streamed into New Orleans, one must truly be amazed that so much need and misery still prevail. Why is this so? We hope that this question will be answered to the benefit of the suffering in a future summer of terror. It would be sad if this did not happen.

The Nurse

Just as in the case of particular individuals, the history of nations is made remarkable not only by extraordinarily great deeds but also by lowly tasks carried out by silent sufferers. In fact, great and mighty deeds that appear at first glance to be worthy of praise often darken and fade into the background on closer examination—since their motives are found to have an impure basis. This is the case with those men who found it easy during the late epidemic to win an eminent name because of their wealth. They earned the enviable name of philanthropists to their suffering fellow man, just as does the tyrant who exploits and robs his people through his entire life but distributes money and food to the poor during a famine or some other disaster. These philanthropists from the "upper-ten" class were often such base persons, despite their great donations to charitable institutions, that whatever they gave with one hand they sought to win back again with the other, double or triple. Their names had to glitter in the newspapers, and the amounts that they had sacrificed on the altar of poverty and misery had to be precisely reported. Would they have given a cent under any other circumstances? The best and noblest philanthropists were certainly those who personally visited the hovels of the poor in this time, without having their deeds trumpeted forth in the journals; they did far more good with their direct help than those pseudophilanthropists who found it more comfortable and less perilous to simply give money to associations that help the miserable. Yet doing so would still be excusable, since not everyone is born a Samaritan, and they can put their idiosyncrasies aside—and we know how dangerous idiosyncrasies can be in an epidemic—but the fact they did not care whether these funds were spent to aid the poor is the stone that we cast at them. It must bear down on their conscience like a ton when it strikes them, if they even possess a conscience in this matter. Some examples will expose some of the ambiguity of their gifts and will also take away much of the false glamour with which the English newspaper mill has gilded their names.

A certain Joshua W∗ gave the Howard Association the sum of two hundred and fifty dollars for the suffering of New Orleans.* One would say

*The *Howard Association* takes its name from the famous English philanthropist [John] Howard, who died in Cork in 1809 [Ed.: 1726–90, Howard died in Russia]. He had taken

that it is a fine and noble deed for this man to contribute to a fund that will aid and rescue the poor sick of this city—it is good that Joshua W* did not neglect to give of his surplus to the needy; indeed, it is also good that during the dreadful tribulations caused by yellow fever he remained in the city, although he had the means to travel to the furthest corner of the world and avoid all danger. So those persons who have never had the honor of knowing him will judge him solely on the fact that he put two hundred and fifty dollars in the coffers of the Howard Association. Nevermind that he gave only in order that his renown should not lag behind that of other rich cohorts and moral Don Quixotes and that he should be celebrated in the newspapers. Mr. Joshua was in fact one of those whose cruelty and greed has brought about the death of whole families.

Mr. Joshua, to be precise, owns a great number of houses whose roomy and well-ventilated apartments remained virtually empty through the entire epidemic because his propertied renters had left the city. At the same

---

upon himself a complete reorganization of prisons and poorhouses. Despite the immense difficulties he had to struggle with at first, his exertions and principled persistence were crowned with the most brilliant success, and on his deathbed this selfless philanthropist was consoled by his sympathy for humanity which he had inspired in the hearts of his countrymen. Unfortunately, we must confess that this sympathy has been little preserved in Howard's own country in the last quarter-century. Particularly in the most recent times, genuinely materialist theories have surfaced and in some cases been brought into practice, theories that completely undermine humanity in the guise of economics. The core of these consists of the following maxim: "The rich have no need to support the poor; everyone should look to his own needs as he can; public welfare is an abomination that supports indolence and every vice." Yet we are getting away from the point, and we must return to the society in New Orleans that has adopted the name of the English philanthropist. The Howard Association was incorporated with a charter from the legislature on 28 February 1842. The act of incorporation says: "Since several philanthropic citizens of New Orleans have organized a society (which has existed since the epidemic of 1837) with the intent of supporting poor persons, especially poor sick persons in time of epidemic, and in the expectation that the usefulness and influence of this society will be significantly increased by the possession of the powers which charters grant to other charitable institutions, be it resolved that, etc., etc."

This society originally consisted of Messrs. J. W. Andrews, G. Kursheedt, J. P. Bredlove, and F. W. Leslie.

It possesses all the privileges of incorporated societies and according to law must have a president, two vice presidents, a secretary, a treasurer, and nine directors. These officers are elected on 1 June of every year. The charter of the society has a duration of twenty years, and, since it has been in effect for eleven years (as of June 1853), only nine years are left to it. The charter will expire in 1862. [Ed.: See Elizabeth Wisner, "The Howard Association of New Orleans," *Social Science Review* 41 (1967): 411-18.]

time, he also has miserable, pitiable tenements, true filth-holes that have not been improved or cleaned in ages. Just living in one of these places is injurious to health and leads to yellow fever, even without an epidemic in the city. These tenements are too old and dilapidated for the owner to expend anything on them. The boards are half-rotted, and the timbers on which these fever-factories stand are stuck in muck yards deep. Add to this the sweepings and refuse from preparing sea rations in neighboring houses, and the portrait of this paradise of a residence is complete. But Mr. Joshua understands how to make money from filth. During this dreadful yellow fever season, these tenements, numbering six to eight in number, were all rented to poor families who obviously could not afford his larger houses. If Mr. Joshua really had the sense of charity that his donation to the Howard Association was supposed to prove, why did he not take the poor families out of these open graves and put them into his healthier houses, which stood empty the entire summer? Well, that would be asking too much, the narrow-minded rabble of land-speculators will declare; how can anyone demand that he lose rent on account of some poor families who would be injured by staying in his tenements? Hasn't he done enough by giving two hundred and fifty dollars to the Howard Association? This rabble is right, yes—but Mr. Joshua has not won as much rent from his swamp-holes as he might have hoped. Between 23 and 29 July, all of his renters succumbed to the disease, and the few old mattresses and broken chairs that he found as inventory could not even be auctioned as he had hoped. That is one of your Croesuses, New Orleans, who clothes himself in the mask of philanthropy in a terrible time! Is Mr. Joshua W* a murderer or not?

The apartment we saw Gertrude enter with Lorie, the raftman's daughter, was in a similar tenement, only a bit roomier and not so deeply mired in the muck. The dreadful and extraordinary circumstances that led to the deprivation into which the count's family had descended for a second time will be imparted to the reader in a later chapter.

Alerted by the sound of the door opening, a woman with her head pointed at the door half-raised her body from a narrow cot, which was covered by a hole-pitted mosquito net.

"It's you at last, my dear child?" she called out in a painful and concerned tone to Gertrude, who could barely stay on her feet but still lurched toward the bed from which the voice came.

"Mother, I went to several doctors, but none wanted to come with me if I didn't pay in advance—now I have no idea what to do—"

"Oh my good child, you have heated yourself too much, give your mother a kiss and lie down with Amelie and rest a bit; otherwise you will get sick, too."

"Come, Gertrude," a weak child's voice now called out, "Mother is right, lie down with me—I am not as sick as the others. But bring me a glass of ice water, I am so thirsty."

Gertrude was only too aware that she was already sick, but the ardent child said nothing so as not to frighten her mother. After she gave her mother a kiss, she sank down on the mattress on the floor beside her mother's bed, which served as little Amelie's sickbed.

A cheap candle burned on the mantel, alongside several empty mustard cans and some jars still containing a little castor oil. That was the total pharmacopeia that the count's family could afford; Gertrude had brought the doctor's prescriptions back from the nearby pharmacy unfilled, since the few cents they'd given gave her had not been enough to pay for the medicine. In a rude tone, the pharmacist had demanded either payment or a ticket and an order from a physician of the Howard Association, and when Gertrude had asked for more information about the association, he'd shoved the prescription back at her and told her to take it to another pharmacy. It was not even worth his time to tell her where to go to get tickets.*

The room in which Melanie, the mother, now resided with her children was miserable. Gertrude would now sleep here for the first time. She had remained awake entire nights until now; if her eyes had closed due to exhaustion, she had dozed where she sat.

Before this unfortunate family had moved in, the apartment had been held by a black washerwoman who also practiced a horizontal profession. Next to this room was a board enclosure that only received the dignity of being called a living space by the fact that human beings were present. The enclosure was roomy enough. What its earlier use had been will not be

*We are not exaggerating here. Hundreds of such cases occurred during the epidemic. One shudders to think of the hard-heartedness some pharmacists showed the poor. The tyranny with which they insisted on the collection of tickets exceeds all belief. Besides the fact that the druggists, with few exceptions, set down very unreal prices and thus won outrageous profits, after the yellow fever was gone, bills were later presented to the Howard Association, fabricated by certain quacks, which brought them sums they could never have won honestly. But that's how you make money! Many repaired their shaken finances through this maneuver, and with another summer like the one just past they would become stinking rich. The intentions of the Howard Association were good, the principles excellent—but it must be understood that the alleviation of misery is not so much a question of how much money flows into the coffers but how it is controlled.

mentioned here. It would be a sin against the feelings that beset us in the face of so much misery and tribulation.

A girl's voice sounded feverishly from this enclosure, which received only a narrow ray of light from the candle burning in the front room.

"Mother! Suzie is not moving; I have also called Father and Hugo twice, but I've heard nothing—"

"Great God!" Melanie cried out as she tried to raise herself from her cot. But she still sank back down.

"Mother, Mother! I am afraid—is Gertrude with you? Bring the light in, I cannot stand up—I am so weak." the girl's voice repeated.

"Gertrude!" Melanie gave a great effort to raise her tall body from the bed, but again it was in vain. "Gertrude, take the candle to Constanze."

The answer was a mere whimper.

"Amelie!" Melanie cried out. "Amelie! Is Gertrude sleeping?"

"Mother, dear Mother, I think I'm dying—" was the answer from the sickbed where Gertrude and Amelie lay.

The unfortunate mother let loose with a cry of pain that would have broken the hardest heart.

At the same moment, a half-dressed girl rushed in from the enclosure and grabbed for the candle, taking it with her. For an instant, fear had driven Constanze into that state of terror in which a feverish person can become virtually uncontrollable. Even though she had not even been able to stand up a moment ago, now it seemed as if her feet had wings.

This impulse never lasted for long.

For a few moments it was as still as death as Constanze rushed from the front room into the enclosure with the burned-down candle.

Wasn't anyone in the family able to make a move, even a cry of pain?

Had Melanie forgotten Constanze's cry of concern, and why had Constanze asked for the candle? Why was there this dreadful pause?

We can see nothing here, where Gertrude and Amelie are lying, since Constanze has taken the candle away.

So let's go where the light is—let's look into the enclosure.

There stands Constanze with the candle in her shaking right hand next to the pitiful bed on which the old count, her father, lies with Hugo. Hugo has turned his face to his father's. They are looking at each other, yet they are not awake. They lie there so peacefully, yet they are not sleeping. Both of them have their mouths wide open, and yet they are not speaking. How could they speak, since they are no longer breathing? No sound passes their blue-black lips.

Cease your dreadful pantomime, Constanze! Let your tears run down, and make some sort of sound for your lost father and brother! Let us weep with you, but do not continue to stand there and do nothing!

Your mother in the next room is not moving, but she is listening for your first word, your first call; she wants to know why you took the candle, Constanze!

Then the eldest daughter of the count turns from her father and brother and looks at her bed, where she had been lying with her youngest sister, with Suzie.

The same pantomime yet again, Constanze? Don't be concerned that a drop from your candle will drop on Suzie's cheek. Your little sister will not feel it any more.

It is your good luck, pen, that you have portrayed an elevated tragedy, that you have not stooped to scratch out common terms such as *black vomit* and the like. It is your good luck that you do not use the profane language of a physician.

People have tears and cannot weep; they have a heart and feel nothing; they have words, but those die on their lips—that is the problem with the greatest pain. The tears, the heart, and the words only begin once the pain has become a memory. So Constanze stepped out of the enclosure to her mother's bed. The tall, noble figure of Melanie erected itself, now a mourning Niobe, and she heard her daughter say: "Mother! Father, Brother, and Suzie are no more." The mother had already suspected what her daughter had to say when she returned with the candle. It was no longer a surprise.

The curse of yellow fever often strikes swiftly and unexpectedly, and someone who is fresh and alert today can be dead tomorrow.

Just as a beautiful garden announces its presence with its magical aroma, even when the entire night heaven is covered with black clouds, just as the fresh images of flowers entice us and draw our senses into fairy tale lands, so also that house, that chamber, called—even where the throttling angel of plague had swung his shining scythe. But here there are no blossoms in whose depths we can linger; here we are driven back by a primal warning force, and disgust and horror rises in those who had been driven to madness by unspeakable pain only moments before. That is the fearful curse of this plague! One is driven back by disgust, and even where one should feel sympathy, aversion rises along with its cold sweat and the stench of corpses. This is why Constanze did not reenter the enclosure; rather, she simply went to the door and quietly closed it. Mother saw this, but she said nothing. Both of them could have only one thought: "They have died, and they are calling us soon to be with them."

A wagon halted outside.

At once the door opened and a young man entered, followed by a small girl in poor clothing.

It was Lorie with a physician from the Howard Association.

As soon as Lorie became aware of the hopeless situation of her friend Gertrude's relatives were involved, she rushed off to get help at a nearby branch of the Howard Association. To be sure, she also had an obligation to return to the people she served as an attendant and for whom she had been hauling the ice block, which now lay in the count's family's apartment, melted by now to quite a small piece. But her childish heart commanded her to care first for her former playmate and her parents and siblings. Attendants were a rarity during this time, and it was usually necessary to pay a great deal to satisfy their—not unjust—demands. They were often taken by the illness themselves before they could be of the least assistance to their charges.

So it was the same in private houses as in public charitable institutions. The protecting hand had to be paid, and one received only if one had something to give in return.

Thus Lorie, although still quite a child but as capable and energetic as an adult, had been taken on by a prosperous family after their domestics died, one after another, of yellow fever. Her own mother had been swept away at the very onset of the epidemic. Lorie had offered her services as a nurse when the head of the family and two of his grown sons lay ill with the disease. She was promised three dollars a day, certainly very good pay for such a young thing as Lorie. She gave up this service in order to help her friend Gertrude, and in her enthusiasm she did not give a thought for the trouble she caused the other family. She couldn't earn anything from the count's family—still, how can children think about money when their heart leads? That is an adult prerogative.

Lorie had been fortunate enough to find an energetic and conscientious physician. If she had come a half-hour later, she might have found one of those physicians who, rather than serving their patients, preferred to be paid by the association while they relax at the lake in happy *dolce far niente.* It is rare for a young physician to inspire the confidence necessary for healing, all the more so if their youth is supplemented by an uncourtly manner. There is a good reason for that. Most physicians who are too young have neither the experience that comes only through years of a trying practice nor that noble jewel called conscientiousness. This is particularly the case with physicians in our city. If a person starts out as a quack and saves one out of twenty patients—even by accident—then one can treat even an experienced physician with disdain. The physician who came with Lorie was not, however, in this category. Despite his youth, he was a physician of splendid renown, a yellow fever specialist par excellence. He had not only had good luck with those in the grips of the illness but also had developed a splendid routine with all the other illnesses that arose in our oppressive climate.

The doctor stood for a few moments in horror as he became aware of the untold misery revealed before him. He had visited many hovels of poverty during this dreadful time, but it had never shaken him so much as this one. Constanze lay stretched out on the half-rotted boards next to the foot of her mother's cot. She had fallen on the spot after she had brought her mother the message of death. Her right hand was clenched on her breast, while her left hand rested on her glowing forehead. All of her blood had gone to her breasts, her head, and the upper extremities, and there the wild currents rushed about like a sea of fire. From her stomach down to her feet, she was as cold as ice. Her lower body seemed already dead, while her upper body was being consumed by the glowing mixture that rushed about in it. The physician found the mother, Gertrude, and Amelie in the same condition. The two younger girls, particularly Gertrude, were hallucinating. Several times she called out Lorie's name. In an instant, the practiced glance of the physician correctly determined that two of the patients had been treated but that the treatment had been interrupted. There was no mention of the doctor who had been called at first but stayed away when his second demand for payment had not been met. Now all four lay in the most dreadful fever, and there was no time to appraise negligent treatment. Since neither paper nor ink was available, the physician tore a sheet from his pocketbook and wrote a prescription. Then he gave Lorie the most precise instructions on what she was to do after he had departed and she had returned from the pharmacy with the medicine. He also promised to return in two hours and bring a nurse, in case she could not bear the burden. He saw only too well that it was too late, that a supernatural miracle would be needed for Constanze and her mother to recover. Salvation was only possible for Gertrude and Amelie. Despite that, the conscientious young man could not deny any of the patients anything and had to do everything in his power.

When the doctor came down to the street and started to enter his carriage, he was amazed to find a man sitting in it, holding the reins in his hands.

"You are a doctor?" the man declared in a commanding tone.

"Yes," the young physician replied with shock, stepping on a spoke of the front wheel.

“I had already determined that from the miserable coach—it is good that I found it,” he declared.

“But sir, what are you doing? What do you want? Who gave you permission to sit in my carriage and hold the reins of my horse? Get out, or tell me what you really intend to do.”

Instead of replying, the man gave the physician such a dreadful blow on the forehead that he fell back without a sound on the sharp curb of one of the stones that divide the sidewalk from the street. At the same instant, a small, bent figure crossed the street to the carriage.

“Hurry, abbé,” the man in the carriage said, “the dogs of the watch are at our heels.” He reached over and hauled up the small figure by the collars, dropping him in the seat. Then the carriage rattled down the street.

When the doctor awoke from his swoon, he found himself in the hands of two watchmen, who bore him away despite all his protests and assurances. They took the poor man to be a suspicious person, a conviction that would have been dropped if they had simply looked at him carefully. They would later learn that their officiousness had been out of place.

• • •

By about midnight, dreadful weather had set in. There was a heavy, depressing rain that poured down on the uneven, broken pavement, and within a few moments the part of the street on which the miserable tenement of our unfortunate family lay was under water. Despite the ceaseless rain, the air was so humid that even those with the healthiest natures felt half sick and were beset by the most painful feelings. Yes, often it seemed as if all the air had been pumped out of the city. The depressing, warm rain appeared as lifeless as the monotonous dark gray night sky, in which no distinct cloud gave the slightest sign of movement—in short, it was perfectly treacherous fever weather.

On this night, the disease raged at its worst. Because the humidity in the room was intolerable, Lorie had opened the only window, outside of which a deteriorated shutter of blistered green paint hung only by a loose nail. She would have liked to have opened the door as well, but she worried that it would attract the curious, who might see her at work and disturb her. For in these days there were many worthless wanderers who would boldly walk through any open door under the pretext of helping those ill of fever and then would do the most dreadful things. Lorie had heard many stories about such rabble, so she thought it better to keep the door closed until the physician, whose unfortunate situation was unknown to her, should return.

Lorie had much trouble with her patients. It was easy enough with Constanze and her mother, who needed bandages on their stomachs with a large piece of ice, to drive the blood that had settled in their upper torso into their lower torso. They even took the quinine that she had obtained on the doctor's order without complaint. But Gertrude and Amelie would simply not be still. The former appeared not even to know Lorie any more. She had continuous hallucinations about Lorie, and she spoke her friend's name time and again, but when Lorie drew too near she screamed and stamped her hands and feet, thinking there was a stranger near who wished to do her harm. Lorie wept bitter tears over this. She was not able to give Gertrude so much as a drop of the medicine the physician had prescribed. Only with great difficulty did she manage to get her into a position to place her feet in a mustard bath. Good-hearted, complaisant Lorie also managed the same maneuver with Amelie, encountering only rather mild resistance.

The little nurse had great trouble preparing the bath itself. The few slats that lay in the corner of the chimney, which Gertrude had brought the day before from the cooper's shop, burned too quickly for her to warm the water more than halfway. So Lorie found herself in a serious quandary. Then she recalled having stumbled over a board that was on the counter right by the door. With great trouble, she managed to split it into several pieces using a long, rusty table knife. These were still too long, so she broke them several times over her knee and then laid them in the chimney in a little pile. But it was still a considerable time before she managed to get the wood to burn, for it was rather moist and produced dreadful smoke.

After long, hard effort and patient waiting, she finally managed to get a fire going to procure hot water for the bath.

The little well-intentioned thing still did not have peace for a moment. Ice bandages had to be changed constantly, and the soaked cloths had to be unwrapped so others, which were not plentiful, could be applied. She had to get new cloths because otherwise the available ice would have been used up too quickly. So she moved from one patient to another, applying fresh ice, now here, now there. Often her eyes closed, and she would have loved to sleep for an hour, but she always overcame her fatigue and did her duty.

Good, poor Lorie! Out of love for you, I hope there is a heaven where you will receive your due. Out of love for you, I would create a God who would see your efforts and give you angel's wings. For people, little Lorie, only respect splendid, outstanding deeds. The poor child, who works so alone among those stricken by fever and fulfills her duties so truly—such a poor child is not worthy of respect among people. They are disgusting, and Mr. Joshua W* is their man, since he gave two hundred and fifty dollars to the Howard Association for the poor sick of the city—he is named, praised, and lionized! People are that way, and they cannot change.

As little as Lorie wanted to, and as much as she feared to, she finally had to open the chamber door. What drove her to this was not so much the humidity as it was a repellent miasma that had begun to spread in the room, seeping through the closed door. At first Lorie paid it no heed, for she knew nothing of the enclosure and thought that the room in which her patients were located was the only one they occupied. Once she thought about it, it seemed odd to her that neither the old count nor Hugo and Suzie were there, but the condition of her sick charges did not permit her to ask them about it. And so she forgot it at once. But now her eyes fell on that door leading to the enclosure, where the dreadful disease had been resting for the night. "Where does this door lead?" the good little girl asked herself. Perhaps it led to a kitchen or to a yard where there was a cistern from which she could draw water? And this nurse needed water very badly, for she had used the last drop. So she thought and considered. After making fresh bandages for the sick persons, she approached the door on her toes. She took the empty bucket in her left hand. Quietly she opened the door and looked in with extended neck—but it was very dark inside. She could not make out anything but the end of a mattress that lay by the wall, touching the threshold.

She felt nauseous and stepped back; she touched the back of her head with her right hand and let the bucket fall. The mother heard the fall and attempted to raise herself up. It also awoke Constanze from a feverish dream. It was not a loud fall—it was only a bucket falling to the floor, but persons so sick hear the smallest sound. Gertrude, on the other hand, heard nothing.

She was still hallucinating. And Amelie? Who knows why she did not hear it?

Outside at the same instant there was a loud splash in the water that had gathered around the tenement from the constant rain. Then two men rushed in; one, a gaunt man with long, pitch-black hair and a luxuriant beard of the same color, called to the other: "Close the door, abbé—we are safe here!"

How It Happened

The stream of life drives us into such a Charybdis of trouble and pain that everyone has felt the need at times to stop still and simply weep. But fortunately the tears do not flow for long, and soon irony lets out its Homeric peal of laughter. So we often see Democritus and Heraclitus joining hands, and it is good that this is so.

We had to weep at Aunty Celestine's pitiable bier—but then we concluded that drama and had a good laugh at the Hamburg Mill. Now we find the count's family in deep misfortune for the second time. And once more we must stop and weep without knowing the cause that conjured up this hopeless misery.

Hadn't all the arrangements been made to return Jenny and Frida to the arms of the count's family? And wasn't the count's family to cross Lake Pontchartrain, where they were to receive a joyous welcome, as we already know? What strange and dreadful events befell them? The sympathetic reader might well have asked this when we entered the impoverished tenement—or even before that, when we saw Gertrude wandering about, so poor and abandoned, seeking a doctor! Listen, then, to how it happened:

Two days before the scheduled departure across Lake Pontchartrain, Lady Evans-Stuart held a party in her residence on Annunciation Square,[3] in honor of the birthday of her daughter, the angelic beauty Dudley. Present were the prince of Württemberg, Countess Jenny R*, Count Lajos Est*** and spouse, the Countesses Constanze and Gertrude, Baroness Alma de Saint Marie-Église and her niece Claudine, and a captain of the United States Army who happened to be in New Orleans and had been presented as an old acquaintance to the elderly Scotswoman by the prince of Württemberg.

In keeping with old Scottish custom, the daughter of the house, Miss Dudley, acted as hostess. It was a marvel to see how this angelic being, who one could not imagine doing anything save kneeling before an altar, was able to observe the finest points of protocol in this high society. Dudley was dressed in snowy white. Through her hair was woven a string of pearls that would have made a princess boast. About her sparkling white neck, through which one could follow the coursing of the blood in her veins, lay a small, golden dove holding a cross set with diamonds. The mother was dressed as simply as the daughter, save that she had chosen a dark color suitable to her age, an ensemble that pleased the captain very much. He appreciated her clothing all the more in contrast to the overdone and garish dresses he had disliked upon the much older women in Washington. To be sure, the old Scottish woman still wore a form of mourning in honor of her late husband, which she had sworn to do until her death, but the very fact that, unlike many coquettishly inclined women who exploited this situation to announce their return to flirting, her dignity of dress was a touchstone of her noble, respectable attitude. Lady Evans-Stuart sat on a sofa of dark green satin, with Prince Paul of Württemberg at her right. He wore a dark blue demifrock with yellow metal buttons and narrow trousers of the finest white cloth. On his left breast could be seen the Grand Cross of a prince of the royal house, half hidden by his lapels. The prince had chosen this decoration to show the captain his esteem for the uniform of the United States. The captain had the fine tact to understand this gesture. He, like the others already named, sat to the side of the sofa in such a way that their chairs formed a semicircle. We should also pay attention to how they are dressed. On the right of the prince of Württemberg, who sat with Lady Evans-Stuart on the sofa, was Countess Frida, whose husband sat on the opposite side, to the left of Lady Evans-Stuart. Countess Frida wore a black barège dress decorated with black silken stripes on the bias that reached below her knee and ran in circles about her dress at narrowing intervals. Her pale face showed her deep mourning even more thoroughly than this dress. In her luxurious, full hair was set a white camellia of the most unsullied purity. The flower was set to one side, and it seemed to be kissing the blonde's startlingly white head. Her sister, who sat next to the captain, was dressed in the same way, but with the slight difference, hardly discernable, that the sleeves of her dress were wider at the front, so that her whole arm was visible with the slightest movement. She had a dark red camellia, instead of white, in her raven-black hair.

Count Lajos Est***, who, like his wife, was dressed in deep mourning because of their dead child, aroused the greatest interest in the old Scotswoman from the moment he appeared. He was no less marveled at in silence by the captain and the old baroness of Saint Marie, who, among her other jewelry, was dripping with diamonds and bore a large signet ring engraved with a coat of arms. Her niece Claudine, the unhappy young woman and, as we know, Orleana's bosom friend, wore fresh, bright colors that made an unfortunate contrast with her pale, suffering features. She also stood out for having attached to her bosom a nosegay of pansies, the sign of a lesbian. Her light brown hair was parted, as usual, à la fleur-de-Marie, and shone like pure silk.

The little Countess Gertrude, with her German forget-me-not eyes and her fabled golden Lorelei hair, sat in her sky-blue dress with its low-cut bodice next to Miss Dudley.

Countess Gertrude and her sister Constanze each wore a small artificial rose of black crepe as a sign of their sympathy for the deep mourning of Count Lajos and his wife. The prince of Württemberg also wore a small strip of crepe in the buttonhole of his coat.

Countess Constanze looked exceptionally fine in her dark red crepe dress with its high bodice. The fresh color of her face, together with the chestnut-brown of her hair, complimented her clothes in a warming ensemble.

The company, which assembled in the grand salon after a stroll in the garden following dinner, carried on its conversation in French. Miss Dudley had been instructed by her mother to make the first introductions in French, as the language proper for the day. This had been done in part out of courtesy to His Royal Highness, whose French was better than his English, and partly because of the old Baroness Alma de Saint Marie-Église, who could not understand a word of English—for in the high French clique within which she moved exclusively, the English language was utterly despised.

The baroness of Saint Marie, who had often visited Lady Evans-Stuart in past years, had avoided her friend completely from the moment Abbé Debreuil took formal charge of the household. The old baroness was mightily upset with the abbé over some matter that she never mentioned, and once she saw that the abbé was influencing not only Lady Evans-Stuart's heart and thoughts but the entire household, she vowed to never set foot in her friend's home again. Now that the abbé had been completely discredited and removed from the house due to the efforts of Prince Paul, she dared to visit Lady Evans-Stuart, or Cornelia, as she called her old friend, once more, often passing the entire day with her. So she had been invited to the party along with her niece, and she had been presented to the prince for the first time. Likewise, she and her niece were new acquaintances to the other guests as well. The Scotswoman was the only person present who knew of Claudine's unhappy relationship with Albert, and she had not known the young architect at all. It was utterly unknown to the prince of Württemberg that Albert had ever been married; that was due to the fact that Albert himself had never breathed a word of it, no matter how often he came to the sisters' lovable cottage, the sole place where the prince had happened to meet him. Claudine had been presented to the prince and the others as the widowed Madame de Lesuire—she did not use her husband's name. This was how the old baroness wished it, and the Scotswoman naturally had no objection.

Lady Evans-Stuart, who loved and appreciated her friend despite the baroness's cramped aristocratic ways and her generally peculiar manners, was making use of her daughter's birthday celebration to present the baroness and her niece to the prince of Württemberg as well as to the other guests. She hoped to create a friendly coterie that would win new and promising reinforcement when the count's family joined them across the lake. All of her earlier friends and visitors, who had sought her company more or less due to her wealth alone and of whom she could count legions before the appearance of the Abbé Dubreuil in her house, were either no longer in New Orleans or hesitated to return to a sphere from which they had been so rudely ejected years ago owing to the whim, or rather the command, of a Catholic priest. Baroness Alma de Saint Marie was the only one who had sought out old Cornelia, accompanied by her niece, as soon as she heard of the abbé's dismissal.

The conversation, which began as a lively crossfire of colorful inspirations and mutual gallantries, suddenly took a more serious and interesting turn when the captain—whether accidentally or on purpose—steered discussion toward the history of the city of New Orleans. He spoke of the time when that portion of the Mississippi that bordered the present Second District bore the name of St. Louis Fleuve and the entire city contained no more than two hundred residents.*

On this occasion he touched upon a theme that drew the close attention of the entire company. He spoke of the first appearance of the yellow fever in New Orleans in 1769, and he rejected the assumption that this disease had been introduced by a British ship that had arrived with a cargo of slaves from the west coast of Africa.

"You do not appear to be an abolitionist, Captain," the prince of Württemberg remarked at this point.

"How did you come to this perilous question, Prince?" the captain asked tensely.

*That is, from 1718 to 1727. At that time, Mr. Bienville was the Governor of Lousiana Province, and he was the person who chose the present (left) side of the river as the chief settlement, to which the name of *Nouvelle Orléans* was given. By 1723 New Orleans already had one hundred cabins, which lay scattered irregularly about. There were four residences, a storehouse constructed out of shipwrecked materials, and a structure called a shed but used as a chapel. In that year the population was not more than two hundred.

"Because you oppose the notion that we have the importation of slaves to thank for this," the prince of Württemberg asserted.

"Now I understand you, Prince—you are of the opinion that, if I were an abolitionist, I would like to believe that slavery was to blame for yellow fever."

"To be sure," the prince responded. "But since you so boldly cast doubt on the correctness of the common opinion that yellow fever came with a slave ship, I would not harbor the least suspicion that you are an abolitionist."

"In fact, Prince," the captain responded cheerfully, "nothing gets past German logic, and we Americans would have trouble winning if we challenged German philosophers to combat."

Claudine, who sat between Frida and Constanze, turned slightly to the latter and softly asked, "Could you perhaps explain to me, my dear countess, what an 'abolitionist' is?"

"I regret very much," she responded, "but the term is utterly unknown to me—by the way, I find it very boring and ungallant of these two gentlemen to talk about such incomprehensible things in the presence of us ladies. I also marvel that Lady Evans-Stuart, our dear hostess, who otherwise is so attentive, has not protested against the crude actions of the prince and the captain—"

The Hungarian, who had heard the secretive whispering of the two ladies but was unable to understand a word, looked directly into Constanze's face to discover what the secretiveness was all about. He was always sharp and earnest when it came to reading faces, and he became immediately aware that the ladies were becoming tired of this turn in the discourse.

"Madame," he turned to the old Scotswoman with a loud voice, "be so good as to look over there—Madame de Lesuire and Countess Constanze appear to be trying to conjure up a revolution."

Claudine and Constanze were quite startled when they suddenly heard their names being called out loud. Claudine raised her head high and fixed a stare on the Hungarian which said loud and clear: "You, my dear count, are shameless; we were introduced only a few hours ago, and you already dare to make me the target of your special attentions in the presence of such a select company!" And Claudine's aunt, the old Baroness de Saint Marie Église, turned as red as a firecracker as she thought: "This whippersnapper of a Hungarian count has no place in this company—I cannot imagine how this person could ever have awakened the least interest in me." Constanze had no thoughts at all but simply glanced from the prince to the old Scotswoman in discomfort.

"The ladies are conjuring up a revolution?" the prince of Württemberg and the captain asked in jocular tones, and they stared first at the Hungarian and then at the ladies mentioned.

"What other thing is possible?" the Hungarian asked. "How could you expect the ladies to carry on a conversation over the effect of a cargo of slaves? For, I must confess, I myself do not feel so comfortable with that sort of discussion—and on account of the ladies—"

With the exception of Gertrude and Dudley, who were still disputing among themselves over the garter, the entire company was completely confused by these words. Frida thought she would sink through the floor from embarrassment.

The Hungarian calmly stood up, grabbed his armchair by its back, and rolled it right across the salon to the place where Countess Gertrude and Dudley were sitting. There he sat himself down in the chair ingenuously, oblivious to the notion that he might have any obligation to anyone else in the company.

If the company had been confused before, now they felt utterly disoriented.

Most fortunately, the captain possessed enough intellectual awareness and ability to turn the conversation in such a way as to avoid the confrontation which otherwise would have been inevitable. Without taking any notice of the Hungarian whatsoever, the captain asked the ladies on behalf of himself and the prince for forgiveness if they had been troubled by the introduction of this subject, and he promised that the error committed by himself and the prince would be made good at once if the ladies would be so good as to give him their attention now.

This succeeded. The long faces vanished, and all eyes turned to the man who had managed so quickly and skillfully to reverse the painful silence that had been setting in.

Only Frida might have had a reason to say anything—quietly, in her wonted gentle way, about her husband's conduct.

"Since the conversation was about the yellow fever," the captain said, "I will tell this high company an extremely interesting story of my experience last year on my expedition in search of the source of the Red River. But before I begin, let me ask a question of my sympathetic listeners." In truth, the captain was well aware of how to get his listeners' attentions and make even the indifferent curious.

"And what would this question be?" they all asked, without exception. But they asked this only with their eyes.

"Ladies and gentlemen, have you ever heard anything about the *Mantis religiosa?*" the captain asked, quite clearly, yet in a mysterious tone, so that even the flaccid face of the Hungarian showed momentary interest.

"I know it, Captain!" Gertrude cried out in a lively voice, while the crystal voice of Miss Dudley sounded: "I know it too—there are many *Mantis religiosa* in our garden—"

The prince of Württemberg could barely suppress a hearty laugh over the rival zeal of the two young women. He turned to Lady Evans-Stuart with a pleased expression and said: "See, Madame, how attentive Angel and Psyche are tonight!"

"Forget not Genius, too, Your Royal Highness!" Constanze declared with gusto: "I trapped two *Mantis religiosa* for you yesterday evening."

"Trapped?" the captain puzzled quietly. "What sort of *Mantis religiosa* could that be that the good young ladies are describing?"

"My God, if only the young people would have the patience to wait until we adults have spoken!" the old baroness de Saint Marie dogmatized, rubbing the coat of arms on her finger as if wisdom was supposed to arise from it.

"We must excuse them," the prince of Württemberg retorted, "youth has the right to be precocious."

The old Scotswoman had too fine, too clever a tact to be upset by the prince's words. This was not the case with the baroness of Saint-Marie-Église. She was extremely upset, and she stared in rage at the prince.

Claudine de Lesuire stared down at her pansies and joined her aunt in irritation.

The prince, however, to put an end to all the sparring, and to give the captain an opportunity to tell his story, which was certainly interesting, turned to him with the words: "You asked whether we had heard anything about the *Mantis religiosa*? The *Mantis religiosa* is the Latin name for a type of insect which is called a *wandelndes Blatt* or a *Gottesanbeterin* in German, since this creature looks like a leaf on one side, while from the other side it always raises its front legs in the air, folded together, as if it were trying to pray."[4]

"Yes, yes, that's it!" Gertrude and Dudley joined in together.

"I can see," the captain interrupted, with the most amiable manner in the world, "that our high company has not yet heard of the *Mantis religiosa* that will play such a great role in my narrative; for it is not an insect but a plant, a plant that only grows close to the source of the Red River, and which during some years is supposed to have the dreadful capacity to cause the plague of yellow fever—"

One can easily imagine that such a mysterious declaration met with no further objections and that everyone pressed the captain to fulfill his promise.

The captain, who is surely already recognized by the reader as Captain Marcy of the Red River expedition, now described the preparations he had made on the command of the United States government to seek the source of the Red River, and he quickly came to speak of his meeting with Emil and Lucy, who the reader already knows.

"It is a demonstration that I have not described both the young people wrongly," he said, among other things, "that they were intimately acquainted with the mysterious personality of this Cagliostro of the New World,[5] who they called Hiram."

"But permit me, my dear captain," the prince of Württemberg interrupted, "did you already have a description of this person you could compare with that the two young people gave you? Or are you perhaps in possession of a certain manuscript, which I had thought was only in my own hands, or rather—do you have a transcription of a certain manuscript, which made you acquainted with this dreadful man?"

The captain appeared shocked. Instead of answering the prince's question, he turned to him with a question of his own: "You possess a manuscript with references to this Hiram? Prince, you could perform a great service for our government in Washington—"

"I had no idea what to do with the manuscript—I have it from the estate of the former president of the University of Louisiana, the member of the French Convention, Joseph Lakanal; it has the strange title, 'Narratives of an Ursuline Novice in New Orleans'—a promising title, isn't it, ladies? Isn't it, Captain?"

Lady Evans-Stuart assumed a mysterious manner that clearly signaled she was acquainted with the manuscript of the patriarch of Mobile.

"But you found nothing about the *Mantis religiosa* in the manuscript—otherwise you would have said right away that it was a plant?" Captain Marcy asked the prince.

The prince of Württemberg admitted it.

"But then what is your source for the existence of this Cagliostro, Hiram, allowing you to recognize the description of the two young people to be correct?" the old Scotswoman asked Captain Marcy.

"In the archives of our government in Washington there is an old issue of the *Moniteur* in which this Hiram is accused,* among other things, of en-

* *Le Moniteur* was the first newspaper to appear in New Orleans. It began in 1794, and most of its subscribers were overseas, particularly in France and Spain. It was the elo-

dangering the lives of the inhabitants of New Orleans by throwing the seeds of a poisonous plant known only to him into the cisterns. This accusation is repeated in a warrant for his arrest, which describes this Cagliostro precisely as the two young people described him."

"Perhaps they had the same issue of the *Moniteur* in hand and pulled one over on you, Captain Marcy," Lajos mocked. "So much humbug is done in this country, and one could hardly blame the two vagabonds if they used your *Mantis religiosa,* as you call it, to make some money . . . By the way, I forbid you to call this cad a Cagliostro. So far as I know, Cagliostro was not a poisoner but a mere innocent gold-maker who never managed to find the philosopher's stone, although he is supposed to have attained great age—"

Frida gave her husband an indescribably moving look. If she had been at his side, she would have whispered: "But Lajos, I beg of you, pull yourself together!"

It was really not the Hungarian's habit to be so demonstrative and careless. On the contrary, he always proved himself to be the astute man of the world in such situations, and he had a very good reputation for this, particularly with Constanze and Dudley, as well as with the prince of Württemberg and the old Scotswoman. And so the last two named grew very uncomfortable over the fact that his conduct should prove so tactless and unrestrained this very day, when he met the captain and the baroness and her niece for the first time; he certainly was making a bad impression on them. Did he perhaps harbor a particular premonition in his head? Or perhaps an inner voice whispered to him: "Let it go, Count Est***, the measure of your crimes and atrocities will soon be full in any case—for the time being, it is no longer worth the trouble to feign having sensitivities. Show yourself as you are so that they are not so surprised when they discover who and what you are. Who knows whether it is still necessary to take precautions—who knows whether you will live to see the death of your wife's old uncle! Let it go, this dissimulation and playacting is just too much of a bother for you! Or are you so reckless, Count Est***, because your dear, evil demon, which has ever spurred you on and led you by the hand, whispers in your ear: 'Now, Lajos, is it perhaps fatal that you have lost the whole

---

quence of this journal, in which several of the leading lights of the day expressed their ideas, that led to the Mississippi's being opened to navigation by citizens of the United States the very next year. This act, arising from the noted Treaty of San Lorenzo, gave the first push for an improvement of trade in the city of New Orleans. One cannot forget that Louisiana only came to the United States in 1803, after it had been given by Spain to France and sold by the latter power to the United States.

treasure of the mill? Wouldn't it be better, perhaps, if you had not burned down the Hamburg Mill, and the clubmen and Lady Merlina and the Pontifex Maximus still lived? Wouldn't you still have your enormous income? Then perhaps your child would still be alive? What now, Lajos?'"

"You are much inclined to satire, today, my dear Count," Lady Evans-Stuart responded to the count's aforementioned misconduct, hoping that the captain would be moved to greater caution.

Lajos, who had perceived the old Scotswoman's finesse at once, did not want to remain with *his* wonted caution, yet he also wanted to demonstrate that he could conduct himself well if he so chose.

With the finest restraint, the Hungarian rose from his deep armchair, bowing slightly to Lady Evans-Stuart, speaking with a Versailles accent: "Madame, if you take the trouble to pay so much attention to me as to try to convince your esteemed guest, Captain Marcy of the United States Army, of the worth of my person, then the only way I can thank you is to recognize your superiority by giving you homage in the manner of the clans of your homeland."

As he spoke the last words, the Hungarian left his place next to the armchair and approached Lady Evans-Stuart. Then he knelt down and graciously kissed her right hand.

"Arise, Earl, and let your banner wave freely from the battlements of our country," Lady Evans-Stuart parried the Hungarian with an historical reference, like for like.

Following this absolution, the Hungarian arose and gave his hand to the captain. He greeted the prince and each of the ladies with the same silent apology.

"He is a splendid man, this Hungarian count," the baroness de Saint Marie declared to herself—for the Hungarian had gazed at her with more than indifference when he offered his hand. "It is only too bad that he was so clumsy before."

In any other situation, the Hungarian's conduct would have been condemned as the most tastelessly theatrical farce. And yet how strange it was! Just as Lajos was rewinning the hearts of everyone with his sudden display of chivalric conduct, there were still two persons who conceived for the first time an inexplicable hostility to him, at the very moment of his gallant ostentation: the prince of Württemberg and—Frida. One glance at the right instant tells us more than the empiricism of the most practiced physiognomy.[6] A shudder ran through Frida's breast for which she could not account—her heart hid an uncanny feeling whose origin she knew not. She wanted to say that she was feeling something for the first time, something she had never felt before. For the first time she did not look at him openly—rather she looked at him several times in furtive glances. Her husband's courtly gallantry, so often a marvel when she was with him in a select company, now appeared repellent, dreadful to her. Her ideas began associating irresistibly with the strange feeling that overcame her when she thought she saw his face, pale as death, the color altered in the reflection from the green lens of the glass lens. The thought occurred to her that he had wept no tears at the death of their unhappy child—and that he had left her alone in her night of pain and shut himself up in his study. Now Lajos no longer appeared to her to be her husband. And now the good Frida no longer heard a word of the conversation that was being conducted in lively terms over the *Mantis religiosa* and Hiram—she was suddenly no longer the quiet, musing thinker she usually was; her imagination pulled her ever further into a labyrinth of distrust. She thought of the planned duel with Karl, of the Doppelgänger and his mate, and in the end she arrived at the most dreadful thought, which was that Lajos was not the man with whom she had crossed the ocean on the *Gutenberg*. The unfortunate woman finally rested on the thought that Lajos had become his own double, whom her sister had seen in the clearing of Ranney's Timber—her heart shrank spasmodically at the thought. May your guardian spirit remain with you, poor, unfortunate woman! Only a step further and you will doubt your own personality. Your cogent spirit departs weeping, and madness calls mockingly within you: Why do you want to desire more than to be the double's wife? So be mine, too, Frida the Doppelgänger! . . .

• • •

So we shall leave the company for a moment in order to direct our steps to another place.

When that dreadful night, when the crimes of an inhuman father were revenged on his own innocent child, had been succeeded by the morning, Lajos sat alone on the sofa of his study—the valise of the murdered Jew was in his hand. He was carefully reviewing the contents, and in particular he was giving his full attentions to that letter from Milwaukee which we have already revealed in a note. He had locked the doors from inside.

"Madness!" he accused himself half-aloud. "The whole story obviously rests on a deception—"

"Just as is the case with the whole story of the money from the mill . . . my dear count, we meet again!"

As if a bolt of lightning had paralyzed his members, the Hungarian looked at the place from which the voice had originated.

"We meet again, count!" and a tall, gaunt figure passed him on its way out the door.

Now *he* leaped as if he had been whipped by the snakey locks of Medusa.

"The door was locked—how did that uncanny old beast manage to come and go? It is ordinary enough to be visited by ghosts in the night, but in the bright light of morning? Nonsense! No one spoke, no one was in the room. Oh you big fool, Lajos, have you suddenly become such a pitiful hallucinator? It is one of Satan's new properties today that he has become the most sensational of authors, who sees ghosts and spirits in broad daylight? I am amazed that the horse's bust on the mantel doesn't laugh me to scorn, and that the Black Prince doesn't rear out of the picture and stomp me with a couple hooves . . . for such pitiful weakness! And this old, gray beast, who yelled 'Cheating!' in my ears while I was playing dominos, so that I am still half-deaf from it—I'm supposed to have seen and heard *him*? I had long since forgotten him—if it had been the Jew, or my panther of a little wife! Then the nonsense would be excusable—ha, ha, the door is as locked as it ever was—ha, ha, Lady Wilmington, gallant mare, take your riding crop down from there and chastise my little-boy brain, chastise it until the count realizes what value a clear, healthy brain can have. Now, now, stop Satan! What did you say? The story about the money from the mill—stop—if you—? Yet here I'm weighing it in my hand—ragged paper and still a hundred thousand dollars!"

Then the Hungarian suddenly let the banknotes fall as he pressed his brow against a doorpost, as if he were trying to bore through it with all his force. His fists were clenched, and out of his eyes there shone a devilish mockery. What had he seen? What had appeared to him? Anyone may take the banknotes who wants them! Can we explain why?

When the Hungarian had been searching for the treasure under the bed, it was utterly natural for him to think he had found it once he discovered a book of the proper thickness in the cavity of the correct size. It was even more natural that he should entertain not a doubt about the genuineness of the hundred-dollar notes, nor did he undertake a precise examination of them; for since he was sure that the total fortune from the mill was under the master bed, why should he have suspected that some sort of deception was afoot? And yet it was so. Madame Merlina certainly had reasons, which were not groundless, to doubt the honesty of the Italian Lombardi and worry that he might want to come into the exclusive possession of the treasure. It was not in her power to change the hiding place of the money to her own advantage, since she had to be present during every moment of any audit ordered by clubmen of the 99th and 100th degree, a prerogative she could not attempt to change since it was established in the statutes in the mill book. Still, in her caution she developed a great scheme. She had an engraver and illustrator in the Spanish newspaper office, which engraved the club's tickets, reproduce the impression of an old banknote plate that had belonged years before to Jennison's infamous counterfeiting band in Plaquemine, and she had substituted these false hundred-dollar notes for all those of the mill's treasure, which by old agreement was supposed to be kept in an opening under the master bed, covered by a board, until an assembly of the club membership decided otherwise. Meanwhile Merlina had hidden the real treasury of the mill on the top of the bed's canopy, where no one suspected. There had never been an audit, not even a comment by any of the members that one was wanted. So Merlina would make a report, which would be signed by Lombardi, the Pontifex Maximus, then by Lajos, and that had sufficed. Either clubmen had been convinced of Madame Merlina's honesty, or they were hesitant to cast doubt on their trust in her through an audit. Expenditures flowed from her hands into those of the membership, where more care was taken. One finds a similar procedure in certain joint-stock companies or the So-and-So Canal Company: the president is raised above all distrust, but the directors are continually laying for one another. Nevertheless, Merlina had prepared herself in case the membership happened to want assurance of the existence of the fund. It had been her plan to take Lajos into her confidence and to deceive the membership with his help, if the two even allowed the membership to survive too great an increase of the treasury. Perhaps she was waiting for Dubreuil's success with his plot in the house of Lady Evans-Stuart. Lajos had always been the one who had made the greatest impression on her, and it could well have happened that, to make sure she could share the treasure with him, a visitation of the membership would have been made—with tar masks. We have long known how it really came out, however.

When the Hungarian came out of his study about midday and went to the room where the corpse of his child lay, he looked dreadfully disturbed. The certainty that he had murdered so many persons in a single night *to no purpose* had caused a dreadful upheaval. Not that he regretted his many crimes and atrocities—no, it was only the thought of feeling once more utterly poor and having to live for a while from his wife's small property that tormented his spirit, and, even if his mind contemplated the undertaking of a new crime, he realized with a shudder that he lacked the strength to bring the plan to completion. He felt exhausted and sated, and if his demon could not reveal to him some fresh stimulus for some sort of crime he would have no alternative but to put a bullet through his brain. Yes, his demon would not even be able to give his spirit its old elasticity with money now—the sated murderer needed an entirely different stimulus. And as this strange father stood for a few moments before his child's corpse—he was alone, observed by no one, since Frida and Jenny were in the garden picking snow-white roses and magnolias for a memorial wreath—Mephisto laid his thin lips on the murderer's scar and whispered these words: "Think of Cleveland the peddler, whose horse bit a piece out of your cheek, think of Lydia Prairiefire, and then of the dark shadow on your child's cheek." And voice seized the father at the very moment when Jenny and Frida entered with wreaths in their hands. He lowered his head on his child's face and let out a cry the sisters took to be a cry of pain but which was really nothing but a miserable curse for which he could find no language.

The body was quietly buried that very day. The prince of Württemberg was the only soul standing at the grave. He had taken on himself the duty of undertaker. He was escorted by no cleric. But as day gave way to night and the cold light of the moon silvered the graves of the cemetery, another soul stood by the little grave weeping bitter tears. "Oh Frida, Frida," sounded a voice heard only by the moon, "even if I am far from you, I am still close to your child." And the man leaned down to the fresh grave and embraced it with his arms, as if he were embracing Frida's child. And if a guardian angel had been at Frida's side, he would have spoken to her at the precise instant the man embraced the grave: "Go to the cemetery, and there you will find a man at your child's grave who loves you without your knowing it and whom you have rejected in favor of your husband." And after Karl had lifted himself from the grave, he looked back at the lovable cottage, in which all the lights had been extinguished except for a single dim lamp.

This happened three weeks before the day the birthday of the angelic Dudley was celebrated in the residence of Lady Evans-Stuart.

• • •

At the very moment they were eagerly discussing the *Mantis religiosa* and Hiram in the residence on Annunciation Square, a slender young man of astonishing beauty, though with rather delicate features, stepped onto the ferry near the French Market. He had missed the signal for departure twice, despite the fact that he had been near the landing at the front of a little ice-cream shop. On the boat he moved restlessly back and forth, impatiently stopping occasionally to cast a searching look at the opposite shore. The few passengers who were with him on the deck observed with almost murderous curiosity the beautiful young man with the long blond hair falling to his shoulders and the large, sky-blue eyes. Everyone's attention was drawn not only by his tall, slender figure but also by the clothes he wore. Other than a short blouse of white silk and a silver belt made up of numberless fine rings, he was without any clothes. He looked as if he had just come from dinner with King Antinous or sitting on the lap of Sardanapalus. A lady who was also on the deck at the time burned with desire at the sight of this mythological figure wandering about naked, violating all the rules of social life.

Many of our lady readers might disbelieve what we have portrayed. But in order to take away the slightest doubt, they only need ask the owner of the ice-cream shop, whose love of truth is celebrated in the entire city. There were also several passengers who saw the beautiful young man on the deck that day.

When the boat landed in Algiers, the young man quickly steered his steps to the area where the charming cottage stood. When he arrived at the garden door, he hesitated for a few moments, looking through the slats at the front entrance, whose bright-green louvered doors let light escape through the arched corridor of trees, seeming to invite him to come into the old, familiar cottage as quickly as possible.

He pressed the latch, but so carefully and softly that the sound made on the inside of the door was only a weak tone that could hardly betray the fact that someone was entering.

He stood once more in the middle of the shadowy grove, contemplating the flowerbeds on either side of the path, planted in the shape of a heart. They were framed with splendid resedas, whose vibrating buds take on the enchantment of polyandria. In the midst of this bed were mysterious nasturtiums, luxuriantly and pleasingly rising on cross-shaped green trellises with gilded heads, their red-flamed glittering hoods always betraying the presence of a German woman. On the sides stood some lychnis, serving as a transition to all-American flowers, which had their best representatives in the rose-colored *Amarillis palustris,* the *Mirabilis jolappa,* or the "four o'-clock." A sensitive observer would recognize in an instant that the beautiful gardeners had been guided by the idea of asserting the German-American element among the flora. This was a moving contribution to that labor of Tantalus by which plants seek to reconcile themselves with these stubborn bipeds.

"How much has changed in the two years I was gone! What innovations! How beautiful and large the trees have grown, which were hardly taller than I was when I left, and now there is an elegant cover for the cistern instead of narrow, uneven boards—and now I see there is also a new kitchen-house.

Albert certainly made the plans for that! Everything is so peaceful and still—my Jenny is certainly taking her afternoon nap with Frida, and perhaps—but may I hope this? Perhaps she is dreaming of her Emil! Oh Jenny, Jenny, had we never set foot on this fateful soil, we would still rather have been driven eternally across the wild seas, even if the *Gutenberg* had never reached its destination . . . and so? Oh God, you will accuse me of infidelity, my Jenny—but the Almighty knows that I have always borne you in my heart and that only an unavoidable fate ever drove me to leave you—"

In the midst of these musings, Emil was suddenly interrupted by a noise from very near.

It was the saucy cook, who was at work picking some eggplants, and when she saw Emil naked before her, she turned red all over, broke through the bushes and cedar branches, and fled to the new kitchen annex.

Amazingly enough, Emil did not consider why the saucy cook had fled from him like a startled deer. Even as the slatternly being fled, he recognized her as a useful spirit the sisters must have engaged during his absence from the lovable cottage. Since he feared that the dumb thing would sound the alarm and bring out everyone in the house, which would rob him of the fun of presenting himself in melancholy serenity, he rushed to the kitchen to find some way to stop the cook's little mouth—if it is possible to speak of anyone from the Lüneburg Heath as having a little mouth—in time.

Everything was peaceful and quiet. It was cool in the garden, since the rays of the sun could not break through the thick darkness of the trees and bushes. The *Mirabilis jalappa* had reopened its blooms—a sign that it was after four. Such a flower clock never deceives.

"Is your mistress at home?" Emil asked the saucy cook, who had tried in vain to prop her body behind the kitchen door, which could only be locked from outside. The sisters had regarded it as unnecessary to provide a latch on the inside.

"No one is at home—go away," Urschl replied as she crept under the kitchen table, where she held her apron in front of her face, knowing the door would give way to a strong push from outside.

"March out of here! If the ladies came, they would wonder what brought us together, you unclothed man, you!" Urschl shouted from under the table, as she continued to hold her apron in front of her face.

It took a great deal of persuading on Emil's part to convince the saucy cook that he was the master of the house and that the Countess Jenny was his wife. Once he had brought Miss Urschl that far, she no longer had the slightest doubt, for while cleaning she had often seen and admired his silhouette, which hung in the drawing room above the mantel; it was his spitting image.

She no longer said "You unclothed man, you," but began addressing him quite courteously as "Count." She crept from her hiding place and shut her little mouth out of sheer amazement and marvel. Now red as a cherry, then as pale as a Barataria oyster, now as hot as a glowing meerschaum pipehead, then cold as pineapple sherbet—she changed color and temperature as Emil questioned her. Incidentally, she always stood with her face half turned away, only casting a furtive eye now and then at the bon-bons of her count and master, bedecked in silky golden down. This is what passes for modesty in modern times, and thus repressed nature has its revenge.

What Emil learned from Urschl was that his parents had been here and, in fact, that they were now across the lake; further, he learned that Lajos had returned, and that the Hungarian's child had been buried three weeks ago, which filled him with a strange mixture of joy and sorrow. It was amazing enough to him that his parents had been so long in America and only now had sought out Jenny and Frida. It particularly surprised him that the prince of Württemberg, who, according to Urschl, had been in the city at the time of their arrival in New Orleans, had kept the whereabouts of Jenny and Frida a secret from his parents and siblings. He learned from the cook that only Constanze and Gertrude had seen the two sisters so far; the reunion with the others was supposed to take place in two days, across the lake. Emil naturally decided at once to join the trip across the lake, but he was tormented by the thought of his earlier relationship with Madame Wilson and his years-long absence from his spouse. It was either by accident or due to delicate caution that Urschl made no mention of Jenny's confinement in Pass Christian.

"The departure is to be the day after tomorrow?" Emil asked the cook, although he had already asked that several times before. The cook confirmed it with a light nod of the head; then she said: "That will be a pleasure, Count, when you go over to the whole grand society there! I can hardly wait for the wonderful life. It is too boring here—year in, year out, we don't see a person, at the most the prince of Württemberg, and he's no fun."

"Don't you like the prince of Württemberg?"

"Yes, yes—as you like it—but I would rather have young, handsome masters around me," Urschl responded, looking rather intensely at her master.

"Aha!" Emil thought to himself. "That's the way it is! The little one seems to me to be a Romantic."

It had become clear that the saucy cook had something in her mind, despite her earlier display of modesty.

Emil suddenly thought of Tiberius and asked: "Tiberius has certainly gone with the ladies? How goes it with the little darkey?"

"Tiberius? Him? He hasn't been here for fourteen days. It's good he's gone—this eternal carousing, the teasing, and the cursing—the life could get quite tiresome after a while. He will soon see that he never had it so good as here. He did precisely what he wanted—I couldn't stand him from the start—no, no, I really have to say that I am very glad that he is finally gone—"

This chatterbox, who, if she did not soon find a man, would have all the potential to become a dreadful Megaera, would have kept on berating and degrading her former black beau, once so beloved, if Emil had not interrupted her. "But where is Tiberius, then, if he isn't here?" he asked in an insistent tone without inquiring into Urschl's outpouring.

"They have sold him to Monsieur Delachaise's plantation," the bold cook abruptly declared.

"Sold?" Emil repeated questioningly, by which one could tell that he was somewhat upset.

"Yes, yes, sold!" she intoned with even more rudeness than before.

One might recall that Tiberius had been a surprise gift from Emil to his wife on her first birthday in the New World. Emil was thus disturbed that his present had passed into other hands in such a prosaic manner, since he flattered himself that she would not have parted with it, a remembrance of him, at any price. This news delivered a painful blow, not so much to his heart as to his pride. To understand this correctly, one must know about certain practices among the Creoles, to which Emil had accustomed his German character immediately after arriving in New Orleans and which he bore on the whole in a quite proper manner.

It was fortunate for Jenny and her sister, by the way, that he was not yet so involved with Madame Wilson then, so that he had the fine tact to choose a Tiberius instead of a Tiberia. But we will briefly explain how Jenny came to give Tiberius away.

After the day that Mephisto had inspired Lajos at his child's coffin to seek out Cleveland the peddler and his mare Lydia Prairiefire, and after he had found them and could begin to destroy them, the Hungarian became most depressed. A thousand plans crossed his brain, but all of them were cast aside as useless. He knew where the mare was, since she was still with Oliver Dubois on St. Charles Street. He had convinced himself of it a few times himself by going into the livery hall, supposedly to look over the horses and choose one to ride. Once he even thought Lydia had recognized him, since when he came too close, she let out such a neigh that the other horses shook their manes in horror and tried to break loose. The Hungarian was shaken, not on account of the mare's unnatural howl but because one of the horsemen looked him over from head to foot with distrust, as if trying to determine if he had somehow attacked Lydia to cause her let out such dreadful neighing. The horseman perhaps knew from experience that there were persons who took pleasure in sneaking into the stalls and driving the horses mad through dreadful, despicable means. Let's just recall how the Italian Lombardi used his secretive "elbow" and "little powder." The Hungarian never set foot in Oliver Dubois's livery stable again, and he also quit seeking information there about Cleveland, the peddler from Illinois.

During these days, the decision was made to cross the lake in the company of the prince of Württemberg and the Evans family, a plan that was hurried all the more by the fact that the fever had already taken a bad turn in the city. The Hungarian, who at first had decided to remain in New Orleans, was persuaded by the prince of Württemberg and the two sisters to promise to join them. Jenny's child, of course, could not come along, so the prince placed it under the sure care of his housekeeper, at his residence on Bayou Road. Jenny wanted to devote her last full day before departure entirely to her child. When the Hungarian had finally decided to go along, there sounded once more in him the old refrain: Money! Money! In order to shine across the Lake, he would need money, a lot of money. He still had several thousand dollars in arson money to collect; but how could he dare to do so, since the creditors of the mill knew full well that Madame Merlina and the clubmen had died in the flames? Why wasn't he satisfied to get off scot-free? How could he threaten them by himself and force them to pay? It was just as well for both sides to be silent. Then his eye fell on Tiberius. It wouldn't be such a bad thing to sell him, he thought. No sooner thought than done! He besieged Frida and Jenny until they finally gave their consent. He took Tiberius the very next day to the auction in Bank's Arcade, where Monsieur de Delachaise bought him for nine hundred dollars. Jenny and Frida still suffered too much from the terrors of that night to consider asking too many questions about the use of the money. They gave the Hungarian free rein with it.

We are now back with Emil and the saucy cook.

Only a little while ago, when she had spied Emil's mythological nudity as she'd been picking eggplants, she had turned red from head to toe and run into the kitchen annex. Then, a few moments later, she became rather cheekier, and she did not shy away from—if rather furtively—catching a glimpse of her master's beautiful bon-bons. And now, as Emil strode toward the marvelous house, she made desperate, distressed faces. The attitude she struck in the kitchen doorway would have done justice to that which the queen of Carthage displayed as she saw the anchor lifted on the ship that bore away Aeneas. Whoever could have seen the slovenly, saucy cook at this moment would have recognized her for an instant as the modern Dido. But, one might protest, how could this Dido-Urschl make such pretensions, and what gave her the right to be so desperate at Emil's departure? Dido-Urschl was experienced enough to know that certain liberties, of which a cook might dream in the kitchen, had no force outside her bailiwick. Under the long, high wash-table there was a laundry basket filled with linen right from the line. She threw herself in on her bottom, not even thinking that this extravagant action had no point. So we leave her and follow Emil.

Since he was now certain there was no one in the entire house, he could go right in. His gait, his manners—in short, everything he now undertook—bore the stamp of the purest naturalness. Watch those who think they are not being observed—then you will either fall in love with them or become their mortal enemies. People are one thing in company, another when alone.

Emil's soft steps had barely reached the upper part of the carpeted stairway leading to the third floor when the despairing cry of a being he had long since forgotten compelled him to beat a brief retreat.

This cry came from none other than our Papchen. He recognized Emil at once, but he was not quite ready to greet him in the accustomed way; rather, he could only make inarticulate noises that were too shrill and words he did not know precisely, which easily led to the conclusion that the two sisters had not been very careful with his training.

"*Señor caballero,* ho, ho, ho!" at first . . .

"Your Jenny loves you from her heart, with sorrow—" was the second verse, and . . .

"*Señor caballero,* ho, ho, ho—no understand!" the third and last, for Papchen let his head sink and did not speak another word, no matter how much Emil petted him and tried to get him to speak.

"Heaven only knows," Emil thought, "what's happened to my dear old Papchen—usually so easy and full of humor, and now he hangs his head and looks down in sorrow."

Papchen was a remarkable bird. He depended on the two sisters heart and soul. If people were happy in the lovely house, then Papchen was happy along with them, which he usually indicated by hopping quickly from ring to ring, sounding out the words he had learned one after another.

If people showed themselves depressed, Papchen went along with that, too, and he would not eat until he saw happy faces around him again. Since that dreadful death, Papchen had become quite mute, and only Emil's longed-for reappearance could shake him momentarily out of his apathy. Then he returned to the same mute sorrow he had taken on.

The first place Emil now sought was his bedroom. He opened the door full of intense expectation. It was here, in this chamber, where he had taken Jenny in his arms so many times; where he had hung about her neck many a night weeping for her to forgive him and to have faith in his undivided love. It was here that he had often covered his wife with passionate kisses while—oh the unhappy error!—he thought of Lucy Wilson. What an unmeasured world of desires and hopes, of torment and pain, of disappointments and errors were held in this little world! Here an angel had kissed the hot tears from his cheek, where the kisses of her competitor had burned shortly before. Here she had created a heaven, and he—possessed by the devil of passion—had made of it a hell. He looked back on his past in his thoughts, and the name *Hiram* shuddered on his lips.

Emil stepped to the bed and pressed his face to the pillows. In the next instant he bolted up. "A man has lain here!" he declared. "That is not my Jenny's bed."

It was the bed in which the Hungarian slept with Frida. The very pillow in which Emil had lovingly pressed his face had supported the skull of the Hungarian, silent and dark, brooding over wild and deadly crimes, at the side of the unhappiest wife the sun had ever shone upon. His bestial head had rested there, with its sodomitic, hyenalike passions, slaughtering with felonious mockery the natural course of thought of a noble, innocent woman.

Emil went to the neighboring room, in which Jenny's bed now stood. He had almost become ill in the Hungarian's bedroom. His chest was constricted by an unexplainable premonition.

There could be no doubt about *this* bed. The pillows garnished with lace, on whose covers were embroidered the entwined letters of his and Jenny's names, the two plumes of sky-blue silk, several blue-white *fleurs de lis,* speckled with lily-white, probably already arranged for the coming night, and several odds and ends on the heavenly night table—all this and much more, which even the gallant pen of the Marquis de Sade would not be able to describe, witnessed to it being Jenny's place of rest.

Emil threw half his body on the bed and covered it with a thousand hot kisses. Then he rose again and sat with his elbows on his knees and his hands on his forehead on the edge of the bed he had renounced for so long.

It was clear he had been weeping bitterly, and he made an effort now to hide the rest of his tears behind his long eyelashes.

An ordinary man would not have been able to do this. Certainly strange thoughts swirled in his head, seeking to form rationally to make a decision, but in vain. Should he remain here until Jenny returned? Should she find him in her bed? Or rather, should he go to Lady Evans-Stuart's and seek his Jenny in the midst of company? What did the etiquette and conventional norms of social life matter to him when it came to the stormy boiling over of his heart? But he still had to take account of one matter, since such a violation would create too great a scandal. For though he assumed that Lady Evans and the entire company with her at this moment would be perfectly familiar with the garb of Olympian majesty and divinity, he still thought it advisable to put on clothing, as was expected in our modern world. He must disguise himself as solid in order to appear as something he was not.

But another question that would be harder to answer imposed itself on Emil: Where was he to get clothing at this moment? The idea of going into a clothing store and buying a coat, trousers, a vest, etc.—he would not do that for all the world; he would rather step utterly naked into Lady Evans-Stuart's salon. Emil had a far too noble, chivalrous sensibilities to be able to go to a clothing store and buy clothes. That was something done by actors, newspaper editors, theater critics, café merchants, rag-pickers, bone-black manufacturers, architects, building inspectors, deputy surveyors, gas-works clerks, and similar demigods.

There was nothing else for Emil to do than to make use of the services of his old personal tailor—which every noble must have. But this fellow lived too far away, and even if he had risked the trip to Frenchmen Street, it would still be a week before he could get his things. Then a grace, costumed as a saleslady of fashion, whispered to him a fortunate thought. No sooner had he decided than he acted to carry out his decision. In the lowest drawer of a German commode, Jenny had preserved his page costume, the same one he'd worn four years before when she fell in love with him at the court chapel. Was it still kept in the same place? Why not? A German woman's love of order is world-famous and is never violated by disaster, domestic confusion, violent passions, or the like. If a place for any object is chosen today, it will still be there in fifty years. Emil did not harbor any doubts about this hypothesis, so he went at once to the commode in question and opened the bottom drawer. There lay the full outfit, wrapped in snow-white linen. As Emil removed the pins that held the linen to the page costume, he revealed the blue uniform, embroidered with silver. Each of the silver buttons, decorated with lions, was separately wrapped in paper, as were the epaulettes, which had been removed carefully so as not to crease the delicate silk. On both sides of the uniform lay the white silken stockings, reaching to the knee, the white kid gloves—one would have sworn they belonged to a maiden of twelve—and the narrow little slippers of sky-blue silk, decorated with silver filigree and fringe. The brief white breeches lay on the bottom, probably so they would not press on the more delicate items of clothing. There were also several white silk handkerchiefs with the coat of arms of the Counts of R* embroidered in gold. Since Emil only had to strip off his short blouse, dressing was very fast. When he stepped before the full-length mirror, tears came to his eyes. If he had not thought of Jenny at that instant, he would have rushed to the mirror and planted a warm kiss on his own lips. One could see that he wanted to do this, but it was better that he abstained, so much he flamed for Jenny. Kissing his image in the mirror would have seemed not unlike a new adultery, and he wanted never to do that again—that was his unshakable decision.

But Emil jumped when he saw a figure rise above his shoulder. He hardly believed his own eyes. When he turned his eyes from the mirror, he stepped back in shock.

The figure was quite oddly dressed. The gaunt silhouette was shrouded in a long, narrow mantle of a dark color, which was closed to the chin by a standing collar and practically touched the ground. The small collars, which turned somewhat inward toward the neck, revealed a lining of dark red; the sleeves extended beyond the middle of the hands, virtually covering them. The mantle was buttoned down along its entire length. His pointed head, dominated by a disproportionately broad and high forehead, was yellow and pale, and his cheeks were hollowed so that one could have laid a flat hand in them. His nose, which arched dramatically outward in the middle, almost touched the fine, almost invisible lips at the end.

Above his eyes, which were completely hidden by green glasses with side-lenses, one could see a pair of bushy, gray eyebrows of uncanny length. Above his forehead ran a blue-red stripe from ear to ear, only slightly covered by gray hair combed forward. This skull must once have been under the scalping knife of an Indian, for that is the standard scalping line, rising from the temples. This man had somehow escaped execution through some fortunate accident.

"Welcome to New Orleans, wanderer from the mesa!" the figure said, placing his emaciated right hand on Emil's shoulder. Only then did Emil recognize whom he had before him. For the clothing the figure wore was so different from what he had worn before that it was impossible to recognize him at once. The dark glasses hid his extraordinary, spectral eyes.

Emil stood calmly in the presence of Hiram. Reverence and pious awe no longer spoke from his eyes. He also no longer bowed as if in the presence of a higher being. His handsome head was held high and free on his pale, full neck, on which the pure gold of his splendid hair sat in disordered, wavy locks.

"Your welcome comes at an inopportune time, man of misfortune—what brought you into my house and disturbed my solitude?" Emil said.

Hiram the Freemason replied: "You are courageous and contrary now, poor Emil, since you know that I have no more power over you. Poor, weak child, you press your hot cheek on your love's pillow and think that you can conjure everything back as it was and bring it into everyday existence—"

"Quit your fruitless talk and entwine other hearts with the mystical threads of your magic! Happy is the lover who has never fallen into your hands and been subjected to your devilish illusions. Were there two more happy mortals on the whole globe than Jenny and I? Where did two hearts love each other more purely and with more enthusiasm? Then you appeared and—"

"Stop, senseless raver! Where did I encounter you when you saw me for the first time? Was it at the side of your Jenny? Hadn't you already alienated her heart from yours? *Who* ordered you to climb out of her bed and into that of Lucy Wilson?"

"Who other than you? You were playing this felonious game with my heart even before I met you—oh, now it is all clear to me, now I understand why an irresistible force always drove me from my true wife into the bosom of Lucy Wilson. Your devilish arts confused my senses and poisoned my heart. How often, when I wandered through the streets in the middle of the night, did I complain to heaven for giving me such an unfaithful heart, which rejected true love and fled into the arms of a whore. But always in vain—all of my begging was in vain! I even left my peaceful home to be with Lucy all the time—on that night I fell into your laid net, and now—tell me that I am a senseless raver—"

"What a commonplace man you have become again since you left the mesa! You howl and thump like a schoolchild who has promised not to do something out of fear of the schoolmaster's rod. You make every earthly effort to deceive your lord that you are guiltless and that I was the one who enticed you into your infidelity and your flippant promiscuity. You appear to have forgotten that you admired and made love to Lucy long before I drew you into the charmed circle of the *Mantis religiosa.* I don't blame you for that, dear, penitent Emil, since my ideas, as you know, are not those of convenience or of an inherited false morality. When it is a matter of humanity as a whole, then one individual can go down to ruin, and a husband can separate from his wife or a child from his parents. Let the husband be unfaithful and the wife a whore, and you will see the good fruits that grow out of this disorder, to the benefit of all mankind. Let all the bonds of family be broken, and you will see how man and woman gird the sword about their loins when the cry is heard: 'Freedom and Equality for *every* race!' Thousands are in our midst who would take up the holy struggle at any moment, if they were not bound by the ties of an ordinary family life. A desperado will begin this revolution, and only a desperado will bring it to a conclusion. Then beauty will raise itself to eternal glory, no more compelled to rub and waste its wild, untamed sensuality within the chains of slavery. Bald Eagle will then no longer hunt and goad to death black prey—he will flee dazzled before the shining sun of *Nigritia*—"

Emil had seated himself on Jenny's bed and in this position had been listening quietly to what Hiram said. But now he rose and interrupted him in a very curt tone: "I never understood you before, and now I understand you even less. What does your nigger business have to do with my situation? Believe and hope whatever you like, but I must ask you to leave my house and never again disturb the peace that prevails in these rooms. You will have no opportunity to drive me mad a second time—your nonsense will not find any sympathy from me. May heaven be thanked that I have finally been freed from the magic, and that I am at last back in the shrine of my spirited, faithful wife. Whether or not Lucy bears the messiah who is to liberate the niggers, I don't care—she can also figure out who will pay for the birth. Who is this Lucy Wilson now, now that magic binding us together has been broken? We had barely returned from the mesa, had hardly set foot on the cursed soil of New Orleans, than she was once again back on the track of a rich man, selling her charms with the greatest boldness, since she assumed that she would starve to death with me. And tell me, could she have become such a loose woman all of a sudden? Wasn't she rotten from childhood, and hasn't all of New Orleans known of that slut Lucy Wilson of the Mulattoes' Settlement? What devil struck me with such blindness? How could I love this money-loving whore, this slippery snake! And how could I leave my faithful, lovable wife?"

"One can see that your higher genius, which was with you in the Atchafalaya Bank and at the source of the Red River, has utterly abandoned you. You strolled though the sanctified plain of the mesa like the son of a god, accompanied with your bacchantic beloved. The beauty of her splendid body, the magic of her passionate eyes, was everything then. You went to sleep every night at her breasts, and when the young morning dawned and Diana Robert brought you your breakfast drink, you seemed so happy and pleased that even the Olympian gods would have envied you. Times have passed, and no sooner are you back in reality than your enervating moral scruples return. Out of the son of a god has come a German Philistine, and I don't wonder that Lucy Wilson has so quickly grown tired of you and sought relief from her tiresome lover in her old promiscuity. You Germans cannot love freely and recklessly, and even if you've caught Venus in your nets for a time, you would rather let her run away, since she cannot stand your weeping and howling, your bites of conscience and mousy philosophizing. Now you will resume legitimate lovemaking with your wife because this will not disturb the peace of your heart. Don't spin fantasies about your nice marriage nest, you have no idea what awaits you, my Emil, and it would be better to leave now than to dream and rave. What drives you to these pillows with such abandon? Rise up and you will see evidence of the fidelity of your wife. Poor Emil, unhappy spouse in his tear-soaked penitential shirt!"

Cagliostro Hiram was right, after a fashion, but the reader has already understood that Emil was still no ordinary person. The magician knew this quite well, but why he spoke this way anyway—who can decipher it? If Emil had been an ordinary German, he would not have sought his salvation in the page's uniform. Just the fact that he was not about to go to a clothing store in order to cover his mythological nudity demonstrates the presence of an extraordinary spirit.

The Philistine would call the magician immoral, and a man of spirit would say he was a blithering old man. Perhaps the sequel will demonstrate that neither the Philistine nor the man of spirit would have hit the nail on the head.

"What drives you to these pillows with such abandon? Rise up and you will see evidence of the fidelity of your wife!"

Without asking, without looking at Hiram, without understanding the import of these words in the slightest, Emil lifted the pillow mechanically—he did this because they had been speaking about it and without the slightest intention of proving anything by this hasty act. But now? Suddenly the scales fell from his eyes, the coral freshness of his lips transformed into the paleness of a corpse, his eyes were glued to the place now uncovered, and he ran both hands through the smooth gold of his Balder-like locks and once more arranged them à la Utgard-Loki. He now turned his eyes from the spot and turned them toward Hiram's long, gaunt form—fear, revenge, distrust raged in his interior, finally breaking out in the words.

"So I still am under your spell, mysterious man! And, poor me, I believed myself to be free of it? Oh, go somewhere else with your arts and do not rob me of my faith in the fidelity of my noble wife with such relish!"

"Poor Emil, you believe in the fidelity of your wife so much that now, when you see it attacked, it all seems so strange that you would rather suspect magic than to try to explain this fact in natural ways. Ever since you and Lucy Wilson took *Mantis religiosa* as an antidote for the yellow fever, you have had nothing to fear from my magic. Even when I spread death and ruin all about, you will remain untouched by it. Everything that happens to you will be the normal result of the confusions and absurdities of everyday life, with nothing at all to do with my personality. I do not have any further reason to test you, since a part of my mission was completed with the prophecy I gave to you and Lucy on the mesa. The Caucasian has impregnated the Ethiopian at the source of the Red River, and the messiah shall rise, whether Lucy leads a fine, decent life or not—but unfortunately the beauty, in which I believed—"

"Finish, finish!" Emil interrupted the source of his torment in a despairing tone. "Tell me instead how this fireman's belt got under the pillow—but I conjure you, tell me the truth and do not torture me with this flood of sarcasms. I conjure you, mysterious man, tell me, tell me, did you materialize this belt here? Tell me, tell me the truth!"

"I would tell you the truth, poor Emil, if I didn't fear that I would lose your understanding by so doing. That is the very reason I came here, to explain the situations in this house. It would not take much for you to lose your head if you were to find someone else's belt in your wife's bed—"

"I conjure you, how did this belt get here? Not a word of complaint or accusation will pass my lips if you tell me the truth." At these words, Emil rose from the bed and placed both his hands on the shoulders of the tall, emaciated figure. Hiram pushed him carefully away from himself and pointed to a chair beside the commode. Without wasting a word, Emil sat down on the chair. Hiram continued standing close to him.

"Do you know the young Architect, Albert R*, Emil?"

With a shaking voice, Emil affirmed this ominous question.

"Have you heard of certain obsessions, elective affinities and the like?"

"Yes—but my God, what does that have to do with it? What are you trying to say?" Emil asked, restlessly moving back and forth on his chair.

"The architect left this belt here in absent-mindedness, though he didn't leave it here on this bed but on the sofa in the next room."

"Stop! I can't stand it—do not accuse my faithful wife—"

"'Of infidelity,' do you want to say?" Hiram interjected.

Emil did not answer. Large tears welled from his eyes and crossed his pale cheeks.

"Don't torment yourself with it, Emil," Hiram continued, "your wife loves Albert and you love Lucy Wilson—now you are even, and no one has any accusations to make against the other. It would be silly for you to demand fidelity from your wife when you have committed infidelity yourself. From now on, you will no longer have to fear your competitor, nor will your wife have to fear hers. If you feel strong enough to return to your wife with love after this revelation, then come with me and I will lead you to her arms."

"I do not want to see her and cannot see her," Emil responded, but as peacefully and rationally as one who has finally come to a conclusion after internal debate and struggle.

"Then you will stay here and await her?" Hiram asked.

"No, I want to leave these rooms at once and never return. It would be better that we never meet again, so that she never knows how much I loved her."

"But what are you going to do? You know that you are still compelled to stay in New Orleans until the plague that has just begun is entirely spent, and much is still destined for you to see and experience—"

"The nights will see me back on the streets of this accursed city, and I will forget my sorrows with carousing."

"For once you are speaking reasonably, Emil—drink and kiss away, 'tis better than your being a whimpering Adonis. Even if your heart wins nothing that way, still your heart at least will remain bright and clear. I wish you good enjoyment, and since you need not be concerned about the horror of the fever, you can live in this city in league with Bacchus and Venus. There is good drinking, kissing, and carousing to be done once your head is free from fear and sentimentality."

Emil had risen from his chair and now appeared to be inspecting his clothes.

"I know," the old man remarked, "what is going on in your inner being: you want to get this plunder off your body so you can be clothed again as an *incroyable.* Here, marvel at my foresight, I have taken care of everything."

With these words, Hiram drew an elegant gentleman's suit from under his mantle, laying it on the bed under Emil's amazed eyes. He did not even forget a precious gold watch, along with various other small accessories to a perfect wardrobe.

"But what use is all of this if I have no money?" Emil said half aloud. "I am still stuck in the mud even with this fine wardrobe."

Hiram again reached carefully under his mantle, withdrawing a small portfolio in black satin, embroidered with obscure signs in silver, and delivered to Emil the sum of five thousand dollars with the remark that this would be enough for the moment.

With the sight of the money, which was in good notes drawn on Citizens' Bank, Emil was greatly relieved.

Whoever thinks this is unlikely underestimates the influence of money.

Jenny and her sister-in-law were forgotten, as were his dear parents across the lake, and an hour later, after he had replaced the page's costume in the commode in the same order in which he had found it and left the lovable cottage, no one would have believed that this young, elegantly clad man had been so long at the side of the most marvelous of all magicians.*

• • •

Two hours after the encounter in the lovable cottage just described, Hiram stood together with a man directly before the front fencing of a grand garden, from whose evergreens and bushes the splendid mansion of Lady Evans-Stuart rose. With the departure of the sun, the rising moon had come into its own domain in the heavens with such a magnificent glow that, once the tint of sunset had departed, the transition from day to night could barely be perceived. Here and there across the uneven pavement on both sides of Annunciation Square rattled a few belated wagons, whose owners sit and sweat year in, year out, on the hard cushion of cotton bales. On the square's green grass some horses and mules, freed from the burdens of the day, grazed quietly and contentedly, while a swarm of youths, drawn

* "The princess of Wolfenbüttel and Monsieur Moldaske had no sooner left us than Hiram entered. The descriptions our esteemed guests, especially Princess Sophie, had given of his character were confirmed to the last detail. Indeed a marvelous man! The most heterogenous visions cross one another in his brain. His overpowering feeling for physical beauty, to which he attributes every imaginable prerogative, often compels him to statements that, should they be realized, would undermine all morality and would obliterate the sacrament of marriage from the ground up. He is a bitter enemy of slavery, which he calls the angel of death to beauty. How he came to such a conclusion is not clear so far. Perhaps it is just an obsession with him. What was recently told at a gathering before our governor concerning a certain Diana Robert, a Negress, borders on the fabulous. She was supposed to be nothing less than the product of his own alchemical creativity. Are we to think that anyone believes in such medieval monsters in our own day? And yet it is so. Raymundus Lullus and Albertus Magnus have not yet passed away. It is our desire to learn something about yellow fever, but this was unfortunately not fulfilled." (From the letter "Clarissa" in Lakanal's *Narrative of an Ursuline Novice in New Orleans.*)

by the glow of the moonlight, sat in tight circles—some by themselves or wandering around—lounging and singing old plantation songs: "Old Folks at Home," "Emma Snow," and "Julius from Kentucky." Young America almost screamed its throat out, but there were also a few who sang quite well:

In New Orleans they shut me in
With hundred more they say,
Some black, some white, some large, some thin
To sell 'em all next day.
I climb the barrel—jump the gate,
And 'scape the guard so lucky,
I go from there to New York State,
And master to Kentucky.

And how prophetic it sounded when the choir intoned:

Oh! Kentucky—it is the land for me,
And surely I'll go there again
When colored folks are free.

And how beautiful the following solo was:

I'm sorry now for master's loss,
And none could feel it greater,
For master he was half a horse,
And half an alligator.
And now I join the Christy band,
The first and the most lucky
Of all the darkies in the land,
From Orleans or Kentucky.

Thus sang young America, and the moon, believing they were tormenting themselves on his behalf, thankfully kissed the mouths of these wild howlers.

As the youths killed time singing and howling on the cool grass of Annunciation Square, plans were being prepared nearby whose dreadful issue would lay the foundations for the complete ruin and destruction of the count's family. Without the events that follow in the house of Lady Evans-Stuart, despite the diabolical sentiments of the Hungarian, the planned journey across Lake Pontchartrain would certainly have taken place, and then, instead of finding them dying in that tumbled-down tenement, we would have seen them greeted and received with universal celebration. But the mysterious old man holds the threads of destiny in his hands, and he is weaving them all into a gigantic shroud, in keeping with his unfathomable will. He had precisely followed the lives of all the persons known to us, unremarked, and now he compels them all onto the magically lit stage of his enchanted kingdom.

Before we enter into the conversation the two men have been carrying on in front of the fence of the Evans-Stuart garden for the last quarter-hour, a brief description of their appearance would not be out of place. The mysterious old man has already been portrayed; we have already described the long, emaciated figure in two distinct metamorphoses, and now we have a third. It is the very transformation of his image in which he was often seen in the summer of 1853, among the Druids, the same lodge that bore him to his grave at the end of that summer of terror. It seems he wished to be buried along with the Grand Master of the Freemasons' Lodge of Louisiana, Mr. Hill. From now on, that is, from the moment he started talking with the other man soon to be described, standing in front of the garden fence, he displays the style of a monseigneur, from whom he had copied the requisite black civilian clothes. His eyes were no longer covered with green glasses, and he also no longer wears a high cap of racoon skin like a trapper or a Rocky Mountain hunter; nor is his body enclosed by a French colonist's mantle with standing collars. White neckbands, black coat, black trousers, and white vest—that sums up the changes that had so quickly transfigured his exterior. The gray head—who would dare number the years that had already passed over his skull—was free, and he had pressed his folding hat under his arm. Just like Cagliostro and the modern pantheist Pierre Leroux,[7] he bore all twenty-seven phrenological organs, equal to the twenty-seven gods of mythology, on the immense circumference of his skull—indicating one who was capable of anything.

The other man is of medium or low stature, and he barely reaches to the breast of the other man. His hair is cut short, and on his face are large, red-brown patches, witnessing to old burns endured and survived. Likewise, his throat displays a scar from either a gunshot or a dull knife. A connoisseur of people could easily read the merchant in the odd movements of his arms and the guiding play of his hands. Though a Scot by birth, his facial type has not the slightest resemblance to that nationality. One would take this man to be an American.

Other than a shirt of irreproachable whiteness and smoothness, he wears a rather improper wardrobe. Yet this is not the result of any lack of money (and the fact that he has money is proved not only by the heavy gold chain and watch but also by the diamond ring that shines from his little finger);

rather, his disorder and dirtiness of attire arose from the peculiarity of people in his trade of dressing poorly even when they have a well-stuffed wallet in their pockets and respectable deposits elsewhere as well. A merchant of that ilk can stand anything but an elegant, modern wardrobe. So far as his age is concerned, he was already well into his forties. He had just hung his wide-brimmed Panama straw hat on a stave of the garden fence. He wiped his raw, brown forehead several times, and now he stands with crossed arms and his back to the fence, next to Hiram, who is now listening to his conversation with renewed attention after an interruption for a few minutes due to the howling of the young men. The French that Hiram speaks would be better used in the Tuileries, while the other man speaks with a bad accent similar to that of a Portuguese Jew in the money markets of Paris. The reader will have little interest in the company among which he adopted this accent, which is frequently encountered in New Orleans.

"It should suffice you to know that I am the one who rescued you," Hiram said.

"You are certainly the most remarkable man I have ever met in my eventful life," the other responded. "If we did not live in such an enlightened time, I could easily conceive that you were an omnipotent magician, such as many who are said once to have existed."

"It all took place quite naturally, sir. I found you lying in that place while I was riding through Looking-Glass Prairie, and I brought you to Shellville, where I quickly brought about your recovery with the aid of several of your acquaintances. Your mare, Lydia, whom you thought had been burned up, had already arrived there two days before. Your friends in Shellville recognized her at once, and since she arrived without you, with your money-belt in her mouth, they feared something had happened to you. So several of them set out at once for your settlement. What they learned there was that you had ridden toward Shellville together with a stranger, so they looked for you in the prairie—without finding you, of course. That it was given to me to rescue you rested on the same accident as the discovery of the murderer, to whom I shall lead you now."

"But how do you know that this Hungarian is my murderer? That is an insoluble riddle to me—"

"Don't concern yourself about this, but just come into the salon when I call for you. He will escape, but we will get him into our hands later. The police should have nothing to do with him—the end of the story would then be a mere hanging, and the rope is no penalty for this monster. He should experience something entirely different. No human head has even conceived the penalty that I have set for him, and this Hungarian count will be the first and the last to receive it."

"What sort of a penalty is that?" Cleveland the peddler asked, since we can call him by his name now.

"Ask no further questions about that, since you will probably be present when he suffers it."

"Well, so I am pushing you concerning things that are to come—but tell me, sir, wouldn't it be better not to let the monster escape this time? Who knows whether we shall ever have him in our hands again or whether, once he has escaped, he won't find some way to put both of us out of the way? Shouldn't we just wait here until the company breaks up, then we can discover where he lives—"

"Cease your objections, sir, I have long known where he is living—do me the honor of following the directions we discussed on our way here."

"You could easily make me object—but I want to follow your wishes. Still, I do wonder—"

"Quiet, sir—just look over there, right by the big Weymouth's pine!"

When the peddler looked at the place indicated, he almost expressed his surprise out loud. But Hiram placed a hand on his mouth at the last moment, warning him to keep silence. "The company will soon return to the grand salon," he said very softly, "wait patiently until then."

The peddler saw the Hungarian, who stood under a splendid Weymouth's pine with Miss Dudley Evans, maintaining a very lively conversation, utterly against his usual inclination. Farther off, at the other end of the garden, shadows fluttered over the garden path, covered by snow-white, fine mussel shells; some of them clung to one another, others parted in order to reunite moments later at another spot. These promenading shadows undoubtedly belonged to the participants in the party that had been given today, as we know, to celebrate the birthday of the angelic daughter of Lady Evans-Stuart.

Here come Prince Paul of Württemberg and the old Scotswoman. They were discussing the *Mantis religiosa* and yellow fever.

Over there, Captain Marcy was escorting the aged Baroness Alma de Saint Marie-Église. The captain was telling her about his Red River Expedition with great enthusiasm. Since the old baroness always wanted to know more and was not satisfied with the data he had given her, the captain was finally compelled to retail the greatest humbug to the lady.

Elsewhere, through a lane of low banana-figs, often standing, then taking a few steps slowly forward, were Countess Jenny and Claudine de Lesuire. They were both widow to the same husband. Yet their conversation turned on flowers alone. The word *man* or *my husband* never emerged. Jenny spoke of honeysuckle, while Claudine grew passionate for pansies. Neither really grasped the other's true passion.

Up on the pinnacle of the high locust tree, the moon was taking a stroll.

Constanze and Gertrude were sitting on the marble edge of a Windsor fountain. They talked about the trip across the lake that lay ahead of them, and in the most painful tones they were discussing their missing brother, whom they so much would have liked to have seen among his parents and siblings, so that the measure of joy would be full. The poor girls! They have no premonition that they have been selected to serve up the bitter cup of sorrow to their loved ones.

Constanze and Gertrude have left a place empty between them. It is for the lovely blonde Frida, who has stepped away only for a moment. Where has she gone? God only knows.

So the shadows promenade, sitting and standing before they finally all return to the grand salon to take a little light refreshment and then say *adieu* for the evening, for a morning party never lasts past nine or ten in the evening.

These have already pulled up in front of the house: The carriage of the Baroness Alma de Saint Marie-Église. The phaeton of Prince Paul of Württemberg. And the state coach of Lady Evans-Stuart, for the convenience of Count Lajos Est*** and the Countesses Jenny and Frida.

The old Scotswoman's garden, as anyone who walks by it can see, has the appearance of a park, owing to its wide expanse and its many bushes, acacias, cedars, and Chinese trees gathered in imaginative groupings. The grand labyrinth of narrow footpaths, which were crossed by broader ways, hid secretive bowers in its dark, dreamlike bosom, from which the aroma from the pitch of foreign pines mingled with the smell of the flora of Louisiana. Here, in such a setting fit for angels, only true love could thrive and be happy. No, such aromas go to the marrow of even the shabbiest devil, seducing him to extravagances and hallucinations such as he has never dreamed. And if this aromatic, dreamy, moonlit setting is able to sprinkle an irresistible magic on a shabby devil's organs of love, wouldn't this be all the more so with a noble devil? A hyena can become a lovesick, raving Adonis—under the right conditions. In the same way, a noble devil can become a noble angel—under the right conditions.

At the instant he stood with Miss Dudley under the Weymouth's pine, Lajos has become something like that.

The fact that the two stood, although they were immediately before a superb bench, showed that they had just arrived at this spot. The moon threw its blinding light through a great, open crown of acacia leaves formed by the intertwining and overlapping of branches. Otherwise, everything was covered in the deepest darkness. Beyond this, above this labyrinth of trees and bushes, the garden was as bright as day. Yet we shall exile our pen to the place indicated, the bright crown of acacias, framed in darkness.

"Look, Count, this is my favorite place—without even knowing it, we have arrived here. Isn't it beautiful and lovely, so hidden and secret? It is only a bit open in that direction, toward the fence, but this opening will also soon vanish, conquered by darkness once the jasmine branches have grown together. That bit of sky above, from which my good old moon looks down, is just enough to make one think of the Creator of this little paradise."

"Miss, this bench calls us to spend a few minutes in your little paradise."

With these words, the Hungarian's eyes looked with gentle persistence on the blue-white, beautiful forehead of his lady.

"How could you say a few minutes? Say the entire night," Dudley responded with her childish directness.

"In your presence, Miss, I could pass months, years, even my entire life—but alone, not a moment. The little bit of sky that looks down, with which you are satisfied, could never fill my own heart. I feel better in broader, freer surroundings, in the presence of the whole sky. But even that is too narrow for me. There are moments for me when I wish I could rise above the limits of the horizon and look down on the entire globe. And if this were granted me, my unappeasable desire would drive me even further. I would wish I could swing around the zodiac, which would crack under the pressure of my ideas."

"That is not pious thought, Count, for we must be satisfied with the limited space in which the wisdom of the Creator has placed us. An overweening spirit among men has ruined much on our beautiful earth."

"You are right, Miss—but who compels us men to take such a high flight?"

When Dudley said nothing, the Hungarian continued.

"Women are most at fault that we men so often harbor perverse thoughts and use our felonious hands to turn a knife against the great spirit of the Universe. Women could easily make us into angels, if they only wished. We men are born troublemakers, and only women are in the position to lead us back to modesty and piety."

Dudley had seated herself on the bench. The Hungarian had taken a position behind her, leaning over the back. They were only inches away from each other. If the conversation became any livelier, their faces could easily have met.

"I do not understand you completely, Count, but it frightens me nonetheless. My God, what are we women to do to save men from pride? And if heaven has really placed this power in our hands, why have women so neglected their duty to turn men into angels?"

"Because most of them suffer from pride of the heart, just as we do from pride of the spirit," the Hungarian declaimed in an almost troubled tone. At the same instant he took one point of his moustache in his mouth and bit on it.

"Pride of the heart, Count? Can the heart be prideful as well?"

"To be sure, Miss. A heart is prideful when it prays to itself and holds itself aloof from other hearts."

"But do women really do that, Count?" Dudley responded, moving a bit closer to the Hungarian as she said it, without meaning to. He stroked the blinding moonlight away from his forehead, letting his long, raven-black hair fall over his face. Now the moon shone on the back of his head, his neck, and his back. He stepped on a frog that had sprung onto the tip of his shoe a moment before, without looking to see what it was.

Outside, in front of the garden fence, Hiram told Cleveland the peddler: "Did you see how he let the hair fall over his face? And do you know why he does that?"

"That is easy to answer, sir. He cannot stand the moonlight."

Hiram remarked, "This is a foretaste of the fate that awaits him."

The peddler looked at him with large eyes but asked no further questions, for the couple under the acacia crown captured his total attention.

Dudley had to wait rather long for an answer to her question. She was about to repeat it when the Hungarian began to answer.

"It is painful for me to tell you the truth, Miss," he said. "Women so eagerly close the shrine of their hearts, and even once they have permitted us entry to this holy temple, their pride drives them to expel us in the next moment with the scourge of egoism. So we must not and cannot become anything other than devils—"

"Count, Count! Do not speak so presumptuously—think of Him who holds sway above us and hears such speech only with pain."

Silence on both sides. The moonlight greedily hovered about the spine of the man who leaned over the back of the bench, often springing to Dudley's profile so that she moved first one way, then another. Her right hand lay on the back of the bench, under the Hungarian's face.

Silence on both sides—until Dudley drew back her hand with an anxious cry. "But my God, Count, you are weeping?" she gasped, looking into the Hungarian's face with confusion.

Tears had fallen on Dudley's hand; that was why she'd drawn it back so quickly.

Was the Hungarian really weeping? And was he, this person, weeping the first tears in his life?

The author is now poised before a dreadful abyss. One more stroke of the pen and he would depict an angel and a devil coupled in the most infamous act of nature that had ever occurred in such a place.

Outside, in front of the garden, Hiram and Cleveland the peddler turned around, with their backs to the picket fence.

"Fortunately, she will die of yellow fever," the first said.

Peddler Cleveland folded his arms and shuddered: "Do whatever you want with the fellow. I will have nothing to do with him . . . he would be capable—"

"Go with me into the salon when the company leaves the garden—I have to have you with me," Hiram declared, in a tone that unnerved the peddler.

"Why should I go with you, since he will escape us anyway, as you said yourself?"

"Good, then you will be one of the first the plague takes away."

"Sir, I am beginning to be most afraid of you—"

"You can only save your life by coming along. Your appearance in Lady Evans-Stuart's salon is necessary to create a scene that will liberate two beautiful women from the distresses of their hearts."

The peddler shook his head pensively, but he promised to obey.

• • •

Why did the widespread boughs of the Weymouth pine not fall down on him? Why did the locust not put out his eyes with its great, sharp thorn as he left the garden? Could nature observe such a crime and leave it unpunished even for a moment? And you flowers, you roses and magnolias, have you lost all modesty, so that you did not even close your buds when he passed by you? And you armored knight of the flora of Louisiana, the hard-riding cactus—why did you not drive your sharp spears into his brain when you saw him approach? In the old Greek times, the sight of such a crime would have raised up a fury in each leaf, and they would have flogged the murderer; Zeus would have sent his thunder and lightning, or he would have bonded the criminal to a gravestone and sent scornful birds to gnaw at his liver—and Flora? She would have poured out hot tears and ordered all her children to put on mourning for the fallen lily Dudley. But such things do not happen anymore. The modern Jupiter has grown powerless, and Flora has lost all modesty. A remarkable time, this!

But stop—the moon, the moon! What have you and Hiram arranged?

We will learn that later.

In Lady Evans-Stuart's grand salon, they had finally returned to a more subdued mood after considerable confusion. Dudley, who was reported to have suddenly fainted at the Hungarian's side during her stroll, was taken to her bed and left there with Constanze and Gertrude, neither of whom wished to part from their friend. The prince of Württemberg had climbed into his phaeton without a word—probably in order to make a personal visit to his physician. At least the company in the salon could not explain his sudden disappearance in any other way. The old Scotswoman, who was usually extremely concerned about her child's welfare, had resumed her duties to her guests as soon as she knew Dudley was in the care of Constanze and Gertrude. She believed that Dudley's condition was simply a matter of a light, harmless fainting spell, the kind that girls of such sensibility often experience at that age. Despite that, she also sustained herself with the thought that the prince had departed so quickly only in order to return with a physician. Besides, the party was nearing its end anyway. The black domestics moved busily in and out, presenting the last dessert on heavy silver plates. Some of them stood behind the chairs and on both sides of the sofas in order to ward off mosquitos with large fans, as the intense glare of three gaslights drew them in from the garden by the thousands. Mosquitos should never be lacking at a party, for they have the good quality of keeping things going in a lively and entertaining manner, even when the conversation stalls.

The company had taken its earlier places. Only those seats occupied by the prince and the three maidens were vacant. So the Hungarian won a place next to Frida. He appeared so placid and cool that even the old Scotswoman began to complain.

"You men are as unfathomable as the depths of the ocean," she said, turning to him. "One would believe, Count, that you were the most indolent man in the world."

"You did me an injustice, Madame, if you ever harbored any doubt about that. I feel myself losing interest more from day to day, and I do better in the company of cretins than in that of spirited persons, in which I now find myself." He put on his black gloves as he spoke, acting out his intention by his manner. "It's late, shall we go?"

"You speak strangely, Count, so strangely that I scarcely know whether to be candid with you."

A Negro entered and announced that two gentlemen where in the waiting room, pressing Madame for permission to enter the salon.

"This is a very unusual time to make visits," Lady Evans-Stuart said, turning to her guests. Then she asked the Negro who the guests were.

"They have not mentioned their names, Madame," was the reply.

"Quite mysterious," Captain Marcy remarked.

"A fool of a Negro," the baroness de Saint Marie softly said to her niece, Claudine, "the fellow announces visitors and doesn't even ask their names."

Countess Jenny turned to Captain Marcy.

"You shall see, Captain, it is none other than the prince with a physician—he loves jokes of that sort."

Lady Evans-Stuart sent the Negro back to ask after the names of the two gentlemen. He returned in a moment and announced: *"Uriah Hiram* and *Sam Cleveland."*

The old Scotswoman shook her head and said in a drawl, "Uriah Hiram and Sam Cleveland? Utterly unknown to me."

"That is certainly the Hiram with the *Mantis religiosa,*" Claudine de Lesuire remarked.

"Don't ask for trouble, baroness," Captain Marcy remarked in a joking manner, "who knows, who knows?"

Lady Evans-Stuart smiled over this observation, but she was still unpleasantly moved by the similarity of the visitor's name to that of the man who had provided so much material for conversation. The same feeling crept up on both the baroness de Saint Marie and Countess Jenny.

Everything passed by Frida unheard. A mute madness that the guests had taken as deep mourning had sent her spirit into other regions for the last two hours.

Either the Hungarian had not been paying attention when the Negro spoke Cleveland's name or the Negro had spoken unclearly; otherwise, one would have expected to see some change, even slight, on his face at the mention of the name. Yet he only mockingly observed: "It is really too bad that his Royal Majesty is not here, he could turn this Uriah Hiram into Hiram the Cagliostro for our entertainment."

"Should we have the mysterious guests enter?" the Scotswoman turned to the guests, and then, turning specifically to the captain, she asked him: "What do you think of this, Captain Marcy?"

"I believe we could risk it," he declared with a smile. "We can hope that the mystery might resolve itself into a joyous surprise."

"Silly nonsense from this Yankee," the Hungarian mumbled to himself, "disgusting formalism!"

The two gentlemen may enter!" Lady Evans-Stuart commanded the Negro.

He left the salon.

Even before the Negro brought his mistress's approval, Hiram said to Cleveland the peddler: "If they deny me entrance, we will go in without permission. Otherwise, remain here until I call for you."

"I am curious how everything will come out. You have brought me into a dubious situation, so I hope that you will try to make it good again," the peddler responded, not yet clear whether he should hold Hiram to be an ordinary necromancer or a being gifted with supernatural powers. He would have been happiest if the mysterious man had left the old Scotswoman's house with him at once, for the mere thought that he was approaching the Hungarian horrified him. Since Hiram had allowed him to see the dreadful scene in the garden under the Weymouth's pine, he had been immeasurably frightened of his attacker, whom he would have been just as happy to let off unpunished. When the Negro brought Lady Evans-Stuart's answer, Hiram reminded the amazed and distressed peddler that he was not to appear until called.

When the Negro saw Hiram depart the waiting room alone, he said to the peddler: "Milady wishes to speak with both gentlemen."

"I know," the peddler replied as he settled in a rocking chair.

The Negro, to whom this conduct seemed strange, and whose suspicions had already been raised by the doubts openly expressed in the salon, left the waiting room but did not let the gentleman in the rocking chair out of his sight for a moment, observing him from the vantage point of his adjoining servant closet.

When Hiram entered the grand salon, everyone rose, with the exception of the Hungarian, who lay more than he sat in his armchair, in a noble manner, though even he made a half-bow from his seat.

That was how imposing the stranger was.

Lady Evans-Stuart left her place on the sofa and approached him, greeting him with an invitation to be seated.

"My name is Uriah Hiram, Madame."

"And what do you want?"

At this she seated herself on the sofa once more, next to her the new arrival. He had seated himself in the place the prince of Württemberg had been.

"I have taken the liberty—"

"Quite well, sir—"

"—upon my visit to the famed city of New Orleans, to visit the residence of Lady Evans, from the famous House of Stuart—"

"Quite flattering, sir," the old Scotswoman interrupted, raising her head a bit higher.

The Hungarian's eyes buzzed like two large lightning bugs about the gigantic, gaunt figure of the new arrival. They soon fell upon Hiram's pale, powerful forehead, and they appeared to measure his entire figure from that base, soon whirring though his bleached hair, now gaping into his eyes.

We want to interpret this play of lightning bugs as quickly as possible.

As soon as Hiram had appeared, the Hungarian's brain became so distressed that it had to surrender. Although, as we know, Hiram wore neither his green glasses nor his long French colonist's mantle, the sharp eyes of the Hungarian could still recognize the man who had so overwhelmed him at dominos in that café on Chartres Street and revealed to him in his own study the worthlessness of the treasure of the mill. What the Hungarian was deciding, what he was going to do in response to this uncanny visit—we will leave that to the devilish laugh that his brain now vomited forth.

"But this is only one," Claudine said to her aunt in a barely audible voice. "Two were announced." That was also what the baroness de Saint Marie recalled.

"—I wished to see for myself the residence of Lady Evans, from the famed House of Stuart, and on this occasion to ask the permission to see Lady Evans-Stuart with my own eyes," the old man continued, allowing the manner of a monseigneur to emerge clearly as he spoke.

The old Scotswoman responded.

"You are certainly not of this country, sir. Your manners as well as your entire attire remind us of portraits of the old Knights of Malta, truly preserved for us by the brush of a Venetian artist."

Lady Evans-Stuart, struck by Hiram's grand fineness, did not want to lag behind him in conduct, and in order to determine Hiram's estate and ancestry without asking him directly, she had hit on the comparison with portraits of the Maltese.

Hiram understood this sign quite well.

"There were times," he said, "when I much resembled a Maltese. Once the Cross of Calatrava glistened on my left breast—"

An unspeakable emotion took control of the old Scotswoman with these words of Hiram. Who knows how, but she had to think in all earnestness of the Hiram who had been such a lively topic of conversation not long ago. The captain thought so at once. The Hungarian thought only that *his* man was here. The notion that this might be the same Hiram Cagliostro did not occur to him.

"A knight of the Order of Calatrava!" the old Scotswoman cried out in marvel. "The Cross of the Order of Calatrava has been buried for a good hundred years."

"Almost a hundred years," Hiram responded. "When Louisiana came to the crown of Spain in 1763, one knight of Calatrava sailed to New Orleans to escape persecution in his homeland. He was also the last of his order."

"And his name?" Lady Evans-Stuart asked.

"Uriah Hiram," the mysterious old man declaimed with a firm voice. "I was then about one hundred sixty years old."

"But sir—I do not know—but excuse me, I do not doubt the rightness of your statement—but how is it possible?" Lady Evans-Stuart asked in great confusion, for she now believed that the Hiram of the *Mantis religiosa* was before her. A nameless dread tightened in her chest.

The brain of the Hungarian convulsed once more. The captain ran his hand into his uniform, reaching for his heart. As decisive, enterprising, and unshakable as this soldier was, he still felt himself cornered. The others, except for Frida, simply marveled at the old man's words.

"He was one hundred sixty years old in 1763?" the baroness de Saint Marie said as she calculated to herself. Jenny did the same, staring at the old man's face.

Claudine de Lesuire was afraid.

"Lady Stuart," Hiram continued, "I beg your pardon, but you provoked my statement yourself by seeking to learn something more about my estate and ancestry."

"Sir, as you will," the lady addressed responded in confusion.

"The very cause that drove me from Spain also compelled me to flee New Orleans—"

No lip moved, but the eyes of those present spoke all the more.

"The Inquisition of those days would have condemned me to death—but fortunately I understood the art of making myself invisible, so that I could reach the place of my birth, the source of the Red River, with safety."

Captain Marcy's whole face turned pale as a corpse. The old Scotswoman also lost her color and appeared to have lost all her presence of mind—as had the baroness de Saint Marie, Claudine de Lesuire and the Countess Jenny. Only the Hungarian suddenly became utterly different—which is to say he came alive.

His brain had ceased to turn inward and suddenly recovered totally. It purged itself through the following logical process: the gray beast said that he'd made himself invisible—such an assertion seems to any reasonable person to be a grandiose trick; whoever committed such a trick was obviously a charlatan, but charlatans are liars; *ergo,* I have nothing to fear from this gray beast.

The Hungarian's conclusion was entirely correct in its own right. He would have had nothing to fear from a liar; but for him there was the dilemma of whether this conclusion could be applied to Hiram.

We know that Hiram had spoken the naked truth when he asserted that he knew the art of making himself invisible to the Inquisition. The document we have already quoted makes that sufficiently clear.

Lady Evans-Stuart and Captain Marcy knew only too well that the facts were precisely as Hiram had presented them.

"But . . . but sir—why did they bring you before the Inquisition at that time?" Lady Evans-Stuart asked with a shaking voice, simply because she realized she had to say something.

"Because I was seen as a malignant sorcerer," Hiram responded abruptly.

"That is impossible," the old Scotswoman responded mechanically.

"Why not?" the Hungarian interjected with the most superficial nonchalance. Then he cheekily said, while staring rudely at Hiram, "*We* would certainly not take it to court if you would make a little presentation of your magical arts—only naturally there should be nothing malignant about it," he said in a mocking tone.

Hiram did not look at him but rather he said to Lady Evans-Stuart: "Madame, if you would permit me to close the festivities of the day with some interesting presentations—"

"Presentations? What sort of presentations?" Lady Evans-Stuart responded.

"Projections—copies, tableaux, polychromes, whatever you call them."

"The fellow really is a charlatan," the Hungarian thought to himself. "To devil with it, it must be that this charlatan is not the gray beast that has already thwarted me several times before—but I cannot deny a certain resemblance. A blunder, to devil with it, Lajos, you've been seeing ghosts again."

Even Captain Marcy was no longer as perplexed. "All of it is humbug!" he thought. "Our spirits were already agitated before he appeared—no wonder that such silly things were put into our heads. If we had not talked all afternoon about such mad nonsense, none of us would have been ready to see anything uncanny here—and that old man at the mouth of Cache Creek was just a spook of my imagination, conjured up by the tales of those two young people. As clear a head as mine, and me, the best mathematician in the United States Corps of Engineers, a hardened hunter of the purest mettle that I am—no, no, it is upsetting that they can dupe me so easily." These were the captain's thoughts.

Hiram had risen from his place on the sofa.

"Sir," the old Scotswoman said quietly, "one of our esteemed guests has stepped away for a moment—please be so good as to delay your presentation until he returns." Lady Evans-Stuart had in fact nodded her approval without really wanting to do so when Hiram had asked her permission to make a presentation.

"You mean the prince of Württemberg?" Hiram asked with emphasis.

"Yes," the old Scotswoman responded with amazement.

"He shall certainly not return," Hiram continued. "I know that it was his intention to visit a physician."

It is not nice to say it, but an author must be loyal to truth—everyone dropped their jaws because Hiram knew of the prince and his intentions.

There was a painful pause. Then the Hungarian abruptly rose and spoke, turning toward the place where the old Scotswoman was seated.

"Madame, would you find it improper if I ask you to step outside for a moment with me?"

At any other time than the present, Lady Evans-Stuart would have upbraided the Hungarian for such coarseness. But now she was happy to hear this direct request.

"Absolutely not," she responded, rising from the sofa. The Hungarian went with her to one of the large glass doors that led to the veranda.

"Something exceedingly opportune, Madame," and he made a movement with his hand toward the veranda.

The Scotswoman mechanically went where he directed. Both of them stood outside. The Hungarian leaned over the iron railing, as did the Scotswoman. The Hungarian brought his face quite close to hers and whispered: "Madame, we must speak very quietly."

"Yes," the Scotswoman said; she was so confused by what had happened that she believed she had to submit to everything and do everything the count demanded of her.

"Everything is proceeding quite naturally, Madame—let the fellow do his magic tricks, and then permit me to throw him out of the house—"

"Count, I beg your pardon, don't do that—one cannot know—"

"One can know perfectly well, Madame—but listen to what I really wanted to tell you: the prince of Württemberg and the captain are real cads—"

"I beg your pardon—"

"Let me speak, Madame, and listen to what I know for certain; the prince and the captain have sent this person to us—"

"Great God, how did you come to such a notion, Count," the Scotswoman interrupted the Hungarian with a shocked manner.

"You are not speaking quietly enough, Madame."

"Yes—yes indeed, count!"

"Well, then listen: the fact that the captain steered discussion this afternoon to his adventurous expedition as well as to someone called Hiram had been worked out in advanced between himself and the prince. They had won over this charlatan ahead of time—do you understand me?"

"Yes, yes, I believe."

"He was to appear suddenly this evening at this command and announce himself by the name of Hiram—well, now do you understand me, Madame?"

"In order to frighten us all?"

"Naturally."

"I can hardly believe that the prince would stoop to such a prank in my house—"

"Why not? Royal Highnesses are no better than other people. First the two of them heated our imaginations with their magic stories, and now they have him appear—that's all!"

Although the Scotswoman was upset about this supposed hoax by the prince and the captain, her face lightened at the thought that Hiram was only a made-up charlatan who had been sent by the prince to scare the company.

"Then it would be no marvel that he knew I expected the prince's return." After some thought she added, "But how did he know the prince was visiting a physician?"

"That is one of this spook's tricks of the trade, Madame—let's calmly await the unfolding of matters, but let's not let on. When we return to the salon, we must appear as if we are really afraid."

"I marvel at your penetration, count," Lady Evans-Stuart said, and she was about to cross the threshold of the glass door when she grasped his arm and pulled him back out on the veranda.

"Something further, Count, before we leave this place," the old Scotswoman whispered.

"Well, what is it?" the Hungarian asked in a quiet but incurious tone.

"Two persons were announced and only one person has appeared—what does that mean, Count, what do *you* think?"

The Hungarian thought a moment, then he asked: "Two? Yes, you're right, I believe I recall that the Negro called out two names—what was the second?"

"Sam—Sam—no, I have really forgotten the name . . ."

"The name is of no importance, Madame—don't torment your memory over it—but I believe this second person will really be the prince."

"Yes, that could be," Lady Evans-Stuart agreed enthusiastically. "Perhaps he will come creeping out of some corner dressed as a ghost in order to cause more fright—no, no, that is just one of the prince's bad jokes. I am only concerned about my dear guests—a sudden fright has often imperiled lives that were otherwise orderly and peaceful."

"Leave it be, Madame, I shall intervene at the proper moment."

"It would be a great relief to me to be able to rely on your discernment and presence of mind."

"Rest assured, Madame!" the Hungarian declared with utter confidence.

Lady Evans-Stuart, who in her utter confusion had not thought to give a word of excuse to Hiram before she had stepped out of the salon with the Hungarian, was now friendliness and courtesy itself when she returned. Naturally this was nothing like petty-bourgeois friendliness and courtesy.

The Hungarian threw himself into his armchair, and if he had been any closer to the table he could actually have put his legs up on it. He even seemed to be considering this, as he stretched out his legs to measure the distance. Anyone could imagine what would have been said, or rather not said but thought, if he had actually carried out this maneuver.

Hiram, who had seated himself on the sofa after the Scotswoman had left the salon, received Lady Evans-Stuart's apologies with short but fine phrases.

Everyone was quite surprised with the Scotswoman's conduct, which had earlier been so confused. It is obvious that everyone thought: "What sort of secret do Count Lajos and Lady Evans-Stuart have?"

Lady Evans-Stuart looked at her watch, small but rich with rubies and pink diamonds, and said to Hiram: "It is five minutes to ten—his Royal Highness shall probably not return. Sir, your generous offer—we all will listen to your presentation with the greatest interest."

These words did not appear to make a good impression on those present, according to the long faces. They would have preferred to hear Lady Evans-Stuart tell the old man in an elegant fashion that he was superfluous.

"I could marry the woman—she makes her points *magnifique,*" the Hungarian said to himself. Then he leaned toward Frida and said softly to her: "Don't say a word, my dear child—as quiet as possible when important things happen. Tell me, how do you like the knight of Calatrava?"

"Lajos, that was not very fine of you—where did you put Lajos if this isn't you?" Frida spoke these words quite clearly. If all the thoughts of those present had not been concentrated on Hiram, her statement would certainly have astonished everyone. As it was, only the Hungarian heard them.

"What are you saying, child?" he said, "The Knight of Calatrava must have infected you—silly talk, what does it mean?"

Frida's conduct certainly would have continued to concern Lajos if his attention had not suddenly been drawn by a marvelous phenomenon.

Long, narrow strips of mist were issuing from Hiram's hands, which he had closed in fists. These strips floated in the direction of the salon door, whose wings had been pulled back, permitting a view of the outside. Now the mist hung before the opening, literally forming a white wall. At the same instant the most pleasant fragrance wafted through the entire salon.

There was a universal "Ah!" of astonishment from the guests. Then there was the deepest silence for a few moments, followed by the most varied expressions of surprise and anxiety. All the lights had been suddenly extinguished, and they sat in the light of the moon, weakened by the drawn window curtains. If there had been no moon, no one could have recognized another, for the shimmering white wall of mist retained its own light and radiated none. It was necessary to produce some sort of light if one wished to operate a camera obscura. Hiram drew just such a device, absurdly small, from his vest pocket and placed it in front of the white, shimmering cloud wall.

If those present had been astounded by the splendid manipulation of mist, particularly by the way the mist had fixed into a flat white wall in the salon doorway—even Lady Evans-Stuart and the Hungarian were not immune despite their conversation on the veranda—now that they recognized the thing the uncanny magician drew out to be a projector, some of the company did their best to suppress a smile.

"I know that thing," Claudine de Lesuire whispered to her aunt, "as a child we often played with it, only ours was bigger than his."

The baroness de Saint Marie agreed, but she still did not understand the strange trick with the mists and the unexpected dousing of all the lights in the house.

The Hungarian, who now sat beside Lady Evans-Stuart on the sofa, said after drawing near to her: "Well, didn't I tell you? A perfectly ordinary charlatan—a child's game with a projector, whatever the old gray fool can think of. The fellow acts as if no one has ever seen one—I would love to throw him out of the house right now."

"That's all well and good, Count," the old Scotswoman hissed, "but the clouds, this remarkable, almost narcotic aroma—the extinction of the lights, so suddenly and without anyone approaching them?"

"That's nothing, Madame. The aroma, these strips of mist—it's nothing but incense. I have seen it done by such mountebanks, often much better. The sudden extinction of the lights? Pah! We could do that, too, if we made preparations to give people a scare."

"I am ready!" Hiram interrupted the whispered, hidden mockery. "Lady Evans-Stuart, you have permitted me to close the celebration this evening in a proper fashion, with the presentation of a number of images that my art is capable of producing?"

"Yes, yes indeed, sir!" the old Scotswoman replied, but with less certainty than she thought she could muster.

"Promise me, Madame, and all who are here, to watch my presentation without the slightest interruption, in case—"

"Sir, whoever you might be," the Hungarian suddenly rose, "that is impertinent language! It should be enough for you that our worthy hostess has consented to show us your black magic show, which every child can see through—whether we interrupt you or not is not your concern."

"Count, calm down, I beg you, leave off—" the old Scotswoman said, as if she expected a nasty conflict. But Hiram did not appear concerned about the Hungarian's words and continued in his dramatic, but not routinely dramatic, tone.

"The total number of images I will show on that wall is a mere five, and they are gathered in my portfolio under the rubric, *Mysteries of New Orleans.*"

First Image

The Confederates of the Atchafalaya Bank

(Hiram inserted the first slide.)

Making a mockery of Newton's *De quadratura curvarum,* the image that flashed on the white wall was an elongated rectangle, a stone colossus of which the audience could perceive nothing at first. Gradually, however, they saw that it was undergoing a metamorphosis—it moved, but what it was becoming was not yet clear. Was it becoming a mausoleum, a pyramid, or a fantastic sculpture? It could well be the last of these, for the straight lines turned into snakes, the flat sides generated curves that clashed with one another like ambitious gladiators. Then the squared forehead of this colossus sprouted a gable, the curves reconciled and united—columns grew from it, the shafts obtained heads, feet—a portico was complete. But it did not remain so for long. The columns moved, seeming to experience a new metamorphosis. They took on life, warm life—had Deucalion been reborn, or did Prometheus risk being punished a second time? These columns are people—not blond or red-haired, not Teutons, not Anglo-Saxons, not Romans, not Indians or Malays—they are Ethiopians, blacker than the storm clouds that chase one another around the head of Atlas, more beautiful than the children of Ophir and the Ivory Coast. These columns are men and women. What had been acanthus leaves has become woolly hair, the snails have become nourishing breasts, and the eggs and staves have become male generative organs, the inexhaustible sources of future power and greatness.

This image belongs to the future; the present sees only the Atchafalaya Bank. Not everyone knows of Hiram and his confederates. Only Abigail, Sarah, old Cato, and the two little children; the two women and Cato are good-natured and grateful. They can never forget their benefactor, who freed them and cared for them to the end of their lives—but that is not enough. They lack the holy feeling for revenge, which has never arisen in them. Why should *we alone* be favored? Why had he, the benefactor of their race, sent Diana Robert? She watches over the two little ones, educating them in his sense. That can be seen inside the Atchafalaya Bank. To the eye of a superficial observer, however, the "allies" look like totally ordinary nigger folk—they do not see the gigantic columns with their threatening capitals.

(The company was extremely bored by this first image, since they saw only the picture and not the meaning of the symbol. The Hungarian even made a bad joke about it.)

It was also in the Atchafalaya Bank that we met Sulla for the first time—but this will only be shown now, in the . . .

Second Image

The Hanged Woman, The Hanged Woman's Son, and the Hangman

(Hiram inserted the second slide.)

The emanation theory was overcome by the undulatory theory, for there could be no question here of the propagation of light in waves. It can be seen on the white wall of clouds and also in how the projector functions.

Cagliostro knew how to fix photographic images on golden plates—an innovation that was buried with him. No Daguerre has managed to recreate it. Through the shimmering haze of incense, he could make his creation take on life, and he laughed and cried with them. In the same way, Hiram had adapted the *Mantis religiosa* to modernize this lost process. His images are even more successful and have more brilliant coloration. There stood a wild mob of people, their beastly faces hungering for blood, surrounding an unfortunate pregnant Negro woman to lead her to the slaughter—without reason, only in response to the accusation of a rabid man. He came from the South and had offered himself as hangman. The projector was really doing a wonderful job. At first glance, who could mistake the face of the slave-breeder Ira B* from Louisiana? The Negro woman is nothing more to him than a wild pig, loaded—or pregnant, as they would say with a human being. What an act of heroism, O noble Ira! You can boast of being a hangman without fear and without reproach.

(The company is upset about this image—including the Hungarian, who agrees that it is improper to show such an image to the group. He hesitates, however, and decides to let the presentation take its course.)

Now the unfortunate Negro woman—Victoria of the White Rose—becomes a mother. The child falls into the midst of the mob—the sovereign people are ashamed of themselves. It is a nightmare of lynch mob justice.

(Lady Evans-Stuart wants to command Hiram to leave the salon that instant—but her words die on her lips. Then she closes her eyes and watches no more. Strange, this offensive scene, the dreadful fate of this Negro woman, makes the blood freeze in their veins—they are offended by the magician's limitless perversity, and yet no one moves. Only the Hungarian clenches his fists and swears to himself, "The old gray beast will pay for it.")

The mob, the hangman, and the hanged woman vanish. Alone on the white wall of mist lies the baby Sulla. He grows before their eyes.

(This phenomenon is less shocking to the company—but the Hungarian's eyes light up and the lightning bug game begins anew. His brain convulses several times in a row, as he recognizes Sulla.)

Hello, hello—what is billowing around the Negro Sulla in the black clouds of dust, what dark ink spits around? Are they coming alive again? There! Lady Merlina, pale mestizas, cholas, zambas, pale chinos—Pharis, Elma, Hyderilla!

Poof! Flown away!

Third Image

The Panthress and the Hyena

(Hiram inserted the third slide.)

This is no optical illusion, just the opposite: *vera ars discendi methodum fluxionum et serierum infinitarum.*[8] One, two, three, four, five, six, seven—stop, no more! What point is there to all this counting? It is enough to see that there is a significant number of beds standing on the white cloud wall. In each of them are cats—stretching, hopping, snoring, frolicking over and under.

(The Hungarian now believed Hiram was more than an ordinary charlatan—he saw in him his old persecutor, his gray beast. He recognized the large dormitory of the Hamburg Mill, where once the pale chino zambo chola ruled. He was rather glad that the magician had enough discretion to display cats instead of women. Still, the heads, the faces of these cats? Still, no one in the company had noticed that yet, not even the Hungarian.)

How well the magician does his work! Truly there has never been a finer projector! Through the dormitory door jumps a panthress. On her appearance, the cats act as if they are sleeping. Now the door of the adjoining chamber opens. It is the Negro Sulla again. The panthress slips into the chamber and shuts the door behind her with her paws.

(Each of the company thinks: "What could that mean? What are they doing in the chamber? A female beast and a Negro man?" Only the Hungarian was not confused.)

Poof! Sulla and the panthress are gone. But the many beds, with the cats in them and over them and under them and between them and next to them, these are still visible on the white cloud-wall.

But there! There slinks a hyena through the salon door and into the dormitory.

("That's a hyena! I have seen them many a time in the zoos," say the onlookers—soon they will have more to say on it.)

The hyena turns to present himself and looks at the company face-to-face. The hyena has the Hungarian's head, pale as death, his high-forehead, his long beard.

("That's too much!" Lady Evans-Stuart cries out, "Sir, enough with your pictures!" The others are shouting that, too—only not the Hungarian, who knows what the image intends. When he sees his own pale image on the ugly neck of a hyena, he starts back—he wants to cry out, but he cannot. He wants to raise himself from his armchair, but he cannot, he is exhausted unto death. Are any of you capable of mustering the will to throw the rascal out, who has so offended the count? Why can't the count do it himself? That is what everyone is thinking, and that's how it remains. The *Mantis religiosa* draws its circle ever tighter.)

Away we go again!

Fourth Image

Elective Affinities

(Hiram inserts the fourth slide.)

Now an entirely different world appears. There is no black person to be seen. The place is Algiers—but the image trembles mightily on the white cloud-wall. We have to wait until it comes to rest. Oh how beautiful it is now! This blooming, enchanting garden! And what stands there in the middle, so secretively placed behind the oleanders, magnolias, orange trees, and china trees? It is the lovable cottage! The most wonderful of all the houses in Algiers. And now, out of the cottage steps a slender blond satyr, with locks of gold and eyes of blue. Beautiful as a dawning day—only a little delicate—and as naked and alabaster-white as his stepbrother Apollo.

("Emil, my Emil!" cries a voice from the audience, and the owner of this voice rises from her seat, stretching her arms out, trying to lunge at the deceptive white cloud-wall.)

("Holy Virgin!" Lady Evans-Stuart cries out, "what is Countess Jenny doing?")

("Damn'd fakir!" hisses Captain Marcy, "that's what he is, Hiram . . . that's the young man who misled me on the Red River.")

(Jenny had to cringe back before she'd gone halfway, for the light emanating from the cloud-wall almost blinded her. She threw herself in her armchair and whimpered, "My Emil, my poor, dear Emil!")

Emil vanishes into the dark shadows of a tree-lined path, and another man steps out of the cottage and stands in the same place.

("My Albert!" cries the same voice that earlier had mourned for Emil, and its owner wants to rush the white cloud-wall. Halfway there she must cringe back again, owing to the blinding light glowing from the wall. She throws herself back in her armchair and mourns, "My dear, sweet husband!")

(But one should look now at Claudine de Lesuire and the baroness de Saint Marie—they have turned white as nuns and are shaking with rage.)

The cottage, the lovable cottage, is gone, together with the garden, Emil, and Albert.

This time the scenery changes very quickly. It is really requires concentration to follow it. There is hardly time to dip a pen.

Toulouse Street? How apropos! The fat, spongelike man with a guitar under his arm—isn't that the Cocker? As he lives and breathes! Now the scoundrel is gone, but the house he stood before opens up. The same man kneels before a marvelous maiden with shining, blue-black hair and large, splendid, antelope-eyes.

("My Orleana! That awful man! Orleana, Orleana!" Claudine cries out, going half-mad before hiding her head in her old aunt's lap.)

Poof! Away like a feather carried away by a breeze while a mattress is being filled.

Now there is the prince of Württemberg. He looks very concerned as he holds a small child in his arm. "Where is Countess Jenny?" he seems to be saying. And when he glances down at the child, he looks at it in a comic manner, as if to say to the little worm, "Dear child, if no one else knows, then at least you should know who your father *really* is."

The elective affinities are gone!

Fifth and Last Image

Reunion to Follow

(Hiram inserts the fifth and last slide.)

The trampling of horses—a snort as from a mucus-filled nostril, a whinny, in between them a true howl from hell, then the weeping of a person—what is coming? Three minutes have passed and still nothing can be seen on the white cloud-wall. What is the matter with the projector? Is the image to be heard and not seen this time?

Now it comes! The scene that had been heard now takes on color and forms itself. A wasted, dreadful locale—everywhere are horse tails and mucous nostrils. One slips on a patch of mucus, and it splashes like a gobbet of rain on the cavalcade of mad huntsmen.

Here it is! This old stud has an arm in its mouth, the mare a leg. A young foal has ripped off the foot of another leg, throws it in the air and catches it again. Clop, clop, here come two other horses, one carrying two thin thighs and the other hindquarters—then others follow with rump, belly, and heart. Are these parts all from the same human being? That's right, a human being.

But the head—can't we see a head? They part and make way for Lydia Prairiefire! She has the head.

It is the same head that earlier sat on the neck of the hyena, but it no longer has a high forehead and a long beard—there is almost no forehead left, and the skull is as naked as a rat's tail, bloody all over, and, what is most disgusting, there is a gaping scar on the cheek. What? Are there two heads? No, but there are four eyes. The two eyes emerging from the gaping scar are fascinating, since they are weeping. They belong to the peddler Cleveland.

(There is a cry of terror, not even excepting Frida this time, whose merciful madness had earlier spared her from fear. The Hungarian did not scream aloud from terror. He was reaching into his pocket, and once it has become still as death, the muffled sound of a pistol-hammer being cocked is heard.)

"J'ai l'honneur—" and Hiram bowed. The lights of the salon flamed bright again.

"S'il vous plaît, Monsieur Cleveland," Hiram called out from the door, turning to the Hungarian and pointing at the entering peddler.

"Count! *Sam Cleveland from Illinois*!"

...

Dear Jenny's heart didn't hurt any more, nor did the splendid blonde Frida's head, since the former had been split by sharp steel and the latter had been smashed by a pistol bullet.

The morning after Hiram's presentation, the two sisters lay next to each other in one coffin. They had often said in life that they wished it so. Constanze and her little sister Gertrude, who knew of this wish, had laid the two sisters next to each other.

Only Jenny's face lay exposed; that of her sister was thickly covered.

Why must they lie together dead? Had these unhappy women done anything to deserve it?

The lowdown dogs of moralism will rush in and draw conclusions that support their ilk. These hounds, if allowed to run at large, would sniff around the deathbed and howl: "One sinned with her heart, the other with her head—it had to happen!"

But we owe the reader some information about the mysterious events of the previous night.

At almost the same instant the peddler Cleveland entered the salon on Hiram's summons, Constanze and Gertrude (who had been looking after the ailing Dudley) were surprised by a loud report.

"That was a shot, Gertrude," Constanze said, and before she finished her words, she heard a second and a third shot.

Dudley in fact lay in a fever, and she was not returning to consciousness from a swoon, as Lady Evans-Stuart, Constanze, and her little sister believed. But she rose from her bed in terror and cried out.

"Where is the shooting? Are you still there, Constanze, Gertrude?"

"Calm down dear Dudley! We are with you," they responded as if from one mouth. Then they listened.

They heard the black servants calling one another by name, then there was a hasty sound of someone running down the stairs—a loud slamming of doors, a violent opening of them, and then a fourth shot that caused the house to shudder from top to bottom.

The sleeping chamber in which Dudley lay, watched over by Constanze and Gertrude, was located in a wing of the Stuart mansion separated from the attic by three broad passageways containing rooms, and thus it was rather far away from the salon where Hiram had conjured up his images. Despite that, even this part of the mansion shook from the last shot.

Constanze rushed to the door, but she opened it only a little, afraid to step out.

"Don't go out, Constanze," Dudley asked, who worried her friend was leaving.

"What could that have been?" Gertrude mused anxiously, laying her blonde head on Dudley's pillow.

"Is it in our house, Constanze?" Dudley asked, dropping her head back on the pillow.

"You are feverish, dear Dudley," Gertrude declared, placing her naked arm on her friend's glowing cheeks.

"Gertrude, it must be a fever. Where am I? Are you still there?" Dudley cried out suddenly.

"Dudley, my dear Dudley! . . . Constanze, come here, look at Dudley," the dear child begged, "see what a fever she has!"

Across the way, beneath the attic, it was finally silent—silent as death. Constanze closed the door again and, without intending to do it, she secured it with the double bar.

"That must have been someplace else," she said. "Still, I thought I could hear the voices of our own servants."

She now stood in front of Dudley's bed.

"Put your hand here again," Gertrude said to her sister, leading her hand to Dudley's hot forehead.

"My God, Dudley, you have a fever?"

"Mother, Mother—help! help! Count Lajos wept—Mother, look at my hand, how the tears burned. Help me, dear Mother—I cannot remove the tears—oh Mother, it hurts so much. Where did my little seat under the Weymouth pine go? I was always your good child, Mother—why do you reject me now? Mother, the abbé killed me—but no, now he's going away—it is the count!" Dudley raved on this dreadful manner for some time.

"Constanze, run down and get Dudley's mother, I'll stay here until you return," Gertrude ordered her sister.

"Good heavens, she says she is so sick—yes, stay Gertrude—Dudley, should I get Mother?" Constanze leaned over Dudley's feverish face before leaving the bedroom with an inexpressibly pained expression.

But she was no sooner out the door than she returned.

Gertrude jumped up in shock when she saw her.

Constanze was as white as death.

"What's happening, Constanze?" Gertrude asked, her whole body shaking. Meanwhile, Dudley was raving once more, more dreadfully than before.

"I couldn't go to the stairs, Gertrude—how glad I am to be back here."

"But what's the matter, Constanze? Don't frighten me so dreadfully! Constanze, tell me—listen to poor Dudley—get . . . oh leave it, I'll get someone myself—but what is the matter?"

Gertrude asked all this in confusion, and when she tried to go to the door herself, her sister held her back, commanding: "Little sister, don't go out—wait a bit until it's gone—oh stay, stay!"

"What is out there, Constanze? Listen to poor Dudley—she wants her mother!"

"I cannot tell you what it was, Gertrude—when I came to the stairs, it pushed me back—"

Dudley resumed her raving, and in such a terrifying manner that the two girls could not do anything but scream.

Constanze did not release Gertrude from her side, although Gertrude wanted to rush out the door despite her sister's strange report. Instead, they hurried together to the window, which gave a clear view of the side of the garden, and called the names of male and female servants.

A Negro who was rushing from the garden into the adjoining courtyard heard Constanze's call for help from the window.

He paused a moment and looked up.

When Constanze noticed this, she called to him.

"What happened downstairs? Was that dreadful shooting at our place? Tell Semiramis and Hannah to come up—I cannot come down, and Miss Dudley is so sick—"

"There's nobody else here but me—the others are all gone, Miss."

"For heaven's sake, what was going on, Tom? Where is everybody? Where is Lady Evans-Stuart? Tell her she should come up, her child is so sick—"

"There's nobody here, Miss," the Negro repeated, then he sobbed, pointing in the direction of the grand salon. "There are still two in there, but they're dead—"

Constanze and Gertrude rushed from the window, and in a moment of extreme agitation they went through the door without the least bit of fear. There was nothing on the stairs to hold them back. As they rushed along they did not notice the thin, fine strips of mist that followed them down the stairs and then vanished down the long corridor into the garden, following a breeze.

Gertrude and Constanze lost their senses when they entered the salon.

Here, in the same place Hiram had stood with his projector, lay dear Jenny:

> . . . as pale, as thin,
> And as immobile,
> As if she had been an Italian statue of marble
> The image of Diana.

A dagger was stuck in her heart, and her hands covered her dead eyes. Don't ask who plunged the deadly steel into her lovely young breast—do not think it was Hiram when you see her lying so. If anyone should tell you who did it now, you would henceforth brand that person a murderer. It is enough to know that she fell victim to romanticism on the cursed soil of America.

She never saw her Emil again—what purpose would that have served, once she had acted out her deformed love for Emil in Albert's embrace?

Over there, right by the legs of the soft armchair where the Hungarian had sat just a short time before, lay the unhappy Frida. Her heart was untouched, but the gold of her marvelous hair no longer wound about her once so splendid head. Don't think of Count Lajos, or you could easily fall into the error that he is the murderer. It is enough for you to know that she fell victim to her fidelity to her husband. She did not see her Karl again, so he never had a chance to convince her of his innocence—yet what purpose would that have served? For he stood at her child's grave, and thoughts of Lajos's Doppelgänger had driven her out of this world and into the dark alleys of madness.

Aunty Celestine and Frida, you are tied together in your madness, and if you ever encounter one another, join hands and say: "We are happy that we're finally dead."

And if Jenny and Frida ever meet, the one will say: "Look, my dear sister, Frida, that was the culmination of my nature as a Don Juan."

And the other: "Console yourself, my dear Jenny—I was the Faust of our sex."

One has an entirely different view of oneself, once dead.

We will not even attempt to describe the two girls' terror and pain at seeing the two women dead. They heard the following confused and partial narrative from the Negro Tom:

"When the tall old man," the Negro continued in his narrative, after he'd told Constanze and Gertrude about announcing Hiram and Cleveland, "went into the salon, the man who gave his name as Sam Cleveland sat down in the rocking chair in the waiting room. That seemed quite strange to me. It did not seem quite right that the old man did not take him in with him. I thought right away that they were up to something bad. For that reason I hid myself right outside the waiting room and looked in the window, and I did not let him out of my sight—for I thought he was up to no good. Semiramis and Hannah, who had just put the hats and shawls of the ladies in order, snuck in behind me and asked what the man in the rocking chair was doing that I should keep watching him. I told them, 'Just you wait, that man is not sitting in that rocking chair to do nothing, he's certainly going to do something bad.' I have no idea why I said that, but it turned out to be true. In the end it took too much time, since the man did nothing but rock and look often at his watch. Semiramis also said to me that I should go to the salon door and see what the tall old man was doing, and if I heard anything then I could come out and tell her.

"The man in the rocking chair did not see me when I stationed myself, and he had no idea what I was doing. Otherwise he would have said to me, 'What are you doing in there, you damn'd nigger, this ain't even your *jour*—Big Billy, Yellow Abram, Jerry, Neptune, and Nelly have it— damn'd Tom.' He then would have said to me, 'The empty sherbet glasses were carried out long ago—go where your place is.' He would have said that if he were a real massa. 'He is some sort of fool, an Irishman from Virginia,' I thought to myself, 'the kind of person who doesn't know what's in fashion.' Then I went out. There were Big Billy, Yellow Abram, Jerry, Neptune, and Nelly—they told me, 'Damn'd black nigger, that's none of your business up here, see that you stay in your own place.' But Yellow Abram did say to me, 'Just look through the salon door, Tom!' I saw absolutely nothing, just as if I had no eyes at all. 'But the door was open,' Kelly said, 'I pulled the wings back myself, and now it's as if they didn't exist.' Then the door opened again, and I could see again, and right then the tall old man stuck his head out in our direction and cried out, *'S'il vous plaît, Monsieur Cleveland!'*

"Then the man from the rocking chair came running in, so I hid behind

Big Billy out of sheer fright. Then all of us, Big Billy, Yellow Abram, Jerry, Neptune, and Nelly, all ran out into the waiting room. Why? We didn't know ourselves. We hadn't been standing there long when we heard a pistol go off, then another and yet another. Everyone in the salon shrieked, and when we began to go in, another pistol shot went off that we thought was aimed at us.

"And now, while I was looking around, the tall old man came out of the salon, with the man from the rocking chair right after him, and after them came Big Billy, Yellow Abram, Jerry, Neptune, and Nelly, and clouds came along with them that almost blinded me, so I ran into the garden in terror and hid. When I heard nothing more, I snuck out here and looked around. But when I came into the salon, there was nothing but the countesses there—they killed them—that is all I know, Misses."

...

Before us lies a rather large packet of letters that could tell us a great deal about Hiram's night. But some of the contents are too compromising for us to dare publish the information contained. In addition—-and this is the main reason we are withholding them—utter silence has been demanded of us as the price for seeing them. What the Negro Tom said has already been given, and that is really all he knew. We also have heard that Gertrude and Constanze performed the last service of love by placing them on one deathbed, something they had ardently desired in life.

We are allowed to make as much use as we desire of one letter, since no discretion was demanded when it was sent to us. The said letter could not have been written by the prince of Württemberg, although it is the clear intention of the writer to make it appear so. Whatever the case, the letter came at the proper moment, since its content fills an important gap in our mysteries.

> When we stopped before Lady Evans-Stuart's mansion, we were greeted by persons totally unknown to us. When I asked for permission to enter, they looked askance. But when I told them my name, I was immediately welcomed. They told me that Dudley had been the first in the house to be taken away by yellow fever. She never saw her mother again, since Lady Evans-Stuart only returned several days later, after her daughter's death. We could not learn where she had been in the meantime. We only noted in her appearance a great distress that terrified us at times. She had not kept any of her Negroes, nor did she allow any to appear. When she learned of her child's death, she did not show the least agitation. Sometimes it seemed to us as if she knew of it already. Now the opinion is voiced in certain circles

that Lady Evans-Stuart had given freedom to all of her Negroes and then shipped them to Liberia.

Captain Marcy told the most incredible things about his visit at Lady Evans-Stuart's, and if the half is true, then we can truly thank our good fortune not to have been present.

He himself asserts that he escaped with his life only with difficulty, and he declares he has lost all desire ever to return to New Orleans. Despite that, he does dare to prepare himself for a new Red River expedition. It is obvious that the captain can be quite brave when he is not in New Orleans. May he succeed in finding the source of the Red River without coming into conflict with supernatural forces. In any case, New Orleans will lose nothing as a result.

So much for the letter.

...

In the meantime, Constanze and Gertrude crossed over the lake and brought their parents and siblings the dreadful story of Hiram's appearance that night and the unhappy end of Jenny and Frida. The initially joyous reunion of the two dear children soon gave way to shock when they told of what had happened, a shock that led the old count and Melanie to serious musings, while Hugo made rumbling oaths and little Amelie cried and complained. And when Melanie asked about the prince, about Lady Evans-Stuart and Dudley, the two children could say nothing more than: "Dear Mother, poor Dudley is dead—we cannot tell you where the prince of Württemberg and Lady Evans-Stuart are, for we have not seen them. Two days after that dreadful night, completely unknown persons came into Lady Evans-Stuart's mansion and drove us out with harsh words. We thought at once of Count Lajos and tried to cross to Algiers to find him and ask him to come here with us. But we could find neither him nor the cottage. The cottage had burned down, and where the beautiful garden once was there is nothing but charred tree-trunks and branches without leaves or blossoms. The neighbors also said that the little German cook perished in the flames. We can tell you neither where Frida's husband is nor how the fire happened. According to what we learned, the fire must have broken out the same night we stayed in Dudley's bedchamber, when there was so much shooting and opening and slamming of doors.

"In our anxiety, we then went to the Bayou Road to seek the prince of Württemberg in his mansion. But instead of him, an old, tall Negro woman met us and told us right away, without being asked, that we sought the prince of Württemberg in vain there, since he had left New Orleans twenty-four hours before. She told us that her name was Diana Robert and that she had orders to admit no one during the day. At night anyone who wished to enter could do so, since she was then with her master, who was not the prince but someone much more important. And so, dear Mother, we made the way to you alone."

What were the unfortunate parents to make of all of Constanze's and Gertrude's strange talk? Let us build a bridge for understanding: pain has its limits just as much as joy. When either of them exceed the limit established by nature, either death or madness comes. Happy is one whose understanding sits like a practiced rider on a horse, keeping it from crossing the most fearsome barriers. Melanie's understanding was solidly in the saddle. There was no fear of it going too far, but still her pain was great. It raved in the most hidden corners of her fine heart when her children brought the news. But her understanding still posed a question: "Could things really have happened as the children said? And if not? Then the children, my Constanze and Gertrude—say it boldly, with understanding—then my children must be mad!" The children might have lied about something joyful, although they had never lied to their parents. Yet that was always possible—but sorrow? Sorrow, pain, and mourning—nobody can lie about such things. So, so—the children must be crazy if what they described did not really happen. Understanding and healthy logic brought about this reasoning—yet the understanding was wrong, fortunately. Melanie would learn on her arrival in New Orleans that the children did not lie. No, never! She would learn that their dreadful news was true.

In the little frame house in Covington where the count's family lived, everything had long since gone to rest, but the people inside remained awake, weeping and hardly speaking a word.

"Children, lie down and may the Almighty grant you the peaceful sleep you need. Lie down, dear children, and do not dwell on your pain. Constanze, Gertrude, follow them and go to bed! Hugo, do it for love of me. Lie down to sleep and stop your silent brooding. Look, children, Amelie has already gone to sleep.

"Constanze, undress Amelie and take her properly to bed—tell her that Mother and Father are already sleeping—then she will undress without protest.

"So, children, be spirited and orderly—Hugo, follow me and the others will follow. Good night, Constanze—sleep well, Gertrude, there, Amelie, it is good of you, Father is already sleeping—good night, Hugo. Before you lie down, do not forget to close the window, the night is wet and unhealthy.

"So, my dear children, all of you rest, and may the Almighty protect you and give you a quiet, peaceful sleep. Look how prettily Suzie is already sleeping, be quiet and do not wake her up. Good night, good night."

This is what Melanie said to her children before she went to her own bedroom, where the old count sat with sunken head on a sofa made by Hugo and Constanze, smoking his good old pipe.

"The children have finally gone to bed, may they sleep better than they did last night," Melanie said, setting herself beside her husband.

The old count set his pipe on the side table and turned his concerned eyes to his wife.

"Well, what did you get out of Constanze and Gertrude? Is it still the same?"

"My dear Ernst, would I hide anything from you?"

"So you still think the same way, Melanie?"

"Oh, this question is too harsh, since you know what I'll say to you."

"But Melanie—can't you explain it any other way? You are so understanding otherwise. Must it be so?"

"Consider, my dear Ernst, how could it possibly be any other way? I have to be amazed that I ever gave the slightest credence to the story the two children told."

"Melanie, I believe that you are wrong this time. Why couldn't it be as they tell us? I have read remarkable things—"

"You've read them, my dear Ernst—but were they true? Think about it a bit. Lady Evans-Stuart and all her Negroes are supposed to have vanished suddenly in the middle of the night? There were supposed to have been four shots fired in the house? Clouds were supposed to have chased after the Negroes? Jenny and Frida are supposed to have been—oh no, no—the cottage in Algiers is supposed to have burned down in the same night, Frida's husband is not to be found, and the prince himself—how is it possible? How could he have left us so suddenly? And yet, if only it were—oh no, if only half of it were true, I would not believe that my dear children—"

Melanie's words were interrupted by a storm of tears. She leaned on her husband, who began to weep himself.

"Melanie—"

"Ernst, don't weep!"

"Woman of my heart, let me weep—Aunty Celestine's prophecy will be fulfilled: our family will meet its ruin on America's soil. Our destiny is that of the Atreids, and all that is needed is that a Clytemnestra take your place at my side."[9]

"Ernst, I should take this badly. You are Melanie's husband and no

Agamemnon at all. Don't conjure up old shades, and let the son of Atreus rest in his grave."

The two spouses were quiet for a few moments, then the old count began again.

"Do you really believe that about the two children, Melanie?"

Melanie's silence gave the count the correct answer to his question.

"Then it is Celestine's heritage—my God, what have Constanze and Gertrude done to deserve a clouded understanding? Melanie, Melanie! Tell me that it isn't so—I will believe it," the count begged with a voice such as she had never heard. Then he put his arm around his wife's slender body and placed his head on her shoulder.

"How loudly your heart beats, my Melanie—can't you hear mine, too?"

"It hammers out an old, sad story—oh, if you had just been silent about Celestine's heritage!" And then Melanie stood up, no longer the tender mother, no longer the quiet, sorrowing Niobe—her face glowed, her eyes danced wildly in their hollows, she raised her arms and let them sink, and then she let out a heart-rending shriek, a sound that bore articulated words.

"Do you know, Ernst? Do you know now?"

The count leaped up in shock, grasping his wife by the hands and crying: "But Melanie, for God's sake, what is the matter with you? What are you trying to say?"

"Do you know what the prince told us about the abbé? Do you know why Celestine, my dear noble sister, went mad?"

"Because he—because—but what are you trying to say? What is terrifying you so? What?"

"Do you know why Constanze and Gertrude have gone mad? Do you know?"

"But Melanie, they are not mad!"

"The dear children have fallen into the abbé's hands! Oh, now I can explain everything to myself! Ernst, Ernst—we have lost our children forever!"

"But Melanie, how did you arrive at such a dreadful thought? The abbé has been gone for some time, and haven't Constanze and Gertrude written cogent and heartfelt letters? You are confused tonight, Melanie, consider it for a while—your pain is driving you too far. And does it have to be the children? Not they! And what they told us could have happened. Melanie, I am coming to my senses only now, as a result of your saying something like that."

How the dear mother deceived herself! And yet, was it any wonder that she made such a connection? The tale Constanze and Gertrude brought them from New Orleans was so strange and sounded so fictional that even the healthiest understanding would have to draw just such a hostile conclusion.

It was only her hot blood that caused Melanie to draw such a dreadful image, it was only her heart that insisted on Aunty Celestine's old story. This agitation *had to* pass away. She thought, grumbled, rejected, and thought further. And the result of all this dreadful torment was what Melanie concluded: that even if the children had really been conscious, and everything had happened as they said, then they at least remained her children, even though they all must mourn the deaths of Jenny and Frida. Yes, during the night it even went so far that the spouses exchanged such a consolation with great resignation.

"We can expect nothing from the present, but everything from the future. When we get to New Orleans, we shall find out."

And the very next morning, when the entire family sat together, neither of the spouses could believe anymore that Constanze and Gertrude had been so unhappy. Melanie's understanding was solidly in the saddle, and her husband was loyal to its strength.

"When we get to New Orleans, we shall find out." They wanted to stay another week in the little farmhouse to await the prince, who was to come across the lake during this time so long as nothing extraordinary held him back or, if they were to give any credence to the statements of Gertrude and Constanze, he hadn't been harmed by some unknown catastrophe. If the prince came, then they would be concerned; if he did not come, they would be the same. In the first case, they would hear only bad news, and in the second case they would learn what had happened late but firsthand.

During this week, Constanze and Gertrude were the sole concern of the two parents when they could find time to be alone with the girls. In some ways the parents gained a great deal as a result of this concentration. Melanie's obsessive worries weakened, but another thought gained force, a thought just as sad if not so hopeless and dreadful. Constanze and Gertrude remained theirs, but they had lost Jenny and Frida.

What a regrettable decision it was to travel to New Orleans with the entire family! To free themselves from the dreadful uncertainty concerning the news their two children had brought them, it would have been enough to send Hugo alone. How different their fate would have been! Then one could declare what the family did not know, which was that the man with the *Mantis religiosa* held their destiny in his hands. Weren't Melanie and the old count Emil's parents? Weren't Hugo, Constanze, Gertrude, and Amelie Emil's siblings? Emil appeared to have escaped his punishment because he had deposited the cell of the future savior of her race in Lucy's body—but his disobedience, his poor fulfillment of his duty after he and Lucy left the upper chambers of the Atchafalaya Bank—O dreadful fate, for this disobedience his dear parents and his innocent siblings were to be punished!

He had already revenged himself on Jenny, who never saw her Emil again. And on Frida, who had trusted a murderer and arsonist until a few hours before her death—he had not allowed her to guess the man she embraced as her spouse. He, the fabled old man, the man with the *Mantis religiosa,* had sent that rat, the same one her husband had pointed out to deceive the Italian Lombardi, into the lovable cottage, to attack her innocent child. And as for Lajos—what the old man plans for him is no longer far away.

Before we watch the unfortunate family arrive in New Orleans, we will present the reader with some interesting historical notes about the Covington farm. This farm, generally known among the denizens of Covington by the name of *Cockroaches' Farm,* had been leased by the prince for two years to three strange-looking persons before the count's family was brought there. The neighborhood folk wracked their brains trying to discover who these three persons were and what was their support, for they did not appear to make the slightest effort to do anything on the farm they had leased. The farm remained as desolate as it had been the day they occupied it through the two whole years.

The Americans living in the area, particularly those in Covington itself, took a great interest in the residents of the farmhouse, which was not a bad-looking cottage. But no one could discover even the smallest fact about them for the simple reason that no one understood their language. Curious visitors were unable to discover anything. They took Germans, Frenchmen, Englishmen, Spaniards, Italians—in short, every imaginable nationality—out to the farm to serve as interpreters. But none succeeding in understanding these strange persons' language or even in guessing what it was. When the prince of Württemberg came to Covington, which was not an unusual event, he was besieged by hundreds and hundreds of questions, and it even happened that the notorious Pompano gang in Covington threatened to burn down his farm and drive its inhabitants away. The prince always assured them that his tenants themselves had no idea who they were and from whence they came. The prince himself would not have discovered the truth if a compatriot of his—who was over forty—had not tracked the story to its source. Soon after this compatriot's first visit to the mysterious residents of the farm, he declared that they were his own countrymen, which is to say that they were "Schwaben." Since the conceited investigator spoke superb English, he immediately translated the name of his countrymen as "cockroaches,"[10] which caused a dreadful sensation among the residents of Covington, for they had never heard of such a nation. They came to the farm in droves to learn about this newly discovered land and to grant it general admiration. The cockroaches finally tired of these endless visits so much that they suddenly vanished one moonlit night and were never seen again.

The prince of Württemberg laughed off his lost rent with a cheerful smile when a trusted friend in Covington wrote to him in New Orleans to inform him of his tenants' disappearance. Since he had discovered the count's family on Washington Avenue in such poor circumstances, it was fine with him that such unthankful riffraff had abandoned the farm so that he could transfer it to the count's family without upsetting his previous commitments.

After the count's family had settled on the Covington farm, everything quickly took on a different appearance. The sun of Louisiana lays to waste just as rapidly as it enlivens. Normally fruitful land produces a jungle of weedy vines of every sort when cultivators slumber, and what had been swampland once more produces palmettos. Our heroes of the sabre did not fear to apply the plow, and they so blunted it with one round that it had to be sharpened again before a second round. These problems impressed themselves on the new farmers at once, and it became clear that they had to be pioneers all over again. With the help of a few Negroes lent by the prince of Württemberg for their first two months, they were soon far enough to show at least a pretty bit of garden to grow vegetables. This was the first goal of their efforts, since nothing could be done with cereals on a small scale. After visiting the surrounding plantations and seeing their complex systems of production, Hugo even argued for starting a sugar plantation, but he was soon told to be quiet. The old count, Melanie, and even the little Amelie worked in the fields, and they only wished that Constanze and Gertrude could return so their workforce could be doubled. They were pleased when the last Negro, which they had kept as a result of the prince's endless encouragement, could be sent back. Some of their vegetables were sold in Covington, and some of them even reached New Orleans by indirect routes. The Cockroaches' Farm not only produced vegetables but also hens, turkeys, and Persian ducks. Hugo also bought a few guinea hens in Covington, but these were more to occupy little Amelie, who could deal with them very well.

The round of activities could be summarized as follows: Out of bed punctually at five, summer and winter, then rustic washing and dressing until quarter after five. The old count would put up Amelie's hair and dress her in a fresh shirt (a new one every day in the summer, every other day in the winter), put on her shoes, and, if there were no laces, he would get a new lace or even take one from his own shoes. During this time, Melanie would set a fire and Hugo would ground coffee. The Yankee clock on the mantel would sound 5:30. Little Amelie would cry out, "Breakfast ready!" And so they ate breakfast. At a quarter to six, the old count would feed the hens, Melanie would milk the cow, Amelie would milk the goats, and Hugo would bring in the gardening tools. With six o'clock, "March! On to work!" This would continue for four hours without a break. Then Hugo would go aside and blow on a cow-horn, which meant lunch—a cold one, of course.

Now Melanie left her work in the garden and began preparing dinner, which was served at two. Three o'clock! Feed the hens and so on, then back to work. At four, Melanie left her work in the garden again and went to the kitchen to fix supper. The Yankee clock struck six. Little Amelie would cry, "Supper ready!"

Hugo then brought the tools under cover and sat down to supper with his parents. At seven o'clock, they would rise from the table. The old count would pull a twig out of a bed of beans or peas and chase the fowl into their nests. If one was missing, which he would know at once since he was in charge of the birds, it is sought until found. If a missing egg-laying fowl could not be not returned, then the old count received only one cup of coffee the next morning instead of two. The count imposed this penalty on himself, and similar penalties were levied on Melanie, Hugo, and Amelie if they failed at their assigned tasks. At 7:30, there was an edifying reading out of the *Southern Cultivator* and *The Soil of the South*. At eight o'clock, free time for entertainment, and so on. By nine o'clock (in winter) and ten o'clock (in summer), the children went to bed.

Father and mother remained up as long as they wished. This is the sole privilege they have preserved for themselves over the children.

This order of work was altered only when Hugo or the count were trading in fowl or vegetables, or when someone was sick or the like.

The Fortunatus-genius of Prince Paul of Württemberg managed to bring considerable change to this monotonous farm life by having a positive influence on the souls of the count's family, bringing irregularity and variation into the rigid schedule of work they had established once and for all. It was about this time that the prince of Württemberg thought it right to cease keeping the whereabouts of Jenny and Frida secret and to make preparations to bring Jenny into the arms of her parents-in-law. For Melanie, this revived the memory of Emil's loss all the more, but she consoled herself that she would soon embrace her recovered daughter-in-law in place of her lost son. They counted the days until Jenny and Frida, escorted by Frida's husband, Count Lajos—whom Melanie was especially interested in meeting—as well as Lady Evans-Stuart and her daughter, Dudley, would cross the lake and witnesses their countryside happiness and quiet satisfaction. For this purpose, the two largest rooms in the farmhouse, which had been used to store fruit, seeds, tools, and the like, were put in order for visitors. Since there were not enough beds for all the guests, Melanie called a family council on a Sunday afternoon, at which her motion that they all surrender their beds to the guests on their arrival was adopted warmly. There was scrubbing and sweeping, sewing and plucking, shoving and pulling, pumping and mixing, quite a sight to see. Even the hens appeared possessed, fulfilling tyrannic measures to assure that the guests did not lack for eggs. In the end the poor hens lost their feathers from all the plucking and tugging, and a good dozen of them refused to lay another egg. The guinea hens, on the other hand, always produced what they were asked to do.

Little Amelie made splendid red silk halters for her gray goats. Yes, she even had the unforgivable idea of locking up the Persian ducks in their own cage so they could not dirty their feet and upset the guests. Hugo taught his little sister at once that locking up the Persian ducks served no purpose, since they had to get themselves dirty if they were to digest anything at all.

Then the longed-for day came at last, when the reunion was to take place. But, adieu—there can be no talk about joy here. For when it appears, it vanishes under horses' hoofs. Yet that doesn't matter, for stupid human beings can always find something to be happy about.

One, two, three days passed, then at last came—the guests? Oh, no—only Constanze and Gertrude with their news about Hiram and that night.

Good night, adieu, dear farmhouse, we'll not see you again. Your residents will not return if they tread the soil of New Orleans, for yellow fever is enticing them thither.

Once they had arrived in New Orleans, the troubled parents confirmed that Constanze and Gertrude had told them the truth about everything, save Hiram's performance that night, whose terrors were beyond their investigation.

"See, Melanie," the count said to his wife on this occasion, "they aren't crazy."

"Thank heaven," the relieved woman responded, "you're right."

Just as the children had said, they found the lovable cottage burned to the ground, the mansion of Lady Evans-Stuart closed up, and no trace of either Count Lajos or the prince of Württemberg. To find the latter, Constanze and Gertrude went with their parents and siblings to Bayou Road. When they arrived at the prince's mansion, they saw the tall old Negress Diana Robert rushing to the barred garden gate. But this time she was not alone, as she had been when Gertrude and Constanze first asked after the prince. She held something living in her thin arms, wrapped in a broad black shawl, which sometimes seemed to grow larger, then smaller. It was impossible to see what it was. As the count's family passed down Bayou Road with empty hands, they encountered a city hearse with not a soul following. Inside were the first victims of yellow fever—foreigners without hearth or home.

"That's not a bad start for yellow fever," a drunk stuttered, almost falling under the wagon's wheels.

In vino veritas.

Here they waited for the omnibus to cross the Bayou Bridge.

The old count and Melanie slowly proceeded on, with Gertrude and Amelie at their sides.

Hugo went to the crossroads with his sister Constanze in order to watch for the omnibus.

"I wish we were already back at our farm," Hugo told his sister, "I am overcome with horror when I think that we will have to spend a night in New Orleans. Besides, yellow fever has broken out, as we have already heard."

Constanze was silent, but she turned an indescribably sad look at her brother. Then a tear stole its way through the darkness of her long lashes.

"You're not weeping, are you, Constanze?" Hugo asked his sister.

"I have good reason to weep, my dear brother."

"We all do, Constanze—"

"Not that, Hugo."

"But why are you weeping, then?"

"I have a premonition, Brother, which I cannot shake. It has pursued me since we left Covington."

"Stop that, Constanze, and quit imagining things—we are unhappy enough. It is entirely unnecessary to torment ourselves with unwholesome premonitions."

"You just said yourself that you shuddered at the thought of spending another night in New Orleans."

"Yes, yes—I did say that, but leave it alone and think about something else."

"Hugo, you'll see that my premonition does not torment me in vain—I felt it before we came to the farm and brought our dreadful news."

"But my dear sister, don't be disturbed if I am a little aggravated at you—you are acting as if we are going to our ruin. What sort of premonition do you have?"

"Hugo, do not be disturbed with me, but you shall see that we are not going to return to our farm—"

"Good, then we'll stay here," Hugo said, acting as if he did not understand his sister.

Repellent laughter interrupted the dear siblings' mournful conversation. When they looked to see where the laughter originated, Hugo said with irritation, "Whatever that tall thing has to laugh about, 'tis as if she were mad."

Diana Robert was standing in front of the fence of the prince's mansion, which could still be seen from the cross street, and she seemed to be reading a placard which caused her to laugh repeatedly.

Then she vanished through the garden gate.

"A moment, Constanze—the omnibus is not coming right away—I will go read that placard and see what that insane person laughed about so much—"

"No, stay here, Brother—what could it be?"

"I'll be right back, Constanze—"

Hugo ran as fast as he could to the appointed place. He read:

DIED

on Friday, the 7th instant, at half past twelve o'clock
of yellow fever:

Mr. Ernest Count of R . . . and his Consort

Mrs. Melanie de Nesebeck

natives of Germany

The members of the family are invited to attend the funeral,
commencing this afternoon, at 3 o'clock, from the

ATCHAFALAYA BANK

opposite to Bank's Arcade, Magazine Street.

. . .

Hugo thought he was dreaming. His right hand pressed convulsively against his forehead, while he held himself up on the garden fence with his left, for he felt quite faint. His eyes searched the ground around him without being able to rise upward. Was this really a dream? Were the demons of his own imagination merely fooling him? Were the words he had just read simply a reflection of his sister's premonition?

Look again, Hugo—get your courage up, perhaps you read it incorrectly!

Hugo dropped his hand from the fence and ran away without lifting his eyes even once.

"An illusion!" he said to himself. But he would easily have recognized an illusion if he had taken the time to go over the death notice again.

Why didn't he do it?

"Why did you stand so long, Brother," Constanze greeted him. "What was on the placard? Brother, you look so disturbed—Hugo, dear Hugo, what's the matter with you?"

"Nothing, Constanze—I'm a little unwell—if only the omnibus would just come."

"I have no idea what's going on, Brother, it has never taken so long—look, Father and Mother will be most impatient—"

The old count, Melanie, Gertrude, and Amelie had just arrived.

"Is Hugo sick?" Melanie asked in a concerned tone, looking at Constanze. Then when she appeared to hesitate, she turned to Hugo.

"Is something wrong, Hugo? You're not getting sick, are you? Tell me, what's wrong?"

Hugo was barraged with similar questions from the old count and his siblings. Hugo said yes—then he said no—then he said he thought it would soon pass.

"Praise God, the omnibus is finally coming!" the little Amelie suddenly said, "Should I run ahead, Mother, and tell the man to stop here?"

"That's not necessary, child," Melanie responded, "the omnibus has to stop here in any case."

The Bayou Bridge omnibus halted at its stopping place longer than usual this time, since it was still awaiting passengers. Then the driver gave up and set out empty.

"Mother, oh how good—there is nobody in it—now we'll all have a good seat. Hugo can put up his feet, since he's not well," little Amelie chattered on, and she was the first at the door, though she had to wait to get in because she could not open the heavy door by herself.

They had hardly gone two blocks when the family's concern about Hugo's distress increased considerably. The ceaseless shaking and jarring of the omnibus caused him such headache that he groaned aloud and expressed the wish to be home at once. The omnibus was also going too slowly, as if the driver had neglected to take care of his mules that day.

Gertrude, who was at Hugo's left, lay her little hand on her brother's forehead and looked with concern into his face. Constanze sat at her brother's right, and she did not release his hands. She brooded over her premonition and thought of the tall Negress's uncanny laughter. The old count had taken little Amelie into his lap. Melanie often turned to Hugo and sent concerned looks at her husband. Little was said, but all the more was thought, considered, and prepared.

So the German Atreids sat until they entered Royal Street. Here the omnibus came across rattling fire engines and a troop of firemen running right across the street in such a mass that it had to stand still for a moment. The delays continued. The mules shied at the loud screaming, pounding, and crowding, and they jumped onto the sidewalk, pulling the wheels of the omnibus to a standstill in the gutter at the side of the road. Melanie, who feared that the mules would run away with the wagon—an unlikely possibility because the present position of the omnibus made for so much resistance—jumped decisively onto the sidewalk and helped the old count dismount. Then she went to the door and literally pulled each of her children off the wagon. Hugo appeared to have forgotten his illness for an instant in the general upset, and he now stood between Constanze and Gertrude, who held his hands.

"Our apartment cannot be very far from here," Melanie remarked as she looked at her children to be sure they were all there.

"I don't know, Melanie," responded the count, who always had trouble orienting himself.

"I know, Mother," little Amelie interjected, "there—the next corner is Orleans Street—we live there, I'm sure!" Amelie was that sure because she had noticed the large shop that displayed so many dolls and other pretty toys.

"Come, children—come, let's hurry," Melanie was saying, as she prepared to pass through a troop of firemen built like athletes, when she hesitated due to a loud "Stop, stop!" This warning came from the puffed lips of an Irish mule-driver, who, owing to his obligations to the owner of the Bayou Bridge Omnibus Line, could not allow his passengers to leave without having paid their fares.

"My God, we forgot to pay the man," Melanie said to her husband as she reached into his vest pocket. The count, quite confused by his forgetfulness, reached into his pocket at the same instant, so that their hands hindered each other. His wallet fell on the ground, and when they leaned down to pick it up, they were crudely shoved away by the crowd. They lost the place where the wallet fell, and the omnibus driver, who had been irritated enough at the outset, now began to curse. The old count, Melanie, and the children were prevented from searching by the press of the crowd, and they were also concerned about losing one another. So it came to pass that, without wishing it, they were pushed from their place and found themselves in front of the fire—and their own apartment.

Amelie saw it and was the first to cry out: "Mother, Father, our place is burning!" There was no chance to get through, since fire hoses and firemen blocked the street. Besides, it would have done no good.

For the few days they were to stay in New Orleans—as they had planned—the family had chosen only a simple boardinghouse, to save money. Fire had broken out there while they were gone, and the other boarders had retrieved their possessions from the voracious fire only at peril of their lives. No one had concerned themselves about the room the count's family occupied. Each saved their own in such a situation, and only thieves were interested in other people's belongings.

But here—look how Melanie is wringing her hands! Listen to her scream! Is it joy or pain that is expressed by this cry? This scream is so extraordinary that everyone who hears it must ask this question.

"Save him, save my Emil!" she called out, and the old count and the children all cried out as well. Even Hugo, who had great difficulty even keeping himself erect, joined in. A young fireman wearing the dark blue uniform of the American No. 2 Company had just emerged from the window, surrounded by flames and holding the large picture in his extended arms, oblivious to the calls from below that he come down from the upper rungs of the ladder. But the warning was in vain. The young fireman was looking only at the picture, and he seemed to mock the flames that stormed around him. If they had asked him, implored him to flee before, now his company swore at their comrade's rashness. Part of the wall on which the ladder propped was already leaning forward. Who wished to mount the ladder to haul the stubborn man down by force? Who still *could* do it?

"Save my Emil—" then suddenly, as Melanie saw the dreadful peril the young man was in, she screamed even louder: "Save yourself!"

A suppressed cry of terror passed through the colorful crowd—the firemen scattered, then regathered around the ruins of the collapsed wall.

The young fireman with the picture lay far beneath it—a glowing heap of stone and snapping flames remained atop him.

Albert's last thoughts were, "My Emil, you were with your Jenny without knowing it."

So Melanie had brought the sole surviving picture of her son from her farm to New Orleans only to lose this, too.

What remained to the count's family but to get back to their farm as quickly as possible? But Hugo's condition did not permit that.

How could they take an expensive apartment if they did not want to make debts? And they needed what little money they had left to take care of the costs of a physician, for Hugo was by now seriously ill. They could tell at once that he had yellow fever. So the old count chose the old, weathered tenement for his family, since they would still be able to pay the small rent even in an emergency.

But we already know *how it turned out.*

Hugo did not tell his parents or his sisters about the baleful death notice. He took that horrid image with him to the grave. This image lay down with him and taunted him in his painful fever, and it closed his eyes for the eternal slumber.

Hugo, the old count, and Suzie were the first to lay down, and they were the first to die.

Their spirits certainly stretched out an arm to their farm in Covington, where they had not been happy but where they had lived comfortably. They wrote, but in vain. Since the prince of Württemberg had vanished in such a mysterious manner, who owned the farm?

The demons resume their dance about the funeral pyre of the Atreids, and we have returned to where we were at the close of the second chapter.

Chapter 4

The Reunion

Recall that, at the instant Lorie let the basin fall, awakening Melanie and Constanze from their fevered sleep, two men quickly entered, one calling to the other, "Close the door, abbé—we are safe here!"

Lorie trembled all over her body when she saw these intruders yelling so noisily. But she was in no condition to say a word to them. She held her head in her two hands as if she feared the fever would break out and set her on fire. She was having one of those dreadful attacks from which even physicians turn away with horror, since they know that it precedes death by a few hours.

"We've reached the right hole, abbé—you can see, there, here—over there! There—don't have such a dumb expression—what is it? Plague! Thunder and lightning, if only the police weren't on our heels."

"Lajos, let's get out of here, I'd rather—"

"You're staying, abbé—I'll crush your Adam's apple—"

"Let me loose, Lajos—you're choking me—"

"So—march on in!"

With these words the Hungarian pushed Abbé Dubreuil into the interior of the tenement, where the corpses of the old count, Hugo, and Suzie lay, and where it was quite dark, since Constanze had put out the light.

And here is an explanation, before we proceed, of how the two came together, since we have not seen the Hungarian since Hiram came that night and we thought Abbé Dubreuil had left town.

On the very night Hiram brought that dreadful tragedy to a conclusion in Lady Evans-Stuart's mansion, the Hungarian rushed hatless, covered with blood from head to toe, down Tchoupitoulas Street to Delord, turning there toward the bank of the Mississippi. It was a marvel that no one stopped him because of his blood-stained face, his disordered hair, his clothing torn in several places, the haste with which he made his way—all of it would have aroused suspicions even in the most indifferent. Indeed, as he went down the wharfs, he noted that he was being followed by two men who doubled their own pace when he hurried up. The Hungarian, growing tired of being chased, suddenly stopped, turning to await his pursuers. They were two privates in the night watch, and he recognized them at once.

"You are too hasty, sirs," he said to them rather rudely. "You are all too conscientious in fulfilling your duties."

The watchmen hardly heard two words before they lowered the billies they had held at the ready. One of them, with full, impertinent red hair and a short, squat stature, extended his hand to the Hungarian and said: "Good times are past, Count—you see that we have to go back to work and chase fellows who look dangerous."

"About the burning of the mill—no question, count, that one of the subordinate clubmen set the fire," remarked the other watchman, a bald, scrawny man who said he was a Creole although every child knew he was a Prussian, that is to say, a German. He was called Tall Jacques in the mill. While the mill was still in operation, he had drawn a lovely salary of five hundred dollars a month from the college of clubmen. In return, he'd been as sharp-eyed as a lynx when it came to guiding the attention of other, more honest watchmen away from the activities of the mill.

"If only I knew where the abbé is hiding," the Hungarian said, "I have heard in various places that he stole money from the bishop and fled on a ship for Rio—that sounds rather improbable, since bishops don't let people steal their money, although the abbé would be bold enough—"

"Count, you don't even know," Tall Jacques declared, still speaking French, "that he's still here?"

"What? That rounder is here? Really? Don't lie to me, Jacques, or I'll arrest you," the Hungarian responded, shifting from a tense to a casual tone.

"To be sure, Count," the redhead confirmed, "he spread the rumor to protect himself from pursuit by the prince of Württemberg."

"Pah, the ass!" the Hungarian cried, "I wouldn't take the effort—he should kill the prince if he knows he is pursuing him. That's a senseless reticence on the abbé's part—he reduces his good reputation through such stupidity," he added ironically. "Still, where is the rounder? He has surely crawled into a hole and is living off his own fat like a marmot."

"He is staying with the Hotoohs," Tall Jacques replied, "he is incredibly upset over the mill being burned down, and since he is always drunk these days he says the dumbest stuff—"

"For example?" asked the Hungarian, who had always been irritated at the abbé's loose lips.

"Oh pah, silly, dumb stuff," Tall Jacques answered, in such an altered tone that the Hungarian knew he was hiding something behind his monosyllabic words.

"What sort of stupidity? Out with it, sirs—I will not take it badly, whatever it is."

Tall Jacques kept his peace, but the redhead answered the Hungarian's question.

"The abbé often says—naturally only when he is drunk—that you, Count, took the treasure of the mill and burned down the whole place. Naturally, when he is drunk, he says perfectly awful things about you."

"That dumb rounder!" the Hungarian declaimed, "if he saw me in this suit he would hesitate to blame such a *coup de main* on me."

"I think so too," Tall Jacques finally spoke. "If you had the treasure of the mill, you would never need to commit a murder again."

"Why do you think that?" the Hungarian calmly asked.

"Count, I was thinking that because you are covered with blood—"

"Damned! Do I appear to be covered with blood? Hell yes—you're right, Jacques—thanks for telling me!" the Hungarian grumbled, for he appeared to have noticed for the first time that he had any blood on him at all.

"Well, farewell, sirs—you may not care for my unappetizing appearance, but tell me, will I be able to get to Canal Street without problem?"

"Yes, certainly," the redhead replied, "everyone along the way knows you, except for one you could silence if you deal with him as you just did with us."

"Mill and garrotte!" the Hungarian called as they parted. That was the password from the old days when the gang had dealt with the watch.

When the Hungarian had departed, the redhead said to Tall Jacques, "He certainly doesn't have the treasure of the mill."

"I believe we should give the count a few dollars more—he would certainly not reject it," Tall Jacques added.

But our pen is pursuing the Hungarian.

He continued right along the riverbank and only made small detours to avoid particular precincts. Numbers 15, 16, and 17 were passed without challenge. At precinct 18 he noticed a man, soon joined by a second, who had stepped down to the riverbank before coming back up. They had seen him approaching rapidly from a long way off, and when he came near one of them went around the precinct to block the suspicious man's way. The Hungarian appeared already to have recognized his own people, for he called out to them openly.

"Mill and garotte!" he called in a lowered tone, rushing past the watch without stopping.

"In such a rush, Count? And so decorated?" the one watchman called to him—but the Hungarian could no longer hear it.

He had already passed precinct 20 with honors.

Then came the precinct about which the redhead and Tall Jacques had warned him.

The Hungarian stood still.

But the watchman did not leave his post, just as they had said. The watchman reached for his weapon in case he needed it.

The Hungarian at first intended to have the watchman come near and then beat him down with his fists—his revolver lay on the blood-smeared carpet of Lady Evans-Stuart's salon. But he suddenly adopted another tactic.

He extended both arms in the air and let loose a dreadful whinny.

The watchman, terrified, turned around and ran as fast as he could, right across the levee into the city.

The watchman would not have run away at an ordinary shout, but he was terrified by the Hungarian's yell. Lajos had learned it from the Hotoohs, who used it as a means of discouraging pursuers; they threw a poisoned knife at the same instant. And this was precisely what had sent the watchman away with the speed of an arrow.

The Hungarian had performed his whinny with great care, and he played his role so well that, as he galloped away, he was the very image of a horse—his long, black hair, which whipped back and forth on his neck, was not that different from a mane. It was just too bad that he had such a problem with Lydia Prairiefire—they would have made a happy couple, such as should appear at least *once* in every novel.

Having arrived at the foot of Canal Street near the Algiers Steam Ferry Landing, the Hungarian halted for a few moments.

It must have been about midnight, if one assumes that Hiram's projector was at work only an hour before and that the tragedy that followed reached its culmination in the next half-hour.

The Hungarian now unbuttoned his trousers and stuffed the flaps of his frock coat into them on both sides. Then he jumped into the flood and beat at the waves with his powerful arms. A practiced swimmer, he did not stamp and push with his feet, which would have tired him out before he reached the Algiers shore. Reaching that goal was no small accomplishment, since the Mississippi is extraordinarily broad at this point; taking into account the diagonal distance, as it must be swum, crossing it would at first seem impossible.

The Hungarian now rushed straightaway to the lovable cottage.

Everything in Algiers appeared dead. The authorities closed the grog shops as early as eight o'clock, since they feared the tumult of rowdies. And when the grog shops are closed, Algiers is as quiet as a cemetery.

Since the two sisters, before leaving for Lady Evans-Stuart's, had ordered the saucy cook to remain up until they returned, she did not risk lying down—although her eyelids had already fallen several times from sheer tiredness. Besides this, she wanted to see the handsome gentleman again; she believed he would return with Lajos and the ladies.

One should recall that Emil had appeared at the lovable cottage the afternoon before Hiram's presentation.

The saucy cook was about to rush out to the garden to watch for her masters. Although the last ferry had run long ago, she thought they might have reserved a boat to take them across. It was about the time Lajos arrived. Urschl raised her masked lantern high and illuminated the Hungarian's face. It was very dark, as the moon had set while the Hungarian was swimming, taking a few favorite little stars with it on its way to bed.

The first thought the saucy cook had on seeing the count soaked to the skin was that the boat had overturned on the crossing and all of them except him had gone to their deaths in the waves. The saucy cook, who had always feared the Hungarian and never dared to direct a word to him unless spoken to, remained entirely quiet, mastering her unspeakable anxiety over the nonappearance of the ladies.

The Hungarian did not appear to be in any sort of a hurry now. He passed down the long garden path with slow, almost hesitant paces.

The saucy cook followed him with the lantern. Her heart beat loudly.

The Hungarian halted in front of the main entry to the cottage.

So did the saucy cook. She thought she should stop—she did not feel she could go ahead of him.

Now the Hungarian went a few steps further.

So did the saucy cook. This was unusual, since she knew that the count no longer had any need of her. He stepped at once into the corridor, where a weak multicolored lamp had been weakly burning the whole night through.

The saucy cook was the last thing on the Hungarian's mind, and he was amazed to see a second shadow beside his on the carpet of the stairway. He quickly turned about, so quickly that the cook jumped and trembled all over her body. The Hungarian's appearance was really hair-raising.

"Dumb troll, roll up in your nest!" he called out in irritation. "I don't need you any more."

"Yes, sir," she said quietly, but she remained standing where she was.

"Didn't you hear? Into your nest!" the Hungarian repeated, looking at the saucy cook.

"Yes, sir!" she said, but she remained where she was.

"Well, what's the matter, what do you want? You're shaking like a leaf," the Hungarian said. He could only guess what was on the cook's mind. Perhaps she wanted to know where the ladies were and whether they would be coming home this evening.

"Lie down in your nest, you don't have anyone more to wait for. Has anyone been here in my absence?"

"Yes, sir."

"So? 'Yes, sir?' Why didn't you tell me right away?"

"Yes, sir!"

The saucy cook was really so confused that she did not know what she was doing.

"Well, hang me, who was here?"

"The young count," the saucy cook whispered.

"What young count?"

"Countess Jenny's young count."

"What sort of dumb nonsense are you chattering?"

"Yes, he was here, Count Emil of Countess Jenny—didn't he come to the party?—I told him that Lady Evans-Stuart—" the saucy cook rolled on without a thought.

One can well imagine that such information piqued the Hungarian's curiosity even more. The saucy cook described everything down to the last hair. Emil's unexpected arrival—the events in Lady Evans-Stuart's mansion—his own situation. Wouldn't it just be better to burn the whole nest down and go to the Hotoohs? This is what he said to himself as he walked upstairs.

In the meantime, the saucy cook had repaired to her chamber next to the kitchen. She pulled a table and chairs in front of the door, crept into bed, and pulled the blankets over her head. Poor woman! She would never see the light of day again.

The first thing the Hungarian did was to wash, shave, and reclothe himself entirely. Then he gathered together all the money available and stuffed it in his pockets. This was no theft, since he knew that Jenny and Frida were no longer alive. Emil would get no more, since the Hungarian had made a solid decision to set the lovable cottage afire. Setting fires had literally become a mania with him, which was easily explained, since he had for some time been the head of one of the most dangerous arsonist gangs. He had a nasty, reprehensible habit of expressing his irritation by setting fires. And he was irritated indeed as he destroyed the lovable cottage by fire.

On the same night he committed this new crime, the Hungarian rowed to New Orleans in the same boat in which Tiberius had often ferried him. He landed far down in the Third Municipality. He did not even tie up his boat when he landed, a sign that he never intended to return to it. Here and there fire bells sounded as he left the riverbank and turned onto the next street. He did not look about. All the more avidly, the fire-reddened heavens looked down on him with coal-black eyes.

In his present clothing, with a cigar in his mouth and a fashionable riding crop in his hand, he looked quite upstanding.

Two watchmen on the next corner asked him what time it was.

The Hungarian drew out his gold cylinder watch with great ceremony and said, "About one-thirty, *messieurs.*" Then he went further and turned onto E∗. One of the watchmen was from the Rhine Palatinate, and he said, "The gentleman is certainly on his way to visit a whore." The other agreed.

The Hungarian suddenly stopped in what is called a common alley without blinds.

"If the abbé is really hiding out with the Hotoohs, as Tall Jacques told me, then I could find refuge with them, too, without a lot of trouble," he grumbled to himself as he crept along the alley. On the right side there was a high wall, and on the left an old, low building, like a warehouse, that had been freshly painted. This building ended roughly in the middle of the alley, where it joined the cross wall.

This part of the wall was called a blinded wall, probably because one was unable to cross it, topped as it was with thousands of pieces of broken glass, and one could not see what was happening on the other side. A door located on the side of the warehouselike building led into two entryways with plain walls and no furniture at all. These entryways also did not have any openings for light, which would have been useless anyway owing to the height of the walls in front of the doors.

The Hungarian had already marveled that he had been able to set foot in the entry without disturbing anyone, and now he was now utterly astounded.

"Strange," he thought to himself, "no one ever entered so freely or undisturbed."

It was utterly dark, so he was unable to see two figures emerging from the western wall of the back entry, remaining half in and half out. They made very little noise, but the Hungarian still heard them. He thought that someone had to be there, for he had always been received. All that was different was that he had not given the first password before entering the passageway.

"We are the yellow and the brown, the women and no fruit!" the Hungarian called out to see if he had heard correctly.

"The Hotoohs protect, the Hotoohs oppress, no women and one fruit!" was the answer, and the Hungarian then heard the expected ball rolling toward him. He bent down and took the ball in his right hand. It drew him forward, and he followed with sure steps until his feet struck the wall from which they had rolled the ball, attached to a thread. He now allowed his riding crop, which he had been carrying between his teeth since he entered the passageway, to fall, and he crept through the entry in the western wall through which the Hotoohs had earlier appeared.

"Whom are you seeking?" one of the two Hotoohs, the one who had rolled the ball at him, asked the Hungarian. They were now at the foot of a narrow stairway leading to the Hotooh chamber.

"I am seeking Abbé Dominique Dubreuil," the Hungarian replied, joining hands with the Hotooh.

"First talk,* then seek," the same man whispered again. It was the whis-

*The language of the Hotoohs is so complex, with such a spectrum of idioms that have distinct meanings, that explaining them would grow to a virtual grammar. Further, the language has the peculiarity that one and the same word can have up to twelve meanings, depending on the tone—now weepy and complaining, now strong, soft, earnest, harsh, etc., decided by the context in each instance. It is virtually impossible to translate every word into another language. So we have translated the Hotooh word *facherin* as "talk." Here the pronunciation must be our guide: the Hotoohs give *facherin* four meanings. It can mean "beat" or "bite," as well as "kiss" and "embrace." The usage, together with the

per of a female animal, called a spark of the god, or spirit, that dwelled in the man's brain.

(Here I apologize to the readers because our pen has cut into the paper and then pressed the cut together so hard that the ink runs down.)

(Ink spots for words. The type for this has never been cast.)

Now the other Hotooh turned to the Hungarian.

"You will not be able to recognize Abbé Dominique Dubreuil when we show him to you."

"How so?" the Hungarian asked as he climbed the stairs with the Hotooh. The other Hotooh crouched below, for he had something else to do.

"Because he has a moustache like you, burned-out clubman," the Hotooh declared, smiling in his fine, mocking manner.

"Is that all?" the Hungarian asked casually. He was talking about the moustache matter. The smile was on account of the "burned-out clubman." He noted that. The redhead and Tall Jacques had spoken the truth when they reported that the abbé said the dumbest things when drunk. What else could the Hotooh be referring to but that he thought the Hungarian had the mill's treasure and had hidden it?

Abbé Dominique Dubreuil really had acquired a formidable moustache, and a beard and sideburns to boot. He was crouching with a horde of Hotooh women when the Hungarian entered the *sanctissimum* with the Hotooh. If the abbé had not coughed, the Hungarian would not have recognized him at first glance. He had so changed in the short time no one had seen him.

This estimable pig had also become quite fat in the meantime, though he had dedicated himself to drink. Other decent persons living among the Hotoohs such as the abbé did would soon have suffered consumption. It is also possible that his once gaunt body was puffed up by dropsy and that he only appeared to be healthy and fat.

The abbé was quite impressed by the unexpected appearance of the former dictator of the Hamburg Mill. He regretted a thousand times that he had cursed him to the Hotoohs so much, but he seemed rather calmed once

---

tone, determines meaning. *Tichel,* which we have translated as "to seek," can also mean "ask" or "wish" just as much as "sleep," "fondle," and "name."

The notorious and unfortunate Alfred Durand, who spent half a year among the Hotoohs and suffered great want in their care, spoke the Hotooh language as well as his native language, which was French. He died because he used the language in the wrong places, however. It was said at the time that he took poison himself as a result of deep melancholy, but it was the Hotoohs who poisoned him and left his corpse on an open street, where it was found early in the morning by a ship's carpenter.

more when he threw Lajos a friendly *"Comment s'en va?"* His peace was disturbed considerably when he heard the Hungarian's decision to remain here permanently. The abbé's anxiety was unnecessary, since the Hungarian did not breathe a word he had heard from Tall Jacques or the redhead, nor did he show that he was upset with Dubreuil. The abbé was also silent about the burning of the mill, since he did not want to conjure up any situation in which his indiscretion might come up. For it remained simply a supposition that the ex-dictator had been the cause of that fateful fire. The Hungarian did not speak of it himself, since it was too touchy. So the two of them remained in continuous check around each other. Once, when the abbé was very drunk—during the reception of a quadroon maiden of fourteen into the Hotooh society—he tried to start talking about the mill (since the Hungarian was so adamant about being silent, the abbé thought his supposition was true), but he quickly let the matter drop. The Hungarian never spoke a word of what had happened on Hiram's night or what had brought him thither. He wanted to howl with the wolves but not take them into his confidence. Only in this way did he believe that he would soon gain control of everything, just as he had done earlier at the mill, particularly with the college of the clubmen. For he had no intention of staying there permanently. He wanted to take over the dictatorship and then use it—to make money. But something else was written in the book of destiny.

We pass over an interval of about ten days.

It was the night we first visited the family suffering from yellow fever in their tenement, and the Hungarian and the abbé had gone out to buy some things for the Hotoohs. No one in the city could recognize the abbé, he was so changed. Besides his great beard, which was enough to make him unrecognizable, he had adopted an artificial hump. He looked exactly like Aesop from the back, not that broken-down, crooked-backed character Dubreuil.

Among other things, they bought a whole set of pill boxes, which the abbé had to stick into his deep pockets. For the Hungarian's pockets were too shallow, he said. The truth was that the Hungarian was just using the abbé as a pack-mule for the expedition.

Soon they were on their way back to the Hotoohs when the Hungarian suddenly remembered that he had forgotten the laudanum. The Hotoohs needed it that very night, so they were compelled to make a small detour.

At the corner of Enghien and Casacalvo Streets, they entered a pharmacy. It was so crowded with persons seeking medicine for fever that they did not have a chance of being served in less than a quarter-hour. To pass the time, the Hungarian read the labels of the tincture bottles on the shelves with an indifferent eye, settling his gaze on only a few of the bottles. The abbé stood on the other side and entertained himself with the roots. But he soon grew tired of that and went to the side where the Hungarian stood. One, two, three persons now left the pharmacy. The pharmacist and his two helpers had their hands full.

"*Tinctura Belladonnæ,*" the Hungarian read half-aloud, then looked at the abbé. "Will it be needed, abbé?"

"For various purposes," the abbé said indifferently.

"Tell me once more, you studied pharmacy, too?"

"That's true," the former first-year student declared.

"Then you could tell me something better than 'for various purposes.'"

"Well, yes—it is used for *erysipelas,*"[11] was the answer.

"Look now, abbé, you don't understand a thing—you are telling me a story."

"Believe it," the abbé responded, "but let's hurry—it will soon be our turn—"

"If I needed belladonna, abbé, do you think he would give it to us?"

"Under no circumstances, even for an equal weight of gold."

"Then we'll take along the whole jar," the Hungarian said decisively. He then turned to the abbé.

"The jar is too high on the shelf. What do you think, abbé? Do you want to climb up and get it?"

"What are you thinking about, Lajos?" the abbé said in shock, but softly and hesitantly, so that even the Hungarian, right next to him, could not hear it clearly.

"Did you understand me, abbé?"

"Lajos, I beg you, avoid a scandal. How could you demand something of me that I would not demand of you, who are so much taller than I—"

"Taller yes, but also larger," the Hungarian interrupted—then, after a short pause, he said: "If you won't do it, abbé, then I'll do it—these people here won't bother me, but take care and follow after me so that no one grabs you, for they have seen us talking."

The abbé mechanically grabbed the Hungarian by his coat as if he wanted to hold him back, and he was about to say, "But the laudanum, Lajos," when the Hungarian climbed up, snatched the belladonna, and rushed out on the street with the whole heavy Pittsburgh jar.

The abbé ran after him. Keeping the Hungarian always in view, he finally was drawing quite close when a part of his hump came off and lodged under his right arm. This restrained him somewhat, while the Hungarian continued to fly, gaining a considerable lead.

"Thieves, robbers, murderers!" then "fire, fire!" people swore, as they screamed and howled after the fleeing men. Then they went on yelling as if the whole city were in peril, "Watch! City rats!"

Such exclamations were raised by people who had no idea what was going on. One cried "Watch!" while a second called "City rat!" and a third cried something quite different, such as "Fire!" and so on.

Members of the watch hate this confused yelling, and with good reason, for they know that such hyperbolic exclamations are often just calls to warn the real fleeing thieves, murderers, or arsonists.

Without this confusion, the Hungarian and the abbé would certainly not have succeeded, despite their swift flight. After the Hungarian had run with his belladonna and the abbé had stormed out of the pharmacy, the cry was raised so successfully that several persons dedicated themselves to the crusade of recovering the poisonous lady. If the watch had already been wearing the crescent moon on their belts, it would have been inexcusable for them not to have caught the thieves. But at that time they did not yet carry those emblems. In these days, it is no longer possible to run away with a *bella donna* unpunished.

Recall that when the physician from the Howard Association left the tenement to get into his carriage, he found a man there who ended a laconic conversation with a blow of his fist to the doctor's forehead before throwing him on the ground. This man was the Hungarian, who had seized the opportunity presented by the empty carriage to enter it and take the reins. One has already heard of the coarse manner in which the Hungarian helped the creeping abbé into the carriage. But the Hungarian was not going to haul his poisonous pharmaceutical mam'sell to the Hotoohs. He drove so fast on rounding a corner that the doctor's carriage hit a lamppost, breaking not one but all four wheels. The harness also broke the horse's jawbone when the carriage suspension collapsed. His coach-driving was at an end.

"Leave the matter be, Lajos," the shaken abbé said, still out of breath. "I believe there is a *Hotooh-Kralle* in the next street—"*

If they had not heard the notorious music of the watch beating away at the very moment the abbé made his suggestion, the Hungarian probably

* *Hotooh-Kralle* (Crahwlla) is a branch operation; the Hotoohs in the Third District have established five, and those in the Second District, one. Fruit is sold there most days. During the summer, a few have tubs filled with icewater that hold bottles or jugs of root beer. They also serve coffee between five and seven in the morning. This takes place in the open, right by the entry to tenements. The branches are closed at sundown.

would have resisted. But now? They could not be sure—they had no friends in the area, and they looked too heated and suspicious. In short, the abbé's suggestion was accepted by the belladonna thief. In the abbé's case it was cowardice that led him to seek asylum—for the Hungarian, it was too monotonous to have another argument, and perhaps he thought the Hotoohs would grow impatient if he remained away too long.

They fled.

Behind them they heard the loud beating of sticks and the snarl of rattles.

Now they splashed through the rainwater and entered—a Hotooh-Kralle? Not at all—they were in the tenement of the count's family.

The abbé had gone the wrong way. They had returned to the same block where they had entered the doctor's carriage.

Was it an accident, or had a higher power driven them here?

And only now, having fled the feverish asylum of the Atreids twice, and after shuffling the deck again and drawing the trump of Hiram's night, and after bringing you through the detour of the Hotoohs and the *bella donna*—only now does the curtain rise on our tragedy, "The Reunion."

• • •

Constanze raised her torso from the bed as the two entered. She recognized the count's voice at once. But she could not understand the words he exchanged with Abbé Dubreuil, since they had used Hotooh language. In the first moment of her surprise she lay her right hand on her glowing forehead as if she were thinking of words or as if she feared that this sudden appearance were only a dream. Then she gathered all her strength and lifted herself up. At the same instant the count also recognized her.

"Countess Constanze!" he cried out, "what does this mean? You here? And what—"

Constanze is moving her lips—only inarticulate sounds issue forth. She throws back her arms, looks at the count, then turns to the face of her mother, who seems half sleeping and half waking. Her movements become ever more violent. It is clear that she would like to be able to speak, to call out—but instead she simply presses her hands to her mouth several times and then expels such a terrifying shriek that the Hungarian takes another step back, Melanie rises up in shock, and the abbé staggers over the threshold of the back room with wobbly knees.

"Mother!" Constanze would like to call out, "that is Count Lajos, that is Frida's husband, who was to come to the farm, and whose acquaintance you were anxious to make—look, Mother, that is Count Lajos, of whom I told you so much, and who was thought to be lost—look, Mother, that is the unhappy father of a child who died such a dreadful death—"

Constanze would have loved to say to the count: "Where did you go on that dreadful night? Why did you not come to visit Gertrude and me? Why didn't you come visit us at the farm? Did you perhaps see the prince, or were you with him? But then, how did you get here? You come too late, Count Lajos—look in there, you'll find Father, Brother, and Little Sister, and then you can look around here. Isn't it true, Count Lajos, that since the last time we met we have become quite unhappy?"

That is probably what Constanze would have said to her mother and to Lajos, had she been able to speak.

Yet the appearance of the Hungarian was too unexpected, too sudden. She remained silent.

The abbé knew with one glance where he was, before the Hungarian even suspected. Hadn't he already seen Melanie in their impoverished dwelling on Washington Avenue, with Constanze as well? Hadn't he seen the latter with Miss Dudley? Trusting his changed appearance, he left the threshold and took his place behind the Hungarian.

Melanie now saw the two of them.

"My Constanze—what is this? Who are these men? Speak, Constanze—what do these men want here?"

The poor, unhappy girl no longer heard her mother's question—she had sunk down on her side of the bed. The throttling angel of fever had decided that it was her time.

The Hungarian and the abbé watched Constanze's dreadful end.

"I'm going out," the abbé said, and he glided through the door—not the one to the street but the one into the rear room where the corpses of the count, Hugo, and Suzie lay. Let us leave him to grope about in the darkness. Perhaps he will touch something cold—and if that is the case, then he will fall to the ground in terror and give up his spirit, for it would be too much of a shock for such a coward.

Melanie, you most unhappy of all mothers, climb back into your bed—you can hardly stay on your feet. Do you really believe the fever has left you because you can rise again? Oh, do not trust this deceptive enemy, who attacks and murders when you least expect it. Look, over there lies dear Lorie—even a few minutes ago she put cooling cloths on your brow. I tell you, unhappy mother, don't trust the fever! Lie down!

Look, Constanze is already dead.

Be careful of your white feet, Melanie. If you step there, they will take on an ugly color. Gertrude and Amelie, too? Just shudder, Melanie. Look—dead too. You will go there soon, too—but Melanie, you are acting as if you were the only living being in your apartment. Now, look, now you are going in to see!

The Hungarian had been thinking to himself as this was going on—he had been thinking a great deal. Who knows what kept him rooted to one place, why he did not flee?

Dead people cannot be looked at for long. It makes the eyes so tired. And you cannot kiss them, either, when they have died *that* way. Melanie wants to get back in her bed, and she no longer thinks of her husband, or of the men she'd asked Constanze about earlier. Then she feels a hand on her bare shoulder, her shoulder so glowing with heat and the hand so bitterly cold. She started, and, as she turned, her lips grazed the scar on the Hungarian's cheek.

This scar! Those eyes! Melanie can only have one thought: she has before her the same man who grabbed the money from her hands during the fire, as she bore Emil's picture in her arms—the originator of all her misery, the murderer of her entire family was before her.

She did not know what she was doing. Instead of removing her lips from the scar, she pressed them down harder and tore at the Hungarian's long hair with both hands. He allowed her to do it. He had already recognized Melanie as that woman even before he'd put his hand on her shoulder. He had guessed that she was also the mother of Constanze and Gertrude and the female head of the count's family he was to visit together with Lady Evans-Stuart and the prince of Württemberg—and it was actually on his lips to tell her who he was—then Melanie pulled him to the floor, and as he pulled himself suddenly away he left much of his hair in her hands.

She never learned that the Hungarian was also Frida's husband. So she never learn that Frida's husband was the thief and arsonist.

The Hungarian then thought of the abbé. He took the light from the mantel and went into the rear room. Since he was not looking at his own feet, he stepped on the abbé. He was dead.

And now the Hungarian closed his eyes for a moment. Without anyone telling him to do it, he walked on his toes out of the back room and put the light, now merely a stump, back in its place.

What was holding him here? It was not as if he had anything further to do.

What was he thinking about now? Did he want to stay here? Now he is going, yes—and now he is staying. He thought to himself, "Outside there are people standing at the door, I can hear their soft speech, occasionally growing somewhat louder."

In came *Uriah Hiram, Sam Cleveland from Illinois, and the young Count Emil.*

Chapter 5

The Journey to the Place of Execution

Those were sad days and horrible nights between 14 July and 27 August. There were few sunny days and an almost continuous dripping from the evening sky. And whenever the sun managed to cut through the filthy clouds, a hail of burning arrows descended on a poor, anxious mankind. The moon did not make things much better when it showed itself once more after several nights. Those who rushed from their oppressive apartments into the open to enjoy its light quickly returned complaining of headache. Yes, many even remarked that more people died on those nights the moon stood in the heavens. The adventurous complex of clouds that was displayed, particularly in the middle of August in the night sky, was no less distressing than the sun and moon. On each occasion, its metamorphoses were always the same. First a massive black cloud would arise from the region where the Mississippi emptied its floods into the Gulf. It remained motionless for several minutes, appearing like a weathered block of stone thrown by some long-dead giant into one of our cypress swamps. Then the inorganic physiognomy of this colossus vanished, as it began flying wider and wider afield, then over our town, where it then came to rest above the Freemasons' Hall.

Then it was impossible to be mistaken. Everyone knew that this apparent colossus of stone was a giant, black cloud. About it were broad circles of unblemished, dark blue night sky, and in the very center sparkled fifteen stars. At the border of this circle of light stretched a fine, dirty mist that hung all the way to the horizon, where it was intermingled with large balls of black cloud. From these flashed lightning, followed by powerful thunderclaps, which made the giant cloud over the Freemasons' Hall tremble. And what image presented itself then? Thousands, hundreds of thousands of black fists sprang out of the giant black cloud, splintering it in the same instant. From out of the dark chaos the white clouds now separated, flying to one side, while the dark portion, from which the black fists had sprung, fled to the other border of the heavens. The fifteen sparkling stars were now situated between the white and the black clouds, which multiplied themselves into hundreds of thousands on each side. Then there was a remarkable spectacle. The black clouds advanced and flew with the speed of the wind at the fifteen stars, pushing at them as if to pry them from the heaven and send them down to earth by the sheer weight of numbers. The white clouds did not appear to tolerate this. They descended on the blacks, precipitating a terrific fight. It was as if they were armed, carrying long knives and dreadful firearms, for one saw flashes of lightning and heard uninterrupted explosions and groans. Then no more could be observed, for the combatants were veiled by thick smoke.

The powder haze flew away, and the white clouds appeared to have won, for there were still hundreds of thousands of them around the illuminated circle—only a few thousand of the black ones remained. The others, appearing to be dead, sank into the fine, dirty clouds about the horizon, where they were received by flashing lightning and powerful thunderclaps. The victors—for it appeared the white clouds were so—bore the conquered behind them, still displaying their black fists.

This complex of clouds now flew from one end of the city to the other, until the illuminated circle over the Freemasons' Hall narrowed to the point where not a single star could be seen. The Hotoohs call this phenomenon, which appeared often in 1847 and 1853, the *wild hunters of the South.*

So we pass along, running up and down all the streets, but nowhere will we find a happy face. Long memorial columns of Odd Fellows and Freemasons, or of firemen and militia companies, or occasionally of Turners march past us along the way. There is not a carriage to be found to take a trip to refresh ourselves, for they are all on their way to the burial grounds. One can hardly even find a proper hearse to take our coffin away. All the gold runs into the bag of the undertaker, but the throttling angel of fever strikes this overcharging beast to the ground as well, and in the end he has nothing.

We will not linger at the haberdashers, since the provisioning of black hats, lace, and veils provides us with no joy. The eternal monotony of white flowers has also not really uplifted us for a long time.

But here! What? A cannon shot? Is Sevastopol being bombarded,[12] or is there a slave rebellion? We quickly turn the next corner to see what's happening. There is a real cannon, and beside it a real cannoneer. We wonder for a long while. Has his excellency the governor of Louisiana died? Aren't the Eighth of January or the Fourth of July long since past? And Washington's Birthday cannot be celebrated today, either—so we have to ask the cannoneer for information.

"Sir, for what purpose is all this shooting?"

"The fathers of our city have commanded us to shoot away the yellow fever."

On the next day half a dozen newsboys run between our legs. We take a *Delta* from one of them. The list of the dead? Here it is—*three hundred twenty dead!* That was all we wanted to know. We throw the *Delta* away and think to ourselves, "So that's the effectiveness of firing a cannon!"

And since we are already quite tired, we take our seat in an omnibus. Not a soul there. We let ourselves be carried on without any goal, just so long as the trip provides some sort of diversion. But soon we tire of traveling, even more than we had of walking. We pull the cord and in our confusion give the driver a quarter eagle instead of a dime.[13] The driver, who already has the plague in his brain, throws the gold piece away and says, "To hell with this dime, it has the yellow fever!"

Now we have arrived at the right place. There can be no discussion of boredom here. Such an amphitheater as the one displayed to us would not even be within the powers of Don Rica to build. It is bordered by Prytany, Plaquemine, and Sixth Streets and Washington Avenue. Who does not know it, the infamous Lafayette Cemetery?[14]

Sanitation? Our mayor is supposed to do this all himself? How could you ask that? To enter there, you need courage and a bottle, not just the bottle alone.

We are very curious, and if these miserable hearses continue to block the entry we will have to beat the mules or climb the walls. Smack, smack—will you let us in? But we don't want to beat the poor mules any more. We should really be happy to see something alive in this place.

So—well, now we are sitting on the high cemetery wall, and since it is not entirely deteriorated it will hold us for a while. We have not brought along a bottle of scent, for we actually thought we could tolerate such a dreadful pestilential stink in the middle of the city. Over there they are shooting off cannons to ward off yellow fever, and here this sort of garbage is thrown at it? But how are we to operate without a bottle of scent? We don't want to jump down, so we continue to sit on the wall. Lacking anything better, we pluck some hairs from the meager tail of a mule we can reach and stuff them up our nostrils. But that is not adequate. Here—these black bunches of feathers on the hearse are easier to reach. We grab a rather large bunch of feathers and press them against our nostrils. That works excellently—in fact, it is an antidote that has never before been cited. Using this mule-hair-feather-moustache, we now sit on the gray cemetery wall and look down on:

Seventy-five coffins. But that would be nothing if these coffins were decently under the earth—at least three feet under. But they had a mere two inches of mud thrown on them, and because it rained last night these coffins have risen up and cracked open. There they lie once more under the open sky: men, women, and children. And since death knows no shame, they are posing in a most improper manner.[15]

Five hundred coffins and only three gravediggers. These coffins have been unloaded and are being organized. But who is there to dig a hole? Only three gravediggers? Why didn't the corporation send its Negroes here to put the corpses away? Aren't Negroes virtually born to such work? The corporation has long since ceased sending its Negroes here—for the dangerous work can often lead to their being stricken by the illness, and then the corporation would lose an average of twelve hundred dollars apiece. It is better to have a pestilential stench over the entire neighborhood than a deficit in the pocket. And only three gravediggers!

Who are the three gravediggers, and how do they work? The three gravediggers are desperate young men. They not only have no money, they also have nothing to eat. This is why, when they heard the high wages paid for digging graves, they took it at once. Twice the pestilential stench has driven them back, and twice they have come back. Five to ten dollars for *one grave!* For such payment a desperado will gamble his already precarious life. Only twenty such graves and our money worries are over, the three men assure one another. They tried it—but once one, two, three holes have been dug, the courage sinks and all strength ebbs away. We should get good and drunk, one of them declares. This motion is carried, and in a minute the desperate threesome staggers onto the cemetery, drunk, and digs mightily away.

When evening comes, each of them has a hundred dollars in his pocket, which they blow that night—for the next morning they are thrown in the very holes they dug the day before. Do you know who these three desperate men were?

This ragpicker will be a rich man if he stays alive. It embarrasses us to say that it is a German eagerly going over the corpses. The ragpicker is smoking a miserable half-Spanish cigar as he strips clothes from the bloated corpses. Summer trousers, good linen shirt-fronts, and women's dresses—he presses everything together into his bag, and every now and then he finds a little golden ring, a droplet earring, and all sorts of other good wares. This man did not have to get drunk in advance to get to his work, as did the three desperate men. All he needs is the smouldering stump in his mouth, and he is able to gather all these treasures.

Do you recognize this ragpicker from last year? Oh, to be sure—he is sitting in a lawyer's office, and he's pushing a pen. A man can get rich if he can just stay alive.

A city corpse-cart bearing twenty coffins. The drivers do not even go up to the gate of the cemetery. They throw their coffins right over the wall, one after another. Are all the people who lie in this trove of dead persons victims of yellow fever? If the coroner were conscientious, and if he did not automatically issue the verdict "died of yellow fever," one would discover that hardly five of the twenty coffins contained persons who had died of that illness. Then one would soon learn that the pretty cigar seller, Inana M*, had grown tired of her husband and used the excuse of yellow fever to get him out of the way quickly and without arousing attention. Didn't people find it quite natural to say that this or that person had died of yellow fever? Did anyone investigate it more carefully? And how is it with W., father and son? Did they fall victim to the disease, or does Mr. Neveu know better?

Yes, yellow fever was the scapegoat of all murderers and poisoners. Insofar as a person stayed alive himself, that was always the best plan.

But now we hop off our gray cemetery wall, for we have seen enough. We throw away our false moustache as we turn the corner.

We stroll back home, passing hundreds of tar pots that our city fathers, in their wisdom, have ordered lit to fumigate the city and suffocate the yellow fever.

Firing cannons and burning tar!

Didn't anybody know that Hiram was in the city?

...

Flee to your apartment, for it is true, I tell you, the moon has never been so bright in the heavens. His full disk flashes like the shield of Achilles and the fifteen stars surrounding it glitter like the diadem of Cleopatra.

Are you all at home with your women and children? If you survive tonight, then you can call yourself lucky. If the sickness befalls you now, do not bother rushing to your physician.

Are you all home? And now, if you are at home, it will still do you no good. The warning came too late.

You discovered as a child that the moon attracts water, causing ebb and flood.

What is the brain of a human being but a deep ocean, in whose depths monsters prowl? The pearls that can be found in its depths are only the tears of these monsters, who pour them out when the harpoon of a moonbeam strikes them.

The ocean has its ebb and flood, why not the brain?

It would hurt the ocean if the moon left it.

And it hurts the ocean when the moon does not leave it—a dilemma without mercy or pity.

The moonlight beats down on the entire city this night. Only one light, but millions of shadows. We will not concern ourselves with the still shadows that stand and remain but only with those that slither and slide, stamp and tramp, these are the shades we want to get to know. For they are in the midst of a journey to the place of execution.

Along Carondelet Canal the tired wheels of a hearse are creaking. The six black feather bunches wave and wobble as if they have gone to sleep. Only one horse pulls this wagon. At a glance it can be seen that this horse is not used to this sort of duty, that it would much rather fly away with a practiced rider in its saddle. But this is the first and last time it will perform such a task.

Three men are sitting in the wagon.

One of them sits far in the back and wears long, white garb along with heavy iron chains, which have been gathered in his lap. His posture, despite the heavy chains and iron balls, is erect, and he has buckled under only once in the course of the entire long journey. This was when he lifted the chains and balls off of the floor in order to gather them in his lap and his arm was pulled downward when he tried to bring his arms together. There is nothing to see of his face except his eyes, which peer out of two holes in a mask that has been pressed on him. The side bands of the mask cover his ears so tightly that he cannot hear a word of what the two other men are saying to each other as they sit on the opposite corners of the wagon.

One of them bears the black clothing of a monseigneur, while the other is dressed casually, almost like a man of the country.

The one is a tall but gaunt figure, the other has a compact build of less than average height.

Both of them spoke French, but the accents were different.

As they spoke, they often glanced at the man loaded down with chains, who still had not spoken a word, although he was able to speak—the mask did not cover his mouth.

"Your Lydia appears to tire already," the tall figure said to the other man.

"She was tired even when I harnessed her," was the answer.

"That might be—it was no trifle. A struggle for three hours straight without letup—if we had not had to deal with the Hungarian count, it would have been much quicker."

"It was only good that the count was not carrying a weapon, or my Lydia would not be alive now."

"Even if he had had weapons with him, they would have done him no good. I stood at her side."

"He already had his fist in her mouth, he probably wanted to rip her tongue out—"

"He intended to do that, but she crushed his wrist at the right moment."

"The chains and handcuffs must hurt him terribly—but he doesn't want to show it—I want to watch carefully how he acts when he sees that he is to die."

The long, gaunt figure shrugged his shoulders at this remark from the other man. Then he asked: "Well, monsieur Cleveland, how do you like the young Count Emil?"

"I like him a lot—I have never seen a more handsome man in my entire life. Whatever crime he committed that caused you to lead his parents into such a situation as punishment is beyond my comprehension. He looks so innocent and good that if I met him in the course of my travels I would take him to be an angel the Lord had sent me."

"Do you believe that his reunion with his parents and siblings broke his heart?"

"You know, I could not remain in that tenement any longer. His cry of pain on seeing his dead mother, and then—oh, it sends a cold shudder over me even now, when I think of it."

"Do you believe that his reunion with his parents and siblings broke his heart?" he asked a second time.

"I believe it," was the answer, "although I did not see him after that evening—how could it be otherwise?"

"I hardened his heart at the instant that it wanted to break. Emil—and Lucy, of whom I have told you—have to remain alive until their child, to be born next month, reaches his eighteenth year, in the year 1871. They are perhaps to experience what I shall never experience—the rise of a new dawn that will break over the South of the United States.

"If you are to experience it, monsieur Cleveland, then don't forget the year 1871 and the young Toussaint L'Ouverture.

"When I die, Diana Robert will rush to Lucy and Emil and provide them personally with money only for the basic necessities, since their frivolity is limitless—they would squander everything despite all their experiences, and they would neglect the child."

The peddler Cleveland extended to Hiram his right hand, browned by the Louisiana sun, and said: "If I am to experience it, rely on me, for I am an enthusiastic reader of *Uncle Tom's Cabin,*[16] the gospel of the modern age."

Hiram suppressed an ironic smile that played on his thin lips at the peddler's words. He did not criticize this clumsy comparison, since he could see that the man at least was showing good will. There was also a question about whether the peddler would even experience the birth of the yellow savior.

The Carondelet Canal has a remarkable appearance during the months of July and August. Its water is so thickly covered with water plants that,* if lake-killers weren't located here and there,† one could easily mistake it for a long, narrow greensward. Many a stranger has lost his life here by trying to cross this betraying meadow on foot, perhaps not noticing the ships or happening upon it when none were there. No year passes without twenty to fifty corpses being fished out; no one ever learns who they were or whether they found their grave here by accident or were pushed in by criminal hand.

The hearse slowly squealed along the canal; it had arrived in the vicinity of the Tivoli Gardens.

"Command the Hotooh to stop here," Hiram told the peddler Cleveland. "We are there."

Without responding in words, the peddler stretched his head out of the hearse and tapped the Hotooh on the leg.

The Hotooh brought the horse to a halt and called into the wagon.

"Are we to throw him in?"

He received no answer.

The Hungarian—for that was the man encumbered with chains and iron balls—made a short but powerful move at the instant the wagon stopped, causing his fetters to fall to the floor and pull his arms downward suddenly. Then he stood up and looked out of the wagon with a bent back. When he saw the canal, he asked in a cuttingly cold tone, turning so that he could see Hiram and the peddler: "Am I supposed to take a walk there?"

*Known to botanists by the name of *Plantago natans.* Near Bayou St. John there is a species called *More Ranæ.*

†Lake-killers are ships that pass from Lake Pontchartrain to Bayou St. John and from there into the Old Basin.

There was no answer to his question—that is, no positive or negative movements of the head, since the Hungarian could not have understood any other response.

Hiram said to the peddler: "Be very careful when we get out, the man has something up his sleeve."

Tivoli Gardens had been closed for an hour. Because of the few guests who visited in these times, the innkeeper did not think it worth his time to keep his gardens open after midnight. There was a lake-killer moored nearby, right at the bank of the canal. It was an old, mastless schooner that was being kept here in expectation of repairs. Until three days ago, three sailors had been living on it. They were all seized by the sickness at the same time, and, unable to get help there, they fell in the canal in the middle of their fevers. The corpses had floated up quickly and were now lying, grotesquely postured, on the green surface of the canal right next to the bowsprit.

The Hotooh had come down from the driver's box and stood by the hearse doorway.

Hiram got out. The peddler wanted to follow at once.

Then the Hungarian gathered up all his strength and hurled an iron ball, striking Cleveland on the back of his head. The peddler dropped out of the opening of the carriage with a hollow cry, falling to the ground. He was dead.

"I told him," Hiram said to the Hotooh driver, "that the Hungarian had something up his sleeve. It is his fault."

At the same instant, Lydia broke out of her harness and rushed to her master, whose cry she had heard. As if she wanted to bed him down on the pasture, she gripped his clothing with her teeth and carried him—into the canal. Lydia would not have sunk, but she caught her master in her reins so that he pulled her into the depths with him. Hiram held back the Hotooh, who wanted to go to her aid. He said: "It was his own fault—I warned him in advance. When one is traveling to a place of execution, obedience is obligatory."

The Hotooh bowed as if he were expecting a command.

Hiram pushed him to the side. "I do not need you anymore," he said.

The Hotooh paid his respects and ran back toward the city. He was overjoyed that Hiram had not commanded him to haul the hearse back.

The Hungarian was still sitting in the wagon. After he had hurled the ball into the back of the peddler's head, he had set himself quietly in the corner as if nothing had happened. Now Hiram approached him and reached for his face. The Hungarian did not move. He sat there as if all the life had flowed out of him. His hands, his feet, and even his face were ice-cold. Hiram reached again at his face, and when the Hungarian would not move, Hiram removed the mask.

"Count, get out of the wagon. The moon will perform its office as executioner."

"Just to show you that I do not fear you," the cold, living man responded, "I will get out."

Hiram stepped a bit to one side and drew out a small container. From the container he withdrew a piece of glass, about the size of a lens. He held this in front of the Hungarian's face.

The Hungarian wobbled back and forth several times, then he fell to the ground.

Hiram held out the glass once more, and when the Hungarian began to convulse he opened his handcuffs and removed the chains.

"Get up, Count, and follow me on board that schooner."

The Hungarian slowly rose and looked at Hiram, then at the canal, then up at the moon.

Now he felt as weak as a child. His usually muscular arms had withered like those of an old woman. His knees buckled.

"What have you done to me?" he asked Hiram as he followed him onto the schooner without protest.

"Tell me, what have you done to me? What is your intention? Do you want to throw me in?" the Hungarian said repeatedly in a soft, weak tone, which sounded more dreadful than the curses he had earlier expelled.

Hiram was silent.

The Hungarian lay with his back to a ruined sail, as Hiram had commanded him. He lay still and peacefully, as if he expected a gentle slumber to come over him at any moment. Only when he tried to raise himself did he suddenly sense an unbearable pain in his temples. He sank down again at once.

Now, in this instant, the Hungarian's face took on a marvelous clarity. His eyes gleamed in heavenly joy, and a mild, almost childish smile played on his lips.

He folded his hands and looked up at the full disk of the moon.

"How beautiful you are, moon!" he prayed, "oh, let me lie in your light here forever!"

Then the moon sent down a ray at him that looked like a bolt of lightning bathed in water.

This bolt struck the Hungarian on the forehead.

His entire face crumbled, deformed, and changed. By the time Hiram grabbed him by his long hair to drop him in the water, the face of the Hungarian had turned coal-black.

He was dead of moonstroke.

Epilogue

The summer of terror of that ever-memorable year, 1853, had passed. Our poets dipped their pens in the fluid gold of the stars and sank, intoxicated, into the magnolia bosom of her majesty, the Queen of the South. And where earlier only the hearse was to be found, now the troubadour once more stood and played sensuous songs to the loving heart of his lady. The lyre-player once more crept under the window of his returning darling, and he was not averse to taking a small donation at Negro cafés. Every night Columbia's naiads, the tireless levee ladies, dance again and mix with the ant swarm of sleepless sailors doing their best to forget God. They weave them crowns of gumboes and Spanish peppers, and they treat them to kisses and turtle soup. In between, there is the rattle of the tambourine, the chatter and bang of the castanets the whole night through. The same old inns have been revived—no sooner had the gravedigger thrown away his spade, no sooner had the avenging angel of plague disposed of his last victim, than they all filled their cup once more. Still, these are harmless amusements, and death would not have such a lovable little people sorrow on his account.

But *Mene, Tekel, Upharsin!*[1] As if nothing had happened, as if they had forgotten that Hiram the Freemason ever walked the earth, as if they did not know why the dreadful epidemic had murdered half the city, the wholesalers in human flesh continue to drive black gangs to market, and the mercenaries of the South sit once more on horseback, the whips of cattle traders in their hands.

And so it happened at Mardi Gras time in 1854,[2] when a stately brig entered the harbor of New Orleans over whose cabin portholes was written in gold letters the name "Toussant L'Ouverture." No tugboat brought the brig to our riverbank. It flew upstream with trimmed sails, to the astonishment of sailors watching. And the commander of the brig, a native of Haiti, sent a messenger into the city with a note. In it were the words:

> We, Faustinus I, Emperor of Haiti, send the Count Emil R* and his consort, Lucy Wilson, our greetings.
>
> Both of them should come aboard the brig "Toussaint L'Ouverture" without the least delay, leaving their son in New Orleans in the care of Diana Robert. This is according to the codicil of the testament of Hiram,

which was sent to our capital by Diana Robert at the specific command of Hiram. We shall not withhold what is in store for both of you in that testament once you have arrived in our land. Many greetings to Count Emil from the prince of Württemberg, who has been under our protection as interim protector of the imperial jewels since summer 1853. In the same way, many and hearty greetings to Count Emil from his old friend the Cocker, who came to our shores from New Orleans on a tour of the Antilles, and who has been made Supreme Court Staff Trumpeter, out of our regard for his nation.

Faustinus

Just as unexpectedly as the brig "Toussaint L'Ouverture" had appeared in New Orleans harbor, it now flew downstream—with Lucy and Emil on board.

On the same day, as the result of a strange series of events, Cousin Karl, the good-hearted man with solid German eyes, was named chief hostler by the lesbian ladies of New Basin. Orleana had already passed to a better world two weeks before. The sudden disappearance of her bosom-friend Claudine de Lesuire, who had not returned to the Holy Grail since Hiram's night, was the cause of her unexpected death. Ever since that time, pansies have not bloomed in New Orleans.

Ruin awaits him who does not take heed!

Notes

Preface

1. J. Hanno Deiler, in Robert E. Cazden, *A Social History of the German Book Trade in America Before the Civil War* (Columbia, S.C.: Camden House, 1984), 393.

2. Florence M. Jumonville, *Bibliography of New Orleans Imprints 1764–1864* (New Orleans: The Historic New Orleans Collection, 1989).

Introduction

1. J. Hanno Deiler, *Geschichte der New Orleanser deutschen Presse* (New Orleans, 1901), esp. 15–17, reprinted in Karl J. R. Arndt and May E. Olson, eds., *The German Language Press of the Americas,* vol. 3, *Press/Research* (Munich: K. G. Sauer, 1980), 620–59.

2. Munich, Stadtarchiv, PMB 138, Familien-Bogen, Alexander Freiherr von Reitzenstein, fol. 2r. Our author always used the spelling "Reizenstein" in America, though his family came to use "Reitzenstein." I have preserved the author's preference in this edition.

3. A list of these generals was compiled by Lt. Gen. Wilhelm Freiherr von Reitzenstein, *Die Generale von und Freiherrn von Reitzenstein* (completed 1928), typescript kept at Schloss Reitzenstein.

4. Biographical sketch of Christoph Ludwig Freiherr von Reitzenstein (of the Schwarzenstein junior line), *Allgemeine Deutsche Biographie* (Leipzig, 1875–1912), 28, 172. Christoph, who rose from major to colonel with the auxiliaries leased to the British by Margrave Alexander of Ansbach-Bayreuth, served along the Delaware Valley as well as at Yorktown. Friedrich Ernst Georg Ferdinand Freiherr von Reitzenstein (1755–1793) also served in America, marrying a German-American wife, Catharina Elisabetha Schenkmayer (1766–1844) of Fredericktown, Maryland, according to genealogical materials at Schloss Reitzenstein. The novelist David Christoph Seybold incidentally composed a scathing attack on the German mercenary trade entitled *Reizenstein. Die Geschichte eines deutschen Offiziers,* 2 vols. (Leipzig, 1778–79), see Harold Jantz, "German Views of the American Revolution: Some Recovered Sources," *Amerikastudien* 23, no. 1 (1978): 14 (reference from Don Heinrich Tolzmann).

5. Helene Freifrau von Reitzenstein, ed., *Ein Mann und seine Zeit 1797–1890. Erinnerungen von Alexander Freiherr von Reitzenstein-Hartungs* (Eggstätt: Helene Freifrau von Reitzenstein, 1990), 58. Deiler incorrectly gives 1829 as the birth year of Ludwig von Reizenstein (Deiler, *Geschichte,* 16). His given names were Ludwig Maximilian Christoph; see *Almanach de Gotha, Freiherrliche Häuser* (Gotha, 1856), 543.

6. For the arms of the baronial family of Reitzenstein, see Johann Siebmacher, *J. Siebmacher's Grosses und allgemeines Wappenbuch,* ed. Otto Titan von Hefner, vol. 2, pt. 1, *Der Adel des Königreiches Bayern* (Nuremberg: Baser und Raspe, 1856), 53, plate 55; for a sketch of the Barons von Reitzenstein, see *Genealogisches Handbuch des Adels,* vol. 21, *Freiherrliche Häuser,* part A, vol. 3, ed. Hans Friedrich von Ehrenbrook (Marburg an der Lahn: Stark, 1959), 355–86; see also *Genealogisches Handbuch des in Bayern immatrikulierten Adels,* vol. 17 (Neustadt an der Aisch, 1988), 529–35.

7. Reitzenstein, *Ein Mann,* 25, 29.

8. *Hof-und Staatshandbuch des Königreichs Bayern 1846* (Munich, ca. 1846), 69–86; Alexander von Reitzenstein-Hartungs is on 76.

9. Ibid., 60; *Hof-und Staatshandbuch des Königreichs Bayern 1856* (Munich, ca. 1856), 37.

10. Heinz Gollwitzer, *Ludwig I. von Bayern. Königtum im Vormärz. Eine politische Biographie* (Munich: Süddeutscher Verlag, 1987), 585: "Without exception crown officials and highest courtiers under Ludwig I were Catholic, just as was the case with the heads of court agencies."

11. Reitzenstein, *Ein Mann,* 90.

12. Munich, Hauptstaatsarchiv, MF 33832, petition of General-Zoll-Administrator Bever to King Ludwig I, 1 December 1843, fol. 1r–v, and petition of Alexander Freiherr von Reitzenstein to King Ludwig I, 28 September 1845, fol. 1v.

13. Munich, Hauptstaatsarchiv, MF 33832, petition of General-Zoll-Administrator Bever to King Ludwig I, 1 December 1843, fol. 1v–2r, and petition of Alexander Freiherr von Reitzenstein to King Ludwig I, 28 September 1845, fol. 1v.

14. The precise date and place of her death is recorded in the *Stammbuch* of Lt. Gen. Wilhelm Freiherr von Reitzenstein, kept at Schloss Reitzenstein, 57.

15. Ernst Heinrich Kneschke, *Neues Allgemeines Deutsches Adels-Lexicon* (Leipzig, 1860), 2:8; Reitzenstein, *Ein Mann,* 38; Munich, Stadtarchiv, PMB 138, Familien-Bogen, Alexander Freiherr von Reitzenstein, fol. 1r.

16. Reitzenstein, *Ein Mann,* 102–3.

17. Ibid., 106–9.

18. Munich, Stadtarchiv, PMB 138, Familien-Bogen, under Alexander Freiherr von Reitzenstein, fol. 1r, dated 1863, there are twenty-one addresses listed between 1845 and 1863.

19. Reitzenstein, *Ein Mann,* 111; for Ludwig von Reizenstein's registration as a student, see Munich, Universitätsarchiv, *Verzeichniss des Lehrer-Personals u. der sämmtlichen Studirenden an der königl. Ludwigs-Maximilians-Universität München in Sommer-Semester des Studienjahres 1846/47* (Munich, 1847), 35, "Ludwig von Reizenstein, Bar., [Heimath] München; Karlsplatz 29, 3. Etage, Philos."; and *Verzeichniss des Lehrer-Personals u. der sämmtlichen Studirenden an der königl. Ludwigs-Maximilians-Universität München in Winter-Semester des Studienjahres 1847/48* (Munich, 1847), same entry, save that Reizenstein has become a student of the theology faculty. There was no teaching in the summer semester, 1847–48, and he is not in the directory for the winter semester, 1848–49.

20. Munich, Hauptstaatsarchiv, MA 27239, petition of Alexander Freiherr von Reitzenstein to King Ludwig I, dated 22 January 1848, Munich, approved by the king on 31 January 1848. A royal order carrying out the petition, directed to the government of Oberbayern, was issued on 14 March 1848.

21. Reitzenstein, *Ein Mann,* 118.

22. The best general treatment of the adventures of Elizabeth James, née Gilbert, a.k.a. Lola Montez, Countess Landsfeld, in Munich is Heinz Gollwitzer, *Ludwig I. von Bayern,* 668–88. According to Deiler *(Geschichte,* 16), Ludwig "studied in Freising and in 1848 at the University of Munich, where, according to his own statement, he allowed himself to be led astray as a partisan of Lola Montez, and he played a prominent role in the uprising over her, with the result that he lost any hope for a place in Bavarian state service, so that he found himself compelled to emigrate to America in 1849."

23. Munich, Staatsarchiv Oberbayern, RA Fasz. 1155, no. 15902, Präsidial-Acten der königlichen Regierung von Oberbayern: Die Störung der offentlichen Ruhe und Ordnung in München in den Tagen von 7.–11. Februar betr.: . . . [Dieser Faszikel enthält auch die die Studenten-Verbindung Allemannia betreffenden Akten-Produkte]; and no. 15909, Tumultuarische Auftritte in der Hauptstadt München, neuentlich in der Richtung gegen Gräfin Landsfeld Lola Montez, Februar und März 1848.

24. Reitzenstein, *Ein Mann,* 118–19. Frederick W. Egloffstein was a surveyor in St. Louis in the early 1850s, located on the west side of Seventeenth Street north of Biddle Street in 1850, on the north side of Pine Street between Second and Third Streets in 1853 (in partnership with a person named Zwanzigel) and at 100 South Second Street in 1854. See *Green's St. Louis Directory for 1851* (St. Louis: Charles and Hammond, 1850), 115; William L. Montague, ed., *The Saint Louis Directory for 1853–4* (St. Louis: E. A. Lewis, 1853); *The St. Louis Directory for the Years 1854–5* (St. Louis: Chambers and Knapp, 1854).

25. Munich, Stadtarchiv, PMB 138, Familien-Bogen, Alexander Freiherr von Reitzenstein, fol. 2r, notes that Ernst was militarily disciplined on 8 May 1848 for *Untreu* (disloyalty).

26. Deiler, *Geschichte,* 16, quoting the testament of Alexander von Reitzenstein, 23 March 1890.

27. In the city directory entries, Ludwig Reizenstein appears in 1853, 1857, 1866, 1867 and 1868, though there is a suggestion that he might have used "Baron von" in 1858 and 1859. In a second entry in 1867 he appears as L. von Reizenstein, and from 1871 (the year of German unification under Bismarck) he is consistently von Reizenstein. His use of the baronial title in the 1880s is known from George Washington Cable, who spoke of him as a baron.

28. Karl J. R. Andt and May E. Olson, eds., *The German Language Press of the Americas,* vol 1., *U.S.A.* 3d ed. (Munich: Verlag Dokumentation, 1976), 176, 1, 183. Deiler also appeared to believe this ephemeral paper was to be published in New Orleans, despite the title reference to Pekin, Illinois.

29. St. Louis, *Anzeiger des Westens,* weekly edition, 17, no. 28 (1 May 1852): 2, entry for 27 April, "Aus Pekin." "Ludwig Reizenstein" was the secretary (second presiding officer) of the meeting, and he was named first secretary of the organizing committee of the Revolution Society in Pekin, which was to seek affiliation with the American Revolutionary League for Europe headquartered in Philadelphia.

30. The New Orleans city directories that mention Ludwig von Reizenstein are: *Cohen's New Orleans Directory* (New Orleans, 1852), 220; *Mygate & Co.'s Directory* (New Orleans, 1857), 240; *Gardner & Wharton's New Orleans Directory for the Year 1858* (New Orleans, 1857), 261; *Gardner's New Orleans Directory for 1859* (New Orleans, 1858), 249; *Gardner's New Orleans Directory for 1866* (New Orleans, 1866), 370; *Gardner's New Orleans Directory for 1867* (New Orleans, 1867), 329 (two entries); *Gardner's New Orleans Directory for 1868* (New Orleans, 1868), 364; *Edwards' Annual Directory . . . in the City of New Orleans for 1871* (New Orleans, 1871), 622; *Edwards' Annual Directory . . . in the City of New Orleans for 1872* (New Orleans, 1872), 411; *Edwards' Annual Directory . . . in the City of New Orleans for 1873* (New Orleans, 1873), 447; *Soard's New Orleans City Directory for 1874* (New Orleans, 1874), 763; *Soard's New Orleans City Directory for 1875* (New Orleans, 1875), 687; *Soard's New Orleans City Directory for 1876* (New Orleans, 1876), 674; *Soard's New Orleans City Directory for 1877* (New Orleans, 1877), 640; *Soard's New Orleans City Directory for 1878* (New Orleans, 1878), 681; *Soard's New Orleans City Directory for 1879* (New Orleans, 1879), 661; *Soard's New Orleans City Directory for 1880* (New Orleans, 1880), 739; *Soard's New Orleans City Directory for 1881* (New Orleans, 1881), 727; *Soard's New Orleans City Directory for 1882* (New Orleans, 1882), 585; *Soard's New Orleans City Directory for 1883* (New Orleans, 1883), 619; *Soard's New Orleans City Directory for 1884* (New Orleans, 1884), 746; *Soard's New Orleans City Directory for 1885* (New Orleans, 1885), 767.

31. Arndt and Olson, *German Language Press,* 1:181–82; the entry on the *Louisiana Staats-Zeitung* differs with Robert T. Clark, who believed the paper folded in 1864. Robert T. Clark, "The New Orleans German Colony in the Civil War," *Louisiana Historical Quarterly* 20 (1937): 990–1015, also reprinted ibid, 3:661–87.

32. Reizenstein appears as a draftsman in 1852; an architect in 1858, 1859, 1867, 1871, 1872, 1876, 1877, and 1885; an engineer in 1866, 1867, 1882, and 1883; as a "surveyor" in 1873, 1874, 1880, and 1881; and a civil engineer in 1878 and 1884. He is listed without profession in 1857 and 1879, and he is missing from the directories in 1855, 1856, 1860, 1861, and 1870.

33. Reizenstein's residences, from the directories, are as follows: 1853, Common, near Robertson; 1857, Howard at Felicity; 1858–59, 60 Magazine, between Mesonene and Freret; 1866–67, Carondelet near Philip; 1867 (second entry), 49 Exchange Place, residence St. Charles near Jackson, 4th District; 1871, 92 Bolivar; 1872, room 20, 18 Royal, residence 436 Bienville; 1873–74, 436 Bienville; 1875, 378 Bienville; 1876, north side of Gasquet between S. Dolhonde and South Broad; 1878, north side of Bienville between N. Rocheblave and North Dolhonde; 1879,

479 Bienville; 1880–83: north side of Gasquet between S. Dolhonde and South Broad; 1884, 313 Gasquet, 1st District; 1885, 309 Gasquet, 1st District.

34. Deiler, *Geschichte,* 17.

35. Glenn R. Conrad, ed., *A Dictionary of Louisiana Biography* (New Orleans: Louisiana Historical Association; Center for Louisiana Studies of the University of Southwestern Louisiana, 1988), 2:678.

36. See the article on Charles Testut in the *American National Biography* (New York, 1999), 21:48–69, by Caryn Cossé Bell of University of Massachusetts–Lowell. The only known copy of *Les mystères de la Nouvelle-Orléans* (New Orleans, 1852–54) is at the American Antiquarian Society in Worcester, Mass. Volumes 1 and 2 are dated 1852; volume 3 has no cover and hence no clear date, and volume 4 was published in 1854, with comments about the "lapse of time" that had been allowed to pass between volume 3 and 4 (2). Less helpful is Marie Louise Lagarde, "Charles Testut: Critic, Journalist, and Literary Socialist" (M.A. thesis, French Department, Tulane University, 1948), 126–28, since Lagarde never read the novel.

37. *Louisiana Staats-Zeitung,* vol. 5, no. 11, 13 January 1854, 2.

38. Ibid., no. 26, 31 January 1854, 1, incorporating typographical corrections in the following number, 1.

39. *Deutsche Zeitung,* New Orleans, 1 February 1854, 2.

40. *Louisiana Staats-Zeitung,* vol. 5, no. 28, 2 February 1854, 1; no. 32, 7 February 1854, 1; and no. 42, 18 February 1854, 1.

41. Ibid., no. 45, 22 February 1854, 1; and no. 51, 1 March 1854, 1.

42. Ibid., no. 100, 27 April 1854, 1; no. 171, 20 July 1854, 1; no. 228, 24 September 1854, 1; no. 294, 10 December 1854, 1; and vol. 6, no. 54, 4 March 1855, 1.

43. Deiler, *Geschichte,* 15: "Reizenstein later tried to compensate for this literary sin of his youth by buying back the book edition of *The Mysteries,* and even now it is difficult to discover a single copy even with the greatest diligence, since the work is treasured as a curiosity. The archive of the German Society of New Orleans still has a copy, and there are also the relevant volumes of the *Louisiana Staats-Zeitung.*"

44. Clark, "New Orleans German Colony," 998.

45. Conrad, ed., *A Dictionary of Louisiana Biography,* 2:678, gives his unit as First Regiment, Second Brigade, First Division, Louisiana Militia. Sevilla Finley informs me that Reizenstein's name appears on a list marked New Orleans, LA, 8 April 1862, transfering him to the "Sanatary Corps," cited in Andrew B. Booth, *Records of Louisiana Confederate Soldiers and Commanders,* vol. 3, book 2 (1920).

46. Clark, "New Orleans German Colony." Only eight installments were published in the *Deutsche Zeitung,* vol. 14, between late September and 1 December 1861, all on Sundays. There is no evidence it was either continued or subsequently published as a book.

47. *Deutsche Zeitung,* New Orleans, vol. 17, no. 5175, 9 April 1865, and no. 5258, 16 July 1865, mentions that an episode was delayed because editors objected to it and it required revision. The last installment appears in vol. 18, no. 5373, 26 November 1865. Clark, "New Orleans German Colony," 998, mentions the novel

for its description of the shabby treatment given a German-speaking unit in Confederate service.

48. Clark, "New Orleans German Colony," 1014.

49. A copy of this pamphlet is in the Louisiana Collection, Tulane University.

50. See, for example, the series in the *Deutsche Zeitung,* New Orleans, vol. 17, no. 5134, 16 March 1865, 2, "Richterliche Forschungen auf dem Gebiete der Geologie"; no. 5137, 19 March 1865, 2, "An den Mündungen des Mississippi"; no. 5163, 26 March 1865, "Epidemie unter Thieren"; and no. 5169, 2 April 1865, "Der Hydrarchos oder Wasserkönige."

51. On Cable in general, see the article by Thomas J. Richardson in Charles Reagan Wilson and William Ferris, eds., *Encyclopedia of Southern Culture* (Chapel Hill: University of North Carolina Press, 1989), 875–76; and Louis D. Rubin, Jr., *George W. Cable: The Life and Times of a Southern Heretic* (New York: Pegasus, 1969). The best study is Arlin Turner, *George W. Cable: A Biography* (Baton Rouge: Louisiana State University Press, 1966), esp. 113–14.

52. Mattie Russell, "George Washington Cable's Letters in Duke University Library," *Library Notes: A Bulletin Issued for the Friends of Duke University Library,* no. 25 (January, 1951), 1–13. The article was L. von Reizenstein, "A New Moth," *Scribner's Monthly, An Illustrated Magazine for the People* 22 (May–October 1881): 864–65.

53. Cable, *Dr. Sevier* (Boston: Osgood, 1885), esp. 255 ff.

54. Published as one of three novellas in George Washington Cable, *Strong Hearts* (New York: Scribner's, 1899). Cable's daughter, Lucy Leffingwell Cable Bikle, in *George W. Cable: His Life and Letters* (New York: Scribner's, 1928), 77, describes the study of the Cable house at 229 Eighth Street in New Orleans, mentioning "a large glass case of moths and butterflies, given him by the old Baron von Reizenstein, the Entomologist of his later story." The original working title for the novella was "The Old Baron Rodenberg," see Turner, *George W. Cable,* 315.

55. J. Hanno Deiler and all who rely on him give fall 1888 as the time of Reizenstein's death; only Turner (*George W. Cable,* 114), gives 1885. The obituary register at Tulane University Library does not have a listing for Ludwig von Reizenstein, but there is one for Augusta von Reizenstein [née Schröder] in 1886, which describes her as the widow of Ludwig von Reizenstein. In *Soard's 1885 Directory* for New Orleans, Ludwig von Reizenstein is listed as an architect resident at 309 Gasquet in the First District (767), but in *Soard's 1886 Directory* there is no entry. Reitzenstein, *Ein Mann,* 146, gives 1885 as the year of Ludwig von Reizenstein's death. The *Stammbuch* of Lt. Gen. Wilhelm Freiherr von Reitzenstein, at Schloss Rietzenstein, 57, gives the complete date.

56. See Conrad, ed., *A Dictionary of Louisiana Biography,* 2:678; on Cypress Grove Cemetery II, see Mary Louise Christovich, ed., *New Orleans Architecture,* vol. 3, *The Cemeteries* (Gretna, La.: Pelican, 1974), 32.

57. Deiler, *Geschichte,* 16.

58. On the phenomenon of the serial novel, see particularly Hans-Jörg Neu-

schäfer, Dorothee Fritz-El Ahmad, and Klaus-Peter Walter, eds., *Der französische Feuilletonroman. Die Entstehung der Serienliteratur im Medium der Tageszeitung,* Impulse der Forschung, no. 47 (Darmstadt: Wissenschaftliche Buchgesellschaft, 1986). See also Eugène Sue, *Les Mystères de Paris,* ed. Francis Lacassin (Paris: Robert Laffont, 1989), 1–27; Werner Sollors, "Emil Klauprecht's Cincinnati, oder Geheimnisse des Westens (1854–55) and the Beginnings of Urban Realism in America," *In Their Own Words* 3, no. 2 (1986): 161–86, also printed as "Emil Klauprecht's Cincinnati, oder Geheimnisse des Westens, and the Beginnings of Urban Realism in America" in *Queen City Heritage* 42 (1984): 39–48.

59. Attacks by Marx and Engels against Sue are contained in *Die heilige Famile oder Kritik der kritischen Kritik* (Frankfurt am Main, 1844), which can be found in Karl Marx and Friedrich Engels, *Werke,* ed. Institut für Marxismus-Leninismus beim Zentralkommittee der Sozialistischen Einheitspartei Deutschlands (East Berlin: Dietz, 1985), 2:7–223. See also the name index in that volume, 710, where Sue is listed as "französischer Schriftsteller, Verfasser spiessbürgerlich-sentimentaler Romane mit sozialen Themen."

60. *Vorwärts!* 4 (18 January 1844): 2. For a facsimile edition of this journal, with a detailed introduction, see Heinrich Börnstein with L. F. C. Bernays, A. Ruge, H. Heine, K. Marz, and F. Engels, *Vorwärts! Pariser Signale aus Kunst, Wissenschaft, Theater, Musik und geselligen Leben. Ab 3.7.1844: Pariser Deutsche Zeitschrift,* ed. Walter Schmidt (Leipzig: Zentralantiquariat der Deutschen Demokratischen Republik, 1975).

61. Sollors, "Emil Klauprecht's Cincinnati," 177. See Don Heinrich Tolzmann in his preface to Emil Klauprecht, *Cincinnati, or The Mysteries of the West* (New York: Peter Lang, 1996), xxi.

62. Sollors, "Emil Klauprecht's Cincinnati," 178.

63. See George Condoyannis, "German-American Prose Fiction from 1850 to 1914" (Ph.D. diss., Catholic University of America, 1953), and Condoyannis, "German-American Prose Fiction: Synopses of Thirty-Eight Works," *German-American Studies* 4 (1972): 1–126. Also see Peter C. Merrill, "The Serial Novel in the German-American Press of the Nineteenth Century," *Journal of German-American Studies* 13, no. 1 (1978): 16–22; Patricia Herminghouse, "Radicalism and the 'Great Cause': The German-American Serial Novel in the Antebellum Era," in Frank Trommler and Joseph McVeigh, eds., *America and the Germans: An Assessment of a Three-Hundred-Year History,* 2 vols. (Philadelphia: University of Pennsylvania Press, 1985), 1: 306–20; Robert E. Cazden, *A Social History of the German Book Trade in America before the Civil War* , 391–93; and Peter C. Merrill, "Eugène Sue's German-American Imitators," *Schatzkammer der deutschen Sprache, Dichtung und Geschichte* 14, no. 1 (spring 1988): 130–44.

64. Marion Beaujean, "Unterhaltungs-, Familien-, Frauen- und Abenteuerromane," in Horst Albert Glaser, ed., *Deutsche Literatur. Eine Sozialgeschichte,* vol. 6, *Vormärz: Biedermaier, Junges Deutschland, Demokraten 1815–1848* (Reinbek bei Hamburg: Rowohlt, 1980), 162.

65. A copy of the first fascicle of this amazing anonymous novel is in the German Society Library of Philadelphia. It was published at the press of *Der Volksvertreter.* Elliot Schor of Bryn Mawr is still trying to assemble the complete text of this book. At the conference on German-American history and literature at Harvard in September 1998, he announced the discovery of a portion of one additional chapter reprinted in a German-language newspaper outside Philadelphia later in the 1850s, so there is hope that the whole may some day be found.

66. Barbara Lang, *The Process of Immigration in German-American Literature from 1850 to 1900* (Munich: Wilhelm Fink Verlag, 1988), 47; for the German side of the equation, see Juliane Mikoletzky, *Die deutsche Amerika-Auswanderung des 19. Jahrhunderts in der zeitgenössische fiktionalen Literatur* (Tübingen: Niemeyer, 1988).

67. Emil Klauprecht, *Cincinnati* (Cincinnati, 1854–55), Book 2, Chapter 6.

68. Heinrich Börnstein, *Fünfundsiebzig Jahre in der Alten und Neuen Welt. Memoiren eines Unbedeutenden,* 2 vols. (Leipzig: Wigand, 1881; reprint, Zürich: Peter Lang, 1986); on Börnstein, also see Alfred Vagts, "Heinrich Börnstein, Ex- and Repatriate," *Bulletin of the Missouri Historical Society* 12 (1955–56): 105–27, and Vagts, *Deutsch-Amerikanische Rückwanderung,* Beihefte zum Jahrbuch für Amerikastudien, no. 6 (Heidelberg, 1960), esp. 114–16. See also the preface to the reprint of Börnstein's memoirs by Patricia Herminghouse, and her chapter, "Radicalism and the 'Great Cause': The German-American Serial Novel in the Ante-Bellum Era," in Trommler and McVeigh, eds., *America and the Germans,* 1:306–20. See the literature cited in Steven Rowan, with James Neal Primm, *Germans for a Free Missouri: Translations from the St. Louis Radical Press* (Columbia: University of Missouri Press, 1983), and also Rowan, "The Cultural Program of Heinrich Börnstein in St. Louis, 1850–1861," *In Their Own Words* 3, no. 2 (1986): 187–206. Manuscript materials concerning Börnstein are in Vienna in the Archiv der Stadt Wien, at the Theatersammlung, as well as the Handschriftensammlung der österreichischen Nationalbibliothek. I have published a translated edition of Börnstein's Missouri memoirs: Henry Boernstein, *Memoirs of a Nobody: The Missouri Years of an Austrian Radical,* trans. and ed. Steven Rowan (St. Louis: Missouri Historical Society, 1998).

69. Henry Boernstein [Heinrich Börnstein], *The Mysteries of St. Louis,* ed. Steven Rowan and Elizabeth Sims (Chicago: Kerr, 1990), esp. introduction.

70. See Cazden, *A Social History,* 591.

71. George C. Schoolfield, "The Great Cincinnati Novel," *Cincinnati Historical Society Bulletin* 20 (1962): 44, 54. For a general survey of the works of German-American authors, see Don Heinrich Tolzmann, *German-American Literature* (Metuchen, N.J.: Scarecrow Press, 1977).

72. For basic biobibliographical information on Klauprecht, see Robert E. Ward, *A Bio-Bibliography of German-American Writers, 1670–1970* (White Plains, N.Y.: Kraus, 1985). I have recently published a translation of the novel: *Cincinnati, or The Mysteries of the West: Emil Klauprecht's German-American Novel,* trans. Steven Rowan, ed. Don Heinrich Tolzmann, New German-American Studies, no. 10 (New York: Peter Lang, 1996).

73. The revolutionary nature of Reizenstein's treatment is underscored by the fact that Jeannette H. Foster, in *Sex Variant Women in Literature* (1956; Tallahassee, Fl.: Naiad Press, 1985), 63–67, is unable to turn up anything as forthright as Reizenstein in the French literature known to her, let alone English-language literature. The lesbian was usually treated as a lonely aberration.

Memoranda

1. Eugène Sue (1804–57) was author of the immensely popular *Les Mystères de Paris* (1842–43). His Fleur-de-Marie was a well-born girl who was orphaned, sank briefly into prostitution, and was doomed to permanent loss of status despite all efforts of her relatives, the Gerolsteins, to redeem her. See Hans-Jörg Neuschäfer, Dorothee Fritz-El Ahmad, and Klaus-Peter Walter, eds., *Der französische Feuilletonroman. Die Entstehung der Serienliteratur im Medium der Tageszeitung,* Impulse der Forschung, no. 47 (Darmstadt: Wissenschaftliche Buchgesellschaft, 1986), 103–4.

2. Sue's sequel to *Les Mystères de Paris* was *Gérolstein,* which was the basis of Jacques Offenbach's popular *opéra-bouffe* of 1867, *La Grande-duchesse de Gérolstein,* libretto by Henri Meilhac and Ludovic Halévy.

3. The disreputable E. Z. C. Judson, alias Ned Buntline, published a novel entitled *The Mysteries and Miseries of New Orleans,* ca. 1851, concerned chiefly with the events surrounding Narciso Lopez's raid on Cuba in 1851. A copy of the novel is in the Louisiana Collection of Tulane University.

4. See Henry Boernstein (Heinrich Börnstein), *The Mysteries of St. Louis,* trans. Friedrich Münch, ed. Steven Rowan and Elizabeth Sims (Chicago: Kerr, 1990).

5. The author of *Cincinnati, oder Geheimnisse des Westens* (Cincinnati, 1854–55) was Emil Klauprecht. See *Cincinnati, or The Mysteries of the West: Emil Klauprecht's German-American Novel,* trans. Steven Rowan, ed. Don Heinrich Tolzmann, New German-American Studies, no. 10 (New York: Peter Lang, 1996).

6. This purported work by Joseph Lakanal (1762–1845) is unknown to his principal American biographer; see John Charles Dawson, *Lakanal the Regicide: A Biographical and Historical Study of the Career of Joseph Lakanal* (University: University of Alabama Press, 1948).

7. Don Francisco Luis Hector, Baron de Carondelet (François-Louis Hector, Baron de Carondelet et Noyelles), was Spanish Governor of Louisiana, 1791–97; see Joseph G. Dawson, III, *The Louisiana Governors from Iberville to Edwards* (Baton Rouge: Louisiana State University Press, 1990), 64–70.

Prologue

1. Construction on the Atchafalaya Bank on Magazine Street, designed by W. L. Atkinson, was begun in the autumn of 1835 and completed in March 1837, at an expense of $125,000. Its columns were of the Corinthian order. *Gibson's Guide and Directory* (New Orleans, 1838), 320, 322.

2. The Canal Bank was at the northwest corner of Gravier and Magazine Streets, see *Gibson's Guide and Directory* (New Orleans, 1838), 323.

Book I

Book I was published with 107 numbered pages, New Orleans: Druck und Verlag von G. Lugenbühl und E. H. Bölitz, 1854.

1. John McDonogh (1779–1850) was a wealthy New Orleans merchant and philanthropist, noted for his support of Negro repatriation to Africa and free public education.

2. This is a hint at Prince Paul of Württemberg, who becomes a major participant in Book II.

3. J. M. Cassidy, restaurateur, was at 9 Union Street and 107 Gravier Street (*Cohen's New Orleans Directory for 1853* [New Orleans, 1852], 48).

4. J. M. Laborde, an importer of Havana cigars, was located at 18 Royal Street (*Cohen's New Orleans City Directory, 1854* [New Orleans, 1853], 150).

5. Cross-dressing is also an element in Charles Testut, *Les mystères de la Nouvelle-Orléans* (New Orleans, 1852), 2:109: "C'est Lavinia qui m'a habillé—au masculin ou au feminin, comme tu voudras—et elle m'a donné des leçons."

6. January 8th is the anniversary of the Battle of New Orleans in 1815.

7. Algiers is a community directly across the Mississippi from New Orleans, reached by ferry.

8. As noted in the author's prologue, Fleur-de-Marie was the heroine-victim in Eugène Sue's *Les Mystères de Paris.*

9. Moritz Gottlieb Saphir (1745–1858), born Moses Saphir in Hungary, was a widely read Austrian humorist, drama critic, and essayist. Edward Maria Oettinger (1808–72) was a German dramatic novelist, essayist, and humorist, noted for his humorous lampoons of anti-Semites. Louis Schwarz had a German bookstore in 3 and 4 Duncan's Buildings, Exchange Alley (*Cohen's New Orleans Directory,* 1851, 172).

10. The February Revolution in Paris in 1848 led to the overthrow of King Louis-Philippe and the proclamation of a French Republic, which was soon subverted by the rise of Louis Napoléon, who eventually became Emperor Napoléon III.

11. Family columbidae or columbiformae, *Ectopistes migratorius.* This North American pigeon once traveled in vast flocks, but it was sought as food by commercial hunters and became extinct in 1914.

12. Agave, daughter of Cadmus and Harmonia, led a band of bacchantes that ripped her own son Pentheus to shreds, and in her madness she carried his head in triumph (portrayed in Euripides, *Bacchae*), see Konrat Ziegler and Walther Sontheimer, eds., *Der Kleine Pauly* (Munich, 1979), 1:120.

13. Louis Charles Alfred de Musset (1810–57) was a French poet, dramatist, and novelist.

14. "Measured Love" is *Massliebchen,* the daisy. "Male Fidelity," or *Männertreu* was the ironic popular name for a number of flowers whose petals fell quickly, referring usually to the speedwell or the veronica.

15. The character of the "Cocker" has been interpreted as a lampoon of Michael

Hahn (1830–86), later the wartime Governor of Louisiana (1864–65), a prominent German-American politician who was a consistent supporter of the Union and progressive causes in Louisiana (according to J. Hanno Deiler and those who rely on him). The historical Michael Hahn was born the illegitimate son of a widowed woman in the Bavarian town of Klingemünster and orphaned shortly after his arrival in America in 1840. He studied law under Christian Roselius, and he began his political career in 1851 as a member of the New Orleans School Board. In 1854–55 he advertised regularly in the *Louisiana Staats-Zeitung* as a notary public (e.g., vol. 6, no. 34, 9 February 1855). The chief similarities between the Cocker and Hahn consist of physique (Hahn was short and fat, walking with the help of a crutch due to a short leg), name (the Cocker's is Caspar Hahn), and the general notion that both cultivated an image as a "man of the people." Unlike the real Michael Hahn, who was a successful crossover politician, the Cocker knows neither English nor French, and unlike the courageous, scrupulously honest Hahn, the Cocker is a sleazy coward. The Cocker's similarity to Michael Hahn might have struck later readers more than strict contemporaries. See Joseph G. Dawson, III, *The Louisiana Governors from Iberville to Edwards* (Baton Rouge: Louisiana State University Press, 1990), 148–52.

16. "Shellroad Mary," who appears further on in this story, became a character in her own right in another short piece probably also by Reizenstein. A rather irreverent mock obituary appeared in the *Louisiana Staats-Zeitung,* vol. 5, no. 34, 9 February 1854, praising her as "an ornament of the city" for her contributions to the community in the form of numerous fines paid to the Recorder's Court. The article concluded with an epitaph declaring that only a dog and her hairdresser attended the burial.

17. Mrs. Felicia Dorothea Hemans (1793–1835), a popular American poet. Count Emmanuel de Las Cases (1766–1842), a member of the Spanish Las Casas family, published his eight-volume *Mémorial de Sainte-Hélène* in 1823, based on his own diary as a companion of the deposed Emperor Napoléon I on St. Helena Island in the South Atlantic. It was a major source of the Napoleonic legend in the nineteenth century. Johann Wolfgang von Goethe (1749–1832), German poet, dramatist, scientist and author of *Faust,* was the central figure of German classic literature in the nineteenth century.

18. German, "Two fellows crossed the Rhine."

19. A Hecker hat was a type of soft hat popularized by the revolutionary Friedrich Hecker (1811–81), leader of the radical wing in the 1848 revolutions in Baden.

20. The German Society of New Orleans functioned from 1847 to 1928, primarily to aid immigrants settling in or passing through the city. See Reinhart Kondert, "The New Orleans German Society (1847–1928)," *In Their Own Words* 3, no. 2 (summer, 1986): 59–80, with an extensive bibliography. It was located in this period at 42 Toulouse Street (*Cohen's New Orleans Directory for 1853,* 107).

21. An eagle was a ten-dollar gold piece.

22. St. Antoine's was a mortuary chapel on the corner of Rampart and Conti, erected in 1826–27, see *Gibson's City Directory,* 1838, 308.

23. *Anathema* ("let him be condemned") is a Greek word used in church Latin.

24. The Pontalba buildings face Jackson Square on the north and south sides, and they were prestigious residences constructed in the 1850s.

25. A line of ellipses in European novels of the time indicated where a censor had required that a passage be removed. Here it is a literary device, rather like a fade to black in film, to bring a violent or sexual episode to a close.

26. The St. Charles Hotel, built in 1837, was one of the most elegant in New Orleans, containing rooms, restaurants, and a central cupola where slaves were regularly sold. This structure burned down in 1851 and was rebuilt without the great dome. See Robert Reinders, *End of an Era: New Orleans,* 1850–1860 (Gretna, La.: Pelican, 1989), 151–52, 208–9.

27. The Veranda Hotel was on Common Street, at the corner of St. Charles Street (*Cohen's New Orleans Directory for* 1853, 263).

28. Part of Bank's Arcade still stands on Magazine Street, "constructed in the 1830s from designs of Charles Zimpel; it was a three-story block-long brick building . . . Dividing the building was a glassed-in arcade, which ran from Gravier to Natchez streets; the building contained a hotel, offices, the armory of the Washington Artillery (Armory Hall), saloons, a restaurant, and the Tontine, a spacious, lushly decorated coffee house which—at least by one account—could hold 5,000 persons. Combining size with food and drinks, it was, quite naturally, a favorite center for political rallies." Reinders, *End of an Era,* 210–11.

29. Napoléon Bonaparte was first consul of a reorganized French Republic, 1800–1804.

30. Alexandre Dumas père (1802–70), famous author of many serial novels, including *The Three Musketeers* and *The Count of Monte Cristo,* had a black grandmother from Santo Domingo and made much of his African ancestry. As a result, Dumas was a hero to African Americans in the pre–Civil War period. A "Hotel Dumas," described in Emil Klauprecht's novel *Cincinnati,* was an actual free black hotel in Cincinnati in the early 1850s. See Emil Klauprecht, *Cincinnati, or The Mysteries of the West: Emil Klauprecht's German-American Novel,* trans. Steven Rowan, ed. Don Heinrich Tolzmann (New York: Peter Lang, 1996), 283–84.

Book II

Book II was published with 96 numbered pages, New Orleans: Druck und Verlag von G. Lugenbühl und E. H. Bölitz, 1854.

1. Here, as elsewhere, Reizenstein is playing on the politics of the Kingdom of Bavaria.

2. The *St. Anna Damenstift* in Munich was an institution that provided stipends for Catholic noblewomen and maintained a school for young women (which still operates). Ludwig von Reizenstein's eldest sister, Konstanze, was a Stiftsdame at St.

Anna's until she became engaged to be married, when her place was taken by her younger sister, Adolfina. See Helene Freifrau von Reitzenstein, ed., *Ein Mann und seine Zeit 1797–1890. Erinnerungen von Alexander Freiherr von Reitzenstein-Hartungs* (Eggstätt: Helene Freifrau von Reitzenstein, 1990), 102–3.

3. Apollo Street is now Carondelet Street, one block above St. Charles Street (formally Nyades).

4. The Bissell's Island described in the novel is fictional, but Reizenstein locates it precisely near Bissell's Point, an angle of the Mississippi at the foot of East Grand Boulevard, opposite the mouth of the Chain of Rocks Canal. It was originally the location of an estate built in the 1820s by Captain Lewis Bissell, and later of a waterworks and a sewage plant. See "Bissell's Point: A Spot Replete with History," *St. Louis Post-Dispatch,* 2 October 1934. Mosenthein and Gabaret Islands, further upstream, which resemble the island described, are in Illinois. Reizenstein shows intimate knowledge of the St. Louis area in his accounts, a result of his residence there as the apprentice of the surveyor Frederick Egloffstein in the early 1850s.

5. The Lucas and Chouteaus families of St. Louis were wealthy French Creole lineages that continued to be prominent through the era of the Civil War. The Chouteaus were the illegitimate descendants of St. Louis's founder Pierre Laclède through his mistress, Madame Chouteau.

6. Bremen, or New Bremen, was a development laid out by Emil Mallinckrodt, E. C. Angelrodt, and partners north of St. Louis in 1844. It was still an independent municipality in the early 1850s but would soon be annexed by the city of St. Louis. Today the area is usually described as the Hyde Park neighborhood.

7. Jefferson Barracks was a military post established by the War Department in 1826 on part of the commons of the village of Carondelet. It was a marshaling place for expeditions and a depot for cavalry and artillery. During the Civil War, its main function was as the site of a military hospital. William Hyde and Howard L. Coward, eds., *Encyclopedia of the History of St. Louis* (New York, 1899), 2: 1120–22. It was closed as a military facility on 30 June 1946. See "Jefferson Barracks Closes," *Bulletin of the Missouri Historical Society* 2, no. 4 (July 1946): 54–55. It is now managed by the St. Louis County Parks System. See William C. Winter, *The Civil War in St. Louis: A Guided Tour* (St. Louis: Missouri Historical Society, 1994), 4–7.

8. Looking-Glass Prairie lies in southern Illinois, due east of St. Louis, between Lebanon and Trenton, Illinois, commencing at a hill two miles east of Lebanon. This information was provided by David Braswell of Maeystown, Illinois.

9. The bloomer costume, consisting of a skirt reaching to the knees and "Turkish pants," was first introduced by Elizabeth Smith Miller, but it received its name from the feminist reformer Amelia Jenks Bloomer (1818–94), *Appletons' Cyclopaedia of American Biography* (New York, 1898), 1: 296.

10. Meran is in what was once Austrian South Tyrol, now Merano in Alto Adige Province, Italy.

11. The *Schönheitskabinet* was a collection of paintings of legendary and contem-

porary beauties placed by King Ludwig I in his Nymphenburg Palace, in what was then the outskirts of Munich. All of the beauties are clothed in white, except for Ludwig's own Lola Montez.

12. This poem puns on the German name for the daisy, *Massliebchen,* "measured love."

13. Many such illustrations are preserved as a part of the record of sale in the Notarial Archives of Orleans Parish. Ludwig von Reizenstein painted a large number of them himself.

14. Leffingwell and Elliott, real estate brokers, were located at 125 Chestnut Street; see *Green's St. Louis Directory for 1851* (St. Louis: Charles and Hammond, 1850), 211; Hiram W. Leffingwell was a St. Louis land developer who had a major role in the development of Forest Park. See Caroline Laughlin and Catherine Anderson, *Forest Park* (Columbia: University of Missouri Press, 1986).

15. This is a reference to the German lyric poet Heinrich Heine (1797–1856), who was in exile and wasting away of a debilitating disease in Paris.

16. Bettina von Arnim, née Brentano (1785–1859), wife of the Prussian Romantic author Ludwig Achim von Arnim (1781–1831), grew up under the personal influence of Goethe at Weimar, and after her husband's death she supported herself as an author in her own right.

17. Judah Touro (1775–1854), born in Newport, Rhode Island, spent his early years in Jamaica and Boston, moving to New Orleans in 1801. He was severely wounded at the Battle of New Orleans and lived virtually as a recluse while cultivating a large fortune as a merchant. He donated heavily to Jewish causes only in his last years. See *Encyclopedia Judaica* (Jerusalem, 1971), vol. 15, cols. 1288–89.

Book III

Book III was published with 184 numbered pages, New Orleans: Druck und Verlag von G. Lugenbühl und E. H. Bölitz, 1854, and in the *Louisiana Staats-Zeitung,* vol. 5, no. 52, 2 March 1854.

1. Although Ludwig von Reizenstein's mother, Baroness Philippine von Branca (divorced after an estrangement beginning in 1841, when Baron Ludwig was fifteen), was of Italian descent, there is no indication in his father's memoirs that Baron Ludwig visited Italy as a child. The date of the novel's completion (December, 1853) would indicate this encounter should have taken place in 1844.

2. The three municipalities were united in 1852.

3. Christian Dietrich Grabbe (1801–36), Romantic poet and dramatist.

4. H. Schlüter was at 78 Common Street (*Cohen's New Orleans Directory for 1854,* 214).

5. Luisa von Mecklenburg-Strelitz (1776–1810), wife of King Friedrich Wilhelm III of Prussia, was regarded as a style-setter in the Romantic era.

6. The Pelican Warehouse was at the corner of Girod Street and Commerce Street, and Judah Touro lived at 128 Canal Street (*Cohen's New Orleans Directory for 1853,* 207, 258).

7. Paul Wilhelm, Duke of Württemberg (1797–1860) was the son of Duke Friedrich Heinrich, brother of King Friedrich II (ruled as duke 1803–6, as king 1806–16) of Württemberg. His family had ruled in Württemberg since the early twelfth century. After leaving the military in 1817, Duke Paul became an explorer and collector of natural specimens of flora, fauna, and minerals, gathering the largest private collection of his day, although he never managed to publish much about it. He traveled extensively in North America, Mexico, South America, and Africa, making four major American expeditions between 1822 and 1857. See the introduction to Paul Wilhelm, Duke of Württemberg, *Travels in North America, 1822–1824,* trans. W. Robert Niske, ed. Savoie Lottinville (Norman: University of Oklahoma Press, 1973), a translation of Paul's *Erste Reise nach dem nördlichen Amerika in den Jahren 1822 bis 1824* (Stuttgart; Tübingen: Cotta, 1835). The enthusiastic reception accorded Paul by the social elite in New Orleans in October 1853 is said to have been one of the irritations that led Reizenstein to compose this novel. See Robert T. Clark, Jr., "The German Liberals in New Orleans (1840–1860)," *Louisiana Historical Quarterly* 20 (1937): 146, citing J. Hanno Deiler.

8. Speculation on the personal life of Madame de Pontalba was a Reizenstein favorite—at one point he specifically declared that her daughter was *not* the model for his lesbian heroine Orleana, *Louisiana Staats-Zeitung,* vol. 5, no. 42, 18 February 1854, 1. On this complex and troubled woman, see most recently Christina Vella, *Intimate Enemies: The Two Worlds of the Baroness de Pontalba* (Baton Rouge; New Orleans: Louisiana State University Press, 1997).

9. *Inferno,* canto 2, ll. 37–39.

10. Literally, "nuns' little farts."

11. *Junker,* literally "young lord," is the term for a landowning squire in northern Germany and Prussia.

12. The French term *poste restante* is used throughout Continental Europe for general delivery mail, which is left at the post office and called for by the addressee in person.

13. Hermann, Prince von Pückler-Muskau (1785–1871), remembered today for a particular type of frozen dessert named *Fürst Pückler,* was a famous nineteenth-century noble wastrel and conspicuous consumer, noted particularly for bankrupting himself to build a vast decorative garden on his estates.

14. Jeanne, Marquise de Pompadour (1721–64) and Marie, Comtesse du Barry (1746–93) were successive mistresses to Louis XV of France.

15. David Garrick (1717–79), English actor and producer of plays, was noted for his Shakespearean performances; August Wilhelm Iffland (1759–1814) was a major German actor with a "common touch."

16. Justus Baron von Liebig (1803–73), was the founder of organic chemistry; Jean Baptiste Boussinggault (1802–87) was a leading French agricultural chemist.

17. Johann Philipp Rothaan (1785–1853), born in the Netherlands, was the twenty-first superior general of the Society of Jesus (1824–53).

18. Alain René Le Sage (1668–1747), French dramatist and novelist, published

his immensely popular novel, *Le diable boîteaux* (translated into English as *The Devil on Two Sticks*) in 1707. He was noted for his daring description of social turmoil and competition, and he was a major interpreter of Spanish literature for the rest of Europe. Reizenstein returned to this theme in a satirical novel whose serialization began in the *Deutsche Zeitung* on 29 September 1861, *Wie der Teufel in New Orleans ist und die Dächer von den Häusern abdeckt* [The devil in New Orleans, and how he lifts the roofs off houses], based on Le Sage. See Robert T. Clark, Jr., "The New Orleans German Colony in the Civil War," *Louisiana Historical Quarterly* 20 (1937): 1006.

19. This was a common euphemism of the period for pregnancy.

20. Narciso Lopez (1798–1851) led two separate expeditions to end Spanish rule in Cuba and annex it to the United States, the second ending in his arrest and execution. This expedition's aftermath in New Orleans is described in the last book of Emil Klauprecht's novel, *Cincinnati* (1854–55). Ned Buntline (alias Edward Z. C. Judson), *The Mysteries and Miseries of New Orleans* (Philadelphia: T. B. Peterson & Bros., ca. 1851) also dealt with the episode, and Heinrich Börnstein once planned a sequel to *Die Geheimnisse von St. Louis,* entitled *Das Blutbad auf Cuba* (The bloodbath on Cuba).

21. Isabella II, Regnant Queen of Spain, ruled 1833–68.

22. Bertel Thorvaldsen, or Thorwaldsen (1770–1844), Danish sculptor.

23. Ellipses indicate that a portion of the text has been removed for decency's sake. This space obviously was meant to contain a narrative of Merlina's murder and her subsequent sexual assault.

24. This "grail," or assembly, of lesbian women resembles the secretive female "Association des sorts" led by a "queen" and priestesses described by Charles Testut in *Les mystères de la Nouvelle-Orléans* (New Orleans, 1852), 1:34–49 and 2:67, 68, although Testut makes no specific reference to same-sex physical relationships and the proceedings are in French.

Book IV

Book IV was published with 188 numbered pages, New Orleans: Druck und Verlag von G. Lugenbühl und E. H. Bölitz, 1855.

1. In the German text of this passage, Reizenstein uses the erroneous *Crasche-Creek,* but the rest of the account closely adapts Marcy's account of his encampment on Cache Creek. Cache Creek enters the Red River from the north, out of Oklahoma, a few miles west of the mouth of the Big Wichita River. The following episode takes place in what is now Cotton County, Oklahoma.

2. Randolph Barnes Marcy (1812–87), from Massachusetts, graduated from West Point in 1832 and went on to serve in the Black Hawk War and the Mexican War. He was engaged in exploring the Red River in 1852–54, as well as a later expedition to Utah and the Seminole War in Florida. During the Civil War he served as chief-of-staff to his son-in-law, General George B. McClellan, and he achieved the permanent rank of Brigadier General after service in the postwar army. He was a

noted sportsman and author, particularly famed for his guide for westward pioneers, *The Prairie Traveler: A Hand-Book for Overland Expeditions* (Washington, D.C.: War Department, 1859; reprint, Old Saybrook, Conn.: Applewood Press, 1990). His report on the expedition, Randolph B. Marcy, with George B. McClellan, *Exploration of the Red River of Louisiana in the Year 1852*, House of Representatives, 33d Congress, 1st session (Washington, D.C.: A. O. P. Nicholson, Public Printer, 1854) has profuse illustrations, particularly of Palo Duro Canyon. Marcy republished parts of this report in his *Thirty Years of Army Life on the Border* (New York: Harper & Bros., 1866). An edition of the narrative portion of this report appears in Grant Foreman, ed., *Adventure on Red River* (Norman: University of Oklahoma Press, 1937).

3. According to Marcy, the Red River began in Palo Duro Canyon of the Llano Estacado ("staked plain") that extended across the Texas border into New Mexico. He actually had reached 31° 35' 3" N, 101° 55' W, but he placed the source at 34° 40' N, 103° 15' W. See Carl I. Wheat, *Mapping the Transmississippi West 1540–1861*, vol. 3: *From the Mexican War to the Boundary Surveys, 1846–1854* (San Francisco: Institute of Historical Cartography, 1959), 14–16, with the Marcy map of 1853 facing p. 13, description of the map, pp. 327–28.

4. St. Patrick's was on Camp Street, between Julia and Girod Streets. St. Joseph's was on Common Street, opposite the Charity Hospital (*Cohen's New Orleans Directory for 1853* [New Orleans, 1852], 319, 320).

5. Antoine Laurent de Jussieu (1748–1876), was author of a taxonomy of plants published in 1789. Oliver de Serres (1539–1619) was a famous French agronomist.

6. The arms of the Barons von Reitzenstein consist of a red shield with a silver bar running diagonally left to right.

7. *Déjeuner à la fourchette* or *Gabelfrühstück* are terms for brunch, especially Sunday brunch.

8. Themis was the Greek goddess of divine order or law and the elementary obligations of family. In her representations she bore the scales, which later became the symbol of justice itself. See Konrat Ziegler, Walther Sontheimer, and Hans Gärtner, eds., *Der Kleine Pauly* (Munich: Deutscher Taschenbuchverlag, 1979), vol. 5, col. 676.

9. General Arthur Görgey was a charismatic soldier in the Hungarian army who defied Lajos Kossuth, the nationalist leader of the revolution of 1848–49, and undermined his authority. He eventually surrendered himself and his troops to the Russians. See Priscilla Robertson, *Revolutions of 1848: A Social History* (New York: Harper & Row, 1960), 287–303.

10. General Rosza Sandor was a Hungarian revolutionary commander who refused to surrender, managing to maintain himself as a robber chieftain until his capture in 1857. See ibid., 301.

11. Lajos Kossuth (1802–94), escaped via Turkey with his chief supporters and became a popular speaker in the United States on behalf of the Hungarian cause in the 1850s.

12. Lewis Bach's beer house was on 190 N. Fourth Street, *Green's St. Louis Directory for* 1851 (St. Louis, 1850), 38.

13. The *Demokratische Presse,* edited by lawyer Christian Kribben, was published from May 1852 to June 1854. The *Anzeiger des Westens,* then edited by the histrionic Heinrich Börnstein (a.k.a. Henry Boernstein, 1805–92), former cohort of Karl Marx and Friedrich Engels, was the oldest German newspaper west of the Mississippi and was published in one form or another from 1835 to 1912. On Börnstein's stormy career in St. Louis, see the introduction to Henry Boernstein, *The Mysteries of St. Louis,* ed. Steven Rowan and Elizabeth Sims (Chicago: Kerr, 1990), vi–xiv. A translation of part of Boernstein's memoirs was published as *Memoirs of a Nobody: The Missouri Years of an Austrian Radical,* trans. and ed. Steven Rowan (St. Louis: Missouri Historical Society, 1998).

14. Construction on the Old Courthouse, a domed structure occupying the block between Fourth and Fifth Streets and between Market and Chestnut Streets, was begun in 1839 and was still unfinished in 1852 (it was declared completed in 1862). It is now part of the Jefferson National Expansion Historical Park.

15. Planters' House was on the west side of Fourth Street, from Pine Street to Chestnut Street (*Green's St. Louis Directory for* 1851, 276).

16. The Virginia Hotel was on the northwest corner of Main Street and Green Street (ibid., 353).

17. Hyde Park is bound by Salisbury Street, Bremen Street, Blair and Twentieth.

18. Doppelgängers (doubles) were commonplace in Romantic fiction, used to personify the multiple personalities of a protagonist or to trace alternate realities, as any reader of Poe would attest. They function in a manner similar to time paradoxes and alternate realities in the time-travel stories of modern science fiction. They were used with particular dexterity by E. T. A. Hoffmann in his *Die Elixiere des Teufels,* 1815–16.

19. *Alessandro Stradella* was a popular opera in three acts composed by Friedrich von Flotow (1812–83), libretto by Friedrich Riese, based on a French comedy. It was first performed at the Hamburg Stadttheater on 30 December 1844. Its protagonists are the lovers Alessandro Stradella and Leonora; Barbarino and Malvoglio are vagabonds who are hired to kill Stradella but experience a conversion to virtue at the end.

20. Boursier School is listed at 184 St. Peter Street, Second District, in *Cohen's New Orleans Directory for* 1853, 33.

21. Karl Egon, Ritter von Ebert (1801–82) was an Austrian Romantic poet; Nikolaus Lenau was the pen name for Nikolaus Franz Niembsch, Edler von Strehlenau (1802–50), a melancholic Romantic Austrian poet. Gottfried Kinkel (1815–82), a professor at Bonn University, was a leading "Forty-Eighter" and a popular poet and author. His *Otto der Schütz, eine rheinische Geschichte in zwölf Abenteuern* (Stuttgart, 1846) was a bestseller, often reprinted. Kinkel was rescued from a prison in Spandau by his student Carl Schurz, and they both later fled to the United States.

22. Johann Ludwig Tieck (1773–1853) was a German Romantic novelist; Friedrich Leopold, Count du Stolberg (1750–1819) was a noted poet.

23. Karl Peter Heinzen (1809–80) was a leftist emigré who became a major figure in the German-American press after 1848.

24. This is a pun on the title of the late-classical philosophical miscellany, *Noctes Atticae* [*Attic Nights*], by Aullus Gellius.

25. The Odd Fellows' Hall was on Camp Street, at the corner of Lafayette Street (*Cohen's New Orleans Directory for 1853*, 200).

26. The Masonic Hall was at the corner of St. Charles Street and Perdido Street.

27. Latin, "the name is the omen." This is a pun of Highland with the German word *Heiland* (savior). Highland is a town on Looking-Glass Prairie in Madison County, Illinois, that was settled by Swiss immigrants. There is an extensive description of Highland circa 1849–50 in Boernstein, *Memoirs of a Nobody*, 103–18.

28. Castalia or Kastalia was the sacred spring at Delphi, named for a nymph who leapt into it to escape Apollo. The water was used to clean the Delphi temples. Ziegler, Sontheimer, and Gärtner, eds., *Der Kleine Pauly*, vol. 3, col. 150.

29. *Wahlverwandtschaften* (1808), by Johann Wolfgang von Goethe (1749–1832), dealt with the affections a married couple had for two persons outside the marriage.

30. Arthur Thompson's foundry was near the Third District Ferry in Algiers (*Cohen's New Orleans Directory for 1853*, 255).

31. In the early nineteenth century, U.S. letters sent "general delivery" (*poste restante*), without specific home addresses, were held at the post office, and the names of the addressees were published in the newspapers. Those addressed in English were advertised in English-language newspapers, and those addressed in German script were published in the German-language press. In each case, the letter lists were an important reason for reading newspapers. Sometimes the post office would withhold these lists from newspapers that opposed the party currently in power.

Book V

Book V was published with 166 numbered pages, New Orleans: Druck und Verlag von G. Lugenbühl und E. H. Bölitz, 1855.

1. This refers to Senator Stephen A. Douglas (1813–61) of Illinois, who introduced the Kansas-Nebraska Bill in January 1854, upsetting the principles of the Missouri Compromise of 1820, limiting the expansion of slavery in the western territories by calling for "popular sovereignty" over the question of slavery. See Gerald M. Capers, *Stephen A. Douglas: Defender of the Union* (Boston: Little, Brown, 1959), 93. This shows that Reizenstein made at least some additions to the text of the novel after its stated date of completion in December 1853.

2. Yellow fever is a viral disease carried by mosquitos. Within three to six days of being bitten, infected persons develop fever, headache, muscle pain, and dizziness.

The skin often turns yellow, and the victim bleeds from the gums and in the stomach. After an apparent recovery, some victims will experience a sudden return of fever, followed by coma and death. The specific course of the disease was established by Walter Reed, and its viral nature was established in 1927. Until the development of a vaccine in 1937, the only means of control was to suppress the mosquito population. Treatment includes complete bed rest and replacement of lost fluids. See *The Merck Manual of Diagnosis and Therapy,* 15th ed. (Rahway, N.J.: Merck Sharpe & Dohme Research Laboratories, 1987), 189–93. The 1853 outbreak in New Orleans precipitated intense controversy over the proper policy to prevent future epidemics; see particularly Bennet Dowler, *Tableau of the Yellow Fever of 1853 with Topographical, Chronological and Historical Sketches of the Epidemics of New Orleans since their Origins in 1796 Illustrative of the Quarantine Question* (New Orleans, 1854).

3. Annunciation Square was created by the intersection of Camp Street and Felicity Street, fronting Orange and Race Streets.

4. They are referring, of course, to the praying mantis (*Mantis religiosa*).

5. Count Alessandro Cagliostro (1743–95), born Giuseppe Balsamo, was a noted alchemist and imposter who visited London and Paris in 1771 claiming to be the master of a new form of freemasonry. In 1785 he was implicated in the "affair of the golden necklace" involving Marie Antoinette and the Cardinal de Rohan, but he escaped punishment. He was arrested in Rome in 1789, condemned to life imprisonment as a heretic, and died in the custody of the Holy Office. See the article in *Dizionario biografico degli Italiani* (Rome: Istituto della Enciclopedia Italiana, 1963), 5:608–15; see also, but with caution, Pierre Mariel, *Cagliostro* (Paris: Celt, 1973).

6. Physiognomy was the popular nineteenth-century "science" that treated external characteristics as indications of human character.

7. Pierre Leroux (1798–1871), was a French philosopher and leading secular humanist.

8. Latin, "The fine art of teaching the method of calculating infinite series."

9. The House of Atreus was the cursed royal family of Mycene in Homeric Greece. Agamemnon was murdered in his bath by his wife Clytemnestra for having their daughter sacrificed to bring a favorable wind for the Greek fleet to besiege Troy.

10. The German word for cockroach is *Schaben,* which is punned here with *Schwaben,* for "Swabians."

11. Erysipelas is a primary bacterial infection of the skin. See *Merck Manual,* 16th ed. (New York, 1992), 56, 2417.

12. Sevastopol, a fortress in the western part of Russian Crimea, was a major object of siege by allied forces in the Crimean War, which was then going on (1853–56).

13. An eagle was a ten-dollar gold piece, so a quarter-eagle would be valued at $2.50.

14. Of the 12,151 burials during the epidemic, 2,212 took place in Lafayette Cemetery. See J. S. McFarlane, "A Review of the Yellow Fever," in *List of Interrments in all the Cemeteries of New Orleans From the First of May to the First of November, 1853* (New Orleans: True Delta, 1853), xiv.

15. In the newspaper publication, there was a double row of long dashes, representing the lined-up coffins. This was not done in the book version.

16. *Uncle Tom's Cabin* (1851–52), by Harriet Beecher Stowe (1811–96), was one of the major bestsellers of the 1850s and the definitive abolitionist novel. It inspired innumerable stage performances. In Germany, its popularity persisted into this century, and there is even a subway stop in Berlin named *Onkel Toms Hütte.*

Epilogue

1. These are the words of "the handwriting on the wall" described in Daniel, 5:25–28, foretelling disaster to those who persist in sin.

2. Mardis Gras was on 28 February in 1854.